STEEL DRAGON 5

STEEL DRAGON 5

STEEL DRAGONS SERIES™ BOOK 5

KEVIN MCLAUGHLIN

MICHAEL ANDERLE

Copyright © 2020 LMBPN Publishing
Cover Art by Jake @ J Caleb Design
http://jcalebdesign.com / jcalebdesign@gmail.com
Cover copyright © LMBPN Publishing
A Michael Anderle Production

LMBPN Publishing
PMB 196, 2540 South Maryland Pkwy
Las Vegas, NV 89109

First US Edition, August 2020
eBook ISBN: 978-1-64971-126-7
Print ISBN: 978-1-64971-127-4

THE STEEL DRAGON 5 TEAM

Thanks to the JIT Readers

Dave Hicks
Deb Mader
Diane L. Smith
Dorothy Lloyd
Heidi Bauer
Jackey Hankard-Brodie
James Caplan
Jeff Eaton
Jeff Goode
Kerry Mortimer
Paul Westman
Peter Manis
Veronica Stephan-Miller

If we've missed anyone, please let us know!

Editor
The Skyhunter Editing Team

CHAPTER ONE

The view from under the palm tree was stunning, Kristen thought as she burrowed her toes in the hot white sand of the beach. The sun had begun to sink below the horizon and was gradually swallowed by the crystal-clear blue water of the bay. On either side of their small private harbor, more huge-leafed tropical trees shaded flowers and exotic birds that called in excitement at the last rays of sun of the day.

She would have liked to be able to enjoy the scenery, but that wasn't exactly possible when camping out in an enemy base. It was even more difficult when trying to prevent a group of technomages from escaping via magical means. Most importantly, they could not be allowed to access the huge cache of weapons they had stored there that could kill dragons as easily as lead could punch holes in humans.

It seemed ironic that people came to islands like this and paid top dollar to eat tropical fruit and fresh fish from the ocean. Her people did those things merely to survive.

Stonequest flew in from the ocean, a massive tuna in the claws of each of his hindlegs. She sighed with relief. At least they wouldn't go without a meal later.

The night before had been sleepless as well as foodless. They had won a great battle but it wasn't exactly reassuring to incarcerate a group of mages in their own cells. None of them had cooperated either. She knew there had to be food rations stashed somewhere in the World War Two complex of tunnels dug into this tropical volcanic island, but none of the prisoners would say where.

Despite Constance Vigil—the former leader of the technomages—advocating for them all to work together and helping them survive the battle when she could have turned it against them, she claimed she didn't know where any of the food was.

"Any luck with getting intel from Eric?" Kristen asked Jim as they watched Stonequest butcher the tuna with his dragon claws.

"Nah. He's not talking about a damn thing," he said.

"Not even to the Wonderkid?" she teased.

Jim smiled his Wonderkid smile. "I don't think they've heard that I have a reputation to maintain."

"I have good news!" Keith said as he emerged from the jungle. He held a massive cordless phone.

"You've found a weapon we can use to kill the mages one by one if we need to?" Hernandez asked. She had spent her time off building sandcastles, filling them with explosives, and blowing them apart.

"No." The Rookie was unshaken by the gallows humor. "But I do have someone who wants to talk to you, boss." He handed the massive phone to Kristen and she put it to her ear.

"Hello?"

"Oh, dear God, Kristen. I am *so glad* to hear your voice!"

"Brian!" She shouted with delight, instantly encouraged by her brother's voice.

"We're on the job. Call me Zed."

"You called me Kristen. Shouldn't that be *Lady Steel,* Zed?" she replied.

"Okay, that's a fair point. I'll call you the queen of the dragons if you want. I'm only glad to finally talk to you. How did you manage? I saw the plane crash and the satellite feed made it look very bad. The water's clear enough to see the damage. Are you guys okay? Are the technomages dead or gone?"

"One question at a time," Kristen said, although she found his optimism contagious. She knew—logically—that they had been in far more danger than him, but it still felt good to hear his voice.

"Right, right, right," Brian said and attempted to regain control of his composure. "Let's keep it professional. What's your status and how can I help?"

"The main concern is that we found more dragons who were imprisoned here and who need serious help. Lumos is trying his best with them, but they're not doing too well. On top of that, we have captives as well."

"The mages?"

She nodded instinctively before she remembered she was talking on a phone bigger than her head. "Yeah. Some died, but we ended up taking a good number prisoner."

"And the leaders?"

"All shackled." She couldn't help but chuckle. "Constance, Katrina, Havington—who was the douche from Europe—and the local boss, Eric."

"Not too shabby."

"It's not only them," Kristen explained. "There are many rank and file mages too, plus regular human soldiers who were loyal to their cause. We have them all under guard but we barely have the personnel to do it. Plus, it's their base. I'm scared shitless that they know back doors we don't."

"Okay, well, I have someone who wants to talk about getting you out of there and, believe it or not, has already started the process," Brian said.

"How is that possible? We just started talking!"

"I sent your team to that island, remember? And I saw your plane go down. We've been watching from the skies and haven't seen any boats leave, so we assumed you'd still be there."

"Who do you mean by we?"

"Hello, Lady Steel, it's Amythist. I'm glad young Zed has finally reached you through the telephones."

"Amythist, unless this is something urgent, I need to continue my conversation with my intelligence officer."

The old dragon sucked a breath in. "I fear we're not the only people who know about your position and what transpired on that island. Things have…changed."

"What things?" she asked, not at all liking that Amythist was being less than direct. Usually, she was relaxed and open, but she seemed jittery.

"Rumors…movements… Detroit seems…still. I don't like it."

Kristen frowned. "Is there something you need to tell me?" She hoped a direct question might compel the ancient dragon to simply spit it out.

"I have chartered a ship to come and get all of you. A yacht, in fact, and a fast one from a billionaire in Japan, but I feel it will still be too slow. Is there no way you can get home faster?"

"Amythist…" She tried to sound patient, "What *exactly* is going on?" She felt certain the old dragon was hiding something now. It was not a pleasant feeling.

"I don't have anything specific…" Amythist admitted. "Merely a feeling that things are shifting, you could say."

"You chartered a racing yacht because you had a feeling?" She took a breath and tried not to get frustrated.

"My duties have kept me at home with the dragons you have rescued, but as I said, there are rumors. Many dragons have left populated areas—some would say fled."

"They might simply be nervous. They can't know that we've finally captured most of the technomages. The last they saw of them was an attack on Detroit."

"And if that was all I'd noticed, I wouldn't be worried. But in the light of a recent attack, I would think Dragon SWAT teams would increase patrols, but this is not the case."

"No?" A pit grew relentlessly in her stomach as if a demon of dread was scooping her insides out.

"No," Amythist said flatly. "Most of them are no longer at their duty stations. I haven't heard about any training exercises either.

They're all simply…gone. Someplace else. The whole thing stinks. I can feel it, thick in the air, like the calm before a storm."

The demon in her stomach dug the hole even deeper, but she didn't want to convey her concern to Amythist. "I don't think you understand." Kristen tried to sound firm. "We've defeated the bad technomages. It should be done now. There's no one left to attack."

"Believe me, my dear, I am quite relieved that you have finally managed to capture the brutes who performed these barbaric acts on the poor dragons who now call my estate home. However, I am not sure this is the kind of thing that ends so easily." The old dragon sighed. "Although you and your team have done admirably, it cannot be denied and is now quite obvious that humans are a clear and present danger to dragon kind. There were many who wished to end your kind when you discovered how to build castles to defend your-selves against us.

"Later, there were dragons who wished to end your existence when you learned how to fly with your machines and others who saw the atomic bomb as the final straw. Truly, that would have been the end if not for your uncharacteristic restraint with the weapon. But for many, this is too much. With these bullets harvested from our own kind, any human can now kill a dragon. This has not escaped us."

"But how can dragons truly think they'll benefit if they have a war with humans?" she asked.

Amythist tsked, "Not all of this is about logic, my dear. Dragons are ruled by their emotions as much as humans—perhaps more so as we have auras to communicate and influence each other with. I agree with you, of course, that this must all be avoided. But it seems to me as if someone sees their chance evaporating. With every day that passes, the threat of humans rebelling will seem less as the news of your success will spread. That is why you need to be somewhere instead of the middle of nowhere as quickly as possible. Can you think of nothing besides the ship I have sent?"

Despite Amythist being much older than her and somehow even wealthier than she was with the money she'd inherited from the dragon Windlock, she was an investigator, so she did not need to answer. "Make sure the Dragon Council knows of our success here, and Brian—I know you're still listening—make sure the media starts talking about what happened in Detroit as the last hurrah of these terrorists."

"You got it," Brian said.

"Of course, my dear," Amythist said.

"I'll see what else we can come up with on this end," Kristen added, although she was unsure what they could do.

She hoped that news of their success would be enough to calm the factions of dragons who wished to slaughter humanity rather than be served by them. Sadly, she would be lying to herself if she thought it would be enough after all that had happened over the last year.

With a heavy sigh, she ended the call.

"Plans?" Jim asked.

"The old dragon's right," she said. "We need to get off this island and back to the USA ASAP."

CHAPTER TWO

Although her private jet was currently damaged—perhaps irreparably so—and tangled in a coral reef at the bottom of the ocean, Kristen still had hopes that they could get home before anything too terrible happened.

It would merely require a little magic, and she had the perfect people to help.

She found Larry and Amy standing near one of the entrances to the network of underground tunnels that had been excavated into the island over fifty years before.

It looked like a scene out of a sci-fi movie. The girl levitated about ten feet up on her skateboard, while pebbles floated around her in complex whirls and spirals. One massive boulder was suspended too and Larry was seated on top of it.

"Am I interrupting a training session or something?" Kristen asked loudly.

The giant boulder jolted and plummeted and the mage tumbled off. "Jesus, Kristen. Don't scare us like that!"

"Us?" Amy asked, rolled her eyes, and flipped into a series of kicks on the skateboard that would have been absolutely impossible if it had been bound by the laws of gravity. She landed easily and the pebbles that had hovered around her followed and created complex shapes or wobbly stacks on the ground.

"Sorry about that," Larry said and dusted his robes off. "Amy was showing me how to increase my power and I had her practice some finesse drills. What can we do for you?"

"I want to get everyone home. Now, if possible," she said.

"Well, why not simply click your heels together and tell your fairy godmother to whisk you away?" he asked.

"I thought maybe the snarky mage who works for me and used a teleportation spell to get me to this island might be able to keep earning his pay."

It was Amy who answered. "I'm sorry, Kristen, but that's not possible."

"Sure it is. You got me here." She tried to keep a smile on her face.

Larry nodded, "Sure, we got *you* here. Then the damn portal closed and left us all scrambling. And even that nearly killed me."

"But Amy, you're stronger."

"It looks like I've reached my limits, though," the girl said. "Seriously, these portals are difficult to make. I think the only way the mages do it is by working in larger numbers than we've realized. It took everything I had to stop that portal from snapping shut and chopping your tail off. Getting you through again *might* be possible, but getting everyone home? That's not even in the realm of possibility."

"Neither is sending you back alone," Larry interjected. "I know what you're thinking. It's not like you want to go back to the Motor City because you're worried about missing a show. You think something's wrong, don't you?"

Kristen didn't bother to lie about it. "I do, yes. Amythist convinced me that something's happening, and it makes sense that the Masked One would want to strike as soon as possible so everyone's gut reaction is to blame the technomages. If only I can go back, fine."

He shook his head and put his hands on his hips. "This is what I'm talking about. We won't send you back alone. For all we know, the Masked One might have tortured Amythist into saying all that simply to lure you back there. If you get separated from us again, he won't hold back. He'll kill you and you know that."

"And Amythist potentially being tortured is supposed to make me want to wait the weeks it'll take for the ship to reach us here and get back home?"

Larry smirked. "Bad example."

Kristen turned to the other woman. Despite the mage being younger, she was far more powerful. Truly, this decision would be hers. "Tell me you can do something."

"Not gonna happen." Amy folded her arms.

"Can't you charter a jet?" he asked. "Windlock left you everything. It's not like you can't afford it."

"I already talked to Brian about that," Kristen explained. "We would still need to take a boat to the nearest island with an airport, plus hire the jet and a pilot. It would take days, at least."

"So we have to enjoy a tropical paradise for a few days. Is that so bad?" He threw his hands up in frustration.

"It is when we're understaffed, have dangerous prisoners, and the outside world is getting soaked in gasoline by someone who wants to play with matches," Kristen snapped.

"We can't do the portal, Kristen. I'm sorry," Amy said. "Maybe we could do a series of jumps or something? Go from here to another island, take a rest, then do another jump? It would take a day at least, but we could do it. It's too much for the two of us to make the jump in one go."

"That's it!" Larry exclaimed.

"I know that's it. I was explaining that we can't really do it," she said and rolled her eyes again.

"No! Not that. I mean that *two* mages could never do it. But we don't only have two mages." He grinned like a fool.

"I know you got some mages to join us, but none of them are even as strong as you. No offense," Amy added hastily.

"We can use them and we should," Larry said. "But that's not who I'm talking about. What if we get some of the technomages to help? They have more experience with the gates. It *is* their magic trick, after all, I only learned how to do it second-hand by watching the spells they had created."

"But we can't trust them," the girl said. "They worked for Constance."

"The fighting stopped because of Constance," Kristen took a deep breath. She already knew what she would do, and she already didn't like it.

"But if we could get them to help us, we could make a portal that could get us out of here." He sounded hopeful. "They probably know ways to use less energy or something and might have a better idea of how to steer, so to speak. I would never have found the way to this island without that thread of magic Constance left."

"It's not worth the risk." Amy folded her arms.

"That's not your call to make," he said, his gaze on Kristen.

She had already made her mind up. "Let's talk to Constance."

CHAPTER THREE

Kristen, Larry, and Amy entered the complex of tunnels and followed a winding route to the interior where the cells were. It was odd to have taken control of this enemy base that had obviously been in use by the technomages for decades. They walked through rooms where esoteric diagrams and mad scribblings covered the walls —new spells being developed, Larry explained. Their path took them past rooms that held munitions from when the base was first built.

Worst of all, they walked past chambers used to hold dragons captive so the technomages could harvest their body parts to use in the manufacture of their awful bullets. Close by were the work areas where they turned these parts into lethal ammunition.

It was extremely uncomfortable to think that if they were attacked, Kristen and her people were the ones currently in charge of all these horrible resources. Unfortunately, it could not all simply be destroyed —not yet and not if Amythist was right.

Finally, they reached the cells where all the captives were held. Even though they had actively tried to start a world war and all either had dragon blood or even human blood on their hands, she still didn't like keeping them in these surroundings.

She'd been in one of the concrete-floored cells only a few days before, but at least she'd had one to herself. That was a luxury she and her team could not afford the captive mages. Behind rusty bars, seated on cold concrete or leaning against the stone walls, was the techno-mage army.

Almost every gaze stared at Kristen, Larry, and Amy as they passed. The only ones who didn't stare at their captors were those who tried to conjure some trace of magic. Even with her right outside, some of the mages didn't stop in their endeavors to harness the abilities that had been taken from them.

Larry had acted wisely when he prepared to come to the island to rescue Kristen. Before boarding the private jet that took them here, he had gone to Detroit SWAT headquarters and commandeered every anti-magic bracelet they had in their possession.

Now, each technomage was equipped with one. Their magic had been rendered useless and they couldn't remove the restraint. Only Kristen could as she'd been the one to put them all on. One mage had managed to remove his forcibly and his lifeless body had already been taken from the cell and buried at sea. Since then, no one else had tried to break the bracelets.

Kristen walked past them all and ignored their attempts at magic, as useless as they were.

She finally reached the one person who had a cell to herself, stopped, and looked the woman in the eye. "Hello again, Constance Vigil."

Constance smiled like she'd been invited to tea. "We have to stop meeting like this. Although I must say, the last time we met with me in a cell was a little nicer as the glass of *that* cell was more picturesque than these rusty old bars."

"Forgive us your accommodations. They are the best we could manage. The last tenants here didn't exactly prioritize the comforts of their prisoners," she said as a dig at how the technomages had treated the dragons they'd kept there.

"It's always a shame when new management doesn't improve on the problems of the last owner, isn't it?" The woman raised an eyebrow.

"Enough of this bullshit," Amy said. "It stinks badly enough without it."

"We need to know more about the portal magic," Kristen said and nodded to Larry as he was the one who knew what he needed to ask.

"We want to know what kind of shorthand you use in those spells," he said and sounded like he was talking about how to fix a carburetor with a fellow mechanic instead of interrogating a prisoner. "We managed to open one but it took a ton of energy. The way your people have used them shows you have a more efficient process. We want it, if you'd be so kind." He gave her his most charming smile.

The smile the mage returned was as fake as his had been. "Why would the Steel Dragon need to open a portal? I was under the impression you had vast resources at your disposal. Surely a jet can be chartered?"

"Jets don't go fast enough," Kristen stated.

"But why must you travel so quickly?" the prisoner asked.

"That doesn't concern you," Amy said.

"Ah, but it does. Knowing the destination is incredibly important when opening a portal. If you are trying to go to a…say, a battlefield, for example, and you picture something that has already been destroyed, the results can be disastrous."

"How do you know there's a battlefield?" the young mage demanded.

"It was merely a guess, given the Steel Dragon's history," Constance told her. "Also, I can't imagine what else would compel the three of you to come and ask us for help. Can you even trust us? I thought we were your enemy." She let her gaze bore into Kristen, willing her to tell her what was going on.

The thing was, the Steel Dragon didn't think of Constance as the enemy. Not anymore. The mage had called for the fighting to stop and left a thread of magic for Larry and Amy to follow. Plus, she'd removed the magic-dampening bracelet Kristen had been fitted with when she'd been captured. If any of those three things hadn't happened, she had no doubt that it would be her team crammed in these cells instead of Constance's.

Still, she knew she needed to tell her something, but she sure as hell didn't want to tell her everything. "We have reason to believe there'll be another attack and want to be in place to stop it."

The woman frowned. "You've stopped all the technomages. There may be a few more out there, but I promise you there are no more major cells. If you think our people will attack, all I need is a cellphone to make sure it doesn't happen."

Kristen ground her teeth and tried to suppress her aura. She wasn't concerned about mages. It was the Masked One who had her worried now and Constance had given her that name. The technomage leader had told her that her entire organization had probably been manipulated by this secret asshole since before it was even founded. She realized that if she wanted her help to stop the Masked One, her best bet was to come clean.

Her mind made up, she shared what information she had from Amythist with Constance and spared no details, as paltry as they were.

The woman nodded as she related what the old dragon had said and her frown deepened all the while.

"We'll help you with the portal," was the first thing she said when the explanation finished.

"Just like that?" Larry grinned.

"Why?" Kristen asked.

"Too many of those details sync up with what I thought was going on. If the Masked One is trying to cause the war—if a dragon has been behind everything going on from the very beginning—he's not likely to stop because the mages were eliminated. He'll push on with his agenda and simply use different actors for the various parts that must be played should he need to."

"So you really will help us?" she asked again.

"Where do you wish to go?"

"The USA. Detroit, probably."

"Why?" Constance asked.

"I already told—"

"Yes, you did, and I know your intentions and trust them, but this is the first time many of the mages here have laid eyes on the Steel Dragon, let alone heard her speak. Why should they follow you? Please tell me. If not for me, then for them."

"Because we're on the same side," she said. "I know all of you fought to end the tyranny of the dragons. I disagree with your methods but not your reasons. I don't want my parents to live in a world where the mood of a dragon could end their lives. Now it seems the dragons—or one of the bastards, at least—is ready to start the war he wanted you to fight.

"The best-case scenario is a decimation of the human population. Worst-case is complete annihilation. I know all of you fought against me because you thought I was upholding the status quo, but that is not why I fought. I did it only to save lives—the same thing I ask of you today."

Many of the mages stared at her as she said this, but a precious few came to the front of their cells and asked how they could help.

It would have to be enough.

C H A P T E R   F O U R

Back on the beach, Kristen watched carefully while Constance explained to Larry, Amy, a few of the stronger mages from their team, and the two technomages who had agreed to help how to cast the spell.

Although she had tried to explain to both her dragon and human allies that the technomage leader wasn't the threat she once was, they had insisted on precautions.

Stonequest was in dragon form, ready to incinerate all of them if needed. Drew and his SWAT team had guns aimed squarely at the mages' heads. She was impressed that Constance didn't seem to mind. Her two underlings were a little squirmy with the weapons but their leader acted as if being a trigger away from being blown to pieces was all in a day's work. She assumed that for the technomages, at least, it probably was.

"The first and most important thing to understand is that this is by no means an easy spell to cast," the woman explained. "Getting it started is the most difficult part, and my mages practiced it for many years before we ever dared to use it in combat."

"So wherever we end up, that's where we'll be," Larry translated. It was hard to imagine they could teleport somewhere calmer and more tranquil than the tropical beach they now stood on.

"Precisely," Constance said. "Furthermore, when most of us go through, we will be drained. Our powers will start to replenish but we'll need cover when we get through."

"Consider that handled," Stonequest growled.

"Quite." She obliged the dragon with a tight smile.

"What do you mean *most* of us?" Amy said.

"That is the real secret of the spell and the only way we've been able to use these portals effectively." The woman sighed, obviously less than pleased to divulge this secret. After a moment's hesitation, she continued, resolute if less than excited. "Maintaining these portals for any amount of time longer than a few seconds requires that someone remain in place on the island as an anchor for the gate."

"That's bullshit," Amy said. "We've chased all your forces through these more than once."

Constance smiled. "You merely thought you did. Most times we escaped you, one brave soul stayed behind."

"We would have seen them," Kristen said.

"They don't need to be right next to the portal, merely close enough to pour magic into it. I promise you, that is how it is done. But it does depend on the distance and the number of people who have to go through. Short hops and a couple of people can usually happen without an anchor. It depends on how long it has to be held open for. In the battle for Detroit, someone stayed behind in the Motor City and met up with us later. Even when they sprung me from prison, a mage stayed behind to get out on their own."

"We never found them, though," Drew said.

"Indeed. The mages who stayed behind were always skilled in a far simpler spell—self-immolation."

"Unless you think otherwise, boss, I would guess that will not be necessary today," Larry said.

"God, no," Kristen said, aghast at the commitment her foes had to their cause.

"Excellent," he said. "In that case, I'll stay behind and serve as the anchor. I'd like to know how, anyway."

"I can't ask you to do that," she responded quickly.

"Ask what? To hang out for a week or so on a tropical island and take a cruise on a yacht to Detroit? It doesn't sound too bad to me."

"It makes sense," Timeflash said. Although she'd been with them, Kristen constantly almost forgot about her. She'd spent her time almost exclusively with the dragons who had been held captive on the island. "Someone needs to stay with the captive dragons anyway. I don't think it would be smart to haul them through a portal when the alternative is a nice calm cruise where we can practice fishing and basic socializing."

"I don't know…" Kristen said.

"Ah, come on, Lady Steel. It'll be fine." The mage smiled cheerfully. "I'm more of a lover than a fighter anyway, and I have the skill to do this. There is a damn good chance you'll need Amy's firepower more than my finesse. Plus, Timeflash and I can keep an eye on the prisoners until the yacht gets here."

"About that…" The technomage turned to Kristen. "I already mentioned that when we pass through the portal, we will be drained of our powers. I do not know the particulars of what will be on the other side of this gate, but I have never liked going anywhere unprepared. It would be useful to have a few more troops available to help. If Lady Steel would release the rest of my people, they could bolster our force."

She was not thrilled with the idea of simply freeing the people she'd worked to capture almost since she'd known she was a dragon. "How can I trust them?" she asked and not completely rhetorically. "Frankly, Constance, I barely trust *you*. The others are not high on my list of people I would trust to babysit."

"We'd trust you with our lives as well," the woman pointed out.

"You're already trusting your lives to us," Stonequest stated. "Letting you free would change that."

"There is a way to make sure they can't betray us." Larry rubbed his chin and looked at the technomage leader.

Constance eyed him for a moment before realization flashed in her eyes. "No." She said. "No way. It was not a good idea back then and it's not a good idea now."

"What are you talking about?" Kristen asked, quite sure she was demonstrating yet again that she had grown up as a regular human and spent less time in the world of dragons and mages than everyone around her.

"There's a type of rarely used magic called contractual magic," Larry explained.

The woman scoffed. "Rarely used? More like archaic and outdated."

"What is it?" she asked and ignored the snide comment.

"It's a binding spell," he explained. "Once cast, it creates a bond between two people that cannot be broken. Both sides are forced by the magic to fulfill their end of the bargain in question."

"Those who don't are incinerated by the magic if they don't comply," Constance said sourly.

"What's the big deal?" Amy asked. "You said your mages were all trained to light themselves on fire if they were captured. How is this different?" It was a snarky, impolite thing to say—Kristen knew that—but there was also something to it.

"The difference is that no one else would hurt those mages. That was their choice. And we always knew some of them might choose to be captured rather than end their own lives." There was a deep bitterness in Constance's tone that Kristen needed to understand.

"But if both parties agree to this…contract," she began, "how is it something they're forced to do?"

The woman chuckled darkly. "Oh, sweet Kristen Hall. I wish all dragons were as trusting and naïve as you are. Sadly, mutual agreement is not the history of contractual magic."

"Can we cut the mystic crap and tell me how the hell it works?" she snapped.

Larry shrugged and forced a weak grin. "Unfortunately, she's right. It's been used in ages past by dragon lords on their dragon vassals, by human mages to control other humans, and by dragons to control captured mages, among other things."

"But how could it be bad if both parties agreed?" Keith asked.

"It's good to see it's not only the leader that's naïve." Constance sneered. "Obviously, many people will agree to all kinds of things if the alternative is being eaten by a dragon."

"Or being ripped apart by a mage," Stonequest added.

"They're not wrong," Larry concurred. "It has a particularly nasty history since this type of magic has been abused many times in the past. It fell out of style when the magic dampening cuffs were invented. For most situations, those have served the dragons fine. But...well, Windlock and I discussed all this once or twice. I would have agreed to it to be free of my bracelet, but we decided it might ruffle too many scales, so to speak."

"You know how to do it?" Constance asked, obviously incredulous.

"I do," he said simply and for once used less words than he might have needed instead of more.

"How does it work?" Kristen asked.

"Well, the basis of it is a paper contract. You write out the terms, read it out exactly as written, and sign in blood. Once you do that, you cannot break the vows you make or… Well, like Constance said…" He mimed an explosion with his hands. The gesture made her suddenly nostalgic for when she first met him when her world had barely begun to get as complicated as it currently was.

Kristen wasn't sure what to do. She could definitely understand Constance's objections. It wouldn't do for her to bring the mages out one by one and force them to agree to fight for her or be devoured. And it could be used for far worse than that. Now that she knew it could be agreed to under duress, she understood how horribly it could be—and probably had been—used. But it could also be used for good, couldn't it?

"What if everyone who signs is not under duress?" she asked. "What if everyone agrees to it willingly?"

"There are precedents for that," Larry was quick to point out.

"When the United States tried to end its slave trade, a few dragons sided with the abolitionists. They convinced landowners to set their slaves free by agreeing to one of these contracts. The slaver—er, former slavers? Future former slavers?—agreed to it because the dragon signed as well. It meant that if a dragon took a slave, they'd be killed by the spell. Back in those days, that was impossible to even think of."

"Those cases are the exceptions, not the rule," Constance spat.

"But what if Kristen wrote it?" Larry asked, grinning like a fool. "If the contract were written in a way that forced her to be a proper liege and leader, it might make it more palatable to your mages. Hell, I know you might not believe it, but if we could write one of these in terms we all liked, I'd be happy to sign it. I trust her with my life as it is. I'd put it in writing."

"I don't know." Kristen wasn't fond of the idea. "It reeks of mind control. Too many people would lose their free will."

"No, they wouldn't," he was quick to say. "Dragons have far more formidable mind control powers with their auras."

Heartsbane—who had the most powerful aura of anyone Kristen had ever worked with—scoffed but she didn't deny what he said either.

"I've thought about this often over the years. I think that—if done right—it's the way forward. It is more powerful and could be abused, but Kristen, you're the Steel Dragon. You won't abuse it because we won't force anyone to sign. This could be a real move toward equality —a document to prove that everyone on this planet can work together."

"Work together or *die,* you mean," Constance said.

"Well sure, yeah, but we didn't exactly suffer zero casualties capturing this base, and I know some of your mages died too. This way will be better if everyone agrees to it."

"I wouldn't know where to begin to write a contact that we could all agree to," Kristen said and fixed him with a pointed stare.

"Let me see what I can do," Larry said. "Like I said, I've thought about this for much longer than only the last few minutes."

"Fine," she said and he vanished into the tunnels of the complex to locate paper, pens, and possibly something to prick all their fingers.

"Is this how you always work?" the technomage leader asked. "Letting whoever on your team do as they wish?"

"I don't have a problem with democracy," she retorted. "But I'll read this as carefully as your mages will."

"So you will offer it to them?" Constance asked. She seemed both surprised and interested.

"You're right that we could use the additional help if war is about to break out. If there is any way to get your people's help in a way I can be sure I can trust them, I think it's worth a try."

"Even if it means your death if you fail to uphold your end of the contract?"

"I've risked my life every day since I became a cop so might as well get that shit in writing."

The woman chuckled and rolled her eyes. "We'll start working on the portal spell. It will take a little practice for us all to do it efficiently. I look forward to reading this contract."

CHAPTER FIVE

Larry managed to produce a document that was surprisingly impressive.

Kristen read the parts that pertained to her first—the liege was the language of the contract—with particular interest. She was not to ask the signees to do anything that violated their ethics. It didn't mean that if she gave them an order they didn't like, she would explode, only that if something felt *wrong* to them, they could protest. She wasn't concerned about this. These people had done horrible things to dragons, killed humans, and who knew what else? That clause basically meant she couldn't kill them indiscriminately or hurt their families. That was fine with her.

She also had to treat their lives as if they were as valuable as her own and honor a commitment to keep them as safe as possible during a time of war. The contract would expire when the risk of war between humans and dragons was over or the war itself ended, whichever happened first. That was to be agreed to by Kristen and at least half of whoever signed it.

In return for these assurances, the signees were to swear to follow her orders in the spirit in which they were issued. More specifically, they were to dedicate themselves to preventing as many deaths of both dragons and humans as possible. They were to do all they could to prevent war between humanity and dragon kind, and if war did break out, they were to work to end it with as few lives lost on both sides as possible.

It seemed reasonable to her and also like a good way to find out if any of the mages there were actively working for the Masked One. There was no way a mole would sign something like this. Not that it meant anyone who didn't sign was working with the Masked One. Surely qualms could be had with the verbose document. It only meant that those who did sign truly could be trusted.

Larry finally managed to achieve the correct wording on his third attempt. Once Kristen liked what it said and Constance grumbled only minimally, the dragons and human fighters were instructed to unlock the cells and bring all the mages out onto the beach.

Part of her wanted to use the hollowed-out heart of a volcano the mages had used for the center of their operation, but she thought the beach was ultimately more fitting. It was a place of freedom and open horizons, where you could practically see into tomorrow. She hoped the mages saw it that way too.

It took a while for everyone to gather. Kristen stood with her people—the dragons, mages, and humans who had fought alongside her. Across from them, a line of technomages waited with their leaders—Constance, Eric, Havington, and the Iron Dragon Katrina—in front.

Everyone watched and listened as she read the document and the blue sky gave way to the rich colors of a tropical sunset. When she finished, she pricked her finger with the quill of a bird—this was apparently essential to the spell and had cost Emerald an hour of time spent hunting a pelican merely to snatch a tailfeather—and she signed.

She immediately felt some of her energy flow into the paper—it had come from a ream with perforated edges that had been used by printers that were practically obsolete even when she was a kid. Her blood seemed to course through the document to make the words

Larry had written seem to burn into the paper. She also found that the somewhat fragile paper seemed to strengthen with it.

Larry stepped forward to sign next, a grin on his face as he read through the half of the document that pertained to him and all the other signees. Stonequest and Drew were already fighting to be the second signee, and the rest of her friends—human and dragon—were in line behind them. They chuckled and pulled faces at each other as they prepared to prick their fingers.

Suddenly, Drew and Stonequest were lifted off their feet and moved a few feet back before Amy landed beside Kristen. "You saved my life. I always intended to serve you but like you said, we might as well make it official."

The girl signed and Drew and Stonequest followed. Jim wanted to sign next but those remaining wouldn't let him, so they ended up reading it as a group.

Kristen couldn't help but shed a few tears of pride as her friends fought to agree to help her with their very lives. They had all suffered so much for her. Each one of them had spent tears, sweat, blood, and hours and hours of their lives and still, they wanted to give more. It was too much, more than she deserved and more than anyone deserved. She was honored by them and was almost glad to have something to bind her to them—a reminder that their lives were worth as much if not more than her own.

Finally, they had all signed except Hernandez. "You know I might try to make you break this shit simply to watch you blow up, right?" the woman said.

"Anything to make you finally shut up." Kristen laughed and wiped tears from her eyes.

"You can't tell me to do that. It's against my ethics to stop talking shit," Hernandez smiled as she signed and the blood from her signature coursed through the paper and strengthened it further.

Now that her people had signed, Kristen turned to the assembled prisoners. "I want to offer all of you a chance to redeem yourselves. Let's not pretend your actions in the past didn't hurt people, but you'd been fooled—tricked and betrayed.

"Each one of you endeavored to end the machinations of dragons intent on controlling human lives, but Constance has made it clear to me that in fact, your movement was coopted by one of the very dragons you sought to destroy.

"The Masked One has used all of you to stir up a war that neither side will win, simply so he can become more powerful. Everything he has had you do—all the dragon bullets and all the killing—was to hurt humanity, not save it. It was all to give that dragon an excuse to steal more power. The way to peace is not through violence but through peace. Join me!"

Her words drew grumbles and whispers from the prisoners. Looks were cast from one to another while heads shook in subtle disagreements and some jaws hardened. No one looked exactly eager to swear themselves to the dragon they'd worked so hard to destroy for so long.

Kristen had hoped for better, but she couldn't exactly blame them. It couldn't be easy to have a long-time enemy tell you that you had a choice to join her side—and, oh yeah, you've been tricked for ages and your mission is phony and you're not even smart enough to realize you've been had.

Still, she'd hoped for at least a few defectors to join sides with her. She really did believe in the terms Larry had written. Maybe she was simply optimistic, but she had thought the mages might believe too.

"I know how it sounds," Constance said. She stepped forward and away from the technomage leaders before she turned to face the others with her back to Kristen. "I know it's hard to think we've worked to fulfill someone else's dream, but we've all known that dragons are capable of this kind of deception. How many of you know a mage who wished to join our fight but couldn't because a dragon had already thrown a shackle on their wrist and denied them their power?"

A fresh round of mutters and grumbles followed this. Kristen had never thought of that aspect of their organization—that these mages might be fighting for more than merely the idea of equality and might be fighting for people they knew who had done nothing wrong besides having the same powers they had. Powers that—if they were dragons—would have been celebrated but—because they were human mages—were nothing but liabilities.

"We all have," Constance went on. "Every one of us knows of the persuasive powers of dragons. I'll be the first to admit they tricked me. I thought I was in control, but the Steel Dragon is right. All our agitating, all these bullets, and all the dragons we have killed haven't made the world more peaceful but less so. Humankind is closer to being attacked by the dragons than ever. And it's our fault."

"That doesn't make dragons innocent!" Havington hissed. "One lizard tricking us doesn't mean we should sign up with another one."

Kristen made a note of this. Perhaps it was he who often contacted the Masked One. Although she had begun to think that if any of the mages had regular contact with their mysterious puppet master, they probably didn't even realize it.

"I'll join forces with Kristen Hall not because she's the Steel Dragon but because she's still *Kristen Hall.* She's telling the truth about the Masked One, exactly like I thought she would when I told her about his existence."

Gasps indicated that none of the technomages had any prior knowledge of the mysterious dragon and that their leader had not only known but had kept the information from them.

"I know," she said to the tight-jawed, frowning mages, "I should have told you but I didn't. I thought we would be safer if this information wasn't spread. That's the kind of leader I was and that's why I failed you. I'll sign this document because Kristen doesn't lie to her people. She's open and honest and has always fought for the same thing we have. I'll sign to help undo the damage we have done and save as many people as possible before it's too late. That is, if you'll have me," Constance said and directed the last to Kristen.

"If you'll agree to the terms of this contract, I would proudly have you at my side," she said.

"That's better than I deserve." The woman's head was held high with pride, despite her words saying she didn't deserve it. She read the contract aloud, her voice strong and full of emotion, shed a tear when she pricked her finger, and signed. The contract sparkled when she wrote her name. The contract somehow knew she was a powerful mage.

"Once again, I offer all of you a chance at redemption," Kristen said. "There's no shame in acting as you did if you didn't know everything, but now that you do, it has to stop. You can still be heroes if you'll only help us to stop the Masked One and the war he's pushed us all toward."

"I don't see why we should trust you lizards," Havington said. She had no doubt his fists would be wreathed in flame if only he had the power to do so. "Dragons are the problem. This Masked One is a problem. The dragons we've killed were problems. You're a problem. I have no faith that beings who held onto their power for ten thousand years will relinquish it simply because we stop one of their more cretinous members."

"Then don't sign," she said simply. "If you truly believe I'm evil, don't sign. If you think I have caused more damage to humanity than the forces and attitudes I have fought against since the day I learned I was a dragon, then by all means, try to break your restraints and fight us. I won't let you go to kill me, exactly like none of you released the dragons you held in captivity. I won't begrudge you this choice if you make it, but this contract is your path to freedom and equality."

"The terms are fair," Constance said. "I hope you join me but if not, a yacht is on its way. It should be here in a week and you'll be able to cruise home in luxury with the dragons we imprisoned for so long. I know even looking them in the eyes would be too much for me, but if that's what you wish, so be it."

It felt like forever before the first mage broke ranks, but once she did, more than half of the others followed. To Kristen's surprise, the other technomage cell leader, Eric, was willing to sign and even led a group in chorus to recite the contract together as her team had done.

The only notable mage who refused was Havington. He scowled and said he was concerned that if he looked at Kristen the wrong way after signing, he'd explode. She didn't press him. While she thought he was a fool, she didn't want to turn this contract into something that bound people against their will. It would then be nothing more than another weapon. The world had enough of those.

There was one more notable encounter, though.

The Iron Dragon walked up with a scowl. Without her iron skin, Kristen could tell how closely they resembled each other. They had the same red curly hair—although Katrina's was slighter darker—the same freckles, and the same figure. She even thought they had the same shoe size.

"It's hard to look you in the face," the woman said to her.

"I thought the same thing," she responded.

"It's tough because you're a reminder of how weak I would be if I hadn't been raised by Constance. I don't like being reminded of that."

"It must be even worse to have those cuffs on, then, given how I put them on you after I kicked your ass."

Katrina smirked. "Only because we couldn't use our dragon forms."

She offered a mirrored facetious smirk. It was the exact expression she wore when she was trying to one-up someone. "Maybe," she said. "Are you going to sign or what?"

Katrina looked surprised at that. "Wait...you're okay with me signing this? You'd fight *with* me? Even after all our battles?"

Kristen shrugged. "I won't ask you to be my roommate or anything, and God knows I wouldn't take you out for beers anytime soon. But if you can agree to this contract, I'd be glad to have you on our side. You're a strong fighter."

"You got that right," the woman snapped.

"There's no weakness in admitting you're strong," she continued. "I've seen you fight. I know what you can do. Plus, I'd like to learn more about you. Together, we might be able to unlock even more of our powers."

"If this is some kind of trick—"

"You can read the contract again if you like," she said. "But if you think I'm smart enough to trick Constance and your leader Eric, how can you hope to stand against me?"

The Iron Dragon snorted at that, although she looked at the two mage leaders with wide eyes. Kristen saw the same bare trust in Katrina's eyes for the two mages she had as her parents. *How hard that must be,* she thought, *for your parents to also be your boss and for your job to be a terrorist.* She had no doubt that Katrina's life had been far more difficult than her own. Although they seemed to share much of their DNA, they did not share experiences and they would likely never see eye to eye. She hoped that would be enough for her sibling.

"I still don't trust you," Katrina said finally after she'd stared at the contract for what felt like forever. "But I trust them. If you'll have me, I'll sign."

"Are you sure?" she asked.

"My word is as strong as iron," she said with a cheeky smile.

"That's impressive. It's almost as strong as steel," Kristen replied, unable to help herself.

Katrina snorted again but she read the contract aloud, pricked her finger—obviously shocked that a simple knife could hurt her at all because of the cuffs—and signed it as well.

The mages who refused to sign were escorted to their cells. Kristen looked at the people who'd accepted this bond with her as their liege.

"I guess it's time to take those bracelets off."

Despite them not wearing them for very long, when they came off, it was evident that the mages had wilted under the stifling effects of the magic dampening cuffs.

Immediately, they perked up and flexed their magic powers by making dervishes of sand or shapes in the waves. She was pleased to see that none of them tried to test the contract by attacking any of her allies. It seemed a peace had been found, at least for now.

"All right. The first order of business," she said and clapped sharply like all this was perfectly fine and completely normal. "It's time to open that portal."

CHAPTER SIX

"Where to?" Constance asked.

It was a fair question, and one that Kristen didn't have an answer to.

"We need to operate under the assumptions that the Masked One is on the Dragon Council and that he'll try to push for war as soon as possible," she said.

"So we should find the Council and tell them not to listen to whoever the hell is pushing for war," Keith said as if it were so obvious.

"The problem is the Council doesn't exactly post their whereabouts," Stonequest explained. "Even when the world isn't on the precipice of a dragon-human war that could exterminate one or both lifeforms, they're extremely secretive. Do we assume the Masked One is on the North American Council?"

"We do," Constance confirmed.

"Then we can essentially narrow it down to the entire continent of North America," he finished.

"That doesn't exactly help," Hernandez complained.

"We will prepare the portal," Constance said with a nod and excused herself. "Tell us as soon as you have a destination."

"What about someplace like Kansas?" Jim asked. "That's the middle of the continent, give or take. If we go there, we'd be a few hours away from shit hitting the fan instead of days."

"I don't like that," Kristen said. "Hours is more than enough time to raze a city. We need a better plan."

"I think we should go to Detroit," Stonequest said. "Amythist said the SWAT forces have left and since we know the Dragon SWAT forces in Detroit, we can probably determine where they've gone to."

"Where do you think they've gone to?" Beanpole—normally so quiet—asked.

"If I was the Masked One—and I'm not," Heartsbane said, "I would try to mass all the fighting dragons. If he can build a force and convince them to fight together, it wouldn't matter where they're located. If he can make the SWAT teams a cohesive unit, that would be a force more than strong enough to wipe humanity out."

The massive satellite phone in Kristen's hand rang and she answered immediately. It was Brian. "This had better be urgent," she said sharply.

"It is," he said so loudly it caused the old device to feed back. "We have all kinds of activity in Detroit—and not good activity. Dragons have arrived and they're attacking the city! They've already torched Tiger Stadium and it looks like they're moving to the rest of downtown."

"Brian, this is important," she said. "Are they flying in formation? Can you tell?"

"No…no, I don't think so. Does anyone have a phone there? I can send video."

Keith dug one out of his pocket. "Am I the only guy with a water-proof case? Seriously? What do the rest of you do at water parks?"

"This is not the time, Keith!" Kristen snatched the phone from his hand. Brian had already patched a video feed through to it. Dragons swooped and attacked her city—that had been attacked by the damn mages only a week before. If this wasn't the work of the same architect, she would eat her tail.

"Stonequest," she said. "Do you know any of them? Are they Dragon SWAT?"

The dragon watched the screen carefully—far too carefully for her as he took forever—but he finally shook his head. "No. No, those aren't on any SWAT team I've ever met. In fact…" He paused as one swooped low and torched the camera that was recording them. Brian immediately switched to another. His sister guessed that he'd commandeered the city's traffic cameras.

"I've busted that one before—unauthorized duel. He's a lowlife named Coal. Or Char. Something like that. I've sent that asshole to prison twice."

"So it could merely be lowlifes causing trouble," Heartsbane said. "When the cat is away, the mice will play and all that."

"It's possible," Stonequest said.

"I don't care *why* they're attacking, only how we'll stop their asses," Kristen said and scowled when she recognized a dragon as well. It was one of those who had tried to beat her up in prison and who had worked for Obscura. "I guess Stonequest was right. We need to get to Detroit. Timeflash, you'll have to come with us as I think we'll need your abilities. Two of the younger dragons can stay with Larry."

"On it!" Keith shouted and ran down the beach to tell Constance, Larry, and the mages who were working on the portal.

She looked at her assembled team. Although battle-weary from fighting the mages, not one of them looked like they weren't ready for this fight.

"What are our orders?" Stonequest asked.

"We'll believe what Constance said about this being most of the technomages," she said with no better reason to do so other than what her gut told her. "It means I want dragons going through this portal as dragons. Once you're in Detroit, take to the air and try to give the rest of us a few minutes to get through and get clear. From what I saw of Zed's footage, the city's already in trouble, so every second counts."

"What are we waiting for?" Hernandez asked as she clipped grenades to her belt.

Kristen smiled. "I'm waiting for you all to grab your guns and get to that portal. The last one through has to stay here with Larry and listen to his jokes."

A few chuckles followed but mostly, people simply retrieved their gear. The dragons transformed and flew down the beach to where a ring of light was already forming in the red light of the sunset.

Kristen wanted to fight, but she knew she had to stick with her people to issue orders when they first went through.

A little frustrated, she watched as the mages snapped the portal open and there on the beach was Grand River Avenue.

The first thing she noticed about the city was how bright it was. Obviously, if it was sunset in the pacific, it was a different time of day in the Motor City.

The next thing she noticed were the flames. They were everywhere. Already, half the windows in the Michigan Building poured smoke, and the bottom floor seemed to be totally consumed by fires.

Her blood boiled as her city burned.

Any plans to watch as her dragons rushed through went up in flames.

"Come on! We fight today with new allies but that doesn't mean we fight any less hard! Now, what are we waiting for? Chaaaarge!" She transformed into her steel dragon body and led her forces through the portal.

CHAPTER SEVEN

The enemy dragons did not fail to recognize the magical gateway as a threat. As soon as Kristen came through it into downtown Detroit, she felt the heat of dragon flames on her back.

But she was the Steel Dragon. It would take more than a glancing jet of fire to harm her metal scales.

The heat did compromise her aerodynamics, though, so rather than soaring through and above the skyline of Detroit, she was forced to land.

The enemy dragons were poised to take advantage of this turn of events.

One of them drove into her back and she grimaced against the now familiar pain of dragon talons cutting through her steel scales to pierce her flesh.

The wound wasn't deep, fortunately. Her scales could be sliced by dragon talons but they blunted most of the damage. She still had sufficient strength and presence of mind to whip the dragon off her back with the ax-blade on the tip of her tail.

The force when her steel-covered tail pounded into her attacker was enough to launch him violently through the bottom floor of the Michigan Building. He leapt out, grinning and silhouetted by flames.

He was a runty little creature and perhaps a little bigger than half of Kristen's size. Something about his face triggered her memories.

"Didn't I kick your ass in prison?" she asked.

The dragon roared at her—thus proving that yes, she had indeed kicked his ass—and he tried to scramble past her and get to the portal she'd come from.

His foolish defiance had cost him precious seconds, however.

Already, the other SWAT Dragons were coming through. Stonequest knocked the attacker aside with a swipe of his claw and catapulted him into a car that he crushed with the force of his impact. Although he was somewhat diminutive compared to his fellows, he was still more than big enough to deliver that kind of damage. It was a reminder to Kristen that the fight would not be an easy one. Her forces had to protect the city and defeat the dragons. The attackers only had to burn them all.

"Stonequest, cover that portal!" she ordered.

He led Heartsbane, Emerald, Lumos, and Timeflash into a tight circle above the portal. The other less experienced dragons emerged next.

"Choose a target and stick to them. I want dragon on dragon to keep them focused on you and not the city," she ordered.

Despite the strange request—strange to them, anyway, as they were not used to protecting anything but themselves—the dragons obeyed. Each of them targeted one of the marauders and surged with claw and tail as they released blasts of fire that did little except annoy their opponents.

"Stonequest, they need support!"

He nodded and broke away from his other SWAT team members. It was great to have more dragons on their team, but none of the new recruits had much combat experience. Their lack meant they wouldn't be able to do much besides distract their opponents for long.

And much needed to be done.

All over, the city was on fire. Police and firefighters raced frantically to rescue people who were trapped in buildings, cars, or simply frozen in fear. Every human had always known this could happen.

Living in a world with dragons meant you lived on their whims. It was a constant reminder that you were mortal but still, it didn't exactly prepare anyone for six dragons to simply rain fire on a city like it was the end times.

"Holy shit!" Drew shouted as he led the human forces through the portal. "What exactly are we supposed to do about this?"

Kristen was terrified that the question was way too big, but she also knew that as a leader, she had to answer it. "You know some of the cops here. Call your old captain and tell her you're here to help to get people to safety. We'll handle the dragons. I want you to get as many people as you can out of here."

He looked at the smoke-choked, fire-filled sky. "Yes ma'am," he said without batting an eyelid.

As more and more humans came through, Drew issued orders. He'd put everyone in squads long before and now sent those groups to help evacuate buildings and clear escape paths. Any of the enemy dragons who tried to veer away from the battle were met with a storm of bullets.

Kristen hadn't ordered her team to equip with dragon bullets. She probably should have, but she was too concerned about friendly fire problems. Still, the enemy were far more wary of the guns than they would have been a year before. They hesitated when they approached the human forces, which of course gave her dragons time to catch them.

Stonequest in particular was able to seize the opportunity created by one of these hesitations. He powered into the back of a dragon who looked like his skin was made of gravel and held him tightly as the two spun above the city. His adversary couldn't escape but he wasn't about to give in without a fight either. He slashed at his attacker's chest and drew blood. Stonequest didn't flinch. Instead, he kept his dive carefully controlled so they avoided any buildings. Then, at the last moment, he transformed his entire body into marble and landed on top of his opponent.

The force drove the dragon into the street below him, created a massive crater, and left the raider utterly motionless. Whether dead or unconscious, Kristen didn't know and Stonequest didn't seem to care. With one threat neutralized, he launched once again to give chase to another target.

Kristen turned to the portal as the mages—many of them former enemies—came through. Finally, Constance, Katrina, and Eric entered Detroit. Larry waved from the other side as if he were disembarking for a vacation instead of being left in charge of a group of prisoners. The gate closed a moment later and he was gone.

"Mages, I need you to put out as many of these flames as possible."

"You heard the dragon!" Constance said and led her forces away to attack the fires.

Only one didn't follow the order—a man with a mustache who had only begrudgingly signed the contract.

"This is what we were fighting to stop!" he screamed. Electricity crackled from his temples, down his arms, and wound around his knuckles in the shape of barbed wire. "Dragons kill people and we're supposed to serve you? This is fucking crazy! Crazy, I tell you."

Rather than following Constance, he turned on Kristen, no doubt confident that his electrical powers could get through her steel skin.

He managed only about five steps toward her before he exploded. One second, he was a man crackling with power and in the next, he was nothing but a sooty stain on the street.

"Nice job, Steel." Katrina sneered at her, still in her human body. "The first of our mages to die and it was because of your contract."

"Do you want to be next? You promised you wouldn't try to kill me. Do you want to see what happens if you do?" she asked.

Katrina made no response and apparently honored her word far better than the dead mage had. In her moment of hesitation, Kristen took one last opportunity to assess the battle before she decided where she would enter the fight.

The mages were making real progress against the fires. Constance used her power over the winds to smother the flames. Rather than blow wind at the fires, she could use it to keep fresh air away from the flames. This turned raging infernos into smoldering embers that firefighters were then able to extinguish with their hoses.

Eric also seemed to have a favorite kind of magic and used it to extinguish fires. When they'd fought him, he'd thrown a thousand tiny needles at them. He used a similar technique now to rip flaming boards apart and send the embers high into the sky so they burned away as nothing but fireworks washed out in the early morning sun.

Other, less powerful mages worked together to extinguish burning buildings. Those with augmented strength asked firefighters what walls could be punched through to give their hoses better access to the flames. Those with elemental abilities either doused flames or tried to contain them.

It looked like the city would survive if the dragons overhead weren't allowed to do anything else to it.

"Dragon SWAT!" Kristen roared.

"Yes, ma'am?" they replied from wherever they were in the chaos.

"Are you ready to take out the trash?"

They all bellowed an affirmative except Heartsbane, who shouted, "I thought you'd never ask!"

"What about you?" Kristen asked Katrina and watched her reaction carefully. She was still far from trusting the Iron Dragon fully. The spell was in place so she knew she couldn't attack her directly, but she didn't seem as ready to fight with her as Constance was. She still felt like she needed to get to know her sister better before she could offer her real trust.

Thankfully, it seemed that Katrina was more than willing to prove her reliability this time around. "I've spent my entire life protecting humans against dragons who have overstepped their bounds," she growled, looked at the sky, and assumed her dragon shape. "I'm more than happy to stop a few more."

The two took to the air together.

As they gained height, Kristen watched the former members of Dragon SWAT bring the fight to the rogue dragons.

It was an amazing sight.

Before, it had been like watching gulls fight each other. Her new recruits could fight well enough, but so could the rogues. Neither had been able to gain much traction or advantage over the other side.

Now, it was more like watching peregrine falcons hunt pigeons.

The members of Dragon SWAT had been trained for years to fight against dragons and better yet, they knew the tactics of some of those they now fought.

Heartsbane closed in on a long, sinuous dragon who turned in midair and tried to spray her with some kind of viscous sludge. The SWAT dragon clearly had experience with the expectorant as she closed her wings around her face so they were coated in the gunk rather than her face.

She landed to clean the crap from her wings, annoyed but not hurt. "When you said trash, I didn't think you meant literal *slime,*" she groused.

Kristen didn't mind that she was temporarily grounded. It gave her an opportunity to attack a target with Katrina at her side.

"The slimy one is ours," she ordered.

The Iron Dragon nodded.

Together, they pumped their wings between skyscrapers and gained altitude until they were above them. Although they'd never worked together before, there was instant grace to the way the two dragons flew as a unit. Both could turn their bodies to metal but knew not to unless they needed to defend themselves or until they were above another dragon and could use the additional weight to aid in a dive assault.

This meant they moved the same way, tried to gain altitude, and turned their metal skin on and off intermittently to block blasts from the other dragons that battled all around them.

"You use your skin well," Kristen shouted at Katrina as they drew closer to the slime dragon.

"You too. I can almost forget that you have hardly any experience with it. You need to guard your back legs better, by the way. That hip joint can be brutalized if you let it—"

"My back?" Kristen asked and felt the teeth of another dragon sink into her thigh.

It seemed the rogue dragons weren't particularly keen on fighting the law enforcement dragons that some of them had faced and failed against multiple times. Not when there was a dragon present who many had a personal grudge against.

"You coward! You're the piece of shit who tried to shiv me!" she yelled at the dragon clinging desperately to her leg with its teeth.

"Mfuufm moo!" he snarled in return, his mouth full of her flesh that rendered the words unintelligible. Still, it didn't take a linguist to realize that he had used that simplest of all human curses against her—the f-bomb.

She couldn't shake him, though. The bastard had sunk his teeth deep in her leg and her efforts to dislodge him proved futile.

The Iron Dragon plummeted and pounded into his back.

The air was knocked from his lungs and he fell, Katrina on top of him, until she crushed him into the pavement below, her iron body multiplying the force of the blow to lethal levels.

Kristen was thankful. It was always good to have someone stop a dragon from ripping your leg off, but she also realized that it meant Katrina would be out of this for the next couple of minutes. It took time for a metal dragon to gain height, and while she did so, she and the four dragons harrying her were already high above the city.

They attacked with about as much grace as they had in prison. She couldn't be sure if these were the same ones who had attacked her with makeshift prison weapons when she'd been falsely accused and incarcerated without her powers, but she decided she'd go ahead and fight them like they were.

"Metal pipe!" she yelled as if greeting an old friend when a gray-scaled dragon with black, broken-looking teeth led the charge.

She called on the training Lumos had given her, struck out with her tail, and swung it into the joint connecting his wing to his body. Her adversary shrieked in pain when the ax-blade tail connected, then plunged like a bird with a wing broken by a jet plane.

Emerald dove after him and sank his claws into the dragon's back. His talons caused pain but also spared his life when he guided him to the top of a building and forced him to transform.

Three more remained and none seemed inclined to retreat.

"I'm sorry, it's been such a long time. How did I kick your ass?"

Kristen asked a red dragon who left trails of smoke from his wings in his wake.

"I almost choked you to death with a chain, bitch." He directed great plumes of smoke at her. It didn't hurt but it left her blind in a cloud of gas that made it hard to breath and therefore do all the other things breathing made possible. "Now you'll choke for real."

Kristen would have felt bad about her dragon SWAT teammates attacking him if not for two reasons. The first was that the dragon engaged her with as much help as he could get, so why should she do differently? The second was the horrible pun.

Because of these two reasons, she didn't feel bad when she heard a shriek from her formerly smug adversary.

She pumped her wings and finally moved clear of the smoke cloud. Lumos had torn a huge hole in the dragon's wing, captured him with his claws, and now guided him to the top of another building.

The last two dragons didn't seem so keen on a reunion.

With a glance and a pulse of their aura at each other, their intentions became clear.

They wanted to get the fuck out of there.

Unfortunately for them, they decided to do that together. Kristen, Stonequest, Heartsbane, and Timeflash were able to pursue them without having to go in separate directions. It didn't take long to catch up with the first. He must have been injured at some point as one of his wings flapped more sluggishly than the other to slow him sufficiently for them to overtake him easily.

Stonequest took hold of him and said something in the dragon's ear that must have been quite persuasive, because he stopped trying to flee and attempted to glide as he was led to the top of another building.

That left only one dragon. Despite the odds stacked against this one, he continued the attempt to flee and pumped his wings furiously to increase his speed.

Amazingly, it began to outpace Kristen and her team. Maybe his power was quickness or his slighter frame simply allowed him to move faster. Whatever the cause, she thought for a moment that he would elude them and she muttered in frustration.

Moments later, the dragon appeared to simply make impact with an invisible wall.

To her, it looked like something out of a cartoon—like someone had painted a fake sky and the dragon had thought it was open space when in fact it was a decoy colored with ACME paint.

To the dragons—she discovered later—it was far more obvious what had happened. A mage had stepped in.

Kristen saw it too when she thought more clearly. The air had a blue shimmer—the same color of the shields Amy and Larry used to block bullets. The dragon had powered into this barrier and Time-flash grasped him in her talons as he began to fall. The battle was over.

The Steel Dragon coasted Earthward and was met by Amy. This was only a little odd because the girl met her a hundred feet off the ground. She rode her skateboard, which was weirder than if she had been flying. A quirk of the young mage's enormous power was that she couldn't lift herself. She had to stand on other objects or use her clothing.

"I'm sorry it took so long." The girl smirked, fully aware that she had stopped a dragon in its tracks without breaking a sweat. "Constance wasn't kidding about that portal sapping my strength. It took me a full minute to build enough power to stop that asshole."

Kristen soared past the mage and marveled at her power. "Come on. We have a city to put back together."

CHAPTER EIGHT

The chaos of the battle was over and Kristen issued orders to restore the city where they could. The mages had already proven useful in battle but truly seeing them help mend things in the aftermath was an even more inspiring reason for them to be on the side of a peaceful humanity.

Those with telekinetic powers used them to patch brick, stack damaged cars, and move rubble so construction crews would be able to get to work immediately.

Timeflash moved among them in her human form, giving tips to some and asking for help from others. Her power was unique in the dragon world as she could put objects back together in their original condition. She focused on the Michigan building, and Kristen watched in delight as windows mended themselves and smoke billowed into the building to reconstitute itself into chairs, paintings, and furniture.

None of the mages had this skill, but they could augment Timeflash's abilities, and those who helped her looked about as thrilled as Kristen did. It was pure magic to see something completely destroyed returned to its former glory.

Unfortunately, the dragon's powers were anything but limitless.

After fixing the Michigan Building, she was almost spent. She helped get a fire station in working order—although she was unable to remove any of the soot stains there—and could do no more.

Still, between her abilities and the power of the mages, the city returned to something resembling normalcy. Windows still had to be mended and many insurance claims would be filed for wrecked cars, but at least the streets were navigable.

Kristen left the clean-up crew to check on their four prisoners. The two dragons who had been pounded into the ground hadn't survived the impact, but the other four had been taken into custody. They now all wore bracelets that only hours ago had been worn by mages who had tried to kill dragons. Despite the turn of events, none of the four seemed particularly thankful to be captured by mages instead of killed.

They all stood sullenly on the roof of Dragon SWAT headquarters in the old Capital Square building in downtown Detroit. Kristen landed and looked fondly at the rooftop. She couldn't count the number of missions that had begun there, nor how many times she'd been reprimanded by Stonequest when he'd been her boss rather than the other way around.

"Stonequest, is there a reason why we haven't started processing these dragons? I seem to remember some fairly uncomfortable cells they might all find familiar."

"Actually…" He looked alarmed. "There is." The stone dragon gestured toward the rooftop entrance to the building where Atramento stood. The mage looked more exhausted than she had ever seen him. He was master of the Paper Dungeon, the bureaucratic center for Detroit's Dragon SWAT team, and managed much of the paperwork of the Midwest as well.

Kristen couldn't imagine what could have compelled him to leave the station he had always seemed almost obsessed with, especially with the mountain of paperwork that would be needed. They had to process these four dragons as well as the two dead ones, and all the damage they'd caused to the city.

"Atramento?" she asked. "Is everything all right?"

He looked at her, his robes a little limp, and the tattoos on his head, face and hands still made him look otherworldly despite the expression of defeat on his face.

"They said they let me stay because of my service," he said weakly. "Like it was a reward to be left in the wreckage."

"Wreckage?" she asked. It wasn't like him to talk about his well-oiled filing cabinet of a floor as anything but perfection.

"That's all they left. They destroyed any records that had to do with dragon imprisonment. Already, requests have begun to come in for dragons who have been 'falsely imprisoned without paperwork.' It's disgusting." The mage shook his head as if there were no affront worse to society than that of false bureaucratic claims. "Even those I would process. There's a procedure, of course, for missing documents, even if they were…burned. But I can't even do that."

"Why not?" she asked, although she feared she already knew the answer.

Atramento choked out a sob as he raised his wrist. On it, he wore a heavy cuff. "They put this on me. After all I've done, they put this on me." He uttered another sob and did not seem to be doing well at all. She didn't think he'd even noticed that the city had been attacked.

"What is it?" Amy asked and glowered at the cuff in distaste.

"It's a cuff like they use for prisoners. It blocks my magic—all my magic. They came here and ordered every mage to put one on, the brutes. We were already fitted with cuffs that wouldn't let us move against them. They didn't need to do this."

"Who?" Kristen asked.

"Dragons," Atramento told her sharply, his tone venomous.

"Where is everyone else?" Kristen asked.

"They took them all away. I asked where so I could update forwarding addresses, but they wouldn't tell me. Do you know what a nightmare this is? Even with my powers, this would have been difficult to fix, but without them, I…I fear I may be held accountable for a dereliction of duties." He looked more concerned about this black mark on his record than the dragons were at the prospect of being imprisoned. Maybe they knew something she didn't.

"But why take the mages? They can't hurt dragons. That's the whole point of the cuffs," she said. "Do they think they can be used as weapons against people?"

Stonequest shook his head. "I doubt that. It's probably the opposite. They are rounding up every known mage because dragons *don't* trust them, not because they do. They'll keep the mages out of the way so they can't decide to switch sides and fight with the humans during the culling."

The word "culling" made her blood run cold. She knew Stonequest had only said it because he'd heard it used in this context before. He'd endeavored to keep the dragon bullets secrets because he feared this exact outcome. Part of her wished he'd been successful, although the wiser part of her knew the mages had to be stopped and that they were on the only path they could be on.

"But mages can't hurt dragons," Kristen said.

He shrugged. "That used to be the case, but the technomages have proven that some can escape detection. No doubt the other dragons think this means these mages could escape. They must be holding them somewhere to keep them out of the action."

That was a sobering thought. What kind of holding place were all those mages in? If they were detained, was it humanely or had the dragons thrown them in a cell and simply planned to do away with them as well?

She was certain of one thing. This was bigger than the six dragons who had openly attacked the city. While she had expected it to be, she had held out hope that they were simply dragons acting out because SWAT was gone.

"Do you think they're being treated well?" Kristen asked.

Stonequest's expression said very eloquently that he thought this very unlikely. "There's always been talk in the Dragon Council and demands that all the mages be exterminated. They've led two rebellions before this, after all, and were damn close to winning them even without dragon bullets. Now, with the bullets plus Amy's insane power, I'm sure they're taking the threat of mages even more seriously."

"But this is crazy. We finally have the technomages on our side so the dragons move against the other ones?"

"You must remember," Lumos said, "that for centuries, we worked to come to terms with the threats of mages. Ever since the rebellion, dragons were wary. It took considerable time to get past that and suddenly, every living dragon has seen Amy defeat multiple dragons with her power on TV. It's not exactly comforting."

Kristen didn't know what to do with that other than work to find where the mages were so she could ensure they weren't being treated cruelly. Or worse, that they had already been killed. "Do we have any ideas where they could be?"

"Perhaps they took them to the prison where I was held?" Constance stepped forward and asked. "I know the technomages… dispatched the guards, but that prison was both ample in size and well-enchanted. I was not able to escape on my own. Other mages would be unlikely to be able to do so either."

Lumos waved his hand dismissively at the idea. "That location is compromised now. It's been a long time since a dragon prison was publicly discovered, but I can assure you the Dragon Council will have ordered it abandoned or demolished. Now that they are aware that it's known to technomages, they'll treat it as a liability, not an asset. Plus, with the dragon bullets, they'll have to assume some of the human governments know about it as well and that has to be treated as a threat."

The woman looked shocked. "But it must have taken decades to build it and put in all those magic fortifications."

"Centuries, more like," Lumos agreed. "But you have the right of it. It represents a substantial loss to the North American Dragon Council. I'm sure they have at least one other prison on the continent, and it wouldn't be outside the realm of possibility to consider that the mages were sent overseas to another prison. I know there are at least a half dozen like this built around the world. The one in Antarctica is particularly difficult to access."

"So you're saying we have no idea where they've been taken?" Kristen demanded.

"They could be tracked," Atramento said sadly. "If only their magic wasn't completely blocked. Like dragon auras, every mage has a particular…style of magic much like a fingerprint. I know those who were taken well enough to track them but not with them cuffed like that. It's so cruel." He shook his head. "Like putting earplugs and a blindfold on a person after years of loyal service."

Kristen's phone rang and the screen flashed with the secure number of the Dragon Council. She cursed, then answered the call. "This is the Steel Dragon speaking."

"You and your dragons are requested to report in person immediately."

She knew Brian had already verified the number, the voice on the other end, and the encryption on the call, so she could trust this was someone from the Dragon Council. It fit with the general rudeness anyway.

After a grimace of irritation, she couldn't resist a little rudeness of her own. "Where exactly am I supposed to rush off to?"

Her phone beeped and she pulled it away to see that they'd sent her a location. It would be annoying if it weren't impressive. She told herself that the dragon on the other end probably had a team of techies helping her.

"Is this in response to what happened in Detroit? Because I assure you that situation is under control," Kristen said.

"We wish to speak no further over this telephone connection," the dragon said disdainfully. It might have been the leader of the Dragon Council herself, Shimmerclaw, but she couldn't tell because they obviously felt uncomfortable talking on the phone.

"We'll leave immediately," she said.

The line went dead.

Kristen sighed and rubbed her face. She was heartily sick of jumping whenever the Dragon Council said so, but she saw no alternative. If all Dragon SWAT had been called away somewhere, it could only be the Council's doing. They would likely know something about the mages and then there was the issue of the Masked One to consider.

This was likely all his doing if—as Constance and Lumos both suspected—he was a member of the Dragon Council. Hopefully, she could find some clue to his true identity.

"All right, dragons, we're up!" She told the members of Dragon SWAT on the roof. "I want you to round up the rookies, get them circling, and for the love of dragon's fire, I want tight formations. The Council needs to see we're as professional if not more so than any of their other forces."

"For how long?" Stonequest asked.

"We'll leave in ten," she said, realizing what she had to do. It was time to put her full trust in both her new allies and the contract that bound them. "I need to talk to Drew and Amy before we go."

She found Drew in the streets below, helping rescue people from half-collapsed buildings. It pained her to pull him away from the work but managing a group of former enemy mages was a task too important to leave to anyone else.

"So if anything goes wrong, contact Brian and he'll let me know. The contract should hold them, but I don't want to put all my faith in it," she said as she finished explaining the situation.

"Yes, ma'am," Drew said. "Although between you and me, I think we lost the only one who wasn't committed to the cause. Most of the technomages seemed more than willing to defend regular folks from dragons."

"That's good to hear," she said before seeking Amy out.

She found the mage clearing rubble as easily as a regular person might sweep the floor of crumbs. "Amy, I'm going with the dragons. They asked for only dragons to come, but I'd feel much more comfortable if you'd come too."

"Are you expecting trouble?" the girl asked.

"Not really, no, but I would much rather that you come with us to give me peace of mind. It would be better than you staying here and pissing these mages off any further. Remember, that contract binds all of us. That means you too."

"Ah, I wouldn't do anything but show a couple of them how much stronger I am."

"Please don't," she said.

"Fine," Amy replied, her expression sulky.

The necessary orders given, Kristen retrieved her phone and called Brian.

"Zed here…go."

"I need you to keep working on the mage problem," she said. "We need to discover where they're being held."

"Whatever you say, boss, but isn't that why you're going to the Dragon Council?"

"I hope so," she answered, "but they ordered me there. That doesn't necessarily mean they want to give me answers. If they're not forthcoming—"

"We need to find them ourselves," he finished for her.

"Right. I want to trust the dragons but this mage-dragon rivalry is way older and far bigger than I realized. I want a location on these mages before the dragons decide to do something horrible to them."

"You mean if they haven't already," he said.

"Just find the mages," she ordered.

Rather than dwell on the uncomfortable point he'd made, she changed into her dragon form and took to the skies to lead the other dragons on their trip to the Dragon Council.

CHAPTER NINE

Despite Brian checking and rechecking the location the Dragon Council had sent to Kristen, he still couldn't make sense of it. He told her as much as he spoke into an earpiece they'd devised for dragons to wear in flight so they could still use the magic that was cellphones.

It appeared—and she could now confirm this in person—that the location was in the middle of Hudson Bay, north of most of Canada and definitely north of the warm part. The problem was that it wasn't an island. It was merely a position somewhere in the northern part of the bay, far enough offshore that as they flew across Hudson Bay, they saw nothing but glaciers. No land and no coasts were present to indicate anything that might suggest a dragon meeting.

It was so cold that Amy, despite having the magical power to use her skateboard as a levitation device that flew as fast as any of the dragons, asked Kristen if she could ride on her back to warm herself on the hot scales of a dragon beneath her. She didn't mind and thought it was probably smarter to have her riding instead of flying anyway. This entire war had become about mages, after all, and Amy —despite having served her loyally—had killed two dragons at her home and fought off a couple more with her telekinetic powers in

Canada. Much of that had been captured on camera and all of it had made international news.

"Is it possible they want us to meet on a ship?" Kristen asked her dragons.

"I doubt it," Stonequest said, although he didn't sound confident. "Dragons aren't particularly trusting of tech and boats totally count as tech."

"I'm sure there's an island," Lumos said.

"But how could there be?" she asked. "Brian scoured the entire area via satellite. He found nothing."

"Human and dragon eyes can be fooled by means both magic and mundane," the old dragon said. "Do you think your electric eyes are different, even though they're much farther away?"

She snorted a laugh. "I think it's a little ridiculous to think that dragons—beings who you said hardly trust tech—have managed to stop the entire planet from seeing—"

Kristen never finished her sentence as they flew into view of an island that—according to modern science—should not be there at all.

As far as a location to hide on went, this one seemed a good candidate. It was tiny, hardly any larger than the squat, thick-walled castle that covered almost every part of its surface. Truly, more of the island seemed to be towering cliffs than actual land. Seabirds in great numbers clung to the cliffs, no doubt counting the days until they would depart for the south once more. Ice and frost coated the castle's walls, while snow dotted its ramparts.

For a moment, it was lost in a mass of clouds.

Kristen emerged from the clouds to find wings of dragon guards flanking her team.

"Hold your course!" a dragon with a broken horn bellowed at her.

"No problem," she responded as that seemed like the only reasonable thing to say given that so many dragons were now in the sky around them. Changing course would seriously risk a collision with at least one of them.

Four wings—each with a dozen dragons—escorted her force of close to a dozen. They flew on both their left and right, above and below, so her team was boxed in. If the others chose to attack, she knew it wouldn't go well, especially since most of her force were dragons who had signed up to help fight with little combat experience.

"Land at the gate to the castle and take your human form. Any breach of the airspace above the castle will be taken as an act of aggression and will result in retaliation. Do I make myself clear?"

Again, Kristen answered with the obvious, "Yup," and maintained her course. She couldn't help but feel relieved that she'd told Katrina to stay behind. Her thought was that the Iron Dragon might stay true to her word in Detroit where she was surrounded by her allies and Kristen's shit-talking and endearing human friends. Here, though, she couldn't imagine her cooperating so easily.

She descended slowly and landed at the gate in front of the castle, where she transformed into her human form once Amy climbed off her back. It seemed the young woman was wise enough to know to not use her magic powers at this particular juncture. The huge crossbows and massive javelins aimed at them made it quite clear that the dragons prowling the ramparts were more than ready to attack.

One was there waiting for her. "State your name and purpose," he said and his voice boomed despite being in his human form.

"Investigator Kristen Steel." She held her badge out to prove it.

"Ah, it's so nice to see a fellow investigator," he said, examined the badge, and extended his hand for a human-style greeting. "They call me Sharpeye in English. Lady Shimmerclaw is expecting you. Your dragons are expected, of course. If you would all please follow me into the courtyard, refreshments will be provided for your human bodies to eat. We know the flight across the bay is a cold one." His accent sounded like it was from the other side of the Arctic. He studied Amy. "Your…servant is welcome to eat in the courtyard too, although the food is cooked to dragons' taste."

Sharpeye smiled but she understood the implicit threat. *Come inside. Stay in your smaller, weaker body while all these big tough dragons in their dragon bodies watch you from the ramparts. If one of your people sneezes without permission, you're dead.*

"Thank you," Kristen said, not sure what other choice she had. It was obvious they couldn't fight their way out of there, not without casualties. That left talking, which meant that yet again, her people's safety was on her shoulders.

"Excellent." He nodded and gestured for them to follow him inside.

She darted one last look at her team. They seemed wary, but Stonequest gave her a small nod to tell her to continue. They had her back, whatever was coming.

The gate was hauled open by two of the most enormous dragons she had ever seen. It was made of iron at least a couple of feet thick.

"I've never seen so many dragons in one place," Kristen said to Investigator Sharpeye once they'd left the rest of her dragons eating grilled seal and fish.

His eyes twinkled. She wondered what he could see with a name like Sharpeye. "Indeed!" He sounded excited. "What you see is a gathering of all the fighting dragons of this continent! Every—well, nearly every—member of the Dragon SWAT teams from across the country are here as well as every investigator, plus a few informal militias as well. We even have a few dragons from the other continents to help balance our forces globally and better coordinate." He sounded like he was describing a convention instead of a warband.

"Why are they all here? I would think they'd need to be in their stations," she said as they moved farther into the castle. The courtyard being open to the air made much more sense. Much of the structure was dug into the island and grew colder as the icy waters of Hudson Bay pressed in on the stone all around them.

"Gatherings like this are happening on every continent except Antarctica," Sharpeye boasted. "Soon, the dragons will strike and wipe out humanity's militaries and infrastructure. You and your forces have been summoned to join the fight. We still have dragon armor here from the last war. You'll be given first choice, and once you see the selection you can choose other dragons who have served you well enough to have earned the right to wear it."

Kristen stopped dead in her tracks. "I'm not here to enlist in a war against humanity."

"Enlist?" His excitement gave way to confusion. "There is no enlisting in a war like this. You are dragon. You will fight with us. If you do not..." He left the sentence unfinished and smirked as if he knew full well there was no need to complete the threat. She didn't need him to tell her that her people would be killed.

Knowing this would not be solved with Sharpeye, she took her badge out again. "I demand to be brought to the Dragon Council."

He looked wary. "Do you refuse your orders?"

"I do not refuse them, but this cannot proceed as planned without the information I must share with the Council. That is my right as an investigator, is it not?"

For the first time since they'd been talking, Sharpeye scowled at her. "That is your right, of course. Follow me. This way." He spun on his heel and took her up a staircase and down a hall they had already walked past.

"Here we are," he said once they arrived at a pair of massive wooden doors inlaid with gold in the shapes of dragons laying waste to a town. "I will be outside, listening and watching."

She wanted to know how much he'd see from behind closed doors, but she didn't say anything. While she didn't much like this Sharpeye, she also didn't want him to regard her as a threat. Asking about the specifics of his powers seemed like a good way to make him suspicious. His name implied that he might have some kind of ability related to sight, though.

With her shoulders back and her head high, she opened the doors and entered, ready to present her case for stopping—or at least delaying—war with humans. She was ready to face the seven members of the North American Dragon Council as well as members of the other bodies that governed other continents and provinces.

But when she entered, most of the members of the Dragon Council weren't present. Only three dragons were there and the first was the platinum dragon Shimmerclaw.

The second was a dragon by the name of Lord Boneclaw. Kristen didn't know much about him other than that he was one of the oldest dragons on the Council. He was easy to recognize because of the scars on his face. He and Shimmerclaw were both old enough to be The Masked One, according to Lumos anyway.

While she had never met the third, she'd seen him before. He was massive—bigger than Shadowstorm, who'd been huge. She guessed he was more than seven feet tall, with massive shoulders and arms as thick as most bodybuilder's legs, although it was hard to tell since he was seated in an ornate chair. Despite being in his human form, crystalline spikes protruded from his shoulders. He turned to face her and his scowl was made cruel by eyebrows and a thin beard that seemed to both be made of crushed diamonds.

"Greetings, Council…" Kristen said and used her aura to communicate her confusion at only seeing three members when over a hundred dragons were outside preparing for war.

"You still speak to the Full Council," Shimmerclaw said and gestured to a wide monitor and a camera set up on a tripod that was linked to the computer via a cable. It was extremely disorienting for Kristen to see a web camera and a group of attractive human-faced dragons looking at her in this ancient castle. Communicating via carrier pigeon seemed more appropriate for their setting.

"Investigator Steel, it's a pleasure to see you, even given the circumstances." Shimmerclaw greeted her with a slight bow.

"Thank you, my lady and lords. You honor me," she replied and bowed deeply. Lord Boneclaw nodded in appreciation. He had a simpering, weak mouth that looked like it mostly wanted to agree with whatever had been said. The spiked dragon hardly moved his chin in greeting.

"I must say I am surprised. I thought I was coming to find out about the whereabouts of the Dragon SWAT members and the mages who were abducted from my city," she said and focused on keeping her aura from making her seem accusatory.

"No one was abducted," Lord Boneclaw said quickly with a glance at the other two dragons. "They were taken into protective custody. If the humans were clever, they could have bombed that building and all those mages would be dead."

"I still say they should be executed *now*," the other dragon said.

"That would be an act of war, Diamontus," Shimmerclaw said.

"We are at war," Diamontus retorted. "The vote is cast and you and the other cowards lost."

"Now, Diamontus, this is no time to gloat or name-call," Boneclaw said through a plastic smile.

"You voted for war too, Boneclaw. You no longer need to play the ambassador," his colleague growled.

"Forgive me," Kristen said and tried to sound like she meant it. "But why would the Council vote to go to war now? My team was successful on our mission. We finally stopped the technomages."

The scowl on Diamontus' face somehow grew ever darker. "You've delayed the vote long enough, Shimmerclaw. The numbers are against you. We fly, and they burn. What value is democracy if a vote is not honored?"

"What say you, Lord Boneclaw?" Shimmerclaw inquired of the weak-spined Council member.

"You know I didn't support rushing into this war," Boneclaw said and Kristen felt a wave of relief wash over her until he continued. "But...the vote has been cast. I *am* concerned about setting a precedent of overturning a vote. Even if it seems the right thing in this particular situation, I don't think it would be wise to undo centuries of tradition."

"A vote can be cast again if new information is available," the woman said rather stiffly. "Lady Steel, how does your mission fare?"

"We don't have time for this!" Diamontus raged. "Our dragons are massing into armies and preparing for war with humanity. We cannot stop what has already been put into motion."

Shimmerclaw clenched her teeth at this but rather than saying anything, she cast a look at Boneclaw.

The thin, bony man with the scars on his face kept his gaze locked on Kristen. He still had the same agreeable smile on his face but something hard was visible in his eyes. "I would like to hear what the investigator has done," he said.

It was the opportunity she had been waiting for. She exuded confidence with her aura and addressed the Council, mindful that others watched her via the camera. "We have defeated the last of the mage cells. Their weapons have been confiscated and we've recovered the dragons they had raised in their labs and used to make the dragon bullets. The fighting is over and the technomages are finished. *We don't need to go to war!*" She couldn't help but sound excited at the last part. Hopefully, losing her composure for the sake of preventing war would be acceptable to the stiff-backed Dragon Council.

"Well, this is excellent news, indeed!" Shimmerclaw beamed.

"What of their leaders?" Boneclaw asked. "If even one of those at the top is free, they can simply retrain more mages."

"Three of them, including Constance Vigil and the Iron Dragon, entered into a magical contract with me. They can no longer move against dragons unless they're defending regular humans."

"That's poppycock!" Diamontus roared, although he looked intrigued. "No one has convinced a mage to sign a magical contract in centuries."

"No one *had,* sir. I left the document in Detroit, but I assure you their leaders won't move against us."

"And there were only the three?" Boneclaw asked.

"One of them, a mage by the name of Neil Havington, refused to sign. He will be transported via ship with the other mages who wouldn't sign the contract."

The almost skeletal dragon nodded—as if he somehow expected this of Havington—but a moment later, his weak smile returned. "My congratulations on your successes and efforts. I know those mages must have greatly valued their dragon prisoners. I wonder at the wording of this contract if you convinced them to agree to it despite taking their source of weapons away from them."

"The weapons are nothing to them. They simply used them to stand against a force they saw as unbeatable," Kristen explained quickly. "They won't use them again. They can't, not with the contract I bound them to."

"How marvelous," Boneclaw said. "The investigator we put in charge of stopping these mages has now enlisted them for her…what exactly is the point of your force now that you've stopped the mages?"

"Apparently to stand against an unbeatable force!" Diamontus roared as he pushed to his feet and displayed his full height. The massive human suggested how big he must be in his dragon form.

"The Steel Dragon has never moved against dragon kind," Shimmerclaw said placatingly. "She stopped the technomages to protect us. Truly, this is a boon, Lady Steel. I move to vote again based on this new information. This completely changes our calculations." She turned to the camera and the other dragons who'd stopped whatever preparations they were making to watch the exchange.

"But we *have* voted," Boneclaw whined. "Perhaps this can change our tactics, but does this change the threat the mages have created by distributing the weapons to regular humans?"

"Not. At. All." Diamontus punctuated each word with a step toward Kristen. He towered over her and his inhuman eyebrows and beard made him seem all the more intimidating. "Even without the terrorist cells, those bullets are still out there. They make humanity into a deadly threat that must be addressed."

"I agree that the bullets are a threat, my Lord," Kristen responded. "My team has made the recovery of the dragon bullets our top priority now that the mages have been stopped. We've already recovered most of the bullets, and we're diligently working to find more."

"They won't simply leave them where they would be easily located," Boneclaw muttered.

"Of course not, sir." She studied him cautiously. He had seemed neutral when she'd first come in, and he was less overtly in support of war than Diamontus was, but he continued to make points that fueled the hulking, pissed-off dragon. "But I have my best people examining the records the mages left with a fine-toothed comb precisely so they can learn where those bullets have already been distributed to and recover them. I have mages working on this as well as humans skilled in computers. I assure you that within the week, my team will have recovered all the bullets so they can be destroyed."

Shimmerclaw looked relieved. "Well, this changes everything. This information completely alters the status of our relations with the world and warrants new discussion and a new vote."

"No more bureaucracy!" Diamontus raged and kicked a chair with enough force to hurl it against a stone wall to shatter like kindling. "The vote is cast. You cannot undo it!"

She shook her head and her expression reminded Kristen of her mother chewing her brother out for raising his voice at the dinner table. "We have rules in place for reasons precisely like this."

"But you can't simply wield them—"

"I *can* and I *will*," she said and addressed the camera behind her. "I was elected as head of the Council by all of you. We *will* recess to consider this new information for a few hours, then reconvene. If all of you still feel we should go to war, we will of course honor the majority as we always have. But let me remind you that this could well kill many dragons. The previous times we went to war, we lost many of our greatest fighters. If there is no need for that now, must we still do so? I ask all of you to remember the Steel Dragon's record and consider how she has already helped us. I will see you all in three hours."

Diamontus looked furious at this decree but most of the dragons on the screen didn't seem as enraged. Maybe it was merely that she could read the large dragon's aura and not theirs, but they seemed ready to discuss this turn of events.

Kristen was thankful for that.

She tried to look respectful and obedient as she watched the camera while all the dragons turned their connections off. They winked out one by one and left her alone with the three Council members of the group that governed her continent.

"Lady Steel, you have done well," Shimmerclaw said. "I am sure that some dragons will not see the prudence of changing their mind to avoid this conflict—"

"Exactly like *some dragons* didn't see the prudence of voting to stop these humans long before they achieved the capabilities they now possess," Diamontus interjected with an obvious dig at the Council leader.

"But," she continued and her aura revealed no annoyance at being interrupted by him. "Some will surely see this as the blessing it is. I hope your cutting off the head of the enemy will change the minds of those dragons who still use theirs."

"Thank you, my lady," Kristen said. "You honor me."

Shimmerclaw gave her a slight bow. She recognized that for the gesture of respect it was supposed to be.

Neither of the other two Council members said anything immediately so—never one to be good at waiting for any amount of time—she started to talk. "With the Council's blessing, I'll take my team to Detroit. We'll get to work uncovering every last bullet we can and devise a way to destroy them."

The Council leader looked surprised by this and Diamontus looked downright belligerent.

It was Boneclaw who spoke, however. "Please correct me if I'm wrong, Lady Shimmerclaw, but I would imagine it would be better for Lady Steel and the dragons on her force to remain here on the island with us."

"We voted to go to war," Diamontus growled at Kristen. "Lady Shimmerclaw can delay the outcome, but unless the next vote is different than the last one, we are still in agreement to attack humanity. That means you and your dragons *will* fight alongside the rest of us."

"And *if* the Council decides to go ahead with this war—despite this recent happy news"—Boneclaw didn't sound like he was happy at all—"it would be beneficial to have that mage you brought with you here. She'll need to be shackled, of course."

"You can't be serious," Kristen stammered.

Lady Shimmerclaw sighed as she nodded. "Lady Steel…Kristen, if the Dragon Council votes to continue with war, you *must* fight alongside us. If you refuse to do so, you and your team *must* be executed. That is the bond we all share as dragons. We can have our squabbles and duels but when faced with a threat as grave as this, we *must* stand together. To do otherwise would be suicide."

"But—"

"Relax, child. The news you bring is good. I am sure many will change their mind and see the foolishness of going to war against the very beings who have made our lives so good for so long. However…" The word felt like a sword in Kristen's chest. "If we decide to go to war, the lords are correct. You and your dragons must serve. Any attempt to leave will be seen as an act of desertion. You are free to enjoy refreshments and one or two of you may stretch your wings at one time, but for your own safety, do not fly to Detroit. Not when we may very well need your abilities and your fighting force to help us stop the threat the technomages have given to humanity."

She nodded, her eyes wide as she walked into the hallway to begin the return journey to the courtyard. The corridor seemed far colder now than it had before.

CHAPTER TEN

K risten felt physically ill as she left the chamber of the Dragon Council. She could not believe it. Every fiber of her being screamed that this couldn't be true. The Dragon Council had voted to go to *war?* After everything she had done, they'd still decided to go to war against humanity?

Given that she had stopped the technomages, that was what this amounted to. A war on regular human beings. People like her mom and dad who had done nothing their entire lives except try to go unseen by the dragons who trampled the world as they saw fit. In that moment of anger and despondency, it was hard to focus on those dragons who didn't regard humans as expendable tools ripe for culling.

She wished she had extraordinary power now but before she could still her mind and consider the problem calmly, Sharpeye saw her. He lurked in an alcove outside the Council chamber with a knowing look on his face. She felt another wave of nausea flood her stomach and wondered how much he had heard...or seen.

"Then it is settled?" he asked with a northeastern European accent.

"No." She choked around the word and cleared her throat. "No. They'll have another vote based on the information brought."

He deflated visibly. "After so many years I thought… Never mind. It is best to have information, yes? Do you still wish to see the armor so your team can be ready when they vote?"

As she glared at him, she realized for the first time that the dark-green jacket and slacks plus the cropped haircut made him seem ready to fight in a military force. How had she not seen that before?

Kristen pushed the thought aside. She had come to find out about the mages who had been kidnapped from the Dragon SWAT Headquarters building. When she'd set out from Detroit, she'd had no idea that they were this close to war, not with all her recent successes.

"Are you feeling well?" Sharpeye asked. "Your aura is…troubled."

"It's nothing," she snapped and clamped down on her aura. She didn't want to give anyone in this damn place any more information. Not now that she knew what they would do with it. "Can you take me to my force? I need to…uh, brief them."

"Of course, my lady!" He smiled and led her through the halls of the castle to the courtyard on the surface.

Now that she knew the Dragon Council had voted to go to war, it was obvious what all this was about. Those weren't defensive formations but dragons practicing offensive maneuvers. The massive scorpions weren't for her and her paltry band of dragons but for any humans who dared to sail close to this hidden base. The food they'd offered her people hadn't been a kindness but a necessity of war. Well-fed troops could fight harder and longer.

Her stomach lurched and she clamped a hand to her mouth. She would be sick and throw up in front of all her people and these other dragons. She would—no. No, she couldn't be anything but the steel-willed woman they all needed her to be. Now was the time for decisive action.

She transformed into her dragon body and leapt skyward.

"A good idea to survey the other platoons!" Sharpeye shouted at her.

"Where are we going?" Stonequest asked and took his own dragon form to launch after her. It seemed he'd made fast friends with the soldiers there, and why not? He had likely told them about the technomages he'd captured. To the dragons, that probably sounded like the first skirmish of the war to come.

"I want to take a look around. Stay with the troops. I don't want anyone else to go airborne yet," Kristen ordered. She spoke quickly when she recalled what would happen if it so much as appeared that she and her people were deserting.

"Troops? You mean our team?" he teased but he obeyed and made one quick lap before he landed in the courtyard—precisely where the scorpions could shoot him if she messed up.

She knew she couldn't go anywhere, so she simply ascended. She pumped her wings faster until she was able to find the posture that Lumos had taught her. With ease, she caught a thermal that rose above the island—likely caused by the heat of all the damn dragons preparing for war—and soared upward.

When she reached the top of the column of hot air, she didn't stop. She continued to flap her wings until all the dragons below her were no larger than bees in a hive. Her ascent continued until they were gnats, the island was but a beetle on a blue blanket, and all that was beneath her was clouds.

Finally, she levelled out and pumped her wings, but frost had accumulated on the scaled limbs that served as the scaffolding for the leathery membrane which kept her aloft. The spikes on her tail and back had also frosted. The air was thinner up there. She had to focus on the air currents to stay aloft more than she had to at lower elevations. This was possibly a good thing since it kept her attention off the war.

Kristen looked at the clouds below her, knowing what lurked beneath. More dragons than she had ever seen and all of them preparing to kill the human world she had grown up in.

So high above everything, she took a moment to consider her powers. She could transform to steel and dive toward the castle. From this height and with the postures Lumos had shown her, she could gain enough speed to strike the ground with the force of a meteor. She was the Steel Dragon and might survive it—she was impervious and invulnerable. Maybe if she managed to blow them all up, she'd finally be what she felt like—utterly alone.

She took a deep breath and the cold air stung her huge dragon lungs before she sighed. This far down the line, she'd thought she had more or less resolved the conflict about who she was. It hadn't been easy, but she had grown to be proud of the fact that she was a dragon raised by humans who valued both sides of her. She treasured humanity, but her dragon nature had allowed her to be bold in a way that being a human simply couldn't—not in this world anyway. Despite the challenges, she had taken both parts of her identity—the way she was nurtured and her own innate nature—and brought them together into the person she was, a dragon investigator who fought for peace.

But now, a war was brewing and at the drop of a hat, the dragons expected her to fight humans for them? She had thought that dragon society finally recognized her for who she was, not an outsider but someone who had a foot in both worlds. But no. They had merely humored her, apparently, and let her gather a force of her own so they could have a few humans to help them understand the weapons that might be used against them.

It was her personal nightmare.

All this time, she had fought to prevent a war from breaking out between the dragons and the humans they ruled. It felt like she'd been at it forever and war would still come to pass despite everything she had tried to accomplish.

Had she done something wrong? Had she focused too much on her human upbringing and ignored the dragon side of her nature? Perhaps joining the war effort would be a good thing. If she could provide intelligence, she could—

Kristen couldn't even finish the thought.

She could not and would not do this. It was impossible for her to even consider the idea of fighting against humanity. No matter what, she would have no part of the slaughter of an entire species. There weren't two sides to this problem. The dragons, in this instance, were *wrong*. They wanted to slaughter people because humans *might* attack them? That was insanity and it flew against every human right there was. Not that the dragons cared. It seemed even those who might have a more liberal approach had been swept up in the paranoia that currently drove the Council.

No, dammit. She couldn't serve them. There was no way to help a cause that was evil at its core.

Regrettably, that only meant her path forward would be a damned hard one. If she refused to help the dragons, she would turn herself and everyone on her team into targets. She'd have to protect herself, her dragons, her mages, her friends from the Detroit SWAT team, and the humans Jim had persuaded to join them. Nor could she stop the list there. She'd have to protect her parents too, of course. Plus, there were her friends from before she'd joined the police academy. One of them had recently had a baby. She couldn't let little Daynerys Williams get incinerated any more than she could let it happen to her parents.

But was she supposed to stop at the people she knew? What about everyone else with parents in Detroit? What about everyone else with kids? Hell, what about single people without families who merely wanted to get through their day and drink a beer or three with their friends? Were they supposed to burn simply because some old rich dragons had voted on it?

The reality, though, was that she knew she couldn't protect them all. Not from a force as large as the one on this island. Worse, Sharpeye had said there were forces like this gathering all over the world.

Kristen was knocked from her dark thoughts by a glimmer of light rising through the clouds.

The shining scales, gorgeous wings, and mane of platinum blonde hair were immediately recognizable as Lady Shimmerclaw. The old dragon drew alongside her, matched speed with her, and said nothing for a moment. She simply looked at the clouds below them. A flock of gulls or pelicans or something—Kristen didn't know much about birds—flew in a V. Their leader moved to the back of the formation to rest while another took the most difficult position—the point.

After a moment of silence, she gave in to her impatience. "Shouldn't you be deliberating on your decision?"

Shimmerclaw laughed, a sound like wind chimes in the thin air. "I had made my decision before you arrived and your success changes nothing in my calculation."

Kristen couldn't help it and her aura flashed with unease.

That made her companion laugh again. "Relax, Lady Steel. I still feel as I have for centuries. The idea of culling humanity is a morally bankrupt one. The technomage threat was a concern but one you handled. Now they are gone, there is absolutely no reason to go through with this war."

"Do you really feel that way?" she asked.

"You can sense my aura. Can't you tell that is the truth?"

It was her turn to chuckle. "I'm not exactly the best with those."

"Well then, let my tongue echo what my heart should have already made clear to you."

Kristen studied the other dragon as they coasted in the frigid air, high above the clouds. Her aura and her demeanor seemed to indicate that she was telling the truth.

"I will be honest with you because honesty is something I value, even if it is not a trait that all of our Councilors always practice. I see humans as an inferior species to dragons."

Her aura spiked reflexively with anger at this.

"Now, now," Shimmerclaw said mildly. "I told you I was being honest, didn't I? The way I see it, it's obvious. We live for thousands of years and they are lucky to last a hundred. While we can change shape, all they can do is age. We can fly, breathe fire, and sense each other's emotions."

"But that doesn't mean we should exterminate them," Kristen retaliated.

"Of course not." The Council leader clicked her tongue. "Humans are undeniably sentient and unbelievably innovative creatures. Their rights and wants deserve far more attention than they receive. I voted against this war before I had your report, and I'll vote against it again. And since I'm being honest, I feel the notion that humans could somehow be exterminated like a particularly serious infestation of roaches is complete nonsense. They have proven themselves to be fierce and powerful when they work together, and if dragon kind attacks, I am sure they would rally against us."

Kristen could agree with that. "I'm sure people would do more than rally. The force here is impressive but it's hardly enough to wipe out a continent in a few days. Humans will band together, go into hiding, and find ways to hurt dragons if they have to. I've seen some of the anti-dragon weapons that have been developed. It won't be the quick war some of the Council seems to hope for."

Shimmerclaw sighed at that. Her aura made it quite apparent that she felt exactly the same way. "You see, then, why we called for you."

She clenched her jaw so tightly that smoke started to pour from her scaled nostrils. How could Shimmerclaw possibly think that she could do anything to hurt humanity? She *believed* in humanity! She *was* humanity.

"Something is bothering you," her companion said.

"How can you tell?" Her tone was raw and rough.

"You practically slapped me across the face with your aura."

It was true and she smiled. It also might be the last smile she would show to Shimmerclaw. She took a deep breath and tried to calm her nerves so she could say what needed to be said. "I cannot and *will not* be a part of this…this slaughter. It goes against everything I've fought for and everything I believe in."

The other dragon inclined her head to get a better look at her. "Are you telling the head of the Dragon Council that you intend to deliberately go against the orders and commands of the Council simply because you don't like them?" she asked pointedly.

Kristen took another deep breath and answered the only way she knew how—honestly.

"Yes."

She was afraid but said it anyway. Shimmerclaw hadn't attained her position on the Council simply by her oratory skills. Despite Kristen's steel skin, she knew full well that her companion could likely shred her long before she could land safely. And even if she could somehow defeat her—as unlikely as that seemed—there was no way her team could escape the massive force of dragons she had seen.

But she still had to stand up for what she believed. It was the only part of who she was that had always been there. No matter what other parts of her identity shifted—human, dragon, student, cop, investigator, sister, or even sister of an estranged dragon—that core had always been there. Standing up for what she believed in drove her, and she wouldn't join a war that would hurl the world into a doomsday catastrophe.

Even if it meant she might be eviscerated above the clouds.

But Shimmerclaw didn't attack like she feared.

Instead, she laughed. "It's good to see you are speaking honestly, exactly as I said I would."

"Do you mean you won't...eviscerate me?" She couldn't help but smile at the grin on the other dragon's face.

"Eviscerate you? With steel scales across your belly?" The Council leader laughed again, harder this time. "I'd break a claw. No, sweet child. If I wished to end your life, you'd never even see me coming."

Kristen tried to stay calm. The Masked One had fought from the shadows. He'd never let her see him coming. Was Shimmerclaw baiting her? Was she the Masked One and this was all an act?

If it was, the platinum dragon did a damn good job of it. "I'm merely glad to see a dragon thinking things through rather than randomly following orders. You'd be surprised what kinds of things a dragon will agree to if the consequence of not doing so is to lose some of their treasure horde."

They flew on in silence for a moment and she glided beside the old dragon. She didn't honestly think she was the Masked One—Diamontus seemed far more likely in spite of his age—but compared to leading dragon kind in a war, being the Masked One wasn't that bad.

"Can't you do that, then?" she asked finally. "Threaten to take their treasure away if they attack humans unprovoked?"

"Yes. I can and I have," Shimmerclaw said moodily. "I will again too, I suspect. But this is bigger than reparations for hurt humans. A vote to go to war is beyond even my abilities to do more than exert mild influence. Don't get me wrong. I don't want this to happen at all.

Nothing good will come of it for any of the beings on this planet. Dragon, human, and mage, all will suffer. Quite honestly, the monkeys, voles, dolphins, and everything else will suffer too. Those humans have unlocked the powers of destruction with their weapons."

"So tell that to the rest of the dragons. Blood will be shed on both sides if they continue down this road. Oceans of blood!"

"That is why so many have felt compelled to go to war." It didn't sound to her like Shimmerclaw had been the one to compel them. "Even with the mage terrorists all stopped, it'll be very close. It could go either way, which makes this entire situation all the more volatile. At this point, I almost wish I knew I would lose so I could at least prepare. But we won't know until the time has elapsed. Before then, I want to identify as many variables as I can."

"Which is why you're up here with me," Kristen said. It wasn't a question. The answer was obvious.

"You are the biggest variable at the moment, so tell me...if the dragons do elect to pursue war, what will you do?"

"Do you mean personally?"

"Let's start there," Shimmerclaw agreed.

Even though she tried to set aside the topic of what to do with her fighting forces, she didn't know what to say. Part of her—the part of her that signed up to be a cop and accepted the investigator badge that Windlock had given her before he died—wanted to say she would fight. The rest of her knew with certainty that to fight a force like the one below would merely be suicidal.

"I suppose..." she began hesitantly. "I suppose I'd try to help people. I can't let my parents or my brother die by dragon fire. I simply can't. And I can't let my other friends die either. Some of them," she added and thought about Amy, "would fight back but some would need protection. You have to understand that these are the people who have fought with me to make the world a safer place for humans, dragons, and even mages. I can't abandon them."

"Well, that's not much of an issue," her companion said and sounded more like an ancient arrogant dragon as so many of her kin were. "Your...ahem, *adopted* family you could keep, of course.

According to dragon law, they belong to you. I would advise calling them servants, or your butler, or some title besides mother and father as those are somewhat….inaccurate. But the law is clear. A dragon is allowed as many humans as they can support. As long as you provide good conditions for them, the law will protect them, even in times of war. The same applies to your little police force. Dragons have hired human guards for centuries. No one will argue against that."

"So *my* humans will be spared from your slaughter?" she snapped.

Shimmerclaw either didn't notice her frustration—which was unlikely—or she chose to ignore it. "You won't be the only one to retain humans. Dragons have long seen the value in them, even if only to maintain our grounds and cook our food. The course of action that was previously agreed to was not one of total annihilation but of complete subjugation, at which point, new terms and rights would be assigned to the survivors.

"I would expect that as the war rages on, many human countries will simply surrender. Those humans would be allowed to live as long as they agreed to whatever the terms of the surrender were. Your friends and family would be fairly simple to keep."

Kristen looked at her. The dragon looked glum as if she'd only now realized how bad her offer had sounded.

"How many do you think would die?" she asked.

The Council leader looked at her with cool eyes. "As I said, that can only be known once the fighting has begun. I assure you, I'd push for a quick surrender from the major human militaries."

"Millions? Or billions?"

Shimmerclaw took an uncomfortably long time to answer. "I don't think billions is out of the question," she said finally.

Kristen took a deep breath. That was it. She had her answer. It was no longer even a choice, not with numbers like that on the table. "That's very generous of you, but it's not enough. I can't stand idly by and only protect a handful of humans who happen to be precious to me while I allow billions to be slaughtered. I could never forgive myself."

"So then…you *would* fight against your fellow dragons?"

"No! I didn't say that." She roared in frustration. "More than anyone, I have seen what the weapons the technomages have designed can do to dragons. Humans would not hesitate to use those bullets, especially since they are made from dead dragons. Every kill would equate to a new pile of ammunition. And I've met the people who are willing to make and fire them. I'm not so naïve to think that if I sided with the humans, I wouldn't get a bullet in my brain when it was all over."

"You trust the beings who raised you so little?" Shimmerclaw enquired.

She snorted a laugh. "And to think Lumos calls *me* naïve. Surely, Lady Shimmerclaw, you don't trust every single dragon with your life?"

"Surely not," the old dragon conceded. It was clear that she had simply baited her to see what she said. "But if you will not fight on either side and you would not feel comfortable waiting at your base with your loved ones for the war to end, what *will* you do?"

Kristen sighed. She had an answer but not a solution. "I need to find a middle road, a path we can all walk. Dragons, humans, and mages. Hell, I might as well make sure the dolphins are good with it too. I know that sounds optimistic or hopeful or whatever but that's what I've been doing, and it's been working. I wish I could show you and the rest of this Council the contract I got the mages to sign. It's a path for peace!"

"Well, let us hope others see this path while the world is still a place we wish to travel. Come. We've been gone long enough."

She nodded and the two started toward the island. They swung into a spiraling descent toward the castle through the clouds, their vision obscured exactly like their future.

Shimmerclaw didn't dare speak her hopes aloud. The Steel Dragon was already looking for a way out of this, even if it meant forsaking dragon kind itself. She knew the youth were unpredictable, and she'd hate to say something and make her think she was being manipulated.

Not that she thought she could successfully manipulate the girl any more than Windlock had been able to. The Council leader had always been friends with the late investigator, and his death had been a blow—especially since most of their conversations in the end had been about the enigmatic Steel Dragon. He always declared her to be a dragon of considerable power and true grit with the most unlikely of upbringings.

She had agreed with him that she might very well be the person capable of shifting the status quo that had held the world in its vice for centuries. Kristen was undeniably a force of enormous unpredictability and chaos. She had the powers of a dragon but the sensibilities of a human. Despite the two species existing together on the planet for tens of thousands of years, it was the first time such a thing had ever happened. She was unique.

Perhaps the girl might be the one to finally shine light into the shadows the Masked One had cast for all these millennia. Shimmerclaw still didn't know why all her most cunning plans never worked out. She also didn't know the face of the culprit responsible for undoing every push she'd ever made for equality and every plan she'd ever had to truly share the planet.

Over the millennia, she had investigated almost every dragon Councilor there was. She knew the Masked One had to be on one of the Councils. In all her searches, she had discovered a few veiled truths. He always hid his face behind the skull of a recently slaughtered human. Part of his power was that he could move through darkness. He was a fearsome and ruthless fighter. And he enjoyed watching others suffer.

Unfortunately, she didn't know how to catch him, let alone beat him. She knew he was behind the war and that his rumors passed from lips to ears to yet more lips, flowing even without their speaker's knowledge of the damage they did. No one knew where these rumors began like no one knew exactly who was at the center of the movement to go to war.

She had long believed that the Masked One understood dragon culture too well to be undone by it. He—like her—had written many of its rules. Shimmerclaw no longer believed he could be beaten by conventional dragon means. If he could, she would have done so already.

But now, she saw a chance. As soon as the Steel Dragon had emerged from under the hood of the Motor City—one thing she loved about humans was the way they played with language—she had hoped that she might be able to turn the girl on the Masked One.

She'd approved when she'd left the human police force to join Dragon SWAT under the wise guidance of the dragon Stonequest. On Windlock's recommendation, she'd been more than happy to allow her to become an investigator. It had even been satisfying—she'd barely been able to hide her smug amusement from the investigator— that she had waited for him to come to her with the idea.

And now, with Kristen closer than ever to removing the wedge the Masked One was driving ever deeper between humans and dragons, it looked like the Steel Dragon might fail.

Even though she had succeeded beyond everyone's wildest expectations, the vote had already been cast. Dragons would have to believe in the chaos she caused if they were to change their vote, and Shimmerclaw knew very well that the only chaos dragons liked was that caused by their own flames.

But still, there was a chance. With her, there was always a chance.

And right now, Kristen was the only chance the old dragon had.

CHAPTER ELEVEN

Lord Boneclaw retired to his private chambers. As he walked, he kept his shoulders slightly hunched and his gaze fixed below eye-level. He had perfected this posture. To the casual dragon observer, he looked like a slightly disapproving superior. To a fellow Council member, he appeared as a dragon intent on making compromises to keep his place of power.

He had hidden in plain sight like this for thousands of years—the weak-willed, eager to compromise, simpering Lord Boneclaw, whose connections were worth more than whatever dragon powers he had.

When he reached his chamber, he opened the doors, entered, and asked a servant politely for a cup of tea.

The beverage arrived in moments and he proceeded to call every contact he had on any of the other Dragon Councils. Telephones were one thing he could admit were a useful contraption the humans had designed. They were almost as useful as the weapons they'd made with the dead bodies of dragons had proven to be. Those dragon bullets might be what tipped the scales and pushed dragon society to war.

While he certainly hoped so, he didn't say that to anyone he called. Instead, he played a tediously careful game of poker. He bluffed some of the most brash and war-hungry Councilors into thinking he didn't approve of the war, knowing they'd only double-down on their positions in response. Those that were committed to peace, he assured of his wholehearted support once the war broke out.

But in each conversation, he reminded them the consequences of failing to serve. To some, he made it clear that this was a threat but to most, he made it sound like something he also feared.

Those who were on the fence were the most difficult to talk to, of course. To them, he told the truth. Over the last hundred years, humans had developed fighting capabilities far beyond what evolution had given them. He reminded them of dragons who had been gunned down with Gatling guns or shredded by landmines. He brought up dragons who'd been exploded by missiles and even one particularly unfortunate dragon who had been killed by a steam engine.

He always knew of a dragon who the Councilor in question had once known—an ex-lover, a friend, a family member, or similar. He'd bring them up and join them in their sorrow. Then, once he could hear the grief in their voice—not an easy thing to do for a being who was used to communicating emotionally via auras and not tone of voice—he told them what Kristen had told the Council.

She had rescued dragons these mages grew from the egg to harvest for bullets. Even though the horrible, despicable, monstrous mages were now in custody, they had already sold who knew how many crates of these bullets to militaries around the world. He didn't mention that he oversaw a fair number of those transactions, of course, as that didn't help his cause.

Boneclaw told them the Steel Dragon had then done exactly as she had said—she had befriended these technomages. No, worse than that, he seemed to realize every time he spoke with one of these undecided dragons. She had taken them under her wing.

That particular argument was a good one, he thought. He had long felt humans had grown too powerful, but he had been willing to wait for things to develop and now they had. Humans were capable of creating weapons that would allow a child to kill a dragon by simply squeezing a trigger. It was time for action.

The old dragon hoped the others agreed. It was hard to be sure how they would vote given that he couldn't sense their auras or subtly tweak them in the way he wished. This was one of the downsides of being able to talk to so many dragons all across the world. It was a price that had to be paid.

By the end of the three hours, he had done all he could. He had the assurances he needed and could only hope for the outcome to be in his favor. As little as he liked the emotion humans seemed so obsessed with, there it was.

Boneclaw stood and entered his sleeping chamber, his hand to his forehead like all the conversations had given him a headache. There was truth to this. He didn't feel like himself but he never did, not when he had to show his pathetic, scarred face to every damn soul he saw.

What none of them understood was that the flesh and bone of his actual face was the mask. He felt far more comfortable behind a human skull. Although the one locked in a chest in his private chambers wasn't fresh, it was still a great comfort to slip it over his head. The feel of human bone on his bald head and the way the human eye sockets framed the world when he looked through them was inspiring and comforting.

These were the feelings of the Masked One, and he relished finally being himself, even if it was for only a short time. He leaned back in a chair, his headache already washing away with the touch of human bone.

He *had* won. It had taken work but he'd finally got that insufferable Diamontus to push for a vote for war. Due to all his carefully laid plans over the past decades plus the flurry of activity in the last year and managing the technomages to try to eliminate the Steel Dragon, the vote had gone in his favor.

Of course, he had expected it to. He would never have convinced Diamontus to call for the vote if he'd thought there could have been another outcome. The Masked One had enjoyed the sweet taste of victory.

But now it had been dashed from his mouth.

The cursed Steel Dragon might ruin everything. He'd had an inkling of that when her power first appeared. It had been because he'd been aware of her potential that he'd tricked her to go into Mammoth Cave and almost killed her. That was why he'd pushed for the vote to happen while the technomages were still a threat. As long as they were out there, her effectiveness could be called into question. Now that the mages were gone, things had changed.

A little disgruntled, he took a deep breath and savored how the air whistled slightly past the nostrils of the skull he wore. He had to be careful with the selection of his masks. His head was not large and was slightly compressed by years of wearing the skulls—it was where the marks on his face came from too—but still, he had to choose humans with skulls large enough to fit over his head.

The Masked One didn't know how the dragons would react to the Steel Dragon forcing the technomages into contractual magic. He was only glad that she hadn't brought the damn contract. The chances were, if anyone read it, they'd side with the stupid runt.

Although maybe it would have been better if she had brought it. Knowing what he did of her, he did not doubt that she had written rules that would stop her as firmly as they'd stop the mages. A contract like that might be ideal—a noose capable of burning Lady Steel alive or at least bringing her to heel.

But the vote had been called for and he was not about to recommend that the Steel Dragon leave with all her people before the vote was returned.

He had many allies on the Council—or more accurately, Boneclaw knew many people and had convinced a fair number to follow Diamontus. But he wasn't the only dragon with a major power block. He had been playing politics with Shimmerclaw for centuries. Her block was larger than his, at least on the surface.

It would come down to the dragons who were too stubborn, arrogant, independent, or all three to ally themselves with another's leadership.

And he truly did not know which way they would vote.

That meant he could lose and the Dragon Councils might not agree to war.

He could not have that.

The Masked One took out another cellphone. This one did not legally belong to the dragon named Boneclaw and in fact didn't legally belong to anyone. It was like the human skull he now wore. It did not exist, at least not in the consciousnesses of the people who thought they knew how the world worked. There was a time long before when even bringing such a thing to one of the dragon bases had made him nervous, but those fears were long gone.

This entire fortress was made to be secure. It had both dragons defending it as well as magical protections. The point of strongholds like this was to give members of the Dragon Council a refuge they could retreat to and make their decisions in private. Boneclaw and the others seated in their private chambers, attended to by servants and protected by hidden guards, were seen as the epitome of dragon democracy. By sequestering himself before the vote he was, in theory, making his final deliberation.

Lord Boneclaw had a reputation for always waiting until the very end to decide. Even his aides sometimes let rumors slip—all of which the Masked One approved in advance, of course—that he rarely sounded certain of his decisions when he called the other dragons and often emerged from his private chamber with his mind changed.

It was all part of the act and the web he had spun to take power from the dragons foolish enough to give some of it up.

He dialed a number quickly. This time, the voice on the other end of the line didn't belong to a dragon but to a human. A pawn, was how he thought of him, although if he used the terms of the human game of chess he adored so much, surely the man who answered the call wasn't a pawn but something more interesting. A knight perhaps, or a bishop. Pieces that could strike unseen, their paths hidden from all but the sharpest of eyes.

"Your honor," the man said, his voice caught somewhere between fear and amazement. "Did the dragons vote to go to war?"

"Alas, they did," the Masked One said. "And it seems they know of your base as well. It's been set as one of the first targets."

"You're kidding."

"I don't kid, Major," the Masked One replied and infused a little umbrage into his tone. "They know the Third Wing out of Alaska is the closest military base with the force needed to damage their army. There is talk of a preemptive strike."

In truth, the only talk of a preemptive strike had been what he had started as Lord Boneclaw. Of course, Major Miller didn't need to know that.

"This is the worst-case scenario, then," the man said. "We don't have the anti-dragon emplacements fully finished yet. If they attack now, the consequences will be dire. I can scramble jets, but we can't keep enough of them in the air at all times to fight the force of dragons you told us was massing there—that our intelligence has confirmed."

"Your intelligence? Oh, you mean those pesky satellites you placed up where dragons can't reach." The Masked One had expected the major to check on the base once he gave him its location, but he found that he often participated in his plans better if he thought he was outmaneuvering the ancient dragon. He didn't mind the deception, however. "Then you know the size of the force here."

"We do. I guess… I guess this might call for the use of nuclear capabilities—"

"I don't think it needs to come to all that," he said quickly. Even he knew it would be best if the humans were not pressed far enough to use their most powerful weapons. "The dragons have learned that the Steel Dragon has allied with the mages. They are holding a vote now on whether to join forces with their former enemies so they can run over humankind and your armies. They feared the mages, but they do not fear you. A strike now—a *lethal strike*—would prove that you will not be defeated so easily."

"You're talking about a preemptive strike on dragon kind," Major Miller said.

"The alternative is to let the dragons attack you first—something they've already voted to do. You can win this war but not if you give them time to destroy your airfields. I think you can see that letting this conflict escalate too far when you and your soldiers could prevent it is the wisest course of action."

"And I have your assurances that my soldiers—"

"Yes, yes, of course. Strike here before the dragons can reach your base and I will send Diamontus himself to claim it as his property. As long as your troops swear allegiance to him, they will not be harmed by the members of my alliance. Those dragons who wish to ally with mages to attack humanity will not defeat us." He hissed as if to emphasize his claim.

"Yes, sir," the major said, although he didn't sound entirely convinced. "I still can't believe the mages changed sides after all the munitions they provided us with."

"That is because we underestimated the hunger the Steel Dragon has for power," The Masked One replied. "It is my fault, Major. My fault entirely. I have followed her ascension to power, as you well know, and I should have moved sooner. When she took control of a powerful mage and refused to shackle her or release her to anyone else, that should have been the clue I needed to act on.

"She must have aura powers far beyond any dragon I've ever faced," the Masked One let his voice tremble. He knew that Miller would interpret that as fear because that was the persona he had given Boneclaw for all the years he'd used the man in preparation for this moment. In truth, it was rage that made his words shake like a tree in a storm. "She could have killed the leader of the technomages many times but instead, she wore her down and now has made her swear fealty to her. Earlier, she took a mage from another dragon. Worse, she has persuaded humans to fight alongside dragons against both their species. She is a monster, one I should have stopped long ago..." He let his voice trail off.

"We'll stop her now, sir," Major Miller said, his faith in his power restored.

"Thank God for that," the Masked One said and hung up as he heard the major start to give orders to his base.

Military men were so predictable.

CHAPTER TWELVE

Kristen returned to the courtyard, where her dragon friends were training with some of those on guard duty.

It was oddly disorienting after the conversation she'd had with Shimmerclaw. The leader of the North American Dragon Council had made it quite clear that if there was a vote for war, she wouldn't be able to stop these dragons from implementing the decision of the Council.

It meant that in less than an hour, the guards who had given Lumos a spear to practice with against one of their swords might turn their blades on their sparring partner. Those who were now in their dragon shapes, using their breath weapons against Stonequest so they could see how effective or ineffective they were against his stone skin, might turn those same tactics and attacks against him.

It was almost unthinkable to see them all there, joking and eating charred meat, when the decision to eradicate humankind might have already been made in the minds of Council dragons who were not even there.

"Is something on your mind, Lady Steel?" Lumos asked. He stopped beside her, breathing hard from his training session, and leaned on his spear. The old dragon still favored one arm after taking a dragon bullet on the tropical island during the final battle with the technomages.

Still? Kristen shook her head at her choice of words. It had only been days since he was injured, and they now tried to stave off a war so they could hunt a dragon more powerful than any they had ever faced. The whole situation was insane.

When this was all over—and if it didn't end with her and all her friends six feet under—she would give everyone two weeks off and a huge bonus, provided they all spent the time napping.

"Everything's on my mind," she said. "I think I could use something to take my mind off it."

"I have an idea about that." He spun the spear as easily as a drum major might twirl a baton.

Five minutes later, she was engaged in a training session unlike any she'd had before. She had practiced with Lumos whenever they could but thus far, the training had focused primarily on how she could hurt other dragons. He'd taught her early on to target their joints—the armpits, the joints on the wings, and places near appendages where dragon scales were thinner and less tightly packed to allow greater range of motion.

She had done well. Now, when she sparred with him, she won more often than not, although she knew part of this was because he was so old. He wasn't as fast or as strong as he once was, but she hadn't been able to even land a strike when she'd started training with him, so she'd progressed. Also, the Masked One was supposed to be even more ancient than Lumos so hopefully, he'd be a little frail in the hip as well.

Kristen had made that joke to Lumos once, only to have him take her legs out from under her.

He did so now when he struck at her from within a ball of light.

She landed hard and scrambled to her feet. Immediately, she lashed out with the spikes on her tail but the attack sliced through empty space.

"Focus!" Lumos said from somewhere inside the sphere of light he'd created. He used it to hide the outline of his human body. She felt like she was fighting a dragon, but the glowing version of one that stood before her was as ethereal as the wind. The only way he could strike her was if he lashed out with the diamond tipped spear he still wielded.

As if he had somehow read the thought, he thrust the spear forward and between two of her talons, and she yanked her dragon claw away.

Kristen took a deep breath and tried to concentrate. She lashed out at where his strike had come from, but he'd already moved somewhere else inside his bright cocoon. She snorted in frustration. "Can't you hold still?'

"*He* will not hold still," Lumos said. He'd refused to speak of the Masked One directly since they'd been there and feared the enemy's eyes would be everywhere.

"But *you* can." She took another swipe and her claw connected—she *was* improving—but the old dragon scrambled away before she could catch hold of him.

He retaliated with a swift blow to her brow with the butt of the spear. "But I won't!"

Her opponent vanished into his light cloud and she gave chase halfheartedly.

Lumos reappeared and looked concerned. "Is everything all right, Lady Steel? Your heart does not seem to be in this session."

Kristen looked at the guards, who all either watched the horizon or sparred with each other. No one seemed to care that she was training with Lumos, which made what she said next ring false even in her own ears. "He could be watching. I'm worried he'll see our methods."

"Let him see," the old dragon said confidently. "If he knows this is training against the powers he has kept secret for so long, he will know he has finally met his match and will taste fear. But that is not what is bothering you, not if your aura can be believed."

"You're right."

"Do you wish to talk about it?" he asked. "If something clouds your heart, it would cloud your strikes in battle."

She nodded and saw the wisdom in it. That, after all, was why Constance had never killed her. It was also why she had never killed Constance. "But not here."

A few minutes later, they walked outside the castle and threaded along a high ridge that had the castle walls on one side and a sheer drop down the other. If they were to fall, many seabirds would see them plummet toward the sea before they took their dragon shape and flew out across the frigid water.

The wind blew fiercely and great waves pounded upon the rocky shore far below. She would probably have found it miserable if she were a human, but as a dragon with blood as hot as fire and skin as hard as steel, it felt wonderfully refreshing—as if the wind and the waves could wash everything that was troubling her away. Of course, a glance at the sky proved that to be impossible. A large number of dragons were still airborne. No wind or waves would be able to stop them once they were sent to attack humanity.

"I think even dragons cannot hear our words, now," Lumos said.

Kristen agreed, so she told him of the strange conversation she'd had with Shimmerclaw. How it seemed the Council leader trusted her even though she'd said she would disobey orders and how she'd told her that her family and friends could be protected in the event that the war became reality.

"She's quite right about that, at least," he agreed but seemed to be at a loss as to what to say about the rest of it. "Humans who belong to a dragon will be on the 'do not kill' list, for sure. Your wealth is substantial so you could take a great many humans under your protection. I'm sure Amythist would agree to protect some on your behalf as well, and—although my resources are smaller than the great wealth Windlock left you—I too would be more than willing to protect anyone you wish me to."

"That's very kind," she said and felt like she was repeating herself— or worse, like she was reliving the moment. Only this time, the old dragon she respected had been replaced by another who—despite what she had previously thought of them—seemed more than willing to sacrifice billions of people so that a small handful could survive.

"But that's not enough for me. Even if I could protect all of Michigan or the Midwest, or the entire United States, that is not enough. I can't let countries with people—entire continents—be slaughtered so my mom can be safe and still go about her life like nothing is happening. None of the people I love would want that. No decent human being would want that."

"Some of your politicians seem more than willing to—"

"I said no *decent* human," Kristen was quick to point out. "Obviously, certain politicians don't count."

"Of course. Forgive me," Lumos said. "I was only trying to lighten your spirits."

"Yeah, well, the potential slaughter of billions has a way of dampening my mood."

The old dragon cleared his throat and sounded uncomfortable. "Do you plan to help the humans, then? I know their weapons have advanced tremendously, but I still cannot imagine them being able to stop the dragon forces before millions of lives are lost. Even with you —with *us*—helping them, it would not be easy to stop thousands of dragons. It may not be possible."

But she was already shaking her head. "Shimmerclaw asked me that as well, and I'll tell you what I told her. I am dragon now, as much as I am human. Sometimes, it feels like I'm more dragon than human, and it certainly feels like the dragon part of me is still growing. I can't take up arms with human beings who are willing to use dead dragons to slaughter our kind. That's as unconscionable to me as setting fire to human cities. I feel like I need to choose a side, but I also know I can't. Both sides would ask me to identify with a cause I can't believe in."

Lumos nodded and turned to look at the ocean. The droves of seabirds had joined forces with a whale to eat a shoal of tiny fish. The water teemed with creatures as the enormous whale forced the fish to surface, where the birds then forced them down again. Caught in the chaos, the fish had nowhere to go but into the bird's gullets or into the whale's mouth. Those that did escape were snatched up by happy seals.

Kristen felt like she was a sardine being attacked from all sides.

"I have lived a long, long time," he said, his gaze locked on the proliferation of sea life before them. "Over all those centuries, I have come to realize a few things. One of them is that beings don't have multiple pieces that are at internal war, even if it feels like that sometimes. Even those creatures below us, although they may feel they struggle to decide between air and food, have made their mind up. Each of us are driven by a singular force of self that drives our decisions going forward."

"I don't know," she said. "I understand that at our core, all living things want to survive, but I think there's more to it than that. Our opponent isn't operating merely for self-preservation. He has larger goals than that."

"You are correct, of course," he said and tossed his spear to her. She caught it deftly and regarded the ancient dragon expectantly. "We are driven by more than our selfishness." He transformed into his gold dragon form. "We are driven by who we are at our core. That person might change or shift over time, but they are always the same self. The struggle of identity you speak of comes from facing a choice where there appear to be only wrong decisions."

Kristen uttered a weak little chuckle at that. When she did, he lunged at her.

She lifted the spear and pointed at the dragon's neck. He'd taught her a thing or two about fighting dragons in her human body. Over the years, of course, he'd fought humans with the skills to kill dragons. Long before the dragon bullet, the weapon of choice had been a spear tipped with a diamond. She would use it not to attack him but to impale him through the heart or the brain if he came too close.

Her gaze focused on him, she spun the weapon and wedged the butt in the ground so that if he brought his weight down on her, he'd gore himself.

Lumos—training her and thus obviously not willing to risk his life to prove a point to a student—pumped his wings and launched off the cliff. A large flock of seabirds that had already eaten their fill of fish fled from their stone perches when this greatest of all aerial predators flew over them.

"But that's not how life works," he said after he'd come about and now readied himself for his next attack. "Decisions are not a simple choice of yes and no. On and off, as your brother says."

"You mean binary?"

"Exactly." He tried to catch her with his tail, but she was able to get the point of the spear into his golden scales. With a yowl of pain, he snatched his tail away. "Very good! You are becoming much better at anticipating the movements of dragons. That will serve you well."

"Thanks, I guess." Kristen became steel as Lumos tried to blow her over or knock the spear from her hands with a great gust of wind. "But that doesn't tell me which side to join."

"You don't have to fight for the humans or fight for the dragons. You could opt to not fight at all, for instance. Or..." He left his next observation unspoken as he surged into a raking dive at her. The maneuver was impressive but he had underestimated her. She rolled onto her back and drove both legs up into the golden dragon's chest in a powerful kick. "Oof!" He grunted as he flew up and away from her.

"Or what?" she asked him sharply.

The old dragon shrugged. "Or whatever your heart tells you is the right thing to do. I don't know what the best choice will be for you. I wouldn't think to make such a judgement for anyone's life. That's another thing I've learned over my many years on this planet. It's impossible to walk the path of another. I would not dare tell you how to walk yours. However..."

"However, what?" Kristen asked and parried his advances with a few thrusts of the spear when he took to the ground and tried to get past her and deliver a swipe with his claws.

"However, you are the Steel Dragon. One with formidable powers that approach invulnerability, it seems to many of us. Yet you were raised by humans and thus understand their fragility and short lifespans better than we do. You are so very special and no matter what happens, I will continue to follow your lead."

"That's merely a nice way to say you don't know."

"I am sorry to say that indeed, you are correct. But I trust you more than I've ever trusted another. We all do. The decision of what to do with that trust is yours." Lumos took to the air again, caught the wind with his golden wings, and screeched like one of the birds. "Do you want my advice? Forget about everything, live on a cliff face like a seabird, and enjoy some fresh fish!" He elevated to a height at which he could focus on the great shoal of fish that continued to fuel the feast below.

He never got to his meal, though.

Before he could begin his dive, a missile rocketed out of the wispy clouds and pounded into the top of castle. The battlement crumbled into an avalanche that threatened to bury her.

She had barely enough time to throw herself from the cliff and transform into a dragon before another missile struck where she had been moments before.

CHAPTER THIRTEEN

Kristen pumped her wings to catch the air before she plummeted into the frothy sea below. "Lumos!" she screamed.

"I'm fine! Lady Steel, we must get to the others!" he shouted and banked toward the castle and away from another missile that streaked past. This one made it over the castle wall and into the middle of the courtyard. A great ball of fire erupted as it detonated. All the training equipment, cooking fires, and supplies were incinerated in the horrific blast.

The screams of the wounded started almost immediately—no less difficult to hear because they came from dragons.

Two more attacks rocketed toward the stronghold. One of the dragons on a still-standing rampart had the good sense to fire his scorpion at it. She had no idea how a dragon would ever have been able to dodge the impossibly fast crossbow bolt, large enough to skewer an ox, but the old fashioned projectile simply passed the missile and made no impact at all.

As if angry at the dragon for daring to fire upon it, the ordnance drove into the wall immediately below the guard manning the scorpion. The heat and force of the explosion was such that his skin, muscle, and finally bone burned away before the orange ball of flame was gone, leaving only destruction behind it.

"How could they be blindsided like this?" Kristen yelled, shocked to see such death in a place of such power.

"Dragons aren't exactly up to date on tech," Lumos said. His gaze peered in the direction the missiles had come from, looking for more. "They have radar here, but probably not a device with the precision to track incoming missiles. Humans must have fired them from a long way out."

"Keep your eyes open for more," she ordered. "I'll check on our team."

She gained enough elevation to clear the wall and landed inside the courtyard. Her team gathered in a corner, protected by the faint, blue shimmer of Amy's defensive magic. A quick head count confirmed that everyone was fine. That was more than could be said of the rest of the assembled dragons.

With all the smoke from the blasts and the chaos of debris everywhere, she couldn't be sure but thought she counted at least a half-dozen dead dragons.

Six dragons had been killed in the blasts at their own base.

To humans, that might have been manageable losses. To dragons, it was a devastating blow.

"I counted six missiles. Did anyone else get a count?" she asked.

"That sounds right," Emerald said. No one else seemed to have any idea how the blasts had happened.

Six missiles, one per dragon slain. There were probably more dead than that, as the broken stone walls could have easily crushed a dragon to death. It was insane that humans could do all this without even being seen.

Three fighters rocketed overhead, most likely to survey the damage.

"They come to drop more fire!" a dragon yelled, and those who had survived—far more than those who had died—all transformed and leapt skyward.

"No!" Kristen shouted. "That was only a pass to see what they've done. They're too fast to chase. By the time we see them, it's too late."

"Catch them!" a dragon roared and many obeyed, but it soon became obvious that a dragon was no match for the jets. The aircraft most likely traveled faster than five hundred miles an hour. Dragons could maybe go a hundred if it was the right dragon in the right wind. She was damn sure she couldn't go anywhere near that fast.

It seemed she wouldn't have to.

"They're coming back," Amy said, her eyes closed and hands held at her temples. "They'll make another pass."

"Everyone get to safety!" Kristen said as Amy flew to her.

"Where the hell are you two going?" Stonequest demanded. He normally took orders well, so she didn't fault him for his incredulity. She was sure she looked insane and certainly felt it.

"We'll try to stop those planes."

Amy levitated herself onto her back and looked like a doll being snatched up from the ground via invisible strings as she used her clothes to move herself.

"Can you sense them? And can you guide me into their path?" she asked the young mage.

"Keep going up. I'll tell you when we're at their level," the girl shouted over the wind. "Or...you know what? How about we simply stay here?"

"Why?" Kristen demanded but then saw them too. The trio of F-22s each fired another pair of missiles. The ordnance streaked toward them and the rest of the dragons still trying to assemble themselves into some form of useful defense below. "Do you think you could protect the whole island from those missiles?" she asked.

"What? Like if they all blew up? No way in hell," Amy replied.

"Then we'd better stop them before they blow," she said. Without the mage to shield them, their friends were in mortal danger, but she was also the only one who might be able to stop those missiles before they made impact. It was a catch-twenty-two, one that would only be solved by quick thinking and fearless action.

Kristen moved toward the approaching missiles but had no idea how long it would take to reach them. She had no experience battling this type of attack, but she didn't think it would take long.

While she focused on flight, the mage reached out with her powers. Two of the missiles began to tremble and a moment later, nosed toward each other, collided, and exploded. There was no time for celebration, though, as they were instantly outpaced by the other four missiles.

She felt like she'd blinked and the ordnance was upon them. Acting on instinct, she turned and lashed out with the spikes on her tail. She managed to whip a missile with one of her projectile spikes and promised herself she'd thank Lumos for the training later.

Amy had short-circuited the second or caused its fuel to run out or something. It rapidly lost altitude and vanished into the ocean.

Two were left but they were both beyond Kristen and she knew she wouldn't be able to catch up.

"Amy!"

"I know!"

"Amy, they're getting close!"

"Dammit, I know!" the mage screamed and a blast of energy radiated from her. It caught the rear of one of the missiles and tumbled it end over end before it crashed into one of the high cliffs that framed the island. Kristen was shocked by how relieved she was that it wasn't the cliff with all the baby birds on it.

That relief soon turned to horror as the last missile pierced the airspace above the base.

"Amy!"

The young mage's aura slipped into unconsciousness. She'd pushed herself too far and passed out.

It meant it was up to Kristen to— *Too late.*

The projectile struck home in the center of the courtyard and exploded to swallow the dragons in a great ball of flame. She cursed when she realized that it had potentially transformed a rally point for a war she was desperate to prevent into its first battleground.

CHAPTER FOURTEEN

Kristen roared as the destruction below her unfolded. She'd been too slow. If she could have taken to the air a fraction faster, maybe she would have been able to stop all the attacks. In the face of such a calamity, her hopes for a peaceful resolution began to slip away. The dragons would want vengeance for this assault. They'd want war, one which could only end in far too much blood spilled on both sides. She banked to return to the castle, hoping to lend help to those injured within.

Before she could reach the wounded and convince them that retaliation wasn't the way forward, she was attacked.

The three fighter jets raced toward her. Two of them remained high above her and the mage on her back, but the third lowered altitude and spun as it did so. She turned her body to steel, ready to slash one of the wings with her tail, but the pilot opened fire.

Thank goodness, all she had to do was roll to put her belly to face the bullets so Amy would be safe on her back. If they were made of dragon scale, they'd tear through her, which meant she'd fall into the frigid ocean below and the girl might drown. If they were normal bullets, she could protect her friend long enough to wake her.

For a few terrifying seconds, they felt like dragon bullets.

Intense pain erupted where she was struck in the belly. She looked down and each bullet felt like it had punched through her gut but surprisingly, she wasn't bleeding. They were *not* dragon bullets, fortunately, merely regular lead but fired from a military-grade rapid-fire weapon mounted on a jet that was already traveling hundreds of miles per hour.

Despite having steel skin and being a dragon, the fire from a 30mm cannon hurt. If they had been dragon bullets, she would have been shredded but she was still in one piece. For the moment, anyway.

The fighter fired again. He missed her body this time and instead, caught her wings. Although being made of steel, the bullets ripped through the membrane.

Kristen screamed in pain and began to plummet toward the icy water below.

She pushed with her aura in an attempt to wake Amy.

With a groggy, "What the fuck happened?" the mage regained consciousness and was back in the action.

"A little help, please!" she screamed, knowing she sounded desperate from the pain but beyond caring. Amy was one person she could allow to see her fear. "My wing is torn."

"Right!" the girl shouted and Kristen felt her chest lifted by an invisible force. It was odd being lifted by magic because there was no aerodynamics to it. Rather than using momentum to help carry her through the fall and out across the water, Amy simply slowed her fall, reversed its direction, and raised the Steel Dragon once again.

That was all the time she needed to heal her wings. The 30mm bullets had hurt but they were still merely bullets. Because they weren't made of dragon scale, they didn't affect her healing abilities. She didn't know if it meant the missiles that had struck the castle were filled with pieces of dragons or if the explosives inside each warhead were simply powerful enough to kill a dragon outright with a direct strike.

It was not something she wanted the pilots to test any more than they already had.

She looked up as the two fighters raced overhead. The one that had shot her attempted to catch up to the others.

Those in the lead dipped their wings, no doubt to look out their window and make sure the Steel Dragon had found her watery grave beneath Hudson's Bay.

Instead, they saw her flying toward them with Amy on her back and magic swirling around them.

All three fighters increased their speed, either to make a retreat or to get far enough away to come in for another pass.

"They'll get away!" Kristen shouted.

"Not on my watch," the mage replied and gritted her teeth.

There was no recognizable color or shape to the magic she currently used, but its effects were very evident.

The two fighters that tried to sneak away began to nose toward each other. Over such speeds and distances, Amy didn't have the level of control she'd had over the missiles. Both pilots fought her manipulations and each of them went into a series of maneuvers to stop her from taking control.

They had to stay alive, keep moving, and keep away from each other, while all she had to do was push their controls. Inevitably, they overcorrected.

That was all it took. In one moment, three planes struggled to hold their formation and in the next, one of the leaders clipped the other's wing.

Kristen didn't see the actual collision as she was too far away and the fighter jets moved too fast, but she saw the effects.

It reminded her of when Brian had played a game with spaceships that blasted lasers at each other over planets. She—in a fit of rage—had snatched his controller and thrown it down their front steps. The spaceship he'd been controlling tried to move in about a dozen different directions before it exploded.

The jets did the same thing. Their elaborate loops and spins no longer seemed so controlled. One of them spun increasingly fast until the pilot ejected and the plane crashed into the bay. The other never had the chance. The pilot tried to increase speed, but the wings of the craft were already shaking too much and the jet simply exploded.

The third and final fighter who had fired on Kristen did *not* want to remain any longer. They activated the afterburners and the jet surged forward until it cracked the sound barrier and released a sonic boom that made the shape of a parabola splash on the surface of the bay below them. Acceleration continued until it reached Mach 2 and vanished into the far distance where even Amy couldn't follow it.

"I could try to make a portal," the girl said, but she sounded doubtful. "But I don't know where he's going and even if I did, I would probably pass out. You'd have to take him and any of his friends on alone. You know what? I'm not gonna open that portal."

"There are more important things to worry about right now anyway," Kristen said and circled toward the island that had taken the brunt of seven missiles in less then six minutes. She spared one more glance at the pilot who had ejected and now parachuted into the bay. The freezing water would do him in, and she thought he should probably be brought in for questioning. She pushed the idea aside when one of the dragons who hadn't heeded her advice to take cover flew to where the man was falling and ate him.

Appalled by what she'd seen, she soared over the castle. The last missile had struck in the center of the courtyard. From the looks of it, about twenty dragons had not heeded her advice and remained in the open. They'd all been in mid-transformation when the missile detonated, their energy focused on changing their body instead of healing it.

All twenty of them were dead now.

Most had made the transition to their dragon body before they succumbed to the injuries from the heat and force of the blast, but a few had only half-changed. They'd died part human and part dragon. It was like something out of a horror film she would never dare to imagine.

"Stonequest!" Kristen shouted down at the destruction. "Emerald, Heartsbane, Lumos!"

There were many more names of her dragons, but she was most concerned about her old friends.

A pile of rubble shifted and the off-white of Stonequest's marbled skin emerged. Flecks of green and orange gleamed here and there as he pushed the rubble off his back. The rest of her team emerged from beneath his wings, all in human form so they were able to shelter under him.

"Is everyone all right?" she shouted and immediately regretted the absurdity of the question amidst such a grizzly scene.

"Our team is," Stonequest said, his jaw agape as he studied the carnage. Not every dragon had died, however. Those who had been airborne remained on the wing, circled overhead, and alternated between looking for more planes and taking in the destruction below.

Some had taken shelter like her people had. Not all, obviously, but more than those who had died. They now streamed from the ground beneath the castle and entered the desolated courtyard through trapdoors that were no longer hidden. Beyond these apertures, tunnels that had stood for centuries were now little more than ramshackle spaces between shattered piles of cut stone.

"This is all those technomages' fault," a dragon with a huge red neck frill shouted and pointed his talon at Amy.

"They couldn't have done this without the weapons they harvested from our bodies," another yelled, this one with many more talons on each foot than Kristen had.

"These were *not* dragon killing missiles," she told them sharply. "If they were, the loss of life would have been far worse."

"You don't seem to be hurt badly," a third dragon said and retrieved a spear from amongst the debris. In his human form, he still had his dragon wings.

"That's because we have experience fighting these monsters," Stonequest interjected.

"More like because you have a mage to protect you," the dragon with the frill who had spoken first shouted. "How are we supposed to know you didn't orchestrate this attack?"

"I *saved* you!" Amy shouted, her voice magically enhanced so it echoed off the crumbling remains of the castle and caused many of the seabirds to take to the air, screaming as if to accentuate her anger.

"I guess so…" a dragon muttered loudly. "But I still don't see why you're not cuffed."

That drew a chorus of grumbled protests, hear-hears, and unnecessary verbal crap. Kristen had changed into her human form but she donned her steel skin reflexively at their accusations.

"She's worse than any of the mages!"

"My representative called and said that the Steel Dragon made some kind of contract with *all* the technomages, not only this one."

"What if she frees them all?"

"They could build more of these dragon missiles."

There were too many misconceptions to correct at one time. She couldn't clarify them all, not while some of the dragons in their human forms snatched weapons while others changed into their dragon bodies.

"She's supposed to be cuffed," one roared.

"Those are the *rules,*" another added. It seemed they had found a rallying point at last.

"If she won't be cuffed, there's a price to be paid."

"She *saved* all of you. If she'd been cuffed, you would all be dead," Stonequest said and moved to stand in front of Amy. The rest of Kristen's forces surrounded the mage as well. Some took dragon form while others remained as humans. All of them looked like they knew damn well that a fight in the ruins of this castle and in the wake of all this destruction would not be a good thing.

But they also knew that they might have to fight, and they put their shoulders together to protect the woman who had saved them all.

CHAPTER FIFTEEN

One of the agitators growled as he blew smoke from his nose. Another lashed out with his tail. Still another sent a small ball of fire at them.

Kristen's dragon fighters held their position. They ignored the smoke, dodged the tail strike, and deflected the fireball. They knew to not break ranks but they also knew the dragons would continue to test them.

"What the hell is this?" Diamontus bellowed as he emerged from the catacombs beneath the ruins of the castle and took his dragon form.

He was absolutely huge, so big that she thought he should be measured in elephants. It was the only conceivable standard. The big fucking dragon was at least as large as three elephants.

Worse were the blueish, crystalline formations that covered his entire body. She wanted to think that the spikes jutting from his shoulders, the backs of his elbows, and the ridge down his back and his head were as strong as ice. But the dragons' name—Diamontus— spoke of stronger stuff.

"This mage is going about without a cuff," a dragon told him. "We were working to fix that."

"She's in a contract with her master," Diamontus said and nodded at Kristen. He looked pissed about it but he was a Council member, after all, and knew the laws better than most dragons.

"But, sir, no one on her team—*no one*—was hurt," a dragon explained. "What if they were working with the humans who shot their missiles at us?"

"It's an interesting thought," the large dragon growled. "That would of course make them traitors to dragon kind. Where were you prior to the attack?" he demanded of Kristen.

"She was with me, you big buffoon." Shimmerclaw appeared from the clouds, her platinum scales glowing as brightly as the sky itself. "She's tried to *stop* this war, unlike you, Diamontus. She's not allied with the humans any more than you are."

He grumbled but before he could say anything, she spoke again. "This is not the time for bickering. A real enemy has revealed itself. It is time to rethink our defensive capabilities before we are struck with such devastation again. We ought to thank Lady Steel's mage for our lives, not threaten her."

"Not everyone made it out with their life," the dragon with the neck frill pointed out gruffly.

"*None of us* would have made it out with our lives if not for the Steel Dragon and her team. I was in the air when this all happened. I saw it play out. She and her mage offered sage advice—take cover— which those of you who survived all heeded. Thereafter, the mage stopped five of the six explosive projectiles the humans in their airplanes launched at us."

"Do you speak the truth?" Diamontus asked. "She stopped *five* of the weapons that did this?"

"Well, Lady Steel might have helped with one," Shimmerclaw said wryly.

"All this death was caused by *only one* of their missiles?" he demanded.

"No, sir," Emerald said. "There were two volleys and six missiles each. The second time, only one hit but that was when we suffered the most casualties."

"And how many casualties *did* your team suffer?" Diamontus asked.

More calls of "Cuff the mage!" and "Traitor!' followed his thinly veiled accusation.

"Enough of that!" Shimmerclaw roared and made her rage plain with her aura. "We will not exact vengeance on the mage who saved us. Plus, what exactly do you idiots think you can even do to her after what she did to those human weapons?"

"With all due respect, my lady, that's not the right question," Kristen said and watched the dragons still surrounding them cautiously. "They should ask what *she* can do to *them.*"

Most of them growled at this, but Diamontus only laughed a big, hearty guffaw more suited for a tavern than the aftermath of a slaughter. "I like you, Steel Dragon. You have balls of steel, as the humans say." With another laugh, he took his human form and returned to the underground portion of the castle.

"And the rest of you, we need scouting parties in all directions to warn us via aura if more of those jets appear. We all saw the blast radius of these bombs of theirs. I don't want another attack to hurt more dragons. If you have ideas on how to defend ourselves, talk to your commanding officer. Now, people!" Shimmerclaw ordered.

The assembled forces obeyed. Some began to stack stones into some semblance of fortifications. Others took to the sky. Still others—the youngest of them—turned their attention to the damaged radar dish that had protruded from one of the turrets of the castle.

"Lady Steel, I thank you for your protection." The Council leader bowed.

Her heart fluttered in protest. She'd been in dragon society long enough to know a bow like that was a sign of great respect. Too bad she didn't deserve it.

"You honor me, Lady Shimmerclaw, but what victory we had here, as small as it was, belongs to Amy."

"Ah," the old dragon said and turned to the mage with a curious expression on her face. "But of course. If I wish the Steel Dragon's alliance, I should honor her ways. You did well, mage of Lady Steel.

We all owe you a great deal. If there is something I can do for you, simply ask."

"You could start by calling me my name instead of the Steel Dragon's mage."

"Very well, Amy," Shimmerclaw nodded. "And you may call me my given name as well," She uttered a long trumpet from deep within her throat. Kristen had been around dragons long enough to know it was the ancient guttural language dragons spoke before they took to the more complex human tongues. Whether she had meant it as a joke or an insult she couldn't tell, but she elbowed Amy to remind her to show some respect.

"Gee, thanks, but, uh… I'd feel awkward calling the leader of the Dragon Council anything but Lady Shimmerclaw."

"Of course, child. Now, Lady Steel, although this young mage— rather, *Amy*—was quite useful in this defense, I think it might be wise if she and some of your force went…elsewhere. That strike was quite…unfortunately timed."

She nodded. That was the damn truth.

"I fear the vote may not be reversed, not now that your work on the technomages has been overshadowed by this carnage. With tensions being what they are, it might be wise if the mage especially were somewhere else."

Neither Kristen nor Amy complained at Shimmerclaw not using her name in this particular rationalization. After all, dragons still scrutinized her and glowered at her naked wrist.

"She's right. Amy, I want you and all the dragons to get out of here. If this vote doesn't go well…"

"Lady Steel, with respect, I won't follow that order," Stonequest said and stepped closer so he could lower his voice.

"Too bad it's not up to you to question it."

"And if you're taken prisoner when they declare war because we left you here alone, will I be giving orders then?"

"He's right," Heartsbane said. "Most of the dragons here are trying to hide their fury because Shimmerclaw and Diamontus were both against attacking us, and we'd be crazy to leave you here."

Kristen wanted to tell them that they needed to go precisely because it wasn't safe there. The Council might very well vote for war and if they did, she had made it much too clear to Shimmerclaw where she stood. But, of course, she couldn't start talking about mutiny with so many dragon ears listening.

When no alternative presented itself, she accepted their advice. "All right. Emerald, Heartsbane, Stonequest, Lumos. You're with me. Timeflash, I want Amy on your back. The two of you lead the recruits to Detroit."

"Yes, ma'am," Timeflash said, growled something at the younger dragons, loaded Amy, and launched into a southward heading away from this place of pain.

But despite the carnage, the dragons handled it well. Kristen assumed they had been preparing for war so perhaps saw this is as part of the price of the battle they were ready to fight.

She had decided to start helping set up the defenses and perhaps recommend places to shelter in the event of another bomb strike when Shimmerclaw gestured for her to return to the castle.

Her demeanor much calmer than she felt, she followed and traversed the hallways beneath the island again. Once more, the chill from the cold of Hudson Bay seemed to permeate the stone.

A few side halls had collapsed from the explosions above but the main route was clear, except for a little debris here and there. They only came to one place that looked like it had caved in and blocked the path, but someone—likely Diamontus—had cleared the rubble to either side of the corridor.

They entered the Council's chamber. Even there, she could see evidence of the strike that had rocked the castle on the surface. A few stones had fallen from the wall and a layer of dust had drifted to coat every surface. Worse, the camera that had recorded them had fallen and its lens had cracked, so the video they were sending to the other Council members spread across the globe clearly showed the battle damage. It would be impossible to downplay the strike.

Although it seemed that any hope of downplaying anything was long gone.

Diamontus leaned over Boneclaw's shoulder and looked absolutely furious. "I told you we were too slow, Shimmer! Don't say that I didn't!"

"What are you talking about Diamontus? I only asked for a few hours to deliberate."

"He's right, my lady," Boneclaw whined.

"Right about what?"

"There was another attack exactly like this one! It seems humans can war with each other for centuries, but when presented with a threat from *us*, they band together like ants," the massive dragon raged.

"Boneclaw. Explain," Shimmerclaw ordered.

"It is as he said. There has been an attack by humans at the European rally point. Three Russian fighters struck their base with twelve missiles. They had no mage to stop them, though."

"The time for deliberation is over!" Diamontus bellowed. "We go to war—now!"

"That is *not* our call," Shimmerclaw said and her aura overflowed the hall.

"She's right, Diamontus," Boneclaw said. "Which is why I already called for the vote. The time for deliberation is over. Everyone is voting now. We'll have our decision in minutes."

The Council leader sighed, obviously disappointed by this turn of events, but it was clear her hands were tied. "If you'll excuse us, Lady Steel. It is time to do our duty."

CHAPTER SIXTEEN

Kristen felt like she barely had time to catch her breath before the door to the Dragon Council's chamber swung open.

She had positioned herself against the opposite wall so she looked directly into Shimmerclaw's eyes when the doors opened. Although the platinum dragon's aura betrayed nothing, sadness was very clear in her eyes—sadness, disappointment, and dread. She shook her head subtly only once but to Kristen, who waited for the outcome of the vote, and the meaning was as clear as day.

The result had not gone their way. Despite her and her team capturing the last of the technomages, the strikes from the fighter jets had done their job. The dragons had voted to go to war.

"There are preparations to make," Shimmerclaw said to Kristen, although she avoided eye contact. "I need to address the troops. I will *not* allow a slaughter."

Before she could so much as think of a reply, Lord Boneclaw stepped out of the chamber and walked toward her. Something was different about him. Before, he had seemed spineless—or if not spineless exactly, more like an eel than not—as if he could contort into any shape he wished if only to hold onto his power as long as possible.

Now, however, he seemed more like a shark that had smelled blood in the water.

"Lady Steel," he said, his voice not as weak as it had been mere hours before. "I wanted to personally congratulate you and thank you for your service to dragon kind. First, you stopped the technomages and now, you spared this base from most of the destruction."

"Not enough to stop the war, though!" Diamontus said gleefully over the old dragon's shoulder. Kristen studied the hulking brute for a minute and wondered if he was the Masked One, but she dismissed the idea outright.

She had fought that particular dragon. In the dark and in his shadow dragon form, yes, but she had fought him all the same. She felt —no, she knew—there was no way she had faced Diamontus with his crystalline shoulders and abrasive personality. No, the dragon she had fought had been a master of deception. He had not only literally been of shadow but had operated from the darkness, using her lack of knowledge against her. His strategy had been to avoid the light at all costs. To skulk, to creep, to hide, to wait, and to bide his time.

None of those seemed to be traits the massive dragon was capable of. As if to prove her point, he punched a stone wall, cracked it, then ran up the stairs, screaming for battle.

That left her alone with Lord Boneclaw.

"Pardon the interruption," he said. "Diamontus has always been excitable. I'm sure he'll be an incredibly valuable asset in this war, although I see you as a far more useful asset to our team. In fact"—he smiled viciously—"I have already prepared a reward for your service. It will need to be approved by the North American Council, of course, but I have no doubt they'll see things my way. They often do."

"What are you talking about?" Kristen asked and barely kept her disgust from her tone.

"Oh, pardon me. I'm getting ahead of myself," Boneclaw said in his simpering little voice she now saw for the lie it was. "The Council has voted for war. Well, war isn't the term we used, of course. More precisely, we voted to exterminate ninety percent of the human race so as to better remove the threat they represent to dragons."

She gasped. Even though she had already heard it from Shimmerclaw, it still felt like a punch to the gut to hear such horrors stated in such simple terms.

He continued, either oblivious to her stress or reveling in it. "These new weapons they have and the vast number of humans isn't something dragons can tolerate anymore. Their infernal breeding and wanton consumption of resources has been a problem for the last century, of course, but these weapons… Well, let me *thank* you once more for removing the creators of such things from the equation. That helped settle many minds, you know. Where before, dragons had feared the technomages, they now see an opportunity to wipe out the human militaries and destroy or exhaust what supplies of the infernal weapons they have."

"How can you possibly talk of rewards in any of this?" she sputtered.

"Oh, silly me and my tangents!" Boneclaw smiled. "Well, you are one of our most esteemed investigators and already experienced in combat against these dragon bullets and guided missiles. You also know what other strange weapons the humans will devise so I'm pushing to make you a captain in the North American Dragon Army. You will help me lead our people to victory. Isn't that wonderful? And if you do well, who knows? Perhaps you'll have a seat on the Dragon Council one day once these humans have been properly put in their place. You could even oversee their treatment. I know their habits are of unusual interest to you."

In a split-second, everything clicked into place for Kristen. She knew who the Masked One was—a Council member of great age and a man who worked from the shadows with hidden powers. There was no doubt in her mind that she looked her nemesis in the eye.

The Masked One was Lord Boneclaw.

The dragon who had told her he would kill her friends and wear their skulls for masks stood directly in front of her. Worse, he'd tried to give her a promotion to fight in *his* force.

"How did you know that guided missiles were used against the base?"

For the first time since she'd seen him, his careful visage slipped. "What did you say to me?"

"You said I had experience against guided missiles. How did you know that? For that matter, how did those fighters know about this base at all? There must be a dragon informant. I had thought that maybe there was a mole or something but now, I worry the rot goes far higher than that."

"I was *neutral*," Boneclaw—the Masked One because now that she'd thought it, she couldn't unthink it—growled.

"Of course, my lord," she said, although her aura made it obvious to him that it was a lie. "But someone told those fighters' commander about this base. Someone told them they had to strike now or the war wouldn't happen because I had already stopped the technomages. The funny thing about them is that they say a dragon pulled their strings too. Do you think it was Diamontus? He seems to be the smartest of the Council besides Shimmerclaw, and she's obviously soft."

"Diamontus is a *fool*," he hissed but seemed to realize what he was saying. "Maybe you can throw accusations around in the human justice system, but dragons will demand *evidence* for these impossible claims. What evidence do you have?"

"Nothing," she acknowledged. "Circumstantial at best but even those are weak."

"What are you accusing me of, exactly?" He narrowed his eyes.

"Nothing at all, my lord," she was quick to say. She knew dragon law well enough to know that if she outright accused him of wrongdoing, he could challenge her to a duel. If that happened, especially there in these dark tunnels with cracks in the walls that led to unknown places steeped in shadow, she had no doubt that the Masked One would obliterate her, even with all her training from Lumos. She couldn't give him reason to challenge her—not yet and not without evidence.

But Kristen also couldn't let him go without making him sweat a little either, not if she wanted to be able to continue to think of herself as a Detroiter. "I have no idea who could be behind all this, but I promise you this, my lord. I will do everything in my power to bring the truth to light, no matter how deep underground the cave it's hidden in might be." It was a reference to when she was trapped underground by the Masked One and it didn't go unnoticed.

Lord Boneclaw didn't flinch or even so mutch as twitch an eyebrow, but understanding flickered behind his eyes, followed by malice. She knew for certain, then. He was the dragon who had trapped her down there. It was he who had pulled her strings, controlled the technomages, and had pushed for war long before she had joined the Dragon SWAT team in Detroit.

It was him she had to stop.

"I've looked into that investigation—something about being misled to South America and tricked into a cave? Not your greatest work, I must say." His tone had taken on an oily edge and he seemed ready to pull another card out of his sleeve.

"I'm sure you've looked at the facts quite closely," she said.

"Oh, indeed I have. And there's nothing there that will be at all beneficial during a war. This conspiracy theory about a traitorous dragon must end. There will be time enough to ferret out those disloyal to dragon kind when this war is over. For now, Investigator, we need warriors, not detectives. And I happen to know—from extremely close sources—that you are indeed a proficient warrior. I can't wait to see what you can do against the humans."

"Yeah, the thing is, I won't stop. I won't sit idly by when injustice is done." Kristen shrugged. She couldn't believe what a relief it was to finally know the face of her enemy. Although she knew the Masked One could kill her as easily as she could kill a mouse, knowing who he was made her feel like she'd won a victory over him.

"I'm a cop, not a soldier," she said simply. "I never signed up for the army. I signed up to be a cop. My job is to bring the criminals to justice. *Whoever* they are."

"Well, I must say your commitment to your ideals is admirable." He patted her on her shoulder.

She noticed his hands were bony and his knuckles looked like thin leather pulled tightly over too-big bones. How had she not recognized him sooner? All she'd known of the dragon in the cave was that he was bony. His claws had seemed to almost lack flesh and his tail had been more like a spine than anything else. She'd seen Boneclaw take his dragon shape before too. When Constance had tried to blow the Dragon Council up, he'd fled when so many others had chosen to stay. Probably—she now realized—because he had known about the bomb. Hell, if Constance could be believed, this was the asshole who convinced a dragon to allow his offspring to be grown as clones and harvested for weapons.

"But," the Masked One continued. "Even a captain cannot disobey a direct order from a Council member. Neither in peacetime, nor in war."

Kristen rolled her eyes and pushed his hand off her shoulder. She knew he could destroy her in Dragon form, but in their human bodies, she certainly had the strength edge. "Then I'll talk to Shimmerclaw. I'm sure she'll see things my way."

"I'm afraid not. Guards?" He snapped his bony fingers and the guards who stood near the door all moved toward her. "Take her into protective custody. I will not allow you to pursue an investigation that might very well get you killed. If you don't wish to fight, it's not my place to order your execution, but I will not let you accidentally do something to endanger our forces."

She was about to spring into action—she could land some blows and kick him a few times before she reached the safety of the sunshine on the surface—when a guard put a diamond tipped spear to her neck. Her teeth clenched in suppressed fury, she was forced to watch her enemy walk away to direct the war he'd started.

CHAPTER SEVENTEEN

Willing herself to remain calm, Kristen looked at the dragon who held a spear to her neck. Another stood to his left , his hands balled in fists and wrapped in what must have been magic-blocking shackles with a long chain. He looked pissed. She could hear the other two dragons step up behind her. All of them were in human form as there wasn't space in these tunnels for dragon bodies.

"Sorry about this, my lady," the spear-wielder said. "I'm a big fan, honestly, but orders are orders. You can't disobey any more than we can."

"You're right," she said and raised her hands high above her head. "It'd be foolish, especially with four of you. I imagine you've seen all kinds of action."

"You got that right, Steel Bitch," said the dragon with chain and cuffs wound around his knuckles. "We've apprehended rogue drag-ons, blown castles up, and stopped dragon murderers. You name it."

She noted that he didn't say anything about *people.* It was a tiny detail, but she took note of it, nonetheless. Sometimes, small snippets of information made all the difference.

With them distracted, she dropped her hands abruptly and grasped the tip of the spear. The dragon holding it tried to stab her but she pulled it toward her, turned her skin to steel, and leveraged her superior weight to drive the spear-tip up and out of the way. After a quick twist, she now held the spear. The dragon's eyes widened in surprise as the weapon slid from his hands.

"It's always nice to meet a fan." She swung the spear—exactly like she'd practiced with Lumos—and caught him across the temple. He fell heavily. If he were a human, he'd be dead, but his dragon healing powers would likely revive him in moments.

Kristen sensed movement at her back and continued to twirl the spear to use it as a tool to keep her attackers away as much as a weapon for attack. She managed to catch one of them across the face. He yelped in pain and clutched his head. The diamond-tipped spear had cut him across the forehead and blood poured in his eyes, blinding him, if for only a few more moments.

The dragon with the shackles lunged at her. She stabbed the spear at him, but he wrapped it deftly with the chain connecting the two manacles. It was precisely what she had hoped he would do. She tightened her hold on the spear, dug the back of it into the stone floor, and used herself as a fulcrum so she could lift him and thrust him into the ceiling.

He impacted with the stone but seemed to be made of harder stuff than the other two she had already disabled. Instead of collapsing, he grasped the spear and wouldn't allow her to move it again.

Rather than struggle to regain it, she let it go, ran forward, and snatched the cuffs to wrest them away from him.

The dragon obviously knew the strength of the cuffs and didn't release them. Instead, he tried to snap one of them around her wrist.

No matter how many centuries this dragon had to snap handcuffs on people, he didn't have as much experience with them as Kristen did from her time as Detroit cop. She blocked his attempted arrest and managed to get one of the cuffs around his wrist instead.

He wilted immediately, denied access to his dragon powers. She put a boot to his chest and shoved him hard against the far wall.

The last guard rushed her from behind and wrapped her in his arms. She was still steel, however, and he couldn't move her. Instead, she lifted him off the ground and threw him into the wall next to his comrade with the shackles. With a burst of dragon speed, she darted forward and cuffed him. Fortunately, each cuff had the anti-magic enchantment, so both guards could do nothing but nurse their wounds that failed to heal.

Kristen turned to check the two dragons she'd disabled earlier.

The one with the spear fixed her with a calm look. He had taken a bronze horn from his belt. "I like you and I've always liked you. That's why I'll give you to the count of five before I blow this horn."

She didn't even consider taking it from him. Whether he blew it or not, she had to get out of there and she had to do it immediately. Plus, it wouldn't do to further injure a potential ally. "Thank you," she said as she raced down the hall, up the stairs, and into the courtyard, moving as fast as dragon speed could manage.

Before she was even all the way out of the stairwell, she began to change into her dragon form and dropped her steel skin at the same time as she knew she'd need the speed. That didn't stop her from simply exploding what was left of the stone that framed the doorway into the tunnel.

She vaulted skyward as Diamontus yelled to other dragons to bring her down. The Masked One had already seen the possibility of her escaping, then—of course he had—and set the massive dragon against her.

As she pumped her wings to gain height, she set her aura to "get the fuck out of here so you don't fucking die" and bellowed at her friends to follow her. In a blink, Stonequest, Emerald, Heartsbane, and Lumos were airborne and beat their wings furiously to catch up to her.

"What on earth have you gotten us into now?" Lumos inquired as if she had ordered them a particularly unusual appetizer.

"It looks like we're aiding and abetting a fleeing prisoner," Stonequest said as a horn blew from inside the tunnels of the dragon base.

"What the *fuck* did you do?" Heartsbane demanded.

"No time! Fly!" Kristen shouted as she tried to gain even more speed. Even beating her wings as quickly as possible, Lumos was able to outpace her.

"If you get caught, we should know why we're helping you. Did you kill someone?" Emerald asked.

"I wish!" She gasped. "I found out who the Masked One is—he's the Councilor, Lord Boneclaw. He was behind my abduction, probably the technomages, and maybe all the other bad shit too."

"Well, let's fuck him up, then!" Heartsbane replied.

"I don't know if that would be prudent," Lumos said and glanced over his shoulder.

"Yeah, I don't think so," Kristen said. "He has most of the Council in his pocket and ordered me to be taken into protective custody."

"So the vote—" Stonequest started to say.

"Went the wrong way," she finished for him.

"And we're running because you refused to join the war effort," Emerald surmised.

"Flying, but yes," she admitted shortly.

"Kristen, there's no way we can outpace them," Stonequest pointed out. "None of us have speed powers, and those six scouts closing the gap between us obviously do."

"And then there are all the other dragons behind them," Lumos pointed out pragmatically.

"I can't ask you to fight," she said, still breathless. "If you do, you'll all be fugitives until we can stop the Masked One and break up the faction he controls. And that's assuming we can even escape."

"Lady Steel, with respect, you don't *ask* us to do anything," Stonequest said. "You give us orders and we obey. Tell us to abandon you, and we might listen. Tell us to help you, and we definitely will."

She darted a glance at her old Dragon SWAT team. She could see on their faces and feel from their auras that their minds were made up. Not one of them wanted to see her arrested for refusing to go to war.

"In that case," Kristen said firmly. "We're leaving and they can *try* to stop us."

"I think they might do that very thing," Lumos commented dryly and gestured at the scout dragons who had caught up to the team.

When the fight began, it was obvious that the six dragons who attacked them were primarily trained as scouts. They were faster than anyone on her team. They pushed in, darted out of range, and raked the fugitives with their claws before they retreated.

The problem for the scouts was that their blows weren't particularly strong. One of them tried to slice Kristen's wings, and she caught the attacker in the armpit with her ax-blade tail. He tumbled away.

In the time it took her to deliver that strike, both Stonequest and Emerald had each dispatched another scout. They had injured them enough to slow their flight but not badly enough to knock them into the frigid waters below.

Heartsbane tangled with another one. She left her stomach exposed, and the scout took what he thought was an opening. Her powerful aura made the trap convincing and as soon as her adversary moved within range of her claws, she slashed him across his face and he screeched in pain as he flew away.

The two scouts who remained tried to double-team Lumos. They were faster on the wing than the ancient gold dragon, but his strikes seemed to move at the speed of light. Kristen felt like she barely had time to blink before one of the attackers held its eyes, blinded, as it fell toward the water below. The other was covered in scratches and had one especially grievous wound across his back. He pulled away, screeching for reinforcements.

It looked like he would get them, unfortunately.

Although Kristen and her team defeated the scouts easily, she couldn't exactly count that as a victory. They had outnumbered the fugitives but were smaller dragons who were built for quickness and trained for speed.

Her team was all former SWAT. They were strong, muscular dragons who were used to throwing themselves into the middle of fights. She had known they would win.

But it wasn't a win, not really, given that the combat had slowed them enough to let another forty or so very pissed off and very combat-savvy dragons catch up to her force of five.

CHAPTER EIGHTEEN

"Orders, Lady Steel?" Lumos prompted as their pursuers hurried to close in on them.

"Retreat!" Kristen ordered. It was the only sane choice. They were vastly outnumbered and her team was scratched and bruised from the fight with the scouts. No one had been seriously injured, but she knew that in a fight with odds like this one, every tiny little wound would be a factor. They all had too many to even try to defeat the force that approached.

"They're gaining," Emerald said.

It was true and it would only take a couple of them to catch up to them to the end the fight. She wouldn't abandon even one of her dragons, not willingly. But if one of them was caught up in a fight, they'd need to stop and help and the other dragons would be upon them.

It wasn't a fight they could win but what choice was there?

Suddenly, Kristen had an idea. She thought it could work in the short-term but it could have long-term implications. Then again, it seemed that if they didn't get out of this, long-term implications might never be an issue. They usually weren't for the dead.

With no other options, she decided to try it. "Stonequest, catch!" she shouted as she changed from her dragon form to her human one.

Immediately, the wind caught her and she lost her forward momentum. The gusts ripped at her clothes and for a moment, she could see herself splashing into the icy waters below.

Within seconds, Stonequest caught her in a claw and tossed her deftly so she landed gently on his back at the peak of her ascent in a perfect landing. She hoped she didn't piss him off too badly with what she intended to do next.

"What's the plan?" he asked, pumped his wings, and fell into formation behind Lumos, who led their mad rush southward. They still couldn't see the shore, not that it would make any difference to their pursuers whether the fight was over land or water.

Kristen didn't answer as she'd already moved onto the next step. She pulled her cellphone out and called their base in Detroit.

Brian answered on the first ring. "What's going on? Did you avert another world war?" he asked with complete confidence in his sister.

"Not this time!" she replied. "Put Constance on *now.*"

He didn't ask for details and less than three seconds later, the tech-nomage was on the line. "Kristen, is everything all righ—"

"I need a portal to Detroit ASAP. We're heading south from a base over Hudson Bay. Brian can tell you where we were."

"I *knew* they had a base in Hudson Bay!" The woman sounded triumphant.

"Bad shit is going down. I'd like to explain later but will not be able to do that unless you open a portal and get us the hell out here!"

"Okay, okay, but I can't simply open a portal in the middle of nowhere. I need a location to ground me. Somewhere I've been before."

"Just open a damned portal!" Kristen raged.

"I can't! Not without a destination. If I get the location wrong, it could tear you to pieces smaller than atoms."

"There's nothing but water. I...I can see land far off to the...uh, east, I guess," She tried to stay calm while their pursuers unleashed a volley of fireballs. They were still out of range but some of the faster dragons were catching up.

"East is good!" Constance replied quickly. "Before we knew our contact was on the Council, I was looking for dragon bases. I thought there might be one there so I—"

"Can we cut to the chase, please?" she demanded.

"Head to Akulivik Airport! There's a billboard there—God knows why because hardly anyone lives there—for smoked salmon. We'll open the portal right behind it to give you cover. Give us three minutes. Maybe five."

"Behind it?" she repeated in confusion.

The line had already gone dead and a second later, the phone buzzed. Brian—listening as always—had already sent her a location.

"To the left slightly!" she shouted to Lumos. He obliged and changed course while the others followed his lead.

Of course, their pursuers changed direction with them. It would be a close call whether they made it to Constance's coordinates in time or not.

"What's the plan?" the gold dragon asked from the front of the formation.

"Head toward a billboard for smoked salmon at a tiny airport. Constance will open a portal there in about three to five minutes."

"I don't think we have three, let alone five!" Heartsbane said.

"Go!" Kristen shouted.

"We would be faster if you'd stayed in dragon form," Stonequest said and dread crept into his voice. "Zed set you up with a headset. You could have called him from that—"

"I didn't transform to use the phone," she said and drew her pistol.

What she didn't say was that it was loaded with dragon bullets. She took a deep breath. The weapon felt heavy, which was probably only her reluctance. She didn't want to do this. Despite practicing with the damn things, she had never wanted to do what she was about to do. But what choice did she have? If they didn't escape, she had little doubt that they'd either be killed or imprisoned and forced to watch as the world burned.

Not today, she told herself resolutely.

Kristen waited for one of the fastest of their pursuers to get into range, took aim, and fired. Her shot was true and she tagged the dragon in the shoulder at the wing joint. Exactly like Lumos had taught her, she thought with bitter regret.

She had been shot there—in her human form anyway—by a dragon bullet. Her comfort was that she knew the dragon would survive the injury as long as they got the bullet out fast enough.

Unfortunately, she also knew the scream of pain was real because being shot by a dragon bullet hurt beyond anything else.

The dragon shrieked and tried to clutch its wounded shoulder as its wings flapped uselessly in the wind. It plummeted, alive but unable to do anything to preserve its life.

Five of the other dragons who had been the closest of those gaining on her and her team all tucked their wings and dove after their wounded comrade. She didn't know, though, if they did so primarily to save his life or because they didn't want to be the next dragon to take a bullet in the shoulder.

Still, more pursuers were trying to close the gap.

Kristen opened fire on them as well. She landed a hit and another dragon fell.

The gunshots and the dragon falling out of the sky seemed to click in the minds of her pursuers. They broke their formation, desperate to avoid being caught by a bullet. At this point, she was aiming to miss. She didn't want to hurt more of them, not with these weapons and not when she didn't have to. And she certainly didn't want to kill.

But the dragons didn't know that. They all took wild evasive maneuvers every time she fired.

Between shots, she checked her watch. Three minutes had passed, and they were above the coastline. The dragons still followed but less enthusiastically than before. None of them wanted to come close enough for her to hit them with one of the terrible bullets.

"What now?" Lumos asked, still in the point position of their formation.

"Look for a salmon sign."

"Got it." He corrected their trajectory and headed toward the lone billboard at the tiny Akulivik airport. It was horrendous and displayed a skinned salmon over a smoky fire, but its head still had its scales and it smiled with human teeth.

"Fly us through!"

"But what if Constance didn't finish opening the portal?" Emerald asked.

"Then we're fucked," she replied.

"Very well," the old dragon replied. "But I must say, I've never been a fan of smoked fish. I prefer it to be cooked *through*." He roared the last word and launched a great blast of fire that punched through the billboard like a bottle rocket blasting through a piece of paper.

Beyond it, a glowing blue ring made up the edges of the portal and the blessedly familiar sight of her Detroit base was visible in the center.

Lumos went through first, then Heartsbane, Emerald, and finally Stonequest with Kristen on her back. She continued to lay down covering fire to keep the pursuing dragons at bay. They vanished from the frigid air of Akulivik and emerged in the much more temperate climate of Detroit.

The portal was lower at ground level, though, so instead of soaring through and into the skyline of her hometown, Stonequest barely managed to avoid colliding with Emerald's tail. He got tangled in Heartsbane's wings and fell to join the pile of dragons who'd all come to a stop in a tangle of claws, tails and wings.

They were safe—or would be once they closed the portal.

Kristen pulled herself out of the tangle and began to squeeze rounds through the gateway to dissuade the dragons from following them.

Their pursuers seemed to have finally realized that only two of them had been shot and that this was their last chance to catch the Steel Dragon with the odds stacked so firmly against her.

They made no attempt to halt their pursuit.

"Close it! Close the damn portal!" Kristen ordered.

"You heard her, seal it." Constance added her commands. "And make sure it's a clean break. We don't want them to force any mages to follow us."

She had never seen a portal close from this side and had assumed they could simply be released. It seemed there was more to it than that.

The mages chanted and waved their hands as the portal shrunk.

In the last second before a dragon reached it, the gate finally vanished.

They were safe for a few hours at least.

"Uh, Kristen?" Brian said. "I know you're the boss and all, but I think you have some explaining to do."

CHAPTER NINETEEN

Once safely at their base, Kristen ordered everyone inside. They had a very short window in which to plan and prepare and couldn't waste a minute of it.

It was a little nerve wracking to realize that Amy and the dragons she traveled with were still moving south across Hudson Bay, potentially with a force of pissed-off dragons who might locate them, but there was nothing to be done about it. Brian said he was in contact with the mage and that she hadn't sensed any dragons with her magic, nor had any of the dragons accompanying her sensed other dragon auras in pursuit.

After finally discovering who the Masked One was and realizing that she had been in the same room with him quite a few times—as well as shared a cave with him while he hunted her—she knew he could hide his aura even better than Heartsbane. Still, she doubted his powers extended to the other dragons, so she forced herself to stop thinking about them and focused on formulating the plans they'd need going forward.

Still, she glanced constantly out of the northern windows of their base as if she might catch a glimpse of Amy and the young dragons before the scouts on the roof and the drones Brian had patrolling the skies of Detroit.

"What did the Council decide?" Constance asked.

She took a deep breath and hoped that the magic contract the mages had all signed was still fresh enough in their memory to prevent anyone from doing anything rash. "The Dragon Councils voted to go to war with humanity. Their plan is to eradicate ninety percent of the population. If they're not pursuing Amy already—"

"They aren't," Brian said from his bank of monitors hooked up to his surveillance sessions.

"They will be soon," she finished and regarded the technomages warily. No one freaked out, but why would they? They had joined their organization precisely because they feared that dragons might attack humanity and inflict even more pain on humankind than they already had. This probably didn't seem like a surprise to them but more like an eventuality or even an inevitability.

Kristen's old human SWAT teammates seemed far more surprised.

Hernandez summed up their emotions the most succinctly. "Well, that fucking sucks."

"But...we stopped the mages," Keith said and his voice quivered and made him sound like the rookie nickname he hated.

"There was an attack," Stonequest said. "Fighter jets tried to assault the dragon base with a dozen missile attacks."

"Thanks to the Steel Dragon and Amy, they only hit the base with seven of the missiles," Emerald added.

"Needless to say," Kristen went on, "the dragons are fucking pissed."

"Why the hell would the military attack a dragon outpost?" Jim fumed. "The first rule of the armed forces when I served was 'don't make the all-powerful dragons and their legions of mages angry.' What the fuck changed that?"

"The Masked One," she said and explained how she'd finally found out exactly who he was. She described how he'd pushed for this war from behind the scenes and how she was damn near certain he'd ordered the strike but of course, had no proof. "Which is our first priority right now. I need people here at this base to receive Amy and the dragon recruits and make sure this city isn't burned while I'm gone, trying to prove that Lord Boneclaw was behind this."

"That can't be our only priority right now," Constance said, and Kristen felt a pulse of magic between them. It was the contract, flexing its proverbial magic muscles at their disagreement. The technomage felt it too and she seemed dismayed before she continued. "If we want to protect humanity, we need the mages they took prisoner from Dragon SWAT HQ. With this war kicking off, the dragons might decide that having a group of mages locked up isn't as good as simply killing them."

"I can help with that one," Emerald said.

"What's that supposed to mean?" the woman demanded. Kristen could tell by the fire in her eyes that she thought he meant he could help slaughter the mages, which of course couldn't be further from the truth. He had personally worked with the mages they were trying to rescue, and—being younger than most dragons—didn't have his prejudices so deeply ingrained under his scales. It was a small reminder that even though they were a team, it would still take time before everyone meshed.

"I think Emerald means he has intel." Kristen tried to clarify, although she had to admit she was also slightly confused. He'd returned to the base at the same time as her.

"That's right." He nodded. "While Kristen was pissing off one of the most powerful dragons alive, I was shooting the shit with the other dragons in the ranks—the general fighters. I found out from them where the prison is. It's a human-style prison in Nebraska. Tecumseh."

"Spell that," Brian responded quickly and the dragon complied.

"How can you trust that?" the techie asked, his fingers in rapid motion to uncover everything he could on the prison. Kristen knew from experience that he'd have floor plans, visitor logs, and even camera security feeds if the prison wasn't as good at security as he was at breaking through it.

"Call it a feeling," Emerald said. "But I'm telling you the guy wasn't lying. He said he took the mages there and talked a whole ton of shit about how crappy and pathetic the facility was, how it could never hold a dragon, and how it probably wouldn't be able to hold the mages for more than a day. He was working some of the other dragons for laughs. I don't think it was a trick."

"Okay, that's good," Kristen said. "Constance, I want you and your team to formulate a plan with Brian for how to get the mages out of there without any loss of life. When I get back from the base that launched these planes—"

"Alaska!" Brian answered the unasked question. "It was the 3rd Wing out of Alaska. They flew above the clouds so the dragons wouldn't see them coming, but that left them visible to eyes in the sky."

"Right," she continued. "That will be our next move after Alaska."

"Boss, I don't want to disagree but I don't know if the mages can wait," Emerald said.

"I don't think the dragons would execute them in a human prison. The publicity would be bad."

"The time for caring about publicity is over," Katrina said. "The dragons will strike with impunity now."

"It's not that," Emerald said. "Although the Iron Dragon probably has a point on appearances meaning much less than they once did. This guard said they would move mages ASAP. Either that or…" He sliced his fingers across his neck.

"We can't let that happen," Eric said, the leader of the technomages cell that had been on the island base.

"Of course not," Kristen sighed. She didn't want to split up but knew that the time for her being able to do what she wanted was long gone. "We have two missions, so we'll need two teams. Plus, I won't leave this base empty, not with that force in Hudson Bay. Shimmer-claw made it clear my people would be safe—and I assume that still applies given all that's happened—but it means I need dragons and humans on patrol to make it very clear that this whole city counts as my people."

"That will spread us very thin," Drew pointed out.

"Not anymore. We have a bigger force than we used to, remember?" she said and glanced at Constance, Katrina, and Eric. "Constance, your people already busted you out of an ultra-secure magic prison. Do you think they can pull it off a second time?"

"In Nebraska? We'll have to be careful with the armed guards, but yes. If you give me a team of mages and either Katrina or Lumos, we can get those mages out."

"Take Katrina," she said and wondered if she had made the biggest mistake of her time as an investigator or the smartest move ever. The magic contract should bind them all together, but what would happen if someone went against it? They'd seen one mage explode, but would the Iron Dragon take that for the obvious threat it was? Or did she see herself as stronger than that? Kristen sighed. Despite the experiences that might suggest otherwise, she believed in trust and that people could change. She also believed she didn't have much of a damn choice.

"I'll come too," Eric said.

"No, I don't think so," she replied. "I need a powerful mage here. As soon as Amy gets back, I'll bring her with me and Larry is still traveling by boat. The dragons know we used unfettered mages to fight—hell, that's why some of them hate me. We can't leave this base without someone who can give them a show if they decide to come take a peek."

"Understood." He didn't look happy about it but she didn't care. Being happy was not a prerequisite for following orders.

"Butters, Beanpole, I want you two here as well—on the roof and armed with dragon bullets at all times. Is that understood?"

"Yes, ma'am," both men answered. She was happy to see the sniper's leg had finally healed thanks to the mages' help. He was back at one hundred percent.

"Keith, you too. Brian might need your help."

"Yes, ma'am," the Rookie replied. He didn't look any happier about being left at the base than Eric had.

"Hernandez, I want you to go with Constance in case they need demolitions."

"You're asking a former cop to help blow people out of a prison?" the woman asked.

"Is that a problem?"

"More like a dream I never thought I'd live to see fulfilled," the demolitions expert retorted and flashed her a grin.

"With me, I want Lumos, Stonequest, Heartsbane, Jim, and Drew. We'll need Amy, too. Brian, I need you to set up a rendezvous location for her and the jet we'll hire."

"No problem. She will love that," Brian said.

"If it's all the same to you, boss, I'd prefer to stay here," Emerald said. "I know more of our dragons should arrive soon, but Timeflash isn't much of a fighter—no offense—and I think our green wings might need someone in charge."

"Okay, that's a fair point. You'll be in command," she agreed. "Do we have any questions?"

"When do we start?" Constance flashed a smile.

"Five minutes ago."

CHAPTER TWENTY

Not long after, Kristen's team arrived at the airport in Anchorage, Alaska. Taking a portal wasn't a good option because none of the mages knew the area very well, which meant getting out might be a problem. A private jet could fly faster than any dragon could and they might need it to escape, so she chartered one. They could have flown directly into the base, but she knew that could be seen as either aggressive, arrogant—what with the private jet—or both. Kristen decided the ugly brown van they rented would look far less threatening.

They all clambered inside with Drew at the wheel. Amy insisted on riding her skateboard outside the van, however. She used the vehicle to pull her around and give her momentum to do tricks, which she of course augmented with her insane magical powers. Kristen had already seen her accomplish feats she'd only ever seen in videogames. She was currently grinding a pipeline.

Brian's rendezvous point with the mage had worked perfectly. They had flown the jet north, put down on a highway that was under construction and slated to open in a few days, and waited about thirty seconds for Amy to meet them. In mere moments, they were airborne again.

It felt good to know that the dragons the girl had traveled with were already on their way to Detroit. They'd seen no dragons behind them, so at the very least, Emerald would be able to allocate all the dragons to defensive stations and prevent a rout if the enemy was in pursuit.

The enemy, of course, was now—legally—all of dragon kind. It wasn't a pleasant thought.

It was also the reason why Kristen was in a dingy rental van at the entrance to an Air Force base and talking to a guard who looked like he'd swallowed a grenade.

"Hi. My name is Kristen Hall. I'm a dragon investigator and police officer from Detroit. I'd like to come in and ask a few questions."

"I'd like you to put that van in reverse and get the hell out of here, ma'am," the soldier replied and his voice cracked as he raised it to almost a shout. He took deep breaths, obviously aware that he wasn't supposed to yell at people arriving at the gate. "We are on lockdown, ma'am. That means no one comes in. Especially not a dragon and a magic skateboarder."

"Amy!" she snapped.

The young mage shrugged. She'd been doing flip tricks nonstop since they'd arrived—kickflips, heelflips, impossibles, and shove-its, all at blinding speed—and made no effort to stop.

Kristen examined the guard. The poor kid looked very young— like he couldn't drink beer yet young. Plus, he didn't sound like any of the Alaskans they'd met and his accent suggested he was from a city in the east coast like Philadelphia or Baltimore. She was better with midwestern variations. The kid looked like he'd been on the job for all of a day when someone on his base had commanded someone else to start a world war. She could understand why he looked stressed.

"I need to talk to the general here," she explained calmly. "I'm trying to stop people from getting hurt. Can you help us do that?"

"No, ma'am. I'm sorry. Lockdown means lockdown. No exceptions."

Heartsbane leaned forward from the back of the van. "Do you want me to do something about him?"

"No, no, it's fine," she said until the soldier noticed the other dragon.

"Do you have more people in there?"

Kristen nodded politely. "We do. That's why we have a van. To fit more people."

"Like I said, you need to back the hell up. No, wait," the boy said, his expression suddenly one of puzzlement. "You…you want to help?"

She glanced at Heartsbane. It seemed the dragon had already used her mastery of her dragon aura ability to affect the guard's mood. She didn't blame him for following orders. His emotions were already controlling his thoughts so was this any different? It didn't matter, she decided, not in the face of a world war.

"We do," Heartsbane affirmed encouragingly. "And you can be the one who helps." She winked, an enchanting gesture from the beautiful blonde that was her human body. "And you can help *me*—I mean us."

"I can," the guard said.

"Call your base commander and tell him to have you open this gate."

From the tone of voice coming from the other end of the guard's phone, the base commander didn't sound too happy to have dragons arrive on his doorstep. When the guard hung up, however, he opened the gate and let them proceed, albeit with an armored car escorting them as they drove their dilapidated vehicle deeper into the base.

They proceeded directly to the main headquarters. It didn't take a veteran to see that the facility was on high alert. Pilots stood near their fighter jets and tried not to fidget. Others manned anti-aircraft artillery that Kristen could only assume was equipped with dragon bullets. Everyone moved quickly and no one was smiling. But at least they weren't celebrating.

They stopped at the headquarters building and were escorted inside.

"General Peralt, this is the…uh, dragon who came to the gate to see you," the officer who'd guided them through the hallways said. "Kristen Hall, Steel Dragon and Investigator, this is General Samuel Peralt."

The general was fairly short and quite thin, with a narrow black mustache and thin grey hair on his head. Kristen shook his hand cordially. "You're more than welcome to take a seat but maybe your friends want to wait outside?" he asked. She could see fear in his eyes and taste it on his aura.

"That would be fine," she agreed and nodded at Amy and the dragons who had accompanied her. If he tried anything against her personally, she would simply turn to steel and move with the speed her dragon powers granted her. Even if he was armed with dragon bullets, he wouldn't stand a chance. The real threat would come from the others on the base, in which case it was better if her team was already outside. They could more easily eliminate the most immediate threats, namely the jets and the anti-aircraft weapons.

It made her nauseous to think that she was half-subconsciously planning how to disarm an entire military base, but this was her life now.

As her team filed out, Kristen made a quick survey of the general's office. There was a smattering of medal certificates on the walls, including a purple heart, plus photographs of him smiling broadly with different groups of people. Many of them looked like the survivors of wars, possibly people Peralt had liberated or helped in some way. There were no pictures of him with politicians or dragons. That was something she appreciated. Based on his office, General Samuel Peralt seemed like a good, decent officer with a long career doing the best work the military did.

So why had he ordered his jets to fire on the dragon base?

"I know you're here because you're wondering why my jets fired on your base," the general began and cut to the chase.

"We're not here for a whale tour, that's for sure," she said.

Peralt uttered a loud, hugely awkward laugh. Immediately, his aura shifted from one of barely controlled terror to one of lingering fear and a substantial injection of hope.

"Did you give especially bad tours, General?"

"No, no. Nothing like that," he said, took a perfectly folded hand-kerchief out of a pocket, and dabbed the sweat that had appeared on his brow. "I merely assumed that if you're here to roast me alive, you probably wouldn't lead with a joke."

"A number of dragons would certainly support me if I did that. Is there a reason why I should not roast you alive?" she asked and tried to make it sound like a joke.

He forced a chuckle. "Well, for starters, you'd be getting rid of the guy knee-deep in his own investigation into why the hell three of his pilots went off and attacked an island in dwarf territory with live fire."

"Didn't you order that strike?" Kristen asked.

"Hell no!" Peralt declared. "My job for the past decade has been to make sure no one pisses the dwarfs in Canada off and that the dwarfs don't piss anyone off either. That includes dragons, by the way. The *last* thing I want is to be the head of the snake that was thrown into the barn and started all this mess. Honestly, those idiots fired on drag-ons. It's a disgrace."

"It's good to know you didn't command it," she said. Although she wasn't the best when it came to sensing auras, his was very straight-forward. She didn't think he was lying about this. If he had been, he wouldn't have been so scared when she'd arrived.

"Of course I didn't command it. And I'm willing to do what I can to make things right."

"You can start by handing over the surviving pilot for questioning."

His aura clenched along with his jaw. "I'm afraid I can't do that, ma'am."

"And why not?"

"Because that knucklehead broke orders on *my base* with *my jets.* My people are mine to punish, and their actions are mine to investi-gate. I can't simply turn them over to you, even though they probably deserve to be fileted and roasted. It's against protocol." He tried to make it sound like he refused dragons to their face all the time, but she could tell from the sweat on his brow that he didn't.

Kristen could have told him that dragon law trumped human—it was true, after all—but she didn't. Her goal there was, as always, to build bridges between the two cultures, not walls. Still, she wouldn't simply walk away empty handed. "I'd really appreciate your cooperation, General Peralt. That strike was used to justify war against mankind."

The general paled. She didn't blame him and had felt the same way when the vote had crushed her hopes to avoid conflict.

"I have reason to believe a dragon may have been involved in triggering the strike," she continued. "This is a fact-finding mission, not a punitive one. I need answers about this dragon, and I need your help to get them. If you refuse, the blood of billions could be on your hands."

"Jesus, no pressure," Peralt said and rubbed his thin gray hair. "I only… You think a *dragon* did this? Why on earth would a dragon get my fighters to attack their own people?"

"Dragon politics," she said. "You wouldn't want to be involved."

He chuckled again. "You got that right! I hate the monsters in American politics—some of the things they make our men and women in the armed forces do is plain horrible—but *dragons?* Their politicians must be a whole other level of…" He trailed off. "You're… you're not a dragon politician, are you?"

"Not willingly," Kristen grumbled. "But I am trying to stop this war from breaking out, which means I need to be able to show a number of them evidence that is convincing enough to call this off."

Peralt still looked pale but he nodded. "Look, if I knew one of my people was taking orders from a dragon, I'd gladly hand them over to you. That breaks about every military law we have. How about we talk to the pilot together? He didn't tell me much but you seem to be more…persuasive, Investigator."

"You can call me Kristen," she said. He had an honest aura and she liked him. She also knew she needed every ally she could get.

"Then please stop calling me General. Sammy's fine. That's what everyone calls me when I'm not in uniform and since you're a dragon investigator, you must outrank me in almost every way possible. Now, shall we?"

"That'd be great, Sammy."

They exited through the same entrance the team had used and stepped out onto the grounds in front of the base. Sammy frowned at the beat-up rental van they had and offered to let them all ride in the back of an armored car. The dragons jumped at the opportunity a little too quickly. She realized that Jim must have told them to keep their eyes out for dragon munitions and this was the perfect opportunity.

As they drove through the base, every inch of their journey was watched by tense soldiers. They no doubt wondered if the commander of their base was about to be executed in front of them to teach them a lesson.

They found the pilot who escaped in a military cell, which helped calm Kristen's nerves somewhat about the entire situation. She trusted Sammy, but she also knew that auras could be misleading. Finding the pilot under actual arrest and not merely confined to his quarters helped convince her that he and his people were taking everything seriously.

"Jeremy," General Peralt said stiffly, "this is Investigator Kristen... uh, Steel. She's a dragon and is here to find out what I wanted to know. What in the hell could compel you and your two late comrades in arms to go against orders and fire on a dragon base in dwarf country?"

"Yes, sir. Of course, sir. Wait a minute, I know her!" The pilot pointed at Amy. "Holy crap, you are the woman who made Don and Marissa crash, aren't you? I didn't know mages could be that strong. You really scared the shit out of me back there, you know that?"

"Did I?" the girl asked, stepped forward, and made the bars of his cell shake. The dust rose from the floor of his cell as if she were powering up to make him explode.

"Hey, look, I only followed orders!" Jeremy said hastily, moved away from the bars, and tripped over a floating tray of food to fall on his ass.

"Whose orders?" Peralt pressed.

"Yours, sir. Or I thought they were yours. My flight commander gave them to us. He said we wouldn't like it but that our job was our duty, not likes. Miller is always like that."

"And you didn't question the order?" Kristen asked.

"Are you kidding? This is the most dangerous base in the United States," The pilot practically spluttered. "We have Russia on one side, dwarven Canada on the other, and the West Coast to the south of us which is crawling with dragons as everyone knows. General Peralt has trained us to follow orders because questioning them would cost lives. And I'm telling you, these orders looked official." He pushed to his feet and seemed to take in his surroundings again. His gaze looked through the bars to his frowning general, the dragon investigator, and the mage who had stopped both his friends from killing any more dragons. "I can see now that I messed up."

"And who did you say gave you these orders? An officer named Miller?" Kristen asked.

"Yes, ma'am."

"It's no good, Investigator," the general said, no doubt defaulting to her title in front of his soldiers so she'd do the same.

"And why's that, General?"

"Because we already asked Miller about it. He said they came from me. I was trying to determine if he was bullshitting me or if someone had wormed into our computer systems when you arrived."

"This wasn't done by someone with a good understanding of computers," she said, more to Amy and Stonequest than to anyone else. "We need to talk to Miller. Is he also under arrest?"

"No, ma'am," Peralt said and a trace of worry worked into his voice again. "Standard protocol dictates—"

"We're so far past standard protocol that it hurts, General," she said. "I need to talk to Miller, and now."

"Sure. I didn't arrest him, but I had him confined to his home here on base. We can be there in less than ten minutes."

Ten minutes later, they finally found a soldier who hadn't followed orders.

The man's house was empty and his car gone.

The general tried him on the phone, but he was apparently both too guilty and too smart to answer.

The other officers began to examine his computer for clues about where he was headed, but they made no progress.

"I don't see anything that could give us any leads," Drew said. He'd jumped into the hunt, hoping to show these military folk what a good old-fashioned police officer could do to locate a criminal. But he'd come up empty handed, exactly like everyone else.

"It's all right," Amy said and held an extremely loud Hawaiian shirt up. "Is this his?"

One of Peralt's soldiers chuckled. "You're damn straight it is. Miller's always going on about moving to a tropical island when he's done here. He hates the cold."

"I can feel his aura on this," the mage said. "And I can feel him… He's…south… Yes, south of here and moving." She opened her eyes in alarm. "He's moving damn fast!"

"Can you lead us to him?" Kristen asked.

The girl nodded. "Try to keep up." She tossed her skateboard into the air and made it spin effortlessly and twist to land in front of her. Without a glance at the team, she stepped on and accelerated.

"Let's go, people!" Kristen shouted at her dragons, plus Drew and Jim. "Follow that skateboard!"

CHAPTER TWENTY-ONE

Constance had to admit there were advantages to working with the Steel dragon. The facilities, for starters, were much nicer than the old barns and abandoned ranches most of the technomages had come to think of as home. The tech was also notably better.

In less than twenty minutes, Brian had used the most advanced computer she had ever seen to give her everything she'd ever wanted to know about Tecumseh.

It made planning the snatch and grab of the mages feel like child's play.

Based on the security feed he had hacked into, they knew the captives were held in a wing of the prison filled with solitary confinement cells. In a troubling omission of accountability, there were no cameras in that particular part of the prison. Faced with this, they had gone through the video again and confirmed that the mages had been taken into that wing and had never left, so it seemed a reasonable assumption that they were still there.

If they were still alive.

"All right, we'll port into the shower area at the solitary confinement cell block," she told her team. "If anyone needs any more photos to properly understand where this portal is going, check in with Zed."

She found it odd that the prison had cameras in the showers and not in the solitary confinement area, but she had many problems with human society as well as dragon society.

"We'll port in and close the portal behind us. Katrina will get us into the solitary wing. There should only be one guard at this time of day, so we'll have Keisha put him to sleep. Once we release the mages, we can be on our way. Any questions?"

"How long will you be gone?" Emerald asked.

"If all goes according to plan, ten minutes," Constance said.

"Great. Eleven minutes means the shit has hit the fan. that's good to know," he said grimly.

The woman nodded. He had the right of it. "If there are no more questions, let's begin."

Two minutes later, the portal was open and created a rip in the fabric of space that connected the inside of their base in Detroit to the showers in the Tecumseh prison.

Three men with the shoulders of those with nothing to do but push ups and pull ups and tattoos that looked like they belonged in the prison were there to greet them.

"What the fuck?" one of them asked, but the other two shushed him as the Constance led her team of mages, military personnel, and a couple of the young dragons through.

"Guard?" she asked and guessed that these prisoners were not fans of the people who kept them under lock and key.

The prisoner pointed to a bank of toilet stalls, all without doors. "Last one on the left."

"I'm on it," Katrina said.

"Katrina, wait," the technomage said.

But the Iron Dragon didn't listen. She marched to the stall at the end which happened to be the only one that would give the person inside any privacy from the rest of the bathroom.

In a moment, everything went to shit.

"You're not supposed to be in here!" was punctuated by the sound of gunfire. Of course, it meant little to Katrina. Even if she had been a normal dragon, it was unlikely that bullets fired from a pistol would have been able to do more than slow her somewhat. Given that she was the Iron Dragon and had reflexively turned her skin to iron as soon as the man had raised his weapon, she didn't even blink when the bullets struck her.

Instead, she raced forward and vanished into the stall.

The sound of bones breaking, porcelain shattering, and tiles cracking followed and suggested that Katrina had kicked the man through the wall. After a moment, the dragon called to her. "He's still breathing. Orders?"

"Leave him," Constance said. "The Steel Dragon doesn't want fatalities. We don't kill if it's possible to avoid it."

"Have it your way," the dragon said and returned with a ring of keys and a keycard.

"We don't want any trouble," one of the inmates said.

"We won't give you anything but a choice," the technomage said calmly. "You can have these keys and try to lead your fellow inmates in an escape, or you can go back to your cells and stay the hell out of our way."

"Are y'all here to get those magic motherfuckers them dragons brought in?" the man asked, surprisingly cool and confident given that he was butt naked.

Constance nodded.

"Fuck that!" one of the other prisoners said.

"Y'all have at it," said the first one. "We'll be in our cells."

"Very well."

"And lady?"

"Yes?"

"I'd hurry if I were you. Them dragons came through not too long ago and made a ton of noise. We was worried we was gonna miss out on all the excitement, but looks like they're about to get more than they bargained for."

She nodded her thanks and led her team in the direction Zed indicated through her earpiece. They exited the showers into a general-purpose holding room.

"Schematics say the door to the solitary hallway should open with a good old-fashioned metal key," he said in her earpiece.

Constance tossed the ring to one of the Steel Dragon's soldiers who came with them. "You're up."

The man caught it and began to try them one by one.

A scream came from the other side of the door. She recognized it immediately. It was the sound of someone being burned alive by dragon's fire.

"We don't have time for this shit," Katrina said and put her iron foot through the door in front of them.

It shattered completely like a pane of glass that had fallen from the top floor of the Fisher building in Detroit.

On the other side of the door was the type of scene the techno-mage had never seen but had always feared.

Mages were lined up on either side of the hallway, shackled wrist to wrist and in nothing but their underpants. She only recognized them as mages because some of the men had the elaborately shaved beards and heads that most people thought augmented magic power. Both men and women had the swirling tattoos that many shackled mages got in an attempt to reclaim some of the powers the dragons took from them.

Normally, merely seeing those tattoos bothered her but right now, she could see the dragons had already taken away much more than magic powers from some of the mages.

Beyond the prisoners and at the far end of the hallway was a group of dragons in their human forms. Like all of their kind, their human forms were extraordinarily handsome or beautiful and they were dressed exquisitely. In keeping with their habitual attitudes, they seemed high on their power.

In the middle of them stood a small dragon in his reptilian form. In front of him lay a charred pile of corpses. From the height of the pile, she knew that at least a half-dozen mages had died already.

She wouldn't let one more suffer that fate.

"Your blood is impure and tainted with magic," one of the human-shaped dragons said to a mage in front of the firebreather. "For that, you must burn." He didn't seem to have noticed that the door to the cellblock had been kicked open. Constance assumed he had too big an erection at the thought of murdering people to focus on much else.

The dragon inhaled and its eyes and many of its scales glowed as it prepared to incinerate the whimpering mage.

Constance used her power over wind to blast a tornado of swirling air down the hallway. It divided around the mage and struck the inferno launched from the dragon's throat before it could immolate the target.

The flames scattered and quickly ignited the fancy clothes of the dragons at the end of the hall.

"How dare you!" one of them shouted.

"Permission to use lethal force, ma'am?" One of the human troops —not a mage, she was thankful to see—asked.

"Oh, fuck yes."

The battle was quick and its conclusion decisive.

The human soldiers laid down covering fire with dragon bullets. They aimed over the head of the mage who now crouched in a huddled mass on the floor. While they might have killed all the dragons with ease, with the mages lining the hallway, the soldiers couldn't take the risk that someone other than the enemy would be wounded.

Still, their bullets savaged the dragon who had incinerated mages like they were nothing but hotdogs. He died, bleeding out from his neck, and his blood soaked the corpses he'd left of the mages who had sworn to serve dragon kind.

As soon as the human soldiers stopped firing, Katrina raced forward. Her iron body made the hallway shake, and the mages who had still been on their feet fell to their knees or their butts and protected themselves as she stormed through. She reached the other dragons and unleashed a concerted assault. One after the other, they were hurled into the walls of the hallway with enough force to crack the concrete.

But these were dragons, not men. Those she didn't strike retaliated and fought with as much speed as her, plus the ferocious edge granted by terror. Even the few she had flung into the wall quickly recovered.

They all attacked the Iron Dragon.

"Forward!" Constance shouted at her mages. They obeyed, moved down the hallway, and positioned themselves as close to the dragons as they could to eliminate them with blasts of magic.

The two young dragons helping them rushed forward as well. Because of their dragon speed, they reached the fight before the mages did. They managed to draw a few away from Katrina, but that only entangled them in their own fights and made it more difficult for the technomages to target the dragons effectively.

Still, Katrina had been with Constance her entire life. She was a ferocious, powerful fighter, but she was also a tactician. A dragon lunged and she caught his neck in one hand and his groin in the other and threw him over the heads of the two younger dragons who attempted to help her.

He landed heavily directly in front of the technomage team.

In an instant, a bolt of lightning pierced his heart and he was no more.

The Iron Dragon threw another one at them and they dispatched it as efficiently.

"That's enough!" one of the dragons yelled. "Stop or we kill this youngling!"

"Hold up, hold up!" Constance shouted.

The dragon had one of their young dragons by the neck. She could tell by the gleam in his eyes that he knew very well how to kill the dragon if he so desired.

"You're here for the mages?" he asked.

"That's right. Set them free and no more of you dragons have to die."

"You're a real stupid bitch, you know that? A war is on. I'd rather die and bring all these mages with me than let them go."

As if on cue, the alarms blared.

The enemy dragon flinched at the sound, mistaking it for more gunfire or who knew what, and his captive squirmed to loosen his hold.

Katrina sprung into action. She raced past the enemy she had been battling and vaulted forward with a flying kick that put her iron toes through the skull of the dragon who had tried to threaten them.

"I guess I was wrong about that guard back there," Katrina said. "If I had killed him, he wouldn't have activated the alarm." She said this as she focused on dispatching the other dragons.

It didn't take long for her to complete her purpose.

With a younger dragon on the sidelines and the other one holding his neck where he'd been hurt, Katrina and the technomages were able to isolate and kill each of the remaining executioners.

Constance had barely given the order to unshackle the captive mages when gunfire erupted from the doorway.

"Shields!" she ordered.

"But the mages—" one of her mages protested.

"Will be freed. Shields, *now!*"

They obeyed and threw up a shimmering barrier at the entrance to the hallway through which they had entered.

The bullets of the regular prison guards stopped abruptly at the magic shield, much to the surprise and relief of the human soldiers who had been about to be mowed down.

"Don't let those shields down," Constance ordered.

"But if we don't let the shields down, how are our mages supposed to open a portal?" one of the young dragons asked.

"It's simple," Katrina answered and stepped toward the magical barrier that shimmered as it absorbed the force of the bullets. "Let me through and I will kill every single one of these kennel masters."

"No!" their leader replied. "These are human guards whose job is to prevent the escape of prisoners who have broken human laws. We will not slaughter them needlessly."

"Then what? We wait until that gunfire exhausts the powers of our mages, then I watch you all get gunned down in this hallway, and *then* I kill them?" The dragon snorted. "Because that way, even more people die."

"I can blow us out!" one of the Steel Dragon's people said. She recognized the Hispanic woman who seemed to be obsessed with bombs.

"It's too risky," she replied. "And besides, you'd merely get us to another part of the prison."

"No, I can—"

"We can help," one of the captive mages said and pushed to her feet. She was a mess. Both nostrils were bloody and her body was covered in bruises. She still had underwear on but it looked like her bra had been ripped off by dragon claws. "Take these cuffs off and we can help."

"You've never opened a portal before," Constance stated. It was true. No mage outside her organization had except for a few of the Steel Dragon's mages.

"Then we'll hold the barrier against those guns. I don't know if we can do that either but we can try. We'll buy you as much time as we can."

Constance looked at this almost naked bruised woman with respect. "You understand that your jobs at the Detroit dragon SWAT are gone? We'll take you to the Steel Dragon, but she's allied herself with a group of unshackled mages instead of dragon kind."

"I have no problem with the Steel Dragon!" One of the mages coughed. "She used to bring us donuts."

"It sounds better than being slaughtered in here like a herd of pigs," a mage who looked remarkably like a pig ready for slaughter said. He had no clothes on at all. Constance didn't know if his fat gut hanging over his small penis did him any favors or the opposite.

"We're wasting time," Katrina said. "And I will not let you get shot by a team of security guards."

"Get their cuffs," she said to the Iron Dragon, the soldiers, and the dragons and they hurried to comply.

The mages had listened to the exchange. Once released, each of them went to join the mages blocking the door. As the shield was augmented by their magic, the technomages fell back and began to cast the spell to open a portal.

Constance had to help with the portal, of course—she was the most powerful mage present and the most adept at this form of magic —but damn if that fact didn't piss her off. The shackled mages were too battered and too used to having their power inhibited to be of much use. Although they greatly outnumbered her force, they were far weaker. Each of her mages needed three or four of the prisoners to provide the same amount of protection.

Time was against them, and it became a choice between creating the portal and rescuing as many as possible or reinforcing the shield, which would ultimately fail anyway when they wearied and could no longer maintain it.

It was a difficult decision, but she pulled her team away to help with the portal and it wasn't long before bullets began to penetrate the barrier.

There weren't many—one in a hundred or maybe less—but when standing in a large group in a narrow hallway, that was enough to be devastating.

By the time they opened the gateway, another half-dozen of the imprisoned mages were dead. She yelled for the barrier to be taken down and for everyone to run to the portal.

Katrina stepped in to block every bullet that entered the hallway with her combination of dragon speed and iron skin. Still, another mage fell with a bullet in his back. Constance knew the dragon would blame herself for the death.

"Katrina! We're through. Come quickly!" she ordered.

The Iron Dragon roared at the humans—a supremely unnatural experience as the roar of a dragon came from her human throat—before she sprinted through the magical gate. Once in the base, Constance ordered the portal closed and her mages didn't need to be told twice.

They let it shut and sagged to the floor from the exertion.

"How did it go?" Emerald asked. He tried to sound calm but looked flustered at the condition of the mages. And why not? He had worked with these mages and had probably known many of them for years. Now they were in his office, bruised, almost naked, and weeping for their fallen.

"We didn't lose any of our people," Constance said. She'd paid careful attention and not even a regular human soldier or mage had been killed. "We rescued close to eighty mages, although maybe ten or twenty perished there."

"Damn," the dragon said and shook his head in disappointment. "Those are good numbers but this sure doesn't feel like a victory." He turned to the human soldiers in the base as well as some of the dragons. "Get these people clothes, food, and water. We need a medical team in here too, stat."

The technomage leader began to assist the captured mages. She reassured them when she had to and told the others what was happening when she could. All of them agreed to help stop more of the atrocities they had lived through. She knew that they would need time to heal, but if they agreed to the same contract Kristen had convinced her and the other technomages to agree to, these mages would represent a big difference if the Steel Dragon failed on her mission in Alaska to stop the war.

CHAPTER TWENTY-TWO

"Sammy, I hate to be this way but you'll need to climb on my back if you want to continue to be a part of this investigation," Kristen said and transformed into her steel dragon form.

"Are you saying my choices are to ride a dragon and help prevent a war or keep trundling along in our vehicle?"

"Basically, yes. Choose now. Amy's way too fast on that damn skateboard."

Heartsbane had already taken to the sky. Lumos and Stonequest had transformed and Drew and Jim were in the process of climbing onto their respective backs.

"It's not much of a choice for an old pilot like me," the general said and scrambled out of the vehicle they'd traveled in. He marched up to her flank and paused. "Is there a saddle or something or do I—"

"I apologize, General, but there's no time," she said, scooped him up in one hand, and vaulted skyward. When she was about a hundred feet up, she tossed him high enough to be able to do a quick loop and catch him on her back.

"Wooooo-hooooo!" Sammy shouted and sounded like a kid on a rollercoaster.

She raised an eyebrow at that. "You don't mind a little speed?"

"Are you kidding? I haven't flown anything bigger than a Cessna turboprop in years. Have at it."

Kristen obliged, pumped her wings with great vigor to gain height, and switched to the rigid flying style Lumos had taught her in their training sessions. She raced forward but took the time to do a few loops now and then since Lumos, Heartsbane, and Stonequest were in tight formation with Amy and her skateboard.

"This is amazing!" the general shouted.

"If dragons had done this for people for the last hundred years, we might not have a war brewing," she mused as she began to level her flight path to catch up with the others.

"You're not wrong about that," he said. "The most important thing about building long-lasting relationships is both sides seeing that the other has something to offer, even if that is only entertainment. It's not a chore for you to fly?"

"No, not at all," she admitted. "Most dragons love it, actually."

"See? That's even better. It makes it like sharing food. If both sides enjoy the same thing, it doesn't take long before we see each other as us instead of others."

"I like that." She didn't have time to say much else on the topic as she noticed a vehicle speeding down the highway.

Kristen stopped her aerial acrobatics and increased her speed again to join the tight formation that Stonequest, Lumos, and Heartsbane were flying in. "Amy, do you think that's him?"

"Oh yeah," the girl replied from her airborne skateboard.

"All right, then," she said. "Let's keep this tight and clean. He might be spooked but he doesn't need to be, not if he cooperates. Heartsbane, can you make sure he doesn't fear us too much with your aura?"

"I tried boss, but it's too late for that."

"What do you mean?" she asked even as she saw the answer to her own question.

Miller had put his foot on the accelerator. Before, the car—an American made truck with fairly high clearance—had cruised at a fairly safe fifty miles an hour. Now, it accelerated dramatically.

Fifty-five.

Sixty.

Sixty-five.

Seventy.

Eighty.

Ninety.

In moments, the vehicle traveled at a speed of over a hundred miles an hour.

It appeared that Miller was more concerned with speed than caution in his effort to outpace and escape his aerial tail. Kristen might not have been concerned except this was a highway in Alaska. The road was pockmarked with strips of tar where it had been patched year after year. Even with this evidence of maintenance, there were still numerous cracks, fissures, and potholes where water seeped into the grooves of the road every year, froze, and damaged the surface.

The truck hit a slight bump and briefly went airborne. It landed again and the driver managed to keep it from fishtailing too badly and rolling. She knew it was as much from luck as it was from the man's driving skills.

"We can't let him get hurt," she shouted to her team. "If he gets knocked unconscious or worse, we won't find out what we want to know. I need plans and I need them before the road bends in a half mile."

"If you swoop down at him, he'll dodge, I promise you that," Sammy said from her back. "Miller's an accomplished pilot, which is merely another way to say he's arrogant, reckless, and good enough in a jet that the first two don't matter. If you approach him, he'll try to stop you, even if he's driving a truck and not an F-22."

"I can stop him," Amy offered. She looked at her boss from her skateboard and frowned at her skeptical expression. "What?"

"I've seen you 'stop' moving objects. I want this guy alive, not a pancake."

"I don't have to simply stop the truck. I could lift it off the ground and shake it until he falls out like the prize from a pinata."

"Negative," she replied.

"Oh, come on!" Mock offense permeated the girl's voice but she turned to Miller and Kristen could tell from her aura that she was taking this seriously. "I've been working on my precision with Larry's help. I can do this without hurting him."

She took a deep breath when she realized they had very little choice. Besides, she trusted Amy. "Okay. Do what you can."

The mage swooped down on her skateboard, grasped the nose of it, and extended her other hand to direct her magic. There was no way to tell how she was directing it, though, and Kristen frowned as she watched intently.

The first thing she noticed was a flurry of leaves on either side of the road. It looked like a great beast had rushed through the forest on either side of the highway and kicked up the pine needles and decaying leaves in its wake. It was unlikely that Amy was making some type of puppet to scare Miller into stopping as she certainly didn't make it visible and there was no indication as to what had caused the vegetation to flurry. It looked like two creatures had taken parallel paths through either side of the highway and met in front of the truck, except nothing was there.

Her frown became a scowl when the engine began to get even louder. This was despite it not increasing in speed. In fact, rather than accelerating, it seemed to be slowing. Kristen didn't understand it until she saw one of the leaves from the woods fly past the truck, then turn and come right at it. Everything became clear. Amy was throwing a huge amount of wind at the vehicle. More than that, she was thickening the air itself so the force of the wind would work against it and the thicker air would do more of the work to slow the mass of gasoline-powered steel.

It looked like the truck was driving through a hurricane made of molasses. The air was so thick that it no longer picked leaves up and simply pushed against the vehicle while its engine strained louder like it was trying to get out of the world's most elusive mud puddle.

Kristen could feel Miller growing more agitated with her aura. She could feel him pushing harder on the gas and the engine rose in pitch until she—a girl from Detroit who knew a thing or two about cars—could practically hear it redlining.

Something snapped and the engine tried once more to please its lead-footed master before it died.

"I stand corrected," Kristen said as she swooped past Amy and toward the truck. "You're much better at stopping cars now."

She landed and lowered one shoulder to the ground so General Peralt could climb off her back. "I'll take it from here," he said. "I've known Miller for years. He'll listen to me. You guys… Well, I won't lie, you guys will simply freak him out."

His request was reasonable and she nodded. If Miller cooperated, it would make things easier. Besides, he wouldn't be able to run from four dragons and a mage given that they were in the middle of nowhere, miles away from Anchorage or anywhere else.

"Miller! It's General Peralt. I want you to step out of the car so we can talk. You hear me? Go ahead and open the door."

The man complied and lowered one leg to the ground, followed by the other. Before anyone could react, he stepped out with his pistol in hand and aimed it at the general. "You can't stop what we started, sir. The dragons have to go." To punctuate this statement, he leveled the weapon at Sammy's face and pulled the trigger.

As soon as she'd seen the firearm, Kristen had whispered "gun" to Amy, who had nodded in understanding. When the man pulled the trigger, she simply encapsulated him in an orb of shield magic. The bullet struck the shimmering blue wall in front of him and dropped uselessly.

Sammy, not accustomed to magic-wielding mages, dove aside all the same.

Miller's eyes widened as his bullet crumpled to a misshapen lump not three feet from his face. Not one to be dissuaded, he fired a few more rounds before he finally accepted that he wasn't doing anything except giving the girl on the skateboard practice with her skills.

The general pushed to his feet. He'd grazed the palm of one hand and cut a knee on the road when he evaded the shot. Kristen began to understand why this short, skinny general was called Sammy. He was much like a little kid, despite his age and rank.

Miller—now understanding that his chances of survival if he tried to fight were nil—chose the other tactic of the criminally desperate. He tried to run.

"Dragons," Kristen ordered.

In the blink of an eye, Stonequest was in the man's path in his human form.

The soldier skidded to a halt and tried to run in another direction, only to find an old man twirling one of the tips of his mustache in his path. "Going somewhere?" Lumos asked cordially.

"You bastards can't stop him. No one can stop him!" Miller shouted, his voice loud with desperation.

"Boss, is it all right if I make him more agreeable?" Heartsbane asked.

"Yes, please. I thought you tried when he was in the car."

"Even with my skills, it's hard to make someone's emotions change completely. He was scared. If I made him more scared of us, he would only have driven faster. But now..." She fixed her gorgeous blue eyes on Miller and stepped toward him with the perfect posture of dragons. "Now, I want him scared."

The man looked at her in horror. His eyes were wide and sweat pricked on his brow. If he wasn't a trained officer of the US military, Kristen thought he might have pissed himself.

"Please, please...don't hurt me!" Miller pleaded. "I'll tell you anything you want to know but *please* don't do anything to me!"

"Why did you give those orders to attack to those three pilots?" Kristen asked.

"I was told to. I was scared that if I didn't do as he said, the dragons would attack first."

"Didn't do as who said?"

"I don't know his name," he said quickly.

"Did you meet him in person or speak on the phone?"

"Both," Miller shuddered. "He delivered these orders over the phone but I have met him before."

"What did he look like? Did you see his dragon form or his human one?"

"I…neither." The man looked utterly mortified. Despite Heartsbane using her aura to make him fear them, he was still terrified of whoever had given the orders.

"What do you mean by that?" Stonequest asked.

The man studied the four dragons who had him surrounded, the mage who had stopped him, the two humans with handguns trained on his chest, and his general. He decided to come clean. "He wore a human skull on his face and he…he said if I didn't do as he said, he'd wear me next and that he liked the look of my skull. It has space inside despite me not having much brains…that's what he told me."

"Did he give you a name?" Kristen demanded.

Miller shook his head. "I'm sorry. I…I didn't ask."

It was predictable and expected but still frustrating. Boneclaw was unlikely to go around telling everyone about his secret identity, but she didn't expect him to meet people while wearing a skull mask either. She had hoped the soldier had seen a middle man—someone like Diamontus who she could have readily identified.

As it was, they didn't have the smoking gun they needed. Still, it might help. She retrieved her phone and dialed Shimmerclaw.

The platinum dragon answered after a single ring. "Where are you?" she asked as if she'd made the call instead of the other way around.

"I'm on a highway in the middle of nowhere, Alaska," Kristen said, being honest without making an attempt to send her GPS coordinates like a fool.

"Oh, thank goodness." The old dragon sounded relieved. "Lord Boneclaw and Diamontus have their armies on the move. You've been labeled a traitor and Diamontus has issued orders to capture or kill you. I'm sorry. There's nothing I can do. When the dragons brought back the dragon you shot… You didn't really shoot him, did you? With a dragon bullet?"

"I'm sorry, I had to," she said. "But he's okay, right?"

"He was shot in the *wing*," Shimmerclaw said. "He won't fly for days!"

"But he will fly," she insisted, frustrated that even though the Council leader was on her side, she still had the biases of an ancient dragon. Didn't she see that she could have killed not only one but many of the dragons who had followed her? Hitting one in the shoulder was the least harm she could have inflicted on her pursuers.

"So you're not at your base, then?" Shimmerclaw asked.

"No...not currently." Kristen felt a pang of worry in her chest. *But I need to get back there as soon as fucking possible.* "We went to the base where the jets that attacked the dragon rally point came from. We were looking for their motive. A dragon was behind it. I have the general from the base with me right now, actually. He has paperwork to prove that he didn't authorize the strike."

"Do you know who the dragon was? Do you have video?"

"No." She sighed. "No, I don't have anything. The officer who ordered the strike said it came from the Masked One."

"Damn it," Shimmerclaw growled. "That doesn't surprise me, but I can't bring that to the Dragon Council as evidence to stop the war. That damned Masked One. Any time I've brought up his existence, half the Council argues that he's merely a myth, an urban legend as the humans say.

"Would it help if I told you who the Masked One is?" she asked.

"Yes, of course!" The old dragon sounded excited at the prospect. "If we could prove his existence once and for all and demonstrate that he's been working behind the scenes, that might sway the Council."

Kristen took a deep breath. "It's Boneclaw. Lord Boneclaw is the Masked One."

For a much too long moment, Shimmerclaw said nothing. Finally, when she spoke, her voice was painfully doubtful. "That's a very serious accusation, Lady Steel. I've worked with Lord Boneclaw for hundreds of years. Still...I suppose it makes as much sense as anyone else. What kind of evidence do you have to prove this?"

"I don't have anything concrete but I'm certain that—"

"I'm sorry, but that won't be enough to help. He's already labeled you a traitor. If you make any statements about him being the Masked One, most dragons will think you're simply trying to turn the tables on him. Dragons have used the name of the Masked One for exactly that purpose before."

"I'm telling you, it's him."

"I'll look into it," the Council leader said a little stiffly. "In the meantime, you need to take care of yourself. The base… I can't tell you much, but you should get home and quickly."

"Got it, thanks," Kristen snapped and hung up. How could Shimmerclaw not believe her? Lord Boneclaw had all but admitted he was the Masked One. How could Shimmerclaw simply—

But now wasn't the time for that. The old dragon had said she needed to get home. She didn't fail to see the significance of that and called Brian to tell him to get her an extraction point. Taking the plane all the way home would take too long.

"I'm on it," he said. "I'll call you when we have something."

She hung up and turned to General Peralt. "Sammy," she began, "I don't think I need to tell you how serious things are about to get."

"I know." The general nodded. "If it's not too much to ask, I'd appreciate being dropped off at the base. I need to get fighters in the air. If dragons intend to attack humans, we need our boys in the sky and ready to fly."

"Please don't," Kristen implored. "I need you to stand down as long as you can. I need time to see if there's anything I can do to stop this. Your base has already caused dragon casualties. I'm hoping to make it clear that it wasn't the decision of a human, but that will be impossible if your people are fighting more dragons. We need peace, General. That's the only path."

He nodded but didn't look like Sammy any longer. His expression was grim and determined. "I can't make you any promises. I have an oath to uphold."

She nodded. "Fair enough. If we give you a ride back instead of forcing you to walk the entire way with Miller, will you at least wait to receive orders before you scramble your jets?"

"I have to do what I think is best." Peralt sounded conflicted. "If you give us an ultimatum like that, I guess I'll fix the truck."

"Will you?" Amy said as the vehicle flipped upside down, tumbled off the road, and rolled into a tree. She proceeded to pulverize it until both the tree and the truck were nothing but splinters and scrap.

"Well, I still have my phone." Peralt took it out and fixed the mage with a resolute look. The device crushed in his hand as if it were nothing but a beer can. "Well, dang. I guess there's nothing to do but ask for that ride. I'll have to tackle this paperwork too. Miller's account of a dragon interfering in our operations needs to be documented."

"Thank you, Sammy," Kristen said and transformed into her dragon body. Her dragons did the same, loaded the humans on their backs, and returned to the base.

No sooner had they dropped the general and his disgraced officer off than her phone rang. It was Constance.

"Tell me you have a portal ready for us," she said, needing some good news.

"I do. It should be near the Anchorage City Hall. Is that close enough for you?"

"Yes, it is." It was much better news than she had even dared hope for. "I thought you could only open portals to places you had been to or risk tearing us apart at the quantum level."

"Fortunately, we have many new mages with us at the base. One of them lived in Anchorage for a few years. He's more than willing to help."

"Well, that's great."

"Sure."

"Then why don't you sound great?" she asked when she detected bitterness in the woman's voice.

"We successfully saved most of the captured mages." The hard edge to her tone focused on the word "most," which made it abundantly clear that it was not as good as the use of "all."

"What happened?"

"Some of the mages had already been slain. Kristen, it was brutal.

They had them naked and on their knees, begging for their lives before they roasted them alive."

"I understand."

"No, I don't think you do."

"Constance, your mages did horrible things to those captive dragons. You might be able to compartmentalize that, but my dragons cannot. Yet we're all working together. There will be a time to grieve and a time for justice when this is all over. But if we don't all work together right now, there will be justice for no one. Do I make myself clear?"

"You always do," the woman said bitterly. "We'll have the portal open soon. It will be big enough for the plane to fit through."

"Can you do that? I don't want you all drained. We can leave the plane for now." Kristen was relieved that Constance seemed to have put aside her bitterness, if only for the time being.

"We have many new mages on our side to help power it. Most of them won't be any good in combat as they were trained for their entire lives to never harm a dragon or practice offensive spells, but opening a portal is something they can help with. We'll see you in ten minutes. Tell your pilot to fly above city hall. You'll come out near the airport."

"Great, see you soon." She hung up.

They boarded the plane and flew through the portal. It was above City Hall and bigger than any she had seen thus far, exactly as Constance had promised. The pilot barely blinked and they flew through it without fanfare.

Kristen and her team returned to Detroit. They disembarked from the jet and flew immediately to their base.

She had just poured herself a cup of coffee when Brian ran up to her, breathless. "We have incoming. A force of dragons bigger than anything I've ever seen is coming to Detroit!"

"What? When will they be here?"

He tried to smile and failed horribly. "I'd say about forty-five minutes."

CHAPTER TWENTY-THREE

"What do you know about the dragon force en route?" Kristen asked. She didn't want it to be true and thus confirm the warning Shimmerclaw had given her.

Brian hurried his station and brought up a number of screens of radar data. *Great,* she thought. *My brother has either hacked into the US weather service or every military base in the United States.* Given the quality of the data they were looking at, it was probably the latter, which of course would make her a traitor to both human and dragon kind. *Great, just great.* This was turning into a seriously crappy day.

He explained the data quickly. "They've divided their force into three units. One is headed to the west coast, one to the east coast, and the third directly to Detroit."

"Gee, I wonder why they're coming here," Heartsbane said and barely contained her sarcasm.

Kristen rubbed her face and ran hasty mental calculations of how many dragons, mages, and soldiers she now had in her force. "How large is each of these forces?"

"Radar isn't one hundred percent clear, but I'd estimate each one at around a hundred dragons," Brian said and tried to keep his voice neutral. "We can't stop them all," he said more softly. "We simply can't."

"No, no of course not," she agreed, although admitting that broke a part of her. "We don't have the manpower to handle all three, especially since the mages we rescued aren't combat-trained."

"So we merely roll over?" Heartsbane demanded.

"No." Kristen straightened and reminded herself that how she behaved was important not only for her mental health but for her team. She was a leader and needed to act like one. "But the one aimed at our hometown? We can do something about them."

She took a deep breath and what seemed like a thousand battle plans ran through her head in an instant. One thing kept distracting her, though. She knew it wasn't fair. It was selfish—more selfish than she wanted it to be. People would die and there were no ifs about that. She should have been willing to let her people die too, but she couldn't risk her mom and dad remaining out there to get incinerated. "Stonequest, can you go get my parents and bring them here?"

"Uh…hold up, Stone," Brian said and looked both proud and guilty at once.

His sister darted him a look from the corner of her eye. He had never directly contradicted her, not since she'd brought him onto her team. Why did he do so now?

"You're…uh, not the first person I told about the dragon force," he admitted.

"Who the hell would you tell before your commander and your sister?"

"Mom and Dad?" He looked past her. She turned to see Frank and Marty Hall coming down the stairs from the top level of their base.

"Oh, Krissy!" her mom said, ran toward her, and threw her arms around her daughter's neck.

"Hi, Mom," she said when she finally pulled away.

"We were trying to look at the skyline before your little dragon friends show up for this scrap of yours. Did you know this used to be a shoe polish factory?"

Kristen didn't know what was better—that her mom tried to

school her on her own base or the fact that she'd described the coming first true battle of a potential world war as a scrap.

"It wasn't a shoe polish factory, Marty. They made bicycles. The best bicycles in the city."

"Hi, Dad." She threw her arms around the man who'd inspired her to become a cop. He'd inadvertently convinced her to get into all this, become involved with the law, and eventually become a dragon investigator so obsessed with justice that she was willing to go to war for it.

"Hey, Krissy," he said and wound his arms around her. "We're proud of you sweetie, we really are. Now go stop these dragons before they trash our city again."

"Sure, Dad," she said, fighting back tears. One escaped and slid down her cheek.

"I told you two to get down below!" Brian shouted at them.

"We know, *Zed,*" Marty said, using her brother's code name like it was the coolest, most inspiring thing she'd ever heard.

"We merely had to see the Steel Dragon before we went into the bunker," Frank explained. He said "Steel Dragon" like he was naming the title of a superhero movie.

Kristen hugged each of them again before she turned to her assembled team and wondered if they'd be enough to save the city. They had to be. The people, dragons, and mages around her were all Detroit had to defend it.

She sighed. It made no difference that she never wanted to be in the middle of this mess. Her personal mission had been to stop common criminals, thieves, child abusers, rapists...the scum of society. Not in a million years would she have thought that signing up for the police academy would bring her into a direct confrontation with an ancient genocidal maniac of a dragon.

Fortunately, she had not only some of the best fighting dragons out there but also scores of mages and other humans with guns. They could do this. It wouldn't be easy, but they could do this.

"All right, everyone." She addressed her team calmly. They'd all crammed into the main building of her base. Human, dragon, and mage waited for her orders. "I want mixed teams. Guns need to be loaded with dragon bullets. We don't have an unlimited quantity but remember, even wounding a dragon with them should knock them out of the fight, so be careful and aim well."

"Lady Steel," Constance said when she took a breath before moving into the more inspirational part of her speech.

"Yes?" Kristen asked. She tried to not be flustered and told herself that the technomage likely had a reason for the interruption.

"There are huge stockpiles of dragon bullets on the island, along with tons of special weapons like anti-missile systems filled with dragon bullets, dragon-plate grenades, and more. That would be a huge help."

Kristen nodded. That was a damn good reason for interrupting. "Okay. That's good to know. We won't have time to set up anti-missile systems, but I want everything else." Something suddenly occurred to her. "Including the chains you used to bind the dragons. I want every single link of those."

"Why?" the woman asked.

"Trust me," she responded.

Constance nodded and began to work on the portal.

Looking through the gate to the tropical island was almost enough to calm Kristen. It was so damn beautiful. Flowering plants and steamy jungles and pristine beaches hid the fact that the island housed the largest stash of anti-dragon weaponry ever assembled.

Plus, Larry was there, smiling like a fool and wearing nothing but swim-shorts and a flower necklace. "Well, howdy." He beamed. "I wondered if I would get a visit. Did someone have trouble opening a jar of pickles or is this the start of World War Three?"

"The second one," she said.

"Damn. I guess play time's over, my friends!" He shouted to someone they couldn't see through this particular angle of the portal —some of the captured dragons, no doubt. "Do you want me, the guns, the dragons, or all three?"

"All three—" she said before Amythist stepped forward. Given how full the base was, Kristen hadn't even seen the old dragon amongst everyone else.

"I think it might be better if I go there and help these dragons on their voyage home," Amythist said.

"Are you sure?" she asked. "We could use you here."

"I know you think that, but I already fought in one war. I killed so many people. I can't do that again. I want to help and those dragons need help. I'll bring them back with the ship, assuming there is somewhere to bring them back to."

"Y'all fucked up that bad, huh?" Larry asked, shucked his flower necklace, and donned his mage robes. "It's a good thing you called ol' Larry Brockton."

"Old is right," Amy quipped as he stepped through the portal.

"Ah, come here, you lil' squirt. Are you still blasting things or did you learn some self control?"

"If you can't control your tongue, why should I control my magic?" she asked cheekily.

Everyone was glad to see him. Kristen had forgotten how good the mage was for her team's morale. He joked even as he got to work transporting the dragon bullets and munitions to Detroit and giving the newly unshackled mages—most of whom he knew quite well from his time working at the Detroit Dragon SWAT building—tips on how to best use their full potential. It was immediately clear he was a better teacher than Constance as the newcomers suddenly seemed far more useful.

They got the supplies through just in time.

"We have maybe five minutes," Brian said. He'd given them reminders which Kristen had only subconsciously registered, but she focused immediately on his warning. "They're over the suburbs to the north."

"All right. I don't like this at all but we'll have to play the hand we were dealt. That means I want every soldier armed with dragon bullets and every mage working defense."

"What about us dragons?" Emerald asked.

She lifted one of the chains Constance's mages had brought. "We need to get dressed."

CHAPTER TWENTY-FOUR

"I'm sorry, but I won't do it."

Kristen regarded Emerald with growing exasperation. They had to do this if they wanted to survive, and she also knew that she didn't have time to argue with the dragon.

"It doesn't hurt if that's what you're worried about," she said and moved through various actions to show that the chains she had made the mages shackle to her body gave her free range of motion.

"It's not that. It's the damn principle of it. Those chains kept your brothers and sisters—our brothers and sisters—in bondage. They're symbols of slavery—and worse than slavery, of dragons beings used as cattle."

"And now they'll enable us to survive a force that's far larger than our own," she argued, but he remained obdurate.

She shouldn't have been surprised, all things told. Emerald didn't have any special powers like her, Stonequest, Lumos, Heartsbane, or Timeflash. He was a regular dragon, which meant he'd worked damn hard on his aerial combat skills. The others were used to dipping into their unusual powers when they needed to. To them, wearing the chains so human soldiers and mages could ride them without risk of falling off was probably another opportunity to gain an advantage. To Emerald, it meant he wouldn't be able to fly the way he'd trained to.

"Fine. But be careful out there, okay? You won't have a mage to protect you."

"Then it's a good thing I won't need one," he retorted and vaulted skyward.

Kristen watched him go but she didn't have time to worry about him. They had scant minutes before the invading dragons reached downtown Detroit, and she needed to engage the enemy force over Lake St. Clair to minimize damage. Time had run out and they had to launch immediately or lose the chosen battleground.

"Are you sure about this?" Drew asked as he climbed onto her back and clipped himself into the chain harness.

"Hell no," she replied. "But it's our only chance. Are you coming, Jim?"

"I wouldn't dream of missing this." The Wonderkid clambered onto her back and settled comfortably.

Amy levitated using her magic powers on her shoes and took her position near the base of Kristen's tail.

They were ready.

"Dragons, your job is to keep moving. I don't want you to engage, only keep the enemy from destroying this town. The mages and soldiers on your back will keep you safe and eliminate the enemy. Let's show them what it looks like when we join forces."

Her team cheered but it was too quiet because they were so few.

Brian had confirmed via drone that the other force had damn close to a hundred dragons and was led by Diamontus himself. Against that massive force, Kristen had her core team of Dragons from SWAT, plus another twenty of the young dragons who she thought were competent enough to handle being a mobile battle platform. Constance and Eric would be on Katrina and would no doubt make a valuable addition to the battle, but that was the sum total of the defenders. Beyond that, she had soldiers and mages guarding her base from its roof as well as some of the tops of Detroit's tallest skyscrapers. But if her plan to engage the dragons over the lake worked out, they wouldn't see action.

While that was a good thing, it also meant her airborne forces would be even more outnumbered.

"For equality! For a world we can share with *everyone!*" Kristen roared.

"For the Steel Dragon!" Heartsbane bellowed and pulsed her powerful aura so strongly that everyone cheered as loudly as ten men.

They took to the skies and she led her twenty-five mobile assault teams over the lake to engage the enemy. She could already see Diamontus, so massive that he seemed to cast a shadow over all of Eastpointe. He saw her force launch and ordered his dragons over the lake.

"Hold tight to your formation!" Kristen bellowed. "We have one chance at a targeted and unimpeded volley. After that, we need to be careful of friendly fire. Make it count."

The dragons closed on the defenders, and when they were about a hundred yards out—so close they could feel the enemy's auras and smell their dragon breath—Kristen ordered her soldiers to fire.

The crack of a hundred guns rang out over Lake St. Clair.

Perhaps three dozen of Diamontus's forces plummeted. It was difficult to count because once the bullets tore through them they broke their formation and scattered in all directions.

The few who maintained a direct course toward her and her people were rebuffed by magic shields. Their claws couldn't find dragon flesh and their breaths of fire, poison, or whatever other unearthly powers they possessed met the shimmering blue shields of defensive magic.

"Keep moving!" she ordered. "Try to come around for another pass."

Her dragons made it through the enemy ranks without issue or fatalities.

The enemy simply wasn't prepared. They had thought they would fight a group comprised of dragon whelps, younglings, runts, and cowards, plus the Steel and the Iron Dragons. Instead, they were met with a force never seen in history.

Kristen wished she felt better about this, but she didn't.

Watching a quarter of the enemy's forces fall was an indisputable early victory, and yet it felt only like death. She didn't want to kill dragons any more than she wanted dragons to kill people. This was a stupid fight, a pointless battle orchestrated by someone who wasn't even there.

Unfortunately, the reality was that they were forced to fight.

Diamontus had rallied his troops—although he'd lost a third of his force, they still outnumbered hers two to one—and they resumed their assault. This time, they came from different directions. They were already learning how to face the new threat her combined arms approach had created.

"Fire at will!" she shouted and dodged as a dragon tried to rake her guts with its claws.

"Holyyyyyy shiiiiiit!" Drew yelled from her back as he was tossed about and reached the end of the chain that connected him to her harness.

Jim managed to keep himself planted securely and fired shots at the retreating dragon.

The action was almost impossible for her to follow. Gunshots rang out all around her. Dragons exhaled flames that were extinguished by magic with a few exceptions. Many of the screams she heard were far too human. In less than a minute, one of her dragons was struck by friendly fire. He plummeted into the lake below and drowned the mage and three soldiers who'd been strapped to his back. She would forever remember the look in his eyes as the young dragon was swallowed by the lake.

"Where's the Steel Bitch?" Diamontus bellowed.

"Behind you, fool," Kristen responded and located the giant, diamond-encrusted dragon easily in the chaos. He was twice the size of any other dragon present.

He spun to face them but was slow to do so because of his bulk. While he came about, Jim and Drew peppered him with shots. Even one of them should have been enough to disable his powers, but his scales seemed to truly be as hard as diamonds and the bullets shattered uselessly against his back and flank.

"We have to hit him in the joints—armpits, hip joints, that kind of thing," she ordered, mortified that she had to use Lumos' training to teach her soldiers how to slaughter dragons.

That meant she had to face the dragon head-on. She gained some altitude and dove. Seconds before impact, she slashed her claws to strike at his face.

Before the attack completed, a great volley of bullets caught both her and Diamontus. They recoiled instinctively, but she knew she was only bruised, not bloodied.

Kristen looked toward the direction of the shots, ready to see a young dragon who'd made a mistake. Instead, she saw twelve fighter jets rocketing toward the dragon battle.

"Defensive positions! Defensive positions! All mages, block those bullets!" she yelled as more rounds from the fighter jets streaked through the battlefield.

The fighter jets seemed to have a very clear battle plan. Kill. Every. Dragon.

They made no distinction between Kristen and her forces and the dragons under the command of Diamontus.

She ordered her people to fall back, but the jets seemed indifferent. They simply banked, circled for another pass, and fired at anyone who tried to leave the airspace above the lake.

One of her dragons died, then another and another.

The mages were being overwhelmed by the sheer quantity of incoming fire. It was hard enough to stop one bullet or the breath of a dragon. Now, they were supposed to stop hundreds of rounds a minute. If she didn't do something, she knew this battle would become nothing but a slaughter. It wouldn't take many bullets to overwhelm a dragon's healing ability if they didn't have steel skin.

"Katrina! Constance! With us!"

The Iron Dragon flapped her wings and followed her up and out of the battle to the level of the jets.

The fighter aircraft fired at Katrina, but she spun between them and dodged as effortlessly as if this were a videogame. *She really does know how to fight in her dragon form,* Kristen thought.

"The plan boss?" Jim yelled. "I don't have the arsenal to eliminate a fighter jet."

"I do," Amy said and used her magical abilities to nudge two jets into each other.

The Iron Dragon simply got in the way of a third, which collided with her. She survived but the jet did not.

Constance wasn't as quick as Amy but she also used her abilities, although more subtly than the younger and more powerful mage. She seemed to thicken the air around one of the aircraft's engines until it overheated. The pilot pulled away, no doubt to find somewhere to land while they still could.

That left eight. It was too many.

"I don't think I can do that again!" Katrina shouted.

"No shit, you can't do that again," Constance reprimanded her and reminded Kristen that the technomage saw Katrina as a super-powered adopted daughter.

"I don't know if we need to," Jim said. "Look—they're pulling away!"

"Oh, thank God," Kristen said, although God didn't seem to have any place on the battlefield.

She tucked her wings so she could return to the fray. As she descended, she looked at the battle playing out beneath her. It was not a pretty sight. While her mages had focused on protecting their dragons and everyone else on the battlefield from the lumps of lead the jets delivered to destroy every dragon they could, Diamontus' force had regrouped and adjusted their tactics.

They fought in tiny groups of only three or four dragons now. With ruthless efficiency, they moved from dragon to dragon, harried those who still had soldiers on their back to retaliate, and savaged those who didn't. Kristen watched in horror as Diamontus led a force of three dragons to slaughter yet another of her young dragons.

The greatest frustration was that she was still too far out to stop him.

"Amy, can you—"

"I'm trying! Those jets weren't easy to destroy, and Diamontus is strong. Something about his scales seems to block my magic."

She was about to brace herself to witness the enemy leader kill yet another of her people when Emerald appeared. He was considerably faster than the rest of her allies because he didn't have a harness on.

Without slowing, he came out of nowhere and drove into Diamontus's back. The bigger, stronger dragon laughed off the blow until his attacker caught hold of and sank his teeth into one of his wings.

The massive creature roared in pain and swatted him away with his tail, but Emerald didn't give up. He swung into another attack and this time, struck at his face.

His adversary blasted him with fire. It charred his green scales but he remained undeterred.

"Get clear!" Lumos shouted at his teammate. "I'll blind him."

"It won't work!" Emerald responded. "You'll blind the whole damn battlefield."

"Fly away, little sparrow!" Diamontus roared at him. "You have bothered me quite enough."

The smaller dragon roared and surged forward again. His enemy was ready for him and slashed with his diamond tipped claws to open a deep gash across the chest. Kristen could see bone and shuddered.

Despite his wound, he still refused to pull back. Instead, he powered into Diamontus and grasped his throat with his jaws.

"Little sparrow thinks he can bite my neck? My scales are as hard as diamonds, you fool. I cannot be hurt by the likes of you."

Emerald pushed off when he confirmed the truth of this, but he still made no effort to retreat. He couldn't. Everyone else was still fighting. If he let the leader of the invaders rejoin the fray, the momentum of the battle would shift. To keep him occupied, he swooped and circled and finally clamped his tail in his jaws.

"Was that supposed to hurt?" Diamontus laughed. "My tail is pure diamond. It's the hardest part of my body."

His attacker made no reply. He couldn't as he had the other dragon's tail in his mouth. Instead, he spun around the massive body and plunged the tail into Diamontus's chest. A look of shock suffused the dragon's face and he scowled in disbelief.

But still, he wasn't defeated. Emerald had come close to his face, and with the last of his failing strength, Diamontus caught the smaller, younger, weaker dragon's neck in his teeth and bit down.

Emerald didn't stand a chance.

He was merely a normal dragon, after all.

His neck was crushed by the diamond teeth, and he died wrapped in the claws of the foe he shouldn't have been able to defeat. Kristen watched, broken-hearted, as the two of them plummeted into Lake St. Clair—two gems that would forever be buried beneath its waters.

With their leader dead, the opposing force seemed to lose its direction. One of them bellowed an order to retreat and the others hastened to obey.

Her forces gradually resumed their formation and fired a few more shots at the retreating dragons to make sure they understood that they had ammunition to keep fighting. Finally, they were gone.

"Talk to me, Brian. Where are they going?"

"It looks like they're headed to the Upper Peninsula."

"How did we do?"

"Detroit wasn't harmed. But we lost nine dragons, plus more soldiers and mages."

"Goddammit."

"I know, Kristen, but it gets worse."

She took a deep breath and signaled her people to return to base. "How?"

"The other two forces are still heading toward their targets. They had farther to go, but I don't know…I thought if we defeated these guys they'd give up."

Rage and sorrow vied within her and she tasted nothing but blood and ash in her mouth. Cities would burn this day, and there was nothing she could do about it. Worse, it was only a matter of time before the dragons they fought regrouped and returned. Diamontus had been defeated but he wasn't the head of this serpent. The Masked One was.

And then there were the human fighter jets who had intervened. Now that dragons and humans had both engaged in open combat, it was only a matter of time before the entire world fell into war. After all, this had happened over a major city. It meant every damn news outlet there would have footage of the battle. They were surely already doctoring the video to further their own political agendas.

It was a dark day and it would only get darker.

CHAPTER TWENTY-FIVE

Kristen flew over Lake St. Clair. The wind was picking up, so the water was covered with the white peaks of the waves churning across its surface. She couldn't see into its depths. The dragons, humans, and mages who had died on both sides of the battle were hidden from view. It was like it hadn't happened, but it didn't feel that way.

She headed toward her base in Detroit and wished she felt more triumphant given how little damage the city had suffered. Her gambit to draw the invaders out over the lake had been successful. The city was unharmed and many of the people there probably didn't even know how close they'd come to complete annihilation.

Although they would soon because it looked like every news truck, camera man, social media influencer, and human being who had been outside with a cellphone had recorded as much of the combat as they possibly could.

An idea pushed through her reflexive irritation.

She knew it was utterly impossible for her team to win this fight alone, but maybe she could make a mass appeal and change the tone of this whole mess. How far she had come, she thought wryly. In her early days as the Steel Dragon, she had detested meeting the media but now, she thought this was her best option. Although, in her early days, she hadn't been faced with twin dragon forces heading to major metropolises with a grudge and fires in their bellies.

Once above the base, Amy floated herself, Jim, and Drew down to the roof. Kristen continued although she removed the chains she'd used as a harness and dropped them into the base parking lot.

Resolute, she glided to the crowd of reporters gathered nearby hoping for a statement. They wanted a sound bite? She'd give them one, in spades. She landed near them and transformed into her human form. Deliberately, she took her time with the transformation and controlled it with a level of precision that had also been impossible when she'd first discovered her abilities.

She walked forward as she changed, stood upright first, and shrank while a maelstrom of silvery flecks swirled all around her. Cameras clicked as people tried to capture the perfect shot. Within a few steps, she was human-sized, at which point she transformed her arms, legs, and torso into her human body and her dragon head to her human one. Now, she walked forward, a human with a steel tail and dragon wings, a creature of beauty and power.

The reporters were ecstatic. The two vans she was closest to kept their cameras focused on her, while the reporters working with the camera operators spoke excitedly. Other people, bloggers, creators of video diaries, and simply plain regular folk who weren't afraid of dragons came forward too.

A dark-skinned reporter in the front with large sideburns who she knew well from her days on the Detroit SWAT team moved toward her and held his microphone closer to her as he asked, "Kristen Steel, what on Earth is going on? We're getting reports of dragon attacks all over the world."

"I want to tell you everything, Chuck, but not here. I'll hold a press conference outside my base in thirty minutes. You can have the front row aisle seat if you call as many reporters as you possibly can and get them all there before I start."

"I want three questions."

"You can have two."

"Three questions or I don't call the conservative news network. They'll merely spin anything you say to make it sound like you want war anyway."

"You can have your three questions. Call them—everyone. And while you're at it, talk to your boss. I want this on every set in the United States and as many screens as we can get worldwide."

"Four questions," he said but he was smiling, an old joke of theirs.

"I'll see you in thirty minutes."

That gave Kristen a half-hour to stew about what precisely she could say that could make any difference. She wandered through the streets of Detroit toward her base, enjoyed the comfort of her hometown familiarity, and let herself think. When she walked along the river and her gaze lingered on Belle Isle across the water, she considered what to say.

The human fighter planes they had fought had every right to be there engaging the dragon army, of course. They were defending human lives or attempting to, anyway. She couldn't begrudge them that.

But at the same time, she thought as she turned right past the GM Renaissance Center, they weren't helping. Human pilots didn't know how to recognize dragons. She knew that to be true from her days as a dragon. In trying to defend themselves, they became a threat to her force as well as the attacking dragons and cost unnecessary lives. So much could have been avoided.

She wandered past the Guardian Building—knowing she didn't have time to enter and enjoy its amazing interior—as she continued north. An uncomfortable truth settled in, one she'd prefer to ignore. She would have to fight both sides if either one moved toward further unprovoked aggression.

It was a daunting task.

To make it happen, she only had a small force of dragons, mages, and humans. They were incredibly outnumbered by either side—humans *or* dragons. Against both at the same time? They were toast.

Kristen glanced down Michigan Avenue and smelled the familiar odor of dueling Coney Island venues, but she kept walking. Her stomach was already tied in knots and now wasn't the time for food. She couldn't fight both sides. It was impossible and yet, that was exactly what had to happen.

War was not an option, not with the forces on either side so ready and capable of annihilating one another. An all-out war would devastate the planet. But what about a police force? That was a necessity. Someone needed to police *everyone*—humans, dragons, and mages. None of them would have true justice until all three of them did.

She understood damn well that none of the three factions would particularly *like* that—especially the dragons who had spent so much time as top dogs—but it was the only way forward that she could see.

Justice had to be applied equally for all or it would fail as it had done for hundreds of years.

Absorbed in her thoughts, she'd already passed Comerica Park and now veered off toward her base. She checked her watch. Time was up.

Sure enough, outside their stronghold, reporters were grouped closely together and more were arriving while she approached a lectern someone on her team had set up—probably her brother. He must have noticed all the reporters and assumed she had something planned. Or he had been preparing a speech. Either way, she had to step up there and speak. Her stomach twisted as she carefully considered what to say. Everything she'd done so far might crystallize in this moment. No words she'd ever uttered were more important.

"Ladies and Gentlemen, thank you for coming and thank you for tuning in all around the world. I'd like to start by thanking Chuck Wallace from WXYZ for getting everyone here."

Chuck beamed at that, although he also held up four fingers.

Kristen continued. "I don't have much time so I'll simply cut to the chase. The Dragon Council has voted to go to war with humankind."

The reporters—despite years of covering every kind of case imaginable—lost their shit at this. A slew of questions were fired but Kristen only answered Chuck's.

"But why?"

"There are many factors. The technomages I've been working to stop and the proliferation of human weapons, but mostly, it's because they were preemptively attacked by human fighter jets." She held three fingers up to Chuck to show him that counted for one.

"The first thing I need to make absolutely clear is that my force here in Detroit, Michigan, had absolutely nothing to do with that. We lost many of our dragons, humans, and mages in a battle to protect this city from a dragon attack. We will continue to protect peaceful citizens from any aggressor, be they dragon, mage, or human.

"War is not the answer. It will solve nothing and accomplish nothing but ending lives. I will *not* go to war with anyone. I *will*, however, call myself the new sheriff in town. Any force of humans, dragons, or mages that attacks any civilians of any kind will be considered criminals by my team and will be stopped by any means necessary. Those of you who haven't had a chance to watch the battle that happened earlier, or who haven't seen what I and my team have done in Canada, Florence, or here in Detroit, do yourself a favor and watch a few videos. We're not to be taken lightly.

"I will repeat myself in saying that we will *not* go to war. Humans have learned to coexist over the centuries. It's time for everyone else to do the same."

"How can you say that when there are still armed conflicts?" Chuck asked, burning another question.

"It's true that there are still battles being fought between humans around the world, but since World War Two, we have managed to avoid global conflict. Even the Cold War never devolved into all of us simply killing each other. Still, fewer people are involved in conflict now than ever before, which proves that humans can coexist with dragons.

"However, coexistence requires equality. Justice must be the same for all. Laws must be equal for all. Punishments must be equal for all. And war between the races cannot be allowed. It will only end in destruction for all.

"We will *not* join this war but we will stop those foolish enough on either side who think a war can be won. Wars only make death. Going to war is always a losing scenario."

"How do you propose to do all this from here?" Chuck asked and waggled a finger to indicate that he knew he only had one more.

"That's a good question, Chuck. Our force is not large enough to police the planet, nor do I wish to be judge and jury for the entire world. Right now, I invite *all* beings of good heart who want to work for a better future to come together in Michigan to stop this war before it gets out of control.

"Join me here and together, we will build a better future. I think we can all agree that the old future is dead. Humans and mages have proven that they won't live in the shadow of dragons. And dragons, if you're willing to fly to war and destroy this planet we all share, why not come here first and *talk* about what your demands are. As far as I am concerned, the old future is dead, as will be anyone who insists on following it."

Mutters of dissent came from the reporters. Clearly, they didn't quite know what to think of this. From the looks on some of their faces, they were simply concerned what broadcasting this message to every aggressive dragon and military leader in the world might do to Detroit. Leave it a smoking black pit seemed like a fair guess.

"Are you declaring war on the system itself?" Chuck asked.

"No, Chuck. I am *not.* However, as both a cop for the great city of Detroit and a dragon investigator, I am declaring both systems—the one controlled by the Dragon Council and our own human governmental system that lets the most powerful do as they wish while the poor suffer—officially on trial. I will not watch as two factions who each claim to be morally superior rip each other to shreds. Those who insist on fighting will be dealt with. By me, yes, and by the dragons and mages and human soldiers I work with, but also by the thousands of people, mages, and dragons out there who have smelled the rot of our society for decades. If you have felt something is wrong, I ask— no, *implore*—you to come to Detroit. Peace is possible. Look at my team."

Kristen couldn't help but love her team. Stonequest stepped out, as well as Amy on her skateboard, the Iron Dragon, and Constance.

Behind them came dozens more battle-scarred dragons, tired humans, and mages with torn and tattered robes.

"We all used to be enemies. We used to fight each other because of our disagreements instead of trying to find middle ground. As soon we all agreed that no one had to die, we were able to see things from the other's perspective.

"I know this won't be easy. In fact, I know this will be *really fucking hard.*"

A few reporters' eyebrows raised the F-bomb dropped on international television. Chuck only shook his head and laughed.

"But we can do this with your help. *You can do this with our help.* That's what I believe and that's what I need people like you to fight for. I'll have my mage show you how to open a portal to teleport here now. If you're a mage in hiding or a former technomage terrorist, you are welcome as long as you share the beliefs I share. If you're a dragon with a mage under your command, ask them if they want to come, and if they do, break the shackle on their wrist and we'll help them open a portal and get you here.

"I know my enemies can use this technique to attack us but I trust that far more of you will come to help. Please don't prove me wrong."

CHAPTER TWENTY-SIX

She finished her speech, drew a deep breath, and accepted that she'd done all she could. It would have to be enough. Every reporter's hand immediately raised, demanding answers to questions while Constance explained how to make a portal to an audience Kristen prayed was out there.

Fair enough, she thought. Of course they would have questions. She was about to start calling names when she sensed a pulse of aura from Lumos. When she turned to him, he shook his head and gestured hastily toward the north. It didn't take a dragon investigator to realize what he was saying. The enemy dragons had regrouped and returned for another round.

"I know you all have questions," she said and tried not to make it sound like too much like an apology. "But you need to get out of here. The dragons who attacked earlier will be back soon."

"What about other dragons?" a reporter demanded. "Are you concerned that you might have brought every dragon on the continent and maybe beyond down on the Motor City?"

"I'm sure many dragons will see us as a threat," she agreed. "And I'm sorry for that. I truly am. But we have to make a stand. That means all of you need to get out of here."

"You can't make us go!" someone shouted.

"Of course not, but my job is to protect people. That'll be much harder to do if you are all milling around here, waiting for these dragons to appear. I suggest everyone gets underground. If you have a basement, great, go there. If not, find a friend who does, or go to the storm shelters at the schools."

Most of the reporters heeded her advice. They looked shaken by the idea of their city being razed to the ground while they hid beneath it, but they also knew her and her reputation. She wasn't threatening them but trying to protect them. Those who argued only did so because they were scared. She didn't blame them but she hoped they could get over their feelings and head to safety before it cost them their lives.

Kristen left her podium and returned to the grounds of her base. Lumos fell into step beside her.

"How do you think I did?" she asked the old dragon.

He smiled kindly. "I am quite proud of you, young Lady Steel. I don't know how this will all come down in the end, but you showed courage and conviction out there. I'm honored to fight alongside someone who has justice so clearly in their sights. However, I have news to report as well."

"Good news, right?" she said with a phony grin.

"I suppose it's good that we have news at all." He smirked. "Your brother has been...what's the term, chopping? Breaking? Illegally accessing the human radar systems at various airports."

"Hacking."

"What?"

"Never mind," she said. Now was no time for semantics, although she loved that even after a battle, Lumos still struggled with human terms. "What did he find?"

"He has *hacked* the human radar systems at various airports, and he's tracking the east and west flights of dragons." He paused and took a deep breath and she could feel him struggle to gain control of his aura. "They've changed course. They're now coming toward Detroit.

All of them. Brian estimates the total at three times the force we fought off."

"Goddammit," Kristen said. She had known this might happen—that her enemies might hear her message and come for her because of it. But she hadn't expected them to act so soon. She had wanted to go to Lake St. Clair and do something for the fallen dragons. While she knew it was unfair, she especially wanted to do something for Emerald. He wasn't a water dragon and didn't deserve to spend eternity under the waves of the lake. His death had been heroic, and he deserved to be honored as the warrior and officer of peace and justice he was, not forgotten as simply another warrior fallen in battle.

But what could be done?

Kristen looked at her people. There were so few of them. They hadn't lost nearly as many dragons as the enemy during the battle over the lake, but every one from their side who was killed represented a significant loss. They were already outnumbered and now, they would face even greater odds. Worse still, humans and mages didn't have healing abilities. Dragons could attack again and again and heal themselves as long as they got some meat to fuel their power. Her human and mage fighters would need sleep and first aid in a way that dragons simply would not.

Her gaze shifted to Constance and her technomages, all of them in meditation and all of them feeling for other mages around the world trying to open portals to come and join them. The leader had explained that if anyone tried to use the unfamiliar magic, she and her mages would be ready to reel them in, so to speak, but it looked like no one had taken them up on the offer. That put her in another bind. Was it better to leave the woman out of the next battle despite her superlative combat proficiency in hopes that mages would answer their call? Or was that suicide?

She was painfully aware that every single one of her people could die trying to stop this war. And then what? If that happened, she would be dead and that would be a bummer, obviously, but the implications for the rest of the world were far worse. Without her to stand between the power hungry faction of the dragon hierarchy and the military industrial complex, what could stop a world war? The humans and dragons would all but eradicate one another, and they'd probably destroy half the planet in the process. Those who survived would be people so far disconnected from society that it would be like civilization as they knew it was simply erased. Hopefully, whoever—if anyone—managed to come back after the war was destroyed would value equality more than the current power system did.

"Kristen, I can feel your aura and I believe you're looking at this all wrong," Lumos said and drew her away from falling deeper into the pit she'd already let her mind leap into.

"Is there a right way to look at the potential end of human and dragon society?"

"You took a stand. Merely by doing that, you have made a huge difference. The Dragon Council has become calcified in their ways. They do little more than dole out compensation to the survivors of dead humans. It has been many centuries since any dragon dared to take a stand against them. It's unheard of in modern times." He laughed as if she had managed to whip a cream pie into a teacher's face rather than invite a rain of fire on her hometown. "Even if we all die in the field of battle here today, your actions will shake the dragon power structure to its very core. Although I'd rather not die, so let's work on a plan?"

She couldn't help but laugh at him. "Sure. You were starting to make going out in blaze of glory sound good, but yeah, I'd rather survive to eat more pizza and drink more beer."

"I agree, my lady. So, tell me, what does the Steel Dragon think?"

Kristen rubbed her chin as she walked. "Well, I'd rather play this as a defensive action if we can. It would make sense to pull back to an easily defended location. We could try to mount the anti-dragon defenses on our base or maybe see if any of our dragons have a cave we could hide in, but we can't do that."

"It seems sensible, so why not?" Lumos asked, but she had a hunch the old battle master only asked her to make her speak her thoughts aloud.

"Because the dragon army would simply ravage Detroit. If they're coming here, they see us as a threat, which means if they can't find us, they'll still need to make it clear that we are not a threat. The easiest way to demonstrate that to humans would be to raze the city."

"I fear that is correct."

"And if that happens, the humans would have to retaliate. A defensive operation won't work."

"I was waiting for you to come to this conclusion."

"But how can we possibly attack?" Kristen asked aloud. "We were already outnumbered. And now they know that we can use mages and bullets from the backs of dragons. They won't attack in the same huge wings. It'll be a much tougher, bloodier battle."

"Remember that your foe relies on the shadows to fight. For millennia, he has used deception over strength and lies over truth. If we can but illuminate the shadows he hides in, we could have a real advantage," Lumos said.

She wanted to believe him more than anything, but how could she? The Masked One—Boneclaw was his name and she kicked herself for not exposing him when she had the international audience —had already proven himself a powerful foe without fighting at all. He had convinced Diamontus and close to a hundred dragons to attack Detroit instead of the Alaskan base that had scrambled the jets.

But then, of course he'd protected that base. He had been the one to call for an attack to come from there, after all. She sighed and felt like she was still learning the rules of checkers while she played against a chess grand master.

"We'll have to try something he'd never expect," she said slowly.

"Precisely!"

"But what can possibly surprise a dragon who has been around for millennia? He knows everything there is to know about dragon bullets. He practically pioneered their invention. He knows about the technomages and was in contact with them for who knows how long —decades? We can't outsmart something like that."

"You're right, of course. We cannot, but you can. You're the Steel Dragon. More importantly, you're Kristen Hall. You are a dragon of formidable power who was raised in a human world. You are special, a cosmic weight to bring balance on a cosmic scale. You have done things that no one else on this planet has done. You have cooked food like a human, labored like a human, you have probably dangled a string into a pond to catch a fish rather than simply boiling the entire lake. And yet you have flown like a dragon and have tasted the power that flows through our blood."

"Wait, what was that?"

"You have the power of dragons. You know you do. You were strong before I started training you but now, you have what it takes to save this city."

"No, no, no. Not the inspirational bullshit."

Lumos guffawed at that. "It was not *bullshit,* my lady."

"It was, but that's fine," she said, her mind spinning. "You're right, I have been fishing. I remember this one time, sitting in a rowboat with my dad and brother. We must have sat there all day, waiting for a fish to bite our lure—any fish."

"If you hope to use bait, I trust you have a better source than you once did."

"Do you think dragons know much about birds?" Kristen asked.

"Excuse me?" He frowned in confusion.

"That day, while we were trying to catch fish, I remember watching the birds. Every damn bird on that lake must have caught a fish while we finally left with nothing. Do you think dragons know about birds?"

He frowned but he answered the question all the same. "No, my lady. Dragons have never been particularly interested in natural history like humans are. The only animals most of us cared about were the big ones we could eat. We didn't even know eggs could be eaten from chickens until we learned it from humans. I do not think we know much about birds."

"Let's hope not," she said. "I don't want to end up being the fish."

CHAPTER TWENTY-SEVEN

The Masked One couldn't believe it.

It had come as no surprise when the Steel Dragon had run. He knew she had a cowardly streak in her and suspected she'd want to die with the humans she called her parents.

Diamontus had been easily convinced to lead the force himself, and he'd trusted the brute to level the city that the Steel Dragon called home. Yet somehow, the Steel Dragon had defeated a force of more than twice her numbers.

Stormwing called the Masked One after the debacle, his voice shaking so much that he didn't need an aura to tell that the dragon was petrified. It was unbelievable and completely pathetic.

"She attacked us with mages who could blast holes in dragons," Stormwing stammered. "I've never seen anything like it."

"Those weren't mages, you moron. They were dragon bullets," he replied, tried to keep the neutral tones of his alias Lord Boneclaw, and failed.

"Diamontus is dead, killed by a common green dragon. It's impossible but I saw it happen. I'm leading the retreat," Stormwing said.

"No, you fool! Hold your position. I'll come myself."

"But...this whole war was Diamontus's idea. Without him, should we even continue?" the dragon asked and sounded even more frightened.

The Masked One ground his teeth. He couldn't blame him for being such an ignorant moron. The architect of this war was alive and well but of course, no one knew that except him. Although that might need to change. It was a small miracle that the Steel Dragon hadn't called him out already. He assumed she was hoping he'd treasure the secrecy behind his identity.

But no. Centuries of scheming had all led to this point, and she had almost undone him too many times already.

He would lead his forces into battle personally.

"Stay there, get meat, and be ready for when I arrive," he said and disconnected.

As he flew, his thoughts churned and made him soar onward all the faster. The Steel Dragon needed to be destroyed for the benefit of all dragons everywhere. She was already a splinter in his plan, but she hadn't known about him before so he couldn't blame her for his own well-played conspiracy. But now, in spite of the vote, she still insisted on following her pathetic moral code? How dare she stand against what the Council ordered?

This time, he was done playing with Kristen Hall. He would kill her and would do it for dragon kind, but he would also do it for himself.

Finally, he reached the upper peninsula of Michigan and located the dragons he'd sent—under the guise of Diamontus's leadership, of course—to obliterate Kristen and her forces. What he found disgusted him. Instead of acting like the noble beings they were, they behaved like sniveling whelps and whimpered over their wounds while they commiserated with one another over the weaker dragons who'd been killed by inferior beings. It was pathetic and he had no patience for it. He hated them all in that moment—their weakness, their cowardice, and the way they looked at him and then to the north, in the opposite direction of the battle they still had to fight.

"Lord Boneclaw," Stormwing whimpered. "Thank goodness you're here. Did you manage to convince the rest of the Council that this war would not be as easy as Diamontus told us?"

The Masked One sighed. He was faced with a decision. The persona of Lord Boneclaw had served him well for years. It had given him vast riches and significant power. Through secret cunning, it had precipitated this war but it could no longer serve him effectively. That dragon was a dealmaker, more intent on keeping all parties happy than accomplishing any of his own goals. Lord Boneclaw—at least the one all these dragons knew—was not the kind of dragon to lead a force into war.

And yet he had no other option. He wasn't about to transform into his human form and put a human skull on—as much as he'd like to—and it would accomplish nothing even if he did. But he couldn't let Boneclaw continue to be the weak-spined persona he had always been.

Ah well, he thought, *in war, sacrifices must be made.*

"The Council has not surrendered to the Steel Dragon yet," he said and let strength underpin the normally quiet tones of his public persona. "They are shocked, as am I, that Diamontus was defeated, but they are resolute in what must be done. If we retreat now, the Steel Dragon will only be emboldened. People may even believe her and her arrogant message of policing dragon kind. We cannot allow this."

"But the Council—"

"I am the Council now," The Masked One said and drew looks from many of the dragons. "And I—like them—do not think we should let the death of our brothers and sisters go without punishment."

"But, sir, they tore us to pieces."

"We will not attack them in the same formation. We know better than that. Instead, we will flank them and torch her beloved Motor City."

"But why?"

"Because that is her weakness. She cares for humans as if they were something more than the cattle and servants they are. We will twist this against her and force her to see the error in her beliefs or cling to it even to her death."

"But we have fewer numbers than we had for the initial assault."

He smiled at that. "For the time being, this is true. But the Steel Dragon is not the only one who called for aid. Come. Time is of the essence. We must join them in battle. Some of us will die, but when our brothers and sisters arrive in numbers that haven't been seen since the Second Mage War, we will crush them like the insects they are."

At the promise of reinforcements, the dragons cheered.

Not one to lose momentum, the Masked One leapt skyward, roared in rage, and bellowed for the dragons to follow him. They rose as one and torched the forests of Michigan as they passed.

Led by their new leader, they glided over Lake Huron so no human bases would see them coming. When they were ten minutes out, he sent half his forces over land to catch the Steel Dragon and her team in a pincer strike. He wanted the battle to take place over the city. He knew that she and her team of peasant-obsessed morons would try to protect the people instead of focusing on what needed to be done.

Truly, this would have been enough of a reason to battle over the metropolis, but a ball of joy also grew in his stomach at the thought. The idea of torching her beloved city sounded utterly delightful to him. He would turn Detroit to ash to bring him pleasure and her grief. It would be resplendent.

They were close and in only a couple of minutes, it would be theirs. How quiet it looked, waiting there in the sunshine as if this were simply another day. The Steel Dragon had done well to lure the last attackers out over the lake. It had given her city a few precious hours of existence.

No longer, he thought smugly. In another few minutes, the Masked One would level it to the ground. A few hours from now, he would build his throne atop the wreckage.

Out of the corner of his eye, he saw a dragon break formation from one of the smaller wings he'd put them into. The daft creature simply dove and speared directly toward the water.

"What is the meaning of this?" he demanded.

The diving dragon tilted in the air. He didn't seem to be conscious. "Sir?"

"Get him," he ordered and two dragons hastened to obey.

The rescuers streaked after him and caught up easily. They were flying, after all, not plummeting as this one seemed to be and they caught him before he struck the surface of the water.

"And?" the Masked One demanded.

"He's dead!" The dragon sounded panicked.

"Spread out and remain calm," their leader said and scanned the horizon. Could the Steel Dragon have placed defenders at the top of the buildings? It was possible, but he'd seen no flash of light to indicate a sniper attack. He saw nothing and no indication that they faced an ambush.

Another dragon fell from the sky.

"The mages are attacking!" a dragon shouted.

A third screamed in pain and yanked his leg up. It had a hole in it.

"Those are dragon bullets, you fools! Not mages. They're firing at us with long-range weapons." The Masked One was frustrated that these dragons continued to underplay the threat of the dragon bullets. Admittedly, this was because he had hidden their existence for decades and downplayed their significance even after the Steel Dragon had finally exposed them to the eyes of the world. That deception would cost lives today but not his.

"It's the Steel Dragon's human warriors. Where are they?"

A screech answered his question as a storm of dragon bullets rained on them from above.

He had time to look up barely in time to see the Steel Dragon's fighters dive out of the sky. They had hidden in the blinding light of the sun and now savaged through his ranks.

The battle for Detroit had begun.

CHAPTER TWENTY-EIGHT

Kristen had guessed that the Masked One had no idea what a kingfisher was and she was right. It shouldn't have been too much of a surprise that a dragon of shadow didn't think about how someone could use the sun to attack, but it still felt great for a plan to work.

Already, her fighters had eliminated more than ten of the enemy dragons. One advantage of the dragon bullets was that they hurt like hell and—once buried in the flesh of a dragon—limited both their healing and dragon capabilities. This meant that even shots that didn't kill effectively disabled them from active combat.

That was good. While they were attacking Detroit, she wanted to kill as few as possible.

But the time for battle tactics was over. Lord Boneclaw swooped directly at her.

He roared as he approached and lashed out with bony claws and tail. Jim and one of the soldiers he'd brought—a woman good with a sniper rifle who went by the name Nines—were on Kristen's back, and they fired a volley at the old dragon.

With incredible speed, he spun as the bullets came at him and turned the part of his body that was shaded by the top half into shadow. It became a spinning torpedo of dragon and dark mist that tried to strike at her.

But Amy was on her back too. When he tried to swipe across her chest, the mage threw him back. He bellowed in frustration as he and Kristen both circled for another pass.

They closed the distance between them and both exhaled a great blast of flame. In this, she had the disadvantage because although her steel skin was impervious to most dragon fire, the humans on her back were not. She had to twist to keep them safe.

Lord Boneclaw banked into yet another onslaught and she did the same, marveling at how obvious it was now that he and the Masked One were one and the same. His bony claws had struck at her deep in the cave and the same skeletal tail had delivered almost lethal blows. Now that she knew his dual identity, she felt a fool for not realizing it sooner. Right now, though, there was nothing left to do but defeat him and end this war.

They exchanged breaths of fire again. This time, Jim and Nines fired at the Masked One and ruined his attack.

He roared at them, or so Kristen thought, until she saw clouds begin build in the sky. Another dragon lurked there, one with the ability to control weather.

"Katrina! Get rid of that dragon!" she yelled.

The unseen adversary was summoning a thunderstorm but she wasn't worried about fighting in rain. It was the huge, fluffy clouds condensing into existence that terrified her.

As soon as a shadow fell over the Masked One, he vanished into mist.

He reappeared above her and gutted Nines. The top half of her simply fell away, while her legs and waist remained tethered to her back.

"Amy!" she shouted.

"When he takes that mist form, I can't do shit to him," the mage responded.

The sound of Jim's gun firing said he was experiencing the same thing.

Kristen streaked toward a patch of sun. Her opponent harried her and effortlessly evaded Amy and Jim's attacks. She looked up, hoping to see the Iron Dragon defeat the dragon causing the storm-clouds, but a group of four dragons flew interference. Even with her formidable combat prowess, Katrina wasn't able to stop the clouds from forming.

With only a few clouds, the Steel Dragon and the humans on her back were outmatched. Her enemy had his shadow abilities, which meant he was impossible to strike. She surveyed the battle quickly and wondered if it was as desperate as the duel she was currently engaged in.

To her pleasant surprise, it wasn't. Her people were winning. Their initial attack had rattled whatever confidence the Masked One had managed to instill in his forces. Her people were fighting with everything they had, while his were merely trying to stay in the air.

It meant that all she needed to do was buy them time and the battle would be won.

She reached the patch of sun and turned to attack, but she no longer tried to land strikes. It was impossible given the cloud cover, and very soon, some of her dragons would finish their battles and join her. No matter how strong the old dragon was, he wouldn't be able to stand against a force of five, or ten, or twenty dragons.

"You're not fighting as well as you were," he teased. "You're fighting like you're only prolonging the end of your life."

"Actually, I'm prolonging yours. You've lost this battle, Lord Boneclaw—or should I say the Masked One. You may not know it yet, but your forces and my forces do."

To her dismay, he merely laughed. "Oh, you sweet, silly little girl. Did you really think I would use the force of dragons you'd already bested to defeat you?"

She made no response and only unleashed another wave of fire that he dodged by turning to shadow. "Surrender now and we'll start building a prison cell for you instead of a grave."

"There is no prison that could hold me," the Masked One said. "And the only grave that needs to be dug is yours."

"What are you talking about?"

"Look." He pulled back from his attack and pointed to the west. Faint specks in the distance grew slowly in size as they flew closer.

"We can handle more dragons," she snapped in response. "Your forces are almost gone."

"But you didn't look in both directions," Boneclaw said and pointed to the east.

Kristen turned and saw more of the same specs on the horizon. Her earpiece buzzed and she answered immediately.

Brian began to speak. "We have radar picking up two more sets of dragons approaching fast. We're talking minutes, Kristen. They must have dodged a number of the military bases or something."

"How many dragons?"

He drew a sharp breath. "Each force looks twice the size of the first one we fought. We're talking close to five hundred dragons."

"Ah, very good," the Masked One commented in his habitual oily tone. "Did one of your little humans tell you what will happen via telephone? You see, I willingly entered your trap because I had laid one of my own. Now, I will end this little rebellion of yours and return to wiping the human pestilence from the planet."

CHAPTER TWENTY-NINE

"Amy! Get us some separation!" Kristen ordered and the mage obeyed.

Rather than confront the Masked One directly, the girl created a blast of wind that cleared the sky above them. He retreated to the edge of the circle of light, still laughing with thinly veiled triumph.

"Couldn't you have done this sooner?" Jim demanded.

"That dragon's powers are made for this. Mine aren't!" Amy replied. "He keeps making clouds appear even where I blow wind. I can get us a minute maybe."

Kristen used the time to survey the battlefield again.

It wasn't good.

Now that she knew the enemy had reinforcements, it was clear that his troops weren't retreating but instead, leading her warriors ever closer to the city. The intention wasn't only to defeat them but to destroy Detroit itself.

And there wasn't anything she could do about it. She hoped the people of her city had all found somewhere safe. Even dragons couldn't incinerate more than the top foot of the soil. Maybe the people of Detroit could survive this if they were deep enough underground.

She was about to order a retreat to her base. It was the only option, as shitty as it was, because at least that way, they could control the areas of destruction. Unless, of course, the Masked One let them get under cover and simply unleashed his dragons upon Detroit.

There's no other choice, she thought when Brian yelled in her ear.

"Holy shit, Kristen. You are not going to believe this."

"What now?" she asked in disbelief. The force of dragons that approached was already enough to slaughter her team. What more did the enemy need? Given her luck as of late, a nuclear strike didn't seem unreasonable.

"Hold on a sec. Let me patch someone through."

While Kristen was still waiting for the static of the connection to resolve into a voice, a flight of fighter jets punched through the clouds the dragon was forming. In an instant, they opened fire. Her heart dropped with the realization that her warriors were in no position to fight the US Air Force.

In the next moment, a voice came through and she realized that maybe she wouldn't have to.

It was General Samuel "Sammy" Peralt. "I saw your broadcast, Steel Dragon. We hope we're not too late to join the action?"

She watched in amazement, unable to immediately respond as the fighter jets targeted the Masked One's dragons. They didn't have dragon bullets but they had big fucking guns and more than enough ammunition. Dragons tumbled with each fusillade.

"Sammy? How is this possible?"

"We saw your broadcast. I'm putting my entire fighter wing at your disposal for the duration of this crisis. Your tech guy, Zed, has already patched us through to your radio and dropped markers on all your dragons. My pilots won't target them, not if they don't want to scrub toilets for a month."

"What are you doing in a cockpit?" she asked as the jets began to turn the tide of the battle.

He laughed loud and hard. "Are you serious? I wouldn't miss this for anything. It will go down as the most important battle in genera-tions. The big boys might name an aircraft carrier after me."

Although she still hadn't completely processed her good fortune, Kristen gave orders all the same. "Can you divide your fighters and harry the two incoming attack forces? Don't get too close as dragon fire will wreck your aircraft and pilots and we'll need them."

"Yes, ma'am!" he responded, and his jets pulled up and separated into two wings to engage the approaching swarms of dragons.

"You might have made this battle less decisive!" the Masked One roared, "but I will still have my victory. If we lose a few dragons, that will only further my cause. Every death today will inspire a hundred more dragons to rain fire on mankind."

But Peralt wasn't the only one who heard Kristen's call.

On the grounds of her base below, a portal blazed to life.

Constance held it open while mages poured through it. These didn't look like the battle-hardened assassins she had trained in her cells, but given the sheer numbers arriving, that might not matter.

As the mages emerged, Larry showed them how to make defensive barriers. A massive sphere of shimmering blue energy already protected the base and continued to grow. It expanded even more as another portal opened, followed by a third. Mages streamed through them, adding whatever power they had to the barrier, and the entire city was soon under the protective shield. The call for aid had worked.

"This means nothing!" the Masked One roared. "This will only strengthen our cause. We will be forged in battle and come out stronger—"

"Like steel?" she quipped.

He snarled and tried to attack, but Jim blasted a few rounds at him and Amy put a shield up to keep him at bay.

Kristen was ready to push her attack and finish this entire battle. She surged toward him and he turned to face her, and for the first time, she saw fear in his eyes.

She looked to the south and saw a wing of dragons approaching. These, however, didn't fly in any formation. They mostly looked younger, but she saw a few of the older dragons she'd helped along the way. Some of the Midwestern dragons she'd saved from being blown up so long before were there to fulfill their debt.

"Lord Boneclaw!" Decimus Aurelius bellowed and she had wondered why he hadn't been at the Dragon Council meeting on the island in Canada. "End this violence now. This is not the war you asked us to vote for. You spoke of swift victory and compromise, not a slaughter on both sides."

The Masked One roared in fury. He dove at Kristen but Amy hurled him back again with her magic.

The clouds broke and Kristen looked up. Katrina had finally managed to knock the storm dragon out of the sky.

"No matter! We will still end this. Together, my dragons. We fight together and end this."

Kristen didn't even have to give an order. Her dragons and the humans mounted on their backs swooped through the middle of the swarm of dragons who tried to assemble over Detroit. The humans aimed to wound and mages disabled dragons by striking their wings or removing air from around their heads. The enemy force crumbled and broke into dozens of little clusters as many injured dragons fell Earthward.

"Curse you, Steel Bitch!" the Masked One roared, but he turned toward the north where he'd come from, and his forces followed.

She had won the battle but she knew he would strike again. That was fine with her. She knew full well a reckoning would come. Next time, she'd be ready for him.

But not today. They'd already lost so many lives. She had to pay her respects and welcome all those who had made their victory possible.

CHAPTER THIRTY

The raucous cheers of thousands of different people greeted Kristen when she landed in front of her base.

And different didn't begin to describe everyone who was there. Ancient dragons mingled with those so young their human forms had yet to grow facial hair. There were mages of every stripe including old spinsters who'd hid their powers from all except those who ate their cookies and powerful mages who had convinced their dragon masters to come with them. A hundred languages could be heard and a thousand skin tones could be seen.

As she moved through the crowd, thanking leaders of various forces and clasping hands with the people crazy enough to come to help, she knew this fragile peace could not hold. She'd let the Masked One go because she knew how hard it was to pursue a dragon into the dark. But she knew he wouldn't stop, not when confronted with a group of such diversity. The army around her was the antithesis of a dragon-controlled world, a democratic power structure in which everyone looked out for each other instead of those at the top only looking out for how they could rise even higher.

After hundreds of handshakes and thousands of congratulations, Peralt arrived via helicopter.

"I had the boys wait at the planes, just in case, but I had to be here."

"I'm glad you came. I don't think we would have lasted another minute without you back there," she said.

"I'm glad to help. And honestly, it was my duty. In this case, the interests of the USA and your force aligned perfectly."

"Well, thank you for serving your country," she said.

"You're welcome, but that wasn't the only reason. I came because I personally believe in what you are trying to accomplish. That's what got me into a cockpit. You're right. Humans and dragons can wipe each other out or they can learn to coexist. But any coexistence at this point needs to be built on mutual respect. The days when humans were willing to sit under dragons' claws are past, at this point. Especially now that humans have seen how effective their weapons can be against dragons." He couldn't help but grin with his last statement.

Not that she could blame him. This was the first time in history that an air force had ever fought against dragons. Even without dragon bullets, they'd proven themselves to be hugely formidable against the massive airborne warriors. No one would forget that. It would be like forgetting a new continent.

"The problem with mutual respect is that it has to be enforced," Kristen said with a sigh. "It's all well and good to say we'll play nice, but the fact is that not everyone always will. That's when we'll need a police force that can hold all beings accountable. We'll need a fighting force strong enough to deal with the criminals, be they human, mage, dragon, dwarf, or whatever."

"It's a good thing we have one in front of us," he said and gestured at the diverse crowd. "Your force is the perfect nucleus for that. Look at what you've done. I never thought I'd see mages, humans, and dragons gather around a common cause, let alone with people from what looks like every damn country on Earth. How often does that happen? I'd say about never." He winked and the gesture reminded her that he was usually called Sammy.

"I think we can make this more than a one-time thing," Constance said when she approached with the magical scroll where she and Kristen's people had signed their names in service to the cause of stopping warfare between the races. She handed it to the Steel Dragon. "I think it's time to add more names."

"No," Kristen said and studied the huge crowd of people at her base. "I couldn't ask that of all these people. They already risked their lives once."

"Living is a risk," the technomage said. "These people came because they believe in you and what you're trying to accomplish. It's time to turn this simple scroll into an oath that your new organization will follow—a code that demands equality and justice for all sentients on Earth. This can be the blueprint for a way forward. I know it won't be perfect or easy, but…this is what I didn't know I was fighting for all these years. This is the way."

After a moment's thought, she nodded and took the scroll. Nervous but determined, she stood before the entire crowd.

Immediately, a hush fell over those assembled.

She cleared her throat. While she was used to speaking to cameras, the crowd was huge—easily thousands, she thought shakily.

"Thank you all for coming. Without you, today would have been one of the darkest in human or dragon history. Because of you, it's a day of celebration."

A riotous cheer rose from the crowd. It was the sound of survival, one that could only be made by those who had faced their deaths head-on and ran willingly into that danger.

"But our history doesn't end today," she continued when the applause died down. "We need to forge a path forward and I will need your help. I want to ask if any of you here will read the oath on this scroll and sign your name—not to me or for me, but for each other. Together, we can usher in a new dawn. A time of justice for all!"

An enthusiastic chorus of agreement rang from the crowd.

Kristen nodded and thanked them all. In that moment, she realized that although she had never wanted an army, she had one now.

She dared the Masked One to try to do something about it.

CHAPTER THIRTY-ONE

Kristen Hall couldn't believe it had been a week since a force of hundreds of dragons had attacked Detroit. It felt like it had happened only minutes before and at the same time, like months had passed. The city was still scarred from the battle—hurling dragons from the sky had consequences. And yet, after everything the Motor City had been through since she had discovered she was a dragon with the awe-inspiring power to turn her skin to steel, the people there were as quick as ever to get back to normal.

Even her base of operations reflected this strange dichotomy of time. On the one hand, it seemed like they were preparing for battle more than they had before. Her numbers had been hugely bolstered by new volunteers. In her moment of greatest need, she had called for help and people had answered.

Mages, dragons, and human soldiers who were able to hitch a magic ride to the battle had all come to her aid, and more than half of them had remained as part of her self-proclaimed peacekeeping mission. The new—and well-paid—volunteers were being trained by members of her old team. After all, humans, dragons, and mages had never shared a battlefield before—at least not all on the same side—

and she knew it took considerable adjustment to think of a dragon's fire and a mage's innumerable abilities as part of one's arsenal.

Most of the other half of her old force was on ready alert status, watching for anything that might break the fragile peace. She had won the last battle against Boneclaw and his massive force of dragons because her ancient adversary had decided to retreat. Of course, she knew he had only done this to better prepare for his next assault. And if she were in his shoes, she would attack within the next forty-eight hours.

And yet, despite the weight of this unseen, unsensed strike she was all but certain would come from her most dangerous enemy, she was busy arranging folding chairs.

"And you're sure there should be three sections?" Butters asked and rubbed his big belly at the prospect of moving the chairs he'd spent time arranging meticulously. "I think everyone seated together might make the most sense."

"I disagree, Lady Steel," Timeflash said. "Two sections is the most logical. One area for dragons and one for humans."

"No," Kristen was steadfast. "Three sections for three groups. Mages do not see themselves as belonging to dragons, and their needs are different than regular humans. They are their own power-block, and they deserve their own seat at the negotiations table."

"Well, can we at least get one of them to rearrange the furniture?" the sniper whined. "Amy or Larry could do it in less than a minute."

She smiled at him and shook her head. "Sometimes, I wonder if you're a sniper because it's the only job where you get to sit still and snack."

"I'm a sniper because my eyes are as good as any dragon's and my aim is even better." He winked. "But I wouldn't have signed up for the job if I knew decorating was part of the responsibilities."

"I *like* redecorating," Timeflash said and looked around the ground floor of the base. They had transformed it in the week since the battle. The old warehouse had already gone through changes in its long life, from bustling factory to warehouse to dilapidated property, and finally, to the base of operations for Kristen and her team of mages, dragons, and humans. Now, it had to serve as an elegant yet approachable space where peace talks could be held in two days.

Before, the ground floor had been filled with gear, sleeping nooks, surveillance equipment, and an over-used kitchenette. They'd transformed most of it into a large meeting room complete with black drapes for walls and large potted plants Timeflash had insisted on —"Nothing says care and compassion like caring for plants," she'd said. A few smaller rooms had also been partitioned off from the large open floor to create private meeting chambers for each delegation.

Sleeping chambers were set up too, as everyone seemed to anticipate a need for security although of course, everyone thought the threat would come from different sides.

It had been frustrating for Kristen to have to devote so much of her time to this part of the operation. She would have preferred to be outside training the recruits, but she'd been needed there. Everyone else constantly displayed bias toward one group or another. She had been the only one who seemed capable of thinking about all sides, which meant that while her team prepared for war, she was inside rearranging chairs.

"Kristen, we have visitors," her brother Brian said into her earpiece.

"Do they look important?"

"Uh…yes?" he said. "Certainly unique. I'd…well, I think you need to receive them."

"Have someone escort them in." She sighed. There had been visitors all week. Dragons had arrived to highlight points they thought she needed to hear. Mages thanked her or cursed her. Humans tried to get a selfie or sell them security systems more suited to the suburbs than a base like this.

A minute later, there came a sharp knock on the door. She went to answer it and both plastered a smile on her face and filled her dragon aura with confidence.

When she opened it, however, no one was there. She looked left and right but saw no one.

"Excuse me, miss?" said a voice from below her navel.

She looked down to see two burly men with massive beards and extremely bright clothing in far too many colors.

"How can I help you?"

"We're an official delegation from Canada and we demand to see the Steel Dragon."

CHAPTER THIRTY-TWO

The two short, burly, bearded men were dwarves from Canada, she realized somewhat belatedly. Their hats and facial piercings should have given them away. When Kristen had gone to Canada, all the dwarves had looked like these two. Well, not *quite* like them. The members of the deputation were extensively pierced and their hats especially vibrant.

"How may I help you?" she asked.

"Well, we've walked all the way across the bridge. We'd love something to drink for starters," the first said huffily.

"But what we need most is to speak to Kristen Hall, the Steel Dragon," the other said.

She forced her fake smile to grow even wider. "I am Kristen Hall," she said as sweetly as she could.

"I told you she was the Steel Dragon," the first said and clobbered the other across the head with such force that his feet cracked the concrete they were standing on.

"You did *not,* Barmus!" The dwarf rubbed his head. It was a reminder of how strong they were. He had been struck hard enough to crack cement and he hardly seemed hurt. "You said she was a young woman with red hair, piercing eyes, an ample bosom, and...oh...oh yeah, I guess you did."

"Forgive Rupert, my lady," Barmus said and bowed so low his beard touched the ground. "We dwarves have not had to serve as ambassadors for years. Rupert is considered quite the socialite, but I will banish him to Canada if you so desire—"

"No!" Kristen interjected, not wanting anyone, least of all an ambassador, banished on her account. "Please, Barmus, Rupert, come inside. May I offer you something to drink? We have tea, coffee, or perhaps something stronger?" She hadn't meant to offer them alcohol, but with everything going on, she thought a pint of beer sounded amazing right now.

It was a disappointment when Barmus asked for coffee.

She led the ambassadors to one of the smaller meeting rooms they'd set up. The three of them sat and the dwarves both removed their vibrant knitted hats before they clambered into the human-sized chairs.

"Forgive me. If you'd like something more your...uh, height, I'm sure I can find beanbags or something." She felt like she had already ruined this, but ambassadorship was yet another new skill for her to hone on the fly.

"No, no, no, these are fine," Barmus said. "You honor us with such offers."

"We merely wish you'd been so generous when designing these peace talks!" Rupert stated sharply.

A little confused, she was about to ask what exactly he was talking about given that the conference hadn't even begun. At that moment, Timeflash entered with a tray loaded with a pitcher of coffee, mugs, and appropriate accouterments.

The visitors busied themselves fixing their coffees with more sugar than she thought was strictly healthy. She drank it black and hoped the caffeine would help her brain make sense of this bizarre situation. The dwarves sipped their coffee contentedly, then returned their attention to her.

"I must say, the caliber of this coffee only makes me fear that Rupert was indeed right," Barmus began.

"What's wrong with the coffee?" she asked as she thought it was perfect. It always was when Timeflash fixed it.

"A dragon brought it to you unless my nose is mistaken," Rupert said.

"Yes, and?" she prompted, hoping she didn't come across as rude.

"And *dragons* don't do anything for humans!" he countered. "This is exactly why we came. We heard about these peace talks through our sources, yet we never received an invitation."

"And you want to come…for the coffee?" she asked hesitantly.

"No!" Barmus said while Rupert said, "Yes!" at the same time.

"We want to be here to broker peace," Barmus said and cast a glare at the other dwarf.

"Especially now that we see you truly have dragons treating you as equals," Rupert added.

"Oh, I'm sorry, of course," she said and finally grasped what the hell was going on. "I had simply assumed that since no dwarves were part of the war, there wasn't a need to have you here for the peace talks."

"See? Is that not what I told you?" Barmus said and struck his companion so hard that he tumbled backward out of his chair.

"Honestly, there's no need to—" Kristen tried to say before they both waved her off.

Despite being knocked about, Rupert was finally smiling. "Forgive me, Lady Hall. I made false assumptions and made a—what do you humans say?—butt of myself."

She wisely decided not to call him an ass as the phrase dictated.

Barmus stood and bowed cordially. "We feel it is important for a delegation of dwarves to be present. We have a sense that these talks may create a new order in the world. The balance of power is already shifting, and we would prefer to be a part of that shift than be left out of it."

"Of course. It makes perfect sense." She understood entirely. "I apologize for not reaching out to you myself. You will be affected by these changes as much as any other group, even if you do choose to remain neutral most of the time."

"And we wish to remain neutral," the lead ambassador was quick to point out. "We merely wish to have our voices heard and to know what exactly the terms are you all agree to."

"That makes perfect sense to me," she said. "In fact, you being here will make it even more likely that all sides agree to whatever we decide here. As you know, I was raised as a human but am now a dragon investigator and in both societies, dwarves such as yourselves are highly respected. We'd be honored to have your delegation present."

"You honor us, Lady Hall, you truly do," Barmus said. "Now, as for food, we like meat as much as any dragon and bread more than humans. We'll bring what we can of those and some to share, but we'd appreciate you providing beverages and vegetables from the south for our hundred most esteemed dwarves."

"I'm sorry, a hundred?"

"We dwarves like to make these decisions in what's called a century," he said and his bushy eyebrows knitted together.

"You are more than welcome to come and we will provide you with food and beverages, of course, but every other delegation will only have twelve members. In the interests of equality, I'd ask you dwarves to bring the same number. My team will provide security for the event as well as work as mediators. Our hope is that new laws and peace treaties can come out of this meeting. Maybe a new and better future for everyone. If you're a part of it as well, maybe we truly can usher in a new era of global peace."

The two shared a look that seemed to say they thought it quite impossible that so few individuals could work anything out, but after a few twitches of their mustaches, they turned back to her.

"That will be...acceptable," Barmus said. "Although we'd like to say that we think an era of peace may be overly optimistic. We hope that a Great War can be averted, but the thought of laws for peaceful coexistence that humans, dragons, and dwarves can all agree to is somewhat...optimistic."

"Humans, dragons, dwarves, *and* mages," Kristen said. "They will have their own delegation."

The ambassadors glanced at one another but this time, they turned their attention to her much more quickly. "Of course, that makes sense," Barmus said. "A Great War would be bad for everyone, even us and even if we are able to remain neutral. To truly avoid such a calamity, mages must agree to it as well as anyone else. It would be difficult to choose sides between the mages and the dragons."

"Difficult?" she inquired. "But not impossible?"

Their shared look seemed to be a private conversation that she witnessed but wasn't a part of.

"We would not wish to hurt the mages," Rupert said. "We've given mages succor in their times of need and many of them have become part of our society."

A good sign, Kristen thought, until Barmus spoke. "But we would never fight against the dragons. Even with our flame-resistant skin and dwarf strength, to fight the dragons would be folly. If they didn't kill us all, they would surely destroy our way of life. No. We would not join sides in this, which means all sides would lose."

"Okay." She nodded, disappointed that she had no idea which way the dwarves would go and annoyed that her position as self-appointed peacekeeper didn't sway the neutral dwarves to simply side with her. "Your delegation of twelve dwarves needs to be here in two days. We're very honored that you will be here, and I apologize once more for not inviting you sooner."

"Please, you've honored us enough," Barmus said. "We'll be here on time."

"Seriously," Rupert added. "We will wear our luckiest duds to attract the luck we will need if we are to truly build a peace that might last. For everyone's sake."

CHAPTER THIRTY-THREE

The dwarves left as abruptly as they had arrived. Kristen instructed Brian to track them with some of his aerial drones. They left as they said they would by walking across the bridge that linked Detroit and Windsor, Canada. Before she could return to the task of rearranging the already rearranged chairs, she saw Constance approach her.

"That was a dwarf delegation," the technomage said. It almost sounded like it was intended to be a question, but it wasn't. And why would it be? The woman knew the dwarves better than she ever had.

"It was," she admitted. "They want to be part of the talks."

"What did you say?"

"I said yes. I think it will give whatever agreement we come to more weight since the dwarves are neutral. I wish I had thought of inviting them sooner, but at least we'll have an impartial party."

"I hope the dragons see it that way too," Constance replied.

She raised an eyebrow at the former leader of the technomages. "What's that supposed to mean?"

"I'm merely glad they're coming." The woman shrugged. "The dwarves have been stalwart allies of the mages for centuries."

"Do you think so? I thought you led your groups into action

because of how the dragons were treating the mages. The dwarves never intervened."

"They're not stupid. They know they can't attack dragons directly. Their veneer of neutrality has served them well, but they've also made a habit of taking in refugee mages fleeing dragon cruelty. That makes them both friendly and wise, in my mind at least. Like I said, I hope the dragons see them as a neutral party."

"Even if you see them as allies, I won't let anyone agree to any rules that don't govern *everyone.* I won't let you convince the dwarves to ally with the mages against the dragons."

Constance looked cross at the accusation. "My goal has always been *equality.* Nothing more and nothing less. I'm only glad the dwarves are coming because they'll be interested in the same goal."

Kristen wanted to say more but she saw Stonequest and Drew hurrying toward them. "What is going on? You're supposed to be training the new mages with those two." She pointed at the former leaders of Dragon and Detroit's SWAT teams.

"It's lunch." The technomage smiled as if she'd outsmarted the Steel Dragon on the battlefield.

Drew and Stonequest each had a box filled with sandwiches, chips, pickles, and a cookie. The restaurants that did lunch catering had made out like bandits in the last week as she had hired so many more people. It was easier and more efficient for the training sessions to simply feed them instead of leaving everyone to their own devices. The downside was that she hadn't been able to enjoy a meal by herself for a week.

"Hi, boys, what can I do for you?" she asked. It seemed to be her catchphrase these days.

"We came to talk security," Stonequest said and handed a box of food to both women. A small marvel, she thought—a dragon as wise and prestigious as the leader of SWAT delivering lunch to a youngling like her and a former enemy mage. Things like that gave her hope. She assumed the dwarves had seen the same relationship around the coffee.

"That's right," Drew said around a mouthful of turkey sandwich.

"I had hoped that all this training had something to do with security," she said before she began to all but inhale her nacho cheese-flavored chips.

"This meeting will attract some bad attention," Stonequest stated matter of factly. "All sides of this, human, mage, and dragon—"

"And dwarf," Kristen added.

"Wait, dwarves are coming?" he looked puzzled.

"They are now," she confirmed before she crammed more chips into her mouth. "But only twelve. If anything, I think that will make us a bigger target. Having them here will help to hold everyone to whatever we agree to, but it also means there's more incentive to disrupt the meeting."

"But...won't Lord Boneclaw be here?" Drew asked. "You said he's the Masked One. How can he attack us if he's here?"

"That's *if* he arrives," she clarified. "I don't think he will. I think something will come up that prevents his arrival. That's what I want to primarily be prepared for."

"If that's your concern, I don't think we have to worry too much," Stonequest said.

"You can't underestimate him," Constance said. "If this Lord Boneclaw is truly the Masked One."

"He is," Kristen insisted.

"I want to believe you. It was the Masked One who led my techno-mages by a hidden string, after all, but you've yet to present proof."

"Regardless..." Stonequest cut her off. "Lumos has trained like a beast. Whoever the Masked One is, he possesses the ability to change into shadow. Lumos' light powers are the perfect foil for that ability. If he attacks, we'll be ready."

"He won't attack alone, though," Drew said, his mouth still full of sandwich.

"Which is why I think we should pair every dragon with a mage," Constance said smoothly.

"You merely want to keep tabs on my dragons because you don't trust us," Stonequest growled.

The woman didn't object, which to Kristen was essentially a confession. Still, it was perfectly understandable.

"I want Amy on Lumos' back. Together, they should be able to stop the Masked One. Stonequest, if you don't trust the recruits, ask Larry to accompany you. Eric can ride Katrina as well. They work well together, and both signed the contract binding them to our cause. Beyond that, you can all work out the particulars but Constance is right. I want a mage on every dragon flying above the city. It's a powerful combination and symbolic of what we're trying to move toward."

"Next, you'll want a dwarf on our backs too," Stonequest grumbled.

"They're too brightly colored," she said. "It makes them too big a target."

Constance and Stonequest both laughed at that, at least, and it broke some of the ice that always formed between them.

"I also thought the mages could erect a shield barrier around the base to keep everyone out," the woman said.

"We've talked about that before," Drew interjected, his mouth finally empty of food. "But you said it would take too much power."

"That was before," Constance pointed. "Our most powerful mages should be on the backs of the dragons. The recruits won't be ready for combat after only a week, but there are enough of them that we should be able to make a shield that can last for the entire meeting period."

"There's no way you can make a shield last two days!" Stonequest scoffed.

The technomage leader smiled coyly. "You do remember that it was my team, including me, that rediscovered the ability to open tele-portation gates? I assure you, we can make a shield that strong with the new mages."

"How strong would this shield be?" Drew asked. "Would our people be able to get in and out?"

"Not at all," she said. "It would be as hard as stone until we break the casting or it runs out of energy. Because of that, we would need to wait until all the delegates are inside before we turn it on."

"How long would it take to create?" Kristen asked.

"If you wish it to hold for the entire meeting, we should start it after lunch," Constance said.

She nodded. While she didn't much like the idea of being locked inside, it wasn't like she would be alone. Besides, the delegations might be more willing to come to an agreement if they knew they couldn't simply leave the table and refuse to negotiate.

"Talk to me about security inside if we create this dome," she said.

"Sure. Honestly, it won't be much different than if we don't have the dome," Drew said. "I expect there will be some hotheads in this meeting, especially if this asshole Lord Boneclaw comes. I'll have two dozen of my best humans, plus a half-dozen dragons working security. Humans will be armed with dragon bullets as a precaution—something I think we should tell the dragons."

"No way. That'll end these debates before we even begin," Stonequest protested.

"That's the way of the world now," Constance said. "You can't put that technology back in the box."

"Yeah, thanks to you," the dragon retorted.

"What about security for the mages? Did we get cuffs?" Kristen asked and tried to keep the conversation on track.

"We did. Those we freed from that prison were all cuffed. We have way more than the dozen we might need for the delegation. Every one of my soldiers will be equipped with one."

"A wise precaution given the mages' history," Stonequest said.

Constance thankfully didn't argue the point.

"Your brother will be our eyes," Drew continued. "He's finished calibrating the newly installed radar. That won't let anything slip past. He said it should pick up incoming dragons, missiles, planes, or anything else that could threaten the meeting. He told me to tell you..." He sighed and frowned as he tried to remember. "That he could detect a goose with a firecracker up its asshole if he needed to."

Kristen nodded. That was a threat from her childhood. Her

brother had always said he'd put a firecracker up the butts of the Canada geese that called Detroit home if they ever came after his sister. She had been terrified of the giant geese as a child, yet his threat had always calmed her. If he said that now, it meant his system was working perfectly.

"What about threats? Do we have any clues of who might want to crash our party?" she asked.

"Nothing yet. Brian and Keith have been working on that too. They've both scoured the Internet for any warning signs that someone could be plotting something. Neither one of them has turned up anything."

"Which doesn't necessarily mean no one's planning an attack," Constance said.

She nodded. That was true, but it was also good to know Brian and Keith hadn't found anything suspicious. The two of them were both quite adept at shining light into the darkest corners of the Internet. It was a small comfort that they'd found nothing. Or, she reminded herself, nothing yet.

"All right then," she said, having already devoured her sandwich. "It sounds like we're doing all that we can to ensure a secure meeting. Hopefully, with this dome of yours, Constance, all our preparations will be enough. Which means all we have left to do is add another section of chairs for the dwarves."

"Butters said Constance can do that with her magic," Drew said quickly.

The technomage smiled tightly. "I have combat powers and the ability to control the wind. I can't exactly blow the chairs into place."

Kristen smiled and clapped. "It's lucky I have all of you to help me do this the old-fashioned way."

From the expressions on everyone's faces, she might as well have asked them all to put a gun to their heads.

CHAPTER THIRTY-FOUR

The Masked One had lost so many of his favorite toys.

Constance Vigil had been taken from him after years of following his orders without her knowledge.

Katrina, the Iron Dragon, had been taken, even though he had personally argued for her to be created. She was like a daughter to him, a beast of power and destruction, and now, she'd sworn to destroy him.

Diamontus had been killed by a pathetic excuse for a dragon. He'd simply been a common green with no powers who the diamond-crusted dragon should have been able to crush like the insect he was.

Obscura and Shadowstorm had been defeated long before. Those two—despite being gone longer than the rest—might have stung the most as they shared blood with him.

Even his alter ego as Lord Boneclaw was in jeopardy of being destroyed.

All of them had been lost because of the Steel Dragon.

Merely the thought of her filled him with rage. He gestured for a human servant to come to him. The man, a strongly muscled, well-built fellow with the most amazing falsetto voice had the only thing that would calm his master.

The ancient dragon turned into shadow and used a clawed hand to peel the man's skin from his skull in an effortless gesture. He let him bleed out, trying to enjoy the blood shed and the man's high-pitched screams, but even this joy tasted of nothing but ash.

He harvested the man's skull all the same, removed the one that hid the scarred face of Lord Boneclaw, and donned this fresh one. There was something comforting about the coppery smell of fresh blood and the sticky feel of it as it adhered to his head.

Now, finally, he could *think!*

The Steel Bitch hadn't taken everything from him.

There was still Neal Havington, the leader of the technomage cell that had operated in Europe for so long before being forced to flee by the Steel Dragon. The Masked One had thought that he would lose this mage too, but he had not. Havington had refused to sign the Steel Dragon's pathetic little contract and thus earned himself a voyage in the jail cell of a ship from an island in the south Pacific to North America. There, the Steel Dragon planned to put him on trial.

It was almost funny. Was that what she planned to do if she ever caught him? It was a delightfully quaint notion and one rife with opportunities to be exploited.

The first of which was that the boat they traveled on was painfully under-guarded. The Steel Bitch had massed all her forces in Detroit and left only enough people to steer the ship and care for the prisoners.

It was almost too easy to get inside.

The Masked One simply waited for nightfall, when his powers were at their zenith. He'd followed the ship's passage via satellite for days, so he knew exactly where it was. While he couldn't teleport like Constance could, he could move from shadow to shadow at the speed of the darkness, which was as fast as light. It meant that during the nighttime, he had free range of the skies as long as he didn't move too close to the blinding lights of human cities.

But of course, there were no such distractions over the Pacific Ocean. Only a storm on the horizon and that too was his doing. He might have sprung Havington sooner had he not needed the ship to be as close as possible to the United States and the hidden source of the nearby storm to be ready and in position.

But all his preparations were in place now. The Masked One moved through the shadow of night until he was above the ship, then entered through a crack in a doorway so narrow that even a rat couldn't have squeezed through.

He reappeared on the other side of the door, took the form of a human in a robe, and used his shadow powers to fully obscure his face so nothing but the strongest lights could penetrate.

With arrogant confidence, he walked down the stairs and slit the throat of a human guard who had failed to hear him approach. In a split-second, Havington was on his feet with his fists raised as if in a reflexive attempt to ready his magic. In the light cast by the dull overhead lights, the Masked One could see that imprisonment had not been kind to the man. His eyes were sunken from lack of sleep and his normally well-trimmed face was haggard with days of growth. If he had been offered baths, he must have refused them as he had the sickening stench of a dirty mammal about him.

But still, the mage had strength. He raised his hands aggressively, an obvious threat that indicated his willingness to use them, even without his magic.

Boneclaw responded to the gesture as exactly that, held his hands up, and backed away. "No, please—I'm a friend," he said and modulated his voice to sound like an old human instead of a timeless dragon.

"Reveal yourself, then," Havington snapped.

"I wish I could," he replied. "But we both know that our side now has enemies all around us. If you were to be captured, I couldn't risk you knowing my identity. I'm so sorry."

"*If* I was captured? Do you hear yourself? I'm standing behind *fucking iron bars* right now!"

The Masked One stepped toward the door of the cell. The guard had not had the keys, but that didn't matter an iota to him. After all, he had been picking locks since humans invented them. He slipped the sleeve of his robe over the lock so his entire hand was obscured from from the mage's eyes. Then, he simply turned his hand to shadow, felt inside the lock, and solidified parts of his claw to turn the tumblers and release it. He pushed the door to the cell open.

Havington smiled. "There's a nice trick."

"I've followed your exploits," he said, still using the voice of an old, decrepit human. "I even tried to join you once or twice but I… I chickened out."

"What good are you, then?"

He smiled at the challenge. It was particularly futile. He had broken the man out, something he had failed to do for himself, and yet he still acted like he was in control? Ah, the arrogance of humans despite their fragility was a fascinating thing.

"I've studied magic since I was a boy and hid my powers from the dragons so they couldn't enslave me. I thought your team would finally end the dragons' tyrannical rule. What…what happened?"

"It was that Steel Bitch, Kristen Hall."

Perfect, the Masked One thought. That was exactly who he wanted to point this particular weapon at.

"I've heard of her. And in fact, I have another ally who also wishes her dead. That's why I'm here. But we must move quickly."

"We must move quickly?" Havington's anger manifested in his stiff and offended posture. "I've been left to rot in here while you've been hiding and we must move *quickly?* Who are you to demand such things of me?" He took a step toward his rescuer.

Rather than stepping back, he slipped into a shadow and reappeared outside the cell.

The mage raised an eyebrow at that. "You're more powerful than you let on, old man. I've heard of shadow magic but only rumors of it in dragons. How did an old mage learn to do such a thing?"

"I told you, I spent my entire life hiding from these monsters. I'm not a fighter but I am an ally of the dark. It's the only perfect way to hide."

Havington looked down his nose at him. For the briefest of moments, he felt nervous. Shadow powers were rare in the dragon world and unheard of as far as he knew in mages. He couldn't let the man link his powers to the legend of the Masked One. He would have to use his anger to distract him.

"But I can't hide any longer. Even now, we're wasting time," he insisted in his old-man voice.

"Again, you insult me. I've been here for *days.*"

"I would have freed you sooner but I was afraid. Even now, I fear being captured."

"Then why risk it, coward?"

"Because the Steel Dragon is holding peace talks."

That stopped Havington in his tracks. "Between who?"

"The mages, dragons, and humans. I even heard a rumor that the dwarves would be there. If they proceed, we'll never free ourselves of dragon rule. They'll use their aura powers to trick the other sides and we'll all agree to slavery. Please, I came because I need your help."

"We can at least both agree that the dragons ruling this planet need to be put down," the man said. "If my mages agree to false negotiations with them, it could set us back decades."

"Or forever."

He glared at the old man for voicing such impertinence but he didn't disagree. "What are you proposing?"

"I have made an ally. Together, your abilities and his powers could create a distraction that would allow me to disrupt the peace talks from the inside."

"I thought you said you were scared?"

"I am." He let his voice crack in terror. "I'm so very scared. But I've been scared my entire life. If I continue to live in fear, I won't be able to live with myself. I showed you my shadow spells. I will use them as best as I can, but I'll need your help."

"Fireballs won't do much against the force she's assembled," Havington groused.

"What about a firestorm?"

The man smirked. "I thought you said you've studied my powers, old man. You should know that such a show of power is beyond me. Mages cannot control the weather for any extended period of time."

"Yes, but some dragons can."

"Who are you?" Havington demanded.

"Only a friend!" The Masked One cowered and used the very aura the mage had been suspicious of to bolster his confidence and fuel his fury. "Please, *please!* I only got the idea because of you. There is an Iron Dragon who worked with you, is there not?"

"She's a traitor to our cause," the man snapped.

"As are some of your mages," he said. "I only ask you to meet him. He feels the same as you do—that the members of the Dragon Council have held their strength for too long. He wishes to see their end as much as we do. His name is Stormwing and together, his control of the weather and your fire powers would be formidable. I have seen him make storms so powerful that he can control their lightning. I have even seen him make tornados."

Havington's suspicion of the dragon seemed to burn away with the thought of creating a firestorm the size of a tornado. It didn't hurt that the Masked One used his aura to ever so subtly tweak the man's suspicion away. "How can you trust him?"

"He has no love of Shimmerclaw, I know that. But…I'm not asking you to trust him. Stormwing is powerful but not much of a fighter. If he turns on you, I'm sure you could kill him."

"So you say."

With a small smile, hidden when he turned away for a moment, he played his trump card. He gave Havington the gun he'd taken from the guard he'd killed. Both of them knew it was loaded with dragon bullets.

Until that moment, the technomage still harbored suspicions about the mysterious old mage who had come to free him, but when he was offered this weapon, those doubts burned to ash. He took it and didn't even consider aiming it at the old, cowardly mage in front of him. The Masked One had him.

"You said he can make tornados?" Havington asked, checked the magazine of the gun, and smiled at the dragon bullets inside.

"He can. If you could be at the center of one, you could set it ablaze. A swirling pillar of fire ravaging her precious hometown would surely distract the Steel Bitch long enough for me to strike."

The man studied him for a moment. He cursed himself internally because he'd let his emotions get away from him in the heat of the moment. It was foolish, but he wanted that bitch put down like the dog she was.

Fortunately, his companion did too. "Can you get me off this ship?"

"I have a rowboat outside. I'll take you there now. Stormwing is already on his way and we have made arrangements to have a mage ready to remove those cuffs."

They left as effortlessly as the Masked One had entered. Even when he moved Havington through shadow, the mage didn't notice that it was a dragon with him and how could he? The shapeless shadow form looked neither dragon nor human.

He deposited the technomage on the boat. Perfectly timed, Stormwing approached and cracks of lightning silhouetted him against the dark sky.

"I'll see you again when this is over. Together, we'll make sure dragons don't continue their tyranny."

"Consider it so," Havington agreed. "And, old man, whoever you truly are, thank you."

"Oh, no, please. I'll be forever in your debt," he said, thinking about how long he would rule this planet once he finally did away with the Steel Dragon, Shimmerclaw, and everyone else who stood in his way.

CHAPTER THIRTY-FIVE

It was the day of the conference and the previous forty-eight hours had passed in a blur. Kristen didn't know how her team had managed but somehow, they were ready for the delegates to arrive. She fidgeted with the uncomfortable formal dress she wore, wishing she could have opted for more comfortable clothing.

Unfortunately, both Stonequest and Larry insisted that she had to look the part and to dragons, that meant a woman should wear a dress. She tried to get Constance to side with her, but the technomage had only suggested that she wear a robe like her. As much as she didn't want to wear a dress, she wanted to wear a black robe with strange sigils on the back even less. Still, she wished she'd chosen one that showed a little less cleavage.

She stood outside her base, feeling both like eye candy and an ambassador at the same time, and greeted the reps as they arrived. It helped to make her feel a little more comfortable when she reminded herself of the pistol strapped to her thigh beneath the dress and the ability to turn into a steel dragon.

"Constance, is everything in place?" she asked and moved her hands away from her garment's hem with an effort.

"I should ask you that," the woman said and turned her back to the Steel Dragon to welcome a mage who had arrived via a portal.

Although it was a little rude, she knew the technomage was right. Constance acted as the leader of the mage delegation. It wouldn't do for her to seem to have any kind of personal relationship with Kristen.

"Lady Steel, this is Emil Lord. He's worked as a servant to a dragon in South Africa for the last two decades," the woman said stiffly.

"Nice to meet you," Emil said and stepped from the portal.

"Nice to meet you too, Emil," she replied. "Forgive me, Constance. I had thought the mages on your delegation would be free like yourself."

"Emil has worked for mage equality for years. He's written papers and papers on the topic."

"Not that the dragons like that," he said.

"How…commendable," Kristen said.

"Thank you, Lady Steel." He bowed in a well-practiced motion that showed his deference to her as a dragon. "Constance contacted me about these talks and I thought it would be wise if at least half the mages worked for dragons. That way, the dragons could see that this isn't all about rebellion. Some of us have followed their rules and simply want a better way."

"I look forward to hearing more of your perspective in the following days," she said.

Emil bowed once more and turned to greet another mage. This one was not beholden to any dragon and looked more like a witch out of a fairy tale than an ambassador. She'd most likely been in hiding from the dragons for quite some time. Kristen wondered how the twelve mages would agree with each other, let alone the other delegations.

However, once the last member of the twelve-mage delegation arrived, Constance closed her portal and the representatives all seemed friendly enough with each other, despite their different backgrounds.

Kristen watched them all enter as a motorcade of black and almost certainly armored SUVs rolled up to her gate.

The guard let them in and a moment later, she began to greet the human delegation. There were no national leaders—which she understood—but she was still impressed. The Secretary of State from the United States was there, along with the chief ambassador to the dragons. Top diplomats from Russia, China, Germany, France, the UK, Saudi Arabia, Brazil, Kenya, Egypt, and Japan comprised the rest of the human team.

She had felt guilty excluding so many other countries from the meeting—guiltier than the United States government did, given that they'd sent two people while every other country had had to make do with one—but the humans now stepping from the SUVs seemed far more united in purpose than the mage delegation had. Despite being from different countries, they all wore suits. The only exception made for gender was that some of the women wore brighter colors than the men, although even these were subdued. The meaning of the clothes and SUVs was obvious to her. *We are here to get shit done.*

Kristen greeted them warmly, and the humans responded in kind. She wasn't surprised to see that they seemed more optimistic than the mages. After all, it was the humans who had most recently proven what a threat they could be with their fighter jets and dragon bullets. The mages had pioneered that technology and suffered the dragon's retributions for it.

The regular humans had made all the gains of this new paradigm, yet they had not had to suffer for it. On top of that, if these talks fell apart, they knew there were over seven billion of them. That, plus their tools of war, meant they were far less fearful of war than the mages, simply because their numbers gave them an advantage.

She showed them to their section of the meeting room and returned to her post outside as the dwarves arrived—all twelve of them.

That it was the dwarf delegation was painfully obvious. There was their diminutive stature, of course, plus their preposterously long beards. But truly, it was their clothes that helped her identify them immediately. While the humans had gone mostly for blacks, dark-blues, and grays, these seemed to be the only colors the dwarf delegation had avoided.

Every one of them looked like a coloring book left in the hands of a technicolor zealot. The cuts of their clothing were unusual and a far cry from what one might consider a well-fitting suit. Instead, they wore long, elaborate robe-like garments or ponchos, or something she might call a gown if it had been worn by someone without a long beard and shoulders knotted with muscle.

Before she could approach them, Amy dropped from the sky on her skateboard and landed with a massive flip in front of the delegation. Rather than being put out by this admittedly awesome but undoubtedly unprofessional show of athleticism, the dwarves cheered. One of them even ran forward to embrace her.

"Alp? Is that you?" the mage asked and hugged him before he answered.

"It's me, all right," Alp said from somewhere near her navel. "I took out some of my old piercings and put in some new, but it's me all right. How are you? Still risking your life with the Steel Dragon, I see."

"Anything to keep from being bored," Amy replied.

He laughed as if it was an old joke they'd shared many times. "It's good to see you're doing well."

"Thanks to you," she responded, her tone more serious and heavy with gratitude. "I don't know where I would have been without your help. Serving in the mage army or dead, or who knows. I owe you so much."

"Ah, don't mention it. If I had my way, I would have sent you to a fish farm in the far north. Sticking with the Steel Dragon was a wise move, though. You know what, if you do feel bad, you could get us all some beers."

Amy grinned. "You got it. Do you…uh, want me to do something with those cows?"

"That'd be cool," Alp said.

Six of the dwarves had a cow on their shoulders. That each of them could carry one was an impressive show of strength to Kristen.

She could lift one with her dragon powers, of course, but to walk a few miles with it on her shoulders? That was a real show of strength. Or so she thought until the girl lifted all six with her magic telekinesis.

"Kristen, I'll take care of them. You remember Alp, right?"

"I do. It's nice to see you."

He bowed deeply and introduced her to the rest of the delegation. It was a mess of names, but she made sure to note the name of Krot Minestrength, the Prime Minister of Canada. Most of the delegation were members of his cabinet. She also recognized Rupert and Barmus, the ambassadors who had procured the dwarves' presence at the table.

Once introductions were made, the dwarves followed Amy inside. They were a big ball of bright colors and high energy. Kristen was extremely thankful for their arrival. Hopefully, they would defuse some of the tension from this meeting simply by being themselves.

She was forced to wait far longer than she wanted to for the dragon delegation to arrive. It wasn't a surprise, of course. She'd said the convention would start at ten in the morning, so why would the dragons bother to be early? It spoke volumes about their power that even though they had suffered the most losses in the early battles of the war, they still forced all the other delegations to wait for their arrival.

Finally, she got a radio message from Butters. He'd located them from his vantage point on the roof.

"Are there any we recognize?" she asked.

"Yeah, I see the platinum one. She's the leader, right?"

"That's Lady Shimmerclaw, yes."

"I see the one whose ass you saved—Aurelius or something?"

"Decimus Aurelius. Thank God," Kristen said. She knew Shimmerclaw was on her side but having another friendly member was helpful.

"There's another one I don't recognize and a real bony motherfu— Kristen, Lord Boneclaw is coming."

"What?" she snapped, and her aura pulsed out of control before she clamped it down again.

"Yeah, I recognize his bony ass from when we saved them from that bomb. I thought you said he was the Masked One."

"I did," she confirmed. "But I have no proof. I'll...shit!"

The dragons were already circling overhead. She knew their hearing was too good for her to continue this conversation with Butters.

With smooth efficiency, they came in for a landing and settled in a wide formation. The delegation took up far more space than was strictly necessary but that was the way of dragons. They took their time to transform into their human forms so the parking lot of the base was filled with glowing amorphous shapes and flecks of a dozen different colors as dragons shifted bodies.

"Lady Steel, thank you for having us," Shimmerclaw said and acknowledged her with the faintest of nods. Kristen knew the Council leader was on her side, but damn did the old dragon have a good poker face.

"Even if this does prove to be a waste of time," Boneclaw interjected.

Kristen narrowed her eyes at the scarred man. "Lord Boneclaw. I didn't think you'd want to come, given that the topic of conversation will be peace and you recently led an attack on this city."

"The point of these talks is a path forward," he responded icily. "I want to make sure no one agrees to a foolish path."

"Nothing's as foolish as that attack you led on the Steel Dragon." Aurelius smiled his perfect smile at her and took her hand to kiss it as if she were a princess. "Lady Steel, a pleasure. I apologize for the attack Lord Boneclaw led here. I would have stopped it myself if I had not been lured away on urgent matters." These last words were spoken with obvious venom to the ancient dragon.

"Don't blame me for your servants not verifying their messages," Lord Boneclaw retorted.

She could tell this would be as fraught with tension as she'd expected. "And who are the other members of your delegation?"

"This is Lady Jade," Shimmerclaw said. "She is a Councilor from Asia. Not many other dragons were willing to spend their time working with the other…delegations." Kristen wondered if she'd wanted to say "lesser species." "But worry not. I assure you that if the four of us can agree to the terms set forth over the next few days, the rest of the Dragon Councils will agree to them as well."

"Pardon me, Lady Shimmerclaw, but don't you mean the twelve of you?" Kristen tried to gesture politely to the other eight dragons. When she did so, she noticed that these were all dressed in loose-fitting clothing. It still looked formal but in the same way that the uniform of a martial arts champion looked formal. She also noticed that the other eight dragons were armed.

"As I said, the other Councilors did not wish to attend," Lady Shimmerclaw said. "Lord Boneclaw and Lady Jade thought it wise for us to have security."

"Given that these talks precipitated from violence committed against dragons by mage and humans, this was the only way we felt safe," Lady Jade said.

"Speak for yourself." Aurelius rolled his eyes.

"Very well," Kristen said and reminded herself that her security forces were armed with dragon bullets and that these warriors did not appear to be wearing Kevlar. She sincerely hoped it didn't come to violence. "If you'll follow me, we should begin."

"I would like to welcome everyone to what I hope will prove to be a historic meeting. I know this is quite different than the history we all share, but I hope to build the foundation of a truly equitable future over the next few days, and I would like to thank all of you for being here to be a part of that." Kristen thought her opening remarks were fairly decent but apparently, she was wrong.

"A foundation?" a human from France asked. "We were hoping to come to a legally binding agreement—like the bill of rights you Americans are so proud of."

"It makes sense to us," the dwarf prime minister said. The other dwarves all raised steins they had apparently brought from Canada, clinked them together, and sloshed beer everywhere.

She thanked herself silently for creating four separate sections. Even the thought of what a dragon would do if they had beer sloshed on them was harrowing.

"We dragons would like to hear exactly what is being offered by the other delegations," Lady Jade said.

"Being *offered*?" Constance already had her hackles up. "Mages served you as slaves for centuries, and you ask about what is being *offered*? Make no mistake, we are here to dismantle the dragon hierarchy and put something more equitable in its place."

"And why would we agree to our *hierarchy*, as you call it, being dismantled?" Lord Boneclaw asked. Only he and the three dragon Councilors were seated. The dragon warriors remained standing with their hands on their weapons. "Let's be honest. Dragons have the power. Why should we share it when all you've done is threaten us?"

"A question you dragons need to start asking yourselves about your relationship with the United States," the Secretary of State said.

Kristen sighed. At least everything looked professional. The meeting room they were now in was spacious enough to give all the delegations their own zone and thus prevent the brawls that humans, mages, and dragons seemed to want to fight. She wondered if the temporary walls they'd put up for each delegation to have a meeting place would prove to be insufficient.

"Ladies and gentlemen, please. I think it might be wise if we begin by breaking into our groups and finalizing what each delegation is hoping to achieve. Maybe then we can find common—"

Before she could finish, an unnaturally loud knock issued from the front door. It sounded as if a giant tried to kick a path into the base.

"Brian?" she asked into her earpiece.

"I'm working on it!" he said. She could hear his fingers flying over his keyboard through her headset. "There's nothing there but a few birds. Nothing that could have made that noise anyway."

She could see she wasn't the only one on high alert because of the sound. The dragon warriors had drawn their weapons and the mages had all spun a different variety of magic. The humans looked concerned. These were diplomats, after all, not soldiers. The dwarves looked ready and willing to fight.

Kristen told her security team to check the door and hoped they were armed well enough for whatever was out there.

CHAPTER THIRTY-SIX

"Amy?" Kristen said into her earpiece as she stepped away from the lectern at the front of the conference room.

"I don't see anything from up here." Wind whistled in the background, which indicated that she was either flying on a dragon or her levitating skateboard. "But I sense something."

That was an ominous sign. Their plan was to seal the protective dome when the talks broke for lunch, but she wondered if she shouldn't implement it sooner.

"If you'll excuse me for a moment," she told the delegations of humans, dwarves, mages, and dragons.

"Jim, Drew, what do we have?" she asked as she followed her security team to the door.

"Nothing as far as we can tell," Drew said but he had yet to open the door.

She understood. He had a bulletproof vest but she had dragon healing powers plus the ability to turn her skin to steel. She donned her natural steel armor and opened the door.

No one stood on the threshold. She frowned and looked from one side to the other, then paused when someone yelled at her in what had to be the most high-pitched voice she had ever heard.

"We are down here, Lady Steel!"

Kristen looked down and gaped at twelve of the most peculiar beings she'd ever seen. They had the ability to surprise even a woman holding a convention with technicolor dwarves and shape-shifting dragons.

The first thing she noticed about the little beings was their height. They were so small, they made dwarves look like Godzilla. She estimated that the tallest of the group was maybe twelve inches, but most seemed to be only eight or nine inches tall. They were all exceptionally beautiful in an androgynous kind of way. She thought she could tell that the one who spoke was a female, but she wasn't sure if she could distinguish which were males.

They wore their hair long or shorn into—what else?—pixie cuts. High cheekbones, massive eyes, and pointed chins made them all seem vaguely feminine to her, but she had thought all the dwarves were male since they were bearded. Perhaps she needed to work on her gender expectations.

The pixies wore gossamer clothing that shimmered like dew at sunrise. In fact, sunrise was a great way to describe their clothes in general. They were all bright and almost white in shades of blue, yellow, and pink and seemed to be about as transient as they were almost transparent.

"How may I help you?" Kristen said, way too late.

"We are rather upset about not being invited to this conclave," the leader said and elevated to hover in front of her face on wings that looked like they'd been taken from the world's largest dragonfly. She didn't know much about pixies, but she did know that they'd originally been made by human mages, which meant their wings might have indeed been modeled after insects.

Another pixie, this one with the dusky wings of a moth, fluttered to join the first. "Yet again, we pixies have been left out." This one's voice was only slightly lower, but to compare them in pitch was like comparing the notes that came from a piccolo. "A meeting of every race and power on the Earth except us pixies."

The being with the dragonfly wings who had spoken first shook her head sadly at this. "It's like the other races don't think pixies have any thoughts of importance."

"I can assure you this is not the case!" the moth-winged stated. Despite them speaking over each other, neither seemed bothered. To her, it only made it harder to tell them apart. "We have many thoughts to share."

"Important thoughts. On many things," one added from the ground.

"Yes! On many important things," yet another one stated.

"Like buttercups and honeybees." This contributor had bee wings and shouted loudly to be heard. It earned a cheer from the tiny, high-pitched voices of the others.

"Forgive my compatriots," the first said. "We do not think as you do. We do not think so…linearly. But that does not mean we wish to be ignored."

Kristen looked back into the room she had been addressing, already crammed with way too many different ideas and viewpoints. *What could twelve seemingly crazy pixies hurt?* she thought somewhat flippantly. But they were right.

"I apologize, Lady…"

"Dragonfly," the pixie with the dragonfly wings said. "It is not my name but you could never understand our language anyway, so Lady Dragonfly will do."

She wondered if the creature had somehow read her mind. Did she find in her thoughts that her wings were the feature she found most unique? Or was she simply used to dealing with humans?

"Lady Dragonfly, I admit, the oversight was mine. I slighted the dwarves similarly. Since you were not involved in the war, I did not think you would wish to be involved in the peace talks. Allow me to correct the issue. Whom among the pixies should we invite to these talks?"

Lady Dragonfly smiled so wide she had to shut her oversized eyes. "We saw that each delegation had twelve members, so we worked that part out ourselves."

"How did you—"

"Did you think a gathering such as this could be kept secret?" a pixie that appeared to wear a beetle's carapace asked. "We could smell the magic for leagues. Hundreds of leagues."

"Thousands of leagues," said another.

"What's a league?" asked a third.

"Focus!" Lady Dragonfly snapped and all the pixies fluttered their wings and flew into a halfway decent formation. "We've been practicing," she said, either noticing Kristen's stare or reading her mind.

"If you will give us a few moments to prepare you an area," she said in bemusement.

"But of course." The pixie leader streaked past her, followed by the other eleven in her delegation. There was much more to the tiny creatures than insect wings because as they moved, they left trails of sparks in red, yellow, and orange that faded to nothing in their wake. They circled the meeting area and darted about above the heads of the groups.

The dragons looked quite annoyed at the intrusion but they didn't say anything. Kristen often saw pixies at dragon gatherings but she had the feeling dragons saw them like they did everything else—as property or entertainment. Shimmerclaw looked intrigued while Lord Boneclaw didn't look as pissed as she thought he would. No doubt he anticipated the new arrivals creating even more chaos, thus ensuring the status quo would not change.

The humans seemed overwhelmed by the strange creatures. They watched them with open mouths and wide eyes as if she had invited a flight of fireflies to the convention. For all the experience she had with pixies, she might as well have done exactly that.

The mages' reaction was divided, but not along any lines that she could distinguish. Some like both the old witch and Emil Lord seemed delighted to have the pixies, while others seemed wary of the strange creatures. Constance was as inscrutable as always. Kristen vowed yet again to never play poker or any game involving bluffing with the leader of the technomages.

The dwarves were the only delegation that seemed truly delighted to have the pixies there. They smiled fondly as the creatures released their showers of sparks on them and were already fetching chairs and making space for the diminutive delegation.

"We only need two chairs," Lady Dragonfly said to one of the dwarves who rearranged the furniture. Her tone was so solemn, it sounded as if she'd already begun the deliberations.

Kristen used the temporary chaos to pull Larry aside.

"Larry, please tell me you know more than I do about pixies."

"Sure." He grinned. "What exactly do you know?"

"Let's say absolutely zero."

"Zero?"

"Well, not zero. I know they make sparkly things and I know they were made by mages in the First Mage War—"

"Second." He cut her off. "Dwarves were from the First Mage War. Wow, you weren't kidding about the zero."

She looked nervously at the room. The pixies tried to balance three to the back of a chair. This meant they constantly climbed it, then fell and resumed the process, to the amusement of the dwarves.

"Okay, well, the mages made them because the dwarves were a spectacular failure. They had thought that by modifying humans, the dwarves they created would want to join them, but they saw how powerful they were in their own right and didn't want to come into existence simply to be dragon fodder."

"Larry, now is not the time for a history lesson. Tell me about the pixies."

"Right, sorry. The mages decided not to model the new beings on humans, what with their propensity to disagree. They harnessed wild magic itself to create the pixies."

"So should we assume that the pixies will side with either the humans or the mages?"

"No way!" He chuckled. "From the perspective of the mages and the regular humans who joined them in the second war, the pixies were an even greater disappointment than the dwarves."

"Why?"

"Pixies are creatures of wild magic," Larry said and rubbed his chin. "They are pure magic given solid form. As such, they each hold immense power—far more than virtually any human, mage, or dragon."

Kristen felt a sudden pang of fear given that she had had now admitted twelve of them into her base before they'd put up the defensive shield that Constance had planned. "Should we be worried?"

"Um…technically, yes. They have powers to do far beyond what any of us—even Amy—can do. But they're capricious and willful to a fault. They're more likely to use their powers to pull pranks than they are to do anything serious."

"Then why do you think they're here?"

He shrugged. "I don't know. I've never heard of them trying to enter any kind of serious deliberations with anyone. Them merely showing up is anomalous, to say the least."

"But you've seen them before, right? I know they're usually at dragon parties."

"They only go to those because dragons often ask pixies to pull pranks on other dragons, which they love to do. Them being here is odd, and we should watch the little troublemakers carefully." He tried to sound tough, but a smile sneaked through. It seemed the mage had a soft spot for the little beings.

"Lady Steel?" Aurelius asked. "Are we ready?"

Kristen turned to see that the pixies had finally managed to take their places. As promised, they'd only needed two chairs. Three sat on the seat of each one, while another three balanced on the back of the seat. Once the dwarves had stopped laughing, the pixies simply used their wings to keep their balance rather than fall repeatedly.

"Now," she said and moved to stand at the lectern on the small stage in the front of the room again. "Where were we?"

CHAPTER THIRTY-SEVEN

If there was any benefit to having two more delegations at the convention than Kristen had anticipated, it was that the dwarves and pixies remained relatively silent.

The other three factions were far more outspoken about their demands.

After her opening statement, she had dismissed each group to formulate their hopes for the outcome of this meeting.

The humans had been the first to finish their deliberations, which hardly surprised her as human beings had been making treaties with other groups of humans they hated for thousands of years. The delegate from Germany was the one to outline the human position once all five groups reconvened. She didn't know if his slightly aggressive accent and quick speaking would work as a positive or negative for the humans.

"We want nothing short of full equality under the law. Dragons who kill humans should face far more significant penalties than their current laws provide. It is not acceptable that a human who kills a dragon is executed without trial, while a dragon who kills a human is fined and set free."

"And what if the human is killed because they intruded into a dispute between two dragons? Surely a dragon should not be executed for a mistake on the human's part?" Lady Jade interrupted.

"If such events occur, the dragon should be put on trial, exactly as a human would be," the German delegate snapped. "If a dragon has a history of such offenses, that should be held against them."

"All dragons have a history of such offenses, boy," Lord Boneclaw said.

From the sneer on the delegate's face, this was exactly his point.

"Lord Boneclaw has a point," Shimmerclaw added. "We live far longer than you and our shared past with humans is a bloody one. If you wish for peace going forward, past transgressions must be forgiven. That is what you are asking us to do with these mages, is it not?"

"What we are asking is an end to servitude," Constance said and looked imperious in her black robes. "Generations of our people have done nothing more than made the lives of dragons easier. We wish to be masters of our destiny, the same as all free beings on this planet."

"Oh, come now," Lady Jade said. "Many mages are treated well. They are all paid in this day and age, and most are paid handsomely."

Emil Lord spoke quickly, and his South African accent added a different weight to his words. "Payment without the choice of freedom is merely a slightly kinder form of slavery. Wages are simply softer shackles when the fruits of our labor can never be enjoyed without a dragon taking whatever they wish from our efforts."

"Ridiculous!" Lord Boneclaw snapped and the mage delegation all pushed to their feet and demanded that the old dragon apologize. He had done little besides voice such interjections. All of them had been aimed at whatever consensus seemed close to being reached. If there was one person there truly trying to scuttle the whole meeting, it was him. Unfortunately, Kristen didn't know what to do about it. She still didn't have any proof that he was the Masked One and everyone there, even him, was under her protection.

"What is ridiculous…" Constance's voice cut through the hubbub of the room and inspired silence on all sides. "Is that despite decades of service, when the first glimpse of open conflict appeared, you dragons rounded the mages up and imprisoned them."

"That was for their safety," Aurelius protested.

"It was not!" she fumed. "The dragons there treated these mages worse than cattle. They were bound and naked and being executed by dragon fire when I rescued them."

"Dragon fire is the price for mages who shoot us with bullets made of our dead," Lord Boneclaw said as if he wasn't the dragon who had given the technomages the idea to make those bullets. Kristen's hatred for him flared.

Constance, though, snapped before she could speak, "*None* of those mages were part of my group. *Not one.* The mages those dragons intended to burn alive were loyal servants of dragon kind. They were people who kept their heads down and did your paperwork and laundry for a chance at retirement that they knew would probably never come. Your betrayal of those mages was the final straw."

All the mages nodded at this. Magic swirled around some of them and gave their anger form as flames or smoke or shards of energy.

"But dragons were attacked by mages when that happened," Lady Jade said. "What would you have us do, roll over?"

"We would have you stand trial," the secretary of state said. "We would have you answer to your crimes in a court of law."

"And would you consent to a trial by peers?" Boneclaw asked. "That is what your law demands, is it not?"

"You're damn straight it does," the man retorted. "But that doesn't mean that the rich and privileged are only judged by the rich and privileged, nor does it mean that women are only judged by women."

"But you can't expect a dragon to sit through a court case?" Aurelius asked.

"We'd be more than happy to call dragons for jury duty." The Secretary of State seethed.

"Again, what do you offer us?" Lady Jade asked. "Your jets already killed some of our best warriors and now, you want more? Why should we agree to any of your terms?"

Krot Minestrength, the dwarven prime minister, cleared his throat as he stood on his chair to be seen when he spoke. "Dragons, the requests of the humans and mages are not unreasonable. They are not asking to take your gold or your castles, simply for an opportunity for justice. Is it not true that to the person used to privilege, equality feels like oppression?"

"But we are not privileged!" Lady Jade whined as eloquently as Kristen had ever heard someone whine. "We maintain peace in the world. We oversee financial institutions that humans have no interest in. We have responsibilities that the other races have never even thought of."

"Nonsense!" the German diplomat yelled, perhaps emboldened by the promise that no one would be incinerated by dragon fire at these meetings. "You act as if we are trying to make you inferior. We are *not!* We simply wish you to be beholden to the same laws as the rest of us."

Lady Jade snorted. "The same laws? How often does a human get caught between a dwarf battle or a duel for honor amongst pixies?"

No one answered, which she took to mean never.

"Precisely! It does not happen. You try to veil all this in the language of *equality* when the truth is the only group that will lose our status in this world is the dragons."

"Because the dragons are the only filthy murderers," the old witch screamed and pointed a crooked finger at Lady Jade that was clearly loaded with one hell of a curse.

Kristen moved between the woman in her off-colored raggedy clothes and the simpering green dragon in her flawless silk dress.

"Let's break for lunch," she said, hoping the beef the dwarves had brought could avert an international interspecies catastrophe.

CHAPTER THIRTY-EIGHT

The tension in the room was such that when Kristen called for a break, each group subsided stiffly and continued to glower at each other. Rather than advancing to violence, however, the agitation was low enough that everyone was still willing to talk amongst themselves and take a break from the other—in each delegations' eyes—unreasonable groups.

She swallowed a cup of coffee proffered to her by Timeflash and decided to start making the rounds to each group in an attempt to show them all that the aims of everyone else weren't so insane. When she looked around to choose her first destination, she noticed the pixies.

Some of them seemed content to dart about the room and shower everyone with sparks, but Lady Dragonfly and a few of the more conversationally gifted seemed to better understand what was going on. Every other group had their area to retreat to except the pixies.

Kristen sighed and moved to avert this slight to their honor before they simply magicked one of the other groups out of existence. She approached them, still wondering if they could do that when Lady Dragonfly fluttered into her face. With her tiny hands on tiny hips, she was the angriest, cutest little creature she had ever seen.

"Lady Steel!"

"You may call me Kristen and please, if you'd like to come this way, I'll show you to a private area where you may discuss the proceedings."

The pixie's fierce little scowl gave way to a big goofy grin. "You honor us, Lady Steel."

"I hope so," she said and scrambled to think where the pixies could go. She knew they didn't need much room, but she still wanted to give them a space that wouldn't dishonor them. The messy bunks of her team, now all crammed into the upper floors, seemed wildly inappropriate, as did the workout room and the kitchen as, despite her constant threats, it was always messy. Finally, she settled on her office.

She led the delegation down a hall. They darted and bounced off the walls until she stopped smiling at their antics.

When she opened the door to her office, she was pleasantly surprised to find it quite tidy. That made sense, though, as she rarely used it. It was a pleasant room with framed newspaper articles of her exploits on the walls, a filing cabinet she'd inherited from Windlock in one corner, and a big old desk she'd had made by a local carpenter who used wood from old barns. Two of the walls were floor to ceiling windows that looked out over the city. The pixies all raced to the windows and crammed their faces against them as if they'd never been this high before.

"You are welcome to my office. I'll send someone to fetch you when the full meeting gathers together."

"You honor us, Lady Steel." Lady Dragonfly landed on her desk and bowed so deeply her wings brushed the old barn wood. "If we wreck the place, we will put it back together. You have my word."

"Thank…you?" Kristen said and was about to see herself out, but her curiosity overcame her. "If you don't mind me asking…"

"You are welcome to ask any question you like, Lady Steel. Except what Sir Ladybug likes to eat. It's not a question that's pretty to answer."

Sir Ladybug waggled his eyebrows—she had thought he was a lady —in challenge and she tried to ignore him.

"Honestly, that hadn't even occurred to me."

He wilted.

She continued quickly, hoping she hadn't offended him. "I'm curious to know what you think of the meeting so far."

The pixies all buzzed excitedly at the question and made sounds that were somewhere between the tinkle of bells and chirp of crickets. She assumed it was their language, but she began to realize that assuming anything with them was not wise.

After a moment of this, they returned to exploring her office. Lady Dragonfly stood next to a framed picture of her parents. She was only slightly taller than their images. "In truth, my Lady, we aren't quite sure yet. There has been considerable yelling but not much said—from our perspective, of course."

"You're not wrong about that," she agreed. "But I think it's good that at least the humans and mages have laid out their positions. Coming to a consensus will probably take some time. At least that's what I've been led to understand."

"I sense that you, like us, are new to all this talking about things more important than buttercups," Lady Dragonfly said ponderously.

"I am," she admitted. "I'm a cop, or I was. I enforce the laws, I don't make them."

"We understand," the leader said after a chorus of tinkling language from the rest of the pixies.

"We too are not well-suited for this kind of discussion. Unlike humans or dragons, we tend to roam rather than settle anywhere. Sometimes, it seems we have as much in common with butterflies as with the more humanlike races."

"Certainly a more similar sense of humor!" Sir Ladybug added, a statement that would later keep her up at night with the implications in it.

"But we do understand how humans and dragons work. We understand you make rules and you divide the world into realms of control. We are unhappy with our place in the world your two races have built. Much like the dwarves, we feel like an afterthought."

Kristen nodded and tried to process the wisdom this tiny creature offered on her. "If you don't mind me asking, what do you hope to gain from the peace talks? I started these discussions in an effort to stop a war, but with you and dwarves here, I see the potential for so much more. Do you and the pixies have any specific problems I can help address?"

"Lady Steel! You honor us," Lady Dragonfly said yet again and bowed deeply. All the pixies stopped their mad flights around the room and came to bow before her. "You honor us by even asking. Truly, that more than anything else is what we would like to see changed. There are some issues here that we will not have an opinion on, I admit. Property rights, for example, are something we have trouble understanding, but we still wish to have our opinion asked. We do not feel valued in this world. You did not invite us to the peace talks."

"Again, I'm sorry."

"It is fine, Lady Steel. You were only following human and dragon precedent. We are never invited to anything but parties. No one cares about our views."

"So, you want more invitations to things?"

"Yes!" the pixies chorused.

Their leader giggled at her flock. "Yes, we would like to be included in things like this. But we also wish to have protection. Currently, we are not protected by dragons or humans. Dragons are fond of us, at least, and leave us be, but there are many places we simply cannot go without fear of being caught by a human's net or shot with a slingshot. We could, of course, turn the humans to toads, but we do not. Are we thanked for this? Never!"

"Well, what else do you want besides invitations and protections? I think those are both reasonable places to start, but is there more?" she asked.

"I think we want what everyone else wants. Well, we also want humans to stop spraying pesticides on their foods, those fucking morons. But we also want to live free. We want to be treated fairly and be equal to other races."

Kristen nodded. "I think freedom, fairness, and equality are good goals to aim for." She didn't know what to think about the pesticides remark. "I'll help you in any way I can to achieve those goals."

The pixies rocketed around the room to show their appreciation.

CHAPTER THIRTY-NINE

Kristen called for the meeting to reconvene after a half-hour. She had thought the time apart would have cooled everyone's nerves. How wrong she was.

The dragons seemed cooler than before, but she could feel their auras boiling with distrust and anger. The human delegation wore scowls above their folded arms. Malevolent energy swirled in the air above the mage's heads. Even the dwarves seemed to be in a funk. Only the pixies didn't seem upset, and she began to realize that she might not even understand what an upset pixie would look like.

She took the lectern to start the meeting but paused to give a warning instead. "We all came here because we all ostensibly agreed to peace talks. I understand that there are many opinions in this room, but that is no reason to behave without civility to each other. I feel like I need to clarify the rules. Delegates who cannot behave themselves will be removed and their vote will be nullified.

"This meeting has grown into something much more important than I had originally planned. Before, I saw it as a way to move forward, a chance to get people talking. Now, it has become a vital part of the pathway to lasting change for our world. When in history have all five of these groups met together? When in history have we agreed to listen to each other? I know I declared myself sheriff, but surely all of you can see that my team can't enforce the rules for the entire planet."

"We're counting on it," Lord Boneclaw mumbled, but when she darted him a glare, he withered and said nothing further.

"We need rules for how the races will interact. We need laws that we all agree to so that we can all enforce them on each other."

"We have laws," Decimus Aurelius protested. "Dragons have had laws far longer than humans have, in fact. All the races have prospered under them, I might add. Admittedly, they're not perfect, but do we need to throw everything out?"

"You're right, Lord Aurelius, we do have rules. Humans have laws, as do dwarves. But the rules that supersede all the others—the rules of dragons—have failed us."

"How can you say that?" he demanded.

"Those rules were what led to both mage wars. They almost precipitated a third mage war a week ago. Those rules have let dragons grow wealthy and powerful while everyone else has fought for scraps. All of the rules are based on a time when dragons controlled everything else simply because they had overpowered all other groups. Those rules were rules of fear."

Kristen reached into her pocket and pulled out a dragon bullet. She held it up for everyone to see. It didn't look any more threatening than a normal bullet. The casing was the same and the primer was the same. The only difference was that instead of having a bullet made of metal at its tip, it had a bullet made of the off-white material of a dragon's tooth or claw. This particular one was lined with tiny hair-like filaments of what must have been blood vessels when this was still part of a dragon.

"But dragons can no longer rule by fear. Not with these. Twice already, the mages have tried to overthrow the dragon rules of fear. Twice, they failed and twice, they were defeated. Does anyone in this room truly believe that a war fought between these five factions would end in a decisive victory for any side?

"The days of easy victory are over. For better or worse, there is more than one superpower at the table. Humans now have missiles that can blow dragons up. Mages have dragon bullets and who knows what else they can use to fight dragons with. The balance of power has become more even. Dragons, humans, and mages all need to recognize that. We no longer live in a world where dragons can simply have their way. But we won't enter a new era where humans or mages take the place at the top that dragons possessed for so long, either."

The dwarves cheered for that while the pixies streaked about the room, clapping and sending sparks down on the people below them.

"A war would be devastating for all involved. No matter who won, the fighting would destroy the planet and wipe out most of every race. Peace is a better way forward, but peace is harder than war. Peace takes work and it takes compromise. It is something we have to strive for every day. That's what we're all here for."

She sat to loud applause. Even the dragon delegates seemed swayed—except Lord Boneclaw, of course, who sat in his chair stewing in rage while he picked at one of the scars on his face.

The humans spoke first. "Lady Steel makes good points," the Secretary of State began. "After some deliberation, we're willing to agree to the dragons' terms that no crimes committed before this meeting will be held against them. However, we still strongly insist that any murders committed by the dragons in the future will need to be investigated by dragon *and* human teams."

"We can agree to that," Shimmerclaw said.

"We can as well," Constance added. "With the caveat that no one's past crimes, human, mage, dragon, dwarf, or pixie will be held against them."

"Fair enough," Aurelius said.

"But there is still the point of dragons having to surrender so much," Lady Jade said.

"We have an idea for that as well," the man said. "If you dragons agree to pay taxes when you're in human territory, we will agree to set aside up to ten percent of each country by land mass for the exclusive use of dragons. This would be land you can still rule however you see fit. Humans would only enter with travel or work visas and would be beholden to your rules on your land."

"All we have to do is let your governments drain our gold?" Aurelius asked, although he didn't sound particularly upset by the idea.

"That's right. If you're on human land—or dwarf land for that matter—we expect you to pay your fair share."

"We like the sound of that," Krot Minestrength added.

"What about the mages? Where do we fit in all this?" Constance asked.

"You have always been treated as humans by humans, and we would continue to treat you as law-abiding citizens. I can't speak for all the countries here, but the United States would like to create a bureau in the federal government to better understand how mages work, how to educate you—"

"And how to exploit us?" the old witch asked.

The Secretary of State smiled a very American smile. "There are certain business considerations we have never had to consider because magic has been in the domain of dragons for so long. We would need to formulate laws about liability around magic and that kind of thing, but yes, we expect you mages could grow very wealthy under a more equitable system."

Some of the mages didn't seem to care for his suggestion, but most of them liked the idea of becoming respected members of society.

"What about the pixies?" Kristen asked the group. "The dwarves have Canada, their territory governed by their laws, but what about the pixies? Do you also wish for your own land?"

"We do not, Lady Steel," Lady Dragonfly said. "We pixies like to travel, and the idea of having to stay in one area because of an imaginary border will confuse most of us. If it suits the rest of the delegations here, we pixies would like to be able to come and go as we please on the condition that we follow the laws of the land we're on."

"In exchange, we will continue to refrain from turning all of you into toads. Which, for the record, some of you deserve," Sir Ladybug said formally.

"Dwarves, do you have new requests?" Kristen asked.

"We think a court of international law might be necessary. Even if the dragons get some of their own territory, we all know many dragons will continue to want to live amongst the humans. We think there should be a court made up of judges from the races to appeal to if cases cannot be solved locally."

She nodded and tried to pay attention as the conversation slipped into the banalities of bureaucracy. Before long, they discussed tariffs, worker's wages, defense contracts—in other words, the dull day-to-day processes of government that made the world work. Although it was dull to a cop turned dragon investigator, she was pleased to see that this meeting was working.

At the rate they were going, it seemed entirely possible that they might come to the first agreement between the five races. While trade percentages would have to be adjusted and inflation accounted for and courts would need to be rebalanced, all that could come with time.

The brief sense of satisfaction was deceptive, which made her feel quite panicked when Brian came into the room with a look in his eyes that said he didn't have a second to spare.

Kristen excused herself and went to him. "Is everything all right? You know you could have contacted me via headset."

"Yeah, but I thought this merited talking to you in person. There's a bad storm coming."

She smiled weakly. "You don't by any chance mean a regular storm that's particularly strong? Like a summer blizzard or something?"

"I don't know, Kristen. Do normal storms have tornados made of fire at their center?"

CHAPTER FORTY

Kristen excused herself as quickly, politely, and unobtrusively as possible. Unfortunately, it simply wasn't possible to achieve all three of these at once, so the eyes of dragons, mages, dwarves, and humans tracked her as she followed Brian to his security station.

"See?" he said and brought up a grainy picture. "I tried to get close with a drone, but the damn thing was shot by a bolt of lightning and totally fried."

Still, the image it had captured was clear enough to tell that his assessment was right. A huge swirling cloud of fire and smoke powered through the northern suburbs of Detroit and destroyed everything in its path.

"How the hell are we supposed to stop it?" he asked, his voice tight with fear.

"You've done your part, Brian, now get a grip. You've fought bigger shit than this in videogames. Pretend that's what we're doing now."

"Okay, you're right. I've been Diablo himself. I can handle this." Brian took a few deep breaths and seemed to get himself under control.

"Right. Good. Now, I want you to contact all our outside forces and get them active. Make sure the dragons are all paired with mages.

Command goes to Lumos and Amy and next in line is Drew and Stonequest, although I'll want them to lead the evacuation of the civilians before they join the battle. Katrina and Eric need to answer to Lumos—tell Lumos this, not Katrina, for the love of God—but other than him, I want them to have full autonomy. This has to be an attack by dragons and mages. We'll need their experience out there."

"Great, sure, and what will you do?" he asked.

"I'll handle on-site security—keep our butts safe and this conference on track."

That finally made him smile. "There's a fucking flaming tornado coming and you still want to finish your job? That's my sister!"

Now, Kristen had to the almost impossible task of extricating Constance from the meeting so she could lead the mages in creating her barrier spell. She made it as far as, "Constance, can I borrow you for a moment?" before chaos erupted between the delegates.

"We demand to know what is going on," Lord Boneclaw called.

"There seem to be a few…troublemakers approaching," Kristen said. "I merely need Constance for a minute."

"Why do you need a *mage?*" Lady Jade asked.

"Because us mages are the only ones who can make defensive barriers," the technomage said. "Your warriors are more than welcome to go outside for the duration, especially since none of them have said a thing. We wouldn't miss their presence."

"How dare you try to short-seat the dragon delegates!" Lord Boneclaw roared.

"I don't wish that at all," she retorted. "That's why you should allow me to set this barrier up. Once it's done, we could withstand tank blasts and missiles."

"Now wait a minute," said the Secretary of State. "I don't much like the idea of being locked in here by magic, especially given that tanks blasts and missiles are what we would use to get us out. Are you saying we're under attack by a military?"

"No, not at all," Kristen said.

"Then what?" A dwarf asked.

"A tornado of flame," she said quickly and hoped that honesty would make the delegates move a little faster. Again, she proved to be quite wrong.

Everyone began to shout except the pixies, who raced around the room and added to the feeling of panic and chaos.

"Ladies and gentlemen!" she yelled. *"Ladies and gentlemen!"*

A burst of emotional energy struck her. Heartsbane was using her aura to make everyone want to shut the hell up.

"Thank you," Kristen said to the silent room. "Now, I promised you all your safety. Constance will help me to do that. I understand that many of you don't trust her but you all trust me, correct? That's why you're here."

"But you won't be doing the spell," Aurelius protested.

"True. But Constance has bound herself to me with contractual magic. She cannot do anything to harm me. Plus, I might add, the mages have the most to gain from this meeting. It's in her interest to make sure it goes smoothly. We have a bunker in the sub-basement below that was designed for exactly this kind of eventuality. If you would all follow Heartsbane below, we can continue our meeting."

"But how do we know that she didn't do this?" Lord Boneclaw asked.

"Because she's been here the entire time," Shimmerclaw said.

Aurelius chuckled. "Seriously, Lord Boneclaw, that would be like saying *you* made the fire tornado." Aurelius laughed even harder at this while Kristen's blood ran cold.

Of course Lord Boneclaw had done this. He must have set this attack up. Who else would want to derail these talks more than the Masked One? He had probably only come to slow the deliberations and to establish an alibi while whoever he'd convinced to to do his dirty work for him was out there risking their lives.

Oh, how she hated this dragon.

But what could be done? Aurelius was right. Kristen couldn't accuse the dragon of foul play right now, not without opening Constance and herself up to the same accusations.

"If we could please proceed calmly, we can resume the meeting," she said.

Despite the considerable grumbling that followed, no one seemed to have an alternative plan to stop a flaming tornado.

She watched them leave for a moment before she focused on Constance, who stepped outside and led the mages tasked with security to create the defensive shield. Each mage began by casting a simple shield spell around themselves. Their leader moved between them, correcting here and encouraging there.

Once she'd walked the perimeter of the building, she performed a complex series of gestures that blew a wind over the mages. It didn't stir any of their clothes or hair but it did trigger all their defensive shields to mingle. One joined with another until instead of dozens of thin bubbles of protection, one huge one now covered and enveloped the entire base.

The woman returned to Kristen, sweating but looking proud. "They've done well. That will hold for days, even if these assholes drop a meteor on us."

She hoped it didn't come to that. Although she was concerned about the rest of the city, Drew knew what to do. She had to trust her team to do their job while she did hers.

Kristen fell in at the back of the delegates and saw Jim, who proved himself to be the Wonderkid, as usual. He seemed to meet every face —be it pixie, dwarf, dragon, or human—with the same warm smile. His reassurances and jokes were delivered easily and calmly and lowered the tension like he could control it with a thermostat.

She gestured for him to follow as she eased through to the front of the crowd. Once there, they caught up with Heartsbane, who was explaining what was about to happen to the sixty delegates crammed into the hallway.

"This bunker is as secure as anything can be," Heartsbane said and used her aura to pump confidence into the room so everyone would trust her. "We're a good forty feet down, which will protect us from almost anything. But on top of that, we have surrounded the structure with reinforced concrete. The only way in or out is through these doors."

"What if someone needs to use the bathroom?" a dwarf asked.

The dragon struggled to not roll her eyes at the dwarf's tasteless joke and the awkward laughter that came with it.

"There are bathrooms provided," she explained. "Like I said, this is the only way to get in, and it's only keyed to those of us who work security. That means me and the Steel Dragon." She wisely didn't mention that Jim could also get in and out, as humans were much squishier than dragons. "Any questions?"

No one raised their hand, which had to be a first for the entire meeting. Heartsbane nodded, and Kristen wondered if she'd used her aura to make them all feel satisfied. She doubted it. The dragons would have surely noticed and besides, a fire tornado had a way of inspiring people to cooperate.

The door opened, and she led them inside to a very large room with three hallways leading down sets of stairs and deeper into the bunker.

"We'll go directly ahead. We have a communal space there but it's not quite as well decorated," Kristen explained, thinking about the lack of the potted plants Timeflash had arranged upstairs, "but it's big enough to hold all of us."

"What's down the other two ways?" one of the dwarves asked. He seemed quite interested to discover that humans also made use of tunnels.

"We have our armory to the left and storage rooms to the right. However, those areas aren't quite as amenable as the meeting room, so we won't visit them today. Now, if everyone would please follow me."

CHAPTER FORTY-ONE

"Do you have any fancy dragon strategy to destroy this, or should we do it my way?" Amy shouted from Lumos's back as they flew toward the fire tornado and the massive thunderclouds all around it.

"I would quite like to see you dissipate this in its entirety before my wings get wet," he said.

"All right, then." She let the magic inside her course through her muscles and out through her fingertips. "Let's do this!"

The young mage pushed her magic into the storm and used some of the wind techniques that Constance had shown her to dissipate the clouds. Although the fire tornado was at the very center, the thunderheads that stretched for miles all around it pulsed with lightning that struck anything and everything below it. Houses or trees that it touched caught fire, and every new source of flame seemed to only strengthen the tornado.

"It's...it's not working!" she yelled and let the magic drop away before she gave herself a nosebleed thirty seconds into the battle.

"That's strange. I feel mage magic in there," Larry said from Stonequest's back. Both Lumos and Stonequest each led a wing of dragons. On the back of each one was a mage and a human soldier armed with an assault rifle loaded with dragon bullets. But none of that would make any difference if they couldn't see their enemy.

"I feel dragon magic as well," Lumos said. "The storm itself is being fueled by a dragon, I think."

"It makes sense," Stonequest said. "I've met dragons with storm abilities. There was one in the last battle, in fact."

"Stormwing," Katrina said from where she followed Lumos in formation. "He has no love of mages. He's taken many of our number."

"He's a real piece of work," Eric added from the Iron Dragon's back.

"But he doesn't have fire powers, correct?" Lumos asked.

"Not that he used against us," Katrina confirmed.

"I don't think the fire is coming from a dragon at all," Stonequest said as a bolt of lightning cracked not ten feet from his wingtips. "It's too sustained. Even the dragons I know who have fire powers rely on their breath to fuel it."

"I've never seen a mage with powers like this, though," Lumos said.

"No, no, most mages don't, but didn't Havington have fire powers?" Larry asked Katrina and Eric.

"Yes, but he could never have accomplished something like that," Eric said.

"Not alone, no, but if Havington and Stormwing combined their powers, it might create a magical vortex. Both mages and dragons use a specialized form of wild magic. If they combine their powers, they could create something self sustaining that feeds off the ambient magic itself." He sounded both amazed and terrified.

"But why would Havington team up with a dragon?" Katrina demanded. "He *hates* dragons."

"He teamed up with you, didn't he?" Amy asked.

"Because he knew I'd kick his ass if he didn't," she replied.

"Stormwing had no love of mages, either."

"This reeks of the Masked One," Lumos stated grimly. "Think about it. The only way to break these meetings up would be a force like this. Any attempt by one power block alone would be defeated.

He probably arranged for Havington to escape and convinced them both that they had to do this in the interest of their own kind."

"Fools," Larry muttered.

"Fools or not, what the hell do we do about it?" Amy asked. "I can't do shit to these clouds. I guess the dragon magic makes it impossible."

"We'll need to find Stormwing himself," Lumos said.

"And Havington," Larry added. "Right now, their powers are fueling each other's. As long as one keeps going, the other will simply be able to gain strength from the one still standing."

"So where the fuck are they?" Amy asked.

"I can only guess about Stormwing," Katrina said, "but Havington always needed to be the center of attention." With that, she pumped her wings, dropped lower over the city, and headed directly toward the fire tornado.

"What do you say, Lumos? Do you want the storm dragon or the mage?" Amy asked.

"Let's not let them have all the fun. Stonequest, Larry, you'll look for Stormwing?"

"With pleasure," Stonequest replied.

"Right. I hope to see you all in the sunshine very soon," Lumos said. It was more optimistic than anything Amy was thinking.

***

Drew had been through some shit but nothing like this. From his vantage point in the streets of Detroit, it looked like the sky was on fire and trying to eat the Motor City. The worst part was that he knew he couldn't do a damn thing about it. Not directly, anyway. But he could still contribute by rescuing those in its path. He had people to save.

"Come on! This way! There's a shelter under the school," Drew yelled to a couple of young men who ran past. He kept his arm around the old woman who teetered slowly across the street, complaining about the Steel Dragon.

"I don't see why there's all this big hoopla. Ever since she's shown up, this city had more traffic and higher taxes. I can hardly stand it."

"Ma'am, that sounds like a problem for your city council representative. Right now, I'd appreciate it if you could get to the shelter."

"You police are all the same. Always deferring the problems."

"Yes, ma'am," he said before he recruited one of the young men who had joined them to help the old woman.

The kid obliged, but rather than a thank you, the old woman darted a scowl at Drew. "Lazy cop."

He didn't have time to argue. Although Kristen's base was in a mostly unused part of the city—she'd bought the warehouse at a discount price because this wasn't a particularly desirable area—there were still people around. Many had lived in the neighborhood for decades and seen its highs and lows—homeless folk who were down on their luck or those who didn't have anywhere else to go.

Jim had asked Kristen for funds to help revitalize the area, but Drew found he was glad things had been happening so fast that no one had yet moved in. It was hard enough to get the people out as it was. If there were more of them, he didn't want to think about what the casualty count might look like.

Especially now that it was raining fire.

At first, he thought he was imagining it. The clouds above his head were already glowing red. They almost looked more like smoke than water vapor. The lightning pulsed through them like lines of fat in a steak and only made them more ominous. When tiny embers began to fall, he thought at first that it was a mirage or raindrops refracting the red light from above or something like that. But no, he realized. It was fire.

His heart began to pound harder as he went to extinguish the flaming contents of a homeless man's shopping cart. "You have to get to cover, sir. There's a school near here. You need to get underground."

"Are you serious? Do you know how much this stuff is worth? I got well over a thousand dollars worth of radio transistors alone in here."

"I'll give you twenty bucks."

"Deal!" the man said and snatched the proffered twenty.

Drew watched him leave while the contents of his cart continued to burn. He looked at the sky and tried to determine how this was possible. While he understood what Larry had said over the radio—that a dragon and a mage had joined their powers together to make this firestorm—how could they make it rain fire? Even in a world of magic, that was impossible. He had never heard of such a thing.

The flaming rain began to fall harder and he understood that he had been right, after all. It wasn't raining flame. It simply appeared to be. It wasn't flaming water that fell but flaming shingles, flaming pieces of fence, and flaming shoes. The tornado sucked up all the detritus of the Motor City, ignited it, and spread it into the bank of clouds above his head. Then, free of the upward draft of the tornado's violent winds, these burnt pieces of Detroit fell back onto the city to trigger more blazes in a horrible cycle.

To him, this looked even more dangerous than a flaming rain.

"On the double, people! This is about to go from bad to a whole lot worse."

He began to weep as he pounded on door after door, making sure as many people were as safe as could be. Desperation kept him moving. He couldn't face the prospect of them not making it underground, not when the consequences were their cremated remains falling to Earth to ignite their neighbor's house.

Drew looked at the dragons and the mages upon their backs. He prayed they'd be able to stop this assault while there was still a city to protect.

"Katrina, do you think you can get close to that tornado and see what's going on?" Amy asked the Iron Dragon.

"Please. I've flown through storms worse than this. Eric?"

"Don't worry about your eyes. None of these pieces of junk will touch us."

The young mage watched as Katrina surged ahead directly toward the tornado itself.

"She truly is a force to be reckoned with," Lumos said.

Indeed she was. Despite her iron skin, Katrina was fast. She seemed to move twice as fast as she had been, and they hadn't exactly been dilly-dallying. Eric was also damn impressive to watch. He didn't have the power Amy did—no one did—but damn, he certainly had a level of control that even Larry couldn't claim.

Any flaming wreckage that came near them was summarily whisked away or torn to pieces so small they couldn't burn. When Amy had battled Eric when he'd been on the other side of this entire conflict, he'd shown an incredible mastery of moving tiny traces of matter. He'd fought with a veritable swarm of needles and used those same powers now, but defensively. It was a sight to behold.

The duo pushed ever closer to the tornado and reached it without real hindrance.

Katrina didn't hesitate.

"Shield?" she demanded as if she already knew what her rider would say.

Eric grunted an affirmative before a bubble of calm settled around the Iron Dragon. She punched through the tornado with such force that she blasted a hole in the flames themselves. The bottom section of it shook as if it had been disconnected from its power cell in the sky.

"They must be up above!" Amy yelled. "Take us higher."

"Yes, ma'am," Lumos agreed and carried them upwards.

She began to wonder if she would even be needed but pressed on, nonetheless.

Katrina and Eric were so formidable, it seemed like they could indeed destroy a flaming tornado on their own. They punched through it again and made a third pass. Each time, it seemed to shake as if this disruption was more than it could handle.

Amy supposed that it was. After all, most tornados only lasted a few minutes. This one had outlasted them by ten times a tornado's normal lifespan. If Katrina could destabilize it, they would be able to deal with whoever controlled it.

But the Iron Dragon would never get the chance.

On her fourth time around she flew up and almost to Amy's level. As she prepared to dive toward the target, a great boom of thunder echoed in the black-and-red sky above them.

A hundred bolts of lightning erupted from the cloud at the same time. The dragons who had followed Lumos and Stonequest were all struck and more than fifty bolts of lightning still remained.

One caught the Iron Dragon, but she flew on. Another struck her and her iron skin began to glow. When a third impacted with her, Eric slid from her back and fell like a ragdoll. Katrina tried to slow to catch the mage who had protected her when a fourth bolt of lightning struck her horns.

Either her iron skin had finally worn off or the mage had provided far more protection from the blasts than Amy had realized. Without him, this bolt of lightning ended the Iron Dragon's part in this fight.

She screamed in pain as she fell and her muscles convulsed and spasmed before another bolt ravaged one of her wings and sheared it off. The pitch and timbre of her shriek of agony rose in volume and intensity until she pounded into one of Detroit's many warehouses and brought the entire building down with her.

Amy swallowed hard as more bolts of lightning began to crack all around them. "How long can this asshole dragon pal of yours keep this up?" Amy asked Lumos.

"Indefinitely, unfortunately," the golden dragon replied before he descended sharply to below the level of Detroit's skyscrapers. The lightning now struck the lightning rods erected on most of the buildings instead of the dragons who flew beneath them. Using this brief respite, Amy took stock of their team.

Stonequest and Larry were all right, as were three other dragons. Everyone else had been disabled. Hopefully, that was all that had happened to them, but she knew from experience that there would be deaths to mourn when this was all over. For now, though, she chose to focus on best-case scenarios rather than dwell on the negative.

"What the fuck do you mean, indefinitely?" she demanded.

"Storm magic is strange," Lumos explained and glided between the buildings while he watched the flaming tornado that drew ever closer to Kristen's base. "Stormwing controls the clouds, not the lightning. It takes dragons like that a great deal of energy to gather the clouds in preparation, but once they've harnessed them, they're little more than micromanagers. There is tremendous energy in this storm. Stormwing isn't creating it so much as riding it."

"But he struck us with lighting!" Amy said. Indeed, he still seemed to be doing exactly that as bolt after bolt of crackling electrical energy connected with the tips of Detroit's skyline.

"Lighting is merely static electricity on a massive scale. He can cause it to discharge but not aim it. That's why we're safe down here."

"We seem to have different definitions of that word," she quipped.

"Regardless, we must eliminate Stormwing. He won't run out of energy, especially if it is as Larry said and the combination of their powers draws magic in to sustain them."

The young mage rubbed her face, intending to wipe the rain away, but her hands came away grimy with wet ash. She didn't want to think about what that ash was made of.

"If we can't stop the dragon, we have to target the mage," she said.

"What do you propose?" Lumos asked as they banked around a building and over the desolate streets.

"Get me as close to that tornado as you can. If a mage is in there, I can probably overpower him."

"I'll try," the old dragon said and circled another building. Now, instead of flying away from the tornado, they moved toward it.

Amy tried to center herself as lightning cracked all around them and fire fell from the sky. She closed her eyes and brought her hands together while her legs remained firmly wrapped around Lumos's body. She wasn't familiar with fire magic but all mage magic was similar at its core. It was an extension of the will—a sense or a power regular people didn't have, but to those who had the gift, it felt as natural as their body, like an extra arm.

She merely needed to reach past the flames, through the storm, and into the tornado itself. If she could find the part of his body that the mage used to control the fire, she could engage it like a couple of wrestlers in a trial of strength. She didn't need to defeat Havington—if that was truly who was inside the tornado. All she needed to do was to take his attention away from his spell. She had to force him to engage with her instead of focusing on the tornado.

Suddenly, she located him. He was high up in the tornado and almost directly above it and flew with both his powers and the help of the dragon's winds. His attention was focused squarely on the tornado of flame.

Amy intended to change that.

She reached out with her powers and began to push him. The first prize would be to thrust him from his position in the center and force him to feel the winds he didn't have any power over.

It had begun to work when Havington realized what she was doing. He responded to her pushes and prods with a massive fireball, bigger than any she had ever seen.

The young mage tried to block it and succeeded only in breaking it from a sphere into a thousand tongues of flame. But much like a popped water balloon, the broken sphere could still fulfill its original intention.

Amy might have been burned to a crisp if Lumos hadn't spun into a barrel roll and knocked the flames away with his tail. His scales crisped and puckered from the heat, but they began to heal instantly. Fire was never particularly effective against dragons.

He finished his spin and she returned her attention to the tornado, expecting the fire to be extinguished since Havington had expended so much energy on his enormous fireball.

The swirling flames were still there, although one or two parts of the tornado seemed to have temporarily gone out. Before she could draw encouragement from that, it simply reinforced itself with even more heat—far more than Havington should have been capable of.

"It's the wild magic!" Larry shouted from Stonequest's back. "We can't expect to stop only one of them, not with the wild magic fueling their synthesis of powers. We have to stop them both simultaneously or this will never end."

"Well, how do we do that?" she demanded.

"I don't have any fucking idea!" He screamed as Stonequest dodged another lightning bolt. Now that the core of the storm was closer to downtown, some of the lighting strikes were lower. Or maybe it was simply that a few of the lightning rods had been destroyed by the massive onslaught of power. Amy had no idea.

"Well, what the fuck do we do?" she asked Larry, Lumos, and the universe at large.

"Pray," the old dragon said as the flaming tornado incinerated the chain link fence that surrounded Kristen's base.

It moved through the parking lot, scooped cars up like they were nothing but children's toys, and gouged the asphalt. Larry retrieved his radio.

"Lady Steel, we couldn't stop the flaming tornado!" he shouted into the device over the wind and booms of thunder.

"We noticed," Kristen replied although she was hard to hear over the static that Amy assumed was caused by the lightning strikes.

"If you guys can get out, you need to."

"It's too late for that," she said over the radio. "But we're in the bunker. We'll be all right."

As the magical attack moved onto the base, Amy couldn't help but think of the clambake her parents liked to do in Maine every year. They'd go to the beach, dig a great big pit, fill it with clams and seaweed and whatever else they could scavenge from the ocean to eat, and cover it before they built a fire on top. While the flames never touched the clams, they turned out to be cooked perfectly every time.

CHAPTER FORTY-TWO

Even with the thick steel doors to the bunker closed, Kristen could still feel what was happening outside. The frantic updates from Larry didn't much help the feeling of unease in the crowded meeting room either. She had turned the radio down as much as possible and Brian was linked to his equipment on the upper floors via a tablet, but even these two small pieces of technology were hard to conceal in such close quarters.

It was also impossible to hide the fact that the room was slowly but surely heating up. When they'd first come down there, the air was pleasantly cool, if somewhat damp. So deep underground, the bunker was insulated from temperature fluctuations on the surface.

That assurance, however, now proved to be an assumption rather than fact.

Already, the air had risen five or six degrees. The pleasant moisture of the cool room began to shift into stifling humidity. The sixty delegates' body heat didn't help much either.

She had instructed the representatives to discuss the new proposals from the other groups amongst themselves. That had bought her maybe five minutes but now, everyone watched what she was doing out of the corner of their eyes. The pixies didn't even attempt such subtlety. They hovered around her head, poked under her armpit, and flitted underfoot as she tried to determine what exactly the hell was going on up there.

"What can you show me, Brian?"

"The cameras on the outside of the base are still intact—oh shit, there goes one."

Kristen scowled as the view from one the cameras mounted near the parking lot seemed to melt and cut to static. Her brother switched to a camera inside the base itself.

"The wind isn't getting through and neither is any of the debris," he explained. "But the heat is coming through the barrier."

"Well, there's that at least," she said and tried to feign optimism.

That lasted for about three seconds until something snapped in the magic barrier and wind rushed into the room they'd evacuated. In a moment, every single window shattered. In the next, the room they had spent so much time organizing and reorganizing was on fire. She didn't even see any flaming debris get in and start the fires.

It seemed that the heat was so intense that an invisible spark had been all it took to turn the entire room into an inferno. In less than a minute, the black curtains framing the room were gone. The fabric backs to the chairs they had so painstakingly rearranged ignited and the cheap metal began to twist and warp in the heat. Her lectern was already ablaze. A moment later, Brian had to jump between cameras as the interior ones began to melt like the ones outside had.

"Can you show me anything outside?" Kristen asked.

"Only one." He cut to an aerial view of a drone.

"Where's the city?" she asked. All she could see was a great blanket of flame across the landscape. It didn't seem quite right as there were no trees or buildings to break the monotony of roiling, billowing smoke. She couldn't identify any structures that seemed to be burning.

"This is over a mile up. Above the storm."

"Then all that—"

"Is the clouds. The storm is covering the entire city and it looks like the clouds themselves—"

"Are on fire," she finished in horror.

"I never anticipated such an attack," Constance said as she joined them.

"Constance, unless there's anything else you can do right now, I need you to return to your delegation. I can't have everyone coming up here right now during a security crisis."

"This kind of heat is beyond my reckoning. I had anticipated the fast-burning strikes of dragon attacks or the rapid-fire bullets and missile blasts of humans, but nothing like this. It…this shouldn't be possible."

"Then there's nothing you can do?" Brian demanded, his voice both too loud and too high-pitched. It drew the attention that his sister so desperately tried to avoid.

"What do you mean there's nothing she can do?" the human from Egypt demanded. "I thought your dome was supposed to keep us safe."

"Let us out of this magic prison!" a dragon warrior who had not yet spoken shouted. His aura pulsed with anger and triggered a ripple of fury through the tightly packed crowd.

"You dragons won't do anything but save yourselves," a dwarf bellowed and swaggered toward the warrior. "Let us out there, Lady Steel. We were designed to withstand flames. We can withstand the inferno and stop whatever's raging outside."

"You could not withstand this," Constance said.

"Are you calling us dwarves weak?" Rupert demanded.

"Quiet, Rupert!" Barmus shouted and whacked his colleague so hard he tumbled into a mage.

The mage scrambled to his feet in an instant and a swirling cloud of ice particles spun aggressively around his hands. "Don't touch me, dwarf!"

"Everyone, calm down," Heartsbane said, stepped forward, and used her aura to send a wave of tranquility through the room. Unfortunately, it was more like an attempted wave. No doubt she had tried for a lake and ended up with a puddle.

"Don't you use those powers on us, dragon!" one of the mages shouted. This only further pissed the other the mages off, as they hadn't realized that she had been manipulating them.

Kristen stepped into the middle of the room. "I understand that you're all upset and I don't blame you. My team will get this under control, but we cannot do our jobs with all of you fighting down here. I need everyone to go back to their corner of the room, now!"

"Or what?" Lord Boneclaw inquired, all smiles.

"Or I make you—personally," she snapped at the dragon.

"Ah. I merely wanted to make sure we've reduced ourselves to human cavemen, using violence and threats to get our way. Right this way," he said, acting as if he'd won as he retreated to his corner with the other dragons.

Thankfully, the other groups did the same. Slowly, the tension began to seep from the room, although the heat continued to increase. Kristen did a quick headcount and saw that everyone was where they were supposed to be.

Except the pixies.

At first, she hadn't noticed what they were up to. But now that all the groups were in their corners, she realized that no pixies buzzed around her head, showered the room in sparks, or played practical jokes on everyone else in the room.

She didn't see them—accustomed as she was to looking at eye level first, then to the ground second—but she heard them. They were singing. Where before, their language sounded like crickets playing bells or something of that nature, it now had the unmistakable sound of voices humming in chorus.

It was beautiful in an alien kind of way. They had the high voices of children but none of the shyness and harmonized in ways she had never experienced. Hell, they harmonized in ways that might not even be possible for humans to achieve.

Following the sound, she finally located them. All twelve of the little insect-winged creatures were gathered near the ceiling. They had formed a circle and held hands while they sang, but the strangest part was that they glowed. Pixies emitting light was not unusual in itself. After all, these creatures had launched sparks out of their fingertips since they'd arrived. What was strange was the quality of the light.

While before, the sparks had come from outside their bodies, the light now seemed to emanate from within them. It was as if a filament in their chests had been ignited and was now visible through their skin. The glow grew steadily brighter. Soon, the illumination from them was so intense that Kristen could hardly make out their features. They looked like human-shaped lights wrapped in gossamer clothing.

"Lady Dragonfly?" she said.

Neither Lady Dragonfly nor any of the other pixies responded.

"Lady Dragonfly. What are you doing?"

"This reeks of wild magic." Lord Boneclaw sneered and slunk quickly to his corner of the room when she glared at him.

The other dragons—even Shimmerclaw and Aurelius, Kristen's ostensible allies—retreated as well. The four Councilors stood in their corner while the eight warrior dragons put themselves between the ring of glowing pixies and their superiors. All wore looks on their faces that seemed to indicate their certainty that these pixies were as dangerous as a technomage armed with a dragon bullet. For all she knew, they could be.

"Excuse me, Lady Dragonfly. Please tell us what's going on," she said. She wanted to believe they were trying to help, but it certainly did not feel like it. The room was still getting hotter. If anything, the temperature increased at a faster rate than it had before the pixies started their little kumbaya session.

"Constance." She beckoned for the mage to come closer. "Please tell me you know what they are doing."

The technomage raised one hand to her temple and extended the other, her fingers a half-formed claw. She held this pose long enough for the temperature in the room to click up another degree or two. When she opened her eyes, they were wide with shock. Sweat glistened on her brow, although Kristen did not know if it was from the heat or from whatever she had sensed.

"I...I can't tell what it is. The dragons are right, though. It's wild magic."

"Isn't all pixie magic wild magic?" she asked.

"Indeed. But all magic stems from wild magic. I've encountered spells from pixies before and been able to sense their purpose or how they were similar to my own, though. A fire spell is a fire spell is a fire spell, which is what we teach our novice mages, but this is… This is something different. Something unlike anything I've ever seen."

"Great," she said, tried not to sound sarcastic, and failed miserably.

"Also, Kristen," Constance said and swallowed so hard she was worried she'd eaten her tongue.

"What?"

"Whatever they're trying to cast, it's a *huge* spell. It's larger even than the barrier we put around this base, and that took dozens of mages. I think my delegation and I should stop it."

"No, don't," she said, almost surprised at herself for how quickly she had responded. "I don't think they're trying to hurt us. They trust me."

"With all due respect, Kristen, you have no experience with these creatures," Constance insisted. "They don't think like we do. They aren't even exactly made of matter like we are. They could be trying to help in their way, which could be antithetical to our existence. I strongly advise—"

"Let me talk to them," Kristen said and took a step closer.

"I think—"

One of the dwarves stepped forward. She recognized Alp, who both knew Constance and had helped Amy. "Is there a problem here, Lady Steel?" he asked politely.

"I was telling the Steel Dragon that we should stop this spell," the technomage said quickly before Kristen could answer. "We don't know what the pixies are trying to do."

"I think it would be a safe bet to assume they're trying to save us from getting roasted alive," he said and used his brightly colored hat to mop sweat from the part of his face that wasn't hidden by his thick beard. It could not be comfortable to be a dwarf in this heat.

"You can't know that!" Constance fumed.

"I've always valued our friendship," Alp said. "But if you try to hurt those pixies, I will stop you. I've always wanted to see what dwarf skin can do against magical blasts."

"It would be the last thing you see, that's for sure," the woman said petulantly, then turned with a swirl of her cloak and stormed away to her corner and the other mages.

"Lady Dragonfly," Kristen said again and took a step toward the pixies, then another. "Lady Dragonfly, please tell us what's going on. We're all here because we want to work together. That means communicating about what our intentions are—"

She smacked into a magic barrier and scowled as she rubbed the pain from her nose in surprise. Her eyes narrowed at the pixies on the ceiling, who were still a few feet away. She raised a hand to reach toward them but it struck a magical barrier.

"What the hell is going on?" Heartsbane asked and came to the other side of the pixies. She stretched a hand toward the pixies and also encountered the magical barrier. "What the fuck is this?"

"Lady Dragonfly!" Kristen demanded and pounded on the shield. It was different than the swirling blue shield spells the mages cast. This was completely invisible and as hard as granite. She doubted that even her dragon strength would be able to do much to it.

The pixies seemed completely oblivious to what was going on outside the barrier they had erected around themselves. Their humming grew in both volume and pitch. They produced more noise than she thought their small bodies would be capable of and it grew even louder as the heat in the room intensified. By now, at least one representative from every delegation yelled in protest, yet she could hardly hear them. All she could hear was the song of the pixies that increased steadily in volume and pace like a choir gone crazy.

They glowed even more brightly too. Already, they shone with such radiant energy that Kristen couldn't look at them directly. She shielded her eyes and looked away, noticing that Lord Boneclaw sheltered behind the dragon warriors, no doubt because the shadow powers of the Masked Dragon made him hate light. She filed that detail away for later.

But there was nothing she could do for now. The pixies' activity continued to escalate together with the almost unbearable illumination until they were all she and anyone else could focus on. Somehow, the unbearable brightness suddenly flared to indescribable brilliance as their spell reached the peak of its crescendo.

The sound they emitted was as close to angelic as Kristen had ever experienced. Even though there were only twelve pixies, it sounded as if a hundred voices were singing, or a thousand. The notes they sang opened and closed, trading places in rhythms she had never heard but was already intimately familiar with. It was as if they sang the notes of the universe itself.

And the color left her breathless with awe. It was white, yes, but it was every other color too. Reds, yellows, blues, greens, and pinks all flashed past each other in a brilliant kaleidoscope until she lost all track. It surged and bloomed beyond its peak until the spell of the pixies consumed every sense she had.

When she had reached a point where she thought she could endure no more, all the lights went out.

CHAPTER FORTY-THREE

For a moment, Kristen thought she might be dead. Her first thought was, *the pixies tried to take us to heaven but we were all too shitty.* It was silly, brought on by too many melodramatic movies, no doubt. But the sudden lack of light and sound was so completely overwhelming and utterly isolating that she could not help but think that maybe her life was over. She could see nothing but the afterimages of the lights the pixies had flooded the room with. When she tried to listen, she could hear nothing but the hum in her ears that was left from the euphoric music the pixies had been singing.

A sliver of panic stirred but a light flared maybe twenty feet away, and she saw Constance. The mage looked harried. She was sweaty from the heat and her robes were askew. The light orb levitated a few inches above her palm and flickered with her discomfort, then flared a little brighter like a kerosene lantern being adjusted. The technomage looked like she felt—like she was surprised and not entirely relieved to find herself still alive.

In the light it cast, Kristen could see the other mages, the humans, and even the outline of the dragons in their distant corner. She was alive, she decided. If there was an afterlife, she was fairly certain it wouldn't be populated with the members of the convention all drenched in sweat.

The next thing she noticed was that the sound of the room had changed. The pixies were no longer singing or glowing but other sounds were gone too. Most notably, the roar of the storm was gone. Before, it had filled the bottom range of her hearing, a low, dull roar that had subconsciously put everyone on edge.

Now, it was gone.

Not only that, the gentle rattle of the air conditioner and the beeps of the computers tasked with keeping this room secure were also absent. In fact, all she could hear was the breathing of the sixty delegates, plus her security team.

It might have been comforting to hear only this simple proof that everyone in the room was all right, but after the insanity of the light and sound show the pixies had produced, it was uncomfortably underwhelming. She imagined that this was what coming down off of drugs must feel like.

"Ma'am," Jim said as he negotiated a path toward her through the dark. Kristen noticed he hadn't turned his cellphone on to use as a flashlight. "It sounds like the air conditioning is dead. I think we need to crack the door open, otherwise, we'll run out of air mighty quick."

She smiled at the Wonderkid. There was something comforting about being in this room with ancient dragons, powerful mages, strong dwarves, and leaders of the world and still find that the former soldier turned cop was the first person to get his bearings and focus on the simple logistics of survival.

"Sure," she said. "Take Heartsbane and some of your soldiers and see what's happening out there. I don't want anyone to leave this room yet but open the door and post a guard. Don't you have a flashlight on your belt or something?"

"I do, ma'am, but the batteries are dead."

"Somehow, I don't think the Wonderkid forgot to put fresh ones in."

"You know me too well. I checked all the flashlights only two days ago. Whatever those pixies did, I think it knocked out all the power, even the batteries."

Kristen pulled her phone out of her pocket and found that it too was dead. "Okay. Go check on what's happening outside. I'll make sure we're all fine in here."

Jim didn't look like he wanted to obey and leave her, but he nodded and complied without argument.

As hastily as she could—given the reality that counting forty-eight people would never be quickly accomplished—she made a headcount and confirmed that everyone was accounted for. Even Lord Boneclaw, which both calmed her nerves and made her wonder why the shadow dragon didn't use this opportunity to attack. A brief flash of doubt that he was the Masked One passed through her, but she disregarded it as the false idea she knew it to be. All his current inaction proved was that he hadn't anticipated that something would knock the lights out.

"We'll find out what's happening and get this convention back on track," she said to the whole group.

Almost everyone began to grumble in response but at that moment, Jim cracked the door and a blessedly cool gust of air blew into the room. The Wonderkid ignited a bright white flare and stepped into the hallway.

"If you can make light, please do so," Kristen said.

A few mages obliged her with more glowing orbs. Two of the dragons ignited their weapons, which of course put the humans and mages on edge for a moment. When the dragons didn't move their flaming weapons from their corner, everyone remained more or less calm.

She noticed that although all the humans and some members of the dwarf delegation reached into their pockets to retrieve their cellphones for illumination, no screens turned on in the darkness. Whatever the pixies had done had killed the electricity and batteries. She didn't know of technology that could accomplish that. While she had heard of electromagnetic pulses in movies, surely the pixies hadn't created one of those. Why would they? An EMP wouldn't do anything to a tornado.

No, she suspected that whatever they had done was far more unusual than a device from a sci-fi movie. She only hoped the tiny, strange beings had an answer. They didn't seem like the type who normally bothered to explain themselves.

Kristen approached the pixies and her gaze tried to find them in the gloom. They were not where they had previously been on the ceiling. So where were they?

"Kristen, they're hurt," Brian said. She hadn't noticed her brother and realized he now knelt below where their ring had been. He was the only person, mage, dragon, or dwarf who had dared to enter the space the creatures had sealed with magic moments before. The light was dim as no mages were nearby, but there was enough for her to see the distress on his face as she sank to a knee beside him.

All the pixies were on the floor and all were unconscious. Whatever they had done, it had knocked them out cold. It meant she wouldn't have any answers anytime soon.

"Damn it," she cursed to no one in particular.

This was exactly the kind of thing her security force was supposed to prevent. It mattered to her that the pixies had seemingly hurt themselves. If the cool air wafting into the room was any indication, whatever they had done had been to protect everyone down there. They had, in effect, done what had been her job. That the pixies had to step in at all reflected a failure on her part.

She only hoped they weren't dead. If twelve pixies had been able to disable the power in this room and stop the heat from the fire tornado, she didn't want to think what ten times that number could do. Or a hundred. It had been hard enough to talk to the delegation, and Lady Dragonfly had said that the group was one of the more logical groups.

Kristen studied them carefully and extended a hand to the one closest to her, hoping the little creatures had pulses like she did but not at all sure.

"Be careful," Constance warned and levitated her light orb closer so that she could see. Despite offering her magical orb, the techno-mage remained a few steps away. Kristen hoped that in a few moments, the woman would prove to be paranoid and that she would still be alive.

She touched Lady Dragonfly gently. The little pixie was warm to the touch, which was a good sign. Very tenderly, like she was checking on a baby bird, she extended one finger and pressed it gingerly against the tiny chest.

"Oh, thank God, she has a pulse." She checked the others and confirmed that they too were alive.

"It's wonderful to know the little sprites didn't die," Lord Boneclaw said and sounded like he did not think it was at all wonderful.

Kristen hadn't seen him approach and did not like how much darkness flooded this room they shared. "I would think you'd like the darkness," she muttered.

He twisted his scarred face into a sneer. "I don't like things I don't understand. You were the last one to talk to them. We saw you take them away while the rest of us were deliberating. Now tell us, what did they do?"

"My team is investigating and will radio me as soon as they have an answer," she snapped at the dragon councilor.

"Yeah…about that," Brian said. "I don't think that'll happen. All the computers are dead. Like, all of them. I checked a few and it doesn't look like a power surge, more like there's no power at all."

"Could the storm have damaged the powerlines?" Kristen asked.

He looked at her like it was the dumbest thing she'd ever said. After the briefest moment of reflection, she realized it wasn't the smartest question she'd ever asked.

"All the electronics are dead," he said bluntly. "We had backup generators that haven't turned on. My phone is dead and so is my tablet. Even the radios are out. I would say it's fucking weird, but I saw twelve pixies hold hands and sing a song that stopped me from being roasted alive so honestly, losing power is like par for the course at this point."

"So what you're telling me is that my head of intelligence is completely useless right now since you can't use your cameras, drones, the Internet, radios, or anything else?" she asked.

"Er…will this affect my pay?" Brian asked.

"No, because you'll take care of these pixies."

The look on his face was one of pure horror. "I…you remember my bearded dragon, right?"

"You won't leave the pixies in the yard while you chase the ice cream man, will you?"

"Uh…no?" He still looked aghast but he seemed to gain a hold of himself. "There are a few boxes in the supplies room. Maybe I can fix them a little shelter."

"Do that," Kristen said. She turned to the leaders of each delegation. "Constance, Lady Shimmerclaw, Krot Minestrength, Mr. Secretary—would you all like to come with me to investigate?"

"I think Ambassador Johnson will do fine," the Secretary of State said and pushed the chief American ambassador to the dragons forward. The other humans seemed quite happy to send Johnson to see what the fuck had happened.

"Take Alp," Krot Minestrength said, settled in with his dwarves, and kept an eye on the dragons.

Lady Shimmerclaw and Constance—demonstrating true leadership in her opinion—both nodded and followed her to the door.

She led the way out of the room they'd sheltered in and into the hallway that led to the top of the base. It was a supremely uncomfortable feeling to have to do this in person. For months, the entire base had been under the constant surveillance of Brian and a security detail. But now, his cameras were all dead, as was their communication equipment and everything else that was powered by electricity. She simultaneously felt like she'd been thrown into the dark ages and rocketed into a post-apocalyptic future.

The first thing she noticed was how cool it was in the hallway. If anything, she had expected it to be even hotter there than it had been in the room with all the delegates, simply because there was one less layer of insulation. But the opposite was true and a wind whistled through the hallway, howling a pitch that set her on edge.

She almost transformed into a dragon when Brian appeared from the gloom at the end of the hall. A magic ball of light followed him, which was all the more unnerving as he didn't have a magic bone in his body.

"Brian?"

"I found a box for the pixies," he said in a rush and moved past her and into the room.

"They're sentient beings, not grounded bats!" she shouted after him, but he was too nervous to notice his sister.

Kristen watched through the cracked door and past the guards she'd posted as he carefully picked the unconscious pixies up one by one and placed them into the box. That done, he shook out a towel and tucked them in gently. Or, at least, that was what he appeared to do. She couldn't see through the box or much detail in the gloom, even with the orbs of magical light in the meeting room.

"Lady Steel, shall we?" Shimmerclaw asked and gestured down the hallway in front of them.

"Of course." She realized she'd been woolgathering. They proceeded cautiously and remained close together. The wind definitely came from up ahead. It blew in their faces and whipped her red hair from behind her ears and into her face. The cool it brought would have been refreshing after the heat from the tornado, but as they drew closer to the stairs that led to the base, flecks of ash began to appear, drawn into the tunnel with the draft. It was hard to feel refreshed when continually reminded that a force greater than any she had seen before had been unleashed on their city.

They reached the base of the stairs to find the door already open.

"Is it supposed to be that way?" Ambassador Johnson asked.

"I sent Heartsbane and Jim ahead to investigate," she said, as much to herself as to everyone else. "They must have opened it."

Alp, Shimmerclaw, and Constance offered no response. The dwarf simply tightened his hand on the ax he wore at his belt and the mage's floating light orb began to spin in a manner that Kristen and the rest of them found to be rather aggressive. Shimmerclaw seemed nonplussed, but she could transform into a dragon if she needed to and so had no need to panic. She had the same ability, but that didn't stop her from donning her steel skin.

The whistling sound came from the slightly askew door. She pulled it open the rest of the way and the sound stopped. A cool gust blew across them before the wind seemed to die down as if it had only blown to lure them out there.

"Heartsbane?" Kristen called out up the stairs, not proud of herself for sounding scared but also scared and beyond giving too many shits right now. "Jim?"

"Kristen," Jim responded quietly. That he was alive was more of a relief than it should have been. "You need to see this."

They walked up the stairs as if a monster of their nightmares might attack at any moment. Only the human ambassador didn't look like he wanted to fight whatever that might be. She didn't blame him, though. The rest of them were supernatural beings with magic coursing through their veins. She was willing to bet Johnson didn't even have a gun with him.

They reached the top of the stairs without being eaten by a demon or a monstrous clown and discovered that the ground floor was completely trashed. Kristen nodded at the damage, having seen some of it already through Brian's cameras before they failed. All the decorations they'd put up for the convention were destroyed. The curtains had been burned to nothing. Some of the chairs looked like they could be salvaged, but the vast majority were either melted or thrown into each other with such force that they would never seat another butt again.

Broken glass from the windows was scattered everywhere. It was a mess. She sighed, but it wasn't much worse than when they'd bought the location. It would cost both time and money, but new windows could be installed and new chairs could be purchased. The base itself seemed relatively unharmed. It seemed Constance's magic had done a decent enough job of protecting them.

"It looks like a flaming tornado came through here, all right," she said in an attempt at humor to lighten the mood.

"Yeah, but where is it now?" Alp asked, his jaw was hanging open and his gaze focused beyond the building to the outside.

At first, Kristen didn't know what he was talking about. Although she had dragon vision, her eyes had more difficulty piercing the gloom than the dwarf's did. Past the windows, it was as dark as it was inside.

Her heart dropped.

"Why is it dark outside?" she asked no one in particular. "We weren't down there that long. Did the storm knock out the lights to the whole city?"

"More like knocked out the whole city," Heartsbane replied. She also stared out the windows into what looked like the blackest night Kristen had ever seen.

"Constance, can you raise that ball so we can see what's out there?" she asked.

The technomage nodded grimly and complied. She launched her ball of light into the warehouse space and made it grow in size and intensity. In a moment, the dull gloom of the room had transformed into bright areas of light and harsh shadows.

But the darkness outside the base didn't change at all. It simply swallowed the light the woman created as if it were hungry for more. Her heart dropped even deeper into her stomach when she saw what was out there.

Only blackness existed, the utter black of nothingness.

CHAPTER FORTY-FOUR

Amy was desperate. She couldn't get close to the mage inside the tornado and she couldn't find the dragon who created the storm. Already, the base of the tornado had swallowed the building all of her friends were in.

It worked at the magical bubble Constance and her mages had created like the world's most powerful snail trying to pry open a clam. She had no idea if the people inside were already dead. Their radios no longer made contact, which she took as a bad sign.

"We have to do something!" she shouted at Lumos.

"What do you propose?" the golden dragon asked.

"I don't know," she shouted in return. Currently, she wondered if she had the strength to simply lift one of the smaller skyscrapers from downtown and hurl it at the top of the tornado. She had no idea if she had the strength for this and understood that if she did it, there was a chance it would simply turn the entire building into tornado fuel or crush the building below, but she honestly didn't know what else to do.

"I don't know what went into Constance's shield, but I don't see how it could stop all these factors. The wind, the heat, and the physical blows from the debris will wear it down," Lumos said. It did not comfort Amy at all that she could tell the old dragon tried not to sound nervous.

That settled it for her. If a thousands-of-years-old dragon was nervous about the goddamn firestorm, she would heave a building at it or die trying. She knew the sheer force of such an exertion might very well overwhelm her. But the people inside had all risked themselves for her or people like her, confused kids who didn't understand their place in the world. She would not let them get cooked.

Cautiously, she sent tendrils of energy out and began to dig into the foundation of a nearby nine-story hotel. As she wrapped her mind and her magical powers around the pieces she would need to sever to lift the building, a blinding flash and a huge pulse of magic came from the base itself, right at the foot of the tornado.

"What did you do?" Lumos asked in shock.

Amy unwrapped her magical abilities from the structure and narrowed her eyes at the flaming tornado that worked so hard to roast her friends.

Except her friends were no longer there.

The bottom of the tornado now spun over empty air, maybe forty feet off the ground. Instead of the base that was her de facto home beneath them, there was nothing. The upper floors were missing and the main level was gone. Even the basement Kristen had no doubt taken everyone into had vanished. It was as if reality were made of gelato and some godlike ice cream man had simply scooped the facility out of reality itself.

Where a moment before, the base was ravaged by the fire tornado, nothing remained at all. She gaped at an enormous hole in the earth with a few smaller holes in its sides that must have led into sewers, pipes, and the steam tunnels that ran under Detroit that she had always found so creepy.

Now, however, she'd spend a week in a steam tunnel if only to have an explanation for whatever the fuck had happened to the base.

"For the warmth of dragon's breath, did you do that?" Lumos shouted.

"I didn't do it," she said.

"Are you…sure?" he asked. "I sensed you doing something seconds before this happened."

A moment of odd calm followed during which they both simply watched the fire tornado extend its base into the hole where the base had been. So much for her hopes that someone had simply turned it all invisible.

"It wasn't me. I promise," Amy said and shook herself from the stupor she'd fallen into. "I tried to pick that hotel up over there to chuck it at the tornado."

"That does sound more like you…" Lumos said as he banked wide around the magical attack so they could continue to look for the missing base. The tornado seemed to search too. Its flaming base worked inside the giant hole but it found nothing. No delegates materialized in the ember-filled wind and no pieces of familiar equipment were suddenly unearthed. It was like the base had simply ceased to exist.

"I felt…something," she said. It was surreal to be so much at a loss for an explanation for whatever the fuck had happened while a literal firestorm was still in the sky above them, striking lightning onto the city.

"Felt what?" Lumos asked. He seemed to be regaining his sense of urgency more rapidly than she was. It made sense, though. He *had* been alive for thousands of years and had probably seen some shit.

"I felt a pulse of magic immediately before that flash of light. It came from either the base or the bottom of the tornado. I know that much."

"Then we should assume that whatever it was came from inside the base itself," he said.

"What? How can you possibly know that?"

"I can't." The old dragon sounded somber. "But given that the tornado is still raging and looks furious over having lost its intended meal, I think it's safe to guess that neither the mage, the dragon, nor one of their allies are responsible for the disappearance. Otherwise, they'd be celebrating. Whoever did this was probably inside."

"Okay, but what is *this*?" she demanded.

"I don't have any idea either," Larry shouted from Stonequest's back. They had caught up to Lumos and Amy.

"We don't have time to find out, though," Stonequest said.

"What do you *mean* we don't have time?" the girl shouted. "Our friends are gone!"

"And there's not a thing we can do about that," Larry said. "The tornado, on the other hand, needs to be stopped."

Sure enough, the masters of the flaming tornado seemed to reach the same conclusion that Amy and her allies did and began to resume the attack on the city. It took a moment to pull itself up and out of the huge hole it had searched through, but once it was clear, it moved directly toward the downtown skyscrapers. She was suddenly very relieved that she hadn't gone through with her plan to use a skyscraper to try to stop it.

When it struck one, it simply savaged it and hurled burning debris in every direction.

"Shit, you're right. We have to stop it!" Amy shouted.

"Do you have any ideas?" Larry asked.

"Katrina seemed like she might be able to do—"

"That's not an option." Stonequest cut her off. "She was badly injured by that lightning and is out of this fight. It's up to us."

That was not at all what she wanted to hear, but there it was.

"We tried getting closer and we couldn't. The heat was too much," she said and tried to sound strong although despair began to close in.

"Well, if you couldn't, we can't," Larry said and sounded as depressed as she felt. "He'll see us coming and hit us with lightning or a fireball."

"That's it!" Amy said, suddenly knowing what she had to do.

"We need to…let him hit us with a fireball?" Larry asked.

"Not we, *you!*"

"As the dragon carrying the mage toward the tornado, I have to say I object to this plan," Stonequest said.

"Gather all the dragons still airborne and get all of them to make dives at the tornado. Stay safe but keep him occupied. Lumos, how fast do you think you can get us out from under this storm?"

"I can get us above it in less than a minute."

"No!" Amy shouted, surprised how sure she was that this would work. "Stormwing seems to be able to sense the winds of the storm. We need to get out."

The old dragon seemed confused but he looked at the horizon. "Five minutes, if you can hold on."

"Do you hear that, Larry? We need ten."

"He said five."

"Start the clock," Amy shouted and spurred Lumos to start his flight.

"I'm a dragon, not a horse," he joked but he obeyed all the same and pumped his wings. Their speed increased until the wind whipped in her face and the raindrops from the storm stung like hail.

They flew away from the tornado, the lightning, and the clouds until, miles distant, they were once again under clear skies.

"I hope you know what you're doing," the golden dragon said. "I've never fled a battle before."

"Good, because it's time to go in again," she said in triumph.

"What? We did all that to let Larry and Stonequest have some practice? I know they need it, but still."

"For an old fella, you sure can be slow. Fly above the clouds as high as you can. We'll go above the storm, where the dragon can't sense us. Once we get above the tornado, we'll drop down on them."

"You can't possibly know that this will work," Lumos said.

"The fact that a dragon who said he's never run from battle before retreated for five minutes means you don't have a better idea."

He cursed under his breath as he flew them above the clouds and increased their elevation until the air was thin before he began to race toward the center of the storm. Amy willed him to go faster. There was no other option. This *had* to work.

She only wished she felt more certain that it would.

CHAPTER FORTY-FIVE

Kristen, Constance, Shimmerclaw, and Ambassador Johnson all stared out the windows of the base and into the deepest, darkest blackness any of them had ever seen.

Only Alp didn't seem terrified at the void. "I reckon we ought to chuck a rock at it," the dwarf said.

Constance guffawed louder than Kristen had ever heard her. "We are faced with a void more engulfing and complete than any discovered by magic or science and you think we should simply chuck a rock at it?"

He responded with a half-shrug. "I reckon we ought to, yeah."

It was better than any ideas she had right now. Looking at it didn't inspire her. It simply emptied her head as completely as the outside of the base seemed to be. She knelt and picked up a piece of twisted metal—either a part of a broken window frame or the leg of a chair—and threw it out the window. Propelled by her dragon strength and guided by the eyes of a police officer who had spent considerable time on the shooting range, the projectile streaked through the aperture and into the void.

That was her assumption, at least. She couldn't honestly be sure.

As soon as the piece of metal met the darkness it simply vanished.

She was at least somewhat certain of that. It didn't simply become harder to see as it moved away from Constance's light orb. It vanished. One moment, it spun end over end toward the wall of inky darkness and then it was gone, swallowed like a dinosaur that had plunged into a tarpit.

Everyone waited—their breath held—for the piece of metal to end its trajectory and make impact with something. No indication of this came, however. There was no sound that suggested it had encountered either an object, structure, or the ground.

"Hello!" Alp shouted at the top of his lungs, which made Johnson and Constance both jump. Shimmerclaw almost changed into her dragon form in surprise. No resounding dwarf voice echoed in return and no one hollered for him to shut up.

In fact, nothing seemed to come from outside except darkness. There were no sounds and no smells or vibrations of the battle that had raged on the streets of Detroit only moments before. There had been wind in the hallway but now that she had pushed the door wide open, even that had faded. It was if the outside had simply ceased to exist.

Constance took a step forward toward one of the walls as if the void didn't surround every side of the base. "I would like to examine this...darkness for a moment if I may. Would someone else mind doing the lights?"

"Sure." Kristen scrounged around for a moment until she found a piece of unburnt fabric inside a ball of ashes. She wrapped it around the metal leg of a chair.

"Here, I can help with that," Alp said and took the makeshift torch. He pulled a vial of some kind of yellowish gooey oil from his pocket and applied it gently to the fabric. Once the oil was stowed, he retrieved flint and steel, knocked them together in a practiced motion, and ignited the torch.

"I had a lighter," she said and brandished a plastic one.

He shrugged. "Dwarves are trained to be able to find their way out of caves when they're young. We also keep supplies on hand."

"It's a pleasure to know we're in a situation where underground survival skills prove to be useful," Shimmerclaw said but didn't sound pleased.

The problem of illumination solved, Constance let her glowing orb wink out and took a few steps closer to the front door of the base. The door had been ripped off its hinges so they could see outside. It was even more uncomfortable than looking out the windows.

Through the windows, Kristen's brain made a valiant effort to tell her conscious mind that it was simply the night sky but completely devoid of stars, the moon, and the lights of the city. But when she looked through the doorway, that illusion simply didn't work. The blackness began at the edge of the sidewalk that went up to the door. She couldn't tell if it went into the ground as well, simply that the sidewalk seemed to ceased to exist in a spectacularly creepy fashion.

Constance also seemed less than comfortable around the darkness because she did not step through the doorway. Instead, she remained behind the frame as if the almost broken rectangle would provide her with some measure of protection.

She extended one hand and a great gust of wind blew from between her fingers into the wall of black. The void swallowed it as if she had done nothing. It did not move, make a sound, or give any indication that she'd had any effect on it. Undeterred, she lifted a few pieces of rubble with her telekinesis and pushed them slowly into the void. She drew one of them back, and Kristen barely caught a glimpse of it before the woman hurled it into the inky vacuum.

It looked like the part that had gone into the blackness had vanished.

Finally, the technomage closed her eyes and started the now-familiar chant that was used to open a gate for teleportation. But rather than proceeding for the few minutes required to open it, she stopped after only a few seconds. Her eyes jerked open and widened with alarm.

She took a step back, drew a deep breath, and regained her composure. Kristen wondered if she had appeared to lose it to the others present. But to her, after all their time battling and then working together, it was as plain as day that Constance was as scared as hell.

"Well?" Ambassador Johnson asked.

"I've heard of things like this before but never seen them."

"Things like what?" he pressed and revealed his experience as a politician.

"Other dimensions. Places outside of ordinary space and time. The teleportation spell we rediscovered uses such places to function."

"Are you telling us this is some kind of weird magical reality?" Alp asked and gestured at the inky blackness like it was something on his plate he did not particularly want to eat.

"I would not use the word *reality* to describe anything out there, but other than that…yes, you have the gist of it."

"And we're simply supposed to take your word for it?" Johnson demanded as if he hadn't been the one to ask her to explain it.

"I agree with the mage—pardon me, Lady Vigil," Shimmerclaw said with a slight nod of respect to Constance. "Although it has been hundreds of years since I have heard about any kind of breach between the worlds. The last time was—"

"Let me guess," Heartsbane interjected, "during the last mage wars."

Shimmerclaw nodded at the younger dragon. "Some of our youth know their history, anyway. But even though I believe this to be one of those realms, I don't see how we could possibly have ended up in a place like this."

"Could it have been the firestorm?" Jim asked from near the door to the bunker below. He had not come out much farther than a couple of steps. "Even a Marine like me could tell you that was a shit ton of magic. Could they have…I don't know…broken something?"

"I think the firestorm may have been a factor…" Constance said slowly. "If a mage and a dragon teamed up, it's quite likely their combined energies would have invited wild magic to join them."

"No one can invite wild magic," Shimmerclaw huffed. "That's why we call it wild."

"Not intentionally, of course," the technomage said quickly. "But magic is like life. It attracts itself." She snapped her fingers, realization plain on her face. "But those were not the only two spells, were they? There was also the protection spell my mages cast."

"You mean the spell that completely enveloped the base like the bubble of black?" Jim asked.

"Indeed," she said grimly. "The combination of all those forces plus whatever ritual magic the pixies did might have created this…this event."

"So…you don't have any fucking idea what those little pixies did either?" Heartsbane asked.

"I'm afraid not, no. I have tried to make allies of pixies, but they do not ever wish to share their magic with us. They don't use spells like we do. I know that what they did was powerful, and I suspect it had some effect on this…void. Lady Shimmerclaw, perhaps you, in your experience and wisdom, can illuminate the problem?"

The old dragon shook her head. "I have seen pixies do many remarkable things but nothing like this, I'm afraid."

"It sounds like we need to wake them up," Johnson said as if he could delegate himself out of any problem that presented itself.

"We'll let them rest for now," Kristen said and tried not to make it sound too much like an order, even though it totally fucking was. "If Constance is right and their spell somehow…misfired, they'll probably need their rest before they try to fix it. In the meantime, I need to do a damage assessment of this building. If any of you would like to join me, that would be fantastic. But if anyone wants to return to the chamber below, that would also be fine."

"I need to head down and make a report," Johnson said, quick to look away from the blackness outside. He started toward the door to the bunker.

"I think I might also be more useful down below," Shimmerclaw said.

"I wouldn't mind having a poke around," Alp told her.

"I'd like to investigate further," Constance concurred.

The three of them set out to explore the upper floors of the base. It was all much the same as the ground floor—broken glass and everything but the brick walls burnt to hell. The structure itself wasn't completely ruined, and there were odd little pockets where either the wind hadn't penetrated or perhaps Constance's shield had held and the damage was minimal. They found a kitchen in perfect working order, as well as Stonequest's office, but everything else was completely wrecked. Still, with the considerable wealth left to Kristen by Windlock, she could replace it all. It would be a massive inconvenience but at least no one was hurt.

When they reached Brian's computer station upstairs, she paid particularly close attention. His room was one of those that had fared better. Considerable smoke had seeped in and the door had burned off its hinges, but that must have happened late in the chaos as the computers seemed fine.

Except, of course, that none of them worked. They were completely powered down and not even pressing the little glowing switch on the surge protector was able to revive them. For some reason, this tiny detail put her on edge. It felt like absolute proof that they were in uncharted waters.

"I truly wish I could say I understood what happened here," Constance said.

Alp shrugged. "We dwarves say if you dig too deep, you might get burned. Maybe those pixies reached a vein of lava, so to speak."

"I hope not," Kristen muttered and wished she could feel hope right now.

They headed downstairs to inform the others about what they had found.

Shimmerclaw was already most of the way through the first report. "So the pocket dimension we're in is small but seems stable," she said.

While she spoke, Kristen went to check on the pixies.

"They're still out cold," Brian whispered while the dragon continued to talk. "Is it as bad as Shimmerclaw makes it sound?"

"It—wait, what?" She moved her attention from the pixies to the room.

"Although we don't have answers yet, this convention has people from all the major races, so we should have an answer soon. Surely someone here will know what to do," Shimmerclaw stated.

"You're saying that even though we have powerful mages, dragons, and dwarves, none of you know what is going on?" the German human yelled, his voice rising in terror.

"Not quite, no. But if we cannot solve it, surely the people outside will."

"Now you're saying we won't find the answers?" the Russian demanded.

"If we don't, surely someone will," Shimmerclaw said and looked openly annoyed with the humans.

But of course they were freaking out. Kristen knew they were the most out of their depth, what with not being magical in any way. Everyone else at least had some vague inkling of how magic could bend reality. Dragons knew their dragon body went somewhere when they transformed, and dwarves owed their very existence to magic. It was only the humans who didn't have a touching point for this.

Unfortunately, their panic had begun to spread.

Kristen stepped forward, thanked Shimmerclaw for her report, and tried to calm those present. "Look, I understand that this is weird, but we'll get through it. If anyone has any ideas or interest, please speak to Constance Vigil, who will be in charge of this investigation. Everyone else, we need to be prepared to be here for a few days."

The inevitable grumbles followed, but it was the "I don't want to do any work, I'm a powerful diplomat" kind of grumbling instead of the "I'm afraid for my fucking life" kind of grumbling, so that was good.

"We have more than enough supplies for everyone, but the upstairs area was destroyed. We had bunks prepared, but we'll need help to set all that up again. This bunker was not meant to hold this many people and quite frankly, you're all starting to stink."

The dragons laughed at this, but no one else did. She swallowed. So much for humor.

"We'll need food, water, cots, and kerosene lanterns so we can see. Right now, I want mages who aren't helping Constance's investigation to help with light. Dragons and dwarves can help carry stuff, oh—dwarves, could we get some torches?"

In a frantic few movements, the eleven dwarves who had been empty-handed all held one. Even Minestrength, the prime minister, seemed to think it important to have the materials needed to start a fire handy.

"All right, let's get to work moving supplies and cleaning the upstairs. With luck, we'll be all set up when the pixies wake and knock this shield down so we can get back to our deliberations."

Everyone got to work. Kristen had already counted on more than a little luck to make this entire convention work. Now, she doubled down to simply get back to the reality they all knew so well.

She had never been much of a gambler.

CHAPTER FORTY-SIX

The Masked One had expected the flaming tornado created by the mage and storm dragon he'd put together to create chaos at the convention, but even he had failed to anticipate whatever the pixies had done.

He had expected the magic dome Constance made, of course. Over the last year, the mages under Kristen's leadership had been quite adept at using their magical powers to defend themselves. He had not thought they would have failed to block heat itself, but the rules of the universe—even the non-magic rules—were tricky to fully account for.

His plans included the expectation that the mages would defend themselves and in doing so, cut themselves off from the rest of the city. He had hoped that halfway through the deliberations, Kristen would look outside to see nothing but a flaming wasteland where her precious Motor City had been. Now, however, there was nothing outside at all.

More out of habit than any actual distrust, he hadn't believed Shimmerclaw and while she'd been talking, he had slipped above. It would have been impossible for any other being to move as quickly as he did, but he could move at the speed of darkness, which was even faster than light. It was always there behind every pebble and every blade of grass. It had taken him less than three seconds to reach the surface, see that the outside world was indeed nothing but a void of darkness, and return.

Experience and knowledge made sure he understood that the darkness outside the base wouldn't provide him the shelter his powers needed to work. It meant he was trapped in there with the rest of them.

The Masked One didn't like his plans being upended but on the other claw, he was a creature who knew how to seize an opportunity. He was a schemer and a planner, yet he saw the innate value of chaos. In this particular situation, the Steel Dragon was the one most reliant on the plans—they were hers after all—which meant the chaos could belong to him.

She finished her pathetic little pep talk and started to delegate orders like she already thought she controlled the new world order she seemed to be so earnestly intent on creating. The room slowly emptied and he sent the dragon warriors with Lady Jade and Decimus Aurelius while he lingered in the room. He wasn't sure what he might discover, but once the mages left with their spheres of light and the dwarves with their torches, he was sure he could find something of interest.

Unfortunately, the Steel Dragon's runty human "brother" stood at the door and watched him.

The room grew darker but the young man stared into the darkness, his eyes narrowed in suspicion and his distrust clear. The Masked One wanted to eviscerate the primate. He wanted to rip his entrails out and strangle him with them. His instinct was to peel his skin back and harvest his skull. It would be pure pleasure to attack the Steel Dragon while wearing the remains of one of the disgusting beings she had sworn her allegiance to instead of the rightful leaders of this world.

"We're all heading up to help. I need to lock this room," the disgusting, fat mammal said.

He almost lost control at that. The impertinence of this greasy slug! To think that he not only dared tell him what to do but that he said it as if he were nothing but a common cleaning wench. His blood began to boil. What light was still in the room came from the hallway. It was not even close to enough to protect the boy. In a blink, the old shadow dragon could disincorporate and sink his claws deep into his chest. He could almost feel the warmth of his blood on his hands as his victim's heart ceased to beat.

Oh, how he wanted to.

He wanted to so much.

But he wouldn't. Not yet and not now. The Masked One saw the utility of this moment. He was trapped there, yes, but those obnoxious electric lights the humans cowered under were gone. With a little patience, he could accomplish far more than slaughtering one little piggy.

"Of course. Forgive me," he said and did not attempt to hide his disgust from the boy.

Using the practiced, weak-spined posture of Lord Boneclaw, he joined the rest of the crowd struggling to get through the door like a herd of fat cattle.

The boy relaxed, his aura as easy to read as a children's book.

"Thanks. I appreciate your cooperation," he said.

That was not easy to ignore. The arrogance of this whelp!

The Masked One merely nodded and followed the crowd down the hallway toward the surface. By the time he reached the intersection of hallways, the area was already bustling with activity. Dwarves and dragons carried cots and supplies from one hallway up the stairs to the surface. Mages made balls of light dance, casting long shadows that shifted this way and that. Even the humans—ostensibly leaders in their own countries—carried supplies like they were nothing more than ants. He looked at all of them with disdain.

None of them looked at him.

The fat boy who had made sure he left the room was now busily trying to activate some kind of electronic device. No doubt he was having withdrawals from the video pornography humans of his ilk were so obsessed with. The old dragon took a step back into the shadow behind a concrete pillar and vanished.

In a split-second, he was in the corridor outside the storage room where the humans and dragons labored. Even though the mages had balls of light moving up and down the hallway, they made no attempt to erase every shadow. Why would they? As a result, he was able to move from one dark patch to the next, first hiding in the darkness beneath a crate, then in the shadow cast by a moving human.

He entered the storage room and found it as he'd expected. It was filled with predictable survival supplies. Jugs of water. Packets of food. Batteries. Lights that didn't seem to be functioning. Medical supplies. Boring.

The Masked One went back up the hallway to the intersection. A glance at the dullard of a human showed him that he had given up on pleasuring himself and checked on the unconscious pixies once more.

That gave the shadow dragon all the time he needed to vanish into the other hallway.

Part of him had wanted to stay and wring those little pixies' necks, but he knew that such a gesture, even if performed out of the sight of everyone—an unlikely possibility given the current circumstances— would have been in vain. The creatures could be killed, of course. All living things could die. He had spent a century of his life proving this very theory personally.

But the pixies were trickier to kill than most. It had something to do with the wild magic of which they were largely comprised. Crushing one beneath a boot or wringing its neck did little beyond turn them into a shower of sparks. Magic had to be used to kill them. He had done so before using his shadow abilities. What a fun little challenge that had been, but there was no point in doing so now. Especially given that the pixies might be the only beings that could do away with the void they all found themselves in.

Plus, there were other more exciting things to kill than a cluster of glorified magical insects with a child's sense of humor. He focused on what was important and moved deeper into the hall opposite the one with the survival supplies. At the very end, he found a locked door.

He had to admit that at least the Steel Dragon was being appropriately cautious. This room had a touchpad that surely would have demanded his fingerprint if it had power, an electric camera that would have required his retina, and a keyboard for some esoteric password. That there was no power was no impediment to this security system, and the door simply remained locked. It seemed that even if the Steel Dragon herself wanted access to this room, she wouldn't be able to have it at the moment. The steel bolts that made this door as solid as the reinforced concrete on either side of it were stubbornly in place. No power outage could disrupt its purpose.

Too bad for the Steel Dragon's security system that he had never met a door that could hold him. And she had tried so valiantly. It was substantial and the walls around it even more so. In addition, the hallway was fairly small. It would be difficult for a dragon to take their true form and have the space needed to simply demolish it. Even if they could, The Masked One knew that humans were greedy and the Steel Dragon was no different. She might have even rigged the room to destroy its contents if broken into.

Of course, he would not break in. He honestly didn't know if he could—brute force had never been a trait he particularly valued—and he also didn't want to make a noise. Besides, why bother when the room had a door?

This one, like all the others, was made to be opened. In this case, it meant hinges. No thicker or substantial than a shadow, he slipped through the tiny crack that allowed the door to move.

Sometimes, he wondered if even the doors humans put on the rocket ships they sent to space could hold him. Certainly, those on a plane had failed to do so more than once. The problem was that air obeyed the rules of pressure, while his will was a far more determined force than any inanimate matter.

Inside, he discovered he was exactly where he wanted to be.

It was the armory and oh, what an armory it was! No enchanted swords covered these walls. No unbreakable spears rested in wait for their user. The walls there held the most human of all weapons—guns.

Dozens of them—possibly even hundreds. An entire wall was hung with every type of gun a modern murder-obsessed human might wish to possess. There were big ones the Masked One knew could shoot hundreds of bullets with the simple squeeze of a trigger. Others were long and straight and could punch through the many materials humans had devised to stop that very kind of weapon. Some fired bombs. Weapons for wounding instead of killing hung beside those intended to be worn as a show of force and still others designed for concealment.

But truly, it wasn't the weapons that most interested him. It was the crates.

The room was full of them. There were huge ones made of cheap wood and smaller versions of burnished metal. Some were locked while others were nailed shut. All of them sat there, ominous in the shadows. He could almost feel what was inside them. Time had taught him that the death and suffering involved in their creation had a particular flavor, and this room positively reeked of it.

He moved toward one of the crates, one of the few that was in a stack on its own. It reached to his chest and was nailed shut. This, of course, was no impediment to most dragons and him even less so. He simply turned his hand to shadow—relishing the complete and utter darkness of the room he was in—and slipped a claw between the lid of the crate and its four walls. When he turned his hand to its solid state again, he pushed the nails up and out of the wood they had kept closed.

With the lid open, the Masked One rested it on the ground, careful to not make a noise. He then examined the contents.

It was as he expected.

This was where the Steel Dragon stored all the dragon bullets.

For a moment, he felt overwhelmed by the sheer scale of the room. He had expected that the crates were filled with bullets, of course. It had been fairly obvious but still, to be confronted with the truth of it was another thing entirely.

There had to be thousands of bullets there. Tens of thousands. Maybe hundreds if all the large crates were as full as this one was. He had known this many existed. After all, it was he who had convinced Windfire to give the mages his DNA to be used to make the clones that had been harvested to make these bullets. In a way, he was responsible for the contents of this entire room. This was the arsenal the technomages had intended to turn on dragon kind and in doing so, initiate the war he so badly wanted.

If only the Steel Dragon hadn't intervened. The mages would have continued their attacks and the dragons would have responded the only way they knew how—by burning the mages and the very ground they stood on. The mages would then have revealed this massive cache of weapons that had until recently been spread all over the world. The ensuing bloodshed would have left both sides decimated and likely pulled the humans with their weapons of war into the fray as well.

The world would have burned until there was no fuel left. Finally, in the darkness that followed, the Masked One would rebuild a better, more sensible society in which everyone would know their place. Dragons would not be beholden to the rules of bloated, dull-witted Council members. Humans would not have to waste their time competing in a nonsensical economy. He would have found a place for every dragon, mage, human, and dwarf. All would have served his world—a better world rich with the efficiency of darkness—and it would have been good. There would be no more arguing and no more fights and only one leader to appease. He would have sat atop a throne of human skulls made from the discarded masks he could afford to make daily.

Ah, but the Steel Dragon had ruined all of that.

Like a lighthouse blowing out the cool light of a starry night, she had appeared out of nowhere—no, not nowhere. She was one of his experiments turned against him and she'd ruined everything.

Well, almost everything.

These weapons were still there, still asking to fulfill their purpose.

The Masked One went to the wall of weapons and frowned at having so many choices. Yes, guns were the logical evolution of the rock the primate ancestor of humans had first used to slaughter one of their kin. Guns were not weapons befitting a dragon, but how could he refuse one now? After all, he'd done the work to turn them into a tool that could kill dragons as easily as they killed human beings.

With so many choices, the Masked One was almost at a loss. He certainly liked the idea of simply picking up a couple of military-style rifles, loading the magazines, and slaughtering each and every delegate there.

But of course, he wouldn't give in to such fantasies. There were mages about, for one thing, and many of them had proven more than capable of stopping bullets. Plus, if one dragon emerged from the blood bath, it would ruin Lord Boneclaw's reputation as a mediator. Even though that reputation was practically gone, he didn't want to wage his war from anywhere but the shadows. That meant a direct assault was an impossible fantasy.

In turn, it meant stealth would, as usual, be his weapon of choice.

He tested many guns in his hand but in the end, settled for a beautiful little Beretta with a suppressor. It was easy to recognize the weapon from the violent films humans glorified. Satisfied with his choice, he returned to the crate until he found rounds that fit the magazine.

Carefully, he loaded the magazine to capacity with dragon bullets. The little handgun ended up fitting seventeen bullets. Each one—if properly aimed—could kill a dragon. It was an efficient tool of death, the Masked One had to admit, even if he did feel like a brute tucking the gun into a holster he had chosen from an extremely convenient set of choices in the room.

Feeling somewhat smug, he turned into shadow and joined the rest of the delegates. He made sure to grumble when he lifted a couple of jugs of water, and the fat human boy who had lost sight of him saw this and smiled.

Although he wouldn't need a dragon bullet to put him down, he thought he might go ahead and do the boy the honor if the chance presented itself.

CHAPTER FORTY-SEVEN

The air was still above the storm. It was almost frightening how rapidly Amy's pulse dropped and how quickly her breathing returned to normal. The clouds didn't look like a storm of destruction. They didn't look like something straight out of the apocalypse. Instead, they resembled a sunset spread below them. They glowed with reds and oranges and yellows, and the crevices where they weren't filled with fire were rich with dark purples and blues.

It was horrifying that a creation of such violence—a force that was able to destroy a city almost as an afterthought—could be so beautiful. Like the mushroom cloud of a nuclear weapon or the clean lines of a fighter jet, there was an elegance to this force of destruction.

She wanted nothing more than to obliterate it.

"Do you see anything?" she asked Lumos.

"I'm afraid not," the old dragon replied. His eyes were stronger than hers and as they doubled back toward the center of the city, he had kept them trained on the clouds below.

"If he's in the clouds…"

"Then this will never work," he finished for her. "We need to attack without notice. Otherwise, he'll simply strike me with lightning."

"I can stop a bolt of lightning."

"I believe you. But what about two? Or ten? Or a hundred?"

Amy didn't bother to reply. She knew she had limits and although she'd never tested them against lightning, she wasn't particularly optimistic.

A clue she needed distracted her before she could refocus her thoughts.

"Look at those clouds down there. Do you see that?"

"They're beautiful, yes, but that doesn't help us, does it?"

"No, *look*. They're moving in a pattern—do you see? It's like they're circling a drain or something."

Lumos stopped focusing on the space directly below them and looked farther out. She could tell he'd noticed when he almost hiccupped in surprise. "My dear, I think you solved our problem."

The golden dragon adjusted course and his new trajectory took them directly to the center of the swirling clouds.

As they approached, they seemed to rise like foam. He flew above them and a moment later, the two of them stared into a tornado.

At the center, resting atop the clouds like a vulture gliding without flapping its wings, were their targets.

Stormwing's scales were the color of bruised clouds. Rivulets of electricity crackled and popped from his scales. Every time the dragon made a micro-adjustment to his wings, electricity surged from them and lanced the clouds around him. The roar of thunder was constant and deafening.

On his back sat Havington, and the mage truly frightened her more than the dragon did. His robe, normally well-pressed and perfect, was half-burned away, and a horrible tube of flame issued from each hand. These extended past the dragon and were sucked in opposite directions to join the horrible counterclockwise swirl of wind that both swallowed the flames and made them larger. He laughed maniacally as he flicked his fingers to send balls of fire at the other dragons who tried to distract this godlike combination of warriors.

"Should we knock to let them know we're here?" Amy asked.

"Oh, I think it might be better to simply drop in and say hello,"

Lumos replied. He tucked his wings and plunged like a hawk made of lead.

They plummeted from their position in the heavens toward the back of the dragon, gained in speed, and multiplied their force as she pushed him ever faster with her magic.

Seconds before they were about to strike, he uttered an ear-piercing shriek. Stormwing flinched at the sound and rolled to intercept him, which was exactly what the old dragon warrior wanted.

Lumos' claws, already glowing with radiant energy, found his target's chest. They punctured his scales and thrust the dragon from his place above the flaming tornado.

But Stormwing was large and brimmed with power. Lightning cracked and Amy had to shield them from it.

As soon as she did, Havington blasted a ball of fire at her that she deflected.

The fight had only begun and already, they were on the defensive.

She would have to change that. Focused, she reached into the wall of fire that spun all around them, found every trace of shrapnel she could, and gathered tables, car doors, and old tires. The detritus of an entire city was at her fingertips. She threw them at Havington while Lumos and Stormwing fought with tooth and claw.

"You can't defeat us!" the enemy mage yelled hysterically as he threw a series of fireballs at the objects she lobbed at him. He didn't have to drop his tubes of fire to do so. The gesture of a finger was enough in his current state to incinerate a car door. "The forces of magic in this world have deemed our mission a holy one! The magic of the earth fuels this storm."

"Is that right?" Lumos asked and made one of his claws glow as bright as the sun before he raked the other dragon across the face.

The assault made Stormwing release his control of the storm. The golden dragon flew back as gusts of wind that previously hadn't been present in the eye of the tornado buffeted them.

Havington was forced to drop the tubes of fire and hang on to Stormwing or risk being blown off his back.

They had done it. Between them, they had made Stormwing lose his place at the center of the tornado and stopped Havington from powering the flames. Amy paused and waited for the storm to rip itself to pieces.

Inexplicably, it didn't.

The mage, his gaze focused on her, only laughed. "I told you that the powers of the earth fuel this tornado. You cannot stop us." To accentuate his point, he hurled a fireball at her. She deflected it but felt the heat all the same.

Beneath him, Stormwing turned to Lumos. Without warning, lightning surged and blasted the old dragon's wing. His flesh sizzled, but he didn't cry out in pain.

Instead, he smiled. "I haven't been tested like this in years."

"Are you saying we have a chance?" she asked, deflected another fireball, and hurled a crowbar at Havington. He melted it into hot iron droplets that joined the tornado of flame that surrounded them all.

"A slim one," the golden dragon said as the enemy mage threw more balls of fire at him. He was forced to dodge both balls of flame and bolts of lighting.

"They're too strong together. We need to separate them," she said.

"He can't fly like you can," Lumos agreed.

"Do you think we should split up?"

"I think if we can face them one-on-one, we might have a better chance."

Amy nodded, found a sewer lid that swirled in the mad tornado, and jumped from Lumos's back.

As she fell into the center of the tornado, Havington laughed and flung a stream of fireballs at her.

When her feet found the metal disc, his laughter faded.

She rocketed toward him and increased her speed until she launched the metal out from under her. It spun as only a skateboarder could make it spin and cracked the man across the face. He fell from Stormwing's back.

Lumos chose that precise moment to strike. Glowing like a sunrise, the golden dragon powered into his enemy and thrust him away from the mage who had been riding on his back.

Amy called the sewer lid to her as she reached the height of her ascent. She made it fly toward Havington again, who was falling into the tornado.

But rather than continue his descent, he launched a great blast of fire from his hands and used the energy of it to fly.

He streaked toward Amy, a wizard turned Iron Man, and pounded into her with a flaming fist. She tumbled off her support and immediately began to plummet.

The man was falling, too. He needed his hands to fly and the fire punch had cost him elevation. Fortunately, the girl was far more adept at flying than he was and she reached into the maelstrom and retrieved the bumper of a car. She ran across that but her adversary destroyed it and continued his assault against her to demolish all the projectiles she summoned—a table, a chair, and a piece of plywood, which he lit on fire.

All the while, the tornado continued to burn.

Amy fell until her feet found a pillow, of all things. It caught her and she rocketed herself up past Havington and had a moment to see the dragons above her fight.

It was like watching the sun fight the storm.

Lumos glowed with radiant energy. Every strike he made launched white-hot light into the wounds of the other dragon. Stormwing answered with strikes of lighting and deafening booms of thunder.

But the golden dragon's experience was telling. He struck with grace and efficiency, while Stormwing did little beyond hope his lightning strikes connected. Lumos' eyes ignited in a blinding light and suddenly, his opponent couldn't see. He followed through on his advantage and drove into the younger dragon to mangle a wing and thrust him from the sky.

He fell into the tornado, seemingly unconscious.

But Havington had regained his elevation. He rocketed past Amy until he was far above her. Then, like the world's most pissed-off phoenix, he engulfed her in a firestorm.

Flames of red and orange gave way to flames of blue, and for the first time since she'd discovered her magical abilities, she feared for her life. A little panicked, she enveloped herself in a web of shields as fire roiled all around her.

She fell at an alarming speed, riding the pillow like she was a horseman of the apocalypse.

In her fiery cocoon, she couldn't see Lumos, Stormwing, or Havington. All she could see was flames. They ate away at her shield and prevented her from doing anything to stop her fall. She couldn't see the ground either, so had no idea how close it was.

Without warning, the flames dissipated. Above her, Amy could see that Lumos had snatched Havington in his claws. The mage screamed in pain. His hands were blackened and his fingers reduced to stumps. The magic he'd employed had overpowered him.

She let her shield drop and threw every ounce of magic she had into stopping herself from making the inevitable collision with the rapidly approaching earth.

It wasn't enough. She was going too fast and couldn't stop without ripping herself to pieces. All she could do was slow and hope she could survive the impact.

Seconds later, she landed with a whump and remembered that for once, she was riding something more sensible than the hood of a truck or a giant boulder. Her pillow cushioned her fall and hopefully left her with nothing but the world's largest bruise on her ass.

Amy looked around in bemusement and finally realized that the tornado had lost its momentum. Stormwing lay on the ground beside her. His scales were burned from Havington's attack and his body mangled and broken from the fall. He wasn't breathing and without him, the tornado had begun to disintegrate.

If wild magic fueled the storm, it no longer had any control. The tornado broke in two pieces, then into three. Each of these did little more than spin themselves out. The fire that burned within their walls of wind, now denied a source, simply snuffed out.

Lumos landed in the surreal, burned, and battered landscape. He held Havington in his claws and the mage was weeping.

"My hands," the mage said. "My hands...my hands—what have you done to my hands?"

"It isn't anything you need to worry about in the future," Stonequest said and marched toward him like he'd waited for their arrival this entire time. Drew stepped from his back and gently put a pair of magic dampening cuffs on the man's charred and misshapen hands.

Havington wept as the last of the flames in the air extinguished themselves. "My hands," he repeated as if trying to draw more attention to what was left of them. "My hands."

Amy couldn't help but feel sorry for the moron. Maybe something could be done for him but for now, he'd have to suffer for the flames he'd engulfed a city with.

Her attention returned to their base—or rather, the pit where the base should be. Nothing remained beyond a giant hole. Whatever had fueled the flaming tornado had not been responsible for what happened to Kristen and the others. She had no idea what could have taken place but was sure that the attack had not caused the base to vanish.

Despite their victory, she felt only despair.

CHAPTER FORTY-EIGHT

It took about an hour, but they finally had all the delegates more or less settled in. Kristen could not help but see the silver lining in the chaos of this attack. Before, she and her team had spent days trying to determine how to best optimize the space to give everyone privacy from the other delegates.

That was now impossible.

Everyone had a cot—dragon, human, mage, and dwarf. They had cooked one of the cows the dwarves had brought and supplemented the meat with emergency rations. It was an extremely democratic existence in that everyone, from the guards to leader of the dragons herself, had the same meal.

They had given up on any attempt at privacy as well. There were a few tarps and rolls of fabric that Timeflash had purchased with the intention of making uniforms, but it was nowhere near enough to create partitions like they had had before.

What materials they had in the storage area—which wasn't much —had been used to hang over the broken windows to block some of the views of the eternal void that stared at them from outside. That did help everyone's mental state but not enough. They'd cleaned the room, swept the ash, and gathered all the rubble and piled it in one corner. The broken windows weren't that bad but the void on the outside was a constant reminder that they weren't exactly in Michigan.

Still, the tarps helped. Instead of almost every pair of eyes staring out the windows into the thick darkness, there were now a few mumbled conversations. In fact, such a sense of normalcy had returned that people had even begun to start to complain again.

"If this is some kind of a plan to force us to compromise, I don't like it," the Secretary of State said to Kristen.

"I assure you, it's not."

"Good. Because we're not interested in furthering these talks until we know who is responsible for our situation and how we'll get out of it," he said as if they were still in the United States instead of whatever realm their base had been transported to.

"Who is responsible?" Lady Jade demanded. "The real question is who is responsible."

She turned to the beautiful dragon woman in her silk dress. "Lady Jade, if you have a theory about what this place is and how to get out of it—"

"It was the mages who did this, obviously. The dragons and humans were making headway, so the mages did this to stop us from progressing. They used the pixies' magic and are probably planning something even as we speak."

Kristen clenched her teeth as hard as she could to prevent herself from punching her in the face. "That is an extremely serious accusation. Do you have any evidence to back it up?"

"Evidence?" Lady Jade scoffed. "What more evidence do you need? The mage said she made the dome around the facility and only what was inside the dome was transported."

"I think the pixies did the transporting," a dwarf interjected sharply.

"It's exactly like a dwarf to side with the pixies," the dragon snapped.

"Lady Jade, please. He's not siding with them," Shimmerclaw said and unknowingly saved the other dragon's jaw from a punch from

Kristen's fist. "If these mages were capable of feats such as this, do you believe they would have been so reliant on the dragon bullets?"

It was Lady Jade's turn to clench her teeth. The gesture might have looked out of place on the slender, graceful woman but when she made it, her eyes flashed into their dragon form and two dragon teeth jutted from her mouth to make her look more like a serpent than a human.

The Secretary of State swallowed hard and went to make himself busy somewhere else.

"Kristen, please tell me we have an idea about what to do next," Shimmerclaw said. "The talks were progressing better than I had hoped. I fear if we do not resume them soon, all progress will be lost. Have you managed to revive the pixies?"

She shook her head. "I wish. My brother is with them in the bunker, but he hasn't reported anything yet," she said and retrieved her cellphone to check if he'd texted, only to remember that all the electricity in every device had ceased to function.

The Council leader nodded. "I fear they will be our only hope."

"What about the mages?" Decimus Aurelius asked. "Even if this was not their fault, surely they can think of some way to get us out of this mess? I'll say that personally, whoever rescues us from this…this void, will earn my good graces and greater consideration in how I vote."

"Is that supposed to mean you plan to vote against the humans?" the German delegate demanded. "We are the only group who you know cannot free us from this prison."

"We can't free ourselves from this 'no-place' either," the dragon retorted.

"We have all seen dragons change from their reptilian form to their human one. Where does that mass go? Hmm? This does not seem so different to us," the Russian delegate added.

"Who are you calling reptile?" Aurelius asked.

Kristen tried not to sigh. He was one of her best dragon allies but he was still arrogant, demanding, and thin-skinned. They needed to get out of this mess so people could at least go outside to catch their breath.

"Constance, I know you checked earlier, but have you or your mages made any breakthroughs?"

"I'm afraid not, Lady Steel," the technomage said and guided a few of the mages from her delegation away from one of the windows that had not been covered with a tarp.

"Please tell us you've found something," Aurelius said.

"We have eliminated a few avenues of escape, yes," Constance said, which earned groans from everyone in earshot.

"You must understand," she continued, "that we must proceed with the utmost caution. We have tried all our elemental magics, and the… bubble has not responded to any of them."

"The bubble?" Aurelius asked.

"Indeed," the woman said. "I believe that some kind of synthesis of magic created the barrier that protects us from the void. It is a porous barrier, as anything we have put through it has met no resistance, but nothing has come through from the other side. I fear we are in some type of antimatter realm, to use the words of human scientists. The skin or bubble or however you wish to think of what separates us from the void is not indestructible. I don't want to try anything too… aggressive for fear of popping the bubble."

"Well, why not simply pop it?" the German delegate asked. "Lance it like a boil."

"As I said, I believe there is magic of some kind keeping the void out of this base. If we were to destabilize its structural stability, I fear the consequences. For example, a gate spell seems to be the most obvious choice to get us out of here, but I am not sure what that would do to the skin protecting us."

"What could it do?" Kristen asked and wondered if the time for risks was now.

"The worst-case scenario would be that by some effort on our part, we pop or shatter what's protecting us and the dark nothingness out there would simply rush in here and cause all to cease to exist,"

Constance said flatly as if explaining a math theorem in a geometry class rather than the nonexistence of everyone she could see.

"Of course, we can't be sure the void out there would cause all to cease to exist," she continued in the same professorial tone. "It's possible that the skin doesn't exist at all and that we will simply linger in eternal darkness forever. There is no electricity, which seems to indicate that some of the basic rules of the universe don't work here. For all I know, stepping into the void may simply take us to Detroit."

"Have we tried that?" Aurelius asked.

"We have not," the technomage said patiently. "I find that an unlikely possibility, given that no sounds or indications of anything have come from outside. I fear that the most likely possibility is that the pixies tried to take us somewhere but the barrier my mages had erected plus the forces of magic creating that tornado interfered. I think we might be trapped in a kind of in-between."

"Do you have any answers?" the Egyptian delegate demanded.

"I am certain that the stuff out there isn't from the reality we come from. It simply doesn't respond to the types of magic we command. It makes me fairly confident to say that coming into contact with it would be…bad. However, as I said, I'm not sure. I heard Lord Aurelius say freeing us from this place would win his graces. Perhaps a human would like to test this theory? I'm fairly confident that a human walking through it wouldn't destabilize it for the rest of us."

"You mean it would simply make us cease to exist?" the German delegate asked.

"That is my leading hypothesis, yes," Constance agreed. "But I might be wrong."

Considerable grumbling came from the room at this. It seemed almost everyone had listened to their conversation, which wasn't surprising. There was little else to do in this nothing-place. Still, grumbling aside, no one came forward to volunteer to test the theory.

It meant that people would begin to get upset. Kristen didn't care if they were human, dragon, dwarf, or mage, she knew that restlessness did not breed good thinking. She needed them focused on something else.

"I know this is a weird situation, but we don't need to worry," she said and raised her voice to draw the attention of everyone in the room. "We have far more mages outside than we do in here, and I'm sure they're working on what to do even as we speak. Most of you are familiar with my mage, Amy, and the power she controls."

Many heads nodded at that.

Encouraged, she continued. "She won't simply let us vanish. I'm sure that with her power and Larry's experience, we'll be out of here before we know it."

"You can't know that," someone shouted from the back of the room. She guessed it was Boneclaw, still doing what he could to sow doubt and discomfort even when he had no other options to try.

"No, I can't. But we've been in this situation for less than three hours. There's still a very good chance the pixies will wake up and undo this themselves."

"Wake them, then!" a human shouted.

"We'll give them six hours to recuperate, then we will. In the meantime, I suggest we either delegate chores or continue with our peace talks."

A concerted wave of discontented mumbling followed that and almost everyone turned away from her, not interested in chores or peace talks any longer. She would give them a few minutes to avoid the work until they grew restless again, then she'd make them resume the talks. There was simply nothing else to do.

CHAPTER FORTY-NINE

It was easy to lose track while looking at the void. Kristen shook her head to clear the sensation. How many minutes had passed? Five? Ten? However many, it couldn't have been more than an hour, as the delegates were still talking amongst themselves. She shook her head again and wondered what in the hell the void was. As she'd watched it, she'd had a strong sense that it was coming for her. But that was obviously only misplaced emotion. It was still beyond the windows and as dark and silent as ever. No tentacles had come from it and no demons of night had invaded. They were still trapped.

Right now, though, she needed a break from the oppressive black that felt like it was pushing in through the windows. She started walking and headed downstairs, where she found Brian at the intersection of three hallways. A dwarf torch burned next to him, its base taped to the back of a chair.

"Oh, man, am I glad to see you!" he said. "I was getting lonely down here."

"I thought I said for you to wait in the bunker. Why are you out in the hallway?"

"Honestly?" He looked furtively around him as if he didn't want to be overheard. "I was scared. That room is big, and the back of it was all black, even with this torch. At least over here, I can hear you guys…well, when you start to argue anyway. I take it things are not going well?"

"Not really, no," she admitted. "Funny, I had thought that being trapped in a giant bubble of an unknowable void would make everyone start to see eye to eye."

"Yeah, gee, I can't believe that tactic didn't work," Brian said sarcastically.

Kristen smiled. Even in this face of their possible destruction, her brother always had time for snark.

"Well, I don't see much point in you staying here now that we're all set up. You should bring them topside with everyone else."

"Sure! It sounds good to me," he agreed. "But before we go, can I go get some of my computer equipment?"

"I thought it wasn't working," she said as she motioned to Jim to come down the stairs so he could keep an eye on the pixies while she went with her brother to get some of his equipment from the bunker room.

"It's not, but I have some ideas about how to make it functional. It's a longshot, but if I can maybe get something up, we could contact the outside. That's assuming we're not four hundred thousand lightyears across the galaxy or whatever, of course."

"From the way Constance talked, we might not even be in the same universe right now."

"Jesus. You'd think a lifetime of video games and sci-fi movies would prepare me for you to drop that kind of crap in my lap but nope, I'm still as scared as fuck."

"Let's get your equipment."

"Yeah." Brian nodded, tried to look confident, and forgot that Kristen—being a dragon—could read his emotions.

They took the torch off the back of the chair, leaving Jim in the harsh glare of a flare, and moved into the bunker.

The room was exactly as Brian described it—oppressively dark. The torch they held—although it burned brightly—didn't seem to even attempt to pierce the gloom on the far side of the room.

"Not to be like a chicken or whatever, but can you see why I didn't want to go back there?" He pointed at the gloom. "Now, at least, your dragon vision can tell me where the fuck my AC adapter is."

"I…" Kristen rubbed her eyes and tried to blink the darkness away as he walked across the bunker to the dark in the back of the room. Despite him growing closer, his torchlight simply stopped before it reached the back of the space.

"Brian, stop!" She flexed her aura to make him feel terror and stop in his tracks.

"Damn it, Kristen. I'm already scared as hell! Do you have to do that dragon aura crap? You'll make me pee my pants!"

"It's better than you walking into the void."

"What are you talking about?" he asked.

"The reason this room was so dark is because that wall is no longer a wall. It's the same darkness as what is outside the building upstairs."

"Are you serious?" He jumped back and dropped the torch.

"I tend not to joke about primeval forces," she replied and approached the curving wall of darkness slowly. It was the identical thick, inky darkness as what waited outside the windows of the base and the same curtain of black outside the door.

"You're saying that tricked-out shock-resistant laptop I purchased was what—swallowed up by that crap?" Brian asked.

"I guess so, yeah."

"But this crap wasn't here before. Are you saying it's shrinking?" he asked and his voice rose with fear.

"I don't want to, but yeah. Or expanding and our bubble is shrinking. Do you want to try to salvage any of your computer equipment? It looks like there's a little still on this side of it."

"I'm good, thanks," he said. "If it's all cool with you, I'll go back to pixie duty but this time on the main floor, surrounded by a horde of dragons, dwarves, and mages."

"Yeah, Mom would never forgive me if you were eaten by an unfathomable void."

"You *are* joking about primeval forces?"

"It doesn't seem like there's anything else we can do to them," Kristen replied.

They left the bunker to find Jim huddled over the little pixies.

"Please tell me you're watching them do a little pixie dance or something?" Brian asked.

"No, but these little guys don't look good," The Wonderkid looked up and his grim expression hardened further. "You guys don't look good either. Is everything all right?"

"Absolutely not," she said. "I need you and Brian to take these pixies upstairs. Get them in toward the center of the floor and tell everyone else to avoid the edges of the base. I need to talk to the leaders of the delegations."

A few minutes later, she returned to the bunker room, this time with Constance, Shimmerclaw, Minestrength, and the Secretary of State in tow. The human and dwarf each had a torch, and Constance held a glowing orb in each hand. With this much light, it was far more obvious what was happening to the back of the room.

"That wasn't here when we were in here," the Secretary of State said. "I thought you said we were safe inside this bubble or pocket or whatever."

"I said we were safer in here than out there," Constance said and knelt in front of the curving wall of darkness. She held her hands up and sent glowing tendrils out from her fingers into the dark wall. Focused, she attempted this for a long few minutes before she finally shook her head, stood, and stepped away from the void.

"Thoughts?" Shimmerclaw asked her.

"It's the same as the darkness up top," the technomage said. Kristen could kiss her for how calm her voice was. "My spells simply cease to exist as soon as my magic enters the dark region. I can't tell what it is, but the bubble protecting us all from it is definitely shrinking."

"Are you sure the bubble is protecting us?" the Secretary of State asked and his voice shook with fear.

Kristen decided to answer the question herself. She walked to the front of the room and found a broom, approached the wall of darkness, and shoved the broom forward. The bristles on the bottom entered the void and bent slightly before going in fully. It felt as if a wall of sludge was being held back by the magic bubble rather than a void of nothingness. That did not do much for her sense of calm. She pushed the broom in deeper until the bristles were all swallowed. It wasn't exactly easy as there was a fair amount of resistance to her push.

"Be careful," Constance said. "I don't know what will happen if your body touches it, but I'm not exactly optimistic about the outcome. In other words, don't touch."

She nodded and stopped pushing once the dark goo—she couldn't help but think of it as tar or lime or primordial soup now that she'd felt it—covered about a third of the broom. Then, she tried to pull it out.

It did not come easily. It was almost as if the wall of gunk attempted to suck the entire broom out of her hand. As she pulled, she kept her breathing even. She couldn't panic, even if she couldn't completely banish the sensation that her entire base had been swallowed by a creature of the night and they were now in its belly.

"Do you need a hand?" Minestrength asked, which irked her into transforming her skin into steel.

She yanked the broom again and it popped out. Or maybe broke it was a better way to think of it as the part that had vanished into the dark did not reappear. Only the handle they had already been able to see came loose. There was a clean slice where it had touched the goo and she examined it carefully. It was more than clean and looked as if the broom had been burned away or eaten by acid and then polished. There were no splinters in evidence and nothing to indicate that the missing end had ever existed.

Perhaps odder to her was that none of this slimy blackness had come away and stuck to it. It made her think that whatever this crap was, it wasn't something that would respond to any form of assault. It was a complete, slimy force of darkness, and it seemed hungry.

"I think we can agree on one thing at least," Kristen said.

"Wh-what's that?" The Secretary of State stammered.

"We definitely should not touch."

CHAPTER FIFTY

Amy might have fallen deeper into despair if she knew that Kristen was as much at a loss inside the building as she was on the outside.

"What do you make of this?" Larry asked her in the teacher voice she usually appreciated but right now found very fucking annoying.

They stood at the edge of where the base used to be. Or maybe, more accurately, where the base used to exist. Now, there was nothing.

"Okay, there's nothing here. It's like a huge scooped-out hole. Like God or the devil came at it with a galactic ice cream scoop."

"I appreciate the metaphor but I think it's flawed," her companion said.

Lumos and Stonequest chuckled. The dumb dragons were out of their league and couldn't help at all.

"How can you stay so calm when the base is gone?" she demanded.

Larry raised his hands in a gesture of peace. "I only mean that if it were scooped, there would be some evidence of its movement. Like a crater on one side or bent pipes or something, but there isn't."

He was right. The area was clean-cut like the base had been

vanished rather than scooped up. The edges that used to lead to the base were smooth and flawless, almost like they were polished.

"How could Havington possibly have done something like this?" she asked out loud. He had only been able to power the tornado because Stormwing had controlled the wind and atmospheric effects. Plus, as Larry had said, there had been wild magic involved.

"I don't think he did," Larry said ponderously.

"Do you think Stormwing had some secret power?" Stonequest asked.

"No. No, I don't think it was either one of them. This is so much more elegant than a freaking fire tornado. I don't think their kind of magic could have done this."

"But it was magic," Stonequest said stubbornly. "And for some reason, I don't think the mages in there would have disappeared themselves. It had to be those two."

"Think about the motives, though," Larry said. "If Havington was behind this, he would have left as soon as his objective was completed. He wouldn't have stuck around, waiting to be captured. The guy might not be on our side but he's not dumb."

"Okay, but if it wasn't Havington or Stormwing, then who was it?" Amy demanded.

"That's the sixty-four-thousand-dollar question, isn't it?" he said with a waggle of his eyebrows.

"Could the mages have teleported the base away?" Lumos asked. "If they formed a gate and could move it, maybe they could…uh, kind of slice away reality."

Larry had his eyes closed and arms extended toward the hole, so Amy was forced to answer even though magical theory was not her strong suit. "That's not how that spell works. The entire basis of it is connecting to anchored points in space and time. It can't be moved and things can only move through it."

"I have something!" the other mage shouted and eyes snapped open. "Oh, damn it—wait, let me try that again." He closed his eyes.

"Try what again?" Stonequest asked.

"Eureka!" Larry chuckled. "I've always wanted to say that."

"Well, what did you get?" Lumos asked and seemed to translate the Greek but not get the reference.

"I recognized the feel of the power residue. See, magic is not like light. It doesn't simply vanish when you turn the switch off. It's more like water and always leaves a trace behind. You merely have to know how to sop it up."

"What did you sop up, oh wise one?" Amy asked sarcastically.

"It's wild, uncontrolled magic," he said like he thought he was wiser than master Yoda.

"So it was the firestorm?" she asked.

"No, there's wild magic here, but there's an intention to it. If I had to guess—and we most certainly do if we want to save our friends—I'd say this is pixie magic."

"But there were no pixies out here," Stonequest said.

"But there were some inside," Lumos said. "They arrived right before they put the dome up."

"I bet they had something to do with this," Larry said.

"But why would they disappear everyone?" she asked.

"I bet they didn't mean to." The mage rubbed his chin in thought. "I think we can safely assume that the fire tornado caused damage to the inside of the base. Otherwise, we would have had updates from Kristen while the tornado was raging."

"Okay, let's say it was damaged, but so what?" Amy asked.

"Well, the mage spell had failed, so the only other group capable of doing something to stop a magic tornado must have stepped up."

"The pixies," Lumos said.

"Right." Larry nodded.

"But why disappear the base?" she pushed.

"I still say they didn't mean to. Pixies understand even less about magic theory than you do, Amy. No offense."

"Absolutely none taken because I am not a nerd," she replied.

"Right. Well, my guess is that the pixies attempted some kind of defense of their own and their spell maybe interacted with the shields around the base, the firestorm outside, or even both. Somehow, that resulted in what we see now."

"What does magical theory have to do with that?" Amy asked.

"Some spells—well, more specifically, some types of magic—have odd effects. Combining mage, dragon, and pixie magic in the quantities needed to stop a flaming tornado could have had any number of unusual effects. The power here must have tweaked with existence itself."

"Are you saying Kristen and everyone else are… gone?" She scowled. "Like, they don't exist anymore because the pixies don't do their magic theory homework?"

"I don't want to give anyone false hope. That is a possibility." Larry looked glum but not as glum as everyone else.

"But it's not the only possibility, not even kind of," he continued and forced himself to sound positive. "Windlock and I saw different types of magic combined quite a few times, and the only thing that's consistent about mixing magics is that the effect is never predictable. I'll not give up on our team simply because they're not here. There's too much I don't understand about wild magic for me to be sure."

"But if you don't understand it, how are we supposed to find the answers?" Amy asked. "Constance is inside. If she knows a way out, I think she would have used it by now."

"You're right. I don't know nearly enough to solve it on my own. But I know who does."

"Time is money as the humans say," Stonequest said, "Out with it."

"I think it's time we ask some pixies for help," he said with a grin.

CHAPTER FIFTY-ONE

Despite Brian saying that he wanted to be around other people, Kristen had hoped to bring the pixies to her office on the second floor without anyone noticing. But after her time below observing the now shrinking sphere of darkness, any hopes of privacy were gone.

Her brother was near the top of the stairs to the basement level, guarding the cardboard box the pixies slept in. And guarding was the right word for it. Everyone seemed quite eager to share their theories on how the creatures might be able to help their current predicament.

"Let's give them a little shake!" The German delegate shouted, his voice edging into what she could only describe as mad-scientist.

"You shake those pixies and we shake you," a dwarf replied, which of course made the humans all group together and grumble at the dwarves.

"Perhaps the humans have a point, though," Lady Jade said ponderously. "If the pixies are doing this, giving them a...*shake* might wake them up."

"We'll not do anything that might hurt them," Kristen said and put herself between the box and the room of unruly delegates. "I want them to get us out of this as much as everyone, but we simply don't know enough about how their magic works to know if trying to wake them is a good idea."

"For all we know," Constance said, her voice loud enough that the entire room could hear, "they might be in a trance to hold this void at bay. If they are indeed maintaining some kind of protection for us, waking them could very well bring that void inside this base."

That didn't do much to stop the general discontent in the room, but it did get the human delegates and Lady Jade to go back to their spaces.

"Maybe we should take them to your office," Brian said. "I was looking forward to some company but on second thought, I think it might be better to chill with the unconscious pixies than to make small talk and risk our entire existence."

"Good plan," Kristen said and gestured to the leaders of each delegation to follow her upstairs with the pixies.

Shimmerclaw and Constance agreed, but Minestrength and the Secretary of State wanted to stay behind.

"I'll make sure no one follows," Minestrength said and glanced at the human Secretary.

"I think I should stay as well to make sure everyone here feels adequately informed of the situation."

"That's what I wanted to talk to you about," she said. "We need to determine the best way to share this information. I don't want to start a panic."

"We'll hold the fort down here while you three determine our educational strategy," the Secretary of State said.

"Thank you, Mr. Secretary," she replied politely before she, Constance, Shimmerclaw, and Brian with his box of pixies went upstairs.

Once in the privacy of her office, her brother went to fetch a cot. A long moment of silence lingered between the three women while he was gone. It might have been an awkward moment, but the absolute blackness outside her huge windows had a way of filling the gaps in the conversation. She couldn't believe it. Everything was so *black*. It was like they had been taken to the deepest darkest corner of space, a region between galaxies where not even stars burned. It was profoundly troubling, so much so that when Brian entered the room with a cot, all three of the powerful women jumped at the sound.

"Sorry. I should've knocked…but then you would've jumped at the knock…so not sorry, I guess. Sorry about that," he muttered as he set the cot up.

Once it was done, he took out each creature gently from the box, starting with Lady Dragonfly, and laid them out one by one. Once all twelve were out, he took a blanket and tucked them all in. Not one of them stirred while this happened, a disturbing sign. Also troubling was their color.

"Do they look healthy to everybody?" Kristen asked.

Shimmerclaw pursed her lips and shook her head. "I've seen pixies in every shade of skin but none of them have ever been so gray."

"Constance?" Kristen asked.

"I wish I knew more about their constitution and their magic." The technomage sounded slightly ashamed. "As it is, I worry that any of the spells I might cast to invigorate them would either overwhelm their little bodies or cause this dome to shrink even faster than it already is."

"Actually, that's what I wanted to talk to you about," she said. "I think we should tell everyone that the bubble around us is shrinking. What do you think the best way to share that intelligence is?"

Constance and Shimmerclaw shared a look that one day might prove to be one of the most significant in history. There was nothing particularly unusual about it—it was simply the narrow eyes and high eyebrows of shared incredulity. What was unique was who did it. Never before had the political leader of the dragons and the political leader of the mages agreed on a point so quickly or so strongly.

"I don't think we should share that the bubble is shrinking," Constance said.

"Nor do I. All it would do is sow panic."

"Dragons panic?" the woman asked and shattered the brief moment of shared disbelief.

"Dragons like to be able to transform into our true forms," Shimmerclaw said as if it were the most obvious thing in the world. "There is already too little space to allow that. Less space would make some of our warriors start to wonder about how to make more."

"But that's only the dragons," Kristen said, "Surely the mages—"

"Would be even worse," Constance said. "Our entire existence has been one of persecution. We are a paranoid people. We spend our lives looking over our shoulders and hoping to appease dragons, no offense meant to Lady Shimmerclaw."

"None taken. You have made your point clearly and eloquently many times during this convention. It hardly surprises me to hear that a group of rogue mages might think in terms of paranoia when trapped with a party of dragons."

"The humans aren't doing any better," Brian added. "All of them—hell, all of us, me included—are out of our depth here. My sister is a steel dragon and I'm still freaking out. If you tell them that the bubble is getting smaller, it would be chaos."

"I merely don't think we'll be able to keep it quiet," Kristen said. "And if everyone discovers it themselves, we lose what trust we've built with each other."

"It's a fair point but—" Constance didn't get to finish it.

At that moment, it felt as if something reached into Kristen's gut and yanked. The sensation passed quickly. For a second, it felt as if some creature from beyond space and time had grasped one of her internal organs and attempted to remove it before everything returned to normal.

"Did anyone else feel that?" she asked.

"You mean the sensation that Cthulhu kicked me in the nuts?" Brian asked and rubbed his gut.

"It feels as if the magic force that animates the universe was… tightened," Constance said, also rubbing her stomach.

"Indeed," Shimmerclaw said. "It felt like a demon grabbed my spine."

"Shit," Kristen cursed. "If we all felt it, we can bet everyone down below felt it too."

"But what was it?" the Council leader asked.

"I think I know why it feels as if there's less magic," Constance said. She pointed out the windows into the blackness.

It seemed like the blackness was not quite as far away. It was hard to be certain, but Kristen thought that only a few minutes before, it had seemed as if the darkness began a few feet out of the window. Now, it seemed that if she opened the window, it would simply pool in. Still, she moved closer and looked out, up, and around the building she was in.

As she'd seen below, she could almost make out a curve to the darkness as if they were inside a sphere. It curved up and around and cut into the top of the structure. The roof—and all the fancy defense systems they had recently installed—was probably already lost to this non-space.

"Oh, shit, you guys." Brian's voice sounded even worse than Cthulhu kicking him in the nuts.

"What now?" she asked.

"I think I know why the darkness got closer," he said with a sniff and pointed to the cot. Kristen realized what he was talking about immediately.

One of the pixies was dead. Even though they were all unconscious, it was still easy to see that Sir Ladybug had passed on. While the other pixies still had color, he looked as blue-gray as a body from the morgue. As she watched, he seemed to unravel like the matter that held him together was made of string and there was no longer anything to hold all those threads in place. It took less than a second. The body of Sir Ladybug lay motionless, then he unraveled and was no more.

"Oh, dear," Constance said and rushed forward to check on the others. She checked the pulse on each one gently and confirmed that all eleven were still alive. "They seem to be fading as well. I...I can't see them lasting much longer."

"I bet their energy *is* fueling this sphere around us," Brian said. "I bet this place contracted by a twelfth of its original size when that happened."

"But it was already shrinking," Shimmerclaw pointed out.

"Right, which means that keeping out that…that inky shit out there must be killing them. I don't think they'll wake up. Not as long as we're in here."

"Which means we can't expect them to help us get out," Kristen said.

"Damn this," Constance cursed, her voice shaken. "We are trapped in a puzzle. I hate puzzles."

"We need to go downstairs and check on everyone else," she said.

"Agreed," Shimmerclaw said. "I think I should go to the basement and look at the progress down there. I didn't look at the distance of the sphere up here before it contracted, but I think I might be able to estimate down below."

"Estimate what? How much time we have left to live?" Brian asked.

The dragon merely nodded.

"Right. Brian, you'll stay here?" Kristen asked.

He nodded. Kristen, Shimmerclaw, and Constance went down to a scene of chaos.

"I said to not panic!" the Secretary of State yelled and made it clear who had caused the panic and also what exactly everyone was panicking about.

"What the hell are we supposed to do about the walls shrinking?" Decimus Aurelius bellowed.

"Not kill those pixies. They're all that's keeping us alive right now!" a dwarf replied and stepped closer to the dragon. Despite him being less than half the height of the dragon's human form, he did not look at all intimidated.

They weren't the only two close to blows. The old witch mage had some kind of magic swirling around a dragon warrior. Another dragon had his weapon drawn and faced a dwarf with the world's largest hammer. Two humans yelled at a dwarf about land-use codes and he bellowed as loudly in response. All in all, it looked like they were moments away from erupting into the world's smallest but most powerful war. Or maybe not the world's, as she wasn't exactly sure that they were even in the world anymore.

"Tell us this is merely more subterfuge by the humans!" Lady Jade demanded of Shimmerclaw. "The only way they could even earn their right at the bargaining table was by using the weapons the mages made. This…news the human Secretary shared is a ploy. More madness designed to take power away from the dragons."

It seemed everyone was desperate to hear they were overreacting and one by one, the arguments fell away. Those who had been pressed chest to chest, posturing like adolescents pumped up on testosterone, stepped away from each other. All the eyes in the room turned to Shimmerclaw.

"This is no ruse," the Council leader said plainly. "I do not know what Mr. Secretary said, but I can tell you this. The bubble we appear to be inside is indeed shrinking. We had thought it a gradual process, but we cannot be sure it will proceed that way. Everyone here doubtlessly felt a tug a few moments ago—"

"Tug? More like a creature from the depth beneath grabbed my nuts and twisted!" a dwarf shouted, which earned a few snickers and bled a little of the tension out of the room, thank God.

"That was the passing of a pixie," Shimmerclaw said. "Whether they are being drained to create this dome or whether they are simply cut off from the wild magic that fuels them, we do not know. We do know that time is limited and that, if we are to make it out of this, we will have to not panic and work together."

"More empty platitudes."

Kristen fully expected it to be Lord Boneclaw once again stirring up the energy of the room, but it was not. It was one of the dragon warriors, who until now had said nothing and been the perfect image of stoicism.

"I am telling the truth," Lady Shimmerclaw insisted.

"I'm sure you are. Your type always does. Maybe you're not telling the full truth, though. Maybe you're leaving out a key detail, but I'm sure you're telling the truth," the dragon continued and his words slurred almost as if he were drunk. "This whole thing stinks. You bring us all here, lock us in this warehouse, and then the world vanishes? And why? So you can make everyone pretend to be allies.

It's sick. Dragons should rule this world. Dragons are the power that will decide our fate. All of this is merely pissing in the wind."

"That's enough," Decimus Aurelius said to the warrior.

"And you are as bad as she is! The only one of these councilors worth a damn is—"

"He said that was enough," Lord Boneclaw snapped, and the dragon warrior subsided. "I do not like this situation any more than anyone. But I can at least see that we will not survive this if we cannot think our way out of it. Dragons, perhaps we have played too passive a role. If we create some space for ourselves, perhaps we can try to transform and see if we still have the ability. If we do not, that could give us a clue about how sealed off we are in this place."

"It's a fair idea," Shimmerclaw conceded.

"Very well," he said and went about setting the dragons up around the room. The rest of the group had to crowd together to give them space, but that suited Kristen fine. As a dragon transformed, it at least gave the rest of the room something to focus on.

"Lady Shimmerclaw, this might be your chance to slip away," she said.

"Indeed. I thought the same thing."

"Are you sure you'll be able to tell how far it has contracted?"

"I am," the old dragon said and sounded only a tiny bit smug. "I have earned my position primarily by noticing things that go overlooked. To say I pay attention to detail would be something of an understatement."

"Okay. But be careful down there, all right?"

The older dragon smiled as if to say, "I always am."

CHAPTER FIFTY-TWO

One of Shimmerclaw's most glaring weaknesses was that she let her control over her aura drop when she thought she was alone. It was stupid—profoundly so—but there it was. The Masked One didn't blame her for such shortcomings. He understood as he spent so much of his time hiding, concealing his aura, and pretending to be something he was not. It was exhausting and of course, it only worked if it went unnoticed, which was frustrating in its own way.

Still, despite his empathy for his fellow Councilor, he would not do her the courtesy of refusing to taste her emotions. He'd put up with her weakness long enough. Finally, after millennia, that might come to an end.

He vanished into shadow and followed her from the darkness that pressed in all around her. She had only a torch and her dragon sight. Neither would be strong enough to see him. In a place such as this, he might as well be invisible.

It was a curious question about the diminishment of powers in this non-space they occupied. He had pursued many lines of study over his years on this planet, but he—like so many others—did not much care for pixies or see their importance. It seemed this was a miscalculation on his part. But whatever the creatures had done, it had not affected his powers. He could still slip into shadows as easily as always and change his form as effortlessly. His aura powers were beginning to diminish, but they had served their purpose well enough.

Shimmerclaw entered the bunker and approached the back wall. It was as she said. The inky void had come into this place. The Masked One didn't understand why his powers seemed no weaker, given that he couldn't enter the inkiness any more than anyone else could. He'd turned the claw of his left hand to shadow and attempted to enter the space and succeeded only in giving himself a manicure. No, he didn't want to penetrate that dark. It was a job for a different dragon.

"Maybe twenty-two inches," the Council leader muttered and knelt to make marks on the floor with her claw. She scratched a few dozen of these, each a perfect inch apart.

That done, she stood and watched the darkness slowly consume them. It took more than fifteen minutes for the darkness to reach the first mark.

During this entire whole time, the Masked One felt Shimmerclaw. He felt her nervousness and her dread. He felt her hope for this convention slowly rot and putrefy. And he felt her faith in the Steel Dragon.

It was sickening that this dragon was the one who all dragons called leader. She was a spineless worm, more interested in a mongrel runt than her kind.

He had to admit, though, the old bitch was patient. She stood calmly, no doubt counting silently to measure the time. To humans, things like electronics were a necessity for counting time or even measuring lengths. In fact, it seemed with every iteration of technology, the humans became that much more mentally deficient. But to the dragons, modern technology was nothing but a fad. Neither he nor Shimmerclaw needed anything but their brain to count the time.

But it was she who had true patience. When The Masked One heard one of the Steel Dragon's human guards descend the stairs, he couldn't help but investigate.

Well, investigate was a silly way to put it. What he did was form out of shadow, slice their head from their body with one swipe of his claw, and peel the skin from their skull before he tucked the bloody corpse into the darkness. Oh, it did feel good to be honest with himself. He understood why Lady Shimmerclaw did it so often.

An instant later, he returned to his surveillance. It didn't take long to butcher a human. The Council leader was talking to herself. "It's going slowly. At this rate, we should have days." She chuckled, the moron. "I wonder if that will be a good thing or bad."

"Bad, I would think," he said, using Lord Boneclaw's familiar voice.

"Lord Boneclaw!" Shimmerclaw said, clamped down on her aura, and cut off the flood of emotional information she had been giving him.

"Do be careful, Lady Shimmerclaw. I don't think one even as powerful as you would want to fall into this void. I don't think it would be healthy."

"Why are you down here? You said you would lead the dragons in their transformations."

"The shrinking sphere doesn't seem to weaken dragon powers, only the mages. What about you, Shimmerclaw. Do you feel weaker?"

She narrowed her eyes at him as if she managed to decipher the extremely obvious clue he had dropped in her lap.

"No… No, I don't feel any weaker. Do you?" she asked. What kind of fool did she take him for?

"As strong as ever, my lady. I am curious, though, how much longer until we all die?"

Lady Shimmerclaw smirked at that, which put the Masked One on edge. *How much does she understand?* But his worry was unnecessary. Her next remarks proved that she was still painfully oblivious to what was about to happen. "A direct question, Lord Boneclaw? That might be a first for you."

"I've never been trapped in a sphere of darkness before." He wanted to ask whether this was how his victims felt. But that was too obvious, even for this late point in the game. "Have you been honest with us? The mages cannot see a way out of this?"

"Unfortunately, yes, I have been. The mages are not familiar with this type of magic and don't seem to be able to penetrate it."

"Then all hope is lost." *For you.* The Masked One kept the last words to himself.

"Not yet," Shimmerclaw said and hope shone from her aura. "I've seen the Steel Dragon manage miracles on more than one occasion. I never thought she'd have fought off that mage attack on our secret base in the mountains. Do you remember that? We had the entire area closed off. No electricity, nothing but dragons, yet as soon as we took flight, dragons started to die from those infernal bullets."

"I do remember that, yes. This is another level of danger, though, is it not?"

"It is, of course. Even so, if anyone can do it, it's the young Kristen Hall," she said warmly.

"You use her human name?" he asked and his Boneclaw character slipped.

"I do. I think her human upbringing is what gives her the edge. You disagree, though, don't you? That warrior intended to say you were the only Councilor he agreed with."

He sneered at that. Indeed, his aura powers were slipping. He had been the one to work up that dragon's temper, of course, but he hadn't meant to make him so slobberingly stupid. The fool had almost made it clear to even the races without aural powers that Lord Boneclaw was the thorn in this meeting's heel.

"He was out of line."

"Curious, though, was it not?" Shimmerclaw asked, smiling now. "Normally, our warriors are so contained. That's what we teach them, isn't it? To control their bodies, minds, and emotions, and yet, his got away from him. Why do you think that is?" Her aura moved into something fuzzier that suggested suspicion. Curse this! Truly, this proved that dragons were more related to mages and pixie magic than he would have liked to admit. Why else would their auras be suffering?

"Curious," the Masked One grated.

"To think they lasted so long and then snapped. I wonder why. They would benefit from peace between the races."

"Would they?" he asked through clenched teeth.

"We all would. I think Kristen *Hall* will make a wonderful leader." Curse Shimmerclaw. She used the human name on purpose.

"A wonderful leader of what? She does not prioritize dragon kind."

"Of course she doesn't. She sees a true way forward. A chance for real progress. I think before long, we'll all use her human name."

"I would think not," he growled and took a step closer to her.

She moved one leg back and shifted her legs into a braced position. This was a woman who was ready to fight. The foolishness of it all.

"She has done so much, though," she continued as if they were younglings gossiping in the nest. She was *trying* to piss him off. He knew it. "She stopped the assassinations in Detroit. She stopped Death, the dragon assassin who had plagued our kind for years."

"That was quite a blow," he said. Of course, Shimmerclaw didn't know that he'd paid Death for all those years. She couldn't. Right?

"Then she stopped those assassinations in Europe and that out of her element, no less. Very impressive. And her final blow was catching the technomages—all of them."

"Not *all* of them," he growled.

"Oh? It seems their leaders are all here."

"Not Havington."

"Havington? You mean the mage in Florence. How did you know about him?"

"I've read the reports."

"Those reports were classified."

"I have my ways," the Masked One responded coldly. This was not going well. Could she read his aura?

"And you've used them well. Back in the Hudson Bay base, I thought you might have succeeded."

"And would it have been so bad if I had?" he snapped. The guise of Lord Boneclaw had fallen away in the face of this obnoxious questioning.

"A global war? Yes, I think it would have been," Shimmerclaw said as if she were addressing a child.

"We would have won! How can you not see that?"

"The mages are powerful."

"Which is why I ordered them all rounded up. They wouldn't have been able to make that shield that trapped us in here if that Steel Bitch hadn't interfered. And if they hadn't made that shield, Havington and Stormwing would have blown this place to rubble."

"I thought the pairing of the fire mage with Stormwing was a brilliant stroke. Too bad about the pixies throwing that all off."

"You… I don't know what you're talking about." The Masked One snapped the denial.

"Tell me, how did you manage to get them to work together?" Shimmerclaw asked, still in the casual tone of a simple gossip. How he hated her then. "Stormwing was always very much about dragon's preeminence and from the reports I read, Havington was no fan of dragons."

"They both understood that there needs to be a hierarchy with someone at the top. Democracy only leads to chaos. You've done nothing but let our kind plateau with your fake leadership. This world needs a true leader. Havington thought it would be an old mage and Stormwing thought it would be an old dragon."

"Neither of them knew they were working for the Masked One?" Shimmerclaw asked.

He paused for a moment and studied her, wondering how long she'd known—if she'd known or if he could still lie to her about his identity. But, unbidden, he began to laugh. She knew! She finally knew! He felt like she must have felt whenever she let her aura run uncontrolled. He felt liberated, free, and like himself.

The Masked One smiled at Lady Shimmerclaw, wiped tears of joy from his eyes, and nodded. "No. Neither of them ever saw my face. But then, no one does."

"I see your face right now," she said.

"This is but a mask," Lord Boneclaw said. He reached into shadow, retrieved the freshly harvested skull, and put it on his head. Oh, how good it felt to finally wear his mask, his true face.

"That's what the scars are from, then?" she asked in her politest tone.

"Indeed," he admitted, turned one arm to shadow, and closed the heavy steel door behind them.

Now, it was only the two of them, Shimmerclaw's torch, and the darkness.

"You don't think you can defeat me in hand-to-hand combat, do you?" The Council leader smiled. "The size of this room might prevent me from taking my dragon form, but I have prepared for this fight for centuries. Even if I didn't know that Lord Boneclaw was the Masked One, I heard the rumors of his powers. I have prepared for your shadow abilities, Boneclaw. You will find them not particularly effective against my platinum punch."

"Your platinum punch is your greatest threat? Truly?" This amused him no end. "You have spent too much time with the humans. The platinum punch. It sounds like something they'd serve at a bar or the final move of one their wrestlers."

"Do you wish to try it?" Shimmerclaw challenged. Her skin began to sparkle as if each of her skin cells turned slowly into glitter. Every tiny light irritated his face but he was no vampire of human superstitions. He could walk in broad daylight without coming to harm. The platinum dragon would need more than glitter to defeat him.

He regarded her curiously and realized for the first time in millennia that he had underestimated this foe. Truly, she had abilities that might rival his own. "I wonder which of us would win if it came to a fight."

"There is no need to wonder." Her fists were clenched and he wondered if she were ambidextrous.

"Ah, but I worry I will for the next century."

"Do you refuse to fight?" She grinned. "Then you've decided to risk yourself in the void? I wouldn't make such a move but perhaps the blackness will recognize the dark in your soul and embrace you."

"The only one of us to join the void will be you, Lady Shimmerclaw, but your soul will be long departed."

"I tire of your threats—"

"But of course," the Masked One said and drew the suppressed pistol he'd taken from the Steel Dragon's armory. He squeezed the trigger and a bullet made of the tooth harvested from a dragon exploded from the barrel and bored a hole in her chest. She had brought her arms up to block a shadow attack that had never came. They sparkled with the lights of the stars themselves.

Then, they faded.

"Curse you, Boneclaw." She fell to one knee. "I would have... destroyed you." The sparkling lights traced up and down her arms and continued to wink out, one by one, like the clouds of a hurricane covering the gentle glow of the milky way.

"Perhaps. But now, we will never know."

He shot her again, not in the heart but the lung. The bullet missed any bone and continued through her chest. For the briefest moment— a moment imperceptible to human senses but laid bare by the abilities of dragons—he saw through her body and out to the wall of blackness she had been examining. Blood hemorrhaged to fill the hole as she toppled to the floor.

"You're...a fool...Boneclaw," Shimmerclaw sputtered. Blood seeped out of her throat and made her words hard to understand as they were delivered through a mouthful of red.

"If this is some kind of threat, I assure you it's a weak one. You cannot heal, not with a dragon bullet inside you. The second one went right through, but the first would have done you in as surely as the second."

"I'm already dead, you idiot," she said, but it was not a statement made with malice. She sounded as if she were talking to an old friend. The Masked One supposed that, from her perspective, maybe she was. She didn't understand that Lord Boneclaw had never existed except as a disguise for the Masked One to accomplish what he desired.

"Then how, pray tell, have you outsmarted me?" he asked and used the voice of Boneclaw for her benefit.

"You killed me in the Steel Dragon's base. You do realize she's a cop?" The platinum dragon barely managed to say the words over her laughter. Blood pulsed with each guffaw. It was almost enough to make him simply put a bullet through her brain to make her shut up.

"I have followed her career, yes. But I fail to see the relevance. No one will take me to jail or put me on trial. We are trapped in this dimension of shadow—or I am, anyway. You'll be free soon enough."

"The fact that she's a cop means she'll come down here and investigate, idiot. She'll find my body and do human forensics on it. She'll find out who did this and she'll catch you."

It was the Masked One's turn to laugh. Loud and long he laughed. It was so loud that for a moment, he worried that others might hear them. But no, the door was solid.

"What is so funny to you?" Shimmerclaw wheezed.

"Did you think I was joking about sending you into the void?" he asked. "Your corpse will be swallowed by that wall of void in less than an hour."

The look on her face said that no, she had not considered the painfully obvious plan of letting her body simply be swallowed by the dark. "No, please…" Coughs wracked her. She didn't have much time left. "Don't let my body vanish into this force of darkness. Use me for your bullets. Burn me. Anything. Please don't let me simply cease to be!"

He smiled. "As you wish," he said coldly and shot her in the gut. She sprawled back from the blow and landed inches away from the void. "You do make a good point about the firearm, though," he said to her unconscious body and flung the pistol into the hungry darkness. *Good luck getting forensics off that,* he thought as he strolled away to rejoin the other delegates.

It felt simply wonderful to have one less nuisance to deal with. Hopefully, the pestilential Steel Dragon would prove as easy to dispatch.

The Masked one vanished into shadow and snuck upstairs.

CHAPTER FIFTY-THREE

"Where the hell are we supposed to find pixies?" Amy demanded of Larry.

He grinned at her and shrugged, a clear indication that he didn't know. It wasn't much of a surprise. He'd worked for a dragon investigator for years. That didn't exactly leave one time for many hobbies like investigating mythical creatures who happened to be real.

"So what are we supposed to do?" she asked.

"I have some ideas," he said. He hadn't realized that he'd said all that aloud. It happened to him often. His mind raced constantly and his mouth always tried to catch up.

"I'm interested to hear those ideas as well," Stonequest said.

"Well, pixies like wild magic, right?" Larry asked, mostly rhetorically. He tried his best to pay attention to what everyone was saying and more importantly, to what came out of his mouth.

"That much is clear, yes," Lumos said.

"Then we simply need to go to a place of wild magic and we're bound to find some."

"Great. So where are places of wild magic?" Amy asked.

Larry scratched his head. "Ancient forests, pristine waterfalls, smoldering volcanos. That kind of thing."

"We went to a volcano a week ago and I didn't see any pixies," Stonequest said.

"Fair point," the mage conceded.

"Plus, we're in Detroit. The only bodies of water around here are damn polluted. And even the suburbs are as manicured as hell," Amy sounded distraught. "I guess we could go to the great lake."

"Lake Superior," Stonequest said.

"But that would take hours. I don't want to spend that kind of time."

"You're right about that. I think we should do what we can to act as quickly as possible."

"Are you sure we should all go?" Lumos asked. "This could turn out to be…less than efficient. I think perhaps some of us should stay here in case they return."

"I agree. I don't want to leave her to go look for pixies," Amy added quickly.

"We wouldn't be leaving her," Larry protested. "We'd be looking for the only way to help."

"Well, it looks like that'll be only you and me, then," Stonequest said.

He nodded. That would have to do. "Fine, but we still need a wild place."

"What about Lady Amythist?" Lumos asked. "Her gardens are not exactly manicured."

"That's putting it lightly," Stonequest added.

"Plus she's surrounded by forest. There might be pixies there," the golden dragon concluded.

"Better yet, we can call ahead." Stonequest retrieved his phone and dialed Amythist. As it rang, he said, "Can you imagine what we would do without these things?"

Larry chuckled. "Fortunately, I don't think anything could wipe out all the phones."

The call connected. After a few questions, he hung up. "She says there are pixies there. Three live on her land, it seems."

"We'll probably need more than that," Amy said heavily.

"But that's a start," Larry said and tried to sound optimistic. "Let's go. Amy and Lumos, you'll stay here. Are you sure?"

They shared a look, but it was obvious on their faces that yes, they would remain there and wait for the Steel Dragon.

"Let's go, Brockton," Stonequest said. The mage climbed onto his back and they were airborne in moments.

The stone dragon flew as fast as he could. Larry used some of the tricks Constance had shown him to put the wind at their backs.

"Do you think this will work?" the dragon asked.

"Honestly? I have no fucking idea," he said. "But that…hole or whatever the hell it is radiated wild magic. If the pixies weren't responsible for that happening, we are dealing with some force far beyond what I thought this world was even capable of."

"That's not a comforting thought."

"If you want comfort, go back to sleep," Larry said.

"What's that supposed to mean?"

"Oh, it was something Windlock used to say when a case got tough," he said, thinking fondly of his old boss. "Whenever we would hit a block or it would seem like there was no other option and I would say something about quitting. Jokes, mostly, but Windlock didn't have much of a sense of humor. Anyway, his point was that life's not supposed to be easy or comfortable. And that, most of the time, if you feel comfortable, it means you're ignoring what's going on all around you. We could sit at that dome and wait for something to happen but in the end, it might merely lull us into comfort."

"I feel like you lost the thread in there somewhere," Stonequest said with a trace of disdain in his voice.

"Look, let's hope I'm wrong, okay? I hope we can make them all reappear. Because if I am right and we need the pixies' help, this won't exactly be easy."

The time for conversation was over, however. They were above the woods that surrounded Amythist's cottage. A moment later, they descended in slow circles and landed on one of the few patches of open grass large enough to accommodate a dragon.

Amythist came out to meet them, not that she was easy to see. Her gardens were overgrown and unsightly, especially compared to the perfectly manicured estates where most dragons lived. Here, it seemed that the plants didn't so much grow as they fought each other for space to survive.

Beds and paths ran between them, but the beds were so packed with plants that sometimes, it was hard to tell where one ended and another began. Plus, as they walked toward her, they'd come across some specimen of plant that had started to grow in the path between the beds. Rather than plucking it, she had encouraged it to grow. In the beds themselves, flowers proliferated, as did herbs in a hundred different colors. There were also numerous dead plants too, many of them heavy with the husks of seedpods left to fully ripen and harden.

It was as close to wild as Larry could think of and insane to think that it existed only a few miles away from the burned-out urban wasteland they had recently left.

Perhaps the strangest of all, though, was that through this malaise of overgrown shrubs, plants going to seed, untrimmed trees, and abundance of flowers, there were dragons. He couldn't be sure how many slunk about but it didn't take more than one to put him on edge.

He'd already seen at least three and reminded himself of those they had rescued from the island who Amythist had escorted home and taken under her wing like the others they'd liberated from the tech-nomages.

One of them scratched itself under an old oak tree. The other two fought over the carcass of something so large, he thought it might have been a moose.

"My skekleton!" one of the dragons growled in what almost sounded like a toddler's mispronunciation.

"Fine! My meat!" said the other, thus demonstrating which of the two had been rescued earlier and been under Amythist's tutelage longer.

"I saw a young stag in the north forest," Amythist told the two dragons as she ambled through her garden toward Larry and Stonequest, who was still in his dragon body.

"Eww. Who likes stag? This skeleton looks much better!" the

second dragon said. A female, Larry judged, based on her voice and the line of her neck.

The first, a young male who seemed to share the sentiment, bit all the more viciously on the carcass. The female—seemingly disgruntled—flew off.

"That's how you let them settle fights?" Larry asked. "They'll learn might makes right."

"Ah, but you see, Silverwing *likes* stag. She was manipulating Emberbelly into not following her."

He nodded because he'd seen human children pull the same trick a thousand times. "But these aren't children."

Amythist's smile, bright until this moment, wilted like one of her flowers. "No, they are not. Emotionally and intellectually, though, they're not much brighter than children. They were stunted by their lives in captivity. My only hope is to educate them and thus give them a life."

"But they were robbed of their childhood," he said.

"Ah, but dragons live much longer than humans do. If I can get these to mature a little, they could have millennia of fulfilling lives ahead of them. But come now, you didn't tell me what you needed on the phone, only that you needed pixies. What has the Steel Dragon done that she requires the help of my fickle little friends?"

"Can't you summon your pets and we'll tell them?" Stonequest said.

"Pixies are not pets, no matter what some dragons think they are," she snapped and revealed some of the fire that had once earned her the nickname "mage eater." "They are powerful beings in their own right and deserve as much respect as anyone. You must give it to them if you wish them to show it to you."

"Oh, come on. We're both talking about pixies, right? Like, the little guys who will shoot sparks in your drink at parties? They've never shown me any respect." Stonequest sounded bemused as he took his human form.

"But if all you expect is sparks, that is all you will get."

"We have something way bigger than sparks," Larry said. "And not much time to explain it. Can you ask them to come? I haven't seen any in here."

"Just because you cannot see a pixie does not mean they are not around," Amythist said enigmatically.

"All right, so you're saying they can hear us now." The mage paused and played back what he'd said in his head. There was a fair amount to work through. He hoped it had all been good. To Stonequest's credit, the dragon at least looked embarrassed about his remark about the sparks.

"So, you came to see some pixies?" said an extremely high-pitched voice from deep inside a shrub covered in yellow flowers.

"We did, er…ma'am. I think we need your help," Larry replied to the bush.

From deep within the tangle of branches, leaves, and flowers, what had to be the world's largest beetle buzzed out to hover in front of his nose. Except it wasn't a beetle. It had the hard, iridescent purple-and-green carapace of a beetle and the same long, clunky wings, but instead of six prickly legs, it had human arms and legs. In fact, its body didn't seem to be a beetle at all, more like a human wearing a beetle, which somehow made sense to Larry's troubled brain. Its face was undeniably beautiful, he had to admit, and the only odd feature was the too-large eyes. Still, even seeing the pixie, he was no surer of its gender or if it even had one for that matter.

"Well, you could start by not addressing me as an old lady!" the beetle pixie huffed.

"Sorry, sir," he said, a little startled because he'd never realized he could find men, pixies, and even beetles attractive.

"I'm not a man!" the creature huffed.

"Jewel, please, these men need your help," Amythist said with a sly wink at Larry.

"But you said—"

"I said don't call me ma'am." Jewel squealed with laughter. "That doesn't mean I'm a boy. You humans! You don't understand anything about us." More laughter followed. It was high and tinkling like the sound of bells. He decided he rather liked it.

Stonequest, however, did not seem so amused. "We came because we think pixies did something to our friends."

"Well, they probably deserved it." She laughed with genuine amusement and another bell tinkled along with her. Larry saw that another pixie had darted over. This one seemed to have the wings of some kind of fly.

"What did your friends do to the pixies?" the newcomer asked.

"Our friends have vanished," Stonequest explained. "One minute they were in a base, a fire tornado created by a mage and a dragon struck, and then they were gone."

"It sounds like a good thing," the fly pixie joked. Jewel laughed so hard she almost fell out of the air.

"What does this have to do with pixies?" she asked. "It sounds more like dragon and mage boring stuff, blah blah blah. All you guys ever do is blah blah blah, but you never ask pixies for anything except party favors. Did you know Lady Amythist asks us to pollinate her garden? We would never do something so perverse out in the open but we asked the bees to do it. No one else asks us a thing."

"But that's not true!" Stonequest snarled. "Pixies were at these peace talks."

"Is that right?" the fly asked.

"It is," Larry interjected before the dragon could completely ruin any chance they had at getting help. "In fact, we think those pixies did something to make our friends vanish. My guess is that they tried to cast some kind of protection spell."

"Pixies don't use spells," Jewel said matter of factly.

"Okay, sure," he agreed amicably. "See, that's why we need your help. I'm telling you, the wild magic pouring off this the crater had to be from a pixie. I think something went wrong and made our friends vanish."

"So what?" the fly asked.

"Yeah, so what?" Jewel repeated.

"So what, chicken butt?" her companion asked and she fell into giggles.

"Well, I thought that since this was pixie magic gone awry, you pixies could fix it," the mage said.

"It's not our problem, though," the male muttered.

"Not really at all," she echoed. "Pixies do things all the time that have nothing to do with me. Why, only last week, a pixie in Australia did something."

"What did he do, Jewel?" the fly asked.

"How am I supposed to know? He was in Australia!" Both pixies collapsed with laughter, which could prove to be fortuitous as it might have saved Stonequest the effort.

"I knew this would be a waste of time!" the stone dragon fumed. "Pixies, *pah!* What have you ever done for anyone but yourselves?"

"About as much as anyone else has done for us," Jewel retorted and flew directly at his face.

The dragon's reflexes were such that he easily intercepted the pixie. He didn't catch her, however. Instead, her body broke into a thousand tiny sparks that flurried around his hand before they flared into his face with the sound of firecrackers.

The fly, not to be outdone, darted around the dragon's back and used the moment to give him an honest to God wedgie.

"I will turn those two into party décor!" Stonequest fumed, but Larry put a hand on his shoulder and managed to stop him. Not that he could have done anything to the creatures. Both of them—their pranks accomplished—had streaked away into the garden and vanished into hedges. They were gone.

"I told you to treat them with respect." Amythist shook her head.

"Can't you make them come back?" Stonequest asked.

"I can't make them do anything. Your failure to recognize this point is why they left."

"But they might still be here, right?" Larry asked. They couldn't fail. Not like this. Not with so much riding on these bizarre little creatures.

Amythist shrugged.

The mage turned to the garden, tried to locate one of the pixies, and failed. They could be anywhere. In a tangle of weeds, hidden inside a bush, or hiding underneath a bunch of roots—anywhere.

"I knew this was a waste of time," the stone dragon muttered.

"Can you stop with the negativity for a second?" Larry asked him. "Let's go."

"Give me a minute," he said, glad his companion was at least outwardly controlling his temper.

"Pixies, I don't know if you can hear me, but if you can, please listen. I know your kind has been given the short end of the stick, so to speak. You've never been a part of society, and that's not fair. But look, Kristen Hall—that's the Steel Dragon, if you've heard of her—admitted twelve of your kind to the peace talks so the pixies would be represented. But now, she and these twelve of your kind have gone missing. I don't think we'll be able to get them back without your help. So, if it's not too much to ask, could you please help us?"

Jewel reappeared in a flurry of sparks. "We'll do it!"

"Really?" Larry asked. He had thought his speech was all right but had expected it to start a dialogue, not end the conversation.

"We've never heard such kind words before," she said. "And to think you said it twice! Now, what did you want us to do?"

"I...wait, what word are you talking about?" he asked, confused.

"Please. You said please," the fly told him and tinkled with laughter.

"They weren't even listening," Stonequest muttered.

Larry darted him a look that he'd never given a dragon before. Previously, it had been reserved for small children whose parents refused to reprimand them for throwing rocks in the playground. Thank goodness his teammate merely rolled his eyes and shut up.

"They heard what they never had before, isn't that right?" Larry said to the pixies.

"Exactly! Most people simply dismiss us, or order us around, or try to trade us things we don't even understand like green paper with old dead people on it. You are the first person who has ever said please." She was glowing.

"Well, I gotta say it wasn't exactly my idea," he said, hoping this would work. "I learned that kind of respect from Kristen—the dragon who is in trouble right now. She was the one who invited the pixies inside. She fights for equality and now, she needs your help."

"I don't know..." the fly said dubiously.

"Please consider it," Larry continued, not afraid to use the first magic word he'd ever learned. "Just think, of all the dragons you have ever known, how many have given pixies an equal seat at a discussion of real importance?"

It didn't take them long to answer. "No one has. Never never never. Not even Amythist and she's the nicest dragon we know."

The old dragon smiled indulgently at the little creatures. "I am sorry, but we have been over this. I will not tear my cottage down so I can plant a grove of willow trees."

"See!" Jewel said, although at least she no longer sounded frustrated.

"Well, the Steel Dragon has," the mage continued in an attempt to seal the deal. He knew pixies enough to know he could not truly count on their help until they were in Detroit and doing what they needed to do. But he could not lose momentum, not now. "Kristen believes that all living beings are worthy of respect. Dragons, humans, mages, dwarves, and pixies are all at the peace talks. I cannot imagine that it's easy for her to get all those different viewpoints to work together or agree on much of anything, but she's trying. And now, she needs your help."

"She does sound rad," Jewel nodded.

"Freaking rad indeed," the fly added.

"But it still sounds tricky. They disappeared? Maybe that's good. Maybe they went somewhere more fun."

"Somewhere with tons of flowers."

"And bugs!"

"And chocolate!"

"Yeah, chocolate!"

"I suppose that's possible," he said, somewhat terrified by how quickly these odd little beings could get off track. "But if she doesn't come back—if she *dies*—then her voice dies as well. Since I've met her, she's worked to make the world a better place. She's worked to make our world one of real equality. If she dies, I don't know if we'll be able to find someone like her to help again."

"I guess even if she went to the flower, buggy, chocolate dimension, she couldn't help here," Jewel said and sounded serious for the first time.

"Wait, is that a real place?" Stonequest asked.

"That's irrelevant." The mage elbowed him in the ribs. "What matters is that she'll be gone from here. And if she is, the voice for equality will be silenced. She's the first person to value pixie life. Without her... I don't know what to think."

"What's in it for you?" the fly asked and studied the stone dragon.

"He—" Larry tried to answer but the pixies darted about until he shut up. They settled to look at Stonequest.

"Honestly?" the dragon asked.

The pixies nodded.

"Kristen is my friend. She's one of the most amazing people, dragons, and cops I've ever met. Losing her would be bad for these peace talks, but it would be even worse for me. She's changed my life."

"You *like* her!" Jewel giggled.

"What? No!" he protested.

"We'll do it!" the pixies beamed.

"Great! Thank you so much," Larry said quickly.

"Of course!" the pixies responded as if they hadn't spent way too long trying to convince the flighty little creatures.

"If you'll follow us," Larry said as Stonequest transformed into his dragon shape and Larry climbed on his back.

"I will, I will," Jewel said.

"Uh...Fly Guy?" Larry looked at the other one.

"Oh, my gosh, please call me that forever!" the newly named Fly Guy gushed. "I have some very important stuff to do first." In an instant, he was gone.

Larry felt their chances begin to evaporate. He could not see what one pixie could possibly do against the wild magic he had sensed where the base should be.

But there was nothing he could do now.

"Would you like a ride?" Stonequest asked the pixie.

"Yes, please!" Jewel chirped, flew to his back, and sat in front of Larry.

The flight was a frantic one. Both Larry and Stonequest were afraid that every minute spent was another chance to save Kristen and everyone else gone forever. But at least the pixie didn't make them slow their pace. In fact, she made it very clear she hadn't *needed* a ride. She sat on the dragon's back when it suited her, but she spent as much time flitting around Larry's head as if they were back in the garden. And yet she never lost pace, nor was she ever bothered by the wind. Their wild magic did seem to make them creatures not of this world. Larry hoped that would be enough to help.

But, as much as he wanted to hope, he simply did not see how one pixie would be able to unravel this mess.

After what felt like a lifetime—although he knew was merely a long few minutes—they entered the airspace over Detroit. Despite knowing exactly what had happened there and that no one could have fixed it in the time they were gone, it still felt like a knife to his gut to see the destruction.

The fire tornado had done far more than try and fail to swallow Kristen's base. It had destroyed entire streets, incinerated houses that had stood for a hundred years, and toppled skyscrapers. The rampant power had all but destroyed the city. What remained resembled a wasteland more convincing and thorough than any Larry had ever seen in any film. It was a nightmare now, and somehow, he was supposed to find hope in this barren and fire-burned landscape.

"Wow. I have to say, this place is fucked," the pixie said. "That's the word, right?"

"It sure is," he said without humor.

They descended and landed near the giant pit where the base had been. Lumos was in his dragon form and flew loops around the area. His eyes scanned the now blue sky for enemies, and he seemed to reach out with his talons and tail as if he might be able to brush against the vanished base.

Amy sat cross-legged and levitated a few feet above the ground.

Her nose was bleeding and her hair whipped in an unseen, unfelt wind. Larry could tell by her expression that even with her formidable magic skills, she hadn't been able to locate their missing friends.

He climbed off Stonequest's back. The pixie hovered close to him. Stonequest took to the air as mage and pixie approached the vanished base.

"Oh, no," Jewel said in what had to be the most disheartening start to a solution he had ever heard.

"What do you think?" he asked, hoping—praying—that there was more to the pixie's assessment.

"You were right." She nodded. "I can sense wild magic here that was channeled through a pixie. They were sent to another dimension."

"Is there any chance it was the chocolaty flower dimension?" he asked.

"Oh no, not at all. The energy I sense here is not the good kind."

"But you can do something about it, right?"

"By myself?" The stream of giggles that came from the pixie's mouth was in no way encouraging. "Oh, no way, you silly human. I will most certainly not be able to do anything about this on my own."

"What if we help?" Amy asked, stood from her meditative float, and wiped the blood from her nose. She was too pale and had been pushing herself too hard while he was gone. Not that he was surprised.

Jewel shook her head. "You humans need too much rational thought to work your kind of magic. Pixie magic is different. You won't be able to help. I'm so sorry."

"So we're simply supposed to give up because Fly Guy had more important stuff to do?" Larry tried to control his tone but it was damn hard. He'd thought they had a chance, but it seemed they'd failed yet again.

"Yeah, that sums it up. Maybe you should take a nap until he's done," Jewel said. "You humans do that, right? Nap?"

"I will not *nap* right now. Not with my friends in danger."

"There's nothing else for you to do, I'm sorry," she said.

"Well, can't you try something?" Larry asked. "Please?"

"There'd be no point," she said. "I'm sorry. I truly am. Even with a hundred pixies, this would be extremely difficult."

"Then it's a good thing I brought one hundred and one."

Fly Guy appeared in a shower of sparks and buzzed around Larry's head.

"Fly Guy?" the mage asked and tried to wrap his head around the surprise arrival. "I thought you had important stuff to do?"

"I did! I had to gather a group to help."

Pixies appeared from the sky above them, from cracks in the pavement, and from the river they could barely see through the destruction. Some crawled along the earth like roly-polies, while others flew using bug wings. A few jumped like grasshoppers.

"I think it could be the Ink," Jewel said.

"That feels right to me," Fly Guy replied.

"Plus, I think the place they made is diminishing in size."

"Equidistant points or groups?"

"Equidistant points, I would think. Let's stick to a circle, though, rather than trying to make a sphere. The last thing we want is for their space to come back twisted on one of the axes of reality," Jewel said.

"That can get messy," Fly Guy agreed and buzzed off to issue the orders.

The two pixies talked so fast and with such attention to detail that Larry had trouble reconciling them with the same silly beings they had found fluttering in Amythist's garden.

"Do you think you can bring them back?" he asked, daring to hope again.

"We'll try," Jewel said grimly. "But honestly, Fly Guy should have brought more pixies. We don't have time to gather any others, though."

"What will you do?"

In response, the creatures began to sing.

CHAPTER FIFTY-FOUR

Kristen had hoped that the dragon-form tests would have proven something, but as far as she could tell, they didn't. The mages disagreed. They thought it was quite interesting that while their powers continually diminished, the dragons' were largely unaffected. Their aura powers were almost gone—this brought great dismay to Heartsbane, of course, who largely relied on them—but to the rest of the dragons, this was a small sacrifice.

In the space of a few hours, the mages had their powers whittled away while the dragon's strength and healing abilities seemed unaffected. The mages attributed this to dragons fueling their magic from their bodies. Their magic was *baked in*, so to speak, while mages had to channel it every time.

But Kristen found it all fairly tedious. What mattered was that her powers were not diminished, so she could still fight. But, on the other side of the coin, neither were Lord Boneclaw's. He had lurked in his corner of the base and watched the dragons run their tests for the last hour. Even when she had stood to pass food and water out, the Councilor hadn't moved. He smiled constantly at her like he already knew the outcome of these meetings while everyone else had to keep guessing.

Still, he hadn't done anything so it wasn't like she could simply attack him, even if he was being weird. That would be wrong, although he certainly deserved it. But that didn't make bringing him food and water any more pleasant.

"Here, a dozen water bottles," she said and gave the water bottles to one of the warrior dragons. "Someone should be over soon with six MREs, and a dwarf will serve beef. Hey, where is Shimmerclaw?"

She only counted eleven dragons. The Council leader was missing.

"I haven't seen her in a while," Decimus Aurelius said. "I thought you sent her on some errand?"

"I did, but that was ages ago," Kristen said and her gaze flicked to Lord Boneclaw, who continued to watch her.

"I have not seen her," Lady Jade said. "Nor did she participate in the tests."

"That's right," she said when she thought about the dragons who had transformed. "Lord Boneclaw, you didn't participate either, correct?"

"Correct," he said with a wicked grin. "Although you will find my powers are no more diminished than any of the dragons." He said it kindly enough, but she couldn't help but read it as a threat. In fact, she'd be a fool to interpret it as anything else.

"The food will be here in a few minutes," she said to excuse herself. Thinking about it, she hadn't seen Shimmerclaw since she'd been down below. Was she still timing the shrinking of the blackness? She decided to check.

As she crossed the room, she found she had a shadow. Constance was following her.

"I just realized that Lady Shimmerclaw has not returned from when she went below to investigate." The technomage kept her voice low, obviously not wanting the information to spread.

"I'm sure she's paying way too much attention to detail," Kristen said but her voice lacked confidence.

"But of course, and yet I feel I should come downstairs with you all the same."

She glanced at where Lord Boneclaw had been seated but she could not see him. The darkness in that corner was too thick.

They descended the stairway into the darkness of the lightless tunnels beneath the base. Halfway down the steps, when the lights from the torches and magical effects above faded, Constance ignited an orb of glowing light.

They walked through the intersection of the hallways, leaving both the storage area and the armory behind as they ventured deeper beneath the earth. When they reached the door of the bunker section of the basement, the door was closed.

"That's odd," Constance said. "I wonder why she closed it."

"Maybe she didn't want anyone to see her counting on her fingers," she joked but in the darkness, the humor felt flat and fake.

The technomage pushed the door open.

At first, they saw nothing but darkness. The void had moved farther into the bunker, but the light could not pierce it any more than it could before. Shimmerclaw was not visible. She was not in any corner of the room, nor was she near the void or hiding from it. Kristen was about to suggest they check the other parts of the basement when she saw her—or what was left of her.

"Oh, dear God," Constance said as she sent her light orb above the partial corpse of the dragon. The void had already swallowed both of Shimmerclaw's legs, most of her torso, and one of her arms.

It had not, however, swallowed the upper portion of her chest where two bullet holes revealed her cause of death.

"She was murdered," the woman said, her voice heavy with dread. "But by whom? She had enemies in every delegation. I don't think the dwarves would use such a weapon, but humans would seek such an advantage, as would my mages." She shook her head in despair.

"Wait a minute—look at her hand," Kristen said. It looked as if whoever had shot Shimmerclaw hadn't finished the job. Her hand was human no longer but had transformed into a dragon claw. In it, she grasped a bone—no, not grasped, but used it to point back in the direction from which they had entered. She was pointing to her attacker.

"Is it a clue?" Constance asked.

She was way ahead of the technomage. Of course Shimmerclaw hadn't died easily. She had used the last of her strength to share this message in a way that she knew Kristen of all people would understand. In her claw, she held a bone.

Boneclaw.

Lord Boneclaw did this.

Which meant that even if he wasn't the Masked One, he was still a murderer.

"Lord Boneclaw did it," she said. "That's what that means. She must have confronted him and accused him of starting the war."

"But how did he get a weapon? We searched everyone before we got in here."

"It must be one of ours." Kristen slapped her forehead with her palm. "When the power failed, I assumed the weapons would be safe because the vault needs electricity to work but of course, the Masked One can simply move through shadow. Oh, dear God, I've been so stupid."

"Come on. Let us try to bind him," Constance said.

She desperately wanted to agree. Better yet, she wanted to batter Boneclaw's face in, but she'd rushed into so many situations before. Sometimes, it worked out well but often, it didn't. "I don't know if now is the time," she hedged, as much as she hated saying it.

"What? Why not? At least now he can't run away!" The technomage was already pulling magic into a vortex of wind.

"That's true, but I don't know if we can beat him here," she said. She hated this fucking situation so goddamn much. "I can't take my dragon form here. All the training I've done with Lumos…it would all be for nothing."

"You'll have the advantage in your human form."

"I don't know. He can turn to *shadow*, Constance. You haven't fought him like I have. It's not easy."

"But together, surely—"

"Your powers are diminished, aren't they?"

The woman clenched her teeth. "They are."

"Maybe if we could get the rest of the mages to help?" she asked.

Constance shook her head. She looked as pissed as Kristen felt. "No. No, that's not wise. The bubble of magic sheltering them is fragile and weakening. If all the mages used our powers…I wouldn't want to risk shattering this bubble."

"Shit!" she said. "Then we have to wait. We can't take him here, not with all this darkness."

"You don't think he planned it all this way, do you?" The techno-mage sounded so morose it was almost contagious.

"No, he couldn't have. The fire tornado must have been his doing, but to plan all this he needed to plan for the pixies, and I don't see how he could have."

"They are flippant little things, aren't they?" Constance said with a weak smile.

"They are, which means the Masked One could not have planned all this. He probably saw an opportunity to assassinate Shimmerclaw and used it. Goddammit! This is why that asshole's been staring at me."

"Still, we are agreed. We wait?" Constance asked again.

She nodded. While she hated it, she nodded.

Although what they saw next would almost break her resolve.

In the hallway on the way to the armory, they saw Boneclaw's other victim. They almost missed the body as it was beyond the door and as far into the darkness as anything could be.

It was a macabre sight to see a human body with its head severed and the skin shucked and tossed aside like a banana peel.

Worse still was the name on the nametag. Kristen didn't want it to matter. She wanted to feel the same pain for all the people on her team.

But finding Jim Washington's corpse hurt far more than she could have possibly imagined.

"I will kill that son of a bitch," she roared.

"No, Kristen, now is not the time."

"I fucking mean it, Constance. How could he kill *Jim?*"

"He will pay. We'll make him pay. But we talked about this. I'm not at my full strength and there's too much darkness here. He probably left the body here to piss you off."

Kristen tried to calm but it felt like an impossible task. The Masked One had murdered Shimmerclaw and Jim in cold blood in the place where they were supposed to come to a consensus of fairness. He had not only intentionally jeopardized the talks, but he'd also killed any people who might stand in his way. Still, Constance was right. No doubt, he did this so she would attack him unprovoked.

"We have to get out of this fucking bubble," she snapped.

"Agreed," the technomage said. "But until we do, you'll wait."

"I'll try," she said. "But if that asshole so much as looks at me wrong—"

"If something happens, I'll have your back, but we can't let him look like a victim. We have to prove that he did this and have him hung for it—or whatever it is dragons do to each other."

"Yes. Good," she said aloud so maybe she would believe her own words. "Boneclaw will be the first dragon, mage, dwarf, human, or pixie tried in the courts we set up."

"He'll be an example," Constance said.

"Okay. Okay. This fucking sucks but okay. Jesus, how the fuck did he get a gun? I don't even have a fucking gun right now."

"Your armory? Can we go there and arm ourselves?" Constance asked. She was thankful for her companion's cool head.

"The problem is that the armory is set up to keep everyone out in the event of a power outage. I can't get in there. He could because he can turn into a fucking shadow but…goddammit!" Merely the thought of losing Jim was almost too much to bear. Even in his death, he had made sure to take care of her.

"What, Kristen? What is it?"

"Jim planned for this," Kristen muttered and stormed down the hallway toward the room filled with supplies. Constance followed and created another orb that drifted after the Steel Dragon as she moved.

She opened the door to the supply room and looked through all the food, rations, cots, medical equipment, and everything else that was left. Finally, she found it—a crate labeled *CANNED CURED SAUSAGES*.

"Are you planning on…stress eating?" the technomage asked.

Her face set and grim, she ripped the wooden lid off the crate. The nails keeping it shut presented no real resistance for her steel fingers. Inside were six handguns and two hundred dragon scale bullets. She loaded the magazine of her gun, tucked it in her waistband, and gave another to Constance.

"Do you have a plan?" the woman asked.

"We go upstairs as discreetly as possible. We get Heartsbane, Decimus Aurelius, Alp the dwarf, and the German Ambassador since he seems the most trigger happy, and we tell them to come down here one by one. Once we're all armed, we announce the murder and the suspect once we have the Masked One surrounded. Even he can't dodge six bullets fired at him at once."

"Are you sure about that?" Constance asked. "Can we honestly stop him with guns?"

"No. I have no fucking idea," she said. "But I will not go quietly into the dark. I will not let this void eat me while that bastard continues to walk free. Maybe you should tell the mages to ready those light orbs."

"Okay. Give me a half-hour and I'll see who I can get to help. You talk to the people you want to arm and I'll get mages."

"All right. Here we fucking go."

Both women left the supply room and hurried down the dark hallway toward the main room of the base where the others were gathered.

They never made it.

Lord Boneclaw waited for them at the top of the stairs.

CHAPTER FIFTY-FIVE

"Six against one. That might have made this a fair fight," Lord Boneclaw smiled before he vanished into the dark.

"Constance, don't let him go to shadow!" Kristen shouted.

The technomage hurled her ball of light to where he had been, but he was already gone.

He reappeared behind Kristen and laughed.

She turned to steel and tried to punch him, but she faltered.

It wasn't his face she saw, or not all of it anyway. He wore a human skull over the top of his face so only his weak jaw and heartless eyes could be seen. She knew he hadn't had it when he came in, which could only mean one thing.

"That's Jim!" She gasped.

"It *was*," Boneclaw admitted and dodged her sloppy punch easily. He made his leg vanish into shadow and reappear to tangle with hers. It didn't take much of a shove to send her tumbling down the stairs.

But as Kristen fell, she saw that Constance was still at the top of the stairs, a ball of light at the ready. She hurled it at the Masked One.

It had no effect and simply flashed in his face, and the ancient dragon laughed. "If light could defeat me, I would not be the dragon I became," he said and rushed to her with a burst of speed.

She was ready for him, though. The technomage had gone toe to toe with Kristen a few times and she knew how to fight. She could use magic to augment her muscles and give her greater speed and strength. While it was diminished, she still had enough to do that now and she pushed herself to match Boneclaw's insanely fast dragon strikes.

But as she tried to keep up, the light orb she had been powering began to fade and it soon winked out completely.

Kristen heard her body thunk down the stairs when the dragon overpowered her.

"Constance, you have to get up. Constance!" She shook the woman's unconscious body. Thankfully, the mage surfaced and ignited another orb light. It was smaller, though, and less bright than it had been.

She put herself between Boneclaw—the Masked One—and the technomage. "Why? Why do all this now? You might never escape."

"I guess that's part of it," he said. It was hard not to think of him as the Masked One when she looked at the bloody skull he wore. "I didn't want to die with all of you thinking that Lord Boneclaw was behind all this. That was merely an alias, a mask. This is who I am and this is who will destroy you." He sauntered down the stairs as if he were about to attend a gala.

Kristen raised her gun and shot him.

His laughter came from everywhere. It came from the pools of shadow hiding at each step, from the darkness behind the concrete pillars and even from her footprints. Her bullets had done nothing. They could do nothing to his shadow form.

"Constance, we need to get above!" she shouted.

"That would be useful, wouldn't it?" their adversary replied from the darkness and sucker-punched her in the gut. A human would have been dead. Even most dragons would have doubled over in pain, but she was the Steel Dragon. Her steel abs caught the blow and prevented the air from being forced from her lungs.

She threw an elbow down and tried to drive it into the back of his head. She connected but only succeeded in cracking the skull—Jim's skull—and knocking it aside.

"That was a new one, you stupid bitch," he said as he vanished. A clawed hand reappeared from the dark and grasped her by the throat, lifted her from the ground, and strangled her.

But the light orb hovered above them and Kristen could see the Masked One's torso and head connected to his body. She swung a steel foot and kicked him in the side of the head hard enough to make him release her.

"We have to get upstairs!" she shouted to Constance.

The mage nodded and made sure to not let the light orb she had used to make the Masked One solid dissipate. They moved back to back and inched up the steps while he tried to attack them.

Together, they were barely able to hold him back. The light was enough to force him to become solid, which allowed Kristen to strike. Most of the time, he simply moved away but she landed a few blows, which unfortunately didn't seem to hurt him at all.

He was incredibly fast. Any time Constance's orb created a point of darkness that was too close, he slid inside it and lashed out with a claw or the barb of his tail.

Still, they made progress.

Step by step, they pushed up the stairs.

Finally, they were at the top. Kristen grabbed the door and pulled it open.

In that brief moment of distraction, the Masked One shoved one of his bone-clawed hands through Constance's gut.

She shrieked in pain but it was cut short by what sounded like a ruptured lung.

"You bastard!" Kristen screamed.

He lifted the mage, his claw still embedded where he'd punched her, and hurled her into the darkness.

"She's not dead," he said. "But she will be. Do you go down there to save her and risk me finishing your pathetic life off in the dark, or do you leave her to die and go ask your friends for help?"

"I will kill you. Do you understand that?" She used every ounce of speed and strength she had, but it wasn't enough. Despite her efforts, she could not hit what was not there. She could not punch a shadow or choke a silhouette of darkness. Frustrated, she maintained her offensive but her fists found nothing, while Boneclaw hid in the blackness and was able to test her steel skin for weakness.

After a minute of feeling like a child fighting a monster she couldn't see, Kristen sensed a blow directed at her face and she managed to block it barely in time. A moment later, she would have been blind for life and not only because of the dark.

"This is what you do, isn't it? You don't fight and simply try to weaken and terrify. You truly are nothing but a shadow." She hissed her disgust.

"A shadow with claws," Boneclaw said and struck with such ferocity that bloody gashes opened on her steel back.

She cursed and acknowledged that she couldn't defeat him down there. They both knew it, and it meant she had to leave Constance while she went to get help.

Her decision made, she turned swiftly and yanked the door open behind her. The Masked One used the opportunity to stab her in the back of the knee. The pain was intense, but the welcome flood of light coming into the room from above took away the sting.

"Shimmerclaw is dead!" she yelled into the room. "Everyone get into cover. The Masked One—"

"Is who made the void!" Lord Boneclaw shouted from the other side of the room.

Kristen's jaw dropped in disbelief. "No...no, Lord Boneclaw is the Masked One."

"But he's right here!" Lady Jade said and gestured to him. "What is this about Shimmerclaw being dead?"

"She was murdered," Kristen repeated. "So was Jim. Constance is down there too and she needs help. If any of you mages can heal, please hurry. You can't believe him. Lord Bone—"

But before she could reply, a shadow claw thrust out from the darkness of the subterranean floors behind her and hurled her across the room.

"It *is* the Masked One!" Decimus Aurelius shouted and moved toward the attacking limb, but it was already gone.

"What is this?" Emil Lord, the mage scholar demanded. "You dragons brought violence."

"It is one of us who was killed," Lady Jade pointed out.

"Please, this is what he wants," Kristen said before a tail emerged from another inky pool and knocked her across the room.

"Enough of this!" Minestrength bellowed.

He was catapulted into a wall by the shadow dragon.

All the dwarves pushed to their feet, ready to fight. "You dragons always were against us," one of them shouted.

"No, please," Kristen protested.

But it was too late. One of the dwarves attacked one of the dragon warriors, who defended himself with a flaming sword. The sparks that flew from the strike of the blade lit the coat of one of the human ambassadors on fire, who yelled to the mages for help. The mages began to launch balls of energy at the dragons, who deflected them with their swords.

It looked as if it would turn into a mage and dwarf battle against the dragons, but as the mages readied their power, the void outside the room began to shake and tremble. This prompted the dwarves to yell at the mages to stop, who of course ignored them.

Panicked, the dwarves attacked them too and turned the shrinking room into a three-way free for all. Dragons, mages, and dwarves fought each other indiscriminately. The humans tried to stay out of the way. Her security team tried to intervene, but most of them were human. They couldn't do anything to a mage, let alone against the inhuman strength of a dwarf or dragon.

"No, please!" she shouted. The room was now filled with dancing shadows. No one attempted to keep any orbs or flames in consistent places, so the darkness ebbed and flowed, disappeared and reappeared in random places.

And from it, the Masked One attacked Kristen.

Every new pool of darkness that appeared near her seemed to contain him. He struck her with claw after claw, focused on her joints, her neck, and everywhere that Lumos had shown her to be the weak points on a dragon and now transferred to her human body.

She attempted to fight back, but he was too elusive and too fast. It was as Constance had said. This was *his* battlefield. The darkness, the close quarters, and even the chaos of the brawl that now unfolded around them was to *his* advantage. She could not defeat him there. In all honesty, she wasn't sure she could beat him anywhere but knew it wouldn't happen in a corner of a bloody brawl.

Once she'd accepted that realization, she stopped fighting.

While the Masked One continued his attacks, she moved to the center of the room and what was left of the stage. He did not simply let her stroll toward it, of course. He struck her from the shadows of dwarves and from behind and around magical attacks from the mages. His onslaughts pushed her into dragon warriors and shoved her in the ways of spells.

But Kristen soldiered on. She had no other choice and had to get there. The fighting could not be allowed to continue.

As she stumbled forward, she watched the chaos all around her. The dragon warriors gave the mages their all. It took everything their opponents had simply to hold them back. Shimmering shields in different shades of blue tried to absorb and stop the raw brutality of the dragon's blows, but it required immense effort and power.

Even more ominous was the fact that every time a dragon struck the shield of a mage, the void outside rippled. Kristen could almost see the pixies absorbing every one of these blows in their bodies. The tiny creatures still tried to keep the powers both outside and inside the sphere they had created from ripping this bubble of safety apart.

The dwarves tried to help against the dragons, but they did little more than fight to a standstill, which benefited the Masked One. Every second gained was a second closer to him destroying them all.

Finally, Kristen reached the stage. She was bleeding in a dozen different places, her blood a vibrant shade of crimson as it trickled over her steel skin.

"I challenge Lord Boneclaw to a duel!" she shouted at the top of her lungs.

For a moment, nothing happened—or, more accurately, nothing changed. Many things continued to happen as dragons, mages, and dwarves tried to beat the shit out of each other.

"Lady Jade," Kristen bellowed and managed to catch the woman's attention, although it didn't make her loosen the chokehold she now had on a dwarf. "I challenge Lord Boneclaw to a duel! Will you officiate?"

The dragon vaulted upward and turned into what was quite possibly the sexiest dragon body Kristen had ever seen. She breathed green fire, which did an excellent job of making everyone stop fighting. It also highlighted how close the sphere of darkness had come. Already, it had cut corners of the building off. The roof above them was still intact, but it wouldn't be long before it was damaged even more and it tumbled onto them—if it wasn't swallowed by the void first.

"On what grounds?" the jade dragon demanded.

"He's the Masked One."

"That is simply preposterous," Lady Jade replied.

"He killed Lady Shimmerclaw," she said.

"That is no cause for a duel," Lord Boneclaw replied and walked toward her as if he had not attacked her from the shadows this entire time.

"He's right, Lady Steel. That is an issue for our courts to decide."

"Fine, then. According to dragon law, he killed one of my people. I demand a duel as payment."

"You can't prove a thing," Lord Boneclaw said.

"Remove your hood and let people see the ring of blood around your head. It's human blood. Jim's blood."

"Lord Boneclaw, if you please, remove your hood and disprove this nonsense," Lady Jade said.

"I will do no such thing," he replied and stepped into the middle of the room. All the mages and dwarves stepped back and he was left standing in a ring of dragon warriors.

"The blood is proof," Kristen replied. "You can disprove my accusation by simply removing your hood."

"I will not debase myself with such a foolish act."

"Lord Boneclaw, your hood was down earlier," Lady Jade said. "Why do you refuse now? Your honor is at stake."

"Fine!" he roared and dragged his hood down. The dried, coagulated crown of blood was still there. "So I killed a human, so what? He tried to shoot me with a dragon bullet."

"Jim would never—"

"Oh, for fuck's sake. Should we ask him what happened?" Lord Boneclaw sneered. "Admit it—it's your word against mine. There's no proof either way."

"Which means the duel is valid," Lady Jade said. "This will be a duel of your human forms as there is no room to be dragons here."

Everyone else in the room shuffled into their respective corners, ready to watch a fight between two almost legendary dragons.

Kristen, still wounded and extremely weary, stepped down from the podium and entered the ring of spectators. She flexed, used what strength she had to heal her wounds, and wiped the blood away. It made sense to remove the evidence so he wouldn't have target points to deliver additional strikes to already weakened places.

Her adversary did nothing with his shadow powers. Instead, he revealed why Boneclaw was such a believable name for the dragon lord. He extended each forearm until they were twice their natural length. At the end of these, he transformed his fingertips into jagged claws that seemed to be thrice their original size. The skin seemed to peel away so it honestly looked as if she was about to duel with a man with literal bone claws. It wasn't a pleasant image.

But still, this was a duel between their human bodies and she might be able to win.

"The loser is whoever forfeits," Kristen said. "They'll be bound by a magical bracelet until they can be put on trial for Shimmerclaw's murder."

"And if neither of us gives up?" Boneclaw asked.

"Then the law is clear," Lady Jade said. "Neither of you will be tried for the death of the other. If you wish to quit, there is honor in that, but if you wish to push your very limits, no one here will stop you."

"As long as you don't bump into us!" a dwarf shouted, which did nothing to break the tension that lay so thickly in the room.

They joined in battle, entirely focused on one another.

Lord Boneclaw was furiously fast, a whirling, swirling vortex of bone and claws.

His strikes, however, fell on the hard steel of her skin. Sparks flew as she defended herself and looked for an opening. He increased his speed until she almost couldn't see him, but it cost him power and he hadn't yet managed to deliver a decisive strike. When he fought from the dark, he could attack with his full power but there, under the lights of dwarf torches and magical spheres, he was forced to use different tactics.

Kristen could beat him.

She let him come at her and his claws battered her shoulders and forearms until he extended himself too far. Ready for the small opportunity, she rocketed a steel fist into his gut with such force that he sprawled backward.

He was on his feet in a second and resumed his attack to scratch, claw, and try to stab her eyes, but she was steadfast. She waited for another opportunity, and when it presented itself, she head-butted him so hard in the face that it split the skin on his forehead.

Boneclaw landed hard and she strode up to him, put a steel foot on his chest, and crushed him beneath her weight.

The old dragon sneered at her as the wound on his forehead slowly healed, but the blood on his face did not go away. He tried to wipe it out of his eyes, but she applied more pressure.

"Surrender," Kristen said.

"Never." Boneclaw struggled beneath her.

"Everyone here heard you refuse. It means that if I kill you, I win. There will be no repercussions." She applied more pressure until she heard a rib crack.

"Foolish Steel Bitch," he wheezed as she leaned over him and made a critical mistake.

With the action, her body blocked the light that had fallen on him.

Despite the few torches and mage spheres, the only significant light came from above and her form eclipsed it.

Lord Boneclaw vanished and the crowd gasped.

"He is the Masked One," Lady Jade said, her voice suffused with dread.

"Of course I am." He reappeared behind Kristen and in the crowd itself. His tail lanced out and swept her feet out from under her.

The dwarves closest to where he had reappeared tried to catch him but in doing so, they dropped their torches, which had probably been what he wanted.

He struck her again from the shadow. When attacking in this way, his blows were insanely powerful as if he'd traveled at the speed of the darkness itself before he materialized to deliver his attack.

"Mages—light!" Emil Lord bellowed and nine mages responded by making their orbs glow brighter.

"No!" Kristen shouted as the increased light made Boneclaw rematerialize.

Above the base, the void moved closer. Its surface rippled as if each ball of light was a stone thrown into its placid surface.

"If you use too much magic, we'll pop this bubble and die!" she shouted.

"It's better if only the Steel Bitch dies," Boneclaw said and appeared from shadow as the mages dimmed their orbs. He punched Kristen across the jaw hard enough to make her spit blood. She tried to fight back, but in the chaos of the dropped torches and the now powerless mages, it was impossible.

Lord Boneclaw savaged her repeatedly and forced her to heal and use what dragon energy she had to simply stay alive. She tried to absorb his strikes as she had before, but now that he had given up any pretense of hiding what he was, he was too powerful, too fast, and too ruthless.

Still, she had to try. Jim deserved that and more.

She braced, let him pummel her shoulders, and when he drew back to slice at her neck, she threw a steel punch at him with every ounce of strength she had.

The Masked One caught her blow as if she were a child.

"It is a pity you couldn't put up more of a fight," he hissed into her ear as he dragged her close. "But if you find something out there in the void, I'm sure you'll come back to tell the rest of us."

He squeezed her fist so hard it broke the bones in her hand despite her steel skin. With a cruel smirk, he squeezed harder and pierced her hands with his bone claws to skewer her like a lamb shank. The pain was so intense that she let her steel skin drop involuntarily.

That was what Boneclaw must have wanted. As soon as she assumed her regular human skin, he flung her vertically by the hand he had caught with such force that it yanked the shoulder of that arm out of its socket and she careened upward.

She tried to transform into a dragon. Her wings could slow her assent, she thought, or maybe her steel form would be best.

But it was no use. She was too exhausted and powered through the roof of the base to avalanche broken concrete everywhere as she approached the void. At the speed she was going, there was no way to escape it. She would join Shimmerclaw and there wasn't shit she could do but try to stay conscious.

CHAPTER FIFTY-SIX

Amy watched the entire day go by and still, nothing had happened. The pixies continued to sing and they chanted and glowed as they surrounded the area where the base filled with her friends had been. They had started when the sun was overhead and the sky still blue in the aftermath of the firestorm.

Now, the sun was kissing the horizon. The sky was shifting from the washed-out blue of late afternoon to the richer purples of the evening. What clouds were still present glowed red and orange as if they wished to be ignited from within once more. Shadows grew all around them and danced here and there from small fires in the places the mages and dragons who had been tasked with defending Detroit had yet to put out.

She wondered if it might finally be time to help them set the city to rights. She'd remained with the ring of pixies and watched them faithfully as if her presence and her willingness to believe that they could rescue Kristen might be the edge they needed.

So far, nothing had happened.

Miserably, she sagged into a seated position. She lowered her face into her hands and began to cry. Sobs wracked her body as she began to contemplate what her future would look like without the Steel

Dragon. Maybe Lumos would take her on as a servant and at least that way, she wouldn't be hunted until she died. Maybe she could become a recluse.

A sob choked out and made her cough. It was too depressing to focus on that. She wiped her tears and told herself she needed to help extinguish the last of the fires, but when she opened her eyes, something had changed.

The pixies were glowing.

At first, it was only Jewel, but a moment later, another ignited in bright white light. The others mirrored them and each began to glow like stars in the sky at dusk.

"They're doing it!" the young mage shouted to no one in particular.

"Not…yet…" Jewel stopped singing long enough to groan.

Their vibrant bodies began to radiate more light and tendrils of it stretched from each pixie toward the others nearby. It looked as if they tried to grow a sphere of vines made of light over the missing base. It didn't seem to be enough, though. Despite the energy pouring off them, their grasping tendrils of light couldn't quite reach each other.

Out of nowhere, another pixie appeared. He simply flared into existence in a shower of sparks over Amy's head, glanced at his surroundings, and flew to the pixies and began to sing.

Another streaked over her shoulder, and another. They filled the spaces in the ring of pixies and added their voices and their light to the magic.

Others arrived within moments—ten more, twenty, thirty, fifty, a hundred.

"I've never seen so many in one place before," Lumos said as he landed beside Amy.

The tiny creatures continued to arrive until they were able to hold hands as they floated in a circle around the sphere. Beams of light darted from each of their singing mouths, up and over the sphere where the base had been until the entire area was cocooned in light.

Larry ran up, grinning as always. "Are you able to understand what the hell they're doing?"

She shook her head. "I can see it, but that's about it. Anytime I reach out—"

"It slips away. Yep. Me too. I can't trace the paths of energy they're using, but damn if this doesn't look like a spell to me. Some of what they're saying is words in languages and some of it sounds like music. I didn't know such a thing was possible."

"There!" Lumos pointed through the glowing sphere. The flashes and pops of lights were constantly distracting but Amy could see something that appeared to be the outline of where the building used to be. It looked like it was being carved from the light—no that wasn't right. It was more like it was being sanded out of the light. Like the pixies had channeled an enormous blob of pure energy and their voices and powers now brushed away all the extraneous pieces. With almost painful slowness, it gradually became more distinct.

At first, it was only the basic rectangular prism shape of any old warehouse before the windows were carved out of it, then the doors. The fixtures on the roof seemed to be gone or beyond the power of the pixies. Lines etched themselves in light to form the bricks of the building. The panes of glass on the windows became more visible and it was soon apparent that something had broken almost all of them.

A sonic boom and an enormous flash of light made her jump and the building was back. It hung in the sphere it had once filled for the briefest of moments before gravity caught hold and fell two feet into the hole with a loud crunch.

Amy gaped as her mind tried to accept the evidence of her eyes. The pixies had retrieved the base. It was damaged and seemed to be missing some corners, but it was there. Before the sonic boom had plowed through Detroit and shattered windows in its path, Kristen rocketed through the roof of her base and into the sky.

"Lumos!" the young mage shouted, but the dragon was already kneeling so she could climb aboard. She hopped up, using her magic to make her shoes give her extra lift, and landed on the dragon with him already in flight.

Kristen reached the peak of her ascent and began to plummet earthward.

"Kristen!" Amy shouted as Lumos pumped his wings and tried to close the gap.

The golden dragon was too slow, however, and he wouldn't make it. They were too far, and it took too long for a dragon to build speed.

Fortunately, they weren't only dependent on him to save Kristen.

She reached out with her magic and immediately felt the drain of everything she had done earlier but ignored it. Her powers caught hold of her friend and wrapped her in a net of magical shielding. Kristen did not respond and seemed to be unconscious.

But that didn't matter. Amy—as tired as she was—had caught her. She held her aloft until Lumos moved beneath her and let her fall onto the golden dragon's back. With her arms wrapped around her, she felt for her pulse and found it since the steel skin had failed to function.

"Thank goodness. She's all right," she shouted to the dragon.

"She is for now," he said.

She was about to ask what the hell he was talking about when she looked toward the base and saw the reason for his warning.

An enormous pool of shadow boiled out of the building below and transformed into a dragon as it rose. Its laughter was darker than any shadow.

CHAPTER FIFTY-SEVEN

"You need to get Kristen to safety. Get out of here, *now!*" Lumos shouted as he pumped his wings to gain height on the massive shadow that had emerged from the base. It seemed to reach its maximum height and was as big as the fire tornado had been, then began to shrink and solidify into a dragon made of bone and held together with little more than darkness.

"I can help!" Amy shouted, still cradling the unconscious Kristen.

"Yes, by making sure she survives," he shouted and spun into a roll.

Normally, she could hold on to him effortlessly, but she didn't have the magic to do so now. She slipped free, her legs as tired as her magic ability, and retained her hold on her friend. They began to plummet toward an inevitable hard landing.

The young mage cursed as she used what power she had left to slow her descent. It wouldn't be even remotely enough, but as she approached the ground, Larry added his powers to hers and they managed a soft enough landing on the sidewalk.

She tried to use her magic powers to lift herself by her shoes so she could return to the fight, but all she accomplished was to give herself a nosebleed and a splitting headache. The young mage slumped, glad

Kristen was all right but worried that her safety wouldn't last much longer.

Lumos had waited what felt like an eternity for this. As a child, he had been raised on legends of the Masked One—a horrible, cruel beast of a dragon who fought from the shadows using lies. He had dedicated his entire life to becoming a strong enough warrior to defeat him. Ever since he'd discovered his unique dragon powers of light itself, he knew that if the dragon of darkness did exist, he would be the one to have to fight him.

"I've studied for millennia for this day," he shouted as the mass of shadow and darkness took the form of a dragon he had never particularly cared for. "Although I had hoped for an opponent more impressive than Lord Boneclaw. Or do you prefer the Masked One? It must be frustrating to hide your power behind this pathetic little farce of a dragon."

Boneclaw only laughed. "You might have once impressed me, Lumos. Centuries ago but no longer. You've suffered wounds from the dragon bullets and you've lost your edge. You're simply an old, out-of-shape has-been. You're too old to have the strength to defeat me yet still young and inexperienced compared to the plans I've laid."

"It seems logic has left you, Boneclaw. How am I both too young and too old?" The golden dragon turned at the apex of his flight and began to dive toward the solid form of his adversary. The dragon was all long, bony spines and long, vicious claws. There was little meat or muscle on him, which might mean that attacking his weak areas would be easy or that it might be impossible.

"You were born when I had already found a place of leadership, and yet the powers you have that burn so brightly have done nothing but use what strength you once had. Still, you are a warrior of legend, Lumos, or you *were.* Stand aside so I don't have to kill you. Let me flay the skin from the Steel Bitch's human face and wear her skull as my most prized mask. Do you think her bones are made of steel?"

"If you want her, you'll have to go through me first," Lumos bellowed as he plummeted and increased his speed.

"You may not believe me, but I had hoped you would say that," Boneclaw replied.

He roared in response and a light bright as the sun began to glow in his throat. It erupted from the ancient dragon's mouth and cut through the inky darkness that had almost completely encapsulated the base.

Boneclaw roared in frustration. He was completely solid now but far enough away that he was able to avoid the attack.

Lumos dropped past him and banked low over the building. "Get out. Everyone get out of there now!"

The dragons, mages, and dwarves within heeded his advice. They ran from the structure as the old dragon spread his wings and glided over the top.

But the Masked One—he could not believe that after all these years, he had finally discovered the identity of the legendary force of evil—did not simply let him go. He attacked from behind and raked him with claws both long and sharp.

The golden dragon twisted in midair so he now flew upside down, facing his enemy. He readied another blast of light from his throat, but Boneclaw clamped down on his jaws.

Lumos smiled as he made his claws ignite with the same blinding light.

He stabbed his talons into the shadow dragon's chest. Boneclaw screamed in pain and released him as he pulled up and away.

The boney dragon pumped his wings and tried to reach a shadow. They were in the sky, and the sun had yet to set so there were none close by. Even if he made it to one of the darker areas under the clouds, he wouldn't be able to escape.

Lumos followed and the light from his claws intensified until each glowed like a flare. Despite Boneclaw's more advanced age, the dragon had not been lying when he'd claimed to be in better shape. He was much faster too, but the light dragon knew how to fight.

He opened his mouth and unleashed another blinding beam of his power at the Masked One. It caught him squarely in the back. This was no ordinary light of course, but a dragon's fire breath turned into light energy itself. His adversary screamed in pain as his scales burned and evaporated in the blinding energy.

In the next moment, Lumos closed and his claws tore at the other dragon's flanks, joints, neck, and every possible target. The claws made most dragons feel intense, searing heat, but to the Masked One, they seemed far worse. Every slash of light made the shadow dragon bleed dark, inky blood that turned to black vapor as he screamed.

They pounded into a skyscraper, drove through the glass walls, and came to a stop wrapped around some of the concrete pillars that held the interior up.

Boneclaw, wounded but not defeated, thrashed his tail with a practiced motion that shattered the ceiling and shorted all the lights.

In a split-second, he was gone.

Lumos wasted no time. He knew exactly what the Masked One would want to do.

He left the building, spread his wings, and doubled back as he descended to the first and second floors. Once there, he blasted them out with his light breath.

The Masked One roared in frustration as his shadowy form fled the light. He assumed his dragon form and took to the sky as he continued his attempt to escape.

"The sewers? Really? Did you think I wouldn't see that one coming?" Lumos shouted after him.

Despite the injuries the golden dragon had inflicted, the enemy seemed to have healed already. This fight wasn't over yet, even if Lumos did have his opponent on the run.

They played an aerial game of cat and mouse. Every time The Masked One tried to duck inside a building to escape into shadow, he launched a blast of light. Those that didn't impact the dragon directly cut his path off.

"How long can you keep this up?" Boneclaw bellowed.

"Longer than you. In case you hadn't noticed, you're losing."

"Ah yes, but we've only just begun and the sun has set."

Lumos cursed inwardly. It was true. There was still light in the air but there wouldn't be for much longer. He had to end this as soon as possible. Of course, he could not let the Masked One know that. "Unlike you, Boneclaw, my powers are not dependent on my surroundings. I can fry you with light all night long."

His adversary sneered at this—which suited Lumos perfectly—then tucked his wings and plunged toward a stand of trees near the ground.

The golden dragon blasted them all with light but he was slightly too late. His target was gone, vanished into shadow.

He didn't waste a heartbeat, however. The Masked One had made it clear what he thought of the old gold dragon. It was Kristen he was after, not him. Lumos turned on his wing and raced to where Amy had caught their leader and put her on the ground.

He reached them not a moment too soon. As he came around a building and saw Amy patting Kristen's head weakly with a wet towel, a great blob of darkness appeared above them from the shadow of a building.

Enormous claws extended, ready to skewer the two women.

Lumos was in place to avert the attack. He opened his mouth and launched an even stronger blast of light energy. The dark dragon shrieked as the light fell on his back and forced him to coalesce into his solid form. The golden dragon dropped sharply and his claws glowed with energy, ready to end this fight once and for all.

He crashed into the Masked One and missed his throat by inches. Without pause, he drew his head back—his teeth now glowed too— for another strike, but Boneclaw wound his long bony tail around his neck to prevent him from completing the lethal blow.

But he had other options. He dug his claws deeper into the other dragon's sides and his opponent howled in pain before he stabbed his claws into Lumos.

Both ancient dragons were far too stubborn to let go, so they remained locked in a lethal embrace as they fell from the sky and powered through one of the walls of Kristen's base.

Lumos managed to position Boneclaw so his back broke through the brick wall, but the shadow dragon was able to twist so Lumos was the one who pounded into the concrete floor.

For a moment, the golden dragon could see nothing but dust and debris. He had struck the ground with enough force to knock him unconscious for the briefest of moments. Across the base—somehow it was still standing despite now missing a wall—he could see the motionless form of Boneclaw.

It was done, he thought with relief.

He pushed to his feet and looked around the room, sensing for any delegates who had been too stupid to flee. Even though Boneclaw—the Masked One himself—was gone, any people in there would still be in danger. Hell, any *dragons* in here would be in danger. Dropping a building on anyone hurt.

But he didn't sense anyone. Not on this floor anyway, and he had no idea how far his powers could reach underground. It wasn't relevant now, though. They would have time to clear the building and check for survivors once they made sure any people working for Boneclaw were caught and in prison.

Lumos turned to the dragon, thankful that the fight had been as easy as it turned out to be. He had suffered some wounds but keeping the fight in the sky had been a smart move. In the gloom, he could see the broken form of the skeletal dragon. It looked as if one of its arms had sheered off.

From behind him, a claw dug into his spine.

He screamed with pain and then dread as Boneclaw's shadowed form melted away into the dark.

Instinctively, he snatched at the claw behind him but it too was gone. All that remained was the pain.

"You thought that would be enough to defeat *me?*" the Masked One hissed from all around him.

"Face me, you coward!" Lumos shouted into the darkness. He made his eyes glow and released lights into the gloom. They illuminated nothing but rubble and he saw no enemies except for the limitations of his powers. He had lied to Boneclaw about the night and *did* get energy from the sun, exactly like the Masked One drew power from the dark.

"We had the little fight above the city in the rays of the sun, did we not?" his enemy asked from the darkness. "We tried your way. You did not use it as well as you should have."

"So says the dragon hiding in the dark." He spun and flicked his tail at every moving shadow.

"Perhaps you would prefer it if I stop hiding?" A claw appeared from the darkness and slashed across his face with far more force than he had expected. It thrust his head sideways and before he could recover, a disembodied tail stabbed a spine into his side.

Lumos unleashed light to where the tail had been, but the Masked One was too fast. By the time the light illuminated the place, his attacker was gone.

A moment later, claws tore the membrane of one of the golden dragon's wings. He flapped them both and flung the bony dragon back, but it was too late. The damage was done and he would not fly that night.

Still, the enemy refused to attack directly. He continued to strike from the shadows to wear him down, tire him out, and force his dragon healing power to overextend itself.

Finally, Lumos decided he'd had enough.

He'd noticed a pattern to the Masked One's strikes. Feint, feint, strike. Feint, feint, feint, strike. He never initiated more than two or three moves without making contact. Logically, he tried to keep him on edge with the feints but didn't want him to get wise to them. Fortunately, he had already discerned the ploy.

At the Masked One's first feint, Lumos looked at the sky. The gloom was growing as dusk faded and he had to act now.

On the second feint, the golden dragon began to prepare his greatest power.

Luckily, his opponent feinted a third time and gave him time.

At the fourth attack, the one that he expected to be real, he unleashed his assault as soon as he sensed movement from the darkness.

Boneclaw lunged forward and Lumos met his claws with a dazzling flash of light. It came not from his claws or mouth but from every scale of his body. Every pore, every whisker, and every piece of exposed skin radiated light. The room filled with the blinding glow and the Masked One—drawn out as he had been—screeched in pain and clutched his eyes as he stumbled back.

The golden dragon pounced and savaged his adversary's armpit with his claws.

The Masked One roared, but he didn't retaliate and instead, tried to dissolve into shadow. His effort proved futile as the light attack had overwhelmed his abilities. He was trapped in his solid state.

Lumos wasted no more time. He bit the dragon in the neck and a great geyser of blood sprayed into his throat.

This proved to be enough for Boneclaw, who stopped trying to dissolve and began to fight like God had intended dragons to fight.

Claw found claw, tooth found tooth, and tail found tail as the two beasts battled. Like the world's greatest Komodo dragons, they bulldozed their bodies into each other. Their powers were spent. The Masked One could no longer use his ability to vanish and Lumos had used every ounce of light energy he possessed in his grand flash.

What followed was a brutal, bloody brawl. The enemy, for all his bluster about fighting from the shadows, was an adept brawler. He blocked Lumos' most vicious strikes yet let those that would only fall on his scaly flank strike without care.

He was hard to wound because of his skeletal frame. The golden dragon found that he often ripped through the other dragon's skin and scales to find nothing but bone beneath. When he found meat, the Masked One roared in pain, but in the places with nothing but scale and bone, it was as if he felt nothing at all.

They engaged repeatedly with violent clashes. There was no longer any real strategy. Each had to inflict enough damage on the other to overwhelm their ability to heal and cause their body to fail and die. It was not a pretty thing to do.

"You could still surrender," the Masked One hissed. "and serve as my second. You're a better warrior than even Shimmerclaw's boasts made you out to be."

In response, Lumos grasped the dragon by the back of the neck and threw him into one of the three still standing walls. The impact was enough to make bricks crumble and the roof sag even more than it already was, but the shadow dragon wasn't disabled.

He darted into another assault, drove his adversary into the opposite wall, and thrust a barb into his chest that might have killed him if it had gone an inch deeper.

"Your healing power is nearly used up," the Masked One said.

"Take a look at yourself," Lumos retorted.

Both dragons took a moment to assess their wounds. They were bleeding profusely from dozens of injuries. The Masked One had a jagged line across his neck from where Lumos had bitten him, and the golden dragon's scales in front of his heart were healing far too slowly to provide him any real defense.

"You could come willingly," Lumos said.

"Indeed," Boneclaw said and lurched forward to drive him into the wall again. More bricks fell, as did many sections of some kind of piping from the ceiling. If they weren't careful, the entire base would collapse on them. In their current state, that would likely mean death for them both.

The golden dragon took a deep breath. That would be worth it, he decided. If he died ending the reign of terror of the Masked One, he would die with honor.

"What?" his enemy hissed. "Did you wish to take this outside so we don't get crushed?"

"I wouldn't dream of it," he said and lunged forward, ready to finish the fight.

Out of the corner of his eye, Lumos saw the heavy metal door to the basement crack open. Constance Vigil, leader of the technomages, stumbled out, barely held upright by an old woman whom he could only describe as a witch. "Constance! Get out of here!" he shouted.

The woman looked up, confused by the chaos of the surroundings.

The Masked One grinned savagely and hurled a chunk of the wall at his foe. It missed by a wide margin and Lumos was about to gloat when he heard it thump into a wall behind him.

The building had suffered so much damage that it should have fallen a while before, but it decided that this was its moment. The entire roof caved and brought the walls with it.

Lumos lunged toward Constance. She couldn't die, not with an actual peace between dragons and mages so close.

He reached her as the roof struck his back. It crushed him to the floor, but he was an ancient dragon of unthinkable power. He kept his legs strong and protected her and the woman who had rescued her.

Unfortunately, it turned out that he had overestimated how long it took for the Masked One's powers to return. An inky blackness poured through the rubble until a bony tail materialized in front of Lumos' eyes.

It plunged into his chest and speared his heart.

The last thing the golden dragon heard before he died was his enemy gloating and a mage screaming his name.

CHAPTER FIFTY-EIGHT

Ever since Constance had discovered that she possessed the gift of magic, she had given her life to fighting for mage equality. She had changed her name, forsaken her family, and lived in hiding, all so that one day, mages could throw off the oppressive yoke of the dragons.

In the service of this mission, she had killed many dragons and done terrible things to even more. She had imprisoned them, found ways to use them to kill their kin, and reduced them to nothing but their bodies. On her journey, she had learned that some dragons—those who had not been indoctrinated since they were children—could be trusted. Kristen was one. Katrina, the Iron Dragon, was another. But that was the end of her list.

Until now.

She was trapped under a massive pile of rubble. But she was only trapped and not dead because a dragon had sacrificed its—no, *his*—life to save her. That Lumos thought he might have survived made no difference to her. He had seen that she was in danger and came to protect her despite being in what must have been one of the most dangerous fights of his entire life.

And now, his murderer was there—his murderer and her former teacher. She had not known that the man who showed her how to take dragon bones and turn them into weapons was indeed a dragon, but she knew now.

"This was impressive," the Masked One commented and resumed his human form with the scars on his face that she recognized. "To play such a long con, only to distract that dragon at the very last moment. Very impressive."

"What is he talking about?" the witch who had revived her asked.

"Kill her," the dragon said to Constance. "Kill the old woman to prove your loyalty to me. Then, together, we will finish both the Steel Bitch and that pesky little mage you failed to capture and convert to our side."

"This woman saved my life," she said before something else occurred to her. *"Our* side? How can you say that? I have worked my entire life to free the world of dragon oppression."

"We fought with different means for the same ends," he responded and took a step toward her. Shadow billowed behind him as he approached as if it wanted to embrace its master. "The Dragon Council kept their claws on the throats of mages, humans, and dragons for millennia. Now that Shimmerclaw is dead, we can remake the Council. In her place, a mage can reign."

"I would rather die." Constance spat in his face, using her magic to control the blob of phlegm to make sure it landed in his eye.

He flinched at the impact. "That can be arranged!" he snapped and vanished into shadow.

The technomage acted quickly but not quickly enough. She tried to spin a shimmering shield of magic around her and the mage who had saved her, but she was too slow. The darkness lifted the witch high above her and savaged her in the air. Claws assailed the woman from a hundred different directions to shred her piece by piece until all that remained was a skull suspended in the dark. Blood, bone, and viscera rained on Constance, but she didn't let the gore weaken her resolve or her shield. The Masked One might be able to use shadow but he still had to become solid to strike her. If the shield could block bullets, it could block a claw.

"I'm sorry I never showed you my true face," the darkness said as the skull floated to seemingly levitate in front of her.

"I saw it during the peace talks. It's nothing to be proud of," she replied to the darkness all around her.

The Masked One chuckled. "Such a tongue you have. Will you use it to beg for your life before I rip it out? But no, that was not my face, not any more than the shadowed hood I hid inside was. This is my true face."

Beneath the skull, his human body coalesced. In one moment, the skull floated freely and in the next, his body had materialized from the shadow with the skull covering his face. He sighed contentedly as if he'd just had sex or a particularly rich dessert. "It is so difficult hiding who you truly are, is it not?"

"I've found that since I broke ties with you, I no longer have that problem."

"And to think I gave you a chance to join me. I'll enjoy mutilating you. Too bad your skull is too small to wear. It would be a prize rivaled only by the Steel Bitch's."

Without warning, the Masked One attacked.

He gave up all pretense of remaining in his human form. Instead, he evaporated into shadow and rained blow after blow on Constance's shield.

It held and magical energy crackled and sparked every time he struck it. Still, it remained in place, although fissures began to form and her nose trickled blood.

With every strike, she felt the blow as if someone had battered her temple with a hammer. She realized then that her shield would not hold indefinitely.

Calmly, she did what she had trained hundreds of mages to do.

She reached into her robe, drew the handgun loaded with dragon bullets she'd taken from the Steel Dragon's storage room, and fired four shots into the Masked One's gut.

Every single one of them missed.

Her adversary simply turned to shadow and stopped his relentless attack.

He laughed from the darkness and it seemed he was all around her, hidden in plain sight. In the rubble of the base, there were a hundred shadows or even a thousand.

"You cannot defeat me here. Not in the dark," he gloated. "That dragon might have stood a chance if not for him sacrificing himself to save one of my greatest pawns. Oh, the irony is sweet with this one. Perhaps, once I level the world's largest cities and slaughter the vermin who call them home, I'll erect a statue of you as one of my most loyal followers."

"Fine," Constance said, lowered her gun, and scanned the darkness for any sign of him. "Kill me then. I won't join you, so you might as well simply kill me."

"If only all my victims were as wise as you, truly, my job would have been easier."

"I only ask that when you erect that statue…" She saw something move in the darkness. "That you make sure there are spotlights on that bitch!"

With her left hand, she lobbed a sphere of light into the air and illuminated the room with every ounce of strength she had.

The Masked One screamed at the light, coalesced into his solid form, and stood at her two o'clock.

"You fool! The dragon thought he could defeat me with light as well. Now you will have to watch as I eviscerate you!"

"Watch this," she said and fired her gun at him a fifth time.

He was insanely, incredibly, unnaturally fast and leapt back at the moment she began to raise the weapon. But Constance was fast too. Her muscles and reflexes were augmented by magic, so she was able to track him as he moved away from her.

She saw the bullet punch through one of his arms and emerge from the other side with a spray of dragon blood.

His screams almost deafened her. They were high-pitched and horrible, the sound of pure pain and so loud and powerful, they made her want to vomit. Yet she had never heard a sound so sweet.

She pursued the Masked One over piles of rubble, but she was too slow.

By the time she caught up to him, he had melted into nothing but a pool of inky darkness that flowed into a crack in the floor of the base. Constance fired at the darkness for good measure, but like before, it did nothing to him.

CHAPTER FIFTY-NINE

Kristen woke to the sound of Amy crying. Despite the pain she experienced, she couldn't help but feel relief, although she wasn't sure if she was more relieved to be alive or to exist. The last thing she remembered was trying to fight Boneclaw and being thrown up into the void like she was nothing but a ragdoll.

"Amy?" she asked and wondered why the mage sounded so heartbroken when she felt nothing but happiness at seeing stars in the night sky above her.

She sat, feeling like a train had run over her, and looked around. The first thing she saw—the most obvious thing—was that her base had been utterly destroyed. One wall was still standing, but that hardly counted for anything.

The next thing she noticed was that her friends were all around her. Stonequest was there and looked grim. As did Larry, his expression morose. Her security team had set up a perimeter and a quick headcount told her that Drew, Butters, Beanpole, Hernandez, Keith, and Heartsbane were all okay. Timeflash flew overhead. Emerald had died in the last battle over Detroit. It still hurt to think about him, but not as much as it hurt to think about Jim. Someone was missing but her friends had to know.

"Jim—" She choked and Drew nodded.

"We found the body in the rubble," he said.

"Where is Boneclaw?" she asked when she realized who was missing. In her mind, the dragon should have been cuffed.

"The pixies brought you back," Larry said frustratingly and didn't answer her question. "They all vanished as soon as it was done, but they did it. They brought you back and by the look of things, not a moment too soon. As soon as your base reappeared, you rocketed through the roof. Amy barely caught you in time."

Kristen wondered briefly if the effects she had seen during that final brawl had been from the pixies and not the mages. But there was something more pressing on her mind. "Where is *Boneclaw?* He murdered Shimmerclaw in cold blood. We have to bring him to justice."

"Constance told us about your theory," Stonequest said.

"*Theory?*" she sputtered.

"There's no evidence of that except for your word, Lady Steel," he said and didn't sound all that happy about it.

"I can attest to everything the Steel Dragon said," Constance said.

"I know you can and I believe you," Stonequest said. "But under dragon law, a dragon accusing another dragon of murder needs evidence to back up that claim. Testimony from anyone but a dragon does not count."

"Oh, come on. That's ridiculous." Kristen would have said more but her head was swimming. Why was everyone so upset? What was she missing? She felt like her brain attempted to make sense of everything but was still missing a piece.

"It's something I wish the peace talks could have changed."

"Could have?" she asked, her head still spinning.

"They fell apart," Larry explained. "When the bubble broke and everyone was free, they all went home, even the pixies."

"Shimmerclaw's body—"

"Is gone," Stonequest said. "Constance showed me where she fell but most of that room is gone. It's like it was simply…erased, I guess."

"She left a message!" Kristen protested.

"Also gone," he told her.

"Fine, okay, but what about Boneclaw? Did you catch him?"

"No, we didn't," Larry said. "But we'll have to hunt for him another day. Right now—"

"What?" she demanded. "All of you are acting like someone died. I know Shimmerclaw was powerful but she wasn't close, not like Lumos…" Her mouth went dry. "Where is Lumos?"

In response, Constance approached and sat beside her. She looked at her and although the line of her mouth was as firm as ever and the strength in her posture was not at all diminished, she could see that the tough lady was in pain.

"I had always thought you were special because you were raised by people," the woman said as if that explained anything. "But in his final moments, Lumos used his powers to save me—a mage who has done more to hurt dragons than any in hundreds of years."

"Oh, God, no," Kristen said and tears welled in her eyes as she understood why Amy was weeping.

"I'm afraid so," Constance said heavily. "And I do not know if I can bear his sacrifice. I spent my decades thinking of dragons as nothing but enemies. You had begun to change my mind but still, my heart had not fully taken in what it meant that dragons could see us as we see ourselves. With Lumos's sacrifice, I can finally see how blind I was."

A thousand questions poured through her head but the only that reached her lips was, "Where is he?"

Constance's head jerked toward the base.

"Oh, Jesus, he's not still in there?" Her aura flashed with rage but she made no attempt to control it.

"We had to secure the perimeter," Stonequest said. She noticed for the first time that there were mages everywhere, shining lights in a wide circle.

She ignored them as she scrambled past toward the rubble of her base.

His body glowed in the moonlight. He had always been so beautiful, a creature of golden light who was still somehow humble, kind, and friendly to people he could have stepped on if he had been anything but his true self.

From the rubble, a mangled wing, most of his tail, and one leg protruded.

"We can't leave him like this!" Kristen shouted and turned to steel. It felt like a hammer had pounded against her skull when she activated the power. She grasped chunks of concrete and twisted rebar to haul them off the noble dragon who had died fighting for others.

But at least she didn't have to work alone.

Stonequest joined her. Using his dragon form, he was even more efficient than she was. Larry helped too, using his powers to lift and remove rubble. Everyone else joined in and for a few minutes, all that could be heard was the labored breathing of men and women hard at work, the dull thuds of concrete being dropped on more concrete, and the flat clang of rebar.

When his head was finally uncovered, Kristen stopped.

She moved closer, closed his beautiful lifeless eyes, and stroked his long mustache as if he were only sleeping.

"You were a better teacher than I could have hoped for," she said finally. "Not about fighting, though. The Masked One totally kicked my ass."

Keith laughed but no one else did.

"You taught me to be kind. You taught me to care for the inexperienced and the less fortunate. You taught me there are more important things than gold. I don't know what dragons think about the afterlife, but whatever happens, you deserve a good, long rest, Lord Lumos."

She stroked his mustache a while longer until finally, it felt like something left the dragon. His scales didn't fade and his body didn't sag, but it still felt as if he had finally let go.

Kristen went to check on Amy while everyone else said their goodbyes. This was becoming a ritual that was far too common. And there was still Jim's funeral to plan. Oh, dear God, why had she not simply gone into accounting like her mom had wanted?

But she knew why.

She was a cop because she wanted to fight for those who could not fight for themselves.

In the same way, she worked as a dragon because she wanted to share the privilege so many enjoyed.

There were bad cops and bad dragons, but the good ones—the best of them—were real heroes.

But they would never get to be that, not as long as the Masked One went free.

"What will we do now?" Amy asked. "The peace talks fell apart. The Masked One is gone. Maybe we should hide in Nova Scotia with the dwarves."

"We could never hide from him," Kristen said and turned to her team. "Hiding is *his* way. Secrecy is his strength. Now, we know who the Masked One is. A wimpy old dragon named Lord Boneclaw did this today. He took Lumos from us. He's the one we have to stop if we ever want this world to be a more just place. We won't have peace until the Masked One is gone."

She looked at the night sky. Yes, it was filled with darkness, but it was also filled with thousands of twinkling lights, plus the glow of all the mages working together to illuminate it. Some people might have seen an overwhelming blanket of blackness, but she knew that Lumos would have seen something different.

He would have seen the light.

The golden dragon would have seen every pinpoint as a source of hope and every magic orb as a person who was willing to forsake their comfort and their wealth so they could make the world a better place for others.

Some would have no choice but to see the dark. But some—the privileged few and people like Kristen—could *choose* to see either the good or the bad. And they could choose which side to fight for.

"Lumos, I promise you he won't go free," she said to the sky above. "I promise that we will stop the dragon who took you from us. We won't rest until we do. We'll turn over every stone and shine the light in every shadow until he is finally stopped. Then, Lumos, you can finally rest in peace."

CHAPTER SIXTY

The castle looked like it had been built of boulders hewn roughly into squares bigger than any beast. It stood on an island with towering wind-battered cliffs and within, the Global Dragon Council held what might prove to be the very last meeting of its kind.

Lord Boneclaw sat in his human form on a chair too heavy to be lifted by human hands. This was one of the few places in the world that were built by dragons, not humans. He had carved this chair well over a thousand years before and had known when he'd shaped it that one day, he would sit in it and preside over the entire council. When that day came, he would use his power to give dragon kind complete control over the earth. His plan had finally come to fruition.

One of the most satisfying advantages was that he no longer had to pretend to be something he wasn't. The world knew of his shadow powers. They knew he was the Masked One and they didn't care. Even now, he wore the mask of human bone he had hidden for so long. This was his true face. The face of Lord Boneclaw, scarred and worn as it was, was the mask. This skull, freshly harvested as they all were, was what made him feel like himself.

He looked out through the eye sockets of one of the Steel Bitch's dead human servants at the five faces around him. Four of them had worked for him for centuries and owed their position on the Council to him. The other was not even worthy of being called an obstacle. Decimus Aurelius would be stripped of his power as soon as he had secured his position.

"Can you *please* remove that?" Aurelius complained. "It is grotesquely macabre and quite unsightly." His gaze had not left Lord Boneclaw since he'd arrived.

"You would let humans use the bones of our dead to arm the guns that kill our kind—*that almost killed me*—and yet you find it offensive for a dragon to wear one of their skulls?"

"I want those bullets destroyed as much as the next dragon," Aurelius said—which was a lie, he knew. The Council member didn't care about dragons but only about ingratiating himself to the Steel Bitch. "But walking around wearing one of their dead is not how we accomplish this."

"I call this session to order," Ironclaw interrupted. He was a particularly easy to manipulate dragon whom Boneclaw had placated with false power decades before.

Aurelius frowned at the shadow dragon but remained silent. He would follow the rules of this session exactly like he had every other one. All the councilors were slaves to tradition. The Masked One would set them all free and give them a true visionary and a true ruler—*him.*

"Lord Boneclaw, why did you ask us to convene this session?" Ironclaw asked with stiff formality.

"To elect a new Council leader, of course," he all but purred. He knew who the leader would be. He'd made certain of the outcome. Shimmerclaw had already lost her sway, even before her death. The Council had voted to go to war because they already knew on some level that he was right. The humans had wasted enough time pretending to be in control of their future.

With her dead, no one would be able to so much as argue against him. He already knew how this would end. Five to one for Lord Boneclaw. Aurelius would then make a fool of himself and he would strip him of his rank. With him out of the way, he'd appoint two new

Councilors to make up the full seven. A vote would be held giving him —how did the humans put it when they tried to empower their tyrants? Ah yes—executive privileges. He would go to war and finally, the world could be remade. It was almost poetic.

"Well then, perhaps we should move directly to the vote," a dragon by the name of Skywing said. She was a strong fighter and loyal because Boneclaw had saved her from an assassination attempt conducted by mages a few centuries before—he had set the attempt up, of course—but she was a common. There was something about common dragons that he detested. She would be replaced in good time as well and maybe used for breeding to see if something more useful might arise from her bloodline. If not, more bullets could always be made.

"We have an even more pressing matter," Aurelius said.

Boneclaw clenched his jaw. Every Council member had the right to set the agenda for the meeting. Dragons had persisted with unnecessary rituals for millennia. He couldn't wait to do away with them.

"And this is?" Ironclaw asked from beneath his bushy grey mustache.

"An immediate investigation into Lady Shimmerclaw's death," Aurelius stated in an official tone and his regality made him look like an overstuffed imbecile of a bird.

"Oh, come now. Not this again," Lord Boneclaw said dismissively.

"You insult this Council, sir!" the other dragon continued undeterred like a rat chasing cheese. "Kristen Hall, the Steel Dragon, has accused Lord Boneclaw of killing Shimmerclaw. Furthermore, Lord Boneclaw revealed shadow powers the likes of which dragon kind has never seen. He is the Masked One and has manipulated us for years. His assassination of Shimmerclaw is simply the culmination of his plan. We cannot allow this."

"Listen to yourself, sir!" Ironclaw snapped in Boneclaw's defense. "Naming hatchling tales at a Dragon Council meeting."

"His powers are no myth. Ask him yourself." Aurelius fumed and made no effort to hide it.

"Who among us does not have some trait they wish to hide?" Lord

Boneclaw said and raised his bony hands at the assembled dragons. Aurelius held his gaze, but the other four looked away. He kept them under his claw because he knew each of them had a secret they never wanted to be shared.

"He killed Lumos, a brave warrior."

"Who intervened in a duel between myself and the Steel Bi—Dragon." He corrected himself with a smirk. "Come now, old friend. You were there. You saw the Steel Dragon and I duel. Lumos interfered. When he did, his life was forfeit."

"And what of Shimmerclaw's murder?" Aurelius seemed determined to not back down.

"What are we supposed to believe? The Steel Dragon herself has admitted that she did not see the death of Shimmerclaw take place. She said she saw a cryptic message that could be interpreted thousands of ways. Will you take the word of a rookie investigator over the word of the Council member who mentored so many of you?"

Aurelius looked around. Finally, understanding dawned his face. He had thought there were open minds there he might convince but of course, everyone's was already made up. Lord Boneclaw almost felt bad for him. It was sad to watch him finally realize this. Maybe he would have one of the other Councilors vote with him to take away some of the sting. The thought drew an inner chuckle because he knew he would do no such thing.

"I don't think anyone here thinks Lady Shimmerclaw's murder should *not* be investigated," Skywing interjected hastily. She was mousy for a dragon, an extremely unattractive trait, he thought. "But we need leadership in place when we discover exactly what happened there."

"You mean once we determine who pulled the trigger of the gun that killed her," Ironclaw cut in. "Because every party has agreed on that much. She was *shot*. By a gun!"

Boneclaw rolled his eyes. Ironclaw was loyal as a dragon could be but he was dense. How else could she be shot if not by a gun?

"That's a human weapon loaded with bullets designed by mages," the dragon added and puffed his mustache out. "I don't think the Steel

Dragon would have done the killing, of course, but would she have looked the other way?"

"She would *not* have!" Aurelius snapped.

"Of course she wouldn't. We know what kind of dragon she is," Skywing said. "But still, she vowed that the dragons who went there would be safe. She broke that vow. There is no good reason to take her at her word."

"Other than the *truth*," Aurelius insisted, but he had finally read the room and saw where this was going.

"I want to know the truth as much as anyone," Skywing said. "But right now, it's far more important to get leadership in place. With the peace talks delayed by the attack of that dragon and mage, it's clear there are still major threats to dragons. We need to be prepared for war to break out at any moment."

Boneclaw let his eyes smile beneath the skull mask. Skywing was so wonderfully naïve. War wouldn't break out until he made it happen. Which would be shortly after this damn vote was completed.

"The motion to vote for our new council leader has been seconded," Ironclaw intoned solemnly, his expression stern. He was a dragon who knew his place well.

The shadow dragon's ears twitched. He had heard a distant boom as if a great battering ram had pounded against the impregnable stone walls of this dragon fortress. But that was impossible, of course. Most likely, a boulder had simply shifted its position after a few hundred years. It didn't matter. Nothing would matter once the votes were cast.

One of the Councilors—a particularly bloodthirsty female by the name of Bloodblaze who he had come closest to telling the truth about the Masked One—brought the urn forward and put it on the table in the center of them all.

Once in position, the ceramic urn blazed with green flame. Bloodblaze waited for the flames to subside, then reached inside. She retrieved six chits, each of them shaped like the scale of a dragon. The urn was enchanted with a variety of complex spells. It had taken the mages who had built it at the bequest of the dragons quite some time to create them. Nothing like it would ever be produced again because once the mages had finished, he had held a vote to have them and their secrets silenced once and for all.

The green fire prevented anyone but a dragon Councilor from reaching into the urn. How it knew *who* was on the Dragon Council was one of its most impressive features. It displayed its strange powers even further when it only produced six chits instead of seven since the Dragon Council was currently down a member. The scales it had given to Bloodblaze were unusual too, of course. A dragon simply had to exude confidence in their vote using their aura powers and place the chit inside the urn. It would turn to a simulacrum of the scales of the dragon for whom the vote had been cast.

This particular feature had prevented Boneclaw from trying to be the head of the Council for years. He hadn't wanted anyone to know that his true scales faded from the color of old bone to the inky dark of shadow. The last time there had been a vote cast for him, none of the current members had even been on the Council. Only Shimmer-claw had seen the true nature of his powers and she was now dead. These dragons were all about to see his shadow powers, but they already knew about them anyway. Boneclaw could not believe how fortunate he had been. He had expected to seize power but not with the entire council knowing all he could do. Oh, his victory would be sweet indeed.

One by one, the dragons cast their votes. They could only vote for a member of the Council, which meant only the six dragons in the room. If a majority wasn't reached, the two highest votes—or more if there were ties—would then be the only options granted by the urn. This would repeat until there was a victor.

However, Boneclaw knew full well that there would not be any need for this. He would emerge the victor and the only question was whether Decimus would vote for himself or if he was foolish enough to think he had any allies left on the Dragon Council.

He was placing his vote—the final one—into the urn when he heard another of those curious booms from outside the castle. Although this one didn't sound like it came from outside, nor did it particularly sound like the shifting of a boulder. To him, a dragon who had spent some time learning about human weapons and explosives so he could ensure the mages properly weaponized the dragon scales, it sounded uncomfortably familiar.

The other dragons heard it too. Six pairs of sharp eyes turned to look at the heavy wood doors and the steel hinges that supported them.

"Count the votes," he hissed.

"Of course, sir," Lord Ironclaw replied and went to upend the urn.

Before the scales settled on the table, another boom came. This one was so close and so loud that it shook even the massively heavy chairs the dragons were all seated in.

"Go and see whatever this is while we count the votes," Boneclaw ordered the two dragon guards in the room with them.

The guardians went to the massive doors exiting the hall, but as they were about to open them, another explosion rang out. This one was so loud and powerful that it blew the doors off their hinges and hurled the guards back. One of them managed to deflect the door to the side and stay on his feet but the other human-form dragon was trapped beneath his. One of his legs was crushed instantly but the dragon didn't so much as cry out. He simply took a deep breath, grunted with exertion, and lifted the door away.

Boneclaw only noticed this in his peripheral vision, though. His attention was riveted on one thing. The Steel Dragon seemed to suck all the oxygen out of the room as she strode in through the stinking smoke of explosives.

CHAPTER SIXTY-ONE

Kristen allowed herself a moment to scan the scene. And oh, what a sweet moment it was. The doors Hernandez had blown off their hinges knocked the guards back and put an expression on each of their faces that a human might wear if they were asked to fight a grizzly bear.

Better still were the expressions on the faces of the Dragon Council. She didn't know four of them, but all wore similar expressions. They each seemed caught between disbelief at the impertinence of being interrupted and carefully controlled fury in the face of a dangerous foe. The only two who looked different were the dragons she knew.

Decimus Aurelius grinned broadly and he looked almost devilish with his silver hair and eyes that positively twinkled.

Lord Boneclaw's vicious scowl was visible below the skull he wore on his face. She knew whose skull that was, and she would take it from him before this meeting was over.

All the dragons were in their human forms and sat in massive, ornate chairs that looked like they might have been made for dragon bodies. She was certain that the effect was supposed to look intimidating, but to her—someone far more accustomed to people sitting in regular fricking chairs—they looked like a group of children having a tea party at their parents' table.

"Oh, did someone spill the kettle?" Kristen asked and gestured toward the overturned urn and pile of stones or some kind of chits in front of it. She had learned from Shimmerclaw that the urn was only used to vote members onto the Council or to promote them. It meant she'd made it barely in time to stop the vote from happening. She strode forward and sat in the seventh chair at the table—Shimmerclaw's chair, she knew. "Sorry I'm late."

Boneclaw bolted to his feet like he had sat on a tack. "You insolent little slug! What makes you think you can simply blast into a sacred place and interrupt a meeting you have no right to attend? This is outrageous behavior. Who let you through?"

"I have every right to be here. You took something from me and I want it back," she told him icy tones.

Before he could wipe the look of shock off his face from being ordered around, the smoke behind her was sucked out of the room in a swirling vortex that also did a great job of messing up the dragons' perfectly coifed hair. She would have to congratulate Amy on the effect later.

"*Let?*" Hernandez laughed and marched into the meeting hall with Amy one step behind her on one side and Heartsbane on the other. "No one *let* us through! Oh, a couple of those guards tried to tell us we weren't welcome here, but I guess they found Jesus or something because they seem to have seen the error of their ways."

"You will have your titles stripped for interrupting a Council meeting!" Ironclaw bellowed at Kristen and Heartsbane. He ignored the human and mage as per typical arrogant dragon behavior.

"Oh, no, no, no, no, no." Hernandez grinned even more triumphantly. Kristen did too. She doubted a human had *ever* stood up to a group of dragons as powerful as the six in this room. "Lady Heartsbane didn't do a thing. All those booms and bangs you heard? Those were merely variations on the Hernandez special."

"You disgusting worm, you pathetic crawling vermin, you—"

Before Boneclaw could unleash his tirade in full, a few dragon guards raced into the room. Their clothes were torn and scorched. The one in front's face was a bloody, blackened mess. As he spoke, it began to heal from the bomb blast the dragon must have suffered at extremely close range. "We apologize, Council. The explosives were wrapped in baskets of food. We didn't think—"

"Morons, each and every one of you. *Morons!*" Boneclaw fumed.

"They probably wouldn't have fallen for it if you let them have a break now and then," Kristen said. She thought chiding him about worker's rights might further infuriate him and it seemed she was right.

"You interrupt a meeting and dare talk to me about *snacks!*" Boneclaw demanded.

"Indeed." She smiled sweetly and took his statement as a question. "I'm confused because you have something of mine and yet you seem to be having this tea party and forgot to invite me."

"This is not a tea party!" Ironclaw roared and pounded the table so hard it cracked.

"We are voting for a new leader." Decimus Aurelius' wide smile made it quite plain how happy he was to see Kristen.

"Oh, so you've already investigated and punished Shimmerclaw's murderer, then?" she replied. She turned her steely glare to Boneclaw. "But that can't be the case, because her murderer is standing right there."

"That is *quite* enough," he roared. "Guards, seize them! They have invaded a meeting of the Dragon Council. They must be cuffed."

The two guards who had failed to hold the door and the four guards who had failed to steer clear of Hernandez's explosives all moved to remove her forcibly from her seat.

Unfortunately for the six of them, they chose the wrong target.

As soon as any of them came within arm's reach of her, Amy simply plucked them up as effortlessly as a gardener removing snails from a garden. She threw the first four into the hallway before any of them had even realized what was happening. The other two—the dragon with the injured face and one of those who had already faced this squad of four extremely tough women—hesitated.

In the hallway, one of the guards displayed his lack of combat tactics by transforming into a dragon, thus blocking the path for the other three.

Heartsbane turned into a dragon as well—there was far more room inside the meeting room than in the hallway leading to it—and blocked the door. But even that turned out to be unnecessary, given the extent of Amy's powers. The young mage simply lifted the two doors Hernandez had so violently removed and thrust them into the doorframe with such force that they jammed in snugly.

"This is barbarism!" Boneclaw hissed. "Your authority as an investigator in North America comes from the authority of the Dragon Council. We gave it to you and we can strip it away."

"I motion for a vote to remove the rank of investigator from Kristen Steel," a Councilor with eyes the color of blood hissed.

"I second," an old man with a bushy mustache who she recognized as Ironclaw piped in.

"All in favor?" Boneclaw asked.

Five hands went up.

"All opposed?"

Decimus Aurelius raised his hand begrudgingly in the air.

"Five to one. The motion carries," Ironclaw intoned officiously. "Investigator Steel is an investigator for the council no longer."

"You pathetic little worm. As head of this Council, I will *end* you," Boneclaw said.

"But you haven't voted yet," Kristen said. "Those chits are still on the table."

"The vote is done and cast, girl," he snapped. "Look at the scales and tell me what you see."

"I see four that look like pathetic, worn bone that's been dipped in tar and two that look like Decimus Aurelius."

"*Four?*" Boneclaw raged and looked around the room. One of his little peons had disobeyed him. Still, four to two was the same as five to one—a clear majority. "Yes." He calmed. "So you see, I have won."

"Is this true, Aurelius?" Kristen asked.

"I'm afraid so," Aurelius said, although he smiled at her as if he wanted her to understand something. Like he had a message he wanted to convey, something he *needed* her to understand.

"Which means I will ostracize you from dragon society. You will be an outcast. An outlaw. The next time a dragon dies, we *know* who will be behind it and we will send the full force of the dragons to end you. You're no longer an investigator, which means you're no longer welcome here. Now *get out!*" Boneclaw roared.

She listened to his little tirade and realized he was being truthful. The vote had been cast and she was too late. Still, she couldn't help herself and burst into laughter.

CHAPTER SIXTY-TWO

Before, the room had felt like a pressure cooker. It seemed as if there was so much heat, humidity, and pressure in the air that any misstep might have caused the whole castle to explode far more violently than any of Hernandez's explosions.

Kristen's laughter had the opposite effect. It completely drained the room of energy until it felt like they were in a meat locker.

All six pairs of eyes were fixed on her, even Aurelius, who seemed slightly less angry but as shocked as the others.

She only laughed harder as she unpinned the seven-pointed badge from her shirt and tossed it on the table. Although it was only a small piece of metal, its impact seemed to shake the dragons so much that it might as well have been an anchor thrown on the stone slab.

"You're the leader of the Dragon Council now, and the best you can do is take my job away?" She snorted a laugh. "Have the badge. I'm sure you cheap-ass dragons wouldn't want to spring for the cost to make another one anyway."

"The title is also gone," Boneclaw growled.

Her laughter intensified, so much so that hard it hurt. "No…shit… the title…is gone!" After a few deep breaths in the frigid awkwardness of the room, she could at least talk again. "What we're doing has nothing to do with titles. It has nothing to do with a salary or whatever dragons seem to think honor means. We are standing up for *justice.* We are righting wrongs that dragons and *anyone else* commit. We are trying to bring the world back into some kind of balance before you assholes all blow it up."

Boneclaw graced her with a little golf clap. "Very nice. Very inspirational. We could all use a good revolution. But to clarify, who is helping you? A tiny band of humans? Some cowardly mages who have spent their lives in hiding? A paltry handful of dragons."

"We've stopped you before, Boneclaw."

"You have stopped the will of the Council, yes. That is true. But only because the humans came to your aid. No human can help you here. This fortress has stood for a thousand years, and no human weapon, no bomb, no nuclear warhead—*nothing* can break its walls."

"Except me, right?" Hernandez interrupted. "You mean that nothing broke its walls until Hernandez gave it a try."

"Imbecilic fool" he retorted. "All we have to do is make sure none of you ever leave this place and your little rebellion is finished."

Amy, Heartsbane, and Hernandez all took a step closer to Kristen's chair. "Try us," they said as one.

She smiled. They had practiced the move. She found it amusing and even cute but Boneclaw flinched at what she was sure he would call their impertinence.

"Thank you, ladies, but I've got this. Lord Boneclaw—the Masked One—your list of crimes is extensive and horrendous. It was you who began to clone dragons and who taught the technomages how to use their bodies to make weapons."

A female Councilor gasped at this.

Kristen continued. "You did this again and again, created and enslaved dozens of dragons, and spread them around the world so their living bodies could be harvested."

"You have no proof besides the word of the mage who doesn't wish to be executed for her crimes," Boneclaw protested.

"Not a denial, I might point out," Heartsbane said.

"Furthermore," Kristen said. "You have set dragons to the task of destroying the world order. Sebastian Shadowstorm and his mother Obscura—remember them? They were *your* pawns whom you sent to try to destroy Detroit. You could have challenged me to a duel yourself but you didn't. You hid behind catspaws like the coward you are."

"All conjecture!" He pounded a clawed hand on the table.

"What about when you ambushed me in Mammoth Cavern? No other dragon has the shadow powers you possess. None. And then there are the dragons who died because of your schemes. All the blood shed by the technomages is ultimately on your hands. The dragons who were killed by the assassin Death belong to you as well. You killed Lumos when you were engaged in a duel with *me.* You are a monster and a coward, and I will take what is mine from you."

"And what proof do you have? Do you have one shred of solid evidence that dragons might believe?" Boneclaw asked.

"We have proof you killed Lumos, you sick old bastard," Amy said.

"Watch your mouth, human," he growled warningly.

"Or what?" the young mage asked as she stepped forward and her hair whipped in a magic wind. "Will you fight me? I'll take payback for Lumos' death any time you're ready. So you want to know how many dragons had to find out the hard way that my magic is tougher than their scales?"

"This is outrageous!" Ironclaw exclaimed. "For a mage to speak this way—"

"Quiet, Ironclaw," Boneclaw ordered. "Lady Steel was muzzling her little pet."

"I can take him," Amy said. "I know I can."

Kristen shook her head and sent her a glance. *Not now.*

"I demand justice for his crimes," she said to the rest of the Council. "I've learned enough to know that I can't challenge him to a duel for these atrocities. I have a case, I'll present it, and the council will judge."

"I motion for us to do exactly that!" Aurelius said.

No one else followed his lead. Not the female councilor who had seemed upset at the accusations, not the one with blood-red eyes, and not Ironclaw. It seemed every one of them was in Boneclaw's pocket. She would get no succor from them.

"Finc," she said and addressed Boneclaw instead of the other four dragons who avoided her eyes. "Then let's have at it, you old coward. You and me to settle Lumos' score."

He chuckled at her. "You naïve, young, ignorant fool. Dragons do not *settle scores.* There are rules we follow. I will not accept a duel for a reason without honor. Now, it is time you left. No one is interested in investigating these reckless conspiracies, and I will not accept a childish human schoolyard brawl. Your time here is over. You are no longer an investigator so you are no longer welcome. Now, *be gone!*"

"Right, of course. Sorry," Kristen pushed her chair out with an extremely loud and uncomfortable screech from the wood on the floor. "Give me that skull and I'll leave."

Boneclaw laughed. "I will do no such thing."

"Fine. Then I challenge you to a duel for it."

"You truly do not understand how this works, do you?"

"But it's *mine.*" She thumped her chest. "It belonged to one of *my humans.* A sweet, wonderful man by the name of Jim Washington who was *so much better* than you'll ever be. I asked for it to be returned and you refused, so I'll duel you for it."

"This is—"

"Completely legal!" Aurelius interjected. "I knew that human. If that is indeed his skull, she can duel you for it. There are many precedents for exactly this."

"Is it this Washington's skull?" Ironclaw asked.

"It… That's irrelevant!" Boneclaw roared. "He's dead. It's no longer his."

"The rules are clear, my lord," the blood-eyed dragon said in a raspy voice. "But do not worry. You are the leader of the Council now. You were challenged so you may set the terms of this…slaughter." She smiled quite viciously.

"Fine, fine. If the Steel Dragon wants the skull—"

"I want the asshole who took it to be dead, thanks. I asked for it, you refused, and I challenged you to a duel. Now fight me. Coward," Kristen said coldly.

He drew a deep breath. Once. Twice. Three times. Finally, he uttered a fake laugh. "I accept your challenge, of course. It will be pleasant to finally end your insulting insurrection personally. When shall we do it? Oh, that's right. I am the challenged, so the choice is mine. Shall we say three days hence so you have time to get your affairs in order?"

"How about right now, outside the castle?" she countered.

Boneclaw shook his head. "You have challenged a member of a Dragon Council to a duel. There are certain rules about such things and some time is required for preparation. We will not battle in a field like a couple of *commons.*" He spat the last word.

Kristen glanced at Decimus Aurelius who nodded to confirm it.

"Fine," she agreed. "Three days from now. That's seventy-two hours. Which means our fight will take place in broad daylight."

He raised a lip at that but nodded. "That is accurate, of course. I will send you information about the location in half that time."

"You can't expect me to agree to—"

Aurelius cleared his throat. "Those are the rules, Lady Steel. You challenged him, so he chooses the time and place. He cannot make it an unfair arena that grants either of you an advantage."

"I wouldn't dream of such a thing," Boneclaw said. "I would tell you the location now but we must find somewhere private. I will not have the winner of this duel—whoever it may be—mobbed by human paparazzi and dragons wishing to earn the favor of their Councilor. Now that it is settled, let us get back to the meeting. As my first act as leader of the Council, I call for a vote to give me executive power to stop any organizations that are working against the will of Dragon Council."

Decimus Aurelius cleared his throat again.

"What is it now?" Boneclaw snapped.

"You can call for a vote of course, but you cannot be granted any kind of executive power."

"Of course I can. I'm the leader."

"Not yet, you're not," Aurelius said politely. "As you said, challenges have certain rules about them. One is that no dragon can assume a new post while a challenge is pending. This includes the head of the Council, of course, for obvious reasons. So, unfortunately for any executive privileges, the challenge will have to take place before you can be sworn in and granted such rights."

"That rule is hardly essential—"

"That *rule*," Aurelius said firmly, "has stood for centuries. It has prevented dragon Councilors who were not fit to rule because of their past grievances from taking power. To throw it out would be akin to throwing out one of our most honorable traditions. If you do that, we might as well sit with the Steel Dragon, dwarves, the mages, and the pixies to rewrite the rules that govern us all."

"*No one* wishes to do that," the blood-eyed dragon said. "The rules are clear. Boneclaw. You must defeat the Steel Dragon in combat in three days before you can be sworn in."

"If you don't, dragons the world over will revolt. These rules govern every Dragon Council. We can't simply ignore them as we please," Ironclaw insisted.

"Fine," Boneclaw said. "The trash heap this planet has become can wait another three days before it is cleaned. In fact, perhaps this is better. This way, I can wear the Steel Dragon's skull as I rise to become the head of all dragons on Earth. Do me a favor and die in your human form so that your skull may serve as a symbol of unity."

"Do me a favor and choke to death," Kristen replied before she strode out of the council chamber.

CHAPTER SIXTY-THREE

The surface of the island was beautiful. Long grasses whipped in a strong wind that blew so continuously, no trees could grow here. The only thing that broke the rolling vista of hills and rippling grass was the castle, which—despite its enormous size—looked like it had been made of eleven massive stones. There was a simplicity to the landscape that Kristen appreciated. Perhaps it was because her life had grown so complicated.

"Too bad it didn't work," Hernandez said as she gathered all the flashbangs she had buried in the grassy hillside.

"I thought for sure the asshole would tell you he'd fight at dusk," Amy said.

"I should have known he wouldn't be so easy to trick," Heartsbane said. "Still, Kristen, forcing him to fight in broad daylight was a masterful stroke."

"Yeah, I wish I felt better about it. With Lumos gone, I don't know how I'll be able to defeat him. I'd be willing to bet that the venue he names will be watched twenty-four hours a day."

"I might not be able to give him any Hernandez surprises, but you'll think of something. You always do," the explosives expert said.

"Everyone always thinks of something until they don't. Then

they're dead," she said. She hadn't meant it to so sound so morose but that was how she felt.

"There's nothing to be done now but train," Heartsbane said. "I think Stonequest and I can do a decent job of attacking you simultaneously so it feels like the Masked One's strikes. If you're blindfolded as well—"

"It won't make an iota of difference."

Kristen turned to see who had interrupted Heartsbane. Decimus Aurelius strode from the castle, studied the broken doors, and shook his head with a little smirk and continued to approach.

"Aurelius. Thank you for your support." She bowed formally.

"We have no time for pleasantries," he replied. "I know time is short so will make this brief. If I may speak to you in private for a moment?" He glanced at the other three women who stood near her.

They simply stared implacably in response.

"No harm will come to her," he said with a forced smile.

"We know it won't," Hernandez said.

"Because if you try shit, all it will take is a twitch of her aura for me to know," Heartsbane said.

"And then I'll crush you." Amy smiled.

"But of course. If I do anything to this planet's last hope for equality, crush away. Now, Kristen, if you please."

She considered telling the old dragon there was nothing he could say to her that he couldn't say in front of three of her most trusted friends, but she decided he might argue and it would merely waste more time. It wasn't like he would be able to kill her in the time it would take for them to come to her aid. Plus, she trusted him.

They walked up a rolling hill and the grass beat at their waists and thighs. With the constant roar of the wind, it didn't take long until they were well out of earshot. Aurelius was clever. He had walked with the wind instead of against it so their words would be carried out to sea, away from her friends and away from any ears that might have listened from inside the castle.

"I think we're alone," Kristen said.

He looked at her allies once more and nodded his agreement, then turned to her with a stern look on his face. "That was a damn foolish thing you did in there."

"Wait, what?" She was more than a little surprised. "Aren't you glad I stood up to Boneclaw? If I hadn't, he'd be the leader right now. Well…no, I guess *you* could have stood up to him. Why didn't you?"

"The fact that I had not challenged him should have told you something," he replied.

She sucked a breath of air in through her teeth. "Go on."

"You must remember that I am more than a thousand years older than you. I have seen Boneclaw do horrible things, and this was before him allegedly being the Masked One."

"There's nothing alleged—"

"No, of course not. It all makes sense, it truly does. He has never been outright malicious but he's always sided with those who were. Sometimes, he won't do it until the last moment but in the end, he always has. I've long detested him and his methods."

"I know you don't like him or what he's done, so why not take a stand? Letting him get away with his conspiracies for hundreds of years is… Well, I respect you sir, but it's cowardly."

Decimus hung his head and focused his gaze on his feet lost in the windswept grass instead of looking her in the eye. "That is a fair accusation. And, unfortunately, accurate." He took a deep breath. "I have not fought Lord Boneclaw because I know I cannot beat him. Even before you revealed him to be the Masked One and having power over shadow, I could not beat him."

"But Lumos told me stories about you. You're supposed to be a legend!"

"No, no, no." He shook his head. "I am stronger and more powerful than most dragons and I know my way around a duel, but Boneclaw is the legend. He has survived scores of challenges over the centuries. He rose to become a member of the European Council and never lost a challenge to his power there, which is saying something because he was there for a long time, and European dragons like war as much as European humans do. Later, he challenged a North American Councilor and took his place. He eventually rose to the Global Council and never lost a duel there either. It's not from a lack of challenges either. Many have tried to take his title because he *looks* weak. But I assure you, he is not. He is strong and he is vicious."

"I've fought him before."

"And it's a miracle you're still alive. It's a first, to be honest."

"What does that mean?" Her mouth was suddenly dry.

"It means that Boneclaw has killed every single dragon he has faced in single combat except you."

"Excuse me?" Kristen frowned. "I thought duels were fought to mercy. Surely Boneclaw couldn't have lasted this long if every duel he fought was to the death."

"They weren't to the death. That's exactly the problem," Aurelius said. "Duels at this level are almost always decided when one dragon admits defeat. To even attempt to become a Councilor, a dragon needs a considerable amount of wealth. That can't be gathered overnight. Because of this, the dragons who challenge others to become Councilors want certain assurances that the centuries they worked accumulating wealth and clout won't simply be erased if they ever try for more. Death is a possibility in any duel. All dragons accept that, but it's rare."

"Because if dragons couldn't challenge each other for rank without fear of dying every time, the members of the Council would never change," she guessed.

"Exactly. Even the original Dragon Council understood the dangers of other dragons being afraid to challenge for fear of death. Unfortunately, Boneclaw's duels always end up in death anyway."

"But how is that possible if the rules say the duel stops when someone asks for mercy?" Kristen asked. She tried to tell herself this was what she wanted anyway. Without a doubt, Boneclaw had to die. As long as he lived, he would continue to work to bring about a war that would burn the earth to ashes so he could stand atop the smoldering remains.

"Boneclaw always seems to find an excuse to kill them before ending the duel. Always. As in every. Single. Time. Sometimes, it was simply that their wounds were already so grievous that when they asked for the duel to end, they were already dying. That happens in dragon duels often enough—well, not often, but it's certainly not unusual. Other duels with Boneclaw were worse, though. He's ripped a dragon's tongue out so they couldn't ask for mercy. He's crushed windpipes.

"I've seen him trigger an avalanche the moment the other dragon asked for the duel to be over. Boneclaw walked away as a mountain crushed his opponent. I've even seen him simply kill them even after they asked for mercy. He hasn't done that in a long time as the blowback was serious, even for him, but I wouldn't be surprised if he risked the repercussions to murder you. Eventually, word got around and dragons stopped challenging him as much because everyone knew it was tantamount to suicide."

She said nothing and her mouth had formed an "O" shape.

Decimus nodded at her understanding. Her aura made what she was feeling clear to him.

He turned to look at her friends who stood near the edge of the cliff with the wind blowing in their faces. "I hope you understand why I didn't want to have this discussion in front of your friends."

"You think I'll die."

"Unfortunately, I do. You are in quite deep now. I understand you are very powerful—*extremely* powerful for such a young dragon—but I simply do not see how it is possible for you to contend with Boneclaw's strength and experience. And that was before it was made clear that he possessed shadow powers. I have never heard of him using those in a duel. Now that he can openly use them in his arsenal…well, the odds are stacked against you even further."

"But…I trained with Lumos. I've practiced so much. I'm a much better warrior than when I first discovered my powers."

"How much did Lumos' training aid you in your last fight with Boneclaw? From the account I've heard, he had knocked you unconscious before Lumos interfered. For that matter," he continued and bulldozed over the old dragon's memory, "how much did all that knowledge help Lumos?"

"I… He had been in another battle. If it hadn't been nighttime…"

Aurelius shook his head sadly. "Like I said, he's never used his shadow powers before, although I'm sure he will choose a location where he had access to them. Kristen, I believe in you. I truly do. But I have to face the reality that you will die. It is the most likely possibility. Is there some way I can help with your team? If I allied with them, how long do you think they could last?"

"No—no, no, no. I *can* beat him. I must!"

"I want you to. I honestly do. If there's something you can think of, any way I can help, please let me know. I don't want you to fail. If you do, no one will be left to oppose him. I'll try to protect your team, but he's already labeled you as a traitor and a heretic. All the people under your protection will suffer the same fate you do."

"Can't you help me defeat him?" Kristen pleaded.

Aurelius' aura pulsed with shame. "I know my powers and limitations far better than you do, Kristen. I am…I am helpless in this case. But I also understand my place. I cannot beat Boneclaw even without the powers of the Masked One. You must think of some way to defeat him because he will not hold back. I promise you that. If you lose this duel, you lose your life. And yet, as badly outmatched as you are, you are our best hope right now."

"Je-sus," she muttered. "Is there anything else I should know? Any comets heading for Earth? Any global pandemics about to break out soon?"

"Merely that I fully support you, Lady Hall, Steel Dragon." He dug in his pocket and retrieved her investigator's badge. She'd recognize it anywhere as one of the seven points was slightly dented.

"How did you…"

"I palmed it when you threw it on the Council table. That was fantastic, by the way. The looks on their faces." Aurelius grinned. "I hope you can win. I will miss you otherwise. Anyway, you should keep the badge. Windlock gave it to you and even if Boneclaw revoked your position, you should have something of his to remember him by. Maybe, if everything goes bad, it can be left to Larry. I know Windlock always loved that mage like a son."

"Your vote of confidence is inspiring," Kristen wanted to say, but she held her tongue as she pushed through the windswept grass to her friends. By the time she reached them, she had a smile on her face and her feelings hidden from all except the prying powers of Heartsbane.

Melissa Heartsbane looked at her with cold blue eyes and smiled. "That bad, huh?"

CHAPTER SIXTY-FOUR

The trip to Detroit was a somber one. Fortunately, it wasn't particularly long. Once they left the island, Amy called Constance and together, the two mages opened a portal that blazed to life in front of Kristen and Heartsbane's dragon forms and took them home to the Motor City.

They left the frigid air of the North Atlantic and reappeared over the familiar Detroit skyline. Thankfully, it *was* familiar. Timeflash had worked tirelessly with the mages to restore the city to its former glory since the fire tornado had ripped through it. She had done so much already. Most apartment blocks and swathes of public housing had already received her expert attention. Progress had also been made with the private homes as well as some of the more culturally significant parts of the city. Kristen pointed out that her favorite pizza place had stood for decades and that it was a rallying point in the community, so it was early on the list.

One thing that hadn't been fixed was her base. To repair a building of that size required a huge amount of energy, power better spent on housing. It was a simple choice because there was little point in fixing the base without also replacing the gear and tech that had been lost. An apartment block was different. If Timeflash and her mages could restore the walls, roofs, electrical systems, and plumbing, people could resume their lives and refill their homes with new beds, books, and furniture.

Plus, some of the main base was gone. As the sphere the pixies created to protect them shrank, some of the building had been sliced away. Timeflash could put things back to the way they were, but she couldn't recreate matter that had been lost in another dimension.

As a result, they didn't return to the main building but the two smaller ones. One of these had been converted to housing and practically overflowed with occupants. Given the state of the world, everyone wanted to stay close in case World War Three—or would it be Four at this point?—broke out.

Kristen entered her new base of operations to find it crammed with people. Humans, mages, and dragons went about their business with determination. Some were cleaning while others worked on plans to reconstruct the old base. Dragons and mages were airborne and worked on synchronizing their attacks in preparation for another battle. Humans, mages, and dragons crowded into a gun range outside the base. The sound of their weapons served as an appropriate background noise for how everyone felt.

She called for her leaders and oldest friends. Together, they squeezed into a meeting room that didn't even come close to comfortably fitting them all.

Drew, Keith, Butters, and Beanpole were present from her old SWAT team. Jim was gone, which hurt them all. She could see the pain of that recent loss in their eyes. The dragons had fared even worse. Stonequest was present, as was Timeflash—who looked exhausted—but Lumos and Emerald were both gone. In their place stood Katrina, the Iron Dragon, who looked uncomfortable. Larry and Constance—two mages with histories as different as could be—were the only two magic wielders until Amy arrived to join them.

Heartsbane, Hernandez, and Kristen followed the girl into the tight room. They were about to begin when her brother pushed in.

"How'd it go, Krissy?" Brian asked with a grin. He looked at her face and—being her brother—was able to read it far better than anyone could, including the dragons with their aura powers. "That bad, huh?"

Everyone groaned and began to complain and he threw his hands up in protest. "Don't blame me."

"Please at least tell us there is some good news," Timeflash begged.

"There is good news and bad," Kristen said, still standing, and motioned with her arms for everyone to sit and be quiet. "I guess it would make more sense if we start with the good. We were right. Boneclaw was attempting to become the head of the Global Dragon Council."

"Well, of course a pig eats slop!" Butters crowed.

"Did you stop him?" Keith asked and sounded like a little kid asking about the ending for a comic book he had yet to read.

"We did…in a fashion," she said.

Everyone cheered so loudly the cheap light fixtures on the ceiling rattled.

"Now for the bad—" She wasn't quite sure how to say it, so it was both annoying and a relief when Hernandez interjected.

"She had to challenge Boneclaw to a duel to make that shit happen. It goes down in three days, and if our Steel Dragon doesn't stop him, he becomes the dragons' fearless leader."

It was a total bummer to see so many faces filled with joy and excitement fade to disappointment and dread so quickly.

Stonequest cut through the general roar of disapproval. "I *told* you not to do that. Trying to surprise him with flash bombs was bad enough but giving him time to prepare for a proper duel…" He shook his head. "You've survived against him this far because you haven't fought on his terms. When you did in the caves, you were almost killed."

"So the flashbangs didn't work, huh?" Keith asked Hernandez.

"They *would* have," the woman complained. "The old pussy was too scared to leave his castle. You should have seen his face when we burst into the room. It seems I was the first person to ever bust in their old-ass base."

"Maybe this is unfair, but is it possible to lay a trap for him?" Beanpole asked in a rare moment of verbal communication.

"It won't be possible," Stonequest said. "He'll need to announce the location in—you said the duel was in three days?"

Kristen nodded. "Seventy-two hours. It'll be at about noon."

"Then he'll have to give you thirty-six hours warning. But by that point, the area will be under surveillance. There is no way we'll be able to interfere," he said.

"I'm surprised you'd even consider such a thing, Stone," Heartsbane said. "Traps aren't particularly honorable."

"Nothing about fighting the Masked One will be honorable," he pointed out.

"Forgive me, but are you supposed to fight him one-on-one?" Constance asked. "We fought him together, and although my powers were limited at the time, he still showed a formidable amount of power. I do not see how good can come of this."

"What about the arena?" Timeflash asked. "When Heartsbane, Emerald, and I fought him in the caves, we barely got out of there alive, but that was in the dark. You said this fight will be at noon, right?"

"Aurelius said the arena can't give either of them an unfair advantage based on their powers. Is that true, Stone?" Heartsbane asked.

"It is. That means he can't put in electrical transformers since you don't do well with electricity, Kristen." Stonequest said ponderously.

"So it can't be in the dark?" Amy asked.

"Probably not, no," he conceded. "But it seems foolish to think you'll fight somewhere without shadow."

"When they announce the location, can we appeal to make that happen?" Larry asked. He was somewhat familiar with dragon rituals. "Can we make it clear the shadows give him an unfair advantage?"

"It's worth a try," Stonequest said.

"Look, I know none of this is ideal," Kristen conceded. "I had hoped the fight would be done and over with already, but we didn't exactly have many options at the time. I did the only thing I could."

"There's no point in complaining about it now," Drew said. "The question is what you will do to prepare for this fight in three days." He was always the practical one. "From what I've seen, you can already outfight every dragon on our force. How are you supposed to get any better?"

"I can't outfight every dragon," she said and looked at Stonequest, Heartsbane, and Timeflash in turn. She expected the stone dragon to agree with her. He was the best in combat, after all, but he nodded grimly.

"Drew's right about that. I've noticed the way you move after you trained with Lumos. You're a natural warrior, Kristen, there's no doubt about that. I wouldn't want to fight you in earnest, not anymore."

"I'm no fighter," Timeflash said. "I have yet to finish fixing the city and I'm already exhausted."

Kristen turned to Heartsbane. "Honestly, Steel? If you tried to fight me, I'd try to use my aura to convince you otherwise. There is not a dragon alive who *wants* to fight the Steel Dragon. Hell, Boneclaw didn't want to fight you either. He would have given that skull to you and backed out the fight if you'd let him."

"You didn't get it back, then?" Drew asked.

She shook her head. "It was the only thing that achieved the duel. Plus—and I'm sorry if this is the dragon in me coming through— getting Jim's skull back wouldn't have changed much. Boneclaw still butchered him. He still defiled his body and he must still be punished."

Her human team leader nodded, his face grim. "I'll call his mother when we're done here and let her know. It's...tough, but you're right. There is no way the Wonderkid will have an open casket."

His words were followed by a moment of silence pregnant with grief.

Hernandez was the one who broke it. "But...if all these dragons and Boneclaw himself were scared, maybe Kristen has a chance."

All three dragons shook their heads.

"I'm sorry, but beating one of us is nothing like fighting Boneclaw to the death. He's been in hundreds of duels over the centuries," Stonequest explained. "We're cops. We stop unruly dragons but we're not the level of fighter you need to be to sit on the Council. It's a pity about Shimmerclaw. I bet *she* could have beat him."

"Thanks for all your confidence, guys," Kristen said and the sarcasm burned through her words.

"You misunderstand me, Kristen," he said and held his hands up in surrender. "You have to defeat him. You *must*. We simply know that you cannot if you attempt to fight him in a duel of his devising."

"They're saying we need to change the game somehow," Brian said. "You have to level up a new technique and try some different tactics. Try a different controller. That kind of thing."

"Your wisdom never ceases to amaze," she said as the shadow of a dragon passed over their base. "Or maybe we won't have to wait after all."

"That's Amythist," Heartsbane said. She was gifted with aura powers which meant she could identify other dragons more quickly and easily than the others.

"Look, I'll go stretch my legs and say hi," she said. "If anyone has anything—and I mean *anything*—let me know. No idea is too small and no notion too bizarre."

CHAPTER SIXTY-FIVE

Kristen left the base to see Amythist, but the old dragon was having none of it. She took her by the arm—leaning on her like she needed support and wasn't an extremely powerful dragon— and told her to take her inside.

In silence, she led her to the conference room. Most of the group had left but Stonequest, Drew, and Larry were still milling about.

She pulled out a chair for their visitor and the old dragon settled in. Timeflash reappeared a moment later with a fresh pot of tea.

"Lemon balm? Oh, darling, you are too sweet," Amythist said by way of thanks and Timeflash excused herself.

"It's nice to see you, Lady Amythist," Kristen said.

"You too, young lady. You too." When she smiled, the wrinkles on her cheeks multiplied. "Although I do wish the circumstances were better. You have landed yourself in a God-awful mess this time."

"Excuse me?" she asked, certain that Amythist was talking about the duel but also shocked that she could know about it. The challenge had been made less than an hour before. She had thought that with Amy's portal, there was no way the news could have outraced them.

"Oh, don't look so flummoxed, child. I know about the duel. *Everyone* knows about the duel—absolutely *everyone.* We dragons do have telephones, you know, and it's not like the news of late hasn't been worth paying attention to."

"That's true, Lady Amythist," Larry said. "But sometimes, it seems like you always seem to know about everything before most folks around you do. Whatever asshole invented social media must have modeled his algorithm after whatever you do to stay in the loop."

"Well, of course I know about things before most do. When you grow to be as old as I am, the only thing worth anything anymore is information. In fact, my knowing so much is a result of me being old *and* the reason I managed to live this long. All you little whippers could learn a thing or two from me if you wish to last more than a few centuries."

"Gee, thanks," Larry said and rolled his eyes at dragon longevity.

"Maybe your experience could be the thing I need," Kristen said. "Aurelius said that unless I can find some kind of edge against Boneclaw in this duel, I'm toast."

"That is a fair assessment," the old dragon said. "Tell me, what kind of edge do you think you can acquire in three days?"

"Honestly? I'm not sure," she admitted. "My plan was to spend the next three days fighting as much as I can. I thought maybe Katrina might be able to give me the edge I need."

"Your twin? The Iron Dragon?" Stonequest asked.

"She's not my twin," she said. "But Katrina has as much raw power as I do and she's a damn good fighter. Maybe she can push me to my next level."

"Even if she is better than you, it won't make a difference," Amythist scolded. "Learning another way to use your weight in a brawl won't help an iota. And, despite your steel skin, I know you're not dense enough to think it would."

Kristen nodded. She knew their visitor was right. Katrina might be able to make her slightly faster or be able to use her powers to gain a little leverage, but that was the problem. Any edge she gave her would be negligible. She was facing a master duelist and a beast of shadow. To defeat him, she would need more than that.

"But what else can I do?" she implored.

"Why, come with me for a cup of tea, of course. I've almost finished this lemon balm and I have a lovely harvest of dried jasmine at home that is ready for tea."

"I don't think the tea will give me an edge that the Iron Dragon won't."

"Not the tea, no, but the…idea I'd like to share with you might."

Hope bloomed in her chest. "I always forget they called you the Mage Eater. You have a fighting technique you've been sitting on this whole time?"

"No, not exactly. There is, however, something we can try although it will not be easy."

"Nothing about being a dragon has been easy," Kristen said. "I've been blown up, shot, stabbed, and sliced a hundred different ways. I've lost friends. I can take whatever it is."

"That is the very problem, my dear. This will be especially difficult for a headstrong young dragon like yourself. But come along. I would love to have tea while the day is still light."

"And we'll spar tonight?" She tried to make sure. Without a doubt, she admired the old dragon—the work she had done to rehabilitate the captured dragons was nothing short of miraculous—but still, what could Amythist teach her that Lumos couldn't? He had at least *looked* like a fighter. She looked like a little old woman who was too obsessed with tea.

"I would not use that word, but perhaps it's as accurate as any other," the old dragon said. "Do come along. I've finished my tea and all this talk has made me all the more thirsty. Will you come with me? The choice is yours, of course."

"I…sure, I mean, yes. I'll come. But how long do you think this will take? I have three days and I intend to use them as best as I can."

"Well, that all depends on you, doesn't it?" Amythist replied. "It only took me a few centuries to learn what I hope to show you in a few days. I hope your optimism is warranted and that you end up with some time for *sparring,* but I would not hold my breath."

"A few *centuries?*" Kristen asked. She had heard similar proclamations from Lumos about his methods, but they had at least had weeks, not hours.

"I hope you will be a quicker study than I because of course, if you are not, we are quite…what's the human word? Ah yes. Fucked."

She nodded at the dire assessment. That much was true. Still, to put off training with Katrina for the promise of tea seemed irresponsible to say the least.

"Stonequest, what do you think?" she asked.

"If she can offer you some kind of edge, take it," he told her. "Even if she is being cryptic about it."

"Some things cannot be explained but must be shown," Amythist said.

"Larry?"

"We would never have rescued you from that sphere if not for Amythist's help and the pixies," Larry said. "I'd trust the old dragon—no offense, Lady Amythist—with my life, and I've already trusted her with yours. I say go for it."

"All right then. That's good enough for me. Drew?"

"Ma'am, you know I know little and less about any of this. I'd respect these two opinions."

"I'm not asking your opinion. I'm leaving you in charge," Kristen said.

He saluted. "Yes, ma'am! I will do everything I can to keep the peace intact while you go and work on whatever this is but please, don't be too long."

"She'll be back in less than three days." Amythist winked. "I can promise you that. Whether that will be enough time is another question, but the duel is set. Is it not?"

No one answered. They didn't need to.

She followed the old dragon outside and the two took to the air. While she tried to enjoy the short flight to the estate outside Detroit, she'd be lying to herself if she said she did.

CHAPTER SIXTY-SIX

The flight was blessedly quick. They arrived in Amythist's overgrown garden of an estate and the old dragon led Kristen inside her cottage, shushing young dragons out of the way and shooing pixies off as she did so.

Once inside, she was once again astonished by how much Amythist had crammed into the tiny home. Some of it was typical dragon treasure—a few jeweled goblets, a chest with iron hinges and finely wrought gold detail, silver platters, paintings that belonged in museums, and similar items. But bunches of herbs hung from the ceiling, glass jars were crammed full of seeds, and piles of root vegetables rested between collections of insect wings and feathers. Her home was like something out of a fairytale, and the pixies trying to peek through the kitchen window only added to the effect.

"Now," Amythist said, cleared two piles of books, and made two chairs appear out of the mess. "Let me get that jasmine tea."

"Wait, you're serious?" Kristen asked.

"Oh yes," her hostess said from the kitchen. "The jasmine is from my garden and it is divine. I know we dragons are prone to exaggeration, but this is the best harvest I have had in years. It would be a shame to not taste some."

"Well, sure then," she agreed. "And after that, we'll get started?"

"Patience, young one, patience. Tea cannot be rushed, nor can it last longer than the warmth in a cup."

"Er…right," she said and sat.

Amythist poured them each a cup of tea, then sat in the chair next to her. Kristen did not fail to notice that the small table on which the old dragon had poured the beverage was not at all cluttered. It seemed she truly did prioritize her tea.

Her hostess lifted her cup to her lips, took a sip, and smiled. "If you'll give me a moment to gather my thoughts," she said, leaned back, and sipped her tea again. Her smile somehow became even wider.

Kristen sipped hers. It *was* good and tasted like jasmine, which was pleasant, she supposed. She looked at Amythist. The old dragon still had her eyes closed and wore a smile that eased every wrinkle on her face.

A little out of her depth, she sipped her tea again and tried to enjoy the delicate flavor and relax and…clear her mind? It was an odd situation for the Steel Dragon and she didn't know what the hell she was supposed to do. How could she sit there wasting time with everything that was racing through her mind?

Had it been dumb to challenge Boneclaw as she had? In the moment, she had thought it was her only choice. She had hoped that by outlining his crimes, his hold over the Council would crack. After all, Shimmerclaw had managed some semblance of control for a long time. How had he so fully stolen all her allies?

She had known that outlining his crimes would end in conflict but had hoped that others on the Council would lead that battle and they would all then deal with Boneclaw together. But there were so many problems with that. As soon as she had discovered that he had already been elected head of the Council, she should have aborted the plan.

Boneclaw still would have taken power, but her force would not be faced with the murder of their leader in three days. Maybe she could have continued to challenge his power or she could work to change minds. But now, she had three days and her enemy had an easy way out. The duel only had to go the same way every other duel he had ever participated in had.

Of course, the idea that he could only kill her in a duel was a complete fallacy. He could move through shadow the way a bird moved through the air. As far as she could tell, he could kill her anytime he wanted. Nowhere was safe from the *dark.* Even if she took to sleeping in a tanning bed, it wasn't like light hurt the Masked One. It only made him solid. And—as Aurelius had pointed out so firmly— he was quite an adept fighter.

That was the worst part about this entire situation—the threat of Boneclaw being able to kill her anytime he wanted. She *hated* that. Feeling vulnerable twenty-four hours a day sucked.

But challenging him to a duel didn't change that. He could attack her there if he wanted to. She doubted the old woman and her tea would be able to stop him, no matter how complex the bouquet.

Kristen looked at the old dragon. She still sat with her eyes closed and a smile plastered on her face. Had she fallen asleep? Was this a trick? She wanted to say something but she thought of Lumos. Her old mentor would have told her to exercise patience.

Oh, Lumos. Why did you have to die? And on top of it, The Masked One had taken Jim's life too. Their deaths—more than anything— were the impetus for her to try to stop Boneclaw so soon. She missed them both terribly. Jim had truly been the Wonderkid. He was always smiling and always perfect, whether in a shootout or a press conference.

And Lumos…she couldn't believe how much losing the old dragon hurt. He had been gone for only a few days, yet she had felt the ache of losing him grow rather than diminish. If she hadn't lost him, she might have been able to control herself when confronted with Boneclaw wearing Jim's skull like a fucking mask.

Kristen spared another glance at Amythist. This time, the dragon took a sip of tea while she watched, so at least she hadn't fallen asleep. Again, she wanted to clear her throat but thought about her life since she had become a police officer for the Detroit Police Department.

How simple everything had seemed then. She would be a police officer and would assist people who called for help. After a few years of learning how the system worked, she would try to tackle the corruption and racism she knew ran through almost all police departments.

She chuckled quietly. Had her life turned out so different from what she had planned? She had always thought she could be a cop who would make a difference, who would help police the police themselves. Now, she was a dragon who policed dragons. Instead of fighting for people only, she was fighting for all beings everywhere.

Seeing it in those terms made her feel like she at least wasn't completely off base. She still attempted to tackle an institution that was far bigger and older than herself. When all was said and done, she was still merely one person trying to make a difference in a world that could feel indifferent or, at worst, cruel.

Although when she'd been a cop she'd never been asked to sit and sip tea while a serial killer was on the loose.

Finally, she cleared her throat.

Amythist only smiled more widely. Kristen hadn't thought that possible. "This tea will work wonders for your cough," the old dragon said.

"Yep, I think it has," she said and swallowed the rest of it in one gulp. "In fact, I feel rested and recharged and ready to go. Are we ready to start training?"

"Not yet my dear. We still have an entire pot to drink. Wait until you taste your second cup." Amythist winked mysteriously.

"We can't simply sit here, Lady Amythist. We need to do something. I have three days—less now. Less than seventy hours to get ready. Every minute counts."

Amythist sighed, opened her eyes, and looked at a cuckoo clock ticking on the wall.

"My dear, it has been five minutes. You are not in such dire straits that five minutes will make a difference."

"Really? Because every dragon I've talked to has made it very clear that my straits are *extremely dire.*"

"Perhaps I misspoke. You are indeed in trouble, but if you cannot master even a little patience, you will not be able to master anything I show you. If five minutes was too long for you, learning this technique will be extremely difficult."

"Seriously?"

"Seriously indeed. Patience is key to what I show you. It is key to everything. If you are to succeed, you will need every ounce of patience you can muster."

"Okay, fine. If I need to be patient, I'll be patient. Can you at least tell me what kind of technique I'll use so I can focus on that during my"—Kristen sighed—"second cup of tea?"

"Demanding answers is no way to improve your patience, young one, but perhaps you are right. I feel refreshed and ready to show you what I know."

"And that is?" she asked after a pause so long that she thought Amythist might have fallen asleep with her eyes open.

"How to use your magical powers, my dear."

She sighed and shook her head. "Amythist, I already know how to use my powers. Stonequest says I have more control than most dragons, in fact." She turned a single fingertip to steel and showed it to her companion, then made the steel extend down the finger and from there to the others. Once her entire hand was metal, she shifted it into its dragon form so her wrist turned into a steel claw instead of a steel hand.

"That is most impressive," Amythist agreed. "You have far more control over your shifting than most dragons. More than me, certainly. Your control over all your dragon powers is quite impressive."

Kristen ground her teeth. "Then why am I here?"

"You are here precisely because of this control. Your ability to manipulate your steel form and your shifting ability are what give me hope that you can learn more."

"There's more?" she asked.

"Oh yes, child, much more." The old dragon put her teacup down and leaned back in her chair. She extended one old withered hand and turned it palm up and held it there for a moment, breathing in and out as if waiting for something to happen.

And then she summoned a huge ball of light in the palm of her hand.

"Child, there is much more to dragon magic than almost any dragon is aware of."

CHAPTER SIXTY-SEVEN

Kristen almost tumbled out of her chair at the display of power. She most certainly spilled her tea all over herself and soaked the front of her black uniform with fragrant jasmine liquid.

"How did you do that?" she asked, her voice filled with wonder like a child who'd seen something miraculous. "I didn't realize you had light powers like Lumos did. But…how can that help me? This duel is supposed to be one-on-one."

Amythist chuckled. "Oh, child, I would never, *ever* enter in any kind confrontation with Boneclaw. His reputation has preceded him for centuries. I eliminated a few mages in my day, but I'm no duelist."

She swallowed hard. Despite the tea she had been drinking, her throat felt dry. "I'm sorry, but I don't understand. Dragon powers are innate. It's interesting that you have light powers and have kept them hidden, but what am I supposed to do with them? I was born with steel powers. I'll have to use them against the Masked One."

"Is that right?" the old dragon asked. She pointed to her teapot and it lifted off the table and filled her cup. A spoon then elevated and began to stir honey into the beverage. With her other hand, she reached under the teacup. Blue flames ignited in her palm and warmed the delicate china.

"How can you have so many powers?" Kristen asked, trying to understand. "Were you born with all these gifts?"

"No child, that's not the case at all," Amythist said after a sip of her tea.

"Then how?"

"Dragons are magical creatures," the old dragon explained. "We are like pixies, in a way, or dwarves or even mages. Magic is in our bodies. It powers every cell. It suffuses us and we are inseparable from it. But you know this, of course. Should dragon powers be possible by the laws of your human physics?"

"Well, I'm no scientist, but no. Merely the fact that we can fly and also crash through brick walls doesn't hold up. If we had hollow bones like birds, we wouldn't be strong enough to do what we do, but we can still fly."

"Precisely," Amythist agreed. "Our fire is the same. We are not snakes. There is no gland that we must replenish. Well, there is a body part of sorts, but like our entire dragon form, it's steeped in magic and is only possible because of magic. Auras, again, should not strictly be possible by the laws of this world, and yet I can read your confusion as clearly as a book."

"Okay. Fair enough, I guess I knew some of that, but it doesn't explain how you can use these other powers."

"Magic tends to come out in various forms of expression. Some dragons only have the ability to transform to and from human form and breathe fire. In fact, those two powers and some ability to read the emotional auras of others seem to be almost universal among dragons. But of course, these are not the only dragon powers. You have quite an unusual one."

"My ability to turn to steel."

"It should be utterly impossible. I am a gardener and a caretaker of living things. I tend to a few young dragons now and enjoy the pixies in my garden, but over my centuries of life, I have cared for many creatures. Humans, horses, dogs, a seal—briefly, but that's a long story.

"Skin is an organ with many purposes. It regulates heat, protects us from infection, and tells us about our environment. It is a complex, many purposed organ. Replacing it with steel should not be possible, nor should it allow you to still function. You should die simply from having your body heat trapped inside you every time you transform. And then there's the fact that your skin can block bullets and yet you can still move when wearing it. No steel on earth can do this—not steel that's not suffused with magic, that is. Your skin is more like dwarf skin than it is metal. And dwarves, of course, are magic."

"Do all the unusual powers work like this?" Kristen asked.

"But of course. Many dragons have managed to gain enough connection to their innate magic that they can do other things with it. Lumos's light was one such gift. Timeflash's time-warping power is another rather unusual one. Stonequest's rocky exterior, too. These powers are the result of innate magic meshing with the personality of the dragon in question. Only dragons who already have a deep connection with their inner magical self have these abilities."

"That's why some dragons don't gain those powers? They don't… connect with their magical self?"

"Indeed. In truth, the lack of many dragons developing special powers depresses me. Although of course, if every dragon did develop these powers, the last ten thousand years would have been even more complicated than they were."

"But why don't they?"

Amythist shrugged and levitated the tea set into the kitchen. "Quite frankly, I believe it's a lack of imagination. Your friend Emerald—rest his soul—was driven to be as powerful as possible because he was nothing but a common dragon."

"He was as strong a fighter as I've ever seen," she said in defense of her deceased friend. "He beat Diamontus in battle. Not many could have done that."

The old dragon nodded. "Perhaps he wasn't a common after all, then. I know the boy loved to train. He built his physique in both his forms. Perhaps that's how his magic manifested itself. Think about it. Does the amount of weight you lift in your dragon form have much to do with your human body?"

She wanted to say it did and point out that she had trained hard in her human body and that had made her a faster and stronger dragon. But that didn't seem quite right either. "Boneclaw doesn't exactly look like he goes to the gym."

"An unfortunately accurate example." Amythist began to pace. Her eyes twinkled with excitement. Kristen wondered if this was the first time she had ever told anyone about these theories. "Boneclaw has tapped into this power. He may not know it the same way I do, but he understands that the will of a sentient being goes a long way. Emerald had convinced himself that he could train to make himself stronger, and the magic supported that because he believed it so deeply. I don't know how Boneclaw fuels his abilities, but I know they are as strong as any dragon's. This has to do with his confidence."

"Wait, so are you saying Boneclaw might have *willed* his shadow powers into existence?"

The old dragon smiled and clapped her hands excitedly. "You are such a quick study. It took me twenty-two years and thousands of cups of tea to understand what the pixies were trying to tell me. You got it much quicker."

"But then why don't all dragons gain these powers if it's as simple as wanting them?"

"Oh, there's much more to it than simple desire, my dear." Amythist tutted. "Our powers express themselves from our subconscious. In the early days of dragons, there were only commons. No one knows who the first dragon was with special abilities, but I believe it was their discovery that allowed the rest of us to have the gift. Once one dragon discovered they could do more than breathe fire and change shape, others understood that they could too. From there, powers manifested based on subconscious desires. Boneclaw's powers likely manifested from him not wanting to be seen. Lumos was the opposite. He wanted to be a shining light of virtue."

"I first turned to steel to stop a rocket from blowing a friend up," Kristen said thoughtfully. "Do you think if something different had happened—like say one of my friends was thrown into a lake—my powers could have manifested differently?"

"I do!" Her companion's excitement was appealing.

"And you're saying I can gain more powers *now?* Like you have? Simply by willing them into existence?"

"No, my dear. We are not mages. We do not learn our powers from teachers but grow them from our subconscious. Any dragon could gain additional powers if they were instructed properly, but the same instruction won't work for all dragons. Some are simply too attached to their physical forms or the powers they already control to learn more.

"Take Diamontus, for example. He was an extremely powerful, extremely arrogant dragon. Most powers came into existence for dragons in times of great need or great duress. I do not think a trial could exist that would have been able to push that dragon to realize more powers, because he *knew*—subconsciously—that he was the strongest there was. This is the case for most of them. That's why duels end in death or defeat instead of the loser gaining a new ability."

"You said dragons are like the other magical creatures. Does that mean dwarves could learn magic too?" Kristen asked.

"It's an interesting hypothesis and one we might be able to test if all species truly valued each other. I hope that if you can defeat the Masked One, we can begin to ask those questions as a society. What other questions do you have?"

"Only two." She took a deep breath. This one would be a doozy. "Amythist, you said you were there in the beginning, that you remember when all dragons were commons. Does that mean you're one of the oldest dragons alive?"

"It does, child. I am one of the only ones still surviving. I'm older than Boneclaw, you know, and older than that poor boy Lumos too. But that wasn't your question, was it?"

"No, ma'am. My question is—since you were there from the start —do you know where dragons come from? They're not in the fossil record. There are no drawings of them in caves. Sometimes, I don't see how people could have even evolved with dragons flying about. Dinosaurs prevented any mammal bigger than a rat from evolving, so why did dragons let people come into being?"

"Your last question is the more interesting one, although it's flawed. I don't believe dragons let humans come into being at all. I believe it was the opposite."

"Wait, what?"

"I believe that dragons were created by a mage."

"That's impossible—isn't it?"

"It is the only thing that makes sense to me. I don't remember my childhood, exactly like humans. No dragon remembers our earliest years. I don't remember a mother and indeed, there are no dragons older than me. And yet, when I was a girl, there were mages. Humans' gift has always been the power of will. You are the only creatures insane enough to divert a river or build a city."

"Beavers and ants do that," Kristen said, feeling like her brother.

"You're also the only creature who would argue with an unfathomably old dragon who is trying to help you unlock the powers you will need to survive in three days."

"Right, sorry."

"As I was saying," Amythist continued. "It's my belief that exactly like pixies and dwarves, dragons were *created*. I can not guess at the intention but it is all that makes sense to me. Think of the dragon. All of us have a human form. Even the poor souls who were trapped in their dragon bodies by the technomages for their entire lives have a human form. Furthermore, we have always lived *with* people. There is no continent of dragons. We *need* people like dwarves and pixies do because *we are people*."

She wished she had another cup of tea to give herself time to let that sink in. It couldn't be possible…it simply couldn't. Dragons had ruled people since history began. There were stories of them in every human culture because they had always been there. But had they? What if they weren't any older than the earliest parts of human history? What if they were part and parcel of the human story? What if mages had made them—to protect themselves, to inspire awe, to try to become immortal—and the world had lived with the results of that fateful experiment ever since?

For her, it made sense in a way nothing about dragons ever had before. Because where else could they have come from? Mages had proven that they could create new life. They had done it twice in history. Maybe they had done it a third time, even earlier. Perhaps it had also been a war but not one fought between dragons and mages but between mages and the same enemy Boneclaw himself now wished to decimate—the masses of humanity.

And if dragons had come from mages, was it so insane to think that their powers were developed in a process similar to a mage like Amy or Constance gaining new control over their magic? That brought her to her next question.

"But how do you have such a wide variety of powers?" she asked.

Amythist smiled. "I was once a dragon with no powers at all. As I said, we all were, in those early days. A common, as some say today, although I prefer the term vanilla. I could fly, transform, breathe fire, sense other's auras, and that was it. More of these new dragons began to emerge. They had abilities so beautiful it made my heart ache. Some of them could swim to the very bottom of the ocean and see things I could only dream of. Others could tap into the very forces of the earth. There were dragons who could shake the ground beneath our feet or make the wind blow or the rain fall. For centuries—no, millennia—I tried to discover some path to one of these powers—*any* of these powers—and came up with nothing."

"What changed?"

"I made a breakthrough a few centuries ago. It was after the Second Mage War. I was able to touch my inner magic and gradually learned how to use it for a variety of purposes. I can do more than these parlor tricks, but I am still learning and always trying to find new ways to use that power."

"So you brought me here to teach me…parlor tricks?"

"Oh no, dear child. If all goes as I plan, the next three days will be the hardest of your entire life and you will learn things no dragon has ever mastered. That is if you survive."

CHAPTER SIXTY-EIGHT

Amy climbed the stairs to the roof of the base and looked out over the skyline of Detroit. Never, not in a thousand years, had she imagined she might one day stand where she was now and do the things she had done. She grew up in rural Maine in a town with nothing more exciting than a yarn store. After college, she had spent time in big cities but nothing worked out for her. She had been happy to move home and ready to live the life a small town required.

Until she became a mage and Kristen appeared.

She would forever be in the Steel Dragon's debt. She knew that and was content with it. In fact, being in her debt was positive. It meant she had someone to be loyal to and someone to care for and fight alongside.

What had been even more amazing about meeting her was that she wasn't the only new person who came into her life. The young mage found a new family in the Steel Dragon's team. She discovered a group where she belonged and where she mattered. And then Lumos had died and it was all her fault.

Her mind constantly told her that she should have been able to defeat the Masked One. She was the strongest mage in centuries, maybe ever. And yet, when Lumos had gone to fight for Kristen, she had been too tired to do anything about it. Maybe if she had trained harder, or used her powers more carefully, or done something better, Lumos wouldn't be dead.

Amy missed the old gold dragon. She missed how his advice always seemed hopelessly out of date and also perfect for the moment. She missed the way they'd race across the sky and she missed his mustache.

But his death was not the worst thing that could happen. As painful as it was, his death was in the past. Far worse was what might happen in the future. Losing him hurt far more than she had expected it to. If the Masked One killed Kristen too, she didn't know how she would live with herself.

Losing Lumos was painful, but at least she could tell herself that the dragon had led a long life. Millennia, in fact. He'd known what he was getting into and had always wanted to face the Masked One. It was something he'd told her on numerous occasions.

Kristen wasn't like that. She was a regular girl like Amy who had somehow stumbled onto godlike powers. Her whole life lay ahead of her and she wasn't ready to die—how could she be? She had never agreed to have a rival who was thousands of years old and could fight from the very shadows under someone's feet. If the Masked One killed her, Amy knew the pain would be even worse than when Lumos had died.

She could not allow that to come to pass.

As she looked at the twinkling lights of the city and the scant stars in the sky—how different it was from northern Maine, where there were hardly any lights and an uncountable amount of stars—she wrestled constantly with the problem.

History didn't do much to encourage her. Kristen had already fought the Masked One—more than once too. She had fought him in Mammoth Cavern where, if not for the quick action of the other dragons, she would have been defeated. And she had fought him inside the sphere of void space as well. Amy had only seen the aftermath of that battle—her friend's unconscious body being hurled through the roof—but it was more than enough to know the battle hadn't gone well.

Lumos had fought Boneclaw as well and lost. From what she had seen, it hadn't even been that close. The Masked One took a few hits early in the fight, but as soon as the environment changed to suit his abilities, he was able to annihilate the golden dragon despite his formidable fighting prowess. She didn't harbor any illusions that he would play fair in this fight. It meant the odds against Kristen were not good, to put it mildly.

But what could she do? She knew she couldn't intervene in the duel itself. There would be dragons and possibly mages present. Her control of magic was not subtle enough for her to even pretend she could help without anyone noticing. But she had to help her. She couldn't lose her at the hands of Boneclaw, not like she had lost Lumos.

Oh, Lumos, Amy lamented. She looked at the wreckage of the old main building of the base. It was still a messy cairn for a wonderful dragon.

She used her magic to pick herself up by the collar of her shirt—feeling appropriately like a sad puppy—and levitated to the wreckage.

Contractors were supposed to arrive in the morning to begin hauling the debris away so reconstruction could begin. Given that Kristen was supposed to fight the Masked One in three days—two and a half, now—it seemed it might have made more sense for them to delay the construction. Although maybe that would be worse. As it was now, the building was still an artifact of Lumos' and the Masked One's battle. The walls they had thrown each other into were still crushed in the same shapes. The pieces of concrete they'd hurled at each other had been left where they'd fallen.

It was mostly the same, anyway. The old dragon's body had been removed. The space where he had been buried was clear and the rubble was piled neatly alongside. It was, she thought sadly, like a cairn for one of the greatest dragons who ever lived.

Amy moved to the cleared space and knelt on the shattered concrete. Unable to help herself, she began to cry. They'd unburied

Lumos's body to find it bruised and broken. In the morning, when the sun had found it, the old dragon simply evaporated like morning dew. She had tried hard to keep something of him—a keepsake or memento—but she'd come up with nothing. All she had was memories, which were not nearly enough right now.

"Goddammit, why did you have to die?" she asked between the tears. It was so fucking unfair that he had to die. He had been *good*. He had fought for what was right and he'd still lost. Was the universe so cold? To her, it felt like they were in the void space Kristen had described—a dark, desolate universe devoid of hope and light.

She pushed to her feet, knowing that if she didn't, she would simply cry and cry and cry until there were no tears left. Although she needed the release, she didn't have time for that. Kristen didn't have time for that.

The young mage walked closer to where Lumos' body had been and stared at the empty space amongst all the rubble. It almost glowed in the harsh glare of the floodlights that Kristen had ordered set up in an attempt to keep the Masked One—he was merely a stupid dragon named Boneclaw she told herself fiercely—at bay. It almost hurt her eyes, seeing how bright it was up close compared to the night sky. The base was awash with light except for one place.

Near the edge of the cleared area, there was a stone that did not reflect any light at all. She narrowed her eyes and realized that was not quite true. One side of it seemed to be as black as coal or ink, but the tip of the other side was the off-white of bone.

Amy picked it up. It was not a stone at all but a dragon scale. She held it to the light and tried to match it to one of the dragons on the team with no success. It wasn't any of Kristen's closest allies and try as she might, she couldn't match it to any of the other dragons who worked for them either. None of them were black or bone colored.

In a sudden wash of clarity, she realized there was only one dragon it could have come from. Boneclaw must have lost the scale during his fight with Lumos.

How bizarre it was to hold this token of her best friend's foe and her other best friend's killer in her hand. To think that she had proof of his mortality. He *could* be injured. Lumos had done so.

The evil dragon had always been so careful to remain in shadow form most of the time and not allow any parts of his body to fall free and be captured. But the battle with Lumos was intense enough that at least this one scale broke away. Another dragon might feel that this proved Boneclaw's mortality. A dwarf might see it as a chink in his armor. A human might see it as a totem of bad luck.

But Amy was a mage.

She held it in her hand and let her magic flow into it to taste it and feel it. The scale still resonated with his aura and she smiled. She could use it to track him. Of course, she would have to be careful. If she got too close and he was in shadow, she knew how the fight would end. But if she could surprise him and flood him with light the way Lumos had, then…drop a mountain or a skyscraper or something on him, that might do it. Even dragons couldn't withstand everything.

Encouraged by the possibilities, she pushed a little more magic into the scale. She could feel that it wanted to return to its body and pumped magic into the idea to strengthen the desire to be part of the whole that made it. It took patience as she fed these intentions into the scale but finally, she had him.

She could tell where he was.

Her gaze drifted to the North, across Detroit, and beyond the suburbs. Was he in Michigan? Hiding out in the upper peninsula perhaps? Amy didn't want to push the tracking ability too far on the off chance that Boneclaw might be able to sense her coming, but she had what she needed. She could use the scale like a compass to take her to him. With it, she would be able to surprise him enough to overpower him and he would die.

The young mage considered telling someone. Maybe Larry could help her hide her power? Perhaps Stonequest could help her in a fight? But no. She didn't know enough about the rules of the duel to risk anything but the most secret of operations. For all she knew, Kristen's team attacking Boneclaw might nullify the entire duel.

It would be far better if she could catch up to him, kill him, and return undetected. Kristen would go to the duel as planned, Boneclaw wouldn't arrive, and they would have to declare her the victor. It was possible another dragon might fight in his place, but surely none would pose as a big a threat as the shadow dragon.

Amy summoned her skateboard from her room in the base. She felt it roll through a hallway, grind a rail in a stairway, and do a triple kickflip out the window before it glided to her side.

She had to do this, and she had to do it alone.

No more of her friends would die from this monster. Not if the most powerful mage in the world could help it.

Her mind made up, she climbed atop her skateboard, pushed off, and ollied into the sky, following where the scale pointed her. She didn't say goodbye because she would be back in the morning and the world would be a safer place because of it.

CHAPTER SIXTY-NINE

"Are you saying I could do what Lumos could?" Kristen asked Amythist.

"I am saying that if you can master the technique of learning magic, you can do far more than he ever could," the old dragon responded from the kitchen. She had it in her mind to serve cookies and seemed to be tearing the entire kitchen apart trying to locate them.

"I...uh, yeah? That sounds great. I can see how doing more than changing shape and armoring up could give me an edge in the battle against Boneclaw. But are you sure it's possible? He has far more powers than I do and his are incredibly deadly."

"It will be impossible if you cannot let yourself believe, child," Amythist said and returned empty-handed. "A key component—no, *the* key component—will be removing the mental blocks you have in your mind."

"I've already come to terms with being a dragon," she quipped. "Learning how to throw light doesn't sound that insane comparatively."

"A very good point, my dear. A very good point. You grew up

thinking you were a regular human. Learning that you were a dragon and could turn to metal must have been quite a shock to your definition of what was possible. I hope that will be enough."

"Enough?" she asked. "I'm ready. I'm totally on board with learning whatever you can teach me."

"Good. That's very good, but you see even now, your subconscious betrays you. You must learn these techniques. Period. It doesn't matter what I can teach you. It matters what you learn. For this to work, the subconscious blocks you have must be shattered so you can walk through them into new realms of possibility. This is not easily done."

"You said it would be difficult. I accept that. If it's pain, I can take it. Nothing would be more painful than watching the Masked One's destruction sweep across the globe. Please, let me try."

Amythist smiled warmly. "I think you will succeed in this, Kristen, I truly do. But you must understand that it took me centuries to learn everything I have. You don't have that, which means teaching you will necessarily be more difficult."

"I'm ready for anything."

"There are two options. The…easier choice is simply to let me do my best to teach you what I know. I am sure I could teach you some… parlor tricks, as you called them."

"I don't mean to be rude, but we both know I'm going to need as much power as possible."

The old dragon nodded and looked out her window to her front garden. "I know, my dear, I know. That is the problem. I do not know how much you will learn before the three days are up. I'll do my best, of course, but there are limits to what we can do in this realm." She cast a wary glance at her.

At that moment, Kristen understood that this offer was more than she had realized. Amythist wasn't only giving her the opportunity to learn a few new abilities but a chance to see into the very threads of existence that held the universe together.

"Are you talking about other…dimensions or whatever? Because if you are, I'm not afraid. I already went to one, a horrible place of nothing but inky darkness. If…if returning there will somehow…will somehow help, I can do it." Tears came to her eyes as she offered to go back to the place that had taken Jim from her and precipitated the death of Lumos. She didn't want to return to that nothingness, never again and *not ever*. But she would. She would face the void if that meant stopping Boneclaw from realizing his sick fantasy.

"I do not know if you will be asked to return to the in-between place, but it would be wise to assume you will face things that seem far more malicious than the empty maw of nothingness."

"I don't understand. If not there, then where?"

"Come outside with me. You said you are willing, which means that as it is, we are wasting time we both know is in short supply."

"And you'll train me in the garden?" she asked as they walked down the front steps and out into the overgrown garden.

"No, my dear. Our second option is to ask for help. You see, I did not learn about these secrets entirely on my own. I had help from the pixies." Amythist winked and looked at the garden. "Which I guess gives the little cretins the right to steal my cookies!"

The tinkling laughter of the creatures—so reminiscent of bells—came from a particularly overgrown rose bush. A moment later, a cookie launched from somewhere in the thick, thorny stems, and exploded into crumbs on Kristen's face.

"She can't even catch a cookie! What makes you think she can catch on to anything we have to say?" a tiny voice shouted before falling back into laughter.

"Wait, was that a test? I can catch a cookie. Throw another cookie," she demanded, which merely earned more tinkles of laughter from the pixies.

"You cannot demand things of the pixies," Amythist said with an amused shake of her head.

"Then why did they teach you?"

"A very long time ago, I saved a few of them. In return, they helped me learn more about magic. Also, they know I keep my pantry well-stocked with sweets, which always helps."

Kristen clenched her teeth. This was already frustrating. How many hours had passed since Boneclaw first issued his challenge? Now, she was supposed to somehow win the trust of creatures whose idea of being a good person was having a pantry to pilfer? "Are you sure it has to be the pixies? The last time I worked with them, I found their methods to be…less than direct."

The old dragon chuckled. "Pixies are beings made almost entirely from pure magic. They tend to have a deeper understanding of magic in general than either human mages or dragons. We are both physical forms imbued with magic. They are more akin to magic imbued with a physical form. They can teach you things not because they will make them easy to understand but because they will make truths of the universe clear at a fundamental level."

"If the pixies will help, of course I choose them. If they can speed up the process of me learning these new abilities, I might have a chance when I face Boneclaw," she said and tried to pitch the words to the pixie hiding in the rose bush.

"I thought you would say that, my dear, which is wonderful, but you must understand the risks inherent in working with the pixies," Amythist warned her.

"Well…do I have a choice? In less than three days, I have to face one of, if not the most powerful dragon in the world. If my only chance to defeat him is the pixies…well, let's do it."

"Very well. But understand that they will test you and push you. There were times during my trials when I very nearly died. Fighting the Masked One will be a challenge, but it is a challenge you understand fully. He will try to kill you. Period. If the pixies agree to help they will not try to kill you, but they do not quite understand the way our bodies work either. To be successful in the timeframe, I am sure the training will be quite extreme."

"Are you saying the pixies might kill me by accident?"

"I suppose that is the nature of their help, yes. Often, when I felt that I was being pushed the most, they would do nothing but laugh about it. Then, at other times, they would apologize or shower me with treats when I could not understand what I did wrong."

"I understand, but I still don't see what choice I have. It's either try with the pixies and succeed, accidentally get killed by pixies and the world burns, or face Boneclaw without the skills I need, get killed, and the world burns anyway. I *have* to do this. I'll simply have to hope that your insight is enough."

"Very well, child, let us see if they will help you at all."

CHAPTER SEVENTY

"Junebug," Amythist called to the pixie hiding in the rose bush. "I know very well that you were listening to everything that was said here. Can you please fetch a few of your kin to assist us?"

"What's in it for Junebug?" the tiny voice piped from the rose bush.

"Those cookies you stole, for starters."

"Those were good cookies. You need to get more!" the creature replied and emerged like a bottle-rocket. The tiny human form with the wings of a beetle rose on a fountain of sparks until he vanished into the sky above with a pop of light.

"How long until they respond to your summons?" Kristen asked.

"No, my dear. That was not a summons. It was a request. Pixies are never servants," the older dragon explained. "They were created from pure magic by mages during the Second Mage War as a tool to fight dragons. They are very capable of accomplishing that task, something that more dragons should remember."

"Are you saying a pixie could kill me?"

"Perhaps not one, but a band of pixies could certainly kill a dragon if they put their minds to it. Not only that, but they would also be able to eliminate quite a few dragons. The mages could not control the pixies but they managed to trick a few of them. They told them that hunting dragons was a kind of game, and that provided the motivation they needed to slaughter them, even if they did not understand the repercussions of their magic."

"Their magic is that strong?"

"Oh yes. I don't think we've ever seen the full force of their power. When the Second Mage War broke out, we had a taste of what they could do, but once they lost interest in being used as crusaders, they stopped using their magic to its full extent. They are capricious by nature, as wild as the wind. As dangerous as a hurricane when angered, but usually as unnoticed as a gentle breeze."

"Some came to the peace talks," she admitted. "They didn't seem to even understand how to make demands."

Amythist chuckled. "That hardly surprises me. They're more interested in listening to the babble of a brook or chasing a sparrow than they are at planning anything. The flighty little beings are not given to working together on much of anything. They failed as a weapon because they simply weren't interested in fighting dragons, so they didn't. As powerful as they were, the mages who made them couldn't control them, so the whole war fell apart."

Kristen knew the old dragon had a role in the war 'falling apart' as she said, but she didn't press it. If she didn't want to talk much about her actions in darker times, she could respect that.

"Do you think dragons could kill the pixies?" she asked. "Do you think that's why they came to the peace talks—to protect themselves?"

"Dragons *can* kill them. A concentrated blast of fire proved to be fairly effective, especially if the pixie could be stunned or distracted first. But they were almost impossible to catch so their mortalities were rare. I don't know how many there are worldwide, but I know dragons and humans vastly outnumber them. Still, the main reason that dragons have not bothered to hunt the little beings is because few dragons think of them as a threat."

"But you're telling me they are."

"Indeed. Generally, they are pleasant little creatures who know their way around a garden, but they are not to be trifled with. One time, I pulled a patch of yarrow out that they were particularly fond of and they almost ripped my bones from my body."

"That's gruesome!"

"In their mind, that was the closest thing they could do to an animal that would be like having a plant torn out by the roots. Never mind that the yarrow had already bloomed and I had harvested thousands of seeds. They wanted vengeance for that plant."

"How did you stop them?"

"Honestly? I begged for mercy," Amythist said with a shrug. "I reminded them that I saved two of their number and that I wouldn't ever rip a plant out without planning to sow some of its seeds the next season."

Kristen took a deep breath and tried to process all this while she watched the sky and waited for the pixie to return. "How did you save them?"

"There was a mage—this was centuries ago—although he called himself a wizard. He had captured them in some type of jar and I'd hate to guess about how it was made. Although, knowing what we do about the powers of dragon bone, I wouldn't be surprised to find this particular wizard was ahead of his time. Anyway, he called himself a king. First, he took over a village, then the surrounding countryside, and soon, a major city. I went to stop him on account of this country being decidedly anti-king and found that he had magic that far surpassed what a normal mage was capable of. Truly, he had earned the name wizard as his power almost defied logic."

She wondered if she should start calling Amy a wizard, as the young woman seemed to have powers of the logic-defying category.

The old dragon continued. "This jar—or urn, or whatever you wish to call it—he had trapped the pixies inside also worked as a kind of siphon. He used it to trap them and also draw their magic into himself. Their powers became his powers. If he had truly discovered how to use them to their full potential—if this setup had allowed that at all—he might have gone on to rule the world. Honestly, he might rule it still had he succeeded."

"What happened to him?" she asked, knowing full well that her companion had earned the name Mage-Eater long before.

"I didn't eat him if that's what you were thinking." Amythist chuckled. "I attacked his tower—men and their phallic symbols will never cease to amaze me. Can you imagine if women were as obsessed with caves as men are with tall skinny things?—and in my assault, managed to strike it hard enough to knock the urn to the floor. It shattered, the pixies were freed, and they had their vengeance."

"What did they do?"

"I…" She hesitated. "It's fairly grotesque."

Kristen looked at the sky again and saw no sign of the pixies. "I think it would be better if I knew what they were capable of."

The old dragon's face puckered, but she nodded. "Well…they said he had been stealing their energy, so they would steal his. They impaled him with an acorn and made it grow *through* him. Its roots found his veins and traveled along them before they burst from his fingers and toes and anchored him to the ground, while the trunk of a tree grew from his mouth."

"Oh, dear God."

"Oh, there was no god there that day. The wizard didn't die either. He lived that way for quite some time—as long as the pixies were held in captivity as far as I could tell. Any magic he attempted to cast was diverted into the tree. His spells became a new branch, a fresh spray of leaves, or more acorns."

"I guess there's a type of…justice to that," Kristen said. "But it seems cruel."

"Undoubtedly, but the pixies don't understand the world as we do."

She nodded, scanned the sky, and found nothing. "But Amythist, you saved their lives. I haven't done that for any pixies. The only ones I met I couldn't protect. They had to protect *me*, and one of them still died."

"Let us hope they see things differently," Amythist said. She did not do a good job of hiding the concern in her aura.

They were distracted when flashes of light appeared in the sky. One…two…three, then five…eight…a dozen pixies buzzed around the two dragons' heads and showered them in sparks, their laughter tinkling like bells.

One of them broke off from the rest and came to hover in front of Kristen's face.

She recognized the pixie immediately. The creature was beautiful in an androgynous sort of way, with a slender body and great big dragonfly wings sprouting from her back. "Lady Dragonfly?" She didn't know if her being there was good or bad.

But still, she couldn't help but laugh as the other pixies danced about, collided with one another, and made great splashes of sparks. When she laughed, they took this for encouragement and increased the absurdity of their antics.

"Lady Krissy!" Lady Dragonfly said after she dodged the careening flight of a pixie with the wings of a beetle. "You did us a great service and we neglected to say thank you. So, thank you!"

"A great service?" she asked.

"Indeed! You let us into the meeting, a very kind and honorable thing, even if the snacks were less than delicious. Plus, you protected us when we fell unconscious."

"But one of your group was lost," she said.

"It was not your fault! The Void place is a bad place. Its energy is not good for us. Not at all. We are lucky your friends called our friends and got us all out of there."

"It is very good that you came, Lady Dragonfly. Lady Krissy"—Amythist smirked at the nickname—"is in need of your help."

"Oh! Oh yes." The pixie twittered with delight. "This is what humans and dragons do for each other, yes? The scratching of the other's back," she said sagely.

The old dragon wasted no time in explaining the situation. Lady Dragonfly listened intently while the other pixies buzzed about and pilfered stolen cookies from Junebug who had returned to his place in the rose bush.

When she was finished, the pixie spoke. "We know who Boneclaw is. We saw the shadow form he became. None of us pixies like him. He cares little for flowers, insects, or worms. If you must stop him, we would love to help."

"And can you help me acquire these skills in three days?" Kristen asked.

The diminutive creature frowned. "Three times the sun may set and rise, then you must be done?"

"Actually, only twice. On the day of the third sunrise, I need to face Boneclaw at noon when the sun is directly overhead."

"Can you—what is the human word?—reschedule? Three days is not enough time."

Kristen tried to stay standing as she felt her strength leach from her. "I'm sorry. I cannot. So there's no hope, then?"

"There is always hope," Lady Dragonfly said. "If you cannot do rescheduling, then there are things we can do to accelerate your training. But it is—what's the human word?—lethally dangerous."

The other pixies laughed like that was a joke. Maybe they were merely impressed by their comrade's vocabulary.

"If there's any chance at all, I have to take it. If Boneclaw wins, he will set up a new world order even more oppressive than the current one. I know you pixies have never been given the respect you deserve, but if he comes to power fully, you never will."

"That is not true about receiving respect," Lady Dragonfly said and bowed deeply "You have shown us much respect, which is why we will do this, even though it may end your existence."

"I understand," Kristen said.

"No." The pixie flew into her face so her big, oversized eyes and dragonfly wings filled almost all of her vision. "No, you truly do not. You *cannot.* No human or dragon can understand the risks you will face. Neither can we as we never need to face them to achieve our powers."

"If I die doing this, the world is no better off than if I refuse and live. I have to beat Boneclaw. I have to do so for my parents, for my friends, and for the mages I protect. I have to defeat him because if I don't, he will never stop killing. Right now, he wears the skull of one of my friends as a totem of his power. No one will even dare to tell him to remove it. He has killed dragons I loved and has tried to burn my home too many times to count. This dragon is a monster, and I will do anything I can to stop him, even if that means ending my existence."

Lady Dragonfly smiled and wiped a tear from her eye. "Let us hope it does not come to that." She turned to the other pixies who cavorted about Amythist's garden. "Pixies, come. We will take her to the Well!"

The color of their sparks all changed from golds and silvers to purples and reds. They began to swirl counterclockwise in a circle in front of Kristen. Their speed increased until their trails of sparks blended and they were indistinguishable from each other and from their magic.

Then, in the middle of the circle, a cloud began to form. It was white at first but began to darken around the edges while the center began to glow. A gust of wind scattered it, and she looked into a place of mist and purple shadows. She couldn't see much at all but felt a sense of power and dread coming from it.

"If you step through here, your training will begin," Lady Dragonfly said. "This realm is the only place you can go if you wish to make it back before noon on the third day. We very much hope you survive."

Kristen thanked the pixies and Amythist alike for the opportunity.

"Farewell, Kristen Hall, Steel Dragon," Amythist said. "May you become what you must."

She nodded and stepped through the portal while the pixies flew around her. It closed behind her and the way to the old dragon's garden vanished, hopefully not permanently.

CHAPTER SEVENTY-ONE

There was a time when Amy's favorite thing to do with her powers was skateboard. She learned how to telekinetically push and pull on both her shoes and her board and could accomplish breathtaking stunts. While she used to scoff at skateboarding videogames for being able to do physics-defying tricks, she now regularly accomplished those and more.

But she wasn't in the mood for any of that right now. She merely wanted to enjoy the peace.

She flew close to a kilometer up and immediately above a cluster of low clouds that might decide to drop rain on the ground below at some point later in the night. It was quiet, so much more silent than anywhere on the surface of the Earth could be. Once she had filtered out the wind rushing past her ears, there was little to hear. Occasionally, a wolf howled from far below. Sometimes, the sound of a train horn would make it through the clouds.

There was no light either, save for the gentle glow of stars above. The clouds blocked out the light from cities and towns, the gas stations with their fluorescent lights and tall signs proclaiming that they had the cheapest gas and the most filling snacks, and the farmhouses whose lights glared into the dark in an attempt to keep foxes from henhouses.

The young mage was thankful to have a moment like this before the fight that was to come. Part of her regretted not telling anyone she was going, but she knew this had to be the way. Kristen was busy, so she hadn't tried to check in on her. Despite not telling anyone, she had still brought her cellphone, albeit on silent. While she knew facing the Masked One would be hard, she had to do it. She could make light as Constance had shown her, and she could move mountains with her magic if she wished. Together, those powers would be enough to defeat the dragon intent on murdering her best friend. They had to be.

In her hand, she still held the enemy's scale. Boneclaw, she tried to remind herself. She would simply face an old asshole of a dragon. Calling him the Masked One was bullshit. He was an old, cruel bastard, not a boogeyman. His scale gave her a steady ping of his location. She knew she was getting closer but still wasn't quite sure of the distance that remained.

Amy knew how powerful he was, and although she didn't want to let him grow to some mythic figure in her subconscious, she also wanted to make sure she didn't become complacent. She had fought dragons before and won, but she saw how easily this one destroyed his targets. That knowledge reminded her that she needed to be careful. Even then, being careful wouldn't be enough. She needed to be flawless.

Which meant she had to keep her bearings. Thus far, the scale had led her north. She had already crossed the state of Michigan and was out over the Great Lake of the same name. As she flew northward and the upper Michigan peninsula came into view, she tried to estimate how far she still had to go. The sense of Boneclaw's energy coming from the scale had increased, but it hadn't jumped like she had expected it to. That meant she still had a way to go and that he wasn't in the upper peninsula of the state. Based on her perception of the scale, it seemed like he would be found in Canada.

That was somewhat surprising. Most dragons tended to avoid that nation. Amy had fled there when the dragons hunted her and had witnessed dwarves and dragons fight for the first time in a small Canadian town. She'd seen how resilient dwarves were against the powers of most dragons. They were tough, strong, and had skin so flame-retardant that even dragon fire didn't bother them. She also knew that dragon magic often didn't affect them.

Dwarves were a pain for dragons to deal with, but they kept mostly to themselves. As a result, most dragons simply left the whole country alone. But Boneclaw was holed up somewhere in dwarf country. Or, at the very least, he was doing something there. But what? She considered this as she crossed the upper peninsula and flew out across Lake Superior, the largest and coldest of the great lakes.

The young mage pushed through the clouds and estimated that she had a little time before she made landfall again. She rose above the water and into the cool moistness that surrounded her as she moved through a cloud. Her telekinesis kept the water droplets from soaking her clothes and hair, but she still couldn't resist stretching a hand into the cloud and let the droplets condense until they formed a tiny pool in the palm of her hand.

Amy sipped it, relishing the fresh taste of cloud water as she burst through the top and almost missed the dragon who flew through the thick cumulus not far from her.

She might have missed it completely if she had not used her powers to affect the clouds as she passed through them. But something was in there. She felt its wings beating at the droplets to create swirls and vortexes in the mist.

Her heart began to pound, but she forced herself to calm. It couldn't be the Masked One—Boneclaw. It couldn't be him. His scale told her his location was still a long way off. This hidden dragon was almost on top of her so it couldn't be him.

Could it be one of his henchmen? A loyalist? A traitor from Kristen's group?

Her mind raced with the unanswered questions and she swallowed hard and calmed herself. She would have to find out.

Grim but determined, she increased her speed and dove into the nebulous mass using her powers to clear the mist from in front of her.

The clouds separated and she saw the dark, almost black form of a dragon ahead before it barrel-rolled to the right to stay in the cloud bank.

Amy proceeded as if she hadn't noticed. She accelerated and tried to draw herself parallel to where the dragon had been given its current speed. That it hadn't attacked was a good sign. Surely Boneclaw wouldn't waste time pretending to hide in a cloud, but one of his minions might.

There was nothing to be done but find out who it was. If it turned out to be a powerful enemy, she would simply have to take time to rest before she fought Boneclaw. It wasn't a pleasant prospect, but neither was the idea of reaching the enemy's location only to be ambushed from behind.

So, when she felt another vortex travel through the cloud as the dragon pumped its wings to change direction, she blasted a great gust of wind toward the source. It scattered the cloud into nothing but drizzle that fell onto Lake Superior below.

The dragon within—as dark as wrought iron—dropped earthward with the rain droplets.

She smiled. A fight was one thing, but a chase? She would beat anyone in a chase. The young mage grasped the nose of her board and pointed it toward the dragon. She rocketed forward with a telekinetic push of magic until she had caught up with the dark shape.

In the light of the stars, the scales had a metallic sheen and suddenly, she knew where she had seen the dragon before. She decided to grind the dragon's tail.

With a broad grin, she hopped off her board, spun it in an impossible twirl, and landed in a boardslide on the iron scales.

"Get off me!" the dragon roared and twisted in the air to shake the person now doing tricks on its tail.

But gravity and momentum meant little and less to a powerful, well-rested mage like Amy. She continued to grind the dragon's tail as the world spun around her.

"What are you doing here, Katrina?" she demanded of the Iron Dragon.

"I could ask you the same thing!" Katrina retorted and plunged them both into Lake Superior.

The coldness was so frightfully strong and immediate that it took Amy's breath away. For a moment, she simply tried not to breathe as the cold clutched at her chest and forced the warmth from her limbs.

But she was from Maine. Swimming in cold water was considered a fun pastime in the most northern state according to Mainers. She launched out of the water and used her powers to shake every drop of water from her. In a moment, she was dry once more.

She glanced to her right to where Katrina—in her Iron Dragon form, of course—coasted above the choppy waves of the Great Lake. Amy always found it impressive that these bodies of water could mimic the look of the Northern Atlantic, but this hardly seemed the time to comment on the vastness of this particular source of freshwater.

"Why did you follow me?" she asked.

"Where are you going?" Katrina snapped in response.

"That's my business. How did you follow me without me sensing you?"

"I've worked with mages for my entire life. I know how to hide from you, especially when you're distracted. You leaving endangers the team, so it's my business too. Why didn't you tell anyone where you were going?"

"Because it's dangerous and I can't risk other people getting hurt," she said and forced herself to go faster. She caught a wave with her board and exploded off the top of it with a splash of water and went into a backflip.

"You found Boneclaw," the dragon said as she caught up to her. She didn't comment on the impressive trick the girl had accomplished.

Amy sighed. "How did you know?"

"Because you know as well as I do that Kristen doesn't stand a chance against that asshole. The only reason you would ditch your precious dragon buddy is if there was a chance you could help her, and the only thing you could do to help right now is to defeat Boneclaw before she has to."

"Lucky guess," she replied.

"Not really," Katrina responded, although her voice was less hostile. "I wouldn't want to leave Constance unless it meant protecting her life. When I saw you slip away, I knew what you were thinking. I decided you could use backup."

"Why didn't you say anything sooner?"

"If I'd said something too soon, you would have simply told me to stay home."

"You wouldn't have listened."

The Iron Dragon didn't reply immediately. It was a reminder that she had been raised by mages and was not one to underestimate a mage. She fully understood that Amy could obliterate her in battle, even with her iron skin.

"The other reason," she said after a moment, "is because you need my help. I was able to mask my presence from you. That's not good. Boneclaw will be at least as good as I am at using his aura. Probably way better, honestly. If he can sense you and drops off your radar—"

"Yeah, yeah, I'm fucked," she agreed.

"That's putting it mildly." Katrina snickered.

"Are you sure you want to do this?" the mage asked. "Look, if shit goes bad and I have the chance to kill him, I will, no matter the cost."

"I won't go home and I won't try to spare your life either. We're both meaningless in this war. If Kristen loses to him, all the progress Constance made, the cause I have been fighting for since I was a child, is finished. I won't let that happen, even if it means a skateboarder gets crushed."

"Fine, we're in agreement then," she replied.

"Two dead bitches flying," the dragon replied. They were silent for a moment before she spoke. "Come land on my back. You shouldn't waste your powers. You'll need them."

Amy didn't say anything to that. She simply did another flip off a wave, caught the board in one hand, and landed on the dragon's broad back.

The two flew on.

The duo followed Boneclaw's trail to a low mountain somewhere in the western part of Ontario. They approached the landscape at dawn. Rivers and lakes were everywhere and pine trees stood in clusters where there wasn't water. It was remote with not much in the way of houses or other buildings nearby. A few old roads were probably only ever used to harvest timber, and perhaps one or two hiking trails were tucked below. On the whole, it felt quite out of the way.

"Do you sense anything?" Amy asked.

"I don't," the dragon said. "But part of suppressing my aura means I can't sense others as easily. Do you think we're close?"

"I do. Close enough to walk. Do you see that cabin halfway up the mountain?"

"You mean hill?" the dragon clarified.

"Sure, whatever. Do you see it?"

"Yes."

"The scale is drawing me to it. Not precisely to that cabin but somewhere near there. I want to land at the bottom of that *hill* and approach through the forest. Boneclaw is probably watching the sky."

"Which means we might have already been seen and should attack *now*." Katrina didn't look even slightly concerned about the prospect of facing a legendary dragon of nightmare.

"No. Not yet. There's no activity and nothing to tell me he has sensed us. We play this cool as long as we can."

"Fine." Katrina snorted, tucked her wings, and landed in a grove of pine trees. Amy dismounted and her companion took her human form.

They moved through the pine woods as silently as possible. The young mage liked the night, or at least she had. Now, with Boneclaw being able to move through shadow, it felt like a dangerous and alien place. Her teammate didn't look any more comfortable despite being part of an organization of assassins that must have utilized the cover of darkness for years.

The going was easy but slow. The forest was thick with pine needles, which made the ground slick as the needles would move underfoot. Katrina led the way, her dragon vision better able to pierce the shadows.

"Constance made it sound like you guys worked for the Masked One. Did you ever meet him?" Amy asked, not sure how her companion would react.

"Fuck no. If I had, you can be sure I would have seen through his bullshit deceptions. The asshole never cared about mage equality."

Obviously, she thought but saw the wisdom in not saying anything. Instead, she whispered a question. "Do you truly believe in mage equality even though you're a dragon?"

"What the fuck is that supposed to mean?"

"Well, you're a dragon and not merely any dragon but an iron one. That makes you something special. If the dragons do start this war and decimate the human population or whatever, joining their side might make more sense for you."

"As if. I was raised by mages. Constance was practically a mom to me. I've seen the crap they have to deal with and the way dragons walk all over them and humans treat them like pariahs. There will be no equality until we all have equality. That's a central tenet of basic civil rights. I believe in mages with all my heart. Although I do wish you could do something about the crackle of these pine needles."

"Crackle?" she asked. She hadn't heard much of anything.

"It might not sound like much to you but to a dragon, this is as loud as walking through a forest of leaves in the fall."

"Oh, right. I guess I could scatter the needles from our path," she said.

"That won't be enough. You know he'll be able to sense us. Don't play dumb with me. I know you had more of a plan than this." Katrina's smile gleamed in the darkness.

Amy knew she should trust her. The dragon had signed the same contractual magic she had. If she tried to hurt her for any reason other than one that protected innocents, she would be immolated. It was as simple as that.

And yet, she didn't trust her, not with her heart of hearts, anyway. But what choice did she have? She knew Katrina might give her the edge she needed against Boneclaw. They had the same goals, even if the methods they had used to achieve those were different.

"I have been working on something," she said as she wreathed herself in magic.

In theory, this was similar to making one of the shields that stopped bullets. She had to surround herself with a force that stopped things from moving through it. The difference was that she didn't want her power to leak out, so the shield had to work both ways. She also wanted to go unseen. While she hadn't known how to do this at first, she had been inspired by—of all people —Boneclaw.

Her body vanished into the shadow of a tree and her powers wove around her like a cocoon. They protected her, concealed her, and made her invisible as long as she remained in the dark. If she wished to move to another patch of darkness, she simply created a tunnel of the magic cocoon and moved through that. It wasn't quite as elegant as Boneclaw being able to completely vanish into shadow itself—she still had a body—but as long as she was in the dark, she could move about unseen and unheard.

"That's better," Katrina said with a smile. "Much better. Now can you do it to me too?"

The mage knew she had to try. "Step into the darkness at this tree."

The dragon obeyed or tried to, at least.

"Not that one, this one," Amy said and stepped from the shadow to show her where she was.

"Very impressive." The dragon's praise seemed genuine. "Can you move?"

"Yeah, and we need to get a move on, so hurry."

Katrina stepped beside her. The mage wrapped them both in her cocoon of darkness and they continued. They moved through the woods almost without walking. Rather than stepping on the needles, she lifted them with her powers and moved them through the protected tunnels her magic created.

When they passed through light, she could tell the illusion of their invisibility wasn't as strong. But there in the faintly gray light of early dawn, it was strong enough to conceal them even from creeping nocturnal creatures.

They proceeded quickly through the forest to the cabin near the top of the mountain—or hill, or whatever. She conceded that it was closer to a big hill than a mountain, but the fact that it was covered in boulders left by glaciers long receded made it feel like a mountain to her.

They reached the lodge and waited at the edge of the forest in the shadow of a particularly old pine that completely eclipsed them from the light. For five long minutes they waited, but nothing stirred inside. There was no light, no sounds, and nothing that indicated anyone moving within.

"It must be empty. If there was a person in there, I'd sense their aura or hear their breathing," Katrina said.

"Do you sense any auras at all?" Amy asked.

Katrina shook her head. "No, I don't, but that doesn't mean much. We're in dwarf country. There could be an entire village a mile from here and a hundred feet underground and I wouldn't be able to sense a thing."

"Does stone block all auras?" Amy asked.

"I don't know. I was never particularly gifted with my aura, and mages don't have them so I was never able to practice how it worked all that much. It is one of the things mages hated the most about dragons—being able to be manipulated emotionally can be devastating when an ally turns against you for no reason—so I never used it. I'm getting nothing, though, so we should be good."

Or, the girl thought, *Boneclaw is sensing our approach and laughing about it.*

But there was nothing to be done if that was the case. The homestead seemed empty, and they were wrapped in the most protective magic she could manage. They had to go in. Cautiously, they moved to a pile of rocks near the back of the cabin, then slipped along the boulder-strewn hill until they were up against the building. The back wall was shorter than the front as if a lazy lumberjack turned architect thought he could save himself timber and labor by using the hill itself for a wall. Amy wondered constantly if the boulders they had moved past were booby-trapped.

Worse still for her impending sense of doom, Katrina refused to enter the cabin in the cover of darkness. "We stay awake until dawn, then enter in the daytime. If shit goes bad and we are below ground, we need to know the sun is waiting on the surface for us."

She didn't have anything to counter that logic, so they settled for some sleep outside the cabin, although she didn't know if she slept at all between the bouts of worry.

As it transpired, any concerns about it were misplaced. The daylight revealed that the interior was empty. There was no one inside, no dog, and nothing to indicate any danger. It was spartan—one room with a sink under a window on one side, a pantry built out into the room, a bed, a table, and no other signs of amenities. A bear pelt that looked like it had seen better days hung on the back wall.

"Do you notice there's no dust on the table?" Katrina asked before she moved toward a sink. "And look, water is pooling in here. Someone was here recently."

"Couldn't that simply be a leak?"

"Not with everything else that's here," the dragon said as she poked around in the kitchen and raided the tiny pantry. "Half a loaf of bread and a plate in the drying rack. People were here until recently. Today, I'd bet."

Amy was quite thankful in that moment to have Katrina with her. "But if people were here earlier, where are they now?"

"That's what we need to find out."

She nodded, not upset that the dragon was taking the lead so much as that she'd barely given the Iron Dragon the time of day before. She was cleverer than she had given her credit for. "Boneclaw's scale feels like we need to move to the other side of the hill," she said and hoped that was helpful.

"Does it feel like we need to go to the other side or go inside?" Katrina asked.

"How would we go insi—" she started to ask before she stopped herself. "Dwarf country, right."

Her companion continued to move about the room as if it were a cage instead of a single-room cabin built against a mountain. "Tell me, did Constance teach you much about wind magic?"

"A little. Why do you ask?"

"There was something she did if she needed an escape. She would blow wind away from her and feel where there was the least resistance. That place would be an exit because the air could flow. Did she ever teach you how to do that?"

"No," Amy said and closed her eyes to try.

"Don't worry about it then. It took her years and I know you're not exactly experienced—holy shit."

She opened her eyes to see the old raggedy bear pelt rustling. "There's a door behind there or something."

"Constance said that was one of the hardest tricks." Katrina's jaw had practically hit the floor.

"Yeah well, let's hope that's as hard as it gets." The mage used her powers to lift the bear pelt carefully off and lower it to the floor. The back wall was hideous. Someone had thought it needed to be covered by planks of wood even though the rest of the cabin looked great being made from rough-hewn logs.

But as she examined the misshapen, crooked boards that had been haphazardly hammered to the back wall in more detail, she saw that this was no lazy effort. A door was hidden there. It was almost impossible to see among the mismatched boards, but now that she had found a seam across the top, she traced it with her wind. Whoever had built it was clever. They hadn't left the edges straight, so it wasn't a rectangle but something approximately in the shape of one.

"If there are magic traps, you should be able to sense them," Katrina said.

She reached out and traded her breeze for tiny tendrils of telekinetic force. Using these, she felt around the cracks of the door and tested for anything out of the ordinary but found nothing besides the latch.

"I think it's clean," she said to her companion. "I'm going to open it."

"Wait a minute." The dragon put herself between Amy and the door and turned her skin to iron. "All right. Let's hope you're right but if you're not, I'm less squishy."

The young mage pulled the door open with her telekinesis. It swung silently into the cabin and its uneven edges slid cleanly against the matching uneven edge of its frame. Nothing exploded and no electricity or ice erupted. Beyond it was a smooth tunnel cut into the stone and earth of the hill. It didn't look like it had been dug, or not by any human machine anyway. Instead, it appeared that it had simply come into existence or perhaps a part of the hill had slithered away and left this cavity behind. Amy had never seen a hole that was so pretty.

"Dwarves made this," Katrina said and examined the exquisitely made door that was fashioned to look like the world's least exquisitely made wall.

"What would Boneclaw want with dwarves?" the mage asked. But she knew he had something to do with this. As soon as they'd opened the door, she had felt a tiny surge of energy from the scale. Whatever else might be waiting for them down there, he was there too.

"There's only one way to find out," Katrina said and dropped her iron skin so she could move silently down the hall.

"Can't you keep your iron on but leave your feet normal?" Amy asked. "That would be safer."

A rueful scowl told her that this particular skill eluded the Iron Dragon. "That is a talent my...sister is particularly adept at. I can make iron claws but if I leave my feet regular, the weight will snap my ankles like toothpicks."

"Let's not do that, then," she said. "You'll probably need your ankles." *For when this all goes to shit and we have to run like hell,* she thought but yet again, she kept this particular little nugget of pessimism to herself.

CHAPTER SEVENTY-TWO

Kristen walked through the portal and into a place without direction. There was no up or down, no left or right, and only an impenetrable purple fog. She continued to move forward, not walking exactly but pushing on as best she could until the mist began to clear.

The first thing she saw was a massive tree. It towered over her, its roots each as thick as the trunk of the tree in her parents' front yard. The trunk was easily as wide as a dump truck. It rose scores of feet before it divided into hundreds of branches, each heavy with vines, ferns, orchids, and dozens of other plants she could only guess at that were all in different stages of bloom.

Sunlight shone through the branches and as she watched, the sun rose until she could see more of the strange surroundings—was it even a place?— she'd stepped into.

She stood in a clearing in a lush, tropical jungle. Her feet sank into lush grass and she was tempted to remove her shoes, so she did. The feeling of the thick, dewy grass on her bare soles was pleasurable and she looked around to get her bearings. The clearing she was in was surrounded by more of the beautiful trees. It must have been maintained by someone as it was filled with calm pools and gently tinkling streams that ran from one to the other before they emptied into the jungle at the low side of the clearing. Wherever she looked, clumps of gorgeous flowers bloomed in every color she could imagine.

It was overwhelmingly beautiful, especially as the sun seemed to lock into its position behind the first tree she had seen and filled the air with dappled sunlight. Birds and insects called out to each other. In the shadow of the trees and clusters of flowers, animals moved furtively or simply watched her, although she would be hard-pressed to say what any of them were. One halfway up a tree looked much like a monkey, but it had a third eye in the middle of its forehead and darted a tongue longer than any chameleon's out to snatch a ripe piece of fruit off the tree from which it hung.

"What is this place?" she asked and wiped tears from her eyes. She had not realized that she had been crying. It was simply so beautiful there.

"This is our home," Lady Dragonfly said. Kristen had almost forgotten that the pixies she met at Amythist's had come through the portal with her.

"But I thought…" Before she could finish asking her question, all the pixies darted out into the clearing.

They sang and laughed as they flew and the tinkling sound of laughter added itself to the sounds of birds and insects. She decided that the pixie laughter fit perfectly in this place.

From the bushes and trees and even the ponds, other pixies emerged, far more than the twelve she had come with. Another dozen embraced those that had come with her as perhaps a hundred more flitted about the clearing. They cheered in celebration, picked flowers and gave them to the new arrivals, and darted in front of her face to get a good look at her before they vanished in a tinkle of laughter. It was a truly joyous reunion, and she was both honored and flattered to have been allowed to witness it.

Once the twelve pixies she had come with finished making their rounds and greeting all the others, Lady Dragonfly drew herself away from them and flitted closer to Kristen. Truly, she would not have been able to recognize her in the group, but when she spoke, her big brown eyes and shimmering dragonfly wings were immediately familiar.

"Welcome!" the pixie said.

"This is a truly beautiful place," she told her. "Thank you for bringing me to your home."

"I'm very glad to hear that!" Lady Dragonfly beamed. "You are not the first human or dragon to come here, nor are you the first to compliment this world we have cultivated, but it is very good that you —an intersection of dragons and humans—can recognize pixie beauty. We have considerable hope vested in you, Kristen Hall. Your appreciation of this place is a good sign that we have not misplaced our trust."

That was a fairly challenging exchange of information. Kristen wanted to know more about how a world could be so wild and still look cultivated, but the pixies' trust seemed a more pressing matter. She had so many questions. Why her? What did they know about her? Why was she there? Who else had been there? "Trust? I mean, thank you, but what have I done to deserve it? I only met you a few days ago and I didn't exactly keep you safe."

"I hope it is enough to know for now that we trust you. We do not have time to answer all your questions. The day is already moving."

"But the sun—" As she spoke, the sun shifted from its position to directly overhead. It had lingered behind the tree but now, in the span of a few seconds, it appeared to move a distance in the sky that would have taken the sun on earth hours to traverse. "What is this place?"

Lady Dragonfly shook her head. "One day, all will be clear but now, we must hurry. We cannot tarry, not if we are to get you back before you face Boneclaw."

At the mention of the Masked One's true identity, the creatures all around them buzzed angrily. She equated the effect to throwing a rock at a hornet's nest.

But her guide was already moving through the clearing toward one of the pools. She hurried after her. The grass felt wonderful under her bare feet.

The pool they stopped at was breathtakingly beautiful. The bed was lined with stones that all appeared to be worn smooth by the water. It was ringed with alternating clusters of pink and purple flowers. At one end, water trickled off the spout of a stone into the pool and splashed pleasantly. A mass of rocks at the other blocked most of the water but let some pass through and out into a stream to another pool.

"You must get in the water, please," Lady Dragonfly said with a little bow.

"I thought we were on a time crunch?" Kristen said.

"The water is essential to the work that must be done. Please hurry. It is good that you took your shoes off. Your uniform should go too."

"You want me to get naked?" A few of the little creatures fluttered about and she wasn't exactly keen to strip down in front of all of them.

"If you are most comfortable in your skin, that would be best, but you can leave clothes on that are truly yours. The uniform is not, though. It is a symbol of what you and your people are to your world. Keeping it on would make things difficult."

"What things?"

"Please!" Lady Dragonfly said and glanced at the sun overhead. It was still directly above them at the zenith, but Kristen began to realize that this place would not behave the way the regular world did. It seemed like the sun would stay at the noonday position until it no longer wished to do so. Maybe her guide didn't want it to jump too far ahead when it did move.

She nodded and relented in the face of the pixie's imploring tone.

Quickly, she removed the long-sleeved black uniform shirt with its silver trim and her pants. She was left in a pair of panties and a tie-dyed tank top she had made with her mom years before. There was no doubt in her mind that these were indeed *her* clothes.

Kristen thought she might have been uncomfortable, but she realized that the opposite was true. The warm, steamy air of the tropical garden felt appealing on her freckled skin. A blush of sweat rose all over and made her feel slightly slick. There were times she might have hated the sensation but right now, it felt perfect, like the sheen of sweat after a particularly invigorating workout.

She still had no idea what getting into a pool of water had to do with defeating Boneclaw, but she knew time was of the essence and she resolved to do what the pixies requested of her as quickly as she could.

When she stepped into the pool, she expected—or hoped—it would be cool and refreshing but instead, found it rather warm. It was barely at body temperature, or maybe half a degree warmer, and it was like being in a pool of water that had been left in the sun all day.

Focused on the pool rather than the pixies, she lowered herself into the water past her waist and her breasts and up to her neck. Normally, she didn't like to get her red hair wet, but something beckoned her to let her hair down and she did so now so the curly red locks floated on the surface all around her. An added bonus of her thick red hair was that it floated on the surface of the pool and helped to block the view of her breasts which her wet tank top did absolutely nothing to conceal.

For a moment, she forgot about all that. She simply let the water envelop her. It felt marvelous—like a massage, a trip to the jacuzzi, and a good night's sleep all rolled into one.

When she opened her eyes a moment later, a group of pixies was braiding her hair into an elaborate version of French braids, plaited tightly to her head. She also realized that she didn't care in the least that Lady Dragonfly hovered directly in front of her, able to see her body.

"You have probably guessed that we are no longer on earth," the pixie began.

"I had a feeling," Kristen replied. "Is this somewhere like where the base ended up when you all cast the spell?"

Lady Dragonfly shivered despite the warmth of the air. "This is not a place at all like that. That was a no-place, a Void, a zone between places where nothing exists. We had pooled our magic to try to bring the building and everyone in it to safety. Unfortunately, we only made it partway across the Void before our magic was spent and we were trapped there. The pixie who died gave the last of his life-magic trying to hold our little bubble of reality in the Void. We only came home because the efforts of the mass of pixies on Earth managed to bring us back."

"So where we are…it's not in the Void?" she asked.

"All places are in the Void. This place, the Earth, all places. They are all like bubbles floating in the Void. This one is a bubble with far more magic than Earth. That is why we come here to refresh and restore ourselves."

"So you made this as a kind of refuge?" Kristen asked.

Lady Dragonfly laughed. "No, no, no, we did not make this place. Even we pixies do not have the magic needed to create permanent bubbles in the Void. We tried to move your base *through* the Void, but once we were stuck, it took all our strength to simply hold the nothingness at bay. We found this place after we were created on earth. In those days, it was nothing but the purple clouds you first saw. We brought seeds and eggs, convinced the magic to form dirt and water, and spent centuries of earth time growing what you see all around you."

"You've done a spectacular job." She smiled.

"Thank you, Kristen Hall! We are quite pleased with it. In its earliest form, this realm could still heal our wounds, replenish our strength, and erase any aging our bodies underwent on Earth. Now, though, it is so beautiful that many like to come here simply for fun!"

Kristen nodded and didn't fail to notice that the pixies were effectively immortal. Or, at least, they didn't die due to aging because they could come to this sanctuary and rejuvenate themselves whenever they needed to.

"Is this pool doing that to me? It feels wonderful."

"Indeed!" Lady Dragonfly beamed. "This pool will heal any wounds, replenish your strength, and clear your mind for the trial that is to come. This realm has much more magic than Earth, which will make what you must do far easier."

"That's good to hear," she said. "Amythist made it sound like it would be quite the challenge."

"Oh, it will be, Kristen Hall. The energy of this pool will make it easier, but that does not mean it will be easy. Maybe I should have said the energy of this pool and the water here will make it *possible.*"

"You are not to tell her of the water!" another pixie snapped, fluttered overhead, and vanished into a clump of flowers.

"What about the water?" she asked.

"There is no time," Lady Dragonfly said and looked at the sun.

Kristen looked too and noticed that it was no longer overhead. It had slipped down so it now touched the tops of the trees on the opposite side of the clearing.

"We have already wasted too much time," the pixie said as the sky shifted from blue to the rich reds, purples, and violets of sunset.

"But how does time work here?"

"It gives us what it thinks we need," her guide said hurriedly, "and not a moment more. Time marches on here as it does on Earth, although to a tempo that will be harder for you to hear. You must push yourself if you want to succeed. Magic will not allow it any other way. You are the Steel Dragon, and thus you must be hardened to steel. This realm never fails to notice such things. We will have to push you too, harder even than we have pushed others…" She trailed off as if remembering some horror she had worked hard to push out of her mind.

"Others like who?"

"It matters not," Lady Dragonfly said. "There will be serious risks, I must remind you of that. You could lose your life, your mind, or even your powers if you are not what the magic thinks you are. Are you sure you want to try this?"

"Yes. I have to do this. I must. Too many people from all Earth's races are relying on me to end the war and bring peace and balance. I have to find a way to do that. I don't want to lose my life or my powers, but if that's the cost I have to pay to keep my loved ones safe, I'll pay it."

"Very well," the pixie said, took a deep breath, and nodded. "We thank you very much for your service. Please finish your bath. The sun should wait for that at least. When you feel completely refreshed, follow the stream from the pool downhill, away from this grove, and into the jungle. You must keep going until you are asked to stop or forced to stop. Do you understand?"

"Don't take in the sights. Got it," Kristen said, pulled herself from the pool, and reached for her clothes.

"You won't need those," Lady Dragonfly told her and gestured to the uniform.

"You said it will be dangerous, right? I'd rather have something between me and whatever's out there."

"As you wish," her companion said before she vanished on a jet of sparks.

Kristen watched her go, then got dressed. She felt more relaxed and energized than she had in ages—like she had been given a major recharge. Could it all be an effect of the pool or was she already unlocking some of her magic powers? She could not be sure.

With no time to waste, she set off, shirking her boots as she kept her feet in the warm stream. She turned back when she reached the edge of the clearing. "Thank you, pixies! I hope I can complete this and we can all feel more welcome on the Earth when this is over."

"Farewell, Kristen!" Lady Dragonfly called in response. "We will watch over your trials. Good luck and follow the stream. Do not tarry and you will win success this day."

She waved farewell and proceeded downstream.

CHAPTER SEVENTY-THREE

As Kristen proceeded into the jungle, it seemed that perhaps the advice to follow the stream was literal. Beyond the now obviously groomed clearing, the jungle was as thick as any she had seen. The only place where plants didn't fight each other for space was the trickling stream she now followed.

In all honesty, she felt far from certain about how any of this was supposed to help. She reached a log that had fallen into the stream and created a little pool. Undeterred, she swam across it—drenching her uniform as she did so—and climbed over the impediment. Past the tree, the stream widened somewhat. The growth of the jungle was now far enough apart that she could extend her arms and not touch any plants on either side.

Was the log she passed supposed to be an obstacle? Surely not. Was she supposed to be lured into the jungle by the bizarre assortment of plants proliferating on the jungle floor? If that was the test, she felt like she was acing it. Odd fruits hung in the jungle—apples the size of watermelons and things that looked like peaches but were the rich purple of eggplants. None of it seemed particularly alluring to her. If there had been a pizza bush, she might have been tempted, but the jungle—despite its strangeness—grew only fruit.

She kept moving as the stream widened more. It was extremely shallow, so even her bare ankles didn't get wet as she walked along its rocky bed. The gap in the canopy overhead caused by the stream had finally widened enough that she could see the sky. The rich reds, purples, and oranges of sunset emblazoned the broad expanse above her. The sun had been setting for what felt like hours. How did the pixies keep track of anything there when time itself behaved so strangely?

Kristen blinked, and instead of all the colors of an impressionistic painting of a sunset overheard, she saw only the stars. Or what looked like stars at first glance. In the Earth's sky, most stars appeared white to her, with some tinged faintly red or blue.

There, they came in every color of the rainbow. Twinkling dots of purple, orange, green, and yellow added themselves to the regular colors of red and blue. Some of the points of light spun like a cartoon version of a star, while others had tiny rings around them that made them look like ringed planets. It was almost like the pixies had painted the sky to look like that because they hadn't quite understood what stars were.

Kristen shook the oddness of the scene aside as she looked at the path in front of her. It was much harder to see now. The stars emitted light that illuminated the middle of the stream but made no attempt to pierce the darkness of the jungle on either side.

That seemed to follow the logic of the stream being significant but she paused a few moments later. Up ahead and in the shadows of the trees, a star seemed to hover above the water.

She sensed that something was different about it. As she looked at it, she had a strong awareness that she could *feel* it. It was like something about the little mote of light tugged at her gut.

Cautiously, she moved toward it and her feet splashed in the shallow water. As she walked, the star didn't seem to get any closer. It behaved like those in the sky and no matter how many steps she took, it refused to grow larger.

Prompted by some inner instinct, Kristen began to run. She ran in the dark and tried to watch her footing and the light at the same time.

Her pace accelerated as far as her human muscles would allow, and when the light didn't seem to grow any larger, she called on her dragon powers and increased her speed to the superhuman level.

Her body strained to the limit as she raced forward. She no longer watched the stream bed, entirely focused on the mote of light in front of her. For whatever reason, she knew she had to catch it. That it was not a star seemed obvious, and her reason suggested something with an aura. Some kind of a creature or a pixie, perhaps.

Kristen's foot landed on nothing but air and she began to fall. In her haste, she had run over the edge of a waterfall. Her arms spun in circles and she tucked her legs up as she plunged past the light. She was close enough that she might have been able to touch it if she wasn't plummeting toward the water below. Fortunately, the drop wasn't as high as it could have been and she splashed into a pool of water that was much colder than the warm bath she'd enjoyed when she started the journey.

She swam to the surface, broke through the water, and sucked in a breath of air.

To her amazement, the ball of light now floated at the edge of the pool. She trod water and wondered if chasing it had been a mistake when it split in half. Now, instead of one light, there were two. Each of those divided to make four and these separated into eight.

They were now all around her and equally spaced so she could only see four of them at any given time as she spun one way or the other in the water.

Kristen decided to keep moving and swam to the edge of the pool, following the current. The water grew shallow again as she approached a mess of rocks and boulders which served as a kind of a dam to hold the water inside the pool. She climbed onto the rocks and noted that the shape of this pool—a round body of water with rocks blocking the water's egress—was identical to the bath she had started in. That had even had a waterfall, exactly like the pool here did.

Did that mean this wasn't a place at all but some type of magical effect based on the pool where she had begun?

Before she had time to ponder that particular question any further, the balls of light began to approach her. They had moved with her so four of them now floated above the pool behind her while the other four were already above the stream that drained the pool. As they grew closer, she could see that they weren't balls of light at all but some kind of creature.

"Pixies?" she asked cautiously, although they didn't seem quite like pixies.

They had bodies that could vanish into sparks but they still had *bodies.* Lady Dragonfly always looked the same. These were different. They looked more like rough sketches of a body made of white light—like reflections, almost.

"Are you will-o-wisps?" Kristen asked them.

They tinkled in response and sounded like bells. Was that them asking her to stop? She didn't know.

Still, this was the first thing that had happened to her since she'd started moving down the stream. The realm was still in night mode, so she decided to wait the little beings out.

They moved closer still. Now, Kristen could see them even better. They were like little humans made of pure light, both adorable and absolutely beautiful. The circle around her grew tighter until the will-o-wisps were barely an arm's length away.

Unsure of what to do but intrigued by the beings' beauty as well as the gentle pull of *something* she felt emanating from them, she reached out to touch one of them.

The will-o-wisp snarled at her and jolted her outstretched hand with a burst of energy.

She yelped and yanked her hand back. "Pardon me." She tried to apologize, but one of the will-o-wisps jolted her from behind.

Kristen whirled and realized that those behind her had moved quite close. They buzzed about now and darted closer as if they dared each other to see who could attack this big, clumsy intruder.

Her reflex was to turn to steel but she stopped herself. The power felt like electricity, which was never a good combination with her steel skin. Plus, there was the directive to follow the water. If there was another pool ahead, being in her steel mode and unable to swim would not be a good thing.

Instead, she ran.

She swung out at the will-o-wisps that stood in front of the stream. They dodged and she used the opening to race past them. Unfortunately, they did not let her go that easily. They gave chase, flew after her, and launched little jolts of energy at her as she tried to outpace them.

Even with her dragon speed, she couldn't outrun the little bastards. They kept pace and darted in front of her and around her as she tried to evade them. As they moved, they released their blast of energy and giggled every time she cried out in pain.

Not sure what else to do, Kristen transformed into her dragon form. She bounded into the air and spread her wings to fly but was immediately reminded that the canopy was still thick there. She couldn't get above the treetops. There simply was not enough space for her to spread her wings.

She bounded forward and proceeded down the stream with great big leaps. Even with the stride of a dragon, the will-o-wisps easily kept pace.

Finally, she tried something else.

Without warning, she turned on them and unleashed a great blast of fire. The heat was so intense that the trees on either side of the stream ignited. All the water that had been in the area of the blast evaporated instantly. About thirty yards upstream, the water began to trickle through the heated rocks to resume its journey downhill.

The will-o-wisps were unharmed when they emerged from the depths of the jungle. Instead of white light, however, they now glowed red.

"Well, that can't be good," Kristen said as she transformed into her human form, turned her back on the little bastards, and ran like hell.

She reasoned that she was supposed to keep going until something asked her to stop or made her. These little beings tricking her could not count as either one of those options. As she ran, the will-o-wisps pursued and easily kept pace as they jolted her with their bolts.

"I guess the pixies did say there would be risks," she muttered. She tried to increase her dragon speed further but the creatures simply mirrored her.

Although she tried to dodge as best as she could, with eight of the balls of light, it was impossible to avoid them all. They were ever-present like the drone of traffic in Detroit or the smell of pizza at Buddy's. She could practically feel them.

A sudden realization almost made her fall into the rocky stream when she acknowledged that she truly could feel them.

When she had her back to them, she still knew where they were, and when they moved, she knew it. They were magic, of course. If anything, the will-o-wisps seemed to have even more raw magic than the pixies did. But how could she *feel* that? Could she use it somehow?

She continued to sprint downstream, but the next time one of the balls of light darted forward to zap her—it didn't take long, only a couple of seconds—she tried to feel its approach. To her surprise, she could. She felt the will-o-wisp grow closer, felt it charge its odd little jolting power, and felt it strike.

This time, she didn't feel the impact. She dodged at the last moment and the will-o-wisp careened past her.

"Yes!" Kristen couldn't help pumping her fist in celebration, which of course left her open to be zapped by two of the other balls of lights.

Still, she had felt them coming, and even though she hadn't dodged those particular attacks, she had begun to get the hang of it. Finally, it started to make sense why the pixies sent her down this path.

She kept moving down the stream and focused on the magic energy coming from the lights. It was difficult to balance her mind so she could sense all eight of the creatures, but as she concentrated on them, she found she was able to dodge more of their attacks.

Soon, instead of being jolted by every single one whenever they wanted to zap her, she was able to dodge them about half the time. A few minutes later—did minutes exist there?—she was able to dodge almost all their attacks.

Kristen's confidence had increased somewhat when she noticed more lights in the woods.

At first, it was only a couple, but then they doubled, multiplied again, and repeated this at least twice more. As if all operating with the same consciousness, the lights began to converge on her.

CHAPTER SEVENTY-FOUR

"Did you see that light?" Amy whispered into the darkness she had enveloped them in. They had walked through tunnels for what felt like hours. She had no idea how much time had passed and if she had to guess, she'd go with "too much."

"I noticed it about a minute ago, yes," Katrina whispered in response.

"Do you think that's the end of the tunnel?" she asked.

"Is that where Boneclaw's scale is pointing you?"

She nodded.

"Then yes."

They continued cautiously down the strange, almost organic-like tunnel. The darkness was thick there so her magic worked well to shield them from view. As they moved deeper into the hillside, they passed a few passages connected to the one they followed. None of them had light coming from them and none seemed to draw the scale toward them more than the path they were taking, so they pressed on.

A short while later, the young mage heard footsteps.

"Are those in our tunnel?" she asked. It was hard to judge with the rock walls. Everything—even her whispers—seemed to echo.

"I don't know. Will your magic keep us hidden?" Katrina asked.

"Not if they walk right over us," she replied.

"Let's step in there then," the dragon said and Amy moved them through shadow into one of the branching passages.

They waited in the dark for almost a minute, breathing shallowly and trying not to move past the cocoon of magic she had spun to conceal them before they saw who was approaching.

She peered out from the darkness and was shocked to see that the people making the footsteps weren't people at all, but two dwarves.

They hurried past, tramping in heavy boots and making no effort at all to mask their passage. One look was enough to confirm that they didn't look like the dwarves she knew. They still had the big beards but lacked the bright colors the dwarves she had met always wore. Piercings were still prevalent, but they looked more jagged and savage somehow as if they were meant to intimidate rather than beautify their wearer. They vanished down the tunnel the duo had been following, but neither the mage nor the dragon said anything for another minute.

Finally, Amy broke the silence with the softest whisper she could utter. "I can't believe they're dwarves!"

Katrina's scowl was such that even in the darkness, she felt stupid for saying anything. "We're in a dwarf tunnel."

"But I thought it must have been made a long time ago and that Boneclaw was merely using it. Why would dwarves want to work with him?"

"Not all dwarves have the same loyalties. Exactly like dragons have different allegiances and mages have different levels of acquiescence to dragon rule, dwarves come in a variety of political stripes too."

"But to work with Boneclaw?"

"We can't know they were doing that," Katrina said. "For all we know, they're here to kill him like we are."

"Do you think we should follow them?" she asked.

The Iron Dragon stared down the passage for a moment before she shook her head. "No, I don't. Can you determine if any of these side passages will take us closer to Boneclaw? If this is anything like other dwarf mines I've been in, some of these tunnels will go to the same place."

"I'll try," Amy said and attempted to use the scale like a divining rod. Thankfully, it worked. A little way down the big passage, the energy from the scale seemed stronger. "This way."

They proceeded down the new route and walked in silence for a long time. While they walked, the mage's mind raced. What were dwarves doing there?

"Do you think those dwarves might have been here to stop Boneclaw?" Amy asked.

"It's possible. After everything that happened in Detroit, it's not exactly a secret that he's an asshole. It's only… Dwarves aren't particularly stealthy. If they were trying to attack Boneclaw, I don't see how they could get the drop on him."

Katrina paused in the darkness and her gaze stared ahead down the tunnel.

The girl could almost see her ears twitch. "What is it?" she asked.

"I hear voices."

They proceeded with caution. The dragon led the way while Amy tried to ensure that every part of her magic cocoon was intact. They were getting close and she could feel Boneclaw's growing presence much stronger through the scale. But would they be able to get close enough to surprise him?

They went around a slight bend in the passage and she was able to see a light at the end of the tunnel.

"Stick to the walls," Katrina said.

Amy nodded and pressed forward. Neither of the two women even considered stopping now. They had come this far and they had to know what Boneclaw was doing there and how the dwarves were involved. As they crept along the wall and remained far quieter than the voice booming from the end of the hallway in front of them, her mind filled with images of dwarf weapons of war. Would they be able to craft weapons that could hurt dragons? What about the Steel

Dragon? If they could, she did not doubt that Boneclaw would ingratiate himself with them to gain the advantage.

As they neared the end of the tunnel, they began to hear not only one voice but many. It sounded like someone was addressing a group, and the listeners were more than willing to express their agreement with raucous shouts and applause.

With extreme care, they crept forward. No one was in the tunnel they were in, not yet anyway. Amy half-expected someone to jump out in front of them, but whatever was happening at the end of the tunnel seemed to demand the attention of everyone present.

Finally, they reached the end, and the long passage opened into a huge cavern lit with torches spaced around the walls. Their route ended in a little alcove set into the wall high above. They were about fifteen feet above the floor and stared into a circular chamber about fifty feet in diameter.

A large crowd of dwarves had gathered, all seated on the stone floor. The flickering light of the torches made their faces unreadable. All Amy could see was heavily furrowed brows and thick beards. She knew she was still wreathed in shadow, but it also seemed like she might not need that particular protection right now. Every single face stared at a central figure who had his back to the two infiltrators —Boneclaw.

He had come to stand in front of the crowd. The applause and cheers they had heard had been for a dwarf who now gestured at the old dragon and called for even more applause.

After a moment, the dwarf stopped working the crowd and went to sit.

Boneclaw raised his arms to motion for silence.

"This is gonna be good," Katrina said, pushed herself against the opposite wall from her teammate, and kept her body in shadow so she could listen.

Amy knew this was not the time to attack Boneclaw, not in front of all these dwarves who seemed friendly toward him. She decided there was nothing to do but listen.

"Is this everyone?" the dragon demanded. "I expected more than fifty."

"Yes, sir," the dwarf who had introduced him replied with pride. "This is every member of our clan, plus a few members of the seven other closest clans. What you say here today will spread through our communities and soon, more will come to your call."

"Well, I suppose that's something to look forward to then." Boneclaw sneered. "Forgive me, but I had expected more of you." His voice now boomed and echoed off the walls of the chamber. As his words reverberated through the space, the flames from the torches seemed to grow dimmer.

"I had expected that more than fifty dwarves would be tired of living in this cold, hard, northern swamp."

The crowd booed loudly at that. They didn't seem angry at Boneclaw, however, but rather at the situation.

"Who here tires of being frozen six months of the year while the humans and dragons lay claim to the lush tropical lands?" he demanded.

A cheer loud enough to echo down the hallway was the answer.

"Who here tires of not being taken seriously?"

Another loud cheer erupted.

"Who here wishes to have a full place at the global table of negotiations instead of being tossed its frozen scraps?"

Cheers erupted, so loud that a few rocks and flurries of dust fell from the earthen ceiling of the hill.

"You are a strong people, stronger than humans and resistant to magic and dragon powers alike, and yet you have been left to gather ice in the back of the freezer. This time must come to an end. With your help, we will realize this vision. We will remake the world into a place of true equality, a place where dwarves don't have to cede any of their territory to human settlements. A place where leaders can hold intruders and foreigners to the laws of the land."

The cheers were so loud that an actual boulder dislodged from the ceiling. One of the dwarves darted forward and punched it and it shattered before it could do real damage.

"I thought dwarves were content with holding Canada?" Amy whispered to Katrina.

"As far as I knew, they were. I guess some wanted something else, but I wonder what the hell Boneclaw has done to convince them. God, I hope it's not more of this decimation of the human population bullshit."

But they would never have their answers as a yell issued from the passage behind them.

"What the hell is a leg doing here?" a dwarf hollered into the tunnel. He held a rifle comfortably and had it aimed down the tunnel with the casual efficiency of someone who knew exactly how to use their weapon.

Katrina yanked her leg back into shadow, but it was too late.

The dwarf, seeing that the leg was not disembodied but was connected to a body and presumably another leg, fired his weapon.

Amy threw a shield up before the bullet could hit the dragon. She then tried to throw another blast of magic at the dwarf to knock him on his ass—after the gunshot, the sound of a dwarf falling wouldn't exactly alert anyone who hadn't already heard what was going on— but she couldn't. Rather than send their attacker sprawling with the tidal wave of magic she threw at him, he only scooted back. It was as if he was playing in the surf and a particularly strong wave had come, but he'd known what to do about it.

This must have been what Constance had been talking about when she said dwarves were resistant to magic.

The dwarf aimed, this time at the mage.

"Pull him toward us!" Katrina shouted.

"Are you crazy?"

"Just do it!"

She yanked him toward them. He shouted in surprise and stumbled forward. Obviously, he was not prepared to be pulled toward the people he was trying to attack. Still, even unbalancing him wasn't enough to knock him down.

Before the dwarven guard could regain his stability, the dragon turned to iron and spun to strike him in the head with a roundhouse kick.

That was enough to thrust him stumbling down the passage, past the two women, and out into the chamber below. He fell the fifteen feet and landed with an impressively loud thud.

Completely unharmed, he pushed to his feet.

"There's a mage in that hallway! And the Steel Dragon!"

CHAPTER SEVENTY-FIVE

With too many of the bobbing lights, Kristen could do little else but run. Her only hope was that if she stuck to the stream, she might get past them and survive. Even that didn't prove to be easy, unfortunately.

The will-o-wisps emerged from the woods, converged on her, and circled her as she moved. Those that were in front of her didn't get out of her way but used the opportunity to launch their tiny bolts. She was not able to dodge all of them, but she could sense those that had the most magical energy and avoided them. It wasn't much of an edge but it was all she had and she was grateful for it.

She ducked under a group directly ahead, then made the mistake of glancing behind her to see hundreds of the creatures—beings? Manifestations? Evil cousins of the pixies?—and decided that her strategy to run as fast as she could was indeed the right choice.

The way in front of her was mostly clear and while a few of them continued to harry her, she could see them as well as feel them. She evaded those that tried to zap her and decided that her skill was improving. As she raced on and dodged their attacks, she sensed the magic as easily as if it were her own. Was this what the pixies meant when they said this was a realm of magic? Was all magic like this? Connected and running through even opposing forces?

A blast of particularly strong magic struck her in the small of her back and she splashed forward into the stream bed. She hadn't sensed the attack so she still had something to learn about how this magic worked. That point was driven home when two more of the little glowing bastards shocked her while she was down. She turned instinctively to steel, only to draw the ire of a few more of the will-o-wisps. A couple of them shocked her—and yes, it hurt as badly as when she was not steel—so she turned to her regular skin again and stumbled forward.

Again, she moved past the main horde and felt like she was improving in her ability to sense their magic, but she couldn't *do* anything to them. She tried to kick one but it darted clear easily as if it could not only sense her future motions but could also see how they would play out in slow motion. She punched at another and turned her hand to its dragon claw form to swipe at a third, but they evaded her strikes far more effortlessly than she had any of theirs.

It seemed there was nothing she could do to kill them, disable them, or even to slow them. She couldn't even touch them so she gave up her futile attempts and continued to run.

Within moments, however, this also seemed to be a foolhardy plan. Up ahead, more light glowed directly in her path. Was it another wave of the will-o-wisps? If it was, she didn't see how she could hope to survive. She barely managed to avoid the attacks by those already in pursuit. The thought of facing a hundred more...or a thousand? Hell, even ten more might be too much.

But with no other option, Kristen ran on. The will-o-wisps pursuing her did not slow their chase. They did not whisper encouragement or that her trial was almost over. They merely harried and pursued her in a seemingly endless stream of attacks. It was damn annoying, but she grimaced and pushed on.

As she drew closer to the light, it seemed to grow in size and elevate from the water until it hung in the sky like a glowing basketball.

"The sun," she thought, shocked that she hadn't recognized it for what it was when she first saw it. As soon as she had the thought, she realized she could no longer sense the will-o-wisps. Well, that wasn't quite right. She could feel them, but for the first time since she'd tried to touch one of them, they weren't pursuing her.

Kristen looked at her surroundings in shock. Without realizing it, she'd left the jungle. She still stood in the bed of the stream, but rather than meandering through the closely packed trees, it now snaked through a plain. She had left the jungle and it seemed she'd also passed the test as the will-o-wisps had abandoned their pursuit.

"Stop and catch your breath before you go on."

She spun to where a pixie sat on a large stone in the middle of the stream a short distance ahead. It had a mustache so appeared more masculine than most pixies, and carried a long stick with a string dangling from it connected to a cork floating in the stream.

"Who are you?" she asked.

The creature twitched its mustache—an expression she decided to take as a smile. "I'm the fisherman."

"Well, Fisherman, I'm Kristen Hall."

"I know who you are and what you're doing here."

"Oh. Well, can you tell me about those glowing lights that tried to zap the shit out of me?"

"Nope."

"Well, what can you tell me?" she asked and tried not to let her frustration show. She reminded herself that the pixies were trying to help her, even if the form of that help was more than a little strange.

The tiny little fisherman looked over his bushy mustache at her for a long moment, his eyes twinkling with some unspoken secret. He glanced over his shoulder at the sun before he turned back to her. "I reckon you can catch your breath before you go on. The sun will rise higher soon enough, but you go ahead and rest now."

Something pulled at his fishing pole and diverted his attention away from her.

Rest could wait. Feeling the pressure of her looming deadline increase with the rising sun, Kristen set her shoulders and set off down the stream again. It was colder on the plains than it had been in the jungle but no less beautiful. Now, instead of tall, towering trees growing along both banks to block out the sky, rolling fields were filled with waist-high grasses and flowers that swayed in the wind.

The riverbed continued through a field covered by grass that was heavy with seed. In the next moment, her surroundings transitioned into a hill of nothing but sunflowers before it reverted to grassland a short distance later. It was like taking a trip across the Midwest if Americans could live off blades of grass and pollen instead of corn and wheat.

Nothing disturbed the landscape except the occasional boulder. Here and there, one of these giant stones protruded from the grass as if—millennia before—a group of giants had played a game of dice with the stones and left them there to be weathered into their lumpen shapes.

As she walked down the stream—it was deeper there, up to her knees—she thought about what it had taken to reach this place. The will-o-wisps and their magical jolts of energy were the first things that came to mind, of course. But as she walked past the beautiful prairie habitat, she found herself thinking back to her earliest days on the force.

Kristen recalled the first time she'd started to notice that something was different about her. She had been playing airsoft with Drew, the gang, and ol' Jonesy, God rest his soul. They had attacked her and she had been able to use her reflexes to deflect their airsoft pellets with her weapon. It wasn't an easy trick, apparently, but she had been able to do it effortlessly.

From there, her powers had only grown. She had been faster and stronger than her teammates, with keener vision and better reflexes. Was that all a manifestation of magic as Amythist claimed? She had spent a long time wondering why she hadn't recognized that she was a dragon sooner, but perhaps she wasn't asking the right question.

Perhaps she should have wondered how her powers could manifest at all. She had turned to steel to stop a rocket from blowing Jonesy up, although she had failed to save his life. After that incident, she had been told she was a dragon. Would her story have been different if she had been told she was something more? Who was to say? Even with the dragon inside her, fueling her speed and strength and granting her steel skin, it had taken her what felt like forever to transform into her dragon body.

Was that something anyone could realize? Was magic merely another skill that most humans did not bother with? Like playing the piano or training their memories?

Who was to say?

Kristen turned a finger to steel, then her hand, and marveled over how easy that now was. When she had first learned her powers, simply changing to a dragon had been difficult, but with a bevy of brilliant teachers, she had mastered her powers. Although some of those teachers had been less than brilliant.

She had learned from Sebastian Shadowstorm too. At the time, she had not known that he was trying to burn her city to the ground, only that he was willing to take a chance on teaching an outsider. Were his powers derived from the same place as hers? He couldn't turn into shadow like the Masked One could, but he could move through them. Did that mean he had visited there? Or had he simply tapped into that power as well as his ability to control the weather?

These were questions she couldn't answer and never would. Shadowstorm was dead and she'd killed him. At the time, it had seemed necessary but now, faced with the Masked One, she almost longed for the simpler time facing a simpler foe.

Of course, he hadn't been her last. She had also faced Death, an assassin and dragon more proficient with dragon bullets than any of the technomages had been. Against that enemy, she had learned that her powers weren't always that useful. Depending on the threat, different responses were needed.

She had mastered so much. What started with her ability to become steel had spread, changed, and grown. At first, she hadn't known how to do that on command and now, she could feel it when only a fingertip changed to steel.

Wait.

That was new.

Kristen turned another fingertip to steel.

She frowned when she realized she could feel each and every part of her flesh change to metal.

While she had always been able to feel something when she transformed, it was mostly the change of sensation. Skin and steel experienced the world quite differently. What she experienced now was entirely different.

It took a moment before she understood that she could feel the magic powering the transformation. She had never been able to do that before. When she changed her hand to steel, she felt the same kind of tingle. It was odd, but it reminded her of the will-o-wisps in the jungle. This brought the same anticipatory jolt, but while the power that had come from the beings had been painful, the energy that came from her was pleasant, like a cool breeze that didn't quite raise goosebumps.

On impulse, she transformed her entire body to steel and felt the magic flow through her. What had seemed like an inner stream before now felt like a raging river as her body coursed with magic.

But it wasn't only through her. It was around her too. Exactly like she had been able to sense the will-o-wisps, she could sense magic there as well. It was present in the stream as it swirled around her feet and drew her onward. She could see it in the way the grass bent and moved in the wind and heard it beneath the sounds and songs of crickets. It was everywhere in this place. More accurately, it *was* this place. But it was more than that too.

Magic wasn't merely something that came from this realm, she realized. It had to be a fundamental force of the universe. Like gravity or the electromagnetic spectrum but much weirder. It gave her power, but it also gave humans the power to use magic to create the pixies, the dwarves, and even—if Amythist was correct—the dragons. But it did more than that. Magic let a woman imagine what her great-grandchild might look like. It let a man think about a mistake he had made when he was still a boy. Magic let people imagine structures that would take lifetimes to build. It allowed people to transform something as simple as words or sounds into stories and music.

Magic was everywhere but ran closer to the surface there. It was in the grass, the river, and the jagged boulder that broke the flow of the water and created rapids in the formerly placid flowing stream.

Kristen opened her eyes to look at the world around her instead of simply sensing the magic. The terrain had changed. The verdant fields of grass and flowers had given way to dried grasses and flowers that had already gone to seed and withered to nothing at all.

The boulders in the field—once so smooth they were almost friendly—now looked jagged like a giant window of stone had been shattered and the shards left to fall where they wished.

Even the boulders in the river no longer looked smoothed by the water that flowed around them. They were aggressive, blocked her path, and forced her to contend with not only their physical presence but with the turbulent vortexes of water that formed in their path. The water itself—crystal-clear until this point—now had debris from the places where it swirled around the rocks.

In the stream ahead of her, Kristen saw many more of them. The stream—it was now wide enough to call a river—pooled once more at a bank of these jagged, threatening boulders before it cascaded down a series of rapids.

What am I headed toward? she wondered before she proceeded, a little more cautious now. When she passed the bank of jagged rocks, she felt the sun on her neck. It had risen higher in the sky, which meant she was running out of time when she needed it most.

CHAPTER SEVENTY-SIX

"Amy, you have to run," Katrina said.

"I fucking know we have to run, so *come on!*" Amy tugged at the Iron Dragon with her magic, but she was too heavy and too stubborn.

Already, the dwarves below—armed with the most effective of all weapons, the gun—were taking shots at the two women.

"You heard that dwarf. Boneclaw now thinks I'm the Steel Dragon. He won't let us out of here."

"Let has nothing to do with it. Let's go!"

"No, Amy, think about it. If he thinks Kristen was here, he'll call for the duel to be declared void. I don't know much about dragon politics, but I know enough to know that he can do that. It can't happen. I have to fight him."

"No, you don't. He'll kill you."

"He'll kill Kristen if you don't warn her about the dwarves." Amy did not fail to notice that her teammate didn't deny that Boneclaw would indeed try to kill her.

But compared to what she did next, that detail seemed trivial.

"Amy, go," Katrina said as she vaulted out of the alcove and landed in front of Boneclaw.

"Ah, Kristen. The Steel Bitch herself," the old dragon mused as the dwarves rushed forward to seize her.

"I don't have time to wait for this duel, Boneclaw. We do this here and now before you can stack the table against me." It was amazing how much Katrina and Kristen looked alike. In their metal forms, they were almost indistinguishable, and in the low light, the iron could not be distinguished from steel. She only had to pitch her voice up a few notes and she even sounded like Kristen.

"You don't wish the odds to be stacked against you, so you choose to fight me *here?*" he demanded.

"Fight me, you coward." She spat in his face.

Boneclaw smiled from beneath the skull he wore as a mask. "Careful. You might get your dead slave's skull dirty." To the dwarves, he said, "Release her."

The dwarves complied and Katrina wasted no time. She lunged forward with her iron fist cocked and loaded but fell through empty space.

Laughter came from all around the room as her adversary turned to shadow and moved from torch to torch and extinguished them all except for one a dwarf held near her.

His laughter grew louder as she began to scream. At first, her shouts were those of a warrior engaged in deadly combat. She punched and kicked with blows strong enough to hurl any dwarf unfortunate enough to get in her way across the room. But the Masked One wasn't an enemy made of matter. Except for when he wanted to lash out at her, he'd taken his shadow form and her punches couldn't strike him. Worse, her iron skin could not rebuff him.

He fought like he had been training for it. His strikes were aimed at her armpits, the backs of her knees, and her throat, places that by necessity couldn't be as thickly armored. Katrina took these blows as well as she could, but the sheer force of his attacks was wearing her down. Plus, she still tried to fight a shadow. Every punch she threw was with her full strength and every kick was meant to be the last.

But she couldn't land a single blow, not in this place of darkness beneath the earth.

In the next moment, he had her. He sliced the tendons at the back of her legs—already weakened from a flurry of strikes—and she fell to her knees. Boneclaw then forced her mouth open and stabbed down her throat.

Red blood burbled out as she fell face-down on the floor of the chamber. Her body landed with the heavy clank of iron.

She was dead and Amy had watched her die. It was over too quickly for her to do more than raise a little magic to her hands. The mage felt worse than useless, knowing she'd been unable to do a thing to save her ally.

"The Steel Bitch is done for but don't let her mage get away!" Boneclaw bellowed and the dwarves hastened to obey. They vanished into a dozen tunnels with terrifying quickness. She didn't have to wait long to hear their boots tramping through the tunnels as they searched for her.

With no other choices, she fled.

CHAPTER SEVENTY-SEVEN

If Kristen had known that the dead grass and raggedy brush of the spent flowers were the last trace of life she would encounter on her path, she might have tried to appreciate them more. From her vantage point atop a boulder in the river, she could see nothing but the grays and browns of a lifeless, barren landscape. Wasteland might be a fairer description, honestly.

There was nothing except the river—the stream had indisputably widened to a river now—and bare stone, dusty, dead earth, and windswept boulders. The water was almost ice-cold, despite the sun beating on it. That was the only connection it had to its former self. The temperature had dropped consistently as the world became more desolate. She didn't want to think about what the world around her might look like if the stream froze.

To be fair to the stream, though, that might be an improvement. The water had never cleared after its descent down the rapids. Even now, despite the river being almost stagnant in most places, it was muddy and filthy with a slight sheen to its surface. She still followed it but she used her dragon powers to leap from boulder to boulder or to take a few steps on one of its craggy banks. The water looked like what her father had described Lake Erie as looking like decades before—toxic.

Not for the first time, she looked longingly over her shoulder. She could still barely see the jungle she had come from in the distance. Even from miles away, its trees towered and cast shade on all the other organisms and possibly creatures that lived on the jungle floor. She missed it, strangely enough, even though the will-o-wisps had ruined the ambiance.

It felt like *days* since she'd been there. She felt like she had walked through the forest all night, the plains all day, and this barren waste-land for a week, but the sun had yet to set. Did that mean she still had two more days? She had no idea. It was probably foolish to think the sun in this realm had anything to do with the sun at home. She hoped she still had enough time but she began to worry that she didn't.

What frustrated her most was that she hadn't learned anything yet. Okay, so she had learned how to sense magic, but how would that help her? It might let her sense Boneclaw before he attacked, but it wouldn't empower her ability to strike him in his shadow form.

Kristen was beginning to worry that the pixies didn't understand her situation or worse, that Amythist hadn't been honest about her intentions. She paused and tried to shake the dark thoughts from her head. Amythist and the pixies could be trusted and she had to take them at their word but still, how much longer would the sun sit overhead?

As if in response, it shifted so the bottom of it touched a craggy mountain on the horizon. The dust and dirt in the air ignited in reds, oranges, and yellows. It would be beautiful if she wasn't worried it would last for hours and hours.

She sighed and cupped her hands in the dirty water. While she had drunk a fair amount in the jungle and the fields of flowers, nothing had happened. It seemed riskier to drink there, but she remembered how the water had invigorated her and hoped it would continue to do so. She hadn't hungered at all on this trip—was that because all this had taken less than an hour?—but she now began to despair of ever seeing an end to this journey.

The most pressing thing about her situation was the time crunch. She had to master abilities that could give her an edge over Boneclaw before their duel. If she didn't do so in time and faced him anyway, she'd be dead. If she failed to master them and didn't arrive, she had no doubt that he would declare some kind of attack on her, and that wouldn't go well. She *had* to be there on time and with the skills she would need and yet, in this realm, time seemed to be nonexistent.

That made her wonder if she would ever get out of there. She felt so alone and had become quite used to working with others. Yes, she was the Steel Dragon, but she was also someone who had learned that you couldn't succeed in much of anything alone. Why did she try to do so now? It was confusing, to say the least.

Plus, there was the implication that she would have to face Boneclaw alone. Well, more than an implication. She knew she would face him alone, but how well could that go? She had already lost to him multiple times, despite having people helping her every time she had faced him. How could she face him alone and hope to win?

The sunset faded into twilight and her despair deepened. She continued to plod forward, so why did nothing happen? A part of her almost wanted something to come from the shadows that stretched from the boulders she walked between because then, at least, she could face something besides her self-doubt.

If the sun sank any lower, she would be in darkness again. So far, every time the sun had shifted on this journey, something had happened. What was different now? Why was it vanishing when the wasteland all around her remained stubbornly the same?

Could this be a trap? Kristen wondered as she hopped onto another boulder and looked back up the stream. The jungle was completely gone now, vanished into the gloom of twilight and the haze that seemed to fill the air. If it was a trap, she didn't think Amythist had set it. She wouldn't aid Boneclaw, not with the way she had helped the captive dragons.

The pixies, then?

The fact that Amythist trusted them made her want to trust them as well. But maybe this was merely beyond their ability to understand.

If they spent time in this realm, perhaps their sense of time was completely disassociated from what it meant on Earth.

Most people didn't associate with pixies because they were capricious to a fault. She had heard stories of their pranks gone wrong. Hell, the story about what the creatures had done to the wizard who had captured two of them was positively gruesome, but at least they had a reason for that particular incident.

That said, she had heard stories of them doing bizarre things for no reason at all. Sometimes, they thought they were being funny but most of the time, they were simply inscrutable. They were simply more...*alien* than any of the other races on Earth, probably because they were beings of pure magic. Their outlook on the world was bound to be different. She had hoped that difference in perspective would give her the edge she needed. Now, she was scared it might very well doom her.

Resolute, she pressed onward. There was no choice and despite her doubts, she wouldn't simply sit and quit.

The sun—challenging her willpower, perhaps—set completely. The same bizarre stars came out and began to twinkle as she waded on without slowing.

The stream was now barely more than a muddy trickle dribbling between pools. Had she missed some branch of it somewhere along the way? How had a once mighty river changed into this disgusting swamp?

Kristen considered taking her dragon form to travel faster, but something held her back from doing so. It didn't feel right. She had no idea why, but she trusted her intuition. This form—her human form—was her true form. While she might have been a dragon from birth, her parents had raised her as a human baby. This was the body she slept in and the one she laughed and cried in. It seemed like the body to make this spiritual journey of magical awakening in.

The sky had to be taunting her as a dust cloud moved in to obscure the stars and plunge the muddy path into complete and total darkness. Her dragon-powered eyesight was usually more than sufficient, even in low light, but the darkness was so thick that she couldn't see her feet. She had walked along the bank of the stream for a short distance. It wasn't like there were plants to deal with, so it had seemed the most sensible choice, but she now wondered if she would be able to stay near the stream in this darkness. It might make more sense for her to resume wading in the muddy water. At least that way, she would be sure she didn't accidentally lose her way in the dark.

She stepped down the slope of the bank and into the water, but failed to see a rock and struck it with her shin hard enough that she fell.

Instinctively, she turned her body to steel to protect herself. It worked, of course. No matter how jagged the rocks, they were never a match for the Steel Dragon wrapped in metal fueled by healing power.

As she pushed to her feet and tried to wipe the water from her before she turned to her regular skin, she realized she could feel the power flow through her for the steel transformation more clearly than ever. She felt the typical enhanced strength and imperviousness of steel skin, but she now felt so much more. It felt like every part of her was alive with magic and every square inch of skin and every follicle radiated it.

And it was her, she realized.

Magic was simply an extension of herself. It was like her spirit, as her mom would say, or her soul, as her dad would say, or maybe her inner self—Brian's favorite euphemism. *That* was how she changed herself into steel. She—and indeed all people—had an essence to them —a life force, something that made them special and unique from all others. To transform, she simply had to direct the flow into the parts she wanted to change. In fact, she already had that skill tuned so well that she could change only a finger if she wanted.

She could control magic and had done so for a long time. Only now, she knew what it meant.

"Are all dragon powers like this?" Kristen asked the darkness.

As she trudged through the muddy water, she decided to experiment. She was used to drawing the magic of her inner self to power her steel skin, her strength, and her speed, but what about the other dragon powers?

Fire breath and the capability to fly were not abilities in the normal sense of the word. They were only possible because of magic. A dragon would never be able to fly without it, nor would one be able to breathe fire. Maybe she didn't need to be in her dragon form to use those powers.

It occurred to her that she merely *thought* she did.

Perhaps Amythist was right and dragons didn't truly exist and were merely manifestations of what people thought was possible. Once someone had transformed into one, other people thought they were capable of the same thing. If that was true, there was no reason to think the powers could only be used when she was in her dragon form.

Kristen paused and planted her feet in the mud and slime at the bottom of the river. She thought about her dragon breath, that most powerful of dragon attacks, and how it worked in her dragon body. There was no sack of poison that needed to be replenished and no potions that needed to be consumed. One simply had to take a deep breath and think of fire.

She took a deep breath.

Her thoughts focused on the power building in her chest and visualized that the heat would brook no argument and the flames would end any attack against her. She thought about the magic flowing through her and from her. Then, she exhaled.

Disappointingly, nothing happened.

With a heavy sigh, she reminded herself that she did not give up. Nothing like this ever worked on the first attempt. She tried again with no response. At her third attempt, she felt heat in her stomach and as she exhaled, she belched.

Kristen screamed in frustration and punched the surface of the muddy water. Why couldn't this be easier?

She looked at the dark sky and then at the water around her legs. In the dark, they were almost indistinguishable. Nothing was visible to lend some kind of assurance that she was even on the right track.

She frowned and narrowed her eyes into the darkness in search of something that provided a clue of what to do next.

Furtive movements seemed to eddy across the face of the darkness.

"What the hell are those?"

When she peered into the blackness, she realized that her scream of frustration might have been a serious mistake. Something moved toward her and she caught glimpses of sharp teeth. Whatever they were, they looked dark and dangerous, and worst of all, they looked hungry.

CHAPTER SEVENTY-EIGHT

Amy ripped her gaze away from Katrina's corpse and stumbled up the tunnel they—she—was hiding in. Her teammate was dead. The Iron Dragon, a powerful thorn in Kristen's side for so long before she became one of her strongest allies, was dead. Boneclaw had killed her effortlessly as if fighting her had been a game. This was a woman who could go toe to toe with the Steel Dragon herself.

All this raced through her mind as she half-staggered through the passage. She tried to make herself move faster but found it difficult with the tears that blurred her vision. She had to escape and tell Kristen to not go through with this duel. There was no way she would be able to defeat Boneclaw. He was too powerful and too skilled with his powers. She had to get back to warn her or her friend would die.

A dwarf lurched into her path, raised a rifle, and fired. She barely had the common sense to block the shot with her magic and realized belatedly that she had let her shield drop when she saw Katrina die. As she tried to bring it up again, the dwarf took aim and prepared to fire again and she knew she didn't have time.

She hurled a blast of force at him, but the magic rolled off like a wave against a boulder.

"You magic bitch," he cursed as he fired again.

Amy blocked that one too.

The dwarf cursed and turned to the hallway. "I found her! I found the mage!"

It was her turn to swear when she heard boots thudding down the passages toward her. She should have silenced the dwarf and been cleverer in her escape. Worse, she should have saved Katrina.

The dwarf aimed for the third time.

The young mage ripped the gun out of his hands with her magic, bent it in half, and clubbed him across the face with it. He reeled from the blow, but she hadn't even drawn blood. It was a reminder that dwarves were much stronger than humans were.

But they still wore clothes, fortunately.

She lifted him by the back of his shirt and threw him behind her. He landed with a thunk but was not knocked unconscious and simply found his feet and charged toward her.

By now, he was no longer the most important threat she faced. Three more dwarves had entered the tunnel to block her path.

Amy had her head together enough now to block all their shots. She'd practiced that a hundred times. Her powers weren't able to work on her attackers directly, so she ripped a boulder from the wall of the tunnel and hurled it at them. They deflected it as easily as she had deflected their bullets.

As she considered her next strike, she heard a roar from the cavern below. Boneclaw sounded pissed and she knew she had to get out of there without delay. She used her telekinesis to boost herself past the three dwarves, only to find another five racing down the tunnel toward her.

It seemed she wouldn't be able to fight, and running looked more and more difficult. What choice did she still have?

Her thoughts reminded her that her skateboard was still in the tiny shack at the top of the shaft. She tucked into another tunnel to avoid the five—now eight—dwarves who were now ranged against her and called for her skateboard.

Unfortunately, it was too late. She had chosen a tunnel that ended in a dead-end. The dwarves, now nine in total, moved toward her with their guns raised. That they were not shooting was not a good thing. They understood that their bullets wouldn't penetrate her shields, which meant they most likely planned to switch to fists. And those, she thought gloomily, deflected her magic like drizzle off an umbrella.

They mumbled to each other in a language of low tones and falling boulders. Then, as one, they attacked. She faced them with her back against the stone wall and tried to keep them at bay by using her telekinesis to block their paths with boulders. They merely punched through them. They were strong—far stronger than she had thought possible. It seemed all the more frustrating because she hadn't anticipated dwarves being there with Boneclaw.

One of them landed a punch across her face that might have rattled her had she not managed to absorb some of the blow with her magic. But she could tell by the dwarf's expression that he knew he would merely have to hit her more directly on the next strike.

"No, please," she said and held her hands up. "Just… I'd rather you shoot me than beat me to death."

He responded with a grin with more teeth made of stone than bone. "Back up fellas. We gonna fill this mage with holes. Aren't we, my lady?"

"I thought you would offer to take me captive, honestly," Amy replied.

"Why would we do that when Lord Boneclaw killed the Steel Dragon herself? You've already lost this fight and you've already lost the war."

"Actually, *you've* already lost this fight."

The dwarf didn't even have enough time to say, "Huh?" before her skateboard rocketed between his legs and came to rest at her feet. She stepped on the end and popped it into her arm.

"Shoot her!" he shouted when he realized something was amiss.

The dwarves obeyed without hesitation.

It wasn't enough.

Amy tossed her skateboard up and spun it with magic while enveloping it with a shield. That power—combined with the Kevlar grip tape and the titanium trucks she had installed on the custom board—were more than enough to deflect the bullets.

"Get her!" the stone-toothed dwarf shouted. The others rushed forward to pummel her again but it was much too late.

The young mage had already hopped on her board and pushed off. There was no way even the most legendary of skateboarders could have gained much momentum with a single push, but she was not merely any skateboarder. She was a skateboarding mage who had played way too many videogames.

Her push sent her up the wall of the round, organically-shaped tunnel, over the heads of the dwarves, and down the other side of the tunnel to skid to a stop behind them.

"What the hell?" one of her attackers asked as the others fell over each other to turn in the tight tunnel and pursue her.

There was no way they would catch her. With magic to propel her forward and glue her shoes to her board, she was unstoppable. A dwarf jumped into her path and she did a kickflip over his head. Another darted out and she ollied over him too and put her board down on the top of his helmet with enough force to knock him off his feet. A group of three tried to block her so she did the loop-the-loop maneuver again.

"I can't believe I don't have a headcam on right now," she mumbled. "This ride will be fucking legend. Katrina? If you're watching, this is for you."

She reached the main tunnel and rocketed up faster than gravity could have pulled her down in the other direction. The dwarves, quite aware of the grade of their tunnel, sent an avalanche of boulders tumbling down the shaft at her.

Amy had played her fair share of videogames and ollied up, then jumped from one boulder to the next without touching the ground until she was past the avalanche. "Mario taught me that one, bitches!" she shouted.

More shots fired from behind her. She ollied again and threw her board into a three-sixty kickflip to divert the bullets before she landed on the board and continued her meteoritic ascent to the surface.

She could see light now. Not much, only the outline of the fancy door she and Katrina had entered through. Nothing appeared to be in her way either, except something weird sparked on the side of the passage.

A massive explosion catapulted her from her board and into empty space. She snatched her board as she fell and managed to get it under her feet before she landed. When she looked up, fifteen dwarves stood near the door of the house. They had used dynamite to collapse the tunnel beneath her feet.

They fired at her now, which forced her to throw her shields up and reassess how to escape. She had decided to simply rip the house out of the side of the hill behind them when she saw Boneclaw's shadow-dragon head appear in the broken end of the tunnel where she had been.

"Where is she?" he demanded.

Amy didn't wait for the dwarves to give him detailed directions to the mage who was right below his nose. Instead, she turned her board and pushed off down a passage.

Gunshots echoed behind her, followed by the mighty roar of a pissed-off dragon, which suggested that Old Boney had indeed learned where she had been. She willed herself to greater speed. Truthfully, it wasn't that difficult to go at amazing speeds down there as the tunnels were beautifully made with incredibly smooth floors and rounded walls. No gravel flurried from her board to her feet, and any time there was a sharp turn, she could simply ride onto it like an Olympian doing the luge.

She glided up one wall, then another, and didn't slow even when the grade of the tunnel grew even steeper. Her tic-tack progress settled into a smooth, comfortable rhythm that enabled her to accelerate.

But still, she heard Boneclaw behind her. He was gaining. While she rolled as quickly as she could, he could simply turn to shadow and travel through the darkness. The only reason she was still alive was because he had to take his solid form to attack her, and that cost him precious seconds.

It certainly wasn't a big advantage for her, nor would it last. Amy knew enough of the dragon to know he was no fool. She prepared a ball of light in each fist. If she could force him to become solid, that might give her the edge she needed.

Focused on the dragon behind her, the young mage hadn't paid attention when she reached the end of the tunnel. She burst out of the relatively narrow tunnel into a much larger area. It was as wide as the room she had seen Boneclaw and all the dwarves in earlier but much longer. In the middle was a metal train track with a mining cart on it. All around that were dwarves running for their guns.

Amy—completely and unabashedly unable to help herself—did the biggest backflip melon grab she possibly could, landed in a backslide on the rail, and pushed down the tunnel.

Dwarves gave chase on either side, firing shots at her that she blocked by doing kick tricks of one variety or another that deflected the bullets into the walls. She reached a switch in the track and hopped onto the rail that entered a passage that led up instead of down and pushed herself ever faster.

She thought she had finally lost the dwarves when the track came to an end. Relieved, she ollied off the track, did a triple kickflip for good measure, and landed in what must have been some type of concrete drainage pipe. Unfortunately, the dwarves had a better understanding of the geography of their mine than she did and they entered the pipe from both ends.

The young mage careened up one side of the concrete tube, planted her hand on the lip, and lifted the board over her head. The dwarves converged on her at the bottom of the pipe and fired a relentless barrage while she used her free hand and feet to direct her board to block their shots. Finally, when they were all gathered in one big old beautiful group, she dropped the handplant, got her feet back on her board, and bulldozed through the middle of them.

They didn't scatter like she had imagined they would—they were too damn tough—but she knocked enough of them on their butts to be able to swoop down the rest of the concrete drainage tube unmolested.

The ground turned into earth and stone as Amy continued her ascent toward a hole that showed a sky rich with the reds, oranges, and yellows of sunset.

She burst out into the cool evening sky to see she was perhaps a quarter of the way around the hill from the cabin she'd entered through and much closer to the bottom.

A deep breath helped to ease her thudding heart. Happy to have the last rays of the sun shining to protect her, she took her board to the air and started toward home.

Her relief was short-lived, however, as she did not make it far.

Below her, the cabin seemed to become a horrible twisted nightmare of Alice in Wonderland. A huge dragon arm drove through the window and another burst through the front door. After a blast of fire that knocked a hole in the roof, Boneclaw stuck his horrible dragon head out.

He truly was a fearsome-looking beast. His scales were the color of ink but the spikes that jutted from his spine, elbows, shoulder blades, and face were the color of bone. They weren't uniform and were jagged and sharp—like each had been broken in some fight in the past and regrown into a more wicked version of itself.

With a roar of utter rage, he spread his wings and demolished the cabin.

"Oh, fuck this." Amy instinctively rose higher as quickly as she could.

She made it perhaps fifty feet before a claw came out of nowhere and drove into her face.

Without a doubt, she would have been dead if she had let her bulletproof shield drop. As it was, the force of the blow was far stronger than she could endure. It hurled her from the air and she plummeted into the forest below. Her shield—a sphere all around her —impacted the trunk of a tree with enough force to crack it in half, and for a moment her head spun so badly she couldn't use her magic at all.

Boneclaw was strong. Far stronger than any dragon she had faced before.

The young mage wiped her face and shook her head as she tried to orient herself. That moment saved her life as in her confusion, she saw some of the shadows of the trees moving. Boneclaw was there in the darkness of the forest. She stood, stepped onto her board, and rocketed it toward the sky and the sunlight.

"You coward!" the old dragon roared. He followed her as a billowing form of shadow but as soon as he broke through the tree-tops and into the warm glow of the evening sun, he coalesced into his dragon form.

It was only a small improvement, in her estimation.

Her instincts pushed her to greater height and Boneclaw followed.

Once they were well above the forest, she turned to him and lobbed a sphere of force. The dragon batted it aside.

"You may think your powers are strong enough to beat me, but I have faced your kind before. Many, many times." He laughed.

"There's never been anyone like me ever before. And there never will be again," she said. As if to prove her point, she ripped one of the trees out of the forest and launched it from Earth like a spear to puncture Boneclaw's wings.

The dragon roared in pain and fell from the sky, but as soon as he reached the darkness of the forest, he healed and resumed his pursuit.

Amy—never one to avoid using a trick that worked—ripped up tree after tree and hurled them one after the other at her enemy.

The dragon dodged repeatedly and avoided as many as he could.

"Child, you will never defeat me!" Boneclaw sneered before she caught him in the teeth with a tree.

He recovered and exhaled fire at her, which she blocked.

"You will tire, little girl, while I have all the time in the world."

She looked at the sun. It was already halfway below the horizon. He was right, and she knew she had to act now.

With that in mind, she continued to fling more trees.

Boneclaw laughed at this effort and dodged them as they rocketed toward him. He couldn't avoid all of them, though, as she was simply able to throw too many. She had grown up in the forests of Maine and knew how trees worked, how their roots dug in, and where their trunks bent and where they didn't. When she had first manifested her powers, this was how she had done it. She had taken an entire forest and used it to demolish two dragons.

Now, she did the same thing but with a hundred times more control.

The old dragon did an admirable job evading the projectiles. Less than one in twenty trees hit him. But when she threw over a hundred trees, it was enough to beat him senseless.

He plummeted earthward and landed with a thud that flurried pine needles and leaves high into the sky.

Amy raced closer to pick up every tree, rock, stone, or boulder she could and throw them all onto the place where he had crashed.

Unfortunately, her efforts were too late.

Boneclaw laughed from the darkness all around her. She looked at the sky to see that the sun had set.

"Oh, you poor little arrogant mage. Did you honestly think a couple of twigs would hurt me?" he asked from the darkness.

"You were beaten!"

"Your attack was very showy. Very impressive. Maybe instead of harvesting your skull, I'll simply break your mind and use your power."

"Fuck you!" the girl screamed. "I had you beat."

The old dragon laughed even more loudly. "Would you have stayed in the fight if you had been losing? No, I know you needed to be delayed, so I let you knock me around a little. You did well. Some of those strikes hurt—or they did until I healed them."

A claw materialized inches from her shield and delivered a blow that catapulted her away like a hamster inside a plastic bubble. Before she could roll to a stop, he was behind her. This time, he struck her with a whip of his tail so swift that it snapped audibly. She heard the sound seconds before she heard her sphere cracking another tree in half.

"You cannot beat me anymore. You understand this, yes?" Boneclaw teased. "Drop your little shield, kiss my claws, and perhaps I will let you live. Like I said, you are entertaining. I like to be entertained."

Amy picked up stones and branches and hurled them at the darkness. Boneclaw simply wicked away into nothingness. He didn't have to become corporeal anymore, not if he didn't want to. She threw more stones, more of the trees she had already hurled at him, and anything and everything she could.

Her efforts proved futile because nothing could reach him. She couldn't hit shadow.

She wiped the sweat from her face and saw that her nose was bleeding. It was a sure sign that she would run out of power. She had spent far too much on her reckless attacks and it was time to run.

The young mage crouched on her skateboard and rocketed above the trees. Boneclaw's laughter followed and easily kept pace with her, and she began to panic. She could outrace dragons. In the past, she had outraced Kristen many times and even Lumos—God rest his soul —used to complain about how fast she was on her skateboard.

Her enemy was faster and the problem was obvious. He didn't need wings to fly and simply moved through the shadows at the speed of the dark. No matter how fast she pushed herself, it wasn't enough.

In desperation, she picked up trees and boulders and flung them behind her, hoping to land a lucky blow on the dragon and failing repeatedly.

Amy could feel herself running out of magic. She couldn't keep attacking, especially since her strikes only hurt her by draining her energy.

In the next moment, it was time to play defense when Boneclaw materialized a claw and tried to pound her in the face with it.

Her shield caught the blow like it had before and she hurtled back. She was about to reverse direction but he anticipated this. He caught her ball of protection with a claw.

"Let me go!" she said and flung stones at the claw that held her bubble. The dragon laughed and dropped her but he caught her again after she fell much farther than a dragon's body should have been able to stretch.

"I did as you asked," he all but purred from outside her protected space. He turned his head briefly and his long sinuous neck became solid. Amy attacked but he simply laughed and became invisible again. The effort of throwing more rocks at him was taking its toll. She could feel a headache of unbelievable proportions growing. "Now, kiss my claws."

He squeezed the ball of force and she felt it like a vice-grip on her entire body. While he couldn't touch her, not inside her shields, the extra force he applied compelled her to counter, which drained every cell in her body.

Once again, she threw rocks at him, headache and nosebleed be damned. Some of the rocks struck her target this time, but not with enough force to do anything but annoy him.

He thrust the largest one away with a flick of his tail.

"You truly are a fascinating creature. Like an ant that can lift ten times its weight, your strength defies common logic."

"And your weakness is a flashlight so we're both weird," Amy said and flashed a light from her fists.

Boneclaw squinted but he wasn't otherwise injured. "Ah, to say light is my weakness is a failure of your ability to understand my power. It is more like darkness is my strength. I can teach you how I use it to empower me."

"I'd rather die."

"And yet you keep this little bubble around you, so you must wish to live for some reason. Is it because you wish to see what you can truly do with your raw power? I have never seen such an innate gift in your kind before. Not once in all my centuries. You lack finesse, of course, but if you had survived a few more decades, you might have become something truly special."

The old dragon squeezed her then as if he tried to wring all the water out of a sponge.

Amy screamed with the effort it took to keep her shield intact, but she did not yield. She would not.

"Even now, you refuse the release of death. Why?"

"Because I want to live to see you beaten senseless like you deserve."

That pissed the ancient dragon off. He took the ball she was in and hurled it toward the ground. She struck with enough force to make a crater in the earth, but she kept herself anchored in the center of the sphere and refused to let it break.

But Boneclaw was not yet done. He swooped at her, flying insanely fast—impossibly fast for a dragon—and whipped her ball with his tail to launch her skyward. At the peak of her ascent, he appeared from the darkness and smacked her upward again.

The young mage had thought she had traveled miles from the hill where Boneclaw had been recruiting the dwarves, but in two blows, he had knocked her back to where she started.

That was when she felt despair. He was simply so fast and so strong. It took everything she had to simply keep herself from being crushed. How could anyone stand against this monster? Was there even any point in fighting him?

"You are a persistent little insect, I'll give you that," he said, scooped her ball up, and peered inside at her bloody nose and sweat-streaked brow.

Amy suddenly understood why she had to fight. She had to stick it to this asshole, even if it cost her life. People had to stand up to tyrants and especially when the odds were against them and it seemed impossible.

Spurred on by her renewed determination, she made a tiny hole in her shield and hocked a ball of snot, sweat, and blood into Boneclaw's face.

He screeched with disgust. "You impudent little cretin!" he shouted and blasted her sphere with fire. Flames enveloped her and threatened to bake her inside her bubble, although she managed to stop the fire itself from touching her.

When the flames subsided, her enemy was there once more.

"I do not have the time to waste on you right now. I don't know if I would need another ten minutes or a few hours, but I know I could break you."

"You fucking wish."

"You fucking know," he growled.

Amy swallowed hard. He was right, of course. She had to fight the urge to fall unconscious, yet he seemed to have not even broken a sweat.

"But as I said, I do not have the time." With that, Boneclaw entered through the remains of the lodge and descended into the tunnels in the mountain. He moved quickly and with certainty until they reached the chamber where she had first seen him with the dwarves. It was empty now, devoid of people and full of nothing but the darkness.

He dropped her in the middle of the floor and vanished into shadow.

"If you think I'll drop my shield simply because I can't see you, you're dumber than you are ugly."

Boneclaw chuckled. "Ah, you humans do have a gift with your languages. Dumber than ugly. Very clever. But no, I am certain you won't drop that shield of yours. So instead, I'll drop the mountain on you."

"You can't."

"I don't boast," he said as if he had been insulted at a dinner party. "I promise."

With that daunting assurance, he vanished. It was hard for her to tell in the darkness—the only light came from her hands—but it looked as if rather than taking a tunnel, the shadow dragon had slipped into the cracks and crevices of the roof of the cave itself. It looked like water running up through fissures in the earth instead of down.

But that was impossible. To think that Boneclaw could move through cracks like that would mean he could do almost anything. The earth itself could be his refuge. Surely she had imagined it.

But if she had, then she also imagined the sound of cracking stone that rang out through the mountain. She realized that her eyes had told her the truth. He'd slipped away into those cracks, and she had no idea what he intended. As she tried to think how he might accomplish the promise he'd made, a powerful roar echoed in the cavern and the entire mountain collapsed upon her.

CHAPTER SEVENTY-NINE

Kristen did not know what the little creatures were that surrounded her, but she didn't like them.

In the darkness, she couldn't see much beyond a glimpse of a mouth filled with a hundred needle-like teeth here or an open eye—staring and vacant—over there. Sometimes, she saw flashes of tails that looked like something between eel and alligator. She couldn't begin to guess the numbers that darted around her but knew there were too damned many of them. They were either perfectly blended with the darkness or they could move through shadow like Boneclaw had.

She knew she was there to learn how to fight the dragon, but being surrounded by savage little versions of him was not how she expected her training to go. Maybe she had watched too many movie training montages.

The creatures seemed as curious about her as she was about them, although less fearful as they moved closer with each darted exploration. Finally, one of them—overcome with either curiosity or rage—came in close enough to touch her. She tried to dodge but it didn't move like a land creature. It was more like a fish and thus was not bound by the rules of gravity the way she was. It streaked past her leg and slashed her with a spine.

The wound stung like hell. She was used to scratches, but this was on another level. Her logic said that whatever it had barbed her with contained poison.

At least now she knew they were dangerous.

As if they had smelled the blood, the others moved in. They didn't behave like the will-o-wisps had and move together. Instead, these little bastards surged in one at a time, like they were wary of her. Unfortunately, they were still fast enough to inflict injury.

They sliced her arms and legs with their fins, tails, or teeth. In moments, her uniform—already singed by the will-o-wisps and muddy from the stream—was shredded. Slashes of red blood framed in white flesh appeared in the dark, which seemed to only further enrage or excite the shadow eels. Piranhas? Alligators? She wished she could see one of the little bastards so she could at least know how to kill one.

The only good thing about all these tiny slashes was that her dragon healing powers were able to mend the small wounds quickly. The creatures didn't seem particularly upset that their prey was heal-ing, however. They maintained their assault without pause, opened new wounds, and ripped her uniform to tatters.

Kristen punched and kicked at them, but she couldn't connect. She could feel her healing powers start to slow. There were simply too many of them and she would die from a thousand cuts.

She considered running back upstream toward the jungle and the glowing will-o-wisps. They seemed like they might be the natural enemy of these damn shadow eels. Maybe the reason she hadn't seen these creatures of shadow before was because they were enemies with the will-o-wisps.

But the instructions of the pixies had been clear. She had to move forward unless told to stop or forced to. To succeed, she needed to go downstream, which meant she had to get past these little monsters.

She didn't seem to be able to fight them, but fighting the will-o-wisps hadn't been particularly effective either. Maybe she could flee like she had before?

One of the eels stung her on the back of her neck and she decided it was worth a shot. She jumped from one boulder to the next, splashed into the muddy shallows of the river, and stumbled forward through the water.

Her movement seemed to excite the creatures. They intensified their slicing attacks but also increased the frequency of their stings and the potency of their venom. They attacked her legs with enthusiasm and seemed determined to tear apart the things that enabled her to move.

Perhaps that was the point of this test. Maybe sometimes, it was best to stay in her human form and at other times, it was better to face challenges in her dragon body.

Kristen chose the latter now and lost her human form in a shower of silver shards as she dissolved and reformed into her dragon body. She pumped her wings and took to the air, and the gusts from her passage sent the eels scattering and rolling. All she could see of them was their teeth and eyes twisting in search of her, but hey. They didn't exactly look comfortable, so she counted that as a victory.

She soared higher and kept her gaze on the faint glimmer of the muddy river below her. After coming so far, she didn't want to lose track of her path. Then she realized she might not have to worry. Up ahead, she saw a glowing point of light. It seemed to lie in the same direction in which the stream was flowing. Could that be her final destination? Was it the sun, ready to bring in the dawn of the next day? She didn't know, but she liked the look of it much more than what she'd left behind, so she pumped her wings and headed toward it.

Her faint glimmer of hope faded when she realized she wasn't alone. The shadow eels—maybe they were more like bats—surrounded her. They seemed as comfortable up there as they had been below, never a good sign. They closed around her like a school of fish around the bloated corpse of a whale. It didn't matter that she flew as fast as Lumos had taught her. They kept pace effortlessly as if she was still stumbling through the muddy water below.

Kristen was now heartily sick of this place.

The shadow bats swarmed as she flew and she realized how profound a mistake taking to the air had been. Below, she hadn't known how many of the creatures there were, but she had estimated their number at something less than a hundred. In other words, she could conceivably count them.

In the sky, they were able to approach her from all sides and there were far more than a hundred. Before, they had surrounded her human frame but she had been able to keep most of them away although a few slipped through. Up there, despite being in her dragon form, they attacked more often. The swarm was as dense as it had before, except she was much larger. Up there, she seemed to be in their domain.

She pushed on toward the light on the horizon, wishing and praying that it would grow bigger despite it steadfastly refusing to do so. The shadow bats pushed closer and closer, nipping and slashing at her belly, flank, her hard scales, and anywhere they could reach. When their spines didn't penetrate, they didn't get dismayed and wander off like a monkey unable to crack a nut. They merely repeated their onslaught as if certain that their persistence would pay off. When some seemed to grow bored and swoop away, more of the creatures took their places.

Soon—as if they had some kind of hive intelligence and attacked as a single entity rather than individuals—they moved on from the hardest, best-protected areas of her body. No longer did she feel them slash at her steel horns or brush against her claws or her tail. Slowly, as the message spread, they focused on the soft areas, the places behind her knees, her neck, and the gaps between her talons.

Kristen began to panic. She couldn't see her attackers at all. Eyes and teeth flickered in front of her, but she could not see the thousand sources of pain that attempted to kill her. This was exactly like when she had fought the Masked One in the depths beneath the Mammoth

Cave. Her opponent was too fast and too nimble. She had tried to retaliate, but he'd seen her coming. If she couldn't defend herself against these little bats, how could she defeat a beast a thousand times their size and a thousand times more intelligent?

The Masked One would move as these monsters did. He would flap his dark wings like a bat and slither his long tail like an eel, and she would fail in her fight against him. She would be torn to pieces and would fall.

But no, she could not fail.

She didn't believe that, not now and maybe not ever, but she told herself it was true.

There was something she hadn't tried, she realized. She inhaled a breath of air—and almost choked as she sucked one of the shadow beasts in—and exhaled a great breath of fire in front of her and down her belly.

The blast must have caught a hundred of them. In the light of her flames, she could see that they were neither bat nor eel but some kind of ghastly demonic tadpole with wings. They had two stump legs with ragged claws that poked from webbed feet—the fins she had thought belonged to the eels. Their front arms were folded above them in a horribly unnatural configuration that allowed them to work as wings.

Instead of the soft leathery membrane of bats or the feathered sheen of a bird, these wings had the gelatinous membrane of an amphibian. From behind these sprouted a long and sinuous tail that was ridged like a salamander. Their face was wide and broad like a toad's, but with far too many teeth that were far too sharp.

They burned and crisped in her blast of flame, but this did not calm her as she had hoped. Even though she had incinerated a hundred of their number, that didn't account for even a tenth of them, nor a twentieth. The demonic frogs seemed to number in the tens of thousands. Her flame reflected off their eyes like stars. It reflected off their teeth and seemed to fill the sky with needles. They swarmed and moved together like starlings or a school of piranha.

Kristen inhaled and readied herself for another blast of fire but they struck her before she could. A hundred pounded into her face in the first second and a hundred more in the tenth of a second after that. She was pushed back by the sheer mass of the creatures from hell.

She had inhaled for a breath of fire so she exhaled now, but there were too many of the creatures and their hive intelligence was too efficient. Perhaps twenty of them were caught in the blast of flames and fell from their swarm like lifeless slime. Her attackers pushed on her top and bottom jaw, however, so rather than her fire blasting from the end of her mouth as an inferno, it squirted and sputtered between her teeth. More of the creatures burned—there were now so many that anything she did managed to knock a couple from the air—but it wasn't enough. It would never be enough.

As if to confirm that thought, they found her wings.

The creatures sliced and tore at the delicate membranes while she struggled to right herself. It was as if they were jealous that her wings were smooth and chrome while theirs were slimy and mottled. They savaged them with abandon and as Kristen flapped, trying to regain forward momentum, she tore her wings to shreds. Soon all that was left was the bone and muscle frame, as useful in flight as a chicken wing was once it was battered, deep-fried, and served with bleu cheese.

The inevitable result was unavoidable, and she twisted her body so she now pointed to the ground. She knew she would crash, but she could at least direct how she did it. Most importantly, she could not hit her head. She had no doubt that if she was knocked unconscious for a second, the frogs would pack so close onto her body that she would never rise again.

Instead of maintaining her direct plunge toward the earth, she twisted and aimed at one of the largest mud puddles that made up the river below.

Seconds later, she splashed into the pool of water. It was deeper than she had expected but not deep enough that her dragon body failed to pound into the cloying mud at the bottom of the pool. Still, the water probably saved her life and she wasn't knocked out, only rendered senseless for a moment.

She thrashed her tail in pain as the monsters of the night continued to savage her wings. Desperate to escape them, she rolled over, slid the stumps of her wings into the muddy pool, and felt blessed relief, although the monsters now diverted their attack to her belly.

Despite the little demons looking like frogs, they didn't go underwater. She could use that. Hell, she had to use that. She hadn't been able to do shit against them.

The pool was not deep enough to submerge her entire dragon body, so she yet again shirked the form so many in the world saw as the most powerful in existence and became a regular human with regular flesh.

As she stumbled through the muddy pool, the creatures attacked her shoulders and the back of her neck. Some of the fuckers even ripped out locks of her curly red hair.

A moment later, she was in water up to her neck. She dove under the surface, her eyes open wide despite the mud and filth her crash landing had kicked up.

Kristen suddenly recalled the last time she'd had to hide underwater to protect herself against a vastly more powerful killer.

The Masked One had done this to her. Beneath Mammoth cave, in paths that no tourist would ever walk and places so deep that the sightless creatures who called the place home would never know the kiss of the sun or the taste of fresh air, he had forced her to hide underwater. Now, exactly like then, she held her breath while the surface of the water calmed. Her enemy, on the surface side of this fragile defense, waited for her to emerge for air.

Inevitably, she had to take a breath. She stuck her face out of the water and sucked in air while the stinging claws of the monsters sliced at her. One of them cut her nose particularly deeply, and as she plunged under the water, she could feel the murky liquid sting in the wound that was too large to heal quickly.

Had the Masked One been there? Was that how he knew how to fight like this? Did he somehow trick the pixies into letting him go on this very same walk? Had he survived the will-o-wisps only to make allies of these horrible monsters?

Kristen wished she had some of the will-o-wisps now. Light was the only thing that could nullify the Masked One's powers. If the will-o-wisps were there, she might have their help to drive these beasts of shadow back.

Her time was up. She had to breathe. When she had been pinned beneath the surface of that subterranean lake where she had fought the Masked One, she had been able to clear a path by using a blast of fire to illuminate the space. Could she do that now even though she wasn't in her dragon form? Was that what was being asked of her?

Rather than dwell on the questions, she tried to focus on making fire, but the primary part of the process was taking a breath. And every time she tried to do that, the fucking frogs lacerated her face.

She burst to the surface, sucked in air and failed to produce a flame, and suffered the consequences when one of the frogs managed to dig a talon into her eyeball.

The pain was excruciating as if it had injected venom not only into her eye but into the nerves that connected it to her brain. Her mind seemed to burn as the poison coursed through her. She sucked in a lungful of water, to which her body rebelled and instinctively surfaced so it would continue to live despite the mistakes of its master.

The creatures' attack was immediate. They slashed at her head and neck and stung her arms and hands when they broke the surface of the water. She thrashed with dragon speed and managed to strike one of them before it stung her.

It splattered like a frog beneath the tire of a loaded dump truck.

Kristen, half-blind, out of breath, and unable to swim any longer, moved toward shallower water. As she did so, the creatures extended their attacks lower down her body. They targeted her shoulders now, her upper back, her chest, the small of her back, and her abdomen. Those that struck her had to turn solid to do so, and she met them with strikes powered only by her fury and the muscle memory from long training days with Lumos.

It wasn't exactly a weakness, but they were like Boneclaw in that regard. To do physical harm, they had to become physical. She managed to take a deep breath—her body thanked her for this—and focused on some of the techniques Lumos had shown her. She knew she could not attack these little bastards. They were too fast and too numerous, but perhaps she could defend herself.

She started to move through a series of martial arts maneuvers that the old dragon had explained were based on the movements of a dragon. Her legs splashed through the muddy water as she kicked, stepped forward, punched, punched again, jumped back, and kicked again. Her movements were fast enough to keep the surging monsters around her at bay as they tried to find the best place to nip her and continue their meal.

"Come on, you floating lanterns! A little help here!" Kristen shouted desperately.

There was no increased glow on the horizon and no twinkling light. Instead, the cloud of shadow beings around her began to press closer. They were learning the routine she was moving through and in moments, they would begin to probe her for weaknesses again. What had taken the Masked One many hours of her being trapped in a cave to learn, these creatures would learn in moments. Exactly like him, they would study her, dissect her, and defeat her.

Why won't the will-o-wisps help? Kristen thought desperately. She was not a leader above asking for help and thought that working together was the only way forward in almost all aspects of life. The frustrating thing was she could still feel the will-o-wisps. She could sense the way their magic shifted from a calming cool light to a sharp jolt and how they were able to multiply and grow.

But that didn't make any sense.

There were none of them around.

Kristen realized that what she sensed wasn't the will-o-wisps but rather the memory of the feel and flavor of their magic. Did she sense them at all, or did she simply sense the same energy flowing through her body?

She thought back to Amythist's cottage as she moved even faster through her routine. Almost instinctively, she alternated moves and added extra punches or jumps when she could, anything to stop the stinging attacks of these monsters of the dark for a moment longer. The old dragon had first shown her a ball of light. Was there a reason for that? She had tried to make fire in her human form, but maybe there was a reason one had to become a dragon to make fire. There were mages who could use fire—Havington had worked with a dragon to make a fire tornado, after all—but they were rare. Meanwhile, it seemed like almost every mage could make light.

Could she manage to shift her inner dragon magic to something other than steel and speed and strength? Was it possible for her to shift it into the same radiant energy the will-o-wisps had produced?

As she moved through her martial arts maneuvers, she tried. She focused on how she normally made her body turn to steel. During her training, she had practiced keeping her body wrapped in normal skin until right before the impact of a blow. At that point, she would change her knuckles or the tip of her foot to steel and thus increase the devastation of the strike.

It seemed logical to try that now. She attacked, turned to steel, and hoped to splatter the frog demons to gore their allies either ignored or lapped up. As she moved, she tried to center herself on the radiant energy of the will-o-wisps. She attempted to let that same energy flow out from her heart to fill her chest, and from her chest down her veins and nerves to blossom at the points of skin to which she directed it.

All the while, the swarm of monsters attempting to consume her became better at their task. When she threw a punch, they attacked her ribs beneath the striking arm. When she tried a kick, they were ready to attack her thighs with their teeth.

But Kristen had known pain before so she focused on the sensation of light. She breathed and moved while she maintained her focus and then, in the palm of her hand, light flickered.

She smiled and uttered a whoop of joy when she saw it, even

though it only illuminated the hundreds of creatures directly in front of her and failed to drive them back.

Her reaction broke her rhythm, though, and the creatures—already intensely keyed into the rhythm of her movements—coalesced into a massive blob of aggression that pounded into her chest and knocked the air from her lungs. She splashed into the muddy water and sank into the filth at the bottom of the pool, unable to breathe.

CHAPTER EIGHTY

Kristen thrashed in the water. Her lungs screamed at her to take a breath and also to not take another fucking breath of water for the love of God, what was wrong with her?

She both ignored her lungs and heeded their demands, pushed up from the water—it wasn't deep there—and took a breath. The shadow creatures were more than ready. They attacked from all sides and bit every patch of skin she exposed. At this point in the fight, that was essentially all of her skin.

Even though she was now above the water, she could hardly breathe. The slashes and stings were relentless, and her body felt like it was filling with fire. Not in the dragon about to incinerate an enemy way but the "holy crap I'm going to die from a fucking jellyfish" way.

Panicked, she tried to focus on the radiant, glowing energy of warmth and light she had so briefly created in her palm. It was incredibly hard with the relentless onslaught of these thousands of creatures that refused to stop or even pause for a heartbeat. She would die there. Having come all this way, she would die. It was truly a miracle that she wasn't dead already. The pain was so intense that she thought she should have had a heart attack—or even better, a brain aneurysm. At least that would kill her quickly and with less pain. She hoped anyway.

But she wasn't dead, not yet. She was still alive and still fighting against overwhelming odds. Was she alive because part of her still knew she had a chance to survive? She had made a glimmer of light happen and could do it again—had to do it again.

The thought helped her to cease her efforts to retaliate or brush away the attacks of the flying fucking monsters. She focused on her breath and the sensation of glowing light that had come from the will-o-wisps. The fucking flying frogs didn't increase the viciousness of their onslaught because they couldn't. They were already attacking at maximum intensity.

Kristen steadfastly ignored their razor cuts. None of the creatures tried to pierce her organs or tear her head from her neck. They were creatures of venom and poison and hadn't changed tactics yet.

As her breathing settled into a slow rhythm, she tried to find her center—her source of magic. She reached deep inside and located the fount of energy she called on when she needed to become steel or a dragon. In rhythmic succession, she let her body change to steel with her breath and back again. Being made of metal did nothing to slow the strikes or lessen the pain from these creatures so she let the changes come and go with her breath to repeat a process with which she was familiar.

When she felt grounded and confident in what she knew, she thought of the will-o-wisps' energy. She tried to bring the sense of calm and wonder they had inspired when she had first seen them into her heart. Then, she tried to channel that energy into the jolting power they had used to prod her down the river.

At first, nothing happened. The shadow creatures, emboldened by no longer being knocked aside, did increase their attacks. Instead of merely slashing and stinging, one of them latched onto her shoulder and sank its teeth in while it shook its head to drive hundreds of needle-sharp teeth deep into her flesh.

Kristen focused all her energy on her palms as she ripped the being from her shoulder. A flicker of light from her palms was enough to burn her handprint on the frog's rubbery, mottled skin and it released her, hissing and screaming.

But its allies seemed to sense that their prey was attempting to be something other than their next meal. More of them began to bite her. They moved their teeth to saw at her flesh, trying to consume her body while she struggled only partially to fend them off.

Still, she continued trying to ignite the light she knew she needed to survive this.

Her palms flickered and glowed with the dim light of a reading lamp. It wasn't much but was nevertheless bright enough to force the creatures that had buried their teeth in her to let go.

As soon as they did, relief flooded her ragged wounds and her glowing hands flickered and faded to nothing. In the ensuing darkness, a thousand shadow creatures brushed past her. They moved with increasing speed as if whatever controlled the swarm took a great big breath in preparation to blow out the candle's worth of light she had managed to produce.

Reflexively, her magic tried to heal her wounds. She could feel it working through her body, struggling to make sense of the mess of meat and skin the creatures had left in their wake. The healing magic soothed her, both as a relief from her pain and by the energy it had. It possessed a particular essence like her steel skin or dragon magic did. But unlike her dragon magic, this was a form that wanted to go to only one place. Her steel skin was like that too. Yes, she could make only a hand or a fingertip turn to metal, but the easiest application of her ability to steel was to go full steel. It had taken practice to control a hand or a fingertip.

Had she looked at the light magic the wrong way? She had thought the simplest thing to do would be to make the palm of her hand glow. But why had she made that assumption? Turning her entire body to steel was no more difficult than turning a single hand to steel. In fact, it was easier as it took far less concentration and she hadn't needed to master turning her entire body to metal. She had simply done it.

Could she do that now with light?

Kristen took a deep breath as she felt the mass of shadow monsters surge to pound into her and finally end their duel. Instead of trying to make only her palms glow, she tried to make whatever damn part of her that wanted to glow have as much energy as it wanted.

Seconds before the creatures collided and knocked her into the mud for the final time, her chest ignited with light.

More specifically, her heart, but it glowed with such brilliance that her ribcage was dark as her heart shone through her skin and flesh and beat with a strength that had never left her.

The creatures that made impact with her chest screeched and shrieked in pain. Those that touched her burst into sparks and disintegrated into nothing but ash.

She took a breath and tried to send the energy outward. It listened and her veins filled with light. Her arms and legs glowed as light flowed from her heart, down her limbs, through the veins in the back of her hands, and out her fingertips. She screamed when the power of it forced her to open her mouth and a great pillar of light—larger and brighter and more powerful than a spotlight for any show in all of Detroit's musical history—burst from her throat and blazed into the night sky.

The creatures that were caught in this blast of blinding energy burst into ash like the others that had touched her. Those closest to her were the first to go, but the process was far from instantaneous. As more creatures erupted higher up in the column, others saw this and fled into the darkness.

Those that had come close to hurling her into the water now slashed at each other and tried to fight their way through their brethren to safety.

In a moment, the entire swarm was gone. Kristen was left standing on a dark, barren plain surrounded by darkness. She closed her mouth and the pillar above her ceased to exist, but her body still glowed brightly, a beacon of brilliant white light.

But that was okay, she told herself. Those monsters had made her stop but now, she had worked past them. Every limb hurt but somehow, she made herself take a step forward, then another. She continued to follow the river toward the light she had seen in the sky when she had become a dragon and taken to the air.

She continued to glow, which surprised her a little, and because of the light, the barren and desolate place didn't seem so bad.

CHAPTER EIGHTY-ONE

Amy came to slowly as if clawing from a particularly long and dark dream, one in which time seemed to be worth more in the dream world, and rather than having one night of nightmares, it felt like an eternity.

She had fought and she had lost. Then she had tried to escape but she had failed. A friend had died—no, not quite a friend but an ally. In some ways, that was worse.

Disoriented, she blinked and tried to focus on her surroundings but saw nothing. She was awake and could feel her head pounding and dried blood from her nose all over her mouth, but she couldn't see anything. When she sat, she thunked her head on something hard —a rock. It was a rock, she realized, because she was buried beneath a mountain.

How did she get there? She tried to turn to look for a path and only succeeded in whacking her head against another boulder. This time, in addition to the sharp crack of rock on bone, the roar of a thousand stones trying to shift a little deeper and settle more fully was the result. Her movement had alerted the mountain that there was a place to fill. The fleshy little lump and the air she breathed was not even an inconvenience to something like a mountain trying to settle into the bedrock. It would crush her whether she wanted it to or not.

Except the mountain hadn't counted on her being a mage of vast power.

Her first step was to extend a bubble around herself, strengthen it, and reinforce it while the mountain pressed down on her. She was tired and her head hurt, and the effort made her nose start to bleed more despite the already copious amount of dried blood crusted to her face. Still, her bubble held.

"You were always more of a hill, anyway," she muttered to the inanimate stone.

As if in response to this tiny little human foolish enough to goad it, the mountain shifted again but she felt a decrease in pressure, not an increase. Her bubble of magic still held up more than enough stone to crush her if she so much as sneezed, but at least the pressure wasn't such that holding it back would cause a blood vessel in her brain to burst like an overcooked sausage.

It did not fail to cross her mind, however, that she was trapped in more ways than one. On one hand, the mountain of stone above had her thoroughly trapped there. On the other, her mental space was restricted too and she couldn't let her shield's strength slacken at all. She couldn't test other magic without risking the entire mountain shifting and crushing her with less effort than it took a human to crunch a bug.

It wasn't the most relaxing place, she conceded irritably.

She tried to make a gate but simply didn't have the energy. Even if she could drop her shield for the minute it would take to open one, she didn't think she'd be able to manage it. The prospect of opening a gate while holding the mountain back was a futile train of thought.

To make it all worse, Amy already felt short of breath. She didn't know how long she'd been unconscious. It was short enough for the mountain to pause before it finished settling—geologically speaking that could be decades, though, so not the best indicator—but certainly long enough to put a sizable dent in the available oxygen.

That settled it. She couldn't stay there. There simply wasn't air available for that to be any kind of decision. But what to do? She couldn't use any magic except her shield, not if she wanted to be sure to keep herself alive.

After a moment's thought, she decided she had to use the shield.

The young mage felt the ceiling above her. Her shield magic made this possible because it didn't have any real substance. It was thinner than paper, a slender veil of energy and nothing more, so she could easily feel the contours of the ceiling inches above her face even if she could not see it.

She felt around with her hand until she found an area of soil. Carefully and with painfully, tediously, and obnoxiously slow effort, she formed part of her shield into a wedge shape. It pushed into the dirt, then split and expanded so some of the soil fell from the ceiling and into the cavity where she was trapped. She was quite used to stopping bullets while letting air penetrate her shield, so holding the mountain but allowing a little dirt wasn't exactly difficult, although it required more of a deft touch than she had hoped.

Still, she kept at it. She kept pushing up—not straight up but at what she reasoned was something like a forty-five-degree angle. She had no doubt that Boneclaw had left her in the dead center of the mountain to ensure that he killed her. If she took a slanting path, it would probably mean she should be able to climb through the tunnel and it would be a shorter distance.

Amy tried to repeat these two ideas to herself as she pushed her magic farther through the dirt. Before too long, she struck a boulder. Her head was already starting to ache from lack of air and from having to maintain her shield while she inched up the tunnel, but discovering the boulder almost broke her.

Still, it was only a rock. She had lifted rocks, broken rocks, and turned boulders into gravel. This was nothing to her, least of all an impediment. Not to her.

She took a deep breath, focused as much of her energy as she could into a tiny pinprick of her shield, and thrust it forward to drive it through the stone and shear it in half. Quickly, she twisted the shield magic, spun it, and gave it teeth as it bored a hole through the boulder.

As she turned and twisted her magic and wielded her magic like a drill, gravel and dust fell onto her. She tried to push herself against one side of the tunnel she had carved so it would fall past her. When she sneezed once from the gravel, it seemed to almost completely deplete what oxygen was left in the cavity in the stone as she wasn't able to catch her breath properly after that.

Still, she soldiered on and climbed up through the boulder by jamming her hands and knees against the opposite side of the tunnel to her back. She moved in fits and starts and each tiny motion robbed her body of more energy and deprived the space of more oxygen.

Finally, she made it through the boulder and faced nothing but more dirt.

Amy fought the overwhelming sense that she wouldn't be able to do this. She would run out of air and would die down there. Worst of all, she didn't even know what day it was. For all she knew, Kristen might have already battled Boneclaw and lost and this was all in vain.

But no—no it couldn't be. She was hungry but not famished so couldn't have been down there for more than a few hours. Not that it made much difference. Hungry or not, she would still die.

She rested her head against the stone—rest being a kind word for someone who couldn't relax their body for fear of sliding down a tunnel into a grave deep beneath a mountain or relax their mind for fear of a mountain crushing them—but she tried anyway.

As soon as she put her head against the stone, she jerked it up again.

As impossible as it seemed, she had heard something in the stone.

Her senses alert, she placed her head against the rock and heard the sound again. It seemed to be tapping of some kind, regular at first, then a pause followed by taps with longer gaps between them. Another pause ensued before it seemed to start again.

Was there a pattern to it?

Amy tried to hear precisely where it came from, but she couldn't tell. She could only hear it coming through the rock, which didn't mean much. Sound could travel a long way through solid substances, but she didn't know how to use that information to ascertain which way to go.

But did she want to follow the sound?

What if the tapping was Boneclaw's dwarves digging for her? Maybe they had thought she was dead until they heard her labored effort to escape through the stones. Perhaps they were digging a tunnel to finish the job. If she remained quiet, maybe they would think she was dead and leave.

But if she tried to wait them out, she would die of asphyxiation. Waiting them out was simply not an option. Although neither was fighting them, not in her condition. Plus, would Boneclaw make the dwarves spend the time needed to dig her out only to kill her?

He had a duel in less than two days. The dwarves were part of his plan but she was not. And, she remembered bitterly, he had defeated Katrina with consummate ease and no doubt believed he could kill Kristen as easily. He wouldn't miss this duel, not for anything. It would be his victory lap, his proof that only he could carry dragons forward with the respect for customs they all seemed so obsessed with honoring.

Amy decided to trust that whoever made these tapping sounds was either oblivious to what had happened or attempted to mount some kind of rescue.

She waited for it to resume and this time, when she heard it, she repeated the pattern in response by hitting the boulder she was now inside with a hand-sized rock.

Immediately, the tapping stopped.

While she couldn't be sure, she thought she heard muffled shouts before the tapping repeated. It was the same pattern but faster now. It repeated twice, then paused. She tapped a reply.

This time, instead of another attempt to communicate, she heard what sounded like power tools.

The young mage was about to begin using her shield to dig in that direction when the earth around her shifted. It had tolerated her burrowing a little mole hole through its stone and dirt, but a team of people using power tools was too much. The lack of oxygen worsened and it took everything she had simply to hold onto consciousness.

Desperately, she tried to keep her breathing shallow and even and her shield firm as the sound of a drill grew louder.

But they were too late. She had already subsisted on too little oxygen for too long. As the sound of drill drew closer, her vision started to fade around the edges. Even in the darkness, the vertigo and sense of loss of control that came with tunnel vision were still present. She tried to stay conscious but she couldn't. Not even when she saw the head of a drill break into the tunnel ahead of her and felt the moist, cool oxygen-rich air of a properly ventilated tunnel spill over her.

<hr>

When Amy came to, she lay in a bed with rough white sheets on a mattress that felt like it had been stuffed with the world's prickliest straw. The ceiling was low and what little light there was came from a small candle. Even its gentle glow was enough to hurt her eyes after so much time in the dark.

She didn't know how much time had passed, only that her hunger had gone from mildly demanding to fully pissed off.

"Oh, you're up," a low voice said.

When she turned to see her savior, she froze as her gaze settled on a dwarf. Instinctively, she screamed. She had been wrong—Boneclaw's dwarves had come back for her. They had rescued her only to turn her into a magical slave, a servant for his entertainment.

The dwarf screamed in return, his voice rich with terror.

"Why are you screaming?" she shouted.

He simply replied, "Ahhhhh!" and ran out of the room.

Utterly bewildered, she tried to push up in bed and earned herself a legendary headache.

With a grimace, she fought to focus and looked around the spartan room carved into the earth itself. She had barely time to take in her surroundings—the uncomfortable bed, an equally uncomfortable looking overstuffed chair that seemed as if it had been stuffed with gravel, a table that was only a boulder with a flat surface cut and polished onto its top—when someone entered.

"Ah, you're up then," the dwarf said. He or she—Amy didn't know how dwarf gender worked—had a kind and gentle voice.

The young mage forced herself to shove aside her rising panic and instead, to study the newcomer carefully. She knew that not all dwarves were bad. In fact, in her experience, most were quite helpful. This one appeared to be one of those. His beard was braided, and brightly colored beads and cut gems sparkled from where they had been tied into it. He wore a knit hat on his head that had more color than any feature of the room they were currently in. His smile was mostly normal with only a single gold tooth to add a charming imperfection to it. Without a doubt, it was much nicer to look at than the jagged stone teeth of the last dwarves she had seen.

"Where am I?" she asked.

"Oh, sure, sure. A fair question, a fair question." He chuckled. "You're in the town of Ruby. Well, the mines under it, more accurately. I'm Trop. A pleasure."

Trop extended a callused, dirty hand and she shook it gratefully.

"Trop, a pleasure. I'm Amy. Can you tell me how I got here?"

"Of course I can. We saw the massive rockslide destroy that house and thought there might be survivors in there. Although we didn't see any, when we heard your tapping, we came down to find you. I don't know how you managed to get so far beneath the hill! You were almost as deep as some of our old abandoned mines."

"Abandoned? But I saw a group of dwarves in there."

His face darkened. "They're abandoned all the same. A group of murdering, clanless dwarves is the exact reason why ye sometimes have to abandon a mine. It's a crying shame, a crying shame. The truth is, we thought it might have been one of them we heard tapping away, so it was a surprise when we found a girl of yer...uh, that is we noticed that you, uh…"

"You know I'm a mage?" Amy asked and felt like she could implicitly trust this Trop.

"You were practically unconscious and you still threw rocks into the chests of two of our miners. Regular folk don't exactly show their thanks in that way. You…uh, you don't happen to be friends with any of them dwarves, do you? The ones you saw?"

"God no. They were all working for a dragon who has tried to start a world war."

"Boneclaw, eh?" he asked.

"You've heard of him?" She was aghast.

"The whole damn world has, at this point. It's all supposed to be hush-hush, mind you, as hush-hush as anything, but the thing about secrets is that they're more fun to spread than what's widely known and put on the calendar. That Boneclaw will fight the Steel Dragon at noon tomorrow. Or he *was.* And I had hoped she would beat him good."

"Well, we have to help!" Amy said, tried to get out of bed, and crumpled to the floor instead. Her legs screamed in pain. She looked at them to see they were both wrapped in casts. "What have you done to me?"

"Saved your damn legs, you fool girl! We got you out of there as fast as we could but not fast enough. Both your legs are broken. I set them myself, so they'll heal fine—or they would have before you went and put some weight on them like a damn fool."

"But…but Kristen…I have to help."

"There's another rumor that's been going around too, child. You might not like to hear this one, though."

"What is it?" she asked.

"The Steel Dragon is dead. A dragon named Bloodblaze claims to have killed her."

"That's a filthy lie!" Her thoughts raced. Was that the story Boneclaw had spread? Did he still think he'd killed Kristen instead of Katrina?

"I'd like to think so, I honestly would, but no one has seen the Steel Dragon. If she is alive out there somewhere, she's taking her sweet time putting the lie to those rumors."

"I have to—"

"What you need to do is rest. We have a stone soup cooking for you that'll heal those legs nicely, but that's only if you didn't mess up the job I had done on them. Rest now, girl. We'll wake you when it's time."

Amy didn't want to rest, not at all, but when Trop helped her back into bed and checked her legs, clucking in approval, she decided the straw was much less pokey and the sheet was far more comfortable.

CHAPTER EIGHTY-TWO

Kristen had been walking down the stream for what felt like ages. Or, more appropriately, an age—the age of her defeat. She knew that was what it would be after being there for so long. It felt as if she had walked for days and probably weeks. She had no way of knowing how long she'd been there, but it must have been too long already. Her duel with Boneclaw had to have come and gone. She would probably emerge—that is if she ever found an escape from this place—into a world that had been ruled by Boneclaw for years. It was not a pleasant thought.

Still, she pushed on. The glowing light ahead of her hadn't grown bigger for a long time now. Nothing had stopped her from advancing, either.

Not that the hideous frog monsters hadn't tried. A group of them made another attempt even now. They flew in a kind of formation and swooped through the darkness.

She held her glowing palms up and dispatched them with a few deft movements. Those she struck burst to ash and any she missed flew away to regroup and try another strategy. There was no more joy or challenge in fighting them, only exhaustion. At least she had mastered how to more carefully control the light power. In truth, she'd had so much practice it had become almost effortless. She thought her improved skill might have caused the landscape to change so it could teach her a new skill, but that proved to be wishful thinking.

She never tired or, more accurately, never grew sleepy. Sleep and food seemed to be two things her body simply did not need there. When she hungered or felt as if she could not take another step, she drank from the muddy water and was given enough strength to continue for another fifty or five hundred or five thousand paces.

But while she didn't crave sleep, she did crave rest. She was beyond exhausted, utterly wiped out in a way she had not thought possible. It wasn't only that her body ached—and oh, did it ache—it was that she was never able to sleep and rest her mind or stop moving to rest her feet. She had blisters that bled, scabbed, and became calluses, all while she was conscious of them going through the process. Her muscle cramps lasted for what felt like days—not literal days, obviously, as the sun had yet to rise in this confounded place. But it sure felt like it had been that long.

Kristen told herself she had to keep going. The pixies had said to not stop unless she was asked to or forced to. Her exhaustion did neither, so on she went. It was a shame that they had also said to hurry, as she felt like that probably meant she was supposed to do this in less than the months she felt it had taken. Unfortunately, one could never please all the people all the time. Even if they were pixies—especially if they were pixies.

After all that had happened, she wasn't sure if she liked them anymore. Had they taught Boneclaw to become the Masked One? If they hadn't, how else could one explain the striking similarities between him and the needle-teethed creatures? Perhaps the world didn't need explanations. Maybe it was merely a big, long, unending and always unfolding puzzle with no real beginning and no real end.

Then again, maybe it had no point and the only thing that ever mattered to anyone was what someone did with it. She had hoped to make her little corner of the world a better place but instead, was now stuck on this damn mythological pixie journey treadmill. Meanwhile,

Boneclaw had sought only to expand his power and must have been successful already.

It was almost enough to make a girl want to stop.

She paused and looked up, her attention drawn by an odd change. The glowing light on the horizon was no longer in the distance but much closer to her.

Sure it was her imagination, she rubbed the grime and exhaustion from her eyes. When she looked again, the light remained where she'd seen it about fifty feet in front of her. It was on the other side of a wide body of water that looked deep enough to let all the mud and scum settle to the bottom. This was the first blue water she had seen in what felt like forever. It was the first color of any kind she had seen in what felt like forever.

Kristen frowned as the glowing light separated into more motes. Great, another test, she thought with a sigh. What was annoying was that these tests didn't kill her. They merely tortured her endlessly for no apparent reason.

Still, she would fight. What other choice did she have?

"Congratulations!" one of the motes of light hollered as it flew past her head.

It wasn't light at all but a pixie with the wings of a moth and the androgynous features common to most of its species.

Exhausted, delirious, and as dirty as hell, she stumbled down the stream and jumped over a small waterfall to splash into the huge pool of water.

As she swam across—staying above the surface was more of a challenge than it should have been—pixies buzzed around her head to congratulate her, shower her in sparks, and blow her kisses. All of them laughed and the sound of tinkling bells echoed off the barren stone around them.

Except it wasn't barren. Kristen had failed to notice when she had entered the pool that it rested deep inside a giant basin. The walls were high and made of nothing but stone, but trees and vines grew atop them. Rich greens and sprays of pink and blue flowers here and there warmed her heart in a way such blossoms never had before.

She swam slowly and as she moved, her aches and pains began to melt away. It was if the current of the pool drew all the dirt and weight of the world to the bottom so she could simply float across its top.

"You did it, Lady Steel. You did it!" Lady Dragonfly bobbed and wove in front of her, guiding her across the pool until her feet found stone under the water. Kristen stepped onto it and walked into shallower water. She marveled that yet again, she was in a pool of water contained by stone that was fed by a waterfall. Had the pixies built this entire brutal landscape?

"We all wish to congratulate you on your success." Lady Dragonfly beamed.

"Success?" she asked as she dropped to her knees and let the water lap against her. "How can you call that *success?* I almost died and…I didn't even face it bravely. I couldn't stop thinking about fighting Boneclaw in that cave. Those monsters…what were they?"

"They were your fears incarnate," the pixies explained. "And you survived! That is what you had to do—survive. And you did." Lady Dragonfly led the creatures around Kristen's head in a merry show of colorful sparks.

"I barely survived, though. If the fight with Boneclaw is like that—"

"Oh, it will be. It will be. He has always been very strong, even when he—" A dozen pixies buzzed in the face of the one that had started to speak.

"You won, Lady Steel. You did it," Lady Dragonfly said. "You learned to direct the magic within you during the first trial, and you learned to direct it to what you think you will need to fight Boneclaw in the second."

"I…I guess I did… But I took too long, didn't I? It feels like it's been weeks."

The diminutive creature shook her head smugly. "You still have more than enough time. Well, not as much as you'd like, I'm sure, since you had three days to begin with. But you will still be able to return home and rest."

"How is that possible?"

"You followed our instructions. You did not stop except when confronted or asked to. That means the time felt like what you thought it should be but only passed as needed in your home realm."

"I honestly don't see how I could do it. I'm so tired. How am I supposed to face Boneclaw at all? Can I still use those powers?"

"You're using them right now." Lady Dragonfly smiled.

Kristen looked down and saw that her hands were glowing with an inner light. She snorted a laugh. To think she had spent so much time learning to turn this ability on and off and now, she had made her hands glow without even meaning to.

"Does this mean I'll be able to use these powers in my home dimension too?" she asked.

"Oh yes," the pixie said. "Your dimension is not a place devoid of magic. Your Earth is huge and vast, filled with many wonderful creatures that power this energy in all of us. It may not feel like it, but there is more magic there than there is here."

"But why did I have to face those…those things?"

"We apologize for the brutal nature of the trial," Lady Dragonfly looked genuinely ashamed. "If we had years instead of days, we could have been there with you for each trial. You could have faced small pieces of your fears instead of the entire thing at once. We did not wish this, but it is as you said, we had no choice. Not with your battle against Boneclaw looming so close. We will not lose you to him, we cannot. He has already caused us so much shame—"

"And what exactly does that mean?" she asked. "Amythist said that magic comes from human willpower. Does that mean Boneclaw's abilities exist because he *wants* them to? And if that's the case, how did he learn them? Those frog-eel-bat fuckers seemed very much like him. Did he face them too? For that matter, did Lumos face the will-o-wisps?"

"You are not…the first person to come here," Lady Dragonfly said. "When we first came into existence, we were no wiser than the young of any other race. We were not born with the fount of knowledge we now possess," she stated a little imperiously.

Meanwhile, a pixie behind her had a finger shoved so far up its nose Kristen was worried about it getting brain damage.

"We made mistakes and trusted those we should not have. But we were also not the first to come to this place."

"Boneclaw was," she said.

"We cannot say." The pixie leader looked upriver as if she too feared the creatures of the dark that had so brutally assaulted her. "There are rules here, even for us. But know that we are rooting for you, Kristen Hall, Steel Dragon. We wish you to be victorious so maybe our wrongs may be righted, along with many others. We apologize for how hard this was. We wish we had met you sooner and perhaps this could have gone better."

"It's all right," she said and dismissed their concerns. "I'm grateful, honestly. You might have saved my life." She made the light in her hands wink out. Hope flared with the certainty that she could use this. Yes, she could definitely use this.

"It is time, Kristen Hall," Lady Dragonfly said warmly.

She nodded and felt the current pulling at her legs to drag her gently toward the glowing portal. It was time. She stepped through the gateway and into Amythist's garden. The old dragon was there, waiting for her with a fresh pot of tea.

CHAPTER EIGHTY-THREE

Amythist's garden was as Kristen had left it—overgrown, untidy, and absolutely beautiful. It was immensely relaxing to be in a place that didn't actively try to kill her and where insects flew between the flowers instead of magical beings. She didn't see any pixies and for the moment, she was more than all right with that.

"Tea, my child?" the old dragon asked and offered her a steaming cup that smelled of fragrant jasmine.

"Yes, please," she said. "And food, lots of food." She hadn't hungered at all in the other dimension but now that she was back, her hunger returned with a vengeance.

"I'll place an order for some Chinese delivery—and holy shit, Kristen, put some clothes on!" Brian slapped his hands over his eyes and turned away from here. "Oh, gross. Sister boobs. Not cool, Kristen, not cool!"

She looked down and realized that she was indeed practically naked. The shadow creatures had been vicious in their attacks and had turned her clothes to tatters. She had healed with her dragon powers, so instead of looking like she had survived a bloody ordeal, it looked like she was trying to embody a particularly racy music video.

"Here we are, Lady Steel," Stonequest said, took a step forward, and removed the jacket of his uniform for her. She noticed that his eyes were not nearly so averse to seeing her in this state of undress as Brian's were.

Kristen took the jacket, went ahead and stripped out of the last tatters of clothing she wore, and put it on. Her ass still hung out, but honestly, she simply didn't give a shit. She had been clothed more in mud and blood than clothes for her entire ordeal and didn't feel at all uncomfortable with some booty hanging out. At least nothing was trying to stab her with venom.

"How long have you guys been waiting here?" she asked.

"The entire two days," Drew said. His eyes also drifted to the patch of skin between her breasts that was exposed by Stonequest's open jacket. She gave less than zero shits. "Well, Brian has been here more than anyone else."

"And you repay me with gross freckled boobs? Seriously?" her brother shouted. "No, no I don't want to order that. Wait, why would you think freckled boob is a dish? No! No, I don't want that!" he yelled into his phone.

"But we've all taken shifts," Drew said.

"Heartsbane will be pissed she wasn't here," Stonequest said.

The human team leader rolled his eyes. "Hernandez too. Maybe you should open that portal and step through it again when they're both here."

"Yeah, they're both gonna have to deal," she said. "I will not go back there."

"Where was *there* exactly?" Stonequest asked.

"Was it bad? You look exhausted," Drew added.

"It was more difficult than I thought it would be."

"I told you so," Amythist said as she led them all inside to sink into chairs. She gave Kristen puffy pants that looked like they might have been in style in Morocco a hundred years before. Once she took a seat, the old dragon pushed the cup of tea into her hands and she sipped it gratefully.

"So, what was it like?"

"The pixies sent me somewhere strange. It was like another dimension or something."

"Quantum physics says that all the dimensions are wrapped up so we can't visit a different one because we're already—"

"Universe then," she said and cut Brian off. He had finished ordering the food and looked much calmer now that she wore pants although he still eyed her warily.

"How do you know it was a different universe and not merely a different part of our planet?" Drew asked.

"Oh, I'm very damn sure there's nowhere on earth like this," Kristen said and chuckled at the idea that such impossibilities existed in what she thought of as the real world. Doing anything else would send her into nightmares. "It was a place of much more raw magic. Or...well, the pixies said our realm has *more* magic, but this place didn't have much of anything else. I guess it was like a garden they had grown."

"They've been working on it since they were brought into existence," Amythist said with a nod.

"They tried to show me how to use different dragon powers. Or more like tried to activate them through life-threatening tests."

"But that's not possible," Stonequest said.

"That's what I thought too, but it seems it is. In fact, I think there might not even be a difference between dragon powers and mage powers."

The dragon didn't scoff audibly but the look was plain on his face.

"You're all right though?" Drew asked. "You look tired as hell and I can't imagine you did that to your clothes on purpose, but you're okay?"

"I am now. My dragon healing powers—sorry, healing powers— took care of most of the damage. It was a nightmare of the stuff I fear most, but I survived, and the pixies said that was enough to be able to use those powers here."

"Wait, so you managed to harness new dragon powers?" Stonequest asked. He leaned forward in his chair and quietly spilled his tea onto the floor.

"I'm sure she did, and if she can manage to master new abilities, you can manage to not spill tea all over that rug. It's older than most governments, for goodness sake!" Amythist tutted, lifted a rag telekinetically, and used it dab up the spill.

The stone dragon looked at it as if a rock had asked him how to bake a lasagna. "I…you… Pixies are doing that. They must be."

"It's true. I learned how to make light, exactly like a mage," Kristen said. "Here, let me…" She raised her hand and tried to send the magic through her body but it didn't work. "Sorry, let me…" She tried again and this time, attempted to make her entire body glow instead of only her hand. That had been much easier at first, so maybe she needed to start with something like that in this universe as well. But no, she couldn't. The only thing she managed to do was make her stomach grumble.

"I call bullshit," Brian said and pointed at her gut. "You already had that ability. Burping too. Don't pretend the pixies taught you how to burp."

The doorbell rang and he stood to fetch dinner. While he and Amythist went about emptying all the rice and sauce-covered meats and vegetables onto plates so it felt like something more than cheap take out, Kristen tried to activate her powers with no success. She was simply too tired and all she was able to do was give herself a headache.

Stonequest frowned and turned away. She knew the look on his face all too well. It was the look a police officer wore when they knew a murderer would go free because a cop had made a dumb mistake like ruining evidence or entering a home without a warrant. It was a look of defeat.

"Come on, Kristen," Drew said and patted her on the shoulder. "Let's eat."

They sat around a table in Amythist's kitchen that Kristen had not known existed when she had been there in the past. Her friends had cleaned it against the old dragon's protests. For a blessed moment, all was quiet as they passed plates and piled them high with rice, sesame chicken, beef and broccoli, and more eggrolls than were strictly necessary for five people. Or it might have been more than enough if she wasn't there. She ate so fast that she couldn't tell the difference between the different dishes and held her plate in one hand and shoveled food with chopsticks with the other. It was more efficient that way.

"Jesus, Kristen, you look like Dad at an all you can eat buffet ten minutes before it closes," Brian said but he looked impressed. Leave it to a brother to be grossed out by a girl's body but impressed that she could eat more than him.

Finally satiated, she scooted back from the table and stretched for more tea.

Unsurprisingly, everyone else was still eating. While they munched and talked shop about how the reconstruction of the base was coming, she merely leaned back and tried to enjoy the moment. As she listened, she tried to think about what she'd learned, about the sensation of magic, and how each type had its individual variety.

Exactly like she could in the pixie realm, she could feel magic around her. It was no weaker than it had been there but it was much more muffled. There was so much *stuff* in this realm. There was Amythist's ticking clock, the sounds of birds singing at the setting sun, and wind shaking the rafters. Smells of strongly seasoned Chinese food, of delicate jasmine tea, and the slightly off funk her brother got when he was stressed mingled. All the knickknacks in Amythist's house, taken from the world over and different centuries, crowded her senses.

But beneath it all was the same sensation that had been present in the pixie world—one of power and of a warm glow waiting to be harnessed. If she could direct it through herself, she knew she could activate it. After all, she had magic too. All living things did. She had learned that in the pixie realm. If she could use new powers there, she could do it here.

Kristen blinked and looked at the table. Everyone was frozen, their eyes wide and the food either forgotten on their plates or midway to their mouths.

"Uh...you guys?"

"Kristen...you're glowing," Brian said.

"Oh, whatever. Mom used to say that about Dad too when he ate too much. I might be full now but I have a dragon's metabolism."

"No, Kristen, you're *glowing*," Stonequest said, his mouth agape.

"I am?" She looked at her hands. "I am!"

"But...but this changes *everything!*" he said and pushed from the table with such force that he knocked his chair over. He began to pace, seemingly oblivious of the upended chair and the half-plate of Chinese food still steaming where he had been seated.

"This changes everything about dragons. Everything! It means that commons don't have to be that way?"

"You don't have to stay vanilla, no," Amythist said. She used her powers to pick up the chair he had knocked over and scooted it to the table. "Much like human ice cream, there are mix-ins available."

"Thank you for putting this in language I can understand," Drew said, smiling.

"Does this mean that dragons like me can add *more* abilities?" Stonequest continued to pace. "I know dragons can *improve* their powers. Emerald—God rest his soul—did that with his fighting abilities to a level I hadn't previously thought possible, but learning new powers changes everything."

"We know," Kristen and Amythist said in unison.

"I had always assumed that Boneclaw's shadows abilities were inherent to him. Like he was born like Shadowstorm or Obscura, and that he *improved* them. But that's not necessarily the case."

"I don't think anyone is born with specific powers," Kristen said. "Not after what I saw there. I think some people have an easier time tapping into their magic potential, and those are the people who are able to do the most different things."

"Well, sure...uh, that's how mages work from my understanding, but this is *dragons* we're talking about."

She was about to explain that no, this was everyone and that she believed dragons were merely particularly advanced mages when Amythist darted her a look and pulsed her aura to make her feel that no, this was not the time for that.

"I learned from the pixie realm that magic is a form of energy. Like water or electricity, it flows and there are different varieties or flavors."

"Sticking with the ice cream metaphor. I love it," Brian said.

"Making myself glow is much like turning into steel." She raised her hand and turned her fingers to metal one by one. "It's a matter of focusing that energy in a different way."

"And you learned how to do all this there in what? Pixie class?" her brother asked.

Kristen shook her head. "It was more like I was given an example of what was possible. I saw these glowing light beings—like will-o-wisps or whatever. But simply seeing them wasn't enough. The pixies put me through a life or death situation so I could break down the barriers in my subconscious."

"And we're all very glad you survived," Amythist said. "It took me a long time to break my mental barriers. I had feared that with the time crunch, the difficulty would be such that you might very well perish."

"Well, it felt like I was there a long time, but you guys said it was only what, like two days? It felt like much longer than that." Kristen chuckled before her mouth went completely dry. She felt her glowing skin fade as she realized what she had said. "Wait, it's been *two days*."

Everyone nodded.

"But that means that the duel is *tomorrow!*"

Again, everyone nodded.

"Well, shit. It means I need to train! In the pixie realm, I was able to punch and kick with light blasts. If I can't do that here, there's no way I'll defeat Boneclaw."

"What you need to do is *rest,*" Amythist said.

"There's no time!" She pushed to her feet and almost swooned before she clutched the edge of the table.

"Child, there is no choice but to rest. You said yourself that you felt like you were there for weeks. I know better than most that you did not sleep there, nor did you eat. You must have your strength for tomorrow and in this realm, that means going to bed with a full tummy."

"No, I…" Before she could finish, a massive yawn overcame her.

"Well, at least tell me about the duel…" Another yawn followed, not as big but as powerful as the first.

"It can wait until the morning," Drew said, stood quickly, and put a hand on her shoulder to lead her to bed. "Amythist has beds for all of us. We'll sleep here tonight and fly to the location in the morning and declare that the duel is still on."

"Still on?" Kristen asked and stifled yet another yawn. "Why wouldn't it be on? It's only been two days."

He looked at her with heavy eyes. "Kristen… We'll talk about this more in the morning but…well… The whole world thinks you're dead."

She would have asked more but at that point, he had lowered her to a bed and holy shit, did it feel soft after days of walking on stone and through mud.

Wearily, she removed the jacket and wrapped herself in the covers. She was asleep before she had time to piece together how anyone could think she was dead when there was no body.

CHAPTER EIGHTY-FOUR

She woke the next morning to the sounds of bird calls and the whistle of a tea kettle. Kristen squinted at the sunlight streaming past the vines that covered the window in the tiny, overstuffed room she was in. For a minute, she could not remember where she was but she didn't care. She was in a room in a house, and in a bed. Compared to the unending walk she had endured for what felt like a small eternity, that was enough.

Then she remembered she was there because in a few hours, she would have to fight a dragon who plagued her nightmares, and she thrust out of bed into an ungainly heap.

Before she could find her feet, the door to her room opened. Brian, Stonequest, and Drew were all there.

"Is everything all right?" Drew asked.

"Why do you still not have a shirt on?" her brother yelled and ran from the room.

"Yeah, sorry. I remembered that I have to battle the dragon who killed Lumos and Shimmerclaw in like six hours."

"Four hours," he said.

Stonequest tossed her uniform to her and winked.

"*Four* hours?" she asked as she tugged her clothing on. Clean clothes felt *amazing.* "What time is it?"

"Eight in the morning," Drew told her.

"Why didn't anyone wake me?" she demanded.

"Amythist said she would use her mage powers on us if we didn't let you sleep," Stonequest said. Then, more quietly as if he did not quite want to admit it, he added, "She said she'd turn me into a toad."

"And you *believed* her?"

"I didn't think dragons could use *any* magic beyond whatever power they inherently have," the stone dragon protested. "You turned yourself into a flashlight last night. What's so crazy about her turning me into a toad?"

"She can't simply...that magic doesn't... Okay, never mind," she said and hurried to the kitchen.

Amythist was stirring a giant pot of oatmeal, but despite Kristen claiming she liked it runny, the old dragon refused to serve her until it thickened. "Besides," she said with a wink, "it should be done by the time you finish a shower."

"I could stop for takeout on the way to the duel."

"If you think you can face Boneclaw with artificial cheese and cheap, processed meat in your stomach, you are in for a rude awakening," Amythist snapped with as much ferocity as her mother.

She acquiesced and took a shower. As soon as the hot water touched her skin, she appreciated the old dragon's insistence on the ritual. She was grimy with dirt not only from a river but from another dimension. It felt wonderful to wash it all off.

When she emerged from the shower, Heartsbane had joined Stonequest, Drew, and Brian in the kitchen.

"Heartsbane? It's nice to see you," she said, genuinely confused as she sat to eat her oatmeal.

"You can't fight Boneclaw with your hair like that," the new arrival grouched. "If you take your human form, he'll grab you by your scalp."

"Oh. My. God. Melissa Heartsbane, are you here to do my *hair?*" Kristen almost squealed with excitement, although she wasn't one to overly obsess over her hair. She was a cop, which meant most of the time, her long, curly red locks were in a tight, professional bun. There was something deliciously hilarious about Heartsbane, the biggest hardass she knew, arriving early to give her a makeover.

"Shut up and eat your porridge," the dragon snapped. "I'll put your hair in five cornrows. It's gonna hurt like hell."

"I'm a dragon, Heartsbane. I'm sure I can stand you braiding my hair."

It turned out that she could, but not without a fair amount of profanity.

Her meal finished, her hair tightly braided to her skull—even with her dragon healing powers, the braids still felt tight and the skin between them stretched—it was finally time to head to the duel.

"Are you ready, my child?" Amythist asked.

"As ready as I'll ever be, I guess. Do we have time to stop at the base before we go to the place?" Kristen asked.

"I don't think that will be necessary," Stonequest replied as they moved to the front door.

"I had hoped to see—oh." Her mouth fell open as she stepped out of Amythist's front door and saw that all her friends were already there.

Her old team was present. Butters and Beanpole smiled at her from the back. Keith had his phone out and snapped photos while Hernandez stood nearby and rolled her eyes at the Rookie. Timeflash smiled from the lawn, the only dragon in her close core of friends who hadn't already been inside the house. Larry grinned and babbled at Constance, who shushed him when Kristen stepped out onto Amythist's front steps.

"There's a tradition—dragons use it but humans do as well. It's called an honor guard." Stonequest raised an arm to gesture at the assembled group of people. "We're here to make sure nothing happens on the way there."

"We're here because we hope something *does* happen," Hernandez said and everyone laughed.

"Thank you all so much for coming. I'm sorry I was gone for so long. I still don't know if I can beat Boneclaw, but I think I might have a chance now."

"A chance? We all dragged our butts out of bed before brunch time for *a chance?* You'd better defeat this dragon. I was promised celebratory pizza." Butters grinned.

She laughed and looked around but didn't see the young mage. "Amy wasn't able to make it?" Kristen asked.

The team all cast furtive glances at each other. It was Larry who stepped forward with a frown on his face. "We haven't seen Amy or Katrina in two days. They left the night you left and no one has seen or heard from them since. We had… Well, to be honest, we had hoped they were the ace up your sleeve. We hoped you had sent them on some kind of secret mission."

She could tell she'd done a poor job of hiding her surprise at their absence as the faces of all her friends fell.

"No, I didn't send them to do anything. No one has any idea where they went?" she asked. "It's not like Amy to run off."

"Well…" Keith had put his phone away and now wrung his hands. "See, there's been this rumor. A dragon called Bloodblaze claims to have killed the Steel Dragon."

"Obviously, she's lying," she said.

"Right, yeah, except…well, what if she *thought* she was telling the truth?" he said. "The only other dragon with powers anything like yours is Katrina. If Bloodblaze came across her in her dragon form and they battled… But hey, it's only a rumor."

A pit began to form in her stomach. "And what's the rumor about Amy?"

"There isn't one," he said quickly. "But she vanished at around the same time as Katrina, at least as far as we can tell. I think…well, if Katrina was killed, then Amy…"

"We don't know. That's the problem," Constance said as he trailed off and wiped his eyes.

"But this all sounds like nonsense. We need to find Amy. I'm sure that wherever she is, there's a reason she hasn't contacted us."

"There's no time, my child. No time at all," Amythist said. "With this rumor going around, Boneclaw only needs you to be a minute late to declare himself the victor. Any later than that and he'll call you an imposter. You have to focus on your duel."

Kristen clenched her teeth. She didn't like her decisions being taken away from her but liked members of her team being taken away from her even less.

"I won't simply give up on Amy and Katrina. Larry, Timeflash, and Keith, I want you to try to find them. If there's anywhere Boneclaw might have as a hideout or lair, I'll bet they're there."

"Yes, ma'am." They all saluted crisply. Timeflash took her dragon form, Larry and Keith climbed on her back, and the three launched skyward.

"We'll find them!" Larry shouted from the dragon's back. "No matter what it takes, we'll find them. No matter where in the world they might be, we'll track them. If Amy is in trouble, we'll get her out, and if they're not in trouble, we'll let them know that they will be once they get back."

"Thank you, Larry. Just bring them home," Kristen responded.

She watched them go and felt horribly guilty and responsible for both the young women. Amy could have gone off and led a quiet life somewhere in rural Canada but she had brought her into this world. Katrina was her responsibility, too. She had switched to her side and now, it was rumored that the Steel Dragon was dead? If the Iron Dragon was dead, she didn't know if she'd ever forgive herself. She had a bad feeling that if she didn't lead this rescue herself, it wouldn't be a rescue at all. Merely a long search with a depressing surprise at the end.

But she could tell by Stonequest's aura that time was tight. She had to win this duel, and now more than ever. The future depended on it, but she also had to win it for those she'd lost—for Lumos, and Emerald, and God, she had to win it for Jim. She had to win it for Jonesy, and for all the people who had joined her fight only to lose their lives.

"Shall we?" the stone dragon prompted.

"Give me a minute," she said, squared her shoulders, and faced her team. "I don't know what Stonequest told you."

"That you have new magic."

"That you can glow like Lumos."

"That your boobs have freckles."

"Regardless," she snapped, "I don't want anyone to know about those new powers. Has anyone told anyone besides the people here? Keep in mind that your answer is probably the difference between my life and death."

All their heads shook firmly in response. Kristen trusted everyone there enough to take them at their word. "That means no outsiders know, not yet. So I have two advantages. One, if Boneclaw thinks I'm dead, he'll arrive expecting a victory lap, not an actual fight, and two, I have powers he doesn't know about."

"But you can make yourself *glow*," Hernandez said. "Can't you simply fuck him up?"

"Do people step on a trip-line for one of your bombs if they know where it is?" she asked in reply.

The woman grinned. "That's why you're the fucking boss, Red."

"I don't know who will be there. I know the duel itself is supposed to be private, but I also know that if rumors are flying around about me, I wouldn't be surprised to find out that the location has been compromised. If that's the case, I don't want anyone bragging or giving hints about what I can do. I need Boneclaw to stay in the dark."

"Are you sure about that?" Butters asked.

"Of course, I'm sure—oh, ha, ha," Kristen said as she caught the joke. "If Butters is done with his stand-up act, let's get a move on."

Everyone nodded. It was finally time.

Stonequest, Kristen, and Heartsbane took their dragon forms and the humans mounted up. They took to the air and started their journey to a final showdown with Boneclaw while Amythist waved to them from her garden.

"Come back when you're done! If you win, I can make you a cup of tea. If you don't…well, I hear dragons make great garden fertilizer!"

CHAPTER EIGHTY-FIVE

"So, what did Amythist tell you about duels before you left for the pixie world?" Stonequest asked as they flew toward the north side of Detroit.

"Uh…not much, honestly. Let's say nothing at all to be safe."

"All right. Well, we don't have a ton of time," he mumbled.

"Then get talking!"

"Right. Okay, Boneclaw was the dragon who was challenged, so he got to pick the venue. He originally wanted Ford Field, but I talked him out of that. I have been serving as your second. I hope that's fine."

"Of course. But I thought this battle was supposed to be private."

"It is. And it'll be covered so no one can see. He said he wanted it near Detroit for your convenience."

"I thought you said everyone thinks I'm dead."

"There have been rumors of that, yes. I think he wanted the location near Detroit so he could gloat."

"And by gloat you mean level the city."

Stonequest shrugged as he flew on. "That would be my guess, yes. Kristen, you can't let him win."

"I don't plan to," she replied. "But you got it moved from Ford Field?"

"Yes, to an open area of about the same size that's north of the city. Boneclaw insisted it be covered, so we had to foot some of the bill to make a scaffolding. It's not a big deal."

"I don't want to be rude but how could you agree to something covered? I thought the arena couldn't favor one of us."

"It shouldn't. It's basically a huge tent held up by steel girders. The material's not particularly substantial either. It's enough to block viewers but not impervious to fire or anything."

"But it will block the light," Kristen said.

"Yes, but I insisted on lights being on the inside. Decimus Aurelius made Boneclaw agree. So you should be safe from his shadow powers."

"That would be fucking lovely," she said. "Are these duels normally held in private?"

"Yes. Council duels are generally held in remote areas beyond human view. The location for this one is very unusual. It's too close to human homes. Ford Field would have been worse, of course, but this one is still surprisingly close to people."

"He must have already planned his victory parade," she said.

"One way or the other, it looks like people have already noticed."

"What do you mean?" she asked, but he didn't need to answer.

The dome looked like a giant caterpillar. It was more round than rectangular and appeared to be supported by air like a giant bounce house.

Although truly, the dome itself was lost in the crowd all around it. Dragons soared high above it while pixies flitted about between them. Humans were present too. They were much farther away than the dragons but they were all within sight of it. Grills were going and coolers were filled with beer. Like any good sports fan, they hoped for the best and prepared themselves for heartbreak. She was concerned that if she suffered a loss, it would be far more devastating than waiting for the next game. If she lost, it wasn't the fans she worried about torching the city in frustration but the winning dragon's henchmen.

Boneclaw was there too. He stood at the north side of the arena in his human form and surrounded by two dozen dragons. A few of them were Council members, but most looked like guards. She did not appreciate the show of force.

Kristen circled the dome and glided to a clearing where Decimus Aurelius gestured for her to land while he grinned broadly in his dragon form. She and her team settled in quick succession.

Aurelius greeted them warmly. "I'm glad I don't follow the rumors."

"Did you think I would miss this if I had a choice?" she retorted.

"I was concerned that choice had already been made for you. I'm glad to see I was wrong."

"Enough of this. Aurelius is supposed to be an impartial judge, not a cheerleader for this rebel." Boneclaw still wore Jim's skull as a mask, the sick bastard.

"Are you all right, Boneclaw? You look like you've seen a ghost," she said.

"I'm merely surprised you didn't go to the Iron Dragon's funeral after you sent her to her death. I thought your side was all about empathy and all that nonsense."

She would have started the fight then—and tried to, in fact—but Stonequest and Heartsbane each caught her by a shoulder and managed to restrain her.

"You sick fuck," she snapped.

The old dragon smiled from beneath his mask. "Such eloquence. I can see why so many humans look to you as a leader. Compared to most of them, you're quite well-spoken."

"Enough of this, please," Aurelius said and swung his tail sharply in annoyance. "May I go over the rules or do the combatants wish to keep hurling insults?"

"The rules, please. I fear the Steel Dragon may not know them."

Kristen sneered at Boneclaw but remained silent.

"Very well." Aurelius cleared his throat. "Both parties will enter from opposite sides of the arena. Both parties will be naked. No outside weapons or items of any kind are allowed."

"Will that be a problem?" Her opponent smirked as he removed his robe to reveal a frighteningly skinny and surprisingly muscled figure. He had the body of a skeleton with flank steaks for muscles. "I know you were raised by humans. Do you share their prudishness for the natural body?"

She scoffed and stripped. "I was more concerned about your old bony ass. This means you'll have to take that off." She pointed to Jim's skull.

He scowled, removed the skull, and tossed it aside. It might well have broken on impact with the dirt, but a gust of wind buffered it before it landed.

"You almost dropped that. Be careful. I know you might be shaky with age, but try to control yourself." Constance smiled sweetly at him.

His response was a stiff scowl.

"Normally, we don't ask the combatants to remove their clothes until they are about to enter, but I see that won't be a problem here," Aurelius said dryly. "Anyway, as I was saying, the battle must be fought with only each person's natural weapons and abilities. No weapons and no additional items. Nothing beyond what your human and dragon powers give you."

"Can we skip to the part where you tell me how I beat him?" Kristen said.

Boneclaw growled.

Aurelius tried and failed to hide a smile. "Either dragon may yield at any time. If a dragon yields, they have lost and the duel is over, but do not forfeit lightly. If the winner deems the duel unconscionable for any reason, they may kill the loser."

"What constitutes unconscionable?" she asked. She already knew that Boneclaw had killed all his previous opponents.

"Rest assured, Lady Steel, your actions are unconscionable. You flaunt your disgusting human upbringing and will no doubt fight like the crude simian you are."

"Cool. I merely want to make sure no one will give a shit when I kill this old fucker."

"Again, such eloquence."

"As I was saying," Aurelius interjected firmly to halt the exchange of insults. "Those are the rules. The arena is set up for Boneclaw and not the shadow powers he has kept secret for so long, so that should not be an issue."

The two combatants glared at each other and neither betrayed their belief that any precautions to stop Boneclaw from using his abilities would fail.

Aurelius cleared his throat. "Now, before we begin, I must ask— will the parties set aside their arguments and find a peaceful resolution before they engage in this battle? This is your last chance to step aside. Technically, Lord Boneclaw may offer the stolen artifact, and if Lady Steel accepts, there is no need for bloodshed."

"Why not surrender so I can beat your ass out here instead of where no one can see us?" Kristen asked.

"Because I look forward to wearing your skull as my mask. Will you please try to die in your human form so I can use that skull instead of your dragon one?"

"All right then. Lord Boneclaw, you are to enter from the north side. Lady Steel, from the south. Lady Steel, your second will accompany Lord Boneclaw as his second will accompany you to make sure you enter the arena abiding by the rules. Lord Boneclaw, we already know Sir Stonequest is Lady Steel's second. Who will serve as yours?"

"Lady Bloodblaze, of course. I'm sure you've heard of her recent exploits."

A woman with eyes the color of blood separated herself from the dragon guards. They split up and Boneclaw left with Stonequest while the rest of Kristen's friends followed her and Lady Bloodblaze.

"You know who I am, don't you?" Bloodblaze asked. She was so close that she could whisper.

"You're the bitch who killed Katrina."

"No, no, no! I simply took credit for her death so as to not interfere with this duel. I'm the bitch who watched her die and I'm the bitch who will erase every memory of you when you die."

"What did you do with Amy?"

"Who?" The dragon looked confused.

"You dumb bitch. You killed Katrina and left my mage alive? That almost makes me hope Boneclaw does win today. It will piss Amy off enough to target all of you. I'll bet she'll let you watch while she defeats Boneclaw."

Bloodblaze growled as they reached the entrance to the dome.

"You got this, Kristen!" Heartsbane yelled. "Pay no attention to Bloodblaze. She's nothing but a toad anyway."

"Am not!" the dragon retorted.

"We believe in you," Butters said. "And we need you to spring for pizza when this is all over, so don't die!"

"Indeed," Beanpole said.

"Be careful, okay, Red?" Hernandez said.

"Thanks, you guys. I'll be back soon."

"On a gurney," Bloodblaze said, but she didn't do anything to Kristen as she entered the arena, ready for whatever the Masked One would try to do.

CHAPTER EIGHTY-SIX

Kristen strode in through the entrance of the dome with her friends cheering her and Bloodblaze scowling.

She put all that aside. There was nothing to do but focus on the being across from her.

Boneclaw strode in, naked but acting as if he wore a fine suit and sported a crown on his head.

"Welcome!" he declared loudly. "I hope you like the setting."

Quickly, she studied the dome. It was massive, big enough to enclose not only a football field but the stadium itself. The floor was a mess of dirt and stone and looked like it had been roughened during the construction. The dome was made of some type of fabric and supported by huge steel girders. Massive spotlights hung from the girders—six of them—and shone with more than enough light to keep any shadows at bay.

"I'm impressed you're here to face me without any shadows," she said.

"I'm impressed you made it at all. Although I should have realized that all the runts of your litter looked alike."

Kristen was about to lunge at him right then, but Aurelius entered the arena. "Did I miss anything?" he asked but when he saw that they were still in their human forms, he smiled, "Ah, not yet. Very good."

"I thought this would be private," she said.

"All duels need a witness. I will serve as one."

"Bloodblaze would have been more than willing—"

"Your *second* is not an appropriate choice," Aurelius stated firmly.

"Of course." Boneclaw bowed to him. Kristen didn't think she'd ever seen a naked man command the respect of one as well dressed as Aurelius before.

"Both of you find the arena satisfactory?" he asked the combatants.

"Oh, yes. I can't wait to crush Lady Steel against the girders. Tell me, would that make you long for your dead mother's touch?" Boneclaw sneered.

"My mom's not dead."

"Yet," he said as he transformed into his dragon shape. More spike and spine than flesh, he would present a formidable opponent, even without his shadow powers.

"Lady Steel, do you find the arena satisfactory?" Aurelius asked.

"Sure!" she shouted, but she was already changing shape and taking to the air. Boneclaw pumped his wings furiously and swooped with increasing speed around the enclosed space of the arena.

Kristen gave chase and tailed him as closely as she could. "Running already?"

Suddenly, he made a quick loop, spun abruptly, and raked his talons across her spine. "More like setting a trap."

She swung the ax-blade on the tip of her tail at him as he swooped past. It drove him away but made no contact. His strike hadn't done much to her. Her steel scales were strong, only one of the reasons she was such a threat to him.

The next time he tried to divebomb her, she was ready. She turned in mid-air to meet her attacker and they exchanged blows. Again, Boneclaw struck and again, his strikes rebounded off her steel scales without causing much damage. She had more difficulty landing a blow, however. Despite the lights and him being unable to change to shadow, he was still damned fast—too fast to hit, she acknowledged.

By the time she lined up a good skull-cracker with her tail, he had disengaged.

He roared in frustration. "You understand that you would be nothing without me? You wouldn't have even existed. It was I who convinced your father to give you life. I convinced him to share his genetic material."

Kristen roared and surged toward him, temporarily disabling her steel skin so she could fly faster to catch up. She was about to collide with him when he unleashed a powerful blast of fire.

Quickly, she shifted to steel and dodged. The fire roared past and struck one of the lights behind her. The glass on the front of it fissured and cracked, and the light went out. The fabric behind it suffered no such damage from the fire.

"Good job ensuring the fabric was fireproof!" Boneclaw shouted at Aurelius, who gaped at the broken light.

"You can't do that!" she said, still in pursuit.

"Oh, I most certainly can! Tell her, Aurelius. Tell her our ways!"

"Lord Boneclaw is correct. You agreed to the arena, which means that it is now part of the duel. But I must stress that breaking the lights was never part of the plan. There will be consequences."

She could hear the same concern that a wrestling referee might have when someone did an unexpected thing during a match. It wasn't that he wanted her to lose but rather that there was little he could do. If he stopped the duel, Boneclaw would win by default.

That meant she had to end it before her opponent could destroy all the lights. She raced after Boneclaw, caught up to him this time, and raked his back with her talons before he swooped away. But the momentum her strike created hurled him into another light. It broke in a shower of sparks.

"If there are consequences"—Boneclaw laughed—"they must now be doled out to both parties!"

Kristen streaked in pursuit as he swooped past another light. He slowed slightly before she reached him so when he struck her with his tail and missed, it almost looked like an accident when the third light shattered.

The three remaining were not enough to completely illuminate the arena. Where before, not even the stones on the floor had cast a shadow on the dirt around them, there were now large pools of darkness. The tent did too good a job of blocking out the sun.

She followed him to one of the pools of darkness and lunged but was too late.

The leg she had aimed at vanished into shadow, only to reappear behind her and shove her into an ungainly sprawl. It didn't hurt as she was still made of steel, but goddamn, was it embarrassing.

"Boneclaw, enough of that!" Aurelius ordered brusquely.

"The rules are clear, Aurelius," the shadow dragon roared. "I am allowed to use what powers I naturally possess. No more, no less. That means I can use my shadow powers since the Steel Bitch agreed to this arena."

"But you can't—"

"Furthermore," he continued smugly, "we have both broken lights —an unprofessional duel if there has ever been one. Don't worry, though. I'll finish her off soon enough."

"This is preposterous—" the Council witness tried to protest, but Kristen cut him off.

"Fine! He can have his shadow magic." That might have been stupid but Boneclaw still didn't know about her newest powers. If he thought he had the advantage, he might make a mistake. She could use her light powers right away, but she wanted to hold them in reserve. The longer he knew about them, the more he would prepare himself for them. She knew that if he had time to strategize, he would likely win, which meant she had to play his game.

But that didn't mean she couldn't tease him and see what happened.

"I'll let it fly because I intend to kill you, Boneclaw," she said. "And when I do, I'll tell the whole world your dirty little secret."

"What secret?" he asked as he flew past the fourth light and punched it with a clawed hand. "You already told the world I was the Masked One and guess what? They did not care. Dragons are still loyal to me. My greatest secret has become my greatest strength."

Only two lights were left and he now led her to one of them. She kept pace and scratched and clawed at his wings. They were one of the few parts of him he couldn't simply make disappear into shadow because he'd fall from the sky. She managed to gash one and he plummeted...directly into the fifth light.

He laughed as sparks flew all around him.

There was only one light left and she knew that without it, they really would be in Boneclaw's domain. She landed in front of it and put herself between him and the final source of illumination. The dome itself glowed with the faintest of red lights, enough to make her think that when it was lifted, not the countryside of Michigan would be revealed but hell itself.

"Tell me your secret, Steel Bitch. You interest me!" Boneclaw's voice echoed as he approached.

Kristen exhaled a great blast of flame and the dragon pulled up and away. She lost sight of him as soon as her flames jetted out as he had vanished into shadow.

"You're not a gifted dragon with powers granted to you by the universe itself. You're simply a common—or, more likely, merely a shitty mage who found a way into another realm."

The silence was deafening for a brief moment.

Then, Boneclaw materialized in the cone of light in front of her, already in mid-strike.

"You lie!" he said and lashed at her with his tail.

"You're the master of deception, not me!" she retorted and blocked blow after blow but still falling short. He was amazing at avoiding her strikes. His blows suffered in strength because of it, but he was extremely difficult to hit. "You learned this way of fighting in another place—a place of magic. Admit it! Dragons only exist because people like you dared to dream themselves into monsters."

"You've been spending too much time with those damnable pixies," he shouted as he intensified his strikes. They were delivered at incredible speed, some now so vicious they punched through her steel scales and drew blood.

But his commitment to the attack cost him as well. Kristen was able to bite him in the chest with such ferocity that he had to use his shadow powers to escape her. He used the shadow she created from the light to vanish, reappeared just outside her grasp, and flew into the darkness.

She wondered if that had been her chance to beat him and if she had squandered it.

Boneclaw had gone into shadow. She could see nothing of his passage—no wingbeats pushing the cloth of the dome and no scrape of talons on the floor.

But she could feel him.

Calmly, she reached out with her senses—*all* her senses—like she had in the pixie world. She looked for him, yes, but she also smelled, listened, and used her dragon aura. Unhurried, she opened herself like a blossoming flower until she could feel the flow of magic itself.

And there he was. She could *feel* his shadow form and his use of dragon magic in the same way she could feel the light wisps and shadow creatures. He came in low, not flying exactly since his body was made of shadow, but gliding above the ground.

Kristen turned her back to him, both to make him more confident and because the front of dragons was where they were most vulnerable. This way, he couldn't reach her throat, while she would look completely oblivious.

A split-second before he made impact with her, she moved slightly so his blow wasn't as powerful as intended although she still acted like it was. She tumbled across the ground and thrashed like a fouled soccer player.

"The only thing I learned in that place," Boneclaw roared, "was to fear the dark."

With a snort of disdain, he smashed the final light and plunged the entire room into darkness.

He approached her and moved around her like a lion hunting a creature of the savannah not gifted with night vision. She could sense his every move, but she turned her head constantly so he would believe she was blind to his approach. Despite her quiet inner certainty, she hoped she was doing the right thing by holding her light power in reserve to catch him.

Kristen didn't have to wait long.

Her adversary lunged and bulldozed into her. He knocked her over and rolled with her as he tried to savage her gut.

She couldn't take hold of him, not like this, and merely struck at shadows. Finally, she activated her new powers and every scale she had ignited with light.

He screamed as the Steel Dragon—shining like silver—snatched him in her claws.

CHAPTER EIGHTY-SEVEN

Boneclaw—forced into his physical form by the burst of light—stumbled and squirmed to get away from her. It was like watching an eel being taken from its cave in the ocean depths and then being dumped unceremoniously on a rocky beach. He screeched and crawled, his legs thrashing as his tail quivered and tried to propel him away from the light.

"You lying bitch," he whined. "You lied about your powers."

"Fair is fair," Aurelius decreed from somewhere above. "You used your shadow powers despite the arena being made to inhibit them, so she can use these."

Kristen said nothing and kept her scales glowing as she pursued her adversary. She pounced like a bobcat and drove into his chest. Her glowing claws cut wounds in his scales that hissed with smoke as the flesh beneath was cauterized by the intensity of her light.

He whipped at her head with his spiny tail. His spines punctured the side of her head, her neck, and her back, but she heard the telltale snap of his spines breaking on her steel armor. She could take this abuse better than he could.

She bit Boneclaw's armpit and savaged the joint that kept his right arm connected to his body. He screamed in pain, howling and yowling like he had been reduced to his animal state.

"Admit that you're merely a human with an overblown sense of your ego and I'll let you live," she snapped as she released his armpit and brought her tail up for a finishing blow.

He exhaled fire directly into her face.

Blinded, she stumbled back and he slipped away.

Her vision was back in an instant. She'd managed to evade the fire blast sufficiently that her steel scales had blocked most of the damage. But now, Boneclaw was free in the darkness.

Kristen could still sense him, however, a malevolent shadow who moved through the dark like a shark who had yet to put its fin above the surface of the water.

"I don't care where you got these petty little flashlight powers of yours. I will still end you," he raged from the darkness.

Still not ready to reveal the full extent of her powers, she used him speaking as an opportunity to attack. She blasted fire into the darkness, only it emerged not as fire but light. The beam of heat and light was as strong as the sun itself.

She caught Boneclaw in it and he screeched in pain before he dropped away. Unused to being able to blast a form of energy that moved as fast as light, she overcompensated in trying to track her target and lost him in the dark.

The shadow dragon must have sensed how devastating this attack could be and increased his pace as he moved through shadows. She shrugged and used him for target practice.

One solar blast after another shone out of her mouth and made temporary cones of light that started at her face and silhouetted her adversary against the fabric of the tent.

On the third strike, he plummeted and landed hard, wheezing in pain.

Kristen ran toward him, preparing herself for her final attack, but found she was unable to. She wasn't used to calling on this kind of energy. Releasing so many of the blasts in a row had done a good job of depleting her energy reserves. Still, she could feel herself recharging. She merely needed to hold him at bay for a minute or so before she delivered the killing strike.

Boneclaw, sensing his opportunity, faded to shadow once again. She waited and made no effort to attack until he made his move.

His claw turned solid long before he wished it to, so she was able to not only sense it coming but see it as well. She clamped her jaws on his wrist and ensured that her teeth glowed with light.

He howled in pain and rained blows on her, trying to force her to let him go.

One particularly powerful punch in the nose forced her to release, but not before she caught his tail in one of her claws.

The shadow dragon tried to flee in the darkness but couldn't. Her glowing claws pinned him in his material state.

"It looks like we finally have a fair fight," Kristen growled.

Boneclaw responded with a roar of fury and stopped his attempts to flee. He lunged forward and drove into her, and both dragons tumbled across the dirt, thrusting stones this way and that with their enormous momentum.

She focused mostly on not letting him go. Whenever she grasped a new limb, she'd pummel him with her tail or another claw, but she was careful to not release him completely. She couldn't let him vanish into the dark again.

He understood what she was doing and mostly focused on pulverizing whichever limb currently trapped him. But his desperation to escape had begun to take its toll. While he tried to pull free, she cut and sliced at him with her tail. Soon, his wounds stopped healing. His scales, which moments before had faded from bone-white to shadow, were now speckled with his blood. In a straight-up brawl, he could not beat the Steel Dragon. Her scales were simply too strong. That, coupled with her ability to deny him his shadow magic, essentially made the Masked One impotent against her.

And yet, he didn't seem scared, frightened, or even that concerned. He fought fiercely, to be sure, but there was something about his demeanor that Kristen didn't like. It was like watching her brother play a first-person shooter game using only a pistol while his opponents used rocket launchers. Yes, he was losing, but it was like he had yet to fully commit to the game.

But like the player using the rocket launcher, her best choice was to blow the bastard to pieces before he could enact whatever plot he was hatching. She battered his head back with a headbutt. Her steel horns cracked his bone ones and he was thrust back and struck his head on a boulder with enough force to break the stone and draw a messy spurt of blood from his head.

In response, Boneclaw laughed.

She decided she'd had quite enough of this.

Kristen pulled back and let the light energy build into a final blast. She still had his body pinned and would crisp him to nothingness at point-blank range.

"You are strong," he wheezed. "You might have won if this was a fair fight."

"If?" she had time to ask before he shouted, "Now!"

All around the arena, dozens of forms rose from the dirt, perhaps fifty in all. They were short, hulking, bearded people, covered in dirt and stone but reflecting the light that poured off her with stone teeth and metal piercings.

They were dwarves, she realized, and they must have been buried beneath the dirt and stone of the floor.

Still, she could defeat Boneclaw and readied her light blast to deliver the final blow.

She might have managed to do it if not for the weighted steel nets the dwarves fired at her. Three of them caught her in the face and she jerked and jolted with the impacts. Boneclaw thrashed beneath her. Between his strength and the nets, she lost her hold on the dragon.

Kristen pushed to her feet and clawed the nets off her face with enough time to intercept two more launched at her.

"This is against the rules, Lord Boneclaw. You know very well that this will void the duel!" Aurelius shouted from somewhere above. It was a lucky thing she had light powers. If not, it was possible Decimus Aurelius might not have seen the dwarves at all. As it was, this might very well cost her adversary the duel.

"Not true!" the dragon roared from the shadows. "You inspected the arena before we began and the Steel Dragon agreed to it. I gave no orders to these dwarves. I didn't tell them to kill this blasphemous, traitorous bitch. They do so of their own accord."

Despite the new threat closing in on her, she laughed. After calling, "Now," to signal the dwarf attack, he thought he could claim they weren't working for him? She supposed it might work if she failed to win, but it was clear to her he'd never intended to battle her fairly.

The dwarves reinforced Boneclaw's point, though. They did not seem interested in the shadow dragon and their focus was almost entirely on her. They had exhausted their net cannons and now attacked her with a mixture of guns and hammers. She had no doubt that the guns were loaded with dragon bullets and the hammers strong enough to crush her bones beneath her steel skin.

"Come and fight me, Boneclaw, you coward!" she shouted before she vaulted skyward and took flight over the dwarves as gunshots rang out inside the dome.

Her adversary responded immediately. He barreled into her, embraced his material form, and dragged her to the ground with him. They collided with the surface and dislodged dirt and debris.

Kristen tried to twist to reach him where he clung to her back and whispered in her ear. "Aurelius might very well be able to deem this duel unlawful. But I don't care. Rules are for lesser beings. I want you dead, Kristen Hall, Steel Bitch. I will rule this planet, and you are the only thing standing in my way."

"You can't...beat me." She grunted as she spun and thrust Boneclaw into the ground.

"Not alone, no." He coughed. "But we'll let my Dragon Council work out what to do with the particulars of this match. Not to worry. I'm sure sweet Decimus Aurelius will give you an unnecessarily valiant defense. Posthumously, of course."

"I've been shot by dragon bullets before," she snapped. "Even if these dwarves shoot me, I'll still have time enough to kill you."

"Perhaps. Nothing in this world comes without risk," he replied but didn't let her go.

They tumbled and tussled and rolled over one another. While before, she had tried to prevent him from getting away, the tables were now turned. If he could keep her grounded long enough, the dwarves would get within range to take a point-blank shot at her. As it was, they could not yet shoot for fear of killing Boneclaw.

But that was changing fast. The dwarves closed in on the two dragons and Kristen—try as she might—could not land a killing blow. She outmatched him in close combat like this, but he was too wily to allow her a finishing strike. It was like trying to make an eel stand still —an impossibility.

As they struggled, the dwarves drew closer until they were surrounded. Those with hammers closed ranks to form a wall. She knew enough about dwarf physiology to know that if she ran into that, she would be rebuffed despite her size.

Kristen tried desperately to land a blow on Boneclaw but missed every time. He dodged and rolled, turned lethal blows into bone-crushing ones, and bone-crushing ones into nothing but bruises.

And still, the dwarves closed in.

The first tentative gunshots rang out. Boneclaw, reacting to these, let her pin him to the ground. She did so before realizing what she had done—left her giant, glowing, dragon body exposed for every dwarf in the arena to fire upon without risk of hurting her adversary.

The dwarves, more than happy to take advantage of this temporary lapse in tactical combat, unloaded a hurricane of dragon bullets that would punch through her steel skin like it was nothing more than aluminum foil.

CHAPTER EIGHTY-EIGHT

It was impossible to dodge all the bullets in her dragon form, so Kristen changed into her human body. The dwarves, no more accustomed than anyone else to facing a dragon that willingly used their human body, continued to fire as she changed and shrank and became her regular old naked but steel-skinned self.

Boneclaw did not fall for the deception.

He lunged under the storm of bullets and turned into shadow as he prepared to surge into the tiny human female in front of him.

Never one to back down, she lit her fists with light and channeled every ounce of magic she had into her right arm before she threw the strongest punch she had ever landed.

As she unleashed the power, she felt her dragon energy—not only the energy she normally had in her human form but her *full* dragon energy—power the punch. It struck Boneclaw so hard that it cracked a tooth and catapulted him away.

She had him. If she could access her full strength in this body—the one she was more comfortable with—she knew she could win this.

Except she had momentarily forgotten the fifty armed dwarves who now raced toward her. Some of them continued to fire at her while their comrades rushed forward with hammers.

One of them swung early in his enthusiasm and hammered a massive crater into the ground. She swallowed. Dragon power or not, a couple of direct strikes from those hammers would do more than enough damage to make her easy pickings for Boneclaw.

So Kristen didn't let the blows catch her. She remained in her human form and recalled all the hand-to-hand training she had ever done. All the bouts with Drew, Hernandez, and Jonesy, when he was still alive, clicked in with their learned responses. She thought about how dragons had trained her too. Emerald and Lumos had shown her ways to use her powers and even an enemy like Sebastian Shadowstorm had shown her secrets about how her body could be used to win a fight.

She brought all those lessons together now, every trick she had, to become the fastest blur she could. When she had an opportunity, she struck a dwarf and hurled them tumbling away, but it was never enough to knock them out. They were designed to fight dragons. She might be able to beat a few in a fight, but not fifty. Recognizing this, she focused mostly on dodging.

"That's right, you little steel runt, run away. Run away like you did when you were born. Run away to whatever cursed mongrel species gave you those light powers," Boneclaw raged.

Her fists still blazed with light as she dodged and moved past the dwarves. She knew they could see in the dark as well as any dragon, so plunging them all into darkness would give Boneclaw the greatest advantage. She couldn't allow that. Not when she was so close to winning.

Except she wasn't, she realized.

The dwarves had changed everything. She had been ready to fight Boneclaw one-on-one, and dammit, she thought she might have been able to beat him, but these odds were too stacked against her. Even though he wasn't currently attacking, he was still winning.

And it still wasn't enough for the conniving dragon.

A bright flash appeared behind her and daylight flooded the room. It was a gate like the ones Constance used. For a moment, she dared to hope but more dwarves poured through, looking surly and ready for a fight. It was Boneclaw's second round of reinforcements. She was about to beg for the lives of her team in exchange for her own when Amy burst out of the portal, riding her skateboard.

"Amy! Where have you been?" Kristen said, almost breathless with excitement.

"Is that important right now? Me and my buddies are here to help with the rabble. Why are you naked?"

"You would know the answer to that if you had been here," she replied and turned her attention to Boneclaw again.

Amy's dwarves wasted no time and raced into the arena. Armed with pickaxes and shovels, they proved to be a more than formidable force against the hammer-wielding dwarves.

She supported them by blocking bullets with her magic shielding, by doing tricks over stupefied dwarves, and by generally turning the sacred and honorable duel into a real brawl.

"This is unconscionable. She can't use her mage," Boneclaw roared.

"I told her not to do this," Kristen replied, unable to help her laughter.

"We'll sort it all out when this is over." Aurelius chuckled. "Proceed!"

Taking the cue, she vaulted upward and changed into her dragon body. Boneclaw shrieked as the light that poured from her fell on his shadowed form. He tried to run but she pursued, and the glow of her dragon energy preceded her so he was unable to vanish into shadow.

He realized that the time to run was over, turned in midair, and drove into her. Any grace he had displayed earlier was abandoned in favor of raw power.

The two dragons fell from the top of the tent and ripped and gouged each other as they plummeted. Boneclaw—no longer trying to play cunning—slashed a gash across her belly while she ripped his bony scales loose from his sides and spilled his blood with each wound.

Although the impact with the ground hurt her and she heard it crack one of his ribs, neither dragon so much as slowed their attack.

They were all teeth and claw and striking tail. There was no thought, only training honed into the sharpness of instinct.

Kristen swung her tail and brought it down on Boneclaw's spine. She felt his scales and flesh part and the blade on the tip only stopped when she encountered one of his ribs. The shadow dragon convulsed in pain, but he didn't release her or cease his attacks. Instead, he bit her shoulder where her wing was attached like he was trying to bite down on a piece of leather to stop the pain.

She shrieked and tried to push him off, but his teeth only clamped tighter. In response, she savaged his back with her tail, but her strikes lacked focus. Still, she managed to add a smattering of smaller wounds to the massive gash down her opponent's back.

The sound of breaking bone was followed by an intense increase in pain, more than she had even thought possible, and Boneclaw released her wing.

He had ripped it off. The bastard had ripped her entire goddamn wing off.

Her blood flowed like water. She lacked the healing energy to heal the wound but he was suffering too. The gash on his back was not healing. In time, he would die from the wound, but she would die first if she couldn't stop the bleeding.

So, once again, she changed into a human.

Boneclaw laughed, the pitch and timbre of it like something out of nightmare before he tried to gobble the tiny woman in front of him.

Kristen caught his top jaw with her steel fists and threw him back.

Enraged, he tried to melt into shadow but she made her entire steel body glow and his powers refused to manifest.

He lunged at her and she met him blow for blow. When he struck with a claw, she parried with a punch. He lashed with his tail and she kicked its pointed tip away. She could feel power in her—power that had always been there yet had never been hers to command. Dragon powers were merely an extension of her belief in herself. And right now, she believed that she needed to defeat Boneclaw. She believed that more than she had ever believed anything in her life. Everyone she knew and loved counted on her winning. She wouldn't let them down, no matter the cost.

The shadow dragon intensified his strikes and moved faster than the human eye could perceive. She could see him, however, and blocked blow after blow, meeting each strike with a steely defense.

Enraged, Boneclaw leaned back and inhaled a great breath of air. If he could not pulverize her, he would incinerate her.

He exhaled a blast of fire so hot it made the rocks strewn about the room melt like wax.

It would have melted her too but she called on this new font of strength, this well of power she had always felt but only learned how to access in the pixie realm. The wall of fire seemed to move in slow motion as it engulfed her, but she had sensed Amy's shield magic many times.

She called upon the enveloping, protective force the mage had wrapped around her in countless gunfights.

It didn't quite work as she planned, but it worked far beyond her expectations.

Kristen wrapped herself in a glowing shield of radiant white energy that turned Boneclaw's fire into nothing but smoke.

He stumbled back as she approached him, his eyes wide with terror. She moved almost languidly. With this amount of power coursing through her, she could see every twitch he made. She could read every emotion that flickered across his aura. When he roared and struck, she knew what he intended to do. It was revealed plainly in his musculature.

So when he opened his maw wide and swallowed her, plunging the arena into darkness, she didn't panic.

Instead, she let his teeth break upon her steel skin and the inside of his mouth blister from the light energy radiating from her.

When he forced her down his throat—as foolish as that was—she was ready. She could see his heart pulsing through the muscles of his neck and could sense exactly where it was. It was a magical engine, the source of all his power. She punched through the lining of the dragon's throat and placed a hand on Boneclaw's heart.

Like the rest of him, there was nothing but darkness there. When the glowing tips of her fingers touched it, the surface blistered and turned to ash. The shadow dragon screamed—the sound coming from all around her—as he tried to claw out the meal that would prove to be his last.

Kristen tried to pull her hand back from his heart. She had hoped to drive out the dark energy that had taken root there and rotted this dragon from the inside, but her level of control was below novice.

His heart was already dead. The light from her fingertip worked across its surface and charred it like an overcooked steak. No longer pulsing with magic energy, the organ collapsed on itself. It shriveled until it was nothing more than a blackened lump of coal, no bigger than a peach pit.

Tired, triumphant, and thoroughly grossed out from being inside a dragon while she killed it, she punched a hole in the body around her to escape.

Light flooded the arena when she stepped from the corpse. In it, she saw that Amy and her dwarves had rounded up those working for Boneclaw.

Now that she could see them all in the light, it was obvious that this second group of dwarves that had come with Amy was quite different than the first. They wore bright colors and had piercings in a rainbow of hues, unlike the dark, gray-clad dwarves with jagged piercings and stone teeth who had first attacked her.

"Oh, dear God, Kristen!" Amy flipped her skateboard in front of her and streaked closer.

Kristen smiled at her. Why was Amy so worried? Before she could think anything more, she collapsed.

Her eyes fluttered open to see the young mage standing above her, mending a massive gash that ran from her neck to her shoulder. It was the wound Boneclaw had made in her dragon form, too dire to completely vanish in her human body. Amy closed the wound and began setting bones and closing puncture wounds that had been inflicted all over her body. The girl's left nostril started to bleed, then the other, but she did not stop in her duty to the Steel Dragon and Kristen didn't caution her.

She hurt like fuck. If Amy didn't help her, she'd die.

But the healing magic did its work and a few minutes later, she was able to rise from the blood-stained soil, albeit unsteadily.

Still covered in blood and wounds, she left the arena victorious.

CHAPTER EIGHTY-NINE

Kristen walked from the arena and into the bright sun of the afternoon. She held her head high, although her body was worn and injured.

Bloodblaze—Boneclaw's second—saw her first. She expected the dragon to fly into a rage but instead, she only stared slack-jawed until Decimus Aurelius flew over her head. This seemed to shake her from whatever thoughts had seized her, and she turned and strode away.

Trying not to stumble and thus limping, she approached her friends. "It's over," she told them. "Boneclaw is dead."

They cheered and whooped, but the rest of the Dragon Council merely stared in stunned silence.

"But...no one beats Boneclaw," Skywing, a dragon Councilor said.

"No one!" Ironclaw shouted, although he did not sound angry but jubilant.

Then Amy came from the arena on her skateboard. Behind her came the brightly colored dwarves leading those who had helped Boneclaw, tied and gagged and with their toys taken from them.

"But...but this is against the rules!" Ironclaw sputtered.

"Cheat!" Bloodblaze declared.

"No rules were broken!" Decimus Aurelius declared from the sky.

"Boneclaw somehow convinced a group of dwarves to hide under the arena. They tried to interrupt the duel, and might very well have changed the outcome had this mage and her cohort of dwarves not arrived."

"They're not my dwarves," Amy said with a sheepish smile, "and that's not quite what happened."

"Do tell," Bloodblaze demanded angrily like a cat luring you in to pet her before she struck.

"I tracked Boneclaw to Canada."

"To cheat, no doubt," Bloodblaze hissed.

"Perhaps, but he had beat me to it. I found him recruiting dwarves in Canada. He buried me under a mountain and left me for dead, but these dwarves rescued me. I told them what I had seen and they volunteered to help even the fight if it got out of hand."

"We sensed the dwarves burst out through the vibrations underground," one of the dwarves added helpfully.

"We weren't far from here, and we hoped Boneclaw would obey the rules, but when his dwarves joined that fight, we couldn't sit back."

"Indeed not," Aurelius said. "Boneclaw actively recruiting anyone of any species to help in a duel is against our rules and traditions. These actions might have disqualified him, but given that Kristen has defeated him already, I will simply rule that this duel is legal and its effects valid and binding. Do any of my fellow Councilors feel differently?"

"No, no of course not!" Skywing assured him. "Boneclaw tried to cheat and got what was coming to him."

"It's a great dishonor for the old bloke to use dwarves in a duel of this caliber," Ironclaw said.

The other Councilors expressed their agreement as well. Kristen was glad. She had been worried that they had all been in the old shadow dragon's pocket, but they looked more relieved than anything that he was gone.

All of them except Bloodblaze. She and Aurelius held each other's gaze. Neither blinked nor turned away, she in human form and he a dragon.

"If—*if*—what the mage says is true, I suppose Boneclaw did break our traditions," she murmured finally.

"If?" Skywing asked incredulously. "You can read that it's the truth as plain as day on the auras of the mage and all the dwarves, those on both sides."

Bloodblaze turned and studied the dwarves and seemed to sniff their funky, earthy aroma even though she did not move any closer to them. "I suppose."

"That makes it unanimous, then." Aurelius beamed. "I declare Kristen the winner!"

Cheers rang out, not only from her friends but from dragons in the air all around them and the onlooking humans, far enough away that they would not have been able to hear had Aurelius not used his magic to make his voice boom and echo across the field surrounding the arena.

"Let us move to a safer place to decide who will be the next Council Leader now that Boneclaw is dead," Bloodblaze said venomously.

Aurelius smiled like he was holding a winning lottery ticket in his pocket and talking to friends who were in fear of foreclosure on their home. "That won't be necessary."

"Well, of course it is, old chap!" Ironclaw protested. "We need a leader now more than ever. A united front and the ability to make quick decisions are of the utmost importance."

He shook his head. "But we already have a new Council Leader." He glanced at Kristen.

The Council stood dumbly for a moment, not quite registering or perhaps not wanting to register what had happened. It was Stonequest who broke the silence. He gasped, his eyes wide, and hurried to Kristen, where he changed to his human shape and knelt before her.

Skywing seemed to understand next, for she smiled and clasped her hands together in delight. Some of the other Council members nodded as if they too understood what the hell was going on.

Kristen decided to ask exactly that. "What the hell is going on?"

"Boneclaw was the duly elected head of the Council. You saw the scales cast. He won. The only reason he hadn't taken the mantle yet was this pending duel. But now that duel has transpired, and Kristen Hall, the Steel Dragon of the Motor City, won. That means she now owns everything Boneclaw once did. All his property and all his titles."

"You don't mean—" She gasped.

"That includes," Aurelius continued, "the title of leader of the Global Dragon Council."

"But surely this has happened before," she said and tried not to stammer. "If I will have to spend all my time defending myself in duels—"

"You defeated one of the most powerful dragons in history. Boneclaw has never lost a duel *ever*. That is unheard of. Everyone on this Council has lost numerous duels but not him. News of your success is no doubt already traveling via electronic mail and cell phones. I don't think there will be much of a line to challenge you for the role," he replied.

"Even if there was, it's not like you'd lose!" Hernandez shouted and her whole team cheered.

Kristen was stunned. Her team raced forward and lifted her onto their shoulders—embarrassing the shit out of the other dragons present in the process—but she couldn't help but think about how much her life would change.

But it had already changed so much. She had expected to be a police officer and hoped to maybe help a few people in that role. Her desire had been to help fix corruption in a broken system. Never in her wildest dreams had she thought it would mean rising to become an investigator whose job was to police corrupt dragons. But even that hadn't been enough. She had expanded beyond her role to root out the corrupt, racist forces on the Dragon Council itself. She knew this new role as leader of the dragon world would change her life, but would it change her life more than all those other things already had?

She had lost so many people and had almost lost her family too many times to count. All of them sacrificed so much to make this day possible. What better way to honor their memory, bring all the races of Earth together, and stop the war permanently than by taking Shimmerclaw's old post and using that power to bring peace?

"I accept," she finally managed to say, which was in turn drowned out by even more cheering from her friends. Apparently, Butters had expected her to win, as he was shaking cans of beers and cracking them open to spray everyone in celebratory foam.

"And for my first role as Council Leader, I will throw the biggest pizza party Detroit has ever seen!"

<hr>

The party didn't quite spend the million-dollar budget Kristen set aside for it, but it wasn't for lack of trying.

The entire city of Detroit was shut down except for bus drivers, the people who operated the People Mover, and the new train system. Those who had to work were given a ten-thousand-dollar bonus for the evening. It was the first night in the history of the city where every single public servant was on the clock at the same time.

She had her people hire musicians, carnival rides, a banging fireworks display that was run by Hernandez, and a thousand other things to do.

Buddy's Pizza was told to start baking pizzas at six am on the day of the party and to not stop. They outdid themselves, spending the two days prior making unbaked pies that were then sent to every kitchen of every restaurant in the city.

The streets of Detroit ran red with pizza sauce. The gutters ran with spilled beer.

Although she didn't get to see much of all that. It was for the people she served, the people who deserved a little more than a paid federal holiday now and then.

Her time was spent in Buddy's Pizza at the table in the back, where she had first discovered that she had been accepted to the Detroit Special Weapons And Tactics team.

When she entered, it was to more raucous cheers and spilled beer.

She had told everyone to go enjoy the festivities but instead, it looked like they'd all crammed themselves in there to wait for her.

Kristen moved to the back, shaking hands, high-fiving, or receiving hugs every step of the way.

The mages Eric and Constance were at a table by the door, levitating parmesan cheese onto each other's pizza. Both were still a wreck, but Eric had thankfully survived the battle that had almost taken his life. They had viewed Katrina as a daughter of sorts, and her loss at the hands of Boneclaw still weighed on them, even after Amy had gone on a mission to recover her body.

A little deeper in was a large gathering of dwarves, including Alp and the Canadian prime minister. They were outraged that there wasn't pineapple on everyone's pizza.

The pixies were there too, although they chose not to eat the delicious, pan-fried pizza. For some reason, the concept of eating cheese was simply too disgusting for them, so they contented themselves—as they had for centuries—with flitting and darting around and filling the party with multicolored sparks.

Beyond them sat the dragons. Only Heartsbane, Stonequest, and Timeflash were left of the original team. They drank pitchers of beer like they were pints of water while they swapped stories about Lumos and Emerald that would have embarrassed the shit out of them if they were still alive but now seemed oddly respectful.

In the back room, Kristen was greeted by hugs from Amy and Larry, who both saw themselves as her personal mages and considered themselves family, her adopted uncle and sister, respectively.

She hugged them both and thanked them for coming. Amy laughed and Larry started in on a shaggy dog story about how he had nowhere else to be. She realized halfway through that both mages were extremely drunk and politely excused herself by making a ball of light and tricking them into arguing over which of them made it.

At the far end was the loudest damn table in the whole place. Crammed in tightly were Butters, Beanpole, Keith, and Drew. As Kristen said hello, Hernandez burst in and sat too. Her face and hands were black with soot.

"If Kristen asks you, tell her I was here this whole fucking time," the woman said.

"I'll be sure to tell her," she said, which earned riotous laughter from everyone else at the table.

"How does it feel to be the boss of the whole world?" Keith asked.

"It probably doesn't feel too great given that she still has to repeat herself to get you to listen!" Butters quipped, which made Beanpole squirt beer out his nose.

"We're proud of you, Kristen, even if you never did learn how to be a team player." Drew laughed.

"I did *too* learn! I always had Butters cover me."

"You never made that easy," the sniper replied to more laughter.

She chuckled at the knuckleheads—her best friends in the whole damn world—and moved on.

The Washington family sat near her family's table. As macabre as it had been, she had given Jim's mother his skull. It had been a weird, horrible moment forced on them by Boneclaw, but Mrs. Washington had accepted the velvet-lined box with gratitude. She and her husband were both still a mess. Her makeup had tear-streaks and her husband stared at a photo on the wall as if he expected it to talk. She said her hellos and thanked them for Jim's service. It was hard, but they were all better for it. They began to eat, at least.

Kristen doubled back to her old SWAT team and told them to invite the Washingtons to their table. They grumbled and complained but did as she said, and before she had stepped away, she could already hear them regaling Jim's parents with tales of bravery and foolishness his folks had never heard. His mom stopped crying and looked at the cops in shock, while his dad laughed about the antics of the Wonderkid. Jim had never told his parents his most embarrassing stories. His friends and coworkers remedied that situation now and she told herself she'd check in on all them later.

But for now, she went and sat at the table in the back corner between her mom and brother and looked at her dad across a tray of pizza.

"Oh, look who finally decided to show up!" Frank Hall quipped.

"You know the cheese is getting all hard and I don't like it when it's hard."

"Like we haven't all seen you eat cold pizza out of the fridge."

"Don't talk about that in public, Marty!" he fumed.

"Glad you could make it, boss," Brian said with a wink.

"For tonight, it's Kristen. With everything that's happening, I don't think I'll get to do these meals for much longer. So tonight, if it's possible, can I simply be your sister and your daughter?"

"Sweetie, you'll always be our daughter." Her mom began to cry and wiped her eyes with the checkered tablecloth.

"Whatever you say, Kissy-Krissy," Brian said, and made the smooching sounds she had loved when she was all of three years old.

She succeeded in not blushing. Being able to control magic had its perks.

"And we're damn proud of you!" Frank boasted to the whole room. "I was a beat cop for thirty years! Thirty goddamn years!" He stood now and had apparently been drinking without eating, never a good combo. "I never thought either o' my kids would be dumb enough to be a cop, especially not the smart one. No offense, Brian."

"None taken until you called me out!" his son said, aghast that his dad had said that in front of his coworkers.

Frank continued, "I thought she might rise to be a detective, maybe a chief when I was done and gone. Never did I dream she'd become not only a dragon cop but the goddamn president of all the dragons in the world!"

"I'm not president, Dad."

"What you are is an inspiration to all of us, Kristen. You truly are. And I would appreciate it if everyone here in this restaurant would raise their glass in a toast."

Her mom and brother—despite their embarrassment—raised their glasses with pride. Kristen's friends shut the hell up and raised their glasses too, as did Amy and Larry, although they used their magic to do so.

The voices in the next room died down and Kristen knew the dragons and mages were also saluting her. A door slammed open and someone yelled into the night, "Cheers for the Steel Dragon!" She only heard it because of her dragon powers.

Although she wouldn't learn about it until the next morning, the toast spread far wider than the restaurant and the street outside. Drone footage—Brian was, of course, still maintaining a perimeter for security—would later reveal that in that moment, the news of a toast to the Steel Dragon spread like wildfire and every man, woman, and child raised their beer, water, or whatever else was handy to the sky in silent thanks to the woman who had risked her life repeatedly to save them all.

And that's when the party started.

The End

If you loved Steel Dragon, you might also enjoy *Never A Dragon*, the first book in the new Dragon's Daughter Series, coming very soon from Kevin and Michael.

Dragons used to rule the world; those days are over. But humans, mages, and dragons have just begun learning to co-exist without conflict.

Kylara Diamantine has never met another dragon. Raised by her mother apart from the rest of their society without any idea why, she's always been curious about the rest of their species. She wants to get out there, to meet other dragons, to explore! To stretch her wings. Literally.

Be careful what you wish for, they say. They're right.

After a devastating magical attack on their home leaves Ky's mother missing, she's placed at a special school for her protection. A school for dragons - but this year, for the first time, mages will be attending alongside their scaley fellow students to learn more about magic and draconic powers.

The attacker who stole away Kylara's mother isn't finished yet and turns up the heat on the school. Ky's dragon powers keep growing in mysterious ways, but will even that be enough to save her?

Ky is a stranger in a place she doesn't know, under attack and desperate to find her missing mother. She'll need all her courage and strength to survive the tests ahead of her.

Pre-order your copy today and have it delivered the minute the book is published!

KEVIN'S AUTHOR NOTES
AUGUST 25, 2020

And we're done, at long last. Kristen Hall's epic journey is finally complete. After about a million words of adventure, she's reached the pinnacle of success. Saved the world from a horrific war and put a stop to the dragon behind all of it.

Thank you so much for following along with her tale! I hope you've enjoyed every step of the journey. If you loved this book, please leave a review!

I can't tell you how fun it's been working with Michael on these books. Steel Dragon has been a game changer for me in a number of ways. It's the first time I've collaborated on a project with someone else. This series was also a return to urban fantasy for me, since it's been years since I wrote the Blackwell Magic books (my other urban fantasy series). I've now got buckets of additional fantasy story ideas, a number of which I plan on tackling over the next few years. Hey, it's a fun genre to write in!

Now, this might be the end of Kristen's primary tale, but we're definitely not done with the Steel Dragon universe (or the "Children of Tiamat", as Michael and I have begun calling this world we've created together). Next up will be a new series, set about a year after the events of this book. The series will be called "Dragon's Daughter".

The first novel ("Never A Dragon") should be out this autumn, and we'll follow that launch with more books as soon as we can have them ready for you.

Dragon's Daughter will bring back some of our old favorites from this series, so you'll get to see our heroes in a new light as they adapt to new roles. Kristen makes a comeback, as do Amy and Amethyst. We'll probably see a few more old friends return in these books, and possibly some old foes — but I don't want to spoil any surprises, so I'll keep the rest of that to myself for now.

While I've been working with Michael on this, I've also been plugging away at my solo writing as well. Inspired by Steel Dragon, I've gone back in and cleaned up/revamped the Blackwell Magic saga, re-releasing each volume as I get it up to my current writing standards. I've got books one through four done and book five will be out really soon, followed closely by number six. That's as far as I got before, but I've *also* got most of the long-awaited seventh book done, so it will launch shortly after the re-release of the sixth book.

What's next for me? Well, my science fiction fans will probably hunt me down if I don't get the next Starship Satori book done, so that's definitely on my to-do list. I've started a Patreon for a new science fiction LitRPG book I'm writing, releasing two chapters a week. And I've got another *really* cool idea for an urban fantasy series I definitely want to write. Oh, and I also came up with another cool science fiction idea that will probably get done next year.

In short, the life of a writer is never boring. I've pretty much always got more stories I want to work on than there are hours in a day to get them all done. But that's OK! At least I'll never have to worry about running out of ideas, right?

If you'd like to drop me a line, I can be reached at author@kevinomclaughlin.com if you'd like to drop me a letter. I can't always reply to every email I get, but I absolutely do read them all and I try to get back to as many people as possible.

Thanks again for reading these tales. I'll see you over in Dragon's Daughter soon!

MICHAEL'S AUTHOR NOTES
AUGUST 25, 2020

WOOHOO!

It is both bittersweet and joyous that we come to the end of our stories and wrap up this series. We could not have done it without you, the reader, and I could NOT have accomplished it without the amazing Kevin McLaughlin.

I've mentioned before how Kevin and I challenged each other (and still do, more on that in a minute), but I feel like Kevin is a *brother from another mother*.

(I just realized one might say a *sister from another mister* for the opposite. Strange places my mind goes in the middle of these *Author Notes*.)

As we were drawing to a conclusion, Kevin and I spoke about what was next. Frankly, I wasn't sure if Kevin WANTED a next. Why?

Well, I can be annoying sometimes. Just ask my wife if you don't believe me. (Actually, please don't. Let's not provide her any opportunities to share ways an author-husband might frustrate a non-author spouse.)

(*Editor's note: Oh, I feel ya there, big guy! Or rather, I feel The Author's Wife.*)

When you collaborate on projects, you are trying to agree on where the story goes. What's more important: character, plot, tension, humor, or world-building (this is a big one)?

Followed with the big one for our fiction stories… *"Are we going to kill off the parents?"*

No, seriously, this is a big question when creating the backstory for our character and the interactions. Having a character with parents is a bit of a challenge. One not only deals with the protagonist's friends and enemies, but you also bring family dynamics into the story, and the difficulty (for a lot of authors including yours truly) just went up.

Somehow, I have meandered into areas I hadn't intended, and I need to wrap up these *Author Notes.* Suffice it to say, Kevin was happy to do another set with me (whew!), and he has mentioned the series title and the book title.

We have a name, we have a plan, we have a due date for the words to be finished. What we don't have is a cover, but take a look at our Coming Soon cover image.

It has a dragon. *That's all that is needed, am I right?*

Have a fantastic week.

Ad Aeternitatem,

Michael Anderle

Book 3 - Vengeance Over Vanaheim

Book 4 - Hel Hath No Fury

Blackwell Magic Series (Urban Fantasy)

Book 1 - By Darkness Revealed

Book 2 - Ashes Ascendant

Book 3 - Dead In Winter

Book 4 - Claws That Catch

Book 5 - Darkness Awakes

Book 6 - Spellbinding Entanglements

By A Whisker (short story)

The Raven and the Rose - Free novelette for email list fans!

Dead Brittania Series:

Dead Brittania (short prequel story)

Book 1 - King of the Dead

Book 2 - Queen of Demons

Raven's Heart Series (Urban Fantasy)

Book 1 - Stolen Light

Book 2 - Webs in the Dark

Book 3 - Shades of Moonlight

Other Titles:

Over the Moon (SF romance)

Midnight Visitors (Steampunk Cat short story)

Demon Ex Machina (Steampunk Cat short story)

The Coffee Break Novelist (help for writers!)

You Must Write (Heinlein's rules for writers)